Soleil and the March of Death
Book Two

THROUGH THE VALLEY OF FEAR

SARAH L NELSON

Swinging Girl Publishing
171 Lakeview
Grosse Pointe Farms, MI 48236
First Printing, 2022
ISBN (ebook): 978-1-7346672-3-3
ISBN (paperback): 978-1-7346672-5-7
ISBN (hardcover): 978-1-7346672-4-0

Printed in the United States of America

For my mother,

Who understands Soleil

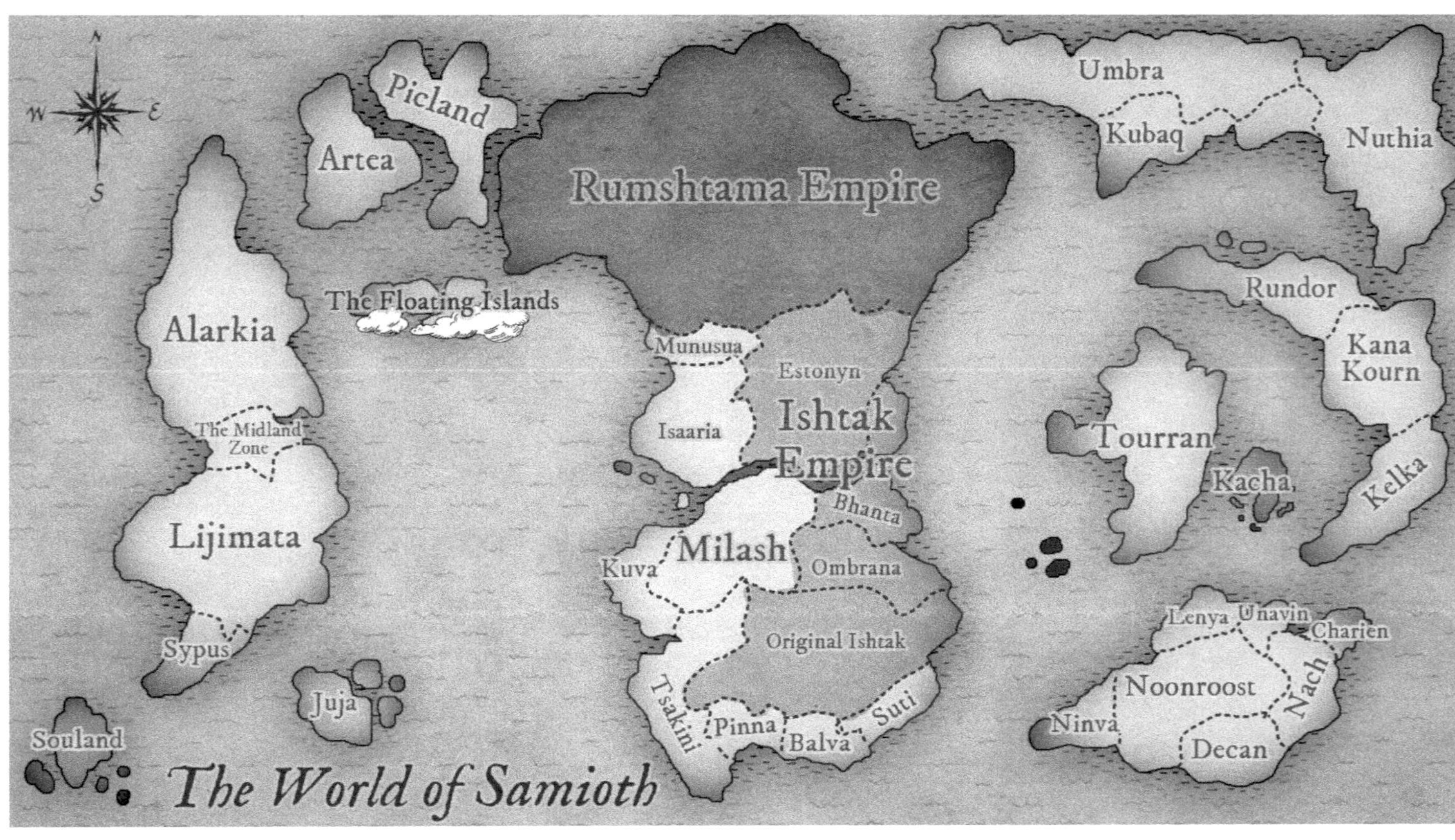

N
W
E
S
Picland
Artea
Rumshtama Empire
Umbra
Kubaq
Nuthia
Alarkia
The Floating Islands
Munusua
Estonyn
Ishtak
Empire
Isaaria
Rundor
Kana
Kourn
The Midland
Zone
Tourran
Kacha
Kelka
Bhanta
Lijimata
Milash
Kuva
Ombrana
Lenya
Unavin
Charien
Original Ishtak
Sypus
Noonroost
Nach
Juja
Tsakini
Pinna
Balva
Suti
Ninva
Decan
Souland
The World of Samioth

Previously…

IN THE COUNTRY OF ISAARIA, royal inheritance is decided by divine-right prophecies, as all magical "flukes" in Isaaria, including that of prophecy, are believed to be bestowed by an Almighty God. Rian, the Laughing Prince of the royal Yakarami family, is determined to be the rightful heir to the throne while still a child. The nature of this prophecy also brings about a betrothal between Rian and Soleil Marson, a Magicsmith with the fluke to create new timelines. Their son is one day meant to rule during a time of peace and prosperity for Isaaria, drawing conjectures about the rule of Rian and Soleil as king and queen before him.

Meanwhile, Soleil's younger sister Lune Marson is chosen to be a *Khashtani* bodyguard for her sister, expected to dedicate her entire life to protect Soleil. A young Soleil and even younger Lune are both left in Isaaria by their parents, about whom not much is currently known.

A *Khashtani* is also chosen for Rian—Taris Qurvo, the son of Khas "Nusk" Qurvo, who was a great *Khashtani* in his own youth. Taris and Lune are trained together by Nusk from the ages of six and ten, respectively, to protect the future king and queen at all costs. Taris' younger siblings Korvaan and Naomi are trained to act as the *Khashtanis'* helpers, called their *khashak.*

As the years progress, Soleil and Rian are eventually crowned and wed, Lune and Taris fall in love—something forbidden for *Khashtani*–and threats against the king and queen appear to diminish significantly. Soleil then decides to release the pair from their *Khashtani* bonds so Lune and Taris might also wed. Disaster strikes at the ceremony, however, as an unidentified assassin kills Rian, leaving Soleil devastated and Lune and Taris guilt-ridden.

A desperate Soleil, pregnant with the prophesized son and petrified to rule alone, creates a new timeline over the old, erasing that future and winding back time to try and save Rian's life. With each failure to save Rian, Soleil creates new timelines over and over, each time going back even farther than before. She is aided by Lune, the Qurvos, Lady Asmer al'Yibna, and a strange man with albinism later revealed to be Soleil's cousin and fellow Magicsmith, Septimus the Memory-Smith. Soleil's current memories of Septimus have been tampered with, leaving him another mystery.

It is concluded Soleil cannot possibly save Rian's life and discover who wants him dead to begin with while still being queen. A plan then forms in which Soleil will be raised by Nusk to act as Rian's *Khashtani* and therefore have greater knowledge of the threats against him. Lune is given to the Carsans family—one of the eight royal families of Isaaria—to stay by Rian's side directly. Asmer, Lune, Rian, Taris and Nusk are given charms created by Septimus and his father to help them remember old timelines and put the clues of these mysterious threats together, but Soleil forgoes one, believing her love for Rian and the pain of losing him so many times over is clouding her judgement. However, centuries pass in a time loop as Rian continues to die at the same time in each iteration.

Unbeknownst to Soleil, Nusk—who was meant to tell her all important information—has rejected her plan. After raising Soleil many times over again, he has come to see her as a daughter. Assuming that her destiny will hold nothing but anguish for Soleil and caring naught for the Prophecy, Nusk has decided the best chance she has of living a good life is to live one apart from Rian. He hopes to find a time loop where he can release Soleil into the world after Rian is crowned king. He also manipulates Rian's parents into keeping Rian's identity as the true heir a secret, triggering a contingency known as Comus Day, when an heir must be chosen for the country through trials. Only the heir of the prophetical Carsans family cannot participate, leaving six potential heirs other than Rian to fight for the throne.

When Taris disagrees with this methodology, Nusk uses his fluke of a silver-tongue to cruelly charm his eldest son: Taris can reveal nothing to Soleil about their discoveries, the possible identities of those after Rian, her own hidden fluke, or her love for Rian. Though it is unclear whether it is as a form of revenge, Taris then insists on secretly marrying Lune in every timeline possible, and trying to create a family. Lune miscarries every pregnancy in every timeline, causing her to become increasingly erratic and uncertain in her convictions.

Meanwhile, Soleil's cousin Septimus has his own apparent reasons for wanting to keep Rian alive—reasons implied to be more cosmic in nature. Disagreeing greatly with Nusk for deviating from the plan, but unable to control him, Septimus allies with Lune and a Lijimi man from the west. He goes about his own dealings in the world, primarily remaining in the west where a war between the counties of Alarkia and Lijimata appears inevitable.

In an unusual timeline, Rian believes Soleil has purposefully interacted with him while posing as a maid and kisses her. He reveals he has known her for a long time, indicating to the oblivious Soleil something is wrong. Septimus appears to force them back in time a day, claiming now is not the right moment for Rian and Soleil to reunite. However, for unclear reasons, Soleil remembers this unwound interaction and becomes suspicious of the life she once knew. Despite Nusk's attempts to circumvent Soleil's discoveries, she begins to keep secrets from him, while learning more about her own past and the potential identities of those aiming to kill Rian.

While some answers remain unclear, Soleil does discover certain truths: first, that several of the other heirs' families have attempted to assassinate Rian to usurp the throne. Second, the country of Lijimata hired Alarkian assassins to kill Rian (who their government deemed the least important heir) to try and force Isaaria to join the war on their side. And third, there is a malevolent organization identified by a firebird and practicing the dark witchcraft art of *Dadj'zcha* who appear to be the main aggressors against Rian.

Rian himself suspects this group may have ties to one of the Families Three; old-blood families with strong magic that were once a force for good. It is a matter of historical fact, in Rian's opinion, that the Grey family became corrupt. Should it be proven they still exist, they are undoubtedly associated with the practice of *Dadj'zcha* and the attempts against his life. However, he is rarely taken seriously even by the academic community, as it is believed the Families Three all died out in decades past.

As Comus Day approaches, Soleil's discoveries push her and Rian closer together until the appearance of a violent young man called General Amerson results in Nusk's death and a serious attempt on Rian's life. Though Soleil manages to dispose of Amerson on two occasions, the firebird organization he is tied to continues to attack Rian. Soleil realizes this organization is bent on manufacturing a war in Isaaria through civil or foreign conflicts: they use *Dadj'zcha* on the other heirs whenever possible to manipulate them into trying to publicly kill one another, stage an assassination of the Milash king leaving evidence tied to Crown Princess Nissa's family, and even attempt to gain control over Aiko Shinya, son of the Tourrannese-Kachin ambassador.

With the help of Lune, the Qurvos, Nissa, and Shinya, Soleil manages to stop a plot involving the Rian's own best friend, Mercer Ralhan, only for a second firebird associate to finish the job. Septimus urges Soleil to go back once again, saying he believes it will take him only two more cycles to solve the necessary equations and possibly save their world. However, he transfers Rian's right to remember past timelines to Korvaan Qurvo, claiming the emotional strain of remembering has been too much for Rian. Soleil returns to the past once more, this time with additional instructions.

In the final timeline thus far, Soleil is raised as a public *Khashtani,* known to Rian. Nusk still trains her and his children. However, Soleil is made a captain and her duties are rotated more fairly between herself and the rest of Rian's guard, including Taris, Korvaan, and another bodyguard, Qhan Khaleem. In this cycle, Naomi is not officially a part of Rian's guard, but stays close while learning to be a doctor.

Some things change, in this cycle: Rian is crowned king, marries Asmer al'Yibna, and adopts a daughter, Ayla, making her his sole heir when Asmer dies young. Other things stay the same: Mercer travels west to help Alarkian refugees and returns to betray Rian, only to be caught and executed; Taris and Lune are both killed while trying to stop the firebird organization from harming Rian and Soleil, and are buried with Soleil not even knowing Lune as her sister. No one can uncover a proper motive for Mercer betraying his closest friend, as he was known as a man uninterested in power, focusing on philanthropic efforts for most of his life.

Nearly twenty years pass, and the world becomes a darker, more dangerous place. Many countries have fallen into war and are left with destabilized governments, hopeless populaces, and smoldering cities. Aiko Shinya, once meant to take his father's place as an ambassador, disappears after returning to Tourran prior to a bloody civil war. Alarkia and Lijimata both tear one another apart, and Milash threatens war against Isaaria while the entire Kachin royal family is seemingly destroyed and the country left in ruins.

At this time, Septimus appears, seeking refuge for himself, his younger sister Teresa, and Teresa's two young children. Knowing Soleil is wary, Septimus returns most of her memories, as well as Rian's, devastating Soleil as she learns harsh truths about herself, Nusk, Taris, and Lune, as well as her parents. A conflicted Soleil demands Korvaan lock her cousins away someplace while she seeks out Rian. The pair comfort one another while speculating if it is possible to save those they have lost.

Whether they will succeed, however, remains to be seen.

One

I WAKE AT THE CHIME OF SEVENTH BELL. The castle may be running on a skeleton staff, yet every hour, on the hour, the bell is pulled. For as long as I can remember, I wake at seventh bell, though I have not trained my body for it specifically. The man in the castle cellar called Septimus claims this is because seventh hour is the hour that I was born, over forty-six years ago, on a cold winter solstice morning. But I have not yet decided whether I trust a thing Septimus says, let alone something so personal.

Currently, he is idling in our wine cellar while I decide what to do about him, the emaciated woman he calls his sister, and his two nephews. Making a decision in regards to him and the rest of my newly found family is what I look forward to least of all, today.

Rising, I make up my bed with quick, practiced movements, pulling the duvet tightly across the mattress until it is perfectly smooth. Then I move to my washroom to dress and wash my face and teeth. To keep it out of my way, I pull my long hair into a twisting braid down my back. Like Rian's hair, mine is now streaked with grey. The youth has been sucked from my face so that my cheekbones stand out severely. I imagine when I meet with folks on Rian's behalf, most are terrified of me. The long scar running from my temple to the bottom of my cheek on the left side of my face does not help, but I hardly asked to be cut in the face by a desperate Mercer Ralhan the morning I went to arrest him for treason. It is a reminder of the duty I have dedicated my entire life to—something Septimus threatens with his mere presence.

The first business of the day finds me reporting to the king's vast chambers, as I have every morning since the time Rian was crowned king. It used to be that Rian practically raced me in our morning preparations, always surprised by my efficiency since his wife Asmer took an hour at least. Now, I am anxious to see if he is awake at all.

After we watched the sunrise, Rian and I went to return inside when he collapsed on me. At first, I thought it was simply a bout of clumsiness; his foot slipping on a wet patch after yesterday morning's snow, perhaps. But no.

When I turned to chuckle at him, and help him to his feet, he did not move. By the time I brought Qhan and Naomi to help me, he was already running a high fever and sweating wildly.

Naomi soothed all worries, promising the fever would break soon, but hours passed, and nothing changed.

Naturally, that was when I stormed downstairs to the wine cellar. Septimus was sleeping there comfortably, like I had sent him to a vacation home by the sea. I interrogated him for several hours, demanding to know what he had done to Rian. He consistently claimed innocence in the situation.

This attempted interrogation resulted in me locking him in the wine cellar in anger and leaving him there overnight. I have already decided that if Rian's fever broke last night, I will question Septimus once more with the promise of happier accommodations if he cooperates. This time, I will bring Qhan with me to keep him honest. If Rian's health remains tenuous, I will leave Septimus in the wine cellar for at least another night.

While I am thinking up the worst of ways to punish my purported cousin, however, the king awaits. I dread entering Rian's rooms to find out, but I know there is no point in prolonging it.

Qhan and Valor stand guard outside Rian's bedroom door. Both are quite haggard, as if Rian's sudden illness has added a decade to them, each. Qhan nods to me and immediately goes to open the door. He does not mention seeing me a matter of hours ago, when Naomi forced me to sleep. I have explained what I can to Nusk about what has happened thus far, but he is so loyal that even if he does not believe me, he will still obey.

Inside Rian's bedroom, Mango looks up at me from his spot curled at the foot of the bed, blinks lazily, then lowers his head back down and folds his wings carefully. He also slept poorly, poor thing. He is so attached to Rian; I am certain he can sense the king's sickness enough to be distressed by it. He has been Rian's constant companion for nearly twenty years, now, and the sunblood dragon loves his master more than anyone or anything else in the world. For a dragon, that is critical.

I hasten to Rian's bedside, where he sleeps, unmoving. For a moment, I am terrified the worst has happened, but he breathes, still. He has encountered sickness before, naturally, though nothing as sudden and devastating as this. It concerns me mainly because I do not know what I will do if Rian fails to recover. Saving his life is my justification for putting my family through a thousand hells. If he dies now, I do not know what I will do.

But then he stirs, and blinks his weary eyes open. I forget how to breathe.

"So-leil?"

"Thank the Almighty," I sigh.

I close my eyes in relief for several seconds before I perch on the side of his bed. Part of me panics, telling me this is entirely inappropriate. But I am not truly Rian's bodyguard, I am his wife.

"How are you?" I say.

"Tired," he mumbles. "Feel terrible."

I feel his forehead. Still hot.

"Did Naomi check your fever?"

"Possibly," he says. "You would have to ask her. I do not recall."

I stroke back his damp bangs. "Oh, what am I going to do with you?"

Rian gives me a weak smile. "I'm afraid I cannot remember this either: was whatever happened yesterday real, or is this just one of the usual fantasies?"

I scoff and roll my eyes at him. "You are a terrible, shameless man."

He prepares for a full bout of banter, but then begins coughing. I worry he might get sick up, but Rian stops me before I can rise and points to the pitcher on his bed-side table. I pour him a glass, help him sit, and drink.

"I'm going to have Naomi come up and look after you," I tell him. "Do you think you could manage to eat, if she brought something simple?"

Rian mumbles something affirmative in nature.

"Good. I'm glad you're awake. I have much to see to today, but if I have the time, I will come back to look in on you later."

I leave his water glass close enough for him to reach it if he likes and then stand to leave. I came here with every intention of making certain Rian was recovering, but despite our fully restored memories, I feel strange while at his bedside. The intimacy feels put on. I can tell myself as many times as I like, based off my memories, that I am Rian's wife, yet it does not feel real.

Despite his weakness, Rian is still quick enough to grab my sleeve.

"Soleil," he whispers. I see the distress in his eyes. "Don't go. Please."

I struggle to find the right answer.

"Stay here, with me," he begs, and the pain in his voice is so palpable that I almost consider doing as he asks.

But I know this is still his fever talking. His eyes are glassy and his cheeks flushed; this panicky, depressed creature is not my husband. He is stronger than that. So, I must do what is necessary to save him, our children, and our country, regardless of how frightened he might be, now, in his sickness.

"Why won't you stay here with me? Stay. Until it is all over," he says.

"Your majesty, this will not end any time soon," I warn him. "And I think you know this as well as I do. We have at least one more lifetime to live—"

"I have grown weary."

"We must endure, your majesty. Once more. We are meant to have children of our own. Aside from Ayla. I will not raise them in a world as dark as this one."

"Soleil," he begs. "I am so tired."

"Our world is ending," I whisper. "Rian. I must find a way to stop this. We must to go back. But this time, we will do it together. You will have me."

He is so pale, the color completely drained from his face, so that he almost does not look like my Rian anymore.

"What if we only make it worse?" he asks, horrified. He shakes, his eyes flickering as they dart about the room. "Soleil, we should not play with time. You might have power over it, but…"

"Yes?" I demand, turning on him.

"Perhaps no one should have that power."

His words stop me from speaking again. I know he is still fevered; I know he is anguished, panicked, and confused. But his words make me think about things I fear are true. Perhaps he is right, part of me whispers. Perhaps I should cut my palms and heels and swear off using my fluke forever.

I tell myself Rian is not considering the consequences of such a thing. He cannot be; otherwise, he should know that denying me of my power would ensure our world fall into unimaginable suffering.

That we never save Lune, and Taris.

That I never meet my son.

I hesitate, then lean down and gently kiss Rian's burning forehead and stroke his sweaty bangs back for a second time. I need to find someone who can help him bathe. Qhan might do it. But if I am going to try and interrogate Septimus again, I will need his truth-sensing abilities.

"I will send Naomi to check on you," I promise Rian. "Stay here and rest for now. I will see you again presently. Be well."

"Sol-eil," I hear him whisper weakly, but I cruelly pretend not to hear him.

I leave in quiet haste. I do not know when it will be time for me to rewind our lives again, or what I will do afterwards, but I have no doubt it will happen. I know I must do so, even if it means going against Rian's wishes.

But first, I need answers. Obviously, this means speaking with Septimus. I am not happy about it, and I wish there were someone else I could ply answers from, but he is the only person who knows all.

Qhan and Korvaan both snap to attention the moment I leave Rian's room. I merely make eye-contact with Qhan and flick my fingers for him to follow me. Korvaan can handle contacting a replacement, for at least the next hour or so. While we walk down to the deepest depths of the palace, I leave word with one of the maids to find Naomi and have her reassess the king's health.

The air cools as we walk down towards the cellar. The palace is warm enough to combat the winter chill easily, but the cellar will have been kept cold. I had not considered that when I chose to sequester Septimus, but given how we find him lounging across several wine barrels, I would say he is comfortable enough.

I should not be surprised, yet here we are. No matter what, this man's feathers remain unruffled. His personality, irritatingly buoyant. Such forced optimism grates on my nerves.

The moment he hears my boots clicking on the stone floor, Septimus takes his time in rising. He turns those pale, white-lashed eyes on me, and it disquiets me that I cannot read his thoughts there.

I refuse to apologize for keeping him here so long, nor do I say anything about his restoring my memories. I do not trust this man, who calls himself my cousin, nor do I trust his wan, sickly sister. But I know that he has answers for me, and I will know what is true, so long as I have Qhan.

Qhan unlocks the wine cellar gate. The two guards I have had keeping watch on Septimus enter first, pulling in a small table and a pair of chairs they had been using to pass the hours comfortably. I want to look Septimus in the eye while I attempt this secondary interrogation. He is a slight man, about my own height, but he somehow still manages to look down on me. It is his arrogance, I believe, that rattles me most.

My alleged cousin watches this arrangement with amusement. He waits until after the guards have finished, leaving me and Qhan with him, before opening his mouth to speak, likely to say something biting.

"Before you say a word, put these on," I order, tossing a pair of Isaarian gloves to him.

Septimus raises an eyebrow. I doubt he can call on any reserves of power after spending two nights away from the moon and a day away from the sun, but I do not know his resilience. He could still have energy in reserve.

Still, he slides the gloves on and makes a show of it; of impressing upon me his so-called obedience.

"Better?" he offers.

"Sit," I order.

"If it pleases you."

I take a seat across the table from him, Qhan standing at my shoulder.

"Bit intimidating, this," Septimus admits.

It is tempting to throw myself out of my seat and haul him up by his lapels, but I manage to control myself.

"I will ask you one last time. What have you done to the king?" I demand, ignoring his comment and cutting straight to the thick of things.

Septimus sighs and rolls his eyes. When he first came here seeking refuge, he was respectful to me, but now he finds me unnecessarily hostile.

"I have said so once and I will say it again: I have done nothing but restore both of your memories. Or, most of your memories."

"Then why is he fevered, confined to his bed?" I demand.

"How should I know?"

"Speculate."

He runs his hands over his face, and thinks. "I suppose, if anything, it is the result of intense mental strain."

I narrow my eyes. "You claim he has done this to himself."

"That is more likely than any other explanation. All I did was give you your memories back. He is the one torturing himself over it."

"But he will recover," I press, trying not to show how desperate I am.

It is more peculiar, having so many forms of love crashing against one another in me, as every time I've fallen in love with Rian has compounded itself in my mind and heart. Every timeline, every kiss, every whisper in the dark as we giggled together as children and caressed each other in marriage assaults me. It is so much to manage; I do not know if I could bear the pain of losing Rian even just once more.

"If he wants to, he will," Septimus shrugs. "This will pass, in time, and eventually be no more than a bad memory."

I glare at him. "I don't know if you've noticed," I say through gritted teeth, "but bad memories seem to have more power than you would presume."

"So it seems," he admits.

"Now, I want the full story from you, from the moment you were born in the first Fate-damned cycle up to now."

"I can tell you approximately half of what you need to know," Septimus offers me, "but that will have to satisfy you for now."

"Give me all or give me nothing," I snap at him. "At this point, you are in no position to refuse me that."

He looks at me, then sighs and barely refrains from rolling his eyes again.

"Well, you see, Soleil, I would rather not give you 'nothing'. I would like to tell you what I can. Clear the air. Answer at least some of the questions I am certain you have. But no matter how much you ask, I will not give you every detail. I would apologize, only, I am not sorry. I know how you would react to some of those facts. For the sake of what is currently best for the world, I cannot tell you everything now. I will not."

I wait for a few moments, examining him in silence, trying to figure a way to call his bluff. There must be some form of leverage I can use over him to get him to talk. I would assume his sister and nephews, but as impetuous as I can be, I restrain myself in that sense. I would rather use them only as a last resort, as I know I could do little to harm them. Should Septimus sense that lack of conviction, I would lose all leverage altogether.

Time, then, for a different approach.

"Let us start simply, then: you claim to be a Magicsmith," I say coolly.

"I am a Magicsmith," he says. "Unfortunately. Trust me, there is nothing I would rather do than surrender my cursed heritage, but there is no denying what one is born with. Best to make use of it and try not to despair too much."

"Well, aren't you the dour fellow."

"Not really," Septimus claims. "I'm past that, for the most part. It merely comes out now and again in bits."

Qhan confirms this is truthful: Septimus is a Magicsmith. Never mind that most people believe Magicsmiths are only folk of legend. Septimus is a Smith, or, he is delusional enough to think he is. But he strikes me as someone far too calculating to claim insanity.

On to the next complication, then.

"You also claim that I am a Magicsmith," I say. "I have no reason to believe that. Even with the memories you have restored."

"But you are. You are a Smith with the ability to create new timelines. The only Smith in the world who has ever been gifted that fluke, in fact; you are quite the individual, Soleil Smith."

"Marson," I correct.

"By your father, yes. But my aunt's name was Olivia Smith. She was your mother," he says.

"I recall. Based on the memories you have released to me," I say. "But as my mother was not present much in my life, and I have no memories of you, I would not count on familial affection helping you out of this scenario."

"That was not my intent in saying so," Septimus says. "I merely thought you would be interested in hearing about our families and how they are associated with one another. Might support my 'claims' that you are a Magicsmith, as you insist on calling them."

"Your father, my mother. Siblings. I think I can manage that."

"There is more to it than that. I thought you wanted to know everything."

"Is this your way of promising to tell me everything?"

"Not even remotely. But about half is better than nothing, is it not?"

I get the feeling that Septimus might easily drive me mad, even without the use of his fluke available. I can't say for certain if he is smarter than me, but I suspect it.

I tap my fingers against the table before us. I like the fact that Septimus is at least conversational, and I know that Qhan will keep him truthful. But he cannot think that he is in any way running this interrogation. I do not want him to think he has the power, here.

"I would like you to answer the following questions for me. Understand?"

Septimus sighs. "It would be much easier if you allowed me to speak at my own pace."

Maybe so, but I am so stubborn it will probably get me killed one day. So, I ignore him and go on as if he never spoke.

"Qhan here will be able to tell if you are lying to me, so there is no point in that. Now, before we move on, I think there is something obvious that needs to be addressed. Where is your sister's husband?" I ask.

Septimus does not look me in the eyes, but replies evasively, "There is a war in the west."

"Dead, then?" I press.

He snorts, his mouth twitching into a barely concealed snarl.

"One can always hope, I suppose. Why do you think it took us so long to come see you?" he continues, when he notices my narrowed eyes. "My sister's husband is not a good man. It took me some time to pry her away from him."

"She wanted to stay?"

He shrugs.

"He terrified her. She married him when she was young and he controlled everything about her life. But then it took some time for her to bear him sons, and whatever meager sweetness he showed her quickly vanished. She has given him two boys, now, but the little one is deformed. Missing an arm. So, in her husband's eyes, she has failed him. He has made no illusions that the child is a burden he would rather not bear, and used that to manipulate my sister. But he went off to war. It took me some time, but I managed to coax her into coming with me, and to bring my nephews with."

I consider what he has said; I had not noticed Teresa's younger son was deformed at all. I must wonder at what variance of monster would dare assign a person's worth, like a god. Teresa's husband, I suppose, if Septimus is to be believed, but I struggle to imagine someone cruel enough that they would threaten to harm their own son over a so-called imperfection.

It is not an impossible story, but it sounds too rehearsed, too carefully reported. Septimus may be a good conversationalist, but there still must be some anxiousness in him, coming here before me and the king of Isaaria and making the claims he has.

"Would you please let me explain in my own way?" Septimus complains again. "It would make this easier for us both. What's the harm? Even if I'm not telling you everything, I'm still giving you information you need."

"No," I say shortly and go on. "So: we are both Smiths, cousins. Your brother-in-law is involved in the war in the west."

"And he is a monster," Septimus adds. "Don't forget that. That is a Fate-damned fact, so long as you are keeping count."

"Which side of the war is he on, then?" I challenge. "I would assume Alarkia, but I want to hear it from you."

I'd thought this would be the simplest of questions for Septimus to answer, but he hesitates and grimaces.

"I told you Teresa and I come from Alarkia, and that is true. Partially. Technically we are Alarkian—mixed blood as we are at this point. But we are also still the purest living line of Magicsmiths left in the world. Which means we're Isaarian-Alarkian, really," he explains.

"That is not an answer to the question asked," I point out.

Septimus thinks, then sighs. "I know you will not appreciate this explanation, but it is the truth, as I hope you will understand. You see, to the west of Alarkia and Lijimata both, behind the mountains, is a hidden country. A forgotten one. Or, at least a fragment of it. Lusch."

I bark a laugh at him automatically. I cannot help myself.

"Lusch?" I repeat. "As in—"

"Yes, the country the Grey family ruled over for hundreds and hundreds of years. Where they still rule, today. Teresa's husband is not on Alarkia or Lijimata's side. He is on the Grey's side."

"The Greys do not exist. And neither does Lusch," I say. "It was magical land that faded like most of the Fae's territory, and all but two of the Floating Islands. Stop using fairy tales as an excuse."

I wait, giving him the chance to amend his answer, but he doesn't. And when I look to Qhan for verification he gives me a hesitant nod.

"Almighty Bless, you're serious," I realize.

Septimus is not amused. "Why-oh-why is it so difficult for you to, well, firstly, listen to me without interrupting, and second, believe what I'm saying? You know I'm not lying," he adds, nodding towards Qhan.

"Qhan's fluke tells me if you're lying or not, but if you've lost your mind, you could only believe you are telling the truth. I suppose the Wolff family is real, too, then?" I challenge him.

I am mocking him because I feel I must. Because the truths he's alluding to admittedly frighten me.

"They were," he confirms. "I met them, once, as a child. In Valeia."

I try my best not to stare at him.

"Valeia does not exist and never did," I claim stubbornly.

Septimus is unimpressed by my insistences. "Oh, yes it did, and it still does. It's under where the last of the Floating Islands hang. Only now it does its best to remain cloaked from the rest of society. The last Queen of Valeia, the last of the Wolff rulers in fact, was considering bringing their society back into the world stage again, but then the Greys struck."

There is such a lament in his tone when he says so, I almost believe him with that alone. But it's a glance at Qhan that forces me to acknowledge the truth in these words.

"What about you, then? Lusch, Valeia, the Floating Islands. Are you going to reveal some secret homeland of the Smith family still exists as well? One previously unknown to everyone?"

"No. Not so far as I'm aware. Teresa and I lived in Lusch and Alarkia, for most of our lives," Septimus explains. "We are—or, *were*, hopefully—'owned' by the Greys. The Smith family has been for generations, now. Their pet Magicsmiths. Whenever they could not procure something from their witchcraft, their *Dadj'zcha*, they forced us to accommodate."

"They are causing the attacks," I say. "Teresa's monsters. Your sister. These Grey people wanted monsters, and had your sister make them."

Septimus scrunches his nose. "In a way. Some of them. Yes," he confirms. "You cannot blame her for them, though," he insists. "She is a gentle soul. Even beyond that, Teresa only accounts for some of the Grey's monsters."

"What is that meant to mean?"

He groans and throws his head back.

"The Greys have had Teresa making monsters for them for some time, now, but not all these 'demon' sightings are her creations. I'm sure your husb—ah…the *king* could confirm this, as the expert, but demons rarely attack people so physically. They prefer to prey on the mind. Tempt people do terrible things. Hang on their backs. They can be seen by some, yes, but…"

"But what?" I demand

Septimus thinks, then attempts to address the issue from a different angle.

"Chronologically speaking: the Greys manufactured political tension to spark violence in the west, between Alarkia and Lijimata. But that was easy for them; the two countries have always had tension. In more peaceful lands, they needed a different approach. So, they had Teresa make monsters to spread fear and panic. And in fear and panic, people lose their heads. They care only about themselves. Do horrible things in the name of self-preservation. And that is what then drew the demons to those areas. Which in turn sparked a vicious cycle of mankind doing terrible, terrible things to one another in fear. Do you understand this?"

"The conclusion you expect me to come to, then, is that the Greys want Rian dead and my son to never exist. That they have manipulated a world filled with war and panic, and have on occasion even attempted to kidnap me so they can control me and make certain I cannot wind back the timeline again. But you refuse to tell me why they're doing any of this," I confirm.

"For now. I'm afraid you would not believe me," Septimus says. "Though you did, once. You were more trusting then. And desperate, maybe."

I stare at him, then look to Qhan. Rian's bodyguard looks just as shocked and confused as I feel, yet when he meets my eyes, he gives a slow nod. Septimus is telling the truth about everything he has said, thus far.

Septimus watches the two of us. He gives us a few moments to settle our thoughts before speaking again.

"The Greys are the enemy you have been unable to defeat," he confirms. "They are the ones who bear the firebird pins. The ones who killed Taris and

Lune Qurvo. They have plans for this world that your son and husband, by merely their *existence,* would thwart. And that is all I can tell you for now. I swear. Anything more, and this all ends in catastrophe."

"But how do you know that?" I ask.

Septimus shrugs. "I'm afraid I need you to trust me, Soleil. And until you do, I cannot tell you the whole story."

"I will not trust you without the whole story," I counter.

This does not sway him.

"Then it seems as if, for now, we are at an impasse. I don't mind staying down here while waiting for you to come to your conclusions," he adds. "Truly, I have suffered worse accommodations. I understand that all this is difficult to take in. Please. Take your time. Well, not too much time, but a day. Once you have processed all this, come see me, and I will tell you more."

I consider his offer and push down my usual fiery temperament. Septimus is not refusing me anything. He is merely insisting he cannot explain this instant. While I may not understand why that is, it is something I can live with. Rian does appear to be on the mend, slow-going as it may be. Now that my anger is starting to ebb, I must admit, Septimus and his little family do not appear threatening. In fact, they came here as refugees.

Though I do not want to trust Septimus—and remain wary of him for the sake of the king, Ayla, and myself—I need time to think. So long as I have Qhan with me whenever I speak with him, I think I can trust what Septimus says enough to use him. Admittedly, I do not know what to do next. I suspect that he does.

"Very well," I agree.

A corner of Septimus' mouth quirks, pleased. But not smug.

"I'll concede you have told me the truth thus far, and that you appear to have no ill will towards the king," I go on. "But I am afraid I do not yet trust you enough to let you leave the wine cellar."

"That is reasonable," he says. "I am a strange man appearing from nowhere, claiming to have all the answers. Come back to see me in time, and I promise, I will tell you more once I know you won't take my knowledge and do something foolish with it. But please look after Teresa and the boys in the interim. None of this is their fault. I would have come to you alone, but there is no safer place for them, in the world, than here. And they needed to escape the Greys."

I narrow my eyes at him, but I see no signal from Qhan indicating that he is lying. "I thought you said that your sister was fleeing her husband."

"Him as well."

I take another ten seconds to stare Septimus down. Yet again I must admit that I do not sense any malice from him. No intent to deceive.

"Very well," I finally repeat, standing. "I promise we will take care of your sister and nephews so long as they are our guests."

Septimus breathes out a sigh. "Thank you. And not to be presumptuous, but to be completely presumptuous: it is actually quite cold down here. Mind sending down a blanket or two?"

I know I ought not glare at him because that is a reasonable request and I cannot think of a way he could possibly use blankets to get into mischief.

"I will have someone come to try and keep you comfortable," I say, and make a mental note to do so. "I suppose you will be wanting to eat as well?"

"If it is not too much trouble. But see to my sister first, if you must choose. She has not been well. And please promise…Well. Teresa has suffered enough. If you want to interrogate someone, question me all you like. But leave her be," Septimus warns me.

"I will question you alone if you'll answer one thing for me honestly and fully right now," I pose. "Otherwise, I'll ask Teresa whatever I feel necessary."

Septimus does not want to bargain with me this way, I can tell, but he is too intrigued to refuse me outright.

"Proceed," he allows, and gestures for me to ask my question. Whether he answers it or not is up to him.

"How did your sister survive her magic-sickness?"

Septimus blinks, startled. I can tell that even Qhan did not expect that question. Of all the things I could have asked, I choose that? But I have my reasons. Teresa Smith is the first person in the world I have known of to not only survive magic-sickness, but appear perfectly normal afterwards, save for a little scarring. I do not know how someone could have saved her from corrupt magic, but I suspect such a thing can only be done with an extremely powerful fluke or, perhaps, even *Dadj'zcha*. Either way, I think the answer will tell me more about the Smiths' pasts than anything Septimus has confirmed so far.

"She…Teresa…Someone saved her," he finally says haltingly.

His reluctance in answering appears to prove my thesis.

"How?"

He grimaces, twisting his face as he tries to find a way to answer me without telling more than he wants to.

"By taking her sickness…and giving it to someone else."

"That is impossible," I say, trying to goad him into giving me more.

"Evidently not," Septimus claims shortly. "There. I answered. Will you promise to leave her be? She is no longer magic-sick, but she is still ill. She cannot be put under strain. Do you understand?"

"I understand she might tell me things you can't or won't," I say, and stand to leave quickly before Septimus can fully realize what that means.

I am by the door when he jumps to his feet, slamming his hands down on the table.

"I answered your question—*honestly*. Leave her be."

"I said 'honestly' and 'fully'," I remind him while I hover in the doorway. "And I think we both know there is much you are withholding from me, even with such a simple question. If you will not tell me who saved your sister's life, I'm sure she will."

He is protesting when Qhan and I leave, but he does not try to stop me. I ignore him and allow Qhan to lock him securely in the cellar. I'll be sure to pass along the order to keep Septimus relatively comfortable and fed well, but I have much to see to today myself. Firstly, seeing about Teresa Smith.

"Captain, are you really going to interrogate the woman?" Qhan asks.

I can tell he does not approve. He has seen Teresa Smith, after all, and she strikes quite the pitiful figure. I cannot imagine anyone suspecting ill of her, at least based on appearances.

"I will not interrogate," I reassure. "But I do want to speak with her. I will guise it all as friendly conversation. If she tells me anything new, then it will be useful for us. But I will not intimidate her."

Qhan is understandably hesitant. He has never refused an order before, and still will not, now, regardless of what I ask him to do. However, I understand why he may feel the urge to protect this woman and her children. After all, he has protected Rian and Ayla for his entire adult life.

Even if Qhan does not understand, there is much at stake here, for me and for Isaaria both. I don't want to think these newcomers are a threat to the king, but I cannot know that for certain. Rian becoming ill was suspiciously timed. Even if I have no proof that Septimus was involved, I need to take care. I have kept Rian alive this long; I refuse to let harm come to him, now.

"They claim to be my cousins, Qhan," I remind him. "My family."

He knows how important that is to me. Even if he cannot understand my newly acquired knowledge about Lune's identity, and what she meant to me, he knows the mystery of my birth parents and how Nusk came to raise me has always troubled me.

"Yes, Captain," he says.

"I will be as fair as I can about it," I promise. "But I have been naïve for too long. I must know of the evils we face. It is for the good of everyone."

"You do not need to justify yourself to me, Captain," Qhan claims, though I'm sure he is relieved.

"Even so. Return to the king," I tell him. "See if he has improved any in the past hour. I will inform you of new developments with the Smiths if necessary. Otherwise, tomorrow, we will try again with Septimus."

"I would be careful with him, Captain," Qhan warns. "He has told nothing but the truth thus far, yet he is concealing much. He knows lying is pointless, so he will withhold information instead for as long as he can."

"And there is no real way to know how much he is withholding. I know," I agree. "We will proceed with caution. But even if he has been sent here to manipulate us, I don't think Septimus is much of a physical threat, now. Nor is his sister. We will keep them gloved, and inside at all times. But there is no reason why we cannot act courteously. If we are good hosts, Septimus might think me 'reasonable' enough to tell us more."

"Very good, Captain."

We part ways. I am sorely tempted to walk Qhan back to the king first, to look in on him myself, but I manage to resist. I am not sure how Rian would react to seeing me again so soon. Given how he wanted nothing more this morning than for me to stay with him, I don't want to torture him.

Qhan will look after him. Naomi will check in on the king dutifully as well. I need to focus on the Smiths. It is the best I can do to help, with my skill set.

I bring two guardsmen to accompany me, though I am not worried about Teresa posing a physical threat. In fact, I am somewhat embarrassed to see her again, since I last had her and her sons locked in an abandoned part of the palace and have not bothered to see to their needs since. Yes, I was angry with Septimus, but Teresa's children are quite young. I should have been more aware of that, and more sensitive to her likely concerns.

I must be careful in the coming hours. I must keep my word to Qhan, and myself, and keep myself in check. While answers are important, I want Teresa to trust me, foremost. If I am too insistent or aggressive—which is to say if I act as I normally would—it will frighten her.

Leaving the guards outside, I unlock the door to the Smiths' room and give a warning knock. Teresa is awake when I enter, but clearly fatigued. She forces herself to stand and bow to me when I make my entrance, yet I can see that every little motion exhausts her.

I observe her for a few moments. It is possible she was astoundingly beautiful, once, but she looks more like a ghost than a fair maiden, now. Her sallow face is gaunt, her coloring ghastly, and her hair dull and thinning. Her lips are chapped, her magic-sickness scars stark against her white face, and there are tiny sores at the corners of her mouth, as if it has been a long time since she has consumed water properly. The bodice of her dress was once covered with delicate fabric flowers and golden piping. It is now more gray than pink, and the gold is flaking off in pieces.

Worst of all, she is so dreadfully thin, it is clear to me she has not eaten well in a long time, perhaps years. My cousin admittedly does host a naturally small frame, but even that is no excuse for how she looks, now. I see her illness in the way her collarbones stand up starkly, her cheekbones jab out, and her bony hands tremble continuously. It occurs to me that I could possibly break her arm as easily as I would snap a twig in the woods.

I should find her a doctor immediately.

Her children look well enough. I suppose she has been working hard to take good care of them. The younger boy is still asleep, curled up on the bed, while the elder sits on the window seat and draws pictures on the glass in the morning frost. He turns away when he hears me enter, and stares at me with those large, dark eyes. Those are his father's eyes, I'd wager, as his mother's and brother's are blue. The caution he observes me with is the sort that should not belong to a boy so young.

"I'm sorry to have kept you waiting," I say to Teresa.

"That's quite all right," she says, so quiet and meek.

When she looks up at me, I find her eyes unfocused. I recall she may need spectacles to see properly, and has lost them.

"Thank you for the lodgings," she says. She sounds as if she truly appreciates it. "It is nice to let the boys sleep in a bed again."

As this portion of the palace had been closed off for years, this room is barely passable for a vagabond in hiding let alone so-called guests. There is no soap in the washroom, the linens have not been cleaned and aired in ages, and the entire place is likely mustier than Teresa and her boys are.

"I'm moving you someplace else," I decided. "I will have someone come with new clothing for you all, as well as toiletries, and you can bathe."

I am off-handed with this generosity, and dismissive, but her cheeks flush pink, and I know she is truly grateful. I can already tell that she has tried to sponge-bathe her sons in the washroom, and she moves carefully, as if she is afraid of dirtying the room simply by standing in it.

"Oh. Thank you," she says, tucking her dirty hair back behind her ears, overly conscious of how she looks. She glances up at me nervously and licks her lips. "Would it be possible…for me to see my brother, soon? I don't know where he is right now, but…"

"I had a nice, long conversation with Septimus earlier today," I say shortly. "You will be seeing him before long, I'm sure. In the meantime: I would like to move you and your sons to more comfortable accommodations."

She is hesitant, as if she wants to press the issue of being reunited with her brother, but then nods.

"I understand," she stammers. "We will go where you want us to."

The way she says it unintentionally insults me.

"It's what will be better for you," I say. "You'll be more comfortable. And I'd wager your boys are hungry, yes? A bath, clothing, food—"

"What do you want me to do?" she interrupts.

"I beg your pardon?"

"What must I do, in exchange?" she presses, her face suddenly taking on a blank look. "You should know now, I will do anything for my children, but I at least want to know, first."

I am too surprised to speak. With every passing second, I know, Teresa's wariness grows, but I'm speechless by her selfless stoicism. It makes me curious about her, but also somewhat afraid of her.

"Nothing."

"Nothing?"

There is both suspicion and surprise in Teresa's tone. Again: she unintentionally insults me. Though, perhaps I deserve it.

"You are our—that is, you are the king's guests, here," I explain. "He has welcomed you here, and has told me to take the greatest care of you."

This is not entirely true, but as I know Rian better than anyone else in the world, I'm sure this is what he'd say if he could currently think straight.

"Where is the king?" Teresa asks.

"At present, that is none of your concern," I say simply. "You will see him when I deem it appropriate and not a moment before."

She looks at the ground and nods.

I know I am already making a mess of things.

"Now, if you don't require much assistance, I can have you moved to your new rooms presently," I say. "I suspect you'll find them a great improvement."

"Of course. Damen," she starts, and her little blue-haired boy leaps up from his seat at the window.

"I'm ready, Mama. I'll get our things," he insists hastily, trying to help her.

The belongings he speaks of are meagre: two small packsacks, and one larger satchel, all practically falling apart. I'll have to have them done away with, and replaced. I'll admit, I'm curious to see what is inside of each.

Teresa, meanwhile, has moved to the bed. She perches on the side of it, and whispers to her younger son, coaxing him, trying to wake him gently. But he is tired, and ornery, having had to endure such a lengthy journey with few of the luxuries I'm sure they're used to, given Teresa's dress. It is ruined, now, but it once must have been the loveliest of things.

I step up beside her when it is clear that, in hopes of not taking up my time much, she is going to try and carry her son.

"Allow me," I offer.

As I am moving them to a much nicer wing, there is something of a walk involved, and Teresa is weak. I think we both know she would be in danger of collapsing, trying to carrying her son. She is hesitant to let me take her place, but acquiesces and thanks me in a humble murmur. The child does not fully wake when I pick him up, and rests his head on my shoulder tiredly.

I lead the way out the door, and though Teresa flinches when she sees the guards, she follows me without mentioning them. Her older son does take her hand, though, to either comfort her or reassure himself. I give my orders to the guards in Isaarian, and I know Teresa is uncomfortable. But now I know she does not speak Isaarian. That will allow me some level of flexibility.

"Come along," I say, and start off, using my long stride to set the pace.

We are quiet as we walk through the halls. My boots and the guards' click impressively, but Teresa's worn-out footwear make mere shuffling sounds. Her gait is tired and dragging. Her son must take half-skip steps every now and again to keep up on his little legs.

As we approach the currently inhabited portions of the palace, Teresa is visibly awed by the grandeur. Her elder son gazes at the decorated ceilings and walls, but does not speak. Occasionally I hear a gasp of surprise from him, but he is mature for his age. He knows to keep his mouth shut, especially around someone like me.

"Have you never seen pictures of the palace before?" I ask.

I had heard previously that Alarkian schools taught decent world history courses and was sure they would at least have some black and white photographs of the palace, given the rise in popularity of photo cameras. It is famous, especially with the Solunium Hub attached.

Teresa shakes her head.

"I remember hearing about the Pyrian Palace as a girl," she says hesitantly. "Our Aunt Liv, she…She told us stories about being here, sometimes. About how beautiful it was."

Olivia. My mother.

"I'm impressed she remembered at all," I say, trying not to be dismissive about it. "Given what else she forgot."

Teresa bites her lower lip.

"She only mentioned she had daughters once," she whispers. "Septimus says it is because she didn't want…for anyone to know about you. For safety."

"Mmm."

There are a few seconds of silence as we continue to walk, before Teresa ducks her head and whispers:

"I'm sorry."

She has startled me enough that I nearly stop walking. It is not that I don't appreciate the apology, as she and her little family did barge into my life and overcomplicate things for me spectacularly. But I suspect that something else has prompted Teresa to say so.

"Pardon?"

"Your mother left to look after my family," she says haltingly. "Sometimes it made me feel as if…as if we stole her from you. And Lune."

I realize, then, that I hate hearing Teresa say my sister's name. That, somehow, I miss Lune, even though I barely knew her to begin with. There is something significant gone from my life, without Lune and Taris present.

I want them here. I want Lune to sing at special events and to banter with Taris. I miss how irritating the two of them could be, in different ways.

I feel reasonable anger towards my mother, but the stronger emotion I resent Teresa for prompting is sorrow.

I loathe trying to manage these new emotions. I am convinced it is Septimus' fault I'm feeling them in the first place. Otherwise, I would not remember Lune enough to miss her.

"My mother made her own choices," I snap, and walk faster.

Two

TERESA AND HER ELDER SON follow me dutifully in silence for the rest of our walk. The suite I have decided upon is unique in that it is a single, large room with an attached washroom. There is a quaint four-person dining set on a dais by the door, a set of small twin beds hidden behind folding cupboards, a living set of sofa and double chairs, plus a marvelous wooden wardrobe and a master bed with canopy that should suit Teresa well enough.

The view from the window-seat is one over the gardens, which have been primed for the winter weather to look particularly enchanting with the snowfall. In fact, a light snow has started this morning, peacefully breaking into the new day.

When Teresa enters and sees the layout of the room, she barely withholds a gasp, and her elder son runs to the window, to see the snow-covered gardens. He drops their bags on the ground heedlessly, amazed by the view.

I look at Teresa's face, and see the perplexed expression, the wariness, her frown. I'd said she was going to experience a change in accommodations, but this is clearly much nicer fare than what she expected.

"Mama?" comes a tiny, nervous voice from my shoulder.

Her younger son has awakened, and is frightened to find himself propped on my hip. I hand him off to Teresa when he reaches for her.

"Damen, get off the window seat, darling," Teresa says quietly.

"He can stay if he so chooses," I say. "These are your rooms, after all."

Teresa does not speak, holding her youngest tightly against her. Her arms are shaking from exhaustion but I doubt she will listen to any advice I give. So, I walk down the steps into the bedroom proper and begin to settle them in, picking up their abandoned bags to hang them on the foot of the bed.

"These should suit your sons," I say, folding back the double doors of the cupboard beds. "And I will have someone come to light the fire; warm the room, some. It has been unoccupied for a long time, now."

Teresa eventually must put her son down. The elder one immediately turns and gestures for his brother to join him.

"Look, Aiden. It is just like home, but better, because we can all be together," he says.

His little brother reaches to take his hand, while looking around. After a while, Aiden nods, as if agreeing, and approving. The children like the room, even if their mother does not trust my good intentions. Fair enough; I approve of Teresa's caution, considering she has two children to look after. Her sons depend on her. She would be foolish to trust me outright.

Damen is eyeing the two closet-beds with some anticipation, clearly wanting to pick one out for himself already. One has blue pillows and bedding, the other, yellow. I cannot tell which one he prefers, but I think it is exciting for him to see how he could close the closet doors and hide himself away in a private little nook.

Teresa notices her son's interest. She hesitates, then walks past me with her shoulders hunched and joins them.

"It's much too early to think about sleep, again," she says with a weak, but light tone. "But let us pick out your beds for you and get you unpacked a little."

The younger boy, now perfectly awake, releases his brother's hand to tug on Teresa's dress. She obliges him, leaning down to his level so he can speak to her.

"Mama, we'll get everything all dirty," he whispers, distressed.

"I will have new clothing brought for you if you'd like to get them washed up," I say before Teresa can reply. "There will be some time, yet, before breakfast. You may as well."

She glances up at me, but I cannot tell if the look in her eyes is grateful or wary. Still, she brings the boys to the washroom, careful to first take their shoes off, as if to keep from possibly dirtying the carpet any further than they may have already.

"I'm afraid your clothes and shoes will have to be disposed of," I admit. "Burned, likely."

Teresa is pained by this idea, for a moment, but then nods. I wonder if she resents the idea of having to do away with something from "home". But she will not argue over something so simple. I'm sure she thinks she will have other, more important battles to fight.

The suite's washroom is large, with proper toiletries, towels, robes, and the like. There are even two sinks, and both a deep ceramic bathtub and a modern shower set in the right-hand corner. The tiles are off-white and gray in style, some with tiny blue fish set in them. Aiden immediately crouches down in awe and pokes at them. I note that I have only ever seen him use his right hand for anything and consider what Septimus said, about him being deformed. I cannot see his left arm, but I know I soon will, given Teresa's intentions.

I make a quick detour, outside the room, to speak to one of the guards and give him some instructions regarding what I'd like some maids to bring in for our weary travelers. I tell him after to check on Septimus, in the basement, to make sure he was seen to as promised.

Back inside the washroom, Aiden is still crouched down tracing the different kinds of fish with a finger. Damen, meanwhile, has helped his mother find several sets of towels, combs, and soaps. He is setting them all in a neat pile on a chair next to the bathing tub.

"Aiden, come here," Teresa says, leaning over to start the water running in the tub. "It's time to get you washed up."

"Mama, did you see the fishes?" he whispers to her, barely noticing me as I stand in the doorway.

"Yes, darling, they are lovely. I'll ask for some paper for you, later, and you can draw them. How about that?"

"Can you draw them? Your pictures are prettier," Aiden says.

Teresa almost smiles. "I'll teach you how to draw them so yours are pretty, too," she promises. "Now, up and over."

"Do not keep your mother waiting," I tell him.

Aiden does not turn to look at me, but immediately scampers over to Teresa.

She begins to help her sons undress, peeling their soiled clothing off and, strangely, folding it all in a neat pile. I warned her it will all have to be burned, and she agreed, which makes the fact that she now still bothers to fold the clothes curious to me.

Teresa leaves the boys' underclothes on, for now, so they are not completely nude, likely because they may be embarrassed in that state in front of me. I cannot help but stare for a few moments, at her younger boy, Aiden. The child's entire left arm is a cheap wooden prosthetic, hinging at the shoulder, elbow, and wrist. The fingers do not move. He appears comfortable with its presence, but lets it flap about as a completely useless appendage: it exists for cosmetic purposes only.

Teresa moves tentatively with me watching her, but pretends as if she is at ease, for her boys' sakes. As the bath fills with water, soaps and oils activating and swirling about, she starts to sponge-clean the children again, as if she is afraid of allowing them into the washtub while so filthy. Once finished, she removes the final pieces of their clothing and, before I can offer to help, lifts both boys into the bath.

Aiden is immediately pleased to be washing. His mother helps him detach his prosthetic to clean it and the stump at his shoulder while he lifts stacks of bubbles onto his brother's head, gives himself a frothy beard, and blows soap suds across the room. Damen is more serious.

"It's fine, Mama. I can do this," he insists, trying to take the soap and washcloths from her. "You can get clean, now, too."

He is trying to be a good son and brother: helpful, and thoughtful. But Teresa hesitates. She is unreasonably nervous and I take note.

"I will wash later," she says uncomfortable, and will not look at me.

"There is a shower there," I say, nodding towards the corner. "I'll watch your boys. Otherwise, you'd have to leave them alone, to wash yourself 'later'," I add. "Something tells me you would rather not do that."

Teresa tightens her mouth as she nods, agreeing with me. But there is still something worrying her. Of her two children, the elder picks up on her nervousness instantly, tuned to it.

"Mama?" Damen asks, a slight anxiety about him. Aiden is too busy using his prosthetic as a bath toy to notice.

Teresa smiles at him, trying to reassure him. "All is well, darling. I'll be right here. It will be so nice for us all to be clean again, won't it?"

The boy surprises me by saying something to his mother in a language I am completely unfamiliar with. Teresa stiffens, her eyes flicking towards me, but then responds cautiously. Her speech is much more halting and uncertain. It oddly sounds as if her son knows whatever language they are speaking better than she does, which posits intriguing implications. I know Septimus claimed they are not exactly from Alarkia. They must, then, be speaking Lusch.

"It will be all right, dear," Teresa reassures, switching back to Alarkian. "I promise. Be good to your brother," she adds, and then goes about collecting the necessary components for her wash.

Teresa waits to undress until she is concealed by the opaque glass of our modern shower unit, no doubt to spare her modesty. It occurs to me too late to offer her assistance in learning the unit's functions, but she manages. Over the shower door cascades layers of her western clothing: her pink dress, the layers of Alarkian petticoats and their soiled hems, her drawers and corsetry. They will go to be burned as well, along with her sons' clothes.

Shortly after she starts the water, a waterfall steam begins to pour from the top of the shower compartment. Damen is doing a good job of cleaning up his brother while Aiden is still preoccupied pretending his prosthetic is a fish. I decide the boys are safe enough in the bath, for now, and decide to take the time to go through their belongings. It has to happen at some point, I know, and I would rather not have to do it under Teresa's watchful eye.

I am careful to keep my ears open, confident they are old enough to take a bath on their own without drowning themselves. So long as I can hear

Damen and Aiden both, they are fine. I will be quick about searching their things in the bedroom and then be back to watch them as soon as I can.

The children's bags carry a few toiletries wrapped together to keep them from getting lost, two changes of clothes, mittens, scarves, and hats, some student's supplies Teresa has clearly tried to use to start their schooling, and little pouches full of spare underclothes and socks. Aiden's packsack has a few personal belongings by means of a small, knit octopus, prayer beads for a tiny child's hands, ointments for his prosthetic and missing arm, what I assume to be his favorite book—with illustrations done by his own mother I note—and a series of hand-written and hand drawn stories that Teresa has kept rolled up and tied together with twine.

Damen also has a book, along with an assortment of natural souvenirs: a series of leaves and flowers he probably thought were pretty, a dried-out daisy crown that reminds me of when I taught Ayla how to make such things, and a handful of pretty rocks that Teresa likely was forced to limit. Instead of further stories written from his mother, however, I find an opened envelope stuffed with five letters. From his father. For each of his birthdays.

I flick my eyes over them in curiosity. There is no signed name, the man only refers to himself as "your father" for Damen's sake. But it does give me some small insight into the man. Much as Septimus has claimed he hopes the fellow is dead, I can say at the very least that he loves his eldest son.

There is not much in Teresa's bag in comparison. Only one other dress, toiletries, underclothes, socks. And a few small, curious items: a small, plain mirror I do not open, a Theebin prayer book with a beautiful image of the Queen of Heaven on the cover, and an expensive-looking Kachin hair pin that I am certain I have seen before, somewhere.

It occurs to me, while I repack their bags, that Septimus did not bring much with him at all, and certainly few personal items, aside from his clothing.

Deciding there is no reason not to let the Smiths keep these belongings, as they are not at all dangerous, I repack the three bags and put them back where I found them. From what I can hear, Aiden is playing with the taps in the bathtub, adding more hot water while Damen tells him not to overfill it.

After returning to the washroom, I fold my arms and wait in the doorway once more as if I had never left. Damen and Aiden are looking much better, now that they are clean. Damen is, I will admit, dutifully looking after his brother, and is careful to scrub clean every inch of himself and the younger boy, including behind their ears. Aiden thinks such a thing is hilarious, but is happy to see all the dirt coming off on the wash cloths. I suspect, of the two boys, he is more sensitive to grime.

I glance at the shower, which is starting to smell sweet with soap. Though her shape is mostly obscured behind the glass, I can at least make out Teresa's outline enough to realize something is odd about it. She is a slim woman, made thinner by their harsh traveling and her previous lifestyle. But her stomach is swollen in just the right place to make me realize after a moment that it is not, in fact, her stomach, but her womb.

She is with child, and she's trying to hide it. By my estimation, she is over half-way there, but her secrecy is helped by the fact that she appears to carry her child low in her abdomen, and the dress she was wearing cut above the curve, almost completely concealing it under the flouncing of her skirts.

If her dress had been fit tighter, closer to her skin, it would have been obvious. But Teresa has carefully mastered that physical illusion. No doubt her well-laced Alarkian corset assisted in the illusion of her falsified waistline.

With the facts all in order, I come to the natural conclusion one might suppose in these circumstances. I rarely boast brilliance, but intelligence is practically optional here: Teresa has three children. Her husband has two.

I'm in the middle of trying to decide how I should confront Teresa about the matter when her sons draw my attention once more.

"Oh, lady?" the elder boy asks. He looks at me with these big, dark eyes, as if partially terrified of me. "We're coming out, now. Don't look. Please?"

"Won't you need help with your brother?" I point out.

"No. I can get him. But really: don't look."

I turn to the side and hold my hand up to block my view, to give them privacy. I am ready to move, in case they slip, but otherwise let them emerge on their own. There is sloshing, as Damen clambers out of the water first, then reaches back in to pull his brother out. I'm worried they'll hurt themselves on the hard tile floor, but they somehow manage.

"Right. You can look, now," Damen says.

I drop my hand to see that he has wrapped a towel around his skinny waist, and is helping his one-armed brother with the same.

They are both small-boned and slim, I note, but as I'm not accustomed to little people in general, it's possible they're normal sized for children with their frames. Either way, I find myself overcome with the fierce desire to feed them until they cannot manage a bite more.

"Your clothes will be here shortly," I tell them.

Damen looks at me for a second, then gives me a short nod. Mimicking his mother's behavior, I note. He pushes his little brother forward towards the sinks and the mirrors. His head barely clears the countertop, so Damen first brushes his brother's hair down and then stands on his tiptoes to fix his own. I would offer to help, but I suspect that would not be appreciated.

"Mama?" Damen calls. "What do I do with Aiden's arm?"

There is an additional splashing of water from the shower. Teresa rinsing her hair out, likely. Or squeezing the excess moisture from it.

"Leave it for now, darling," she says. "I'll help him in a moment."

"Yes, Mama," Damen says.

I feel awkward standing there and waiting for Teresa to finish, so I drain the water out of the washtub. Damen has his brother sit on the floor, and they begin talking about those little tile fish again. I get the feeling, from what I've noticed and what I found in their bags, that Teresa's children are equally interested in the fantastic and natural world around them. Regardless of what she put them through, running with them, she has tried to be a good mother. That is more than evident.

After about another minute, the shower water shuts off. A towel and robe disappear from where they had been flung over the top to hang. Teresa emerges in the robe, her folded towel clasped tightly over her torso. As I've already guessed at what she's trying to hide, I barely give her a glance. But the robe's sleeves and length are short on her, and I notice there are faded bruises up and down her arms that look like they are taking too long to heal. And there is something else; something worse and not too old, yet. A burn wound covers most of her lower left arm, including over the top of her hand.

There is a knock at the suite door; the maids bringing clothes for our guests. The food should be here shortly, I should hope. I allow the two maids entry, holding the door for them as their arms are both full of clothing options and shoes. We will hardly be providing a full wardrobe, but there are at least a few options for Teresa and her sons.

Back in the washroom, I find Aiden with his prosthetic arm reattached and Teresa crouched down near the cupboards under the sinks. I'm about to ask what she's looking for when she pulls out a pair of scissors and gets to work trimming her sons' hair. When finished, she turns the scissors on her own damp locks and cuts about half of it off, so that her hair hangs at her shoulders. It is not an even cut, but I do not offer to help her fix it. I do not think she'd want me that close to her with a pair of scissors.

Once Teresa is finished and allows me her attention once more, I bring forward the maids to present their dress options.

"Clothing for each of you," I say. "Not fitted, but hopefully close enough. There will be night clothes in the drawers of your room, as well."

I have procured for them three pairs of day-clothes, two sets of evening wear, and two sets of night-dress, each, as well as underclothes. I make a note to have a cobbler fit them for proper shoes as soon as possible.

Teresa looks through the day-clothes and selects items for them all. I motion to the maids to pack away everything else. They leave the washroom to do so, but I stay behind, and merely turn my back, until Teresa murmurs that she and the boys are finished dressing. I'd assumed they would require some assistance—Isaarian styles are quite different from western ware, after all—but Teresa manages on her own.

They, all together, look much more presentable now that they are clean and clothed. The boys are dressed in matching blue tunics, embroidered with silver birds, and soft trousers. Both belonged to Aloysius Pike II, Grand Prince Vásan Pike's son, at ages three and five, respectively. The silver Tochia birds belong to the Pike house, after all, but I doubt anyone will mind me borrowing them. His mother, Yvette, kept everything of her son's, as if in the vain hope she may one day have use of the little clothes again. Even I could not have predicted my cousin's children would make use of them.

Teresa, meanwhile, is wearing one of the queen's old gowns: she is a good bit taller than Asmer was, so the dress only reaches her lower calves, but the sleeves were originally intended to be long, and Asmer always preferred a clean, flowing style with few restrictive pieces, even for fashion's sake.

I'd have asked Ayla to lend Teresa some gowns, only Ayla is even shorter than Asmer was, and I know for a fact she does not have anything styled in a manner that might help tastefully conceal a pregnancy.

"One last thing," I say, as Teresa finishes straightening out her son's tunics.

I know it is possible she'll balk at this final request, but I suspect that if I tell her Septimus readily complied, she will as well. The gloves I hold out in offering will suffice for a time, and are versatile enough to match all their clothing options. I will have them fitted for gloves if I can find anyone left to make them. Otherwise, these will have to make-do.

Teresa hesitates in reaching out for the gloves and flicks her eyes at me.

"I understand it is Isaarian custom to wear these," she starts.

"If you're about to ask if they're necessary, I'm afraid they are, in their entirety," I say. "For yourself and your sons."

"No, it's...We will wear them," Teresa promises. "It's only...When are we allowed to not wear them?"

"You must wear them in public or around anyone other than those in your own family," I instruct. "Otherwise, they won't be necessary."

Teresa acquiesces. She first puts on her own, then helps her sons slide on their gloves, even covering the false hand attached to Aiden's prosthetic. She must have explained things to them at an earlier time, because her sons do not complain. They wear their gloves as they are good little Isaarian children, born and raised here.

The boys whisper to their mother in Lusch, giving me glances out of the corner of their eyes. I'm tempted to ask them to speak only in Alarkian, but I suspect if I do that, they will simply stop talking all-together.

Teresa eventually ushers them out of the washroom, and the boys run into the suite. I suspect they are curious and hoping to explore their new home. Teresa is more hesitant in passing by me.

"I...hope you realize that my children are...Well, whatever it is that you suspect myself or Septimus of, my children..." she starts.

"None of you are being put on trial, here," I reassure.

Teresa gives me a short nod, then follows her sons into their suite.

Damen is at the bookshelf, looking through tomes far too old for him. I think he is hoping I notice, and wants to impress upon his hosts how smart he is for his age. Aiden is snuggling his octopus and flipping through the pages his mother made into storybooks for him. Teresa takes a few pained seconds and then chooses to join Aiden. She pulls him close against her and whispers to him as quietly as she can in strained, broken Lusch.

We only must bear this scene for another minute before the food arrives, and I have it arranged on the table, along with place-settings. Teresa and her sons must be starving, but I know from experience that filling a belly with rich, variant food after weeks of eating minimally is a terrible idea. I have selected foods, then, that are relatively simple: eggs, thin slices of simple meats, some bread, soft cheeses, yoghurt, olives, and some plain vegetables. There is a little honey for the yoghurt, but that is all, in terms of sweetness. It occurs to me, briefly, that Teresa's sons might be picky, or used to fancier fare than this, but they do not complain.

"We will have a formal dinner this evening, but this should tide you over. And they can take off the gloves for now," I say.

I watch the boys' eyes widen with delight at the presented food. But they are obedient children, still, and stand by quietly, waiting for their mother to say whether they should sit and eat or not.

"A formal dinner?" Teresa repeats. "With the king?"

I choose my response carefully.

"Perhaps not tonight. He is quite busy. We are moving the court to the Summer Palace," I explain. "We will leave within about a week, and bring you four with. Our country has not been breached—not yet—but the danger is still very present. It's much safer at the Summer Palace, and the king will be able to conduct a more suitable military command from there."

"Oh," Teresa says.

I watch her expression tighten. She thought she would be safe, here, and is not pleased to be traveling again. Now that I know she's with child, I understand why.

She pushes that worry away for another.

"Will Septimus be there?" she asks.

"Your brother will join us when he decides to tell me the whole truth," I say, and for some reason, my words make her flinch.

"He cannot tell you everything," she says.

I raise an eyebrow.

"Cannot, or will not?"

"Cannot."

"Is it a matter of your safety?"

"Yes."

She nervously awaits my answer.

"Well. Then we shall see," I finally say. "He told me he will speak to me again tomorrow, but no sooner," I say, trying not to sound too harsh. "In the meantime, I think it would be best if your sons got the chance to eat some proper food, wouldn't you?"

For a moment, Teresa says nothing. Then there comes a few, quiet words in Lusch and her sons all but run to the table to find their places. I pull one of the chairs away a few paces and sit, while the three of them try to satisfy the gnawing in their stomachs.

The two children are ravenously hungry. In fact, Teresa barely has time to remind them to take off their gloves before Aiden starts begging her to help him fill his plate, and Damen is already helping himself. He's tearing into the bread with his teeth and already has oil on his fingers. I note, then, that there is a blue tattoo on Damen's right hand that I had not previously noticed. An odd design, as if it was meant to be the beginnings of a larger work stretching up his arm. I cannot imagine tattooing such a young child.

I wonder if there is a connection to the burn wound of his mother's.

"Damen, eat slow," Teresa warns, giving her elder son a steady look while she cuts the younger's food for him. "Or else you'll feel sick."

"Yes, Mama. Sorry."

He then proceeds to scarf down his food as quickly as possible.

"Baby, please," Teresa sighs. "I don't want you getting sick up."

Damen responds similarly to before, but his speech is so mumbling I can't tell if he's speaking in Lusch or Alarkian.

"I'm guessing the food is to their liking?" I ask.

Teresa does not notice the potential humor.

"The food is much appreciated. As is everything. But would it be possible... for us to go outside? At some point?" she asks innocently.

I consider this.

"No."

"Oh," she says quietly. She had not expected that answer.

But if little Miss Teresa's sons happen to have powerful flukes like hers, I do not want to invite them in close to Rian and then give them the opportunity to use those gifts against us.

Teresa looks down at the table, at her sons, anywhere but at me. She focuses as much as possible on making certain both her sons are eating a variety from the options provided. I have no doubt that Teresa and Septimus did their best to always make sure that the children were eating the most of the rations while traveling, but it would be difficult to give them everything, considering Teresa's pregnancy.

Regardless, traveling all the way from so-called Lusch to east Isaaria must have taken a toll on them all.

I give them five minutes, then begin.

"Would you mind talking to me, while you eat?" I offer, though Teresa has yet to make a plate up for herself.

She freezes.

"You don't have to answer anything you don't want to," I say, knowing full well that giving her the option to decline will make her feel obligated not to.

Again, such a tactic would not work on Septimus, but I think I can manipulate Teresa that way.

"Oh. Well. I suppose," she says uneasily.

"I only want a few details. Your brother says you have fled your husband," I say, and her eyes flick up at me nervously, as if she thinks my next move will be to send her back.

"Yes," she finally says after a moment. Her voice is so quiet, I can barely hear her, and yet, one could not call it a whisper.

"Was there any specific reason for that?"

Teresa sucks in her lower lip for a second, trying not to glance at her sons. "There were…many reasons," she says shortly.

I will have to be a little more discreet about how I interrogate, then. Teresa might not have much of a backbone, but she is no idiot.

"How long were you married?" I ask, sure that is a simple enough question that she won't mind answering.

"Nine years, as of this past autumn."

"Mmm. It is interesting: you have been married about a decade, now, and yet: only two children. Is your husband away often?"

"I…am usually unwell," she says evasively.

She keeps fiddling with her hands, in her skirt. I can tell I am making her uncomfortable, talking about this, but I both need and want to know everything about these supposed cousins of mine.

"Must we talk about my marriage?" Teresa suddenly says. "I would rather leave that behind, now. For my boys' sakes."

"There is something we need to address first," I say. "And then, perhaps."

Her relief lasts for only a few seconds before I open my mouth again.

"You are expecting a child," I guess, and her brightly flushed cheeks give her away. "And it is not your husband's. That's how your brother finally convinced you to leave him."

Teresa's mouth opens. Then she looks down at the table again, her hands covering her stomach. I'm sure she knew I'd discover her secret sooner or later; she'd just hoped she would not have to discuss it, now.

"Whose child is it," I demand.

I have supposed that the person is either someone of great importance, or someone with features different enough from Teresa and her husband's own that it would be obvious she was disloyal.

She mutters an embarrassed answer so quietly I can barely hear her. I wouldn't push her to talk about this in front of her children, except I know that Teresa will never speak to me if I separate them.

"What was that?" I say.

Teresa sighs, then pushes her hair back away from her face, takes a deep breath, and forces herself to look up at me.

"He said to call him Aiko Shinya," she says.

I feel a chill to hear the name.

"What?"

"He's Tourrannese," she says, oblivious of how wide my eyes have gotten. "He snuck me rare medicine for my Aiden, when Aiden was sick and my husband…"

Aiden has stopped eating, after hearing his name, and looks up as his mother. He does not say anything. I get the feeling he learned early on to almost always stay quiet, for his own sake. Teresa absently strokes his hair, staring at the tablecloth with unfocused eyes. She clears her throat.

"My husband said Aiden needed to learn how to be stronger. That he had to recover on his own. I didn't have any way to pay, since my husband keeps track of everything I own, even every piece of my jewelry, so I…"

She is crying, now, tears sliding freely down her cheeks. Her voice does not break, but I imagine this is from practice: ten years of crying silently so her husband couldn't hear, and now she can do it well enough that her sons will not notice, either.

She shrugs helplessly.

"It was just once," she says, her voice back to a whisper again. "Just once, for the medicine. It was a little frightening, at first. But he was kind to me. I didn't know what else to give him, and I felt so relieved...And then, when I found out I was pregnant, I knew…I could not let my children suffer for the mistakes I've made. I needed to leave, so all three of them might live."

She stops, there, and waits for my reaction. It takes me a few moments to sort out what to say next, as Teresa's answer was not what I expected. But if Teresa is telling the truth, her pregnancy could hold serious consequences not merely for her personal life, but politically for our former eastern allies.

I remember Aiko Shinya. I have met him, in almost every timeline: son of Lord-Ambassador Aiko Renki, polite, rather demure, diplomatic. It is overwhelming, thinking about how he would grow into a vagabond of loose morals, willing to bed a desperate woman pleading for nothing more than the opportunity to save her son.

I am almost convinced it cannot be the Aiko Shinya. The last I had heard of him, he'd turned his back on the rest of Tourran after the war with Kacha.

He'd later joined with several other Ronin and rebelled against Tourran directly, when they outlawed the practice of the Theebin religion. The rebellion ultimately failed, and as of several years ago, no one knew exactly what happened to him.

"Did he have a fluke?" I manage to ask hoarsely.

"I'm sorry?" Teresa says in surprise.

"The man who…" I say, and gesture obscurely towards her stomach, trying not to be crude. "…said to call him Aiko Shinya. Did he have a fluke? An aptitude, I think Alarkians say, yes?"

"Oh," Teresa says. "Yes. I don't know what to call it. Or how to describe it, exactly, but he showed me. The things he touches, he can…Slide? He can touch something and drag it. Alter its properties. I don't know. It's nothing I've ever seen before. It's strange. But beautiful. He made me a flower."

"Fate-dammit," I mutter. "That's definitely Aiko Shinya."

"Oh? Have you heard of him?" Teresa asks, meek and nervous. "I was under the impression he was no one important, just a wanderer."

Teresa trails off when she sees the look on my face.

I continue to stare at her. "You have no idea who Aiko Shinya is?"

She frowns, shaking her head slowly.

"I…I'm sorry," she says. "I…Never had much of an education."

Both her sons are paying full attention to me, now. I doubt Aiden understands much of what we're discussing, but it's possible Damen might.

"Aiko Shinya is the fifth-born child of the Tourrannese ambassador, Lord Aiko Renki and Kachin princess Park Chunya," I say. "After the wars in Tourran and Kacha, no one knows if any of the Kachin royal families are alive. All the royal family of Tourran is dead. All of them except Aiko Shinya. He is the only surviving member of the Tourrannese royal family, which means," I say, pointing at her belly, "that you are now carrying the rightful heir to the Tourrannese Islands in your womb."

Teresa is too pale for the blood to drain from her face, at this point, but she looks horrified by this news. She presses her hands harder against her stomach, as if to protect the child inside.

"It's a girl," she claims. "I can tell."

"That does not matter in Tourran," I say, ignoring the scientific unlikelihood of her knowing her child's sex based off a feeling. "Male or female—that child is the heir."

Teresa's breathing picks up. "Is that important? If Tourran is in ruins?"

"It matters now more than ever before," I say gravely. "With the attempts to keep countries like Tourran in political disarray, it is possible someone might try to kill your child."

Teresa's body is shuddering with every breath. Damen looks vaguely concerned about his mother.

"Some of those people, I'm assuming, are the very ones you ran from," I start. "But there may be additional dangers, for all three of your children, especially—"

Teresa suddenly gives a weak sigh and topples sideways off her chair.

"Mama!" Damen cries, and he and Aiden both rush from the table to their mother's side.

I drop to my knees as well and place a hand near Teresa's nose. She is still breathing, but her skin feels clammy, and she is sweating. The room temperature feels adequate to me, and neither of her sons seem to mind the warmth from the growing fire. So, either her pregnancy is affecting her body temperature, or she is sick. Regardless, it is a relief when one of the guards rushes in; saves me the trouble of having to call for one.

"Send for a doctor immediately," I demand. "Quickly, now. And find Naomi Qurvo!" I add as he rushes out.

Aiden is crying, now, sobbing for his mother. He is trying to shake her awake with only one hand. Damen seems caught between holding and comforting his brother and trying to see what ails his mother.

I don't know how to handle the children, so I do my best to help Teresa. Damen finally decides to grab onto Aiden, helping me by distracting his sobbing little brother. I manage to get my arms under Teresa and bring her down from the dais to the bed.

Damen has started speaking to his brother in Lusch, but whatever he's saying, it is not calming the younger boy much.

It likely takes only a minute or so, but it feels much longer, waiting for Naomi to arrive. Once she finally bursts into the room, I am relieved to see she has brought Ayla and Valor with her. I assume, this is to help occupy the children while we look after their mother. Ayla will be sweet and comforting, and Valor is kind. They will be able to get the boys to stop crying.

"What happened?" Naomi asks, immediately joining me before I can give instructions to Ayla and Valor.

They thankfully take the boys from the room, but I have no idea where they are bringing them or what they plan to do or say. I must focus on Teresa, for now, and hope for the best.

"I may have said things that increased an unexpectedly high level of anxiety, and she fell unconscious," I say to summarize quickly.

"Fate's Fingers. What do you know about her?" Naomi demands, taking Teresa's pulse. "Medically, Captain."

"Well, most important first," I sigh. "She's expecting a child."

Naomi stares at me for a second.

"It's true," I say. "She's confirmed as much."

"Hope's Head, Captain," Naomi curses again. She glances back at Teresa, whose condition is now obvious with her lying on her back. "What are we going to do? This family: they have no papers, no identity, no proof of who they are. They are running from someone, someone important in the west—"

"Next week, we take them to the Summer Palace with us," I interrupt. "If asked, we say they are refugees; we do not specify where they are from or who they are. We keep them under close guard. Secret."

"But Captain, this could put the king in a dangerous position—"

"We are all in danger, now, Naomi. The world is falling around us. We need to find a way to use Septimus and his sister to fix this. They know how to use my fluke, even if I don't. I don't trust them, but I need to learn what they know. I need to find a way to fix this, so we're not just running in loops, over and over again."

Naomi gives me a wary glance, considering. She eventually nods, knowing full-well she is in no position to disagree, but I can feel her critical displeasure.

It is strange, reminding myself that this Naomi does not remember what I do. Does not even remember what Korvaan does. She is still Naomi, but she treats me the way she would an authority figure whom she is uncomfortable with, and that is a painful position to be in, considering.

Beside us, Teresa suddenly sucks in a gasp and flings herself upright. I turn to help, but Naomi is faster, and gently pushes Teresa back against the pillows. From what I can see, my cousin must often wake terrified. Especially now, with her eyes darting around the room, I'm sure she is desperate to know where her children went.

"Calm yourself," Naomi soothes her, letting Teresa grip her arm hard, her fingernails digging in. "You are safe, here. No one will hurt you."

Teresa is not listening. She's shaking, and her eyes are large with terror, but she's too weak to resist Naomi and must lay back down.

"Where are my babies?" she demands hoarsely.

"Your boys are just in the other room," Naomi soothes. "We sent them out to keep them from being frightened. You can see them in just a few minutes; I only want to make sure you are doing well first. Agreed?"

"I want to see them," Teresa whispers. "They must be so scared."

"And you will," Naomi says. "We only want a doctor to take a look at you first. I think seeing a doctor here might scare them even more, don't you?"

Teresa thankfully nods in agreement.

"Let us try to settle you down, some," Naomi says. "How are you feeling?"

"Headache," Teresa mumbles, pressing her fingers against her temples.

"I'll get you some water. Try to relax."

Teresa nods again. "I'm sorry," she whispers. "I'm so sorry."

This surprises Naomi and I both. But while we exchange a look, neither of us know what to say.

We wait for the doctor to arrive. Naomi makes Teresa take controlled sips of water, and says gentle, comforting things to her while sitting at the bedside. I am agitated, wanting to continue my line of questioning but knowing I cannot. Even if it wasn't, clearly, something that effected Teresa poorly, I know Naomi would glare at me if I even dare open my mouth to utter anything other than an apology.

I curse myself. Septimus did warn me, but I thought he was exaggerating.

When the doctor arrives, Teresa is even meeker with him than she has been with me. The way she lets her shoulders curl and keeps her gaze downward makes me think I should have specified to find a female doctor, but I had not considered that at the time, and they are admittedly rarer. I cannot help but bitterly think that Taris might have done a better job at making her feel comfortable while examining her. I recall him comforting Aiko Shinya once in the forest. Despite what one might assume, he was good at that type of interaction.

In his examination, the doctor politely but firmly inquires after my cousin's mild injuries, and the more concerning burn on her arm that he has covered in a salve and wrapped. Teresa evasively claims they are the results of mere accidents and will not explain herself further. I can tell the doctor would like to insist upon answers, but can see as well as Naomi or myself that Teresa is uncomfortable.

Once finished, I step aside with the doctor to ask after his report in Isaarian, while Naomi sits with Teresa again, chatting with her.

"Please tell me she is not deathly ill," I sigh.

"She should be perfectly fine," the doctor says. "It is mainly fatigue and anxiety that has put her in such a state. Her body is weak, and in such a state, her healing is slow. Have her get plenty of rest. Assume a regular, varied diet. And try to relieve whatever might have caused that anxiety."

I nod. "What about the child?"

"The baby appears healthy. So long as you look after her mother, I would not expect any unusual complications."

"It is a girl, then?"

"If I am as accurate as usual, it would appear so. Please call on me, if necessary, particularly if that burn begins to fester," he adds. He hands me a short, written report on Teresa and her baby. "But sleep and decent nutrition should be all she needs."

"Thank you, doctor."

A hesitant knock on the door spares me anything more in terms of farewell. When prompted, the door opens a crack and Ayla's head peeks around. She looks into the room nervously, as if afraid of what she might see.

"Anything you need, Ayla? How are the children?" I say.

"They want to come in and see their mother," Ayla whispers, looking at me nervously. "Is that possible? They are very worried about her."

I sigh. I have done a wonderful job, here. Qhan will be disappointed in me, I suspect, given what I promised him.

"You can bring them in. Thank you, Ayla."

Ayla nods and disappears again. The doctor gathers his things to leave, and Naomi rises from the bed to join me. She speaks to me in Isaarian, and quietly. Even if Teresa could understand us, Naomi has chosen to keep the noise level in the room low. I do not know how effective that is in assisting with stress, but it seems appropriate.

"I am going to return to the king," Naomi says. "Teresa appears properly settled, for now. So long as you promise not to upset her again, I see no reason why I should stay."

She gives me a sharp look. I think back on all the good memories we share and bite my tongue from snapping at her.

"Please, do what you think is best," I say. "If you do not mind, though, I think we will borrow Valor for a while longer. To stay with them, after I leave. The boys seem to like him well enough, and I don't want to take up the princess's time."

She tightens her mouth, but nods shortly before stalking out, nearly bumping directly into her husband and Ayla as they return with the boys. After glancing my way, Valor takes his wife aside in the hall, likely to ask her what has rankled her so. But Ayla follows the boys up to Teresa's side.

Aiden goes to fling himself on the bed, and while he manages to get up on it, Ayla stops him from instantly crawling to his mother. She's gentle with him, and I can tell Aiden, at least, trusts and likes the princess. He listens to her just as much as he would Teresa.

Damen is more cautious. He hovers near the foot of the bed, a large, mature book tucked under an arm. Valor and Ayla must have brought them to the library; it is just down the hall and both boys appear to like reading or being read to. Damen's choice is curious, though. It is a medical tome.

Aiden babbles to his mother in Lusch. She smiles at him and combs through his hair with her fingers before giving a short reply. Damen speaks in Alarkian, though, so we might all understand.

"Mister Valor helped me find a book in the library and I learned about why you didn't feel good," he says. "So that you won't fall over again."

"Oh?" Teresa says. "What did you find out?"

"Loss of con-sci-ous-nus is called sync-cop-ee," he says carefully. "Mostly because of not eating or drinking enough or not breathing good enough. So, you need to remember to breathe, Mama."

Teresa smiles weakly. "Yes, baby, I'll do that. Sorry for frightening you."

Damen readjusts the book under his arm. "That's all right."

I retract my previous statement about Damen reading books too old for him: the boy understands the works he is reading for the most part, even if he can't yet apply it accurately. He truly is quite intelligent.

"Your boy is smart," I compliment, raising an eyebrow.

Teresa does not look at me. "Yes. Our little prodigy," she murmurs, and shudders.

"I started speaking whole sentences when I was two," Damen boasts, excited to tell me so, it seems. "Aiden didn't talk at all until he was almost three."

"Don't show off, darling, that's rude," Teresa says mildly.

"Sorry, Mama."

"You don't need to be sorry, Damen, just mind your manners."

It occurs to me, then—as Valor re-enters the room sans Naomi—that I have not offered Teresa a proper introduction to the two people who have been looking after her children. But I also do not want to overwhelm her, at the moment, and risk having to summon the doctor again. Or, worse, Naomi. As I have a few more questions for her, still, I decide those must take precedence. I need to have enough information to use as leverage when I visit Septimus again.

"Are you able to come back and sit at the table?" I pose to Teresa. "You haven't eaten anything yet."

Teresa thinks for a moment, then nods drowsily.

"Mmhm. Yes. I think so," she says.

I gesture for Ayla to assist me. Valor could carry my cousin with ease, but I don't know if she wants another strange man touching her right now. We help Teresa out of bed and, between the two of us, carry her to the table. Immediately, when we sit Teresa down, Aiden clambers up onto her lap and snuggles with her, having clearly been very worried about his mother.

I serve Teresa a portion of eggs as well as a large slice of bread spread with cheese, and put it in front of her. I place a fork in her hand before taking my own seat across from them.

"Do you want me to leave?" Ayla leans down to whisper to me once Damen and I retake our places.

"That may be best for now. Thank you, princess," I say. "I will come find you shortly."

Ayla nods, says a brief farewell to Aiden, at least, and then slips out the door. Valor stays, but keeps his distance. He knows how to read a situation well and I know he is the right person to stay. Ayla is good with children, but she is the king's daughter, and these are strangers.

I need to protect her interests.

"I would like to first apologize for what happened," I offer to Teresa while she nibbles on her bread. "It was not my intention to make you unwell."

"That's all right," Teresa murmurs, in a way that reminds me of how Damen said it earlier.

"I promise, I'll only bother you for a few minutes more. Afterwards, try to rest. And I'll come to retrieve you all for dinner later today."

She intentionally checks the clock sitting in the far corner, then nods.

"Might I speak with your sons, briefly? To ask them a few things?" I ask, and there's sudden alarm in Teresa's eyes.

"Not alone," she says hastily, holding her younger son tighter.

I am terrified she will fall into a panic again and quickly placate her.

"Of course not," I say. "I would never. But I would like to get to know them a little better, if that's acceptable. You are my cousins, after all."

It is not what Teresa expected me to say, but I have passed her unspoken test. She gives me a nod and tells her sons in Lusch what I assume is some reassurance. Her tone is wrong for it to be a warning; she sounds as if she is genuinely telling them not to be afraid to speak with me.

Still, Aiden looks nervous, and keeps sucking on his lower lip. Best to start with the elder, then.

"Damen, isn't it?" I say in Alarkian, facing him. He nods. "I'm Captain Soleil Marson. Your mother and uncle's cousin. I'm sorry if things have been difficult for you. I hope, moving forward, you will find them much improved."

"That's all right," he says after a moment.

"How old are you, Damen?"

"Five. I'll be six in a few more months. And Aiden's four and a half."

"Ah. Practically an adult already."

I can hear myself. My tone is horrendously awkward. Not at all congenial and friendly as I'm sure Naomi and Ayla might manage. *Or Lune...*

"How was the journey here?" I ask.

Damen barely glances at me.

"Fine," he says. "It was harder on Mother and Aiden then on me."

He is purposefully calling her "mother", now, though I've heard him and Aiden both continually refer to her as "mama". He wants to sound more adult. He's five.

"I'm sure you helped, though," I say, giving him a chance to boast again. I am not helping Teresa's parenting technique, but that is hardly my concern.

The boy does not take the bait.

"I tried," he says, and looks again at his mother, as if to check and see if he had been helpful at all.

"You were both very good," Teresa claims, kissing the top of Aiden's head. "It was a long, hard trip, and you did better than most adults would."

"And how are you finding Isaaria so far?" I ask.

"It's fine," the boy says. "I like the snow. It snows in Lusch, but we couldn't go outside much because everyone worried that we would get sick. We've gotten to go outside lots more here."

"Don't you miss your father?" I ask.

Damen hesitates, then tries to shrug casually.

"Sometimes," he says, but his eyes slid sideways towards his mother. Not as if he's trying to check to see if he's telling the story straight—oh, no. He does not try to meet her eye. Instead, he looks at her stomach.

So, Damen understands, then, that he has a half-sibling on the way who, along with his mother, may be in no small amount of danger if his father discovers the child is not his. As the baby's father is of mixed Tourrannese-Kachin heritage, she will not look anything like Damen and Aiden.

I look to the other boy.

"And what about you, Aiden?" I say, trying my best to sound amicable.

I'm no expert, but I believe I'm failing grandly. Probably my face and demeanor does not help to put the boys at ease. I am nothing like their soft, gentle mother with her sweet, quiet voice. Honestly, I still cannot imagine myself being a good mother, to whatever children Rian and I were meant to have, but I do want them. Something in me at least attempts to soften, around Damen and Aiden. And there is a part of me that I buried deep that likes to imagine holding my own son for the first time, Rian sitting there next to me. He will probably cry with joy, knowing him…

I force myself out of such a foolish daydream.

Aiden does not look at me, but turns and whispers into his mother's ear. I could listen in, if I wanted, but trust Teresa to translate the message accurately. Only, she refuses to coddle her sons that much, I suppose.

"You can tell her yourself," she prompts gently instead, encouraging him. "She's a nice lady."

The fact that my supposed cousin is introducing me in such a way to her children startles me. I have done nothing particularly kind to them, as far as I'm concerned. But Teresa apparently wants her sons to trust me. Interesting.

"I don't miss Daddy," Aiden tells me stoutly. "He likes Damen. He doesn't like me or Mama."

Well, that is certainly illuminating.

Damen's expression darkens as he scowls and, for once, looks at his little brother less than charitably.

"Don't say that," he insists. "He loves Mama."

"He does not!" Aiden cries, as if this is something Damen has tried to convince him of before, but Aiden's seen enough to know better.

"Does so, or else we wouldn't exist! You have to love someone to have a baby with them!"

"You don't hurt people you love!"

"Sometimes you have to! He said so! And Father's one of the greatest men in the entire world, so I think he would know—!"

"Damen, please," Teresa whispers, and he instantly quiets, chagrined.

"Sorry, Mama."

"And Aiden, do not yell at your brother," she adds.

"Sorry, Ma-ma," Aiden repeats. "I won't do it again. *Promise.*"

I tighten my jaw. The way these boys speak frightens me, and I'm not sure if it is because they are aware of so many horrible implications at a young age, or because I'm wondering what my own son might have been like, at this age. Would he be smart like Damen? Endearingly innocent like Aiden? Would he look more like me, or Rian?

Stop it. Stop it. Stop thinking about it.

"Aiden—what makes you think that about your father?" I ask, needing to clear my throat twice to get the whole sentence out.

Teresa is ashamed by what her son says next, but she does not stop him.

"Daddy is mean to Mama. He hit her. I saw. And then she cries."

Teresa covers her mouth with her hand.

"He says mean things to her," Aiden goes on. "I hear. And sometimes he grabs her and doesn't let go, and shakes her. Uncle Jarrod told me Daddy might hurt me sometime, if I'm not good. Or he might hurt Mama more, cuz she'll get in the way. So, we're really, really good. Right, Mama? Damen and I are good?"

He looks to her, and Damen and I do, too. She is crying so hard her shoulders shake, and when Aiden turns his head to her, she pulls him close and presses him to her chest, as if trying to hide her tears from him.

"You're the very best, Aiden," she promises him. "Both of you. The very best children a mother could have."

I am not sure if I should if I should be horrified yet or if I need to save that reaction.

"Who did you marry, Teresa?" I demand.

She shakes her head, still looking down and holding Aiden. "He doesn't matter anymore," she claims. "He is only a man with too much power."

I drag my chair in closer to the table and lean closer. "This is very important, Teresa, I'm going to need you to answer, understand?"

She shifts uncomfortably. "I can't tell you who he is," she insists. "Really, I cannot. I'm sorry. Septimus said."

"I won't make you tell me," I promise. "But for the safety of your family and everyone else in the palace, I need to know: is your husband the sort of man who might try to come after you and your sons? To get you back?"

Teresa's expression goes quickly from relieved to haunted.

"Oh," she says, her voice grave, trembling in warning. "He definitely will."

Three

VALOR IS HAPPY to stay with Teresa and her sons for the rest of the day. I tell him not to allow them outside, but that they can explore approved areas of the castle if they wish, so long as Teresa is not up on her feet too much. He appears at ease with Teresa's children, and his affable nature is the sort they come to trust easily, even in these circumstances. I suspect Valor somewhat regrets that he and Naomi never had children and misses the opportunities that may have provided him with.

With much of the day still at my disposal, I first head upstairs a floor and to the west wing to make good on my word to Ayla. I'm sure she has heard the gossip—even without a full staff, the palace cannot ignore the presence of our guests—but I doubt anyone has had the chance to properly explain to her. All she knows is a handful of people claiming to be my relatives have intruded upon our hospitality and that her father has suddenly taken ill. Even if I cannot tell her things of lives past, she deserves something of an explanation.

Ayla is not a little girl anymore, but an adult woman; the same age, now, as I was when Rian and I should marry. A matter of days ago, one could argue the second most pressing issue in Rian's life, aside from the impending wars around us, might have been the fact Ayla and her not-so-secret admirer might get it into their heads they are not children anymore.

When I knock on her bedroom door, Ayla readily invites me in. She has told me on numerous occasions I never need knock, but I value her privacy more than she does.

Inside Ayla's bedroom, her personality emerges via decorations, presents, furniture, books, and clothing. One might be overstimulated by all the variety, if not prepared. Such lavish grandiosity is nothing new to Rian, given his princely origins, but he neither enjoys nor despised it. It is his every day. Ayla, meanwhile, came from a world where she had to fight for her dinner quite literally before the disgusting conditions of that orphanage came to light and the University sponsored the poor children housed there.

It is easy to forget, sometimes, because Ayla rarely, if ever, speaks of her early years, but it's the little hints that brings it to mind. How she never complains about food she does not like, how every dress made for her is a style she claims to adore, how she still likes to donate half her allowance back to the East High Courts University in thanks. How she is opening her own orphanage with the Pyrian nuns.

Ayla is seated in front of her vanity, peering at her skin, and examining herself from different angles. Anyone else might accuse her of narcissism, but I know the opposite is more likely. Ayla is highly self-critical.

"Oh, Captain Marson," she sighs when she sees me in the mirror. "Do you have any useful skincare tips you'd like to impart? A magical cure-all?"

"I'm afraid not, your majesty," I say apologetically.

"I thought not…I wish my skin would stop being so problematic. I thought this sort of thing would all stop once I was an adult but that wasn't true at all," Ayla says. "Why can't I simply have good skin? It isn't fair."

"It may be from stress, princess," I say. "Or environment. Or…diet: Snacking on too many gifted sweets from Soren Carsans, perhaps?"

Ayla whirls from the vanity, her eyes wide. "You know about that?! …You haven't told my father yet, have you?"

"Princess, of course I know. No present arrives at your doorstep before it's inspected by men I trust. You know that."

Ayla blushes and looks back down at her vanity.

"I suppose that means you've read all the letters, then, too," she mumbles.

"I would never invade your privacy that way," I reassure her. "The letters were tested, for any powdered substances that might have tainted them, but I did not read anything that might have been intended only for your eyes."

Still, Ayla is bright red. Her eyes flick towards one of her drawers, where I know she has stashed all one-hundred and twenty-three of Soren Carsans' letters from over the past few years. She starts fiddling with her hair.

"It's…um…They are only letters," Ayla says, trying to defend herself.

"And I am certain the two of you are only writing appropriate content, considering your correspondences could be intercepted," I say.

Ayla grimaces. "Well. Mostly?"

"That's what I thought. You'll be seeing him again soon," I remind her.

Rian appointed the Carsans as caretakers and retainers of the Summer Palace almost twenty years ago. After the sudden death of the late grand prince Crispin Carsans, Soren graciously took over in his brother's place at only the age of twelve. He has done a good job, I'll admit. And he has come to visit the Pyrian Palace about once a year, maintaining his childhood friendship with Ayla. There was no such visit this year, but as we are moving to the Summer Palace, one did not seem practical at the time.

"I know," Ayla says, still a touch pink.

"If you like, I can...persuade your father into agreeing that you and Soren Carsans are a good match," I offer.

Ayla is surprised at first, but then brightens and smiles. She didn't think this was the direction I planned to take things, but I like Soren Carsans. He has always been a good boy, and a good friend to Ayla. If the two of them have intentions for one another, I am happy enough with the arrangement. I'm glad Ayla has decent taste in men, which is, I'm told at least, not common for princesses. It is also lucky that the marriage would be politically beneficial, given the need to strengthen the king's unstable relationship with the Carsans, and therefore likely to be approved.

"That is because Father believes everything you say," Ayla says.

"I could very easily lead him around by the nose and he would be happy to be fooled," I agree, which is only doubly true now that I know our full history together.

Ayla cannot help but laugh at that one. However, after another second, she continues to think, and her laughter fades.

"I do worry about my father, though," Ayla admits with a frown. "And what will happen with him, once I'm married and gone. Sometimes, I feel like you, Qhan and I are all he has in the world. And if I leave...It will be only the three of you. And it is different, because you are his bodyguards, before anything else."

I struggle with how to answer that. If things go the way I suspect they will, we will likely be starting all over again within a matter of months at most. I know that is no excuse to abandon this reality in its entirety, which is partially why I am offering to help with Soren and Ayla. But my concerns for Rian are primarily regarding whatever he is dealing with day-to-day. For some reason, while I can picture a future for everyone else, there is nothing for me or Rian.

"Your father is something of a reclusive man, princess," I finally say. "But I am certain he'll adapt. You shouldn't let that keep you from your own life."

"I know, I know. But still. It would be nice to know there are more people around for him. I always thought he might be friends with the Qurvos," she sighs. "I think out of any of them he was closest to Taris, but..."

"Really? I had not noticed," I confess.

Ayla shrugs. "I think Father wanted to be friends. But Taris was always very closed off, wasn't he?"

"That he most certainly was," I agree.

I try not to shudder. It is still strange to think about Taris and Lune, let alone hear one of their names. It is both painful and transcendental. As if "Lune" and "Taris" did not exist, but are mere figments of my imagination and childhood loneliness. I need to keep Ayla from mentioning them again, if possible. She has no way of knowing that, in another time, they were her aunt and uncle.

"Look, princess, can I speak to you honestly for a moment?" I say.

"Oh, please do," Ayla says, sitting up straighter.

"If you are interested in Soren Carsans, I would be happy to put in a good word for the two of you once your father has recovered. That said, I would still be cautious about your staying in the same building as Soren. I know that you are a responsible young woman, but sometimes our passions can get the best of us—"

"I-I understand," Ayla stammers, flushing even pinker as she understands the lecture intended. "I am not going to be sneaking around at night."

"Or any time of the day, I should hope."

"Captain!"

Ayla covers her face up with her hands in embarrassment, but she is laughing. I cannot help but smile as well.

"Additionally, I came here to thank you, for helping with the Smith boys," I say carefully. "You did an excellent job of keeping them calm."

"It was no trouble at all. I was happy to help!" the princess insists. "They were such sweet little boys. So concerned about their mother. Are they really your cousins, Captain Marson?" she adds, intrigued, but cautious in asking.

I sigh. "It appears that way, yes."

"It's peculiar," Ayla says, twirling a strand of her hair absently. "I never considered the possibility of you having a family. In my head, you always belonged to ours."

I frown, now wondering if it is possible Ayla has 'memories' of times past.

"Ours?"

Ayla gives me a look. "I am not blind, Captain. I have seen the way my father looks at you. There is more than one reason why he did not want to marry Queen Asmer, Almighty rest her soul."

She is making me mildly uncomfortable, now. I do enjoy mothering Ayla, but it bothers me that she may see me as her mother, in this reality. I do not feel like I have earned that right, especially when Asmer always tried so hard to fulfill that role in Ayla's life. It is as if I've stolen from the dead.

I clear my throat. "Yes. Well. Your father and I have been close, since he was a boy, princess—"

"Why don't the two of you get married already?" Ayla interrupts. "It has been long enough since Asmer died. No one would care. And then he would be happy."

I stare at her, trying to imagine how it is I came here to explain about the Smiths to her, and somehow found myself discussing another topic entirely.

"That is none of your business, princess," I warn her.

"Korvaan says you would be happier, then, too," she says, pressing me.

Korvaan, who I also need to find time to speak with.

"Naturally," I sigh. "Any other advice you wish to impart in regards to how you think I should live my life?"

Ayla takes a moment to consider; precocious girl.

"Only that, if the Smiths really are your cousins, you probably should not be keeping one of them in the wine cellar. I know it's your job to be paranoid, but I don't think they are going to be much of a threat to me or my father."

"I will consider that, princess."

"Oh, and the Smith boys said there is a dinner tonight—I'm assuming I'm invited, and that you will be in attendance?"

I realize, then, that when I came up with the idea of the dinner, I'd forgotten that I have never dined with Rian or Ayla in this universe. I've stood guard over them at plenty of dinners, but never ate with them. I need to sit down and get my head wrapped around these timelines and relationships, or else I'm bound to get myself into unnecessary trouble.

"We will dine together," I say carefully.

Ayla brightens. "Wonderful! I will assemble a list of proper dinner topics that will be appropriate for the children, yet stimulating for their mother, but reveals nothing that would cause you or Qhan distress."

I force myself not to smile; it would not be appropriate given my current concerns. "That sounds agreeable, princess. I shall leave you to it."

She smiles. "And do not fret overmuch. My father will recover. I saw him this morning. He seems better."

I force myself to nod. I have been trying to reassure myself that Rian will make a full recovery, but my fear is what feeds my anger. And my anger is what has kept me from falling apart, particularly in front of Septimus. If I fail to sustain it, I know I will fall apart, possibly as Rian has.

Ayla asks me a few more questions I do not have answers to, regarding the dinner menu she has begun to prepare. I am no expert, but I urge her not to serve overcomplicated dishes. I do not want to make our guests sick. After, I return upstairs, to check in on Rian once more. And to speak with Korvaan.

I send Qhan inside with Rian, who apparently has fallen back asleep but managed to eat something and is improving by the hour. Someone must look after the king, still, while I take up Korvaan's time. While I would like to have both Qhan and Rian present for this conversation, to keep our knowledge base even, I do not wish to wake Rian. The faster he recovers, the better.

"Right, then—you are wearing Rian's ring," I say, startling Korvaan.

"You remember that, now?"

"I remember, I think, everything you do, but from my own perspective," I clarify. "Perhaps a little more. Do you recall Septimus at all?"

Korvaan hesitates, but adjusts. "Only vaguely. I have no distinct memories of *him,* only an idea of who he is, and why it is important for me to trust him. To follow his instructions. But when he appeared, asking after you and the king, I suddenly *knew* who he was."

"Do you have any knowledge of our enemies?" I ask. "Or of where Septimus and Teresa came from?"

Korvaan shakes his head.

"Unfortunately, no. I know Septimus has explained everything before. And I feel as if I should trust him. But there is something in my head telling me I know all I'm meant to. As if it is for my own good."

I sigh. "Septimus put that in your head, I suspect. The only question is, while he has made you think you can trust him, *can* you? Can we?"

Korvaan does not appear to appreciate my skepticism. "If we can't, Soleil, we're in a world of trouble."

Considering what I've recently learned about the Greys, he is not wrong. If Septimus has come here to help us, we have a chance. If he's here to infiltrate the palace and take us apart from the inside, I can't imagine us surviving.

"Worst case, you turn back time and we use Septimus' own tools against him," Korvaan says, offering me a surprisingly useful tactic.

"Well only get the chance to do that once, though," I warn. "Septimus can edit these charms, and change what we remember. If he brings our enemies to our doorstep, and betrays us, I'll have one chance to wind things back before he gets the chance to change our memories."

I consider the few instances I've been able to see Septimus use his fluke.

"The good news," I say, "is I believe he needs to have physical contact to edit, change, remove, or withhold memories. The only way he can use his fluke without physical contact is release memories once more. That is what he did in the throne room."

"We shall keep our distance, then," Korvaan says.

"And if he and Teresa stay inside, they will be too weak to use their flukes, anyways," I add. "Teresa's sons as well."

Though I still need to know what the children's flukes are, I do not think it's the most pressing piece of information.

"Do you have any memories of Aiko Shinya?" I ask.

"Some. Vague ones," Korvaan says. "Why?"

I decide not to keep information from him.

"Teresa is having his child. Regardless of whether we can trust Septimus, Teresa believes her husband will pursue her and her sons. I suspect he will be less than pleased to learn she is carrying another man's child."

Korvaan blinks, startled. "Is…Is Aiko Shinya still alive?"

"He was a few months ago, at least."

"Your family is twisted, Soleil."

I sigh. "Thank you, Korvaan."

"By extension, I suppose, mine as well," he realizes.

This surprises me a little. "...You remember Lune?"

"I meant since I see you as my sister," Korvaan admits. "But, I suppose I remember Lune. She's...Wait, sometimes she is a Carsans' and sometimes she is not? Now that I think of it, it is a little confusing."

"She's my sister, Korvaan. And Taris' wife."

"Oh," Korvaan says, and thinks on it longer. "*Oh!*"

"Exactly."

Korvaan stares, trying to make sense of everything in his head, now, but I don't have the time or energy for suppositions.

"The important thing to do, now," I say, "is to put together a plan moving forward. I believe we will have to start again one last time, and before I do that, we need to know everything we can from Septimus."

"You might need to spend more time in nature, then, to make sure you can use your fluke when we need it," Korvaan says.

"Likely," I agree. "I will be sure to do so before I interview Septimus again. He has 'invited' me to make a second interrogation attempt tomorrow, but I think I will make him wait a few days. I want to make certain he realizes who is really in control, here."

Korvaan is hesitant. "Technically, still him, I think, but you might be able to convince him otherwise, I suppose."

"In the meantime, I want to go through all of Rian's Magicsmith research," I say. "I know I cannot trust Septimus fully, but history won't lie. I want to take a look at those family trees Rian was working on."

"I don't think they're completed," Korvaan warns.

"That does not matter. Every bit helps. I'll be in his study," I add. "I'm leaving my usual duties to you and Qhan; please be sure to tell him. And send someone to come and find me for Ayla's dinner. I may lose track of time."

"Of course, Soleil. I'll make sure you eat," he says, and smiles.

It is nice to hear someone say my first name again, as a friend. While I appreciated the respect title of "Captain Marson", it is impersonal. Too much has happened in my long life for me to pretend as if I have no emotions.

Rian hasn't worked on his Magicsmith research in years, nor has he bothered to store the materials. It is all neatly organized in his study, or, at least, organized in a way that makes sense to Rian. I strike up a match for the fireplace to warm the room, take a seat at Rian's desk, and pull in the chair. On the top of his stack is an old map, with handwritten notes included. Rian has sketched in Old Isaaria, as well as Valeia—or where Valeia is believed to be located, under the Floating Islands. There are several areas that he has sketched in labeled "Lusch?", near the Midland Zone, Kelka, Balvan, Artea, and even to the east of the Rumshtama Empire.

Considering the direction from which the Smiths traveled, I think it is safe to confirm Lusch is in the west, between Alarkia and Lijimata, by the Midland Zone. I have only just started and I've already made a discovery that would shock and awe the entire world. It is strange how that does not feel at all like a victory.

I put the map to the side and pick up the first of Rian's journals.

For the rest of the day, I spend hours poring over Rian's notes and charts. In several of his journals, he has re-written popular Isaarian folktales, adding back in where he believes the Magicsmiths were originally. Some are easy, like the Curse of the Dragon's Tooth, where the names Smith and Grey were merely omitted. Others, Rian struggled with, believing certain Magicsmiths were involved in historical events, but lacking solid proof.

I set aside the journal with the Curse of the Dragon's Tooth, as there is enough space in it to make notes of my own. There are also places where Rian has scribbled iterations of the note "the Seven Eyes of Death?", the hints of which seem to confuse him. I need to ask him or Septimus about that. I do not know if it's pertinent, but Rian's mentioned it enough times for me to think it could be.

It's not long before my head spins, attempting to keep track of all these individuals. It is not only the Smiths I must research, after all, but the Greys and Wolffs as well. Horrible though it sounds, I am relieved the Wolffs are practically extinct at this point. That is one less thing to worry about, in terms of enemies or allies. The only one who may still be alive is Aldrich Wolff, but he is a Wolff by marriage and must be quite old at this point.

It takes some time before I manage to find Rian's family trees. He has several, large charts I need to unfold and spread out on the floor, one or two per family. Each one extends a family tree as much as possible, using dates—general or specific—to help him realize where the gaps are. There is hardly solid proof linking me and Lune to Septimus and Teresa, but from what I can tell based on dates, Rian somehow managed to get as far as the generation my great-great-grandfather may have belonged to. With the Greys, he got even closer. But I do not see any names I recognize.

I am hesitant to desecrate Rian's hard work, but this is important. Leaving space, I begin to draw at the bottom of the Smith's page.

Lune and I are sisters, born to Olivia Smith and from a father whose first name I cannot recall. All I can write for him is "Marson". I marry Rian Yakarami, and we adopt Ayla. Lune marries Taris Qurvo, son of Khas Qurvo, though I do not know Taris' mother's name. That is simple enough.

From there, it becomes challenging.

Septimus has said multiple times that my mother was his father's older sister. I do not recall if he has mentioned his father's name, and I know for a fact Teresa's husband is still to be identified. But I can add in her affair with Shinya, and the resulting child.

I arrange the Grey's family tree off to the left, nearest to Teresa. Whoever her husband is, he is at least connected to the Greys. Perhaps a distant cousin. I don't know how the Wolffs fit into this, yet, but this all has to do with some Families Three malarky. I am sure of it. I recall Rian telling me once that Aldrich Wolff is known for impressive but less than moral reasons, ending the Wolff bloodline. That must be tied into all this somehow, too.

The sun fades early, in winter, making it even more difficult for me to tell what time it is. As promised, Korvaan sends a guard to retrieve me for Ayla's dinner, but I dawdle, my mind still filled with the history of my ancestors. By the time I have joined them in the candle-lit dining room, the food has been served, and Ayla has just finished explaining to Teresa's sons why she says prayers before eating.

Teresa is seated between her sons, and Ayla has put herself on the other side of Aiden at the head of the table. Valor, Naomi and I will sit across from the Smiths. The seat across from Ayla remains empty.

Ayla smiles purposefully when she sees me enter. I have not dressed for the evening the way the rest of them have, but am still in uniform. My hair is falling out of my braid, but I do not think anyone will notice or care.

"Now that we're all here, we can get started," Ayla says as I sit.

"I assume introductions are not necessary?" I say.

"We've taken care of all that," Ayla says cheerfully.

"When is Uncle Septimus coming back?" Damen asks.

His brother's nose barely clears the tabletop.

"Soon," I say. "Now, I think it best we get a few rules out of the way."

Teresa's boys glance at each other in displeasure at the mention of rules, making faces. Teresa herself sits stiffly and tries not to look at me, instead fussing over each of her boys, particularly Aiden, as our food is served.

"As I mentioned earlier," I start. "You will not be permitted outside, at least for now, and I never want to find any of you without your gloves on, outside of your rooms. In a few days, dependent on what Septimus tells me, I may reassess and make some exceptions. You are also confined to this floor of the palace. So long as you are accompanied by Valor, Naomi, or Ayla, you may visit any rooms on this floor including the library, the salons, and the mirror hall."

"Mirror hall?" Damen repeats, perking up some.

"I'll take you tomorrow," Ayla offers. "I think you'll like it."

"Whatever you need, within reason, we would be happy to provide," I continue. "Including any particular foods you enjoy. You will not be left with materials to utilize the fireplaces, but Valor will light a fire for you if you ask. Does that sound fair?"

It takes Teresa a moment to answer, as if she is surprised there are not more rules to follow.

"Yes, I think we can do that," she says slowly.

"I am assigning Naomi and Valor to look after you officially," I say, fully aware that this is news to the pair of them. "If the princess has the time, so desires, and I approve, she may keep you company on occasion."

Teresa nods, looking down at her soup. She keeps playing with her spoon, never lifting it to her mouth, but spinning the contents of her bowl around. Both her sons have dug into their supper with relish, and their mother is too distracted to lecture them on not using their bread to sop up the broth.

"It's been a while since I've had anyone close to my own age to talk to," Ayla adds, trying to meet Teresa's eye. "If you like, we could—"

Teresa suddenly throws her chair back, tossing her napkin on the table. She barely manages to excuse herself before she flees, a hand over her mouth. Everyone else is too shocked to move, but I am quick to leap to my feet and gesture for no one else to rise.

"I will see to her," I say, and hesitate before forcing myself to address the boys. "Do not worry for your mother. I'm sure she's fine. Eat your dinner. We will return shortly."

I can hear Aiden asking Damen something in Lusch as I head out, but from what I can tell, he does not sound panicked. Confused, maybe, but not frightened. Given recent events, they might be too tired for it.

I do not have to go far to find Teresa; even if I could not hear her, there are several concerned servants that have wandered into the hall to point the way. Teresa has run to the nearest washroom, and I find her hunched over, coughing and retching. I immediately move to help stabilize her, holding her hair back for her until she stops gagging. She manages not to be sick up, but likely the nausea remains.

"I'm sorry," she whispers as I help sit her back up against the wall. "It's the smell of the meat, it…"

I frown. We are still on the soup course Ayla has had prepared and there's no meat in it. I don't know what we're meant to eat next, but Teresa can apparently smell it from the kitchen, and it has upset her stomach. It is going to be difficult to get her enough nutrients if she won't eat meat, but at least now I understand the issue.

"It's fine. Don't apologize," I say. "I will let everyone know you are too tired to finish dinner if you would like to go rest. We can have some simple foods sent to your room, later."

Teresa wipes at her mouth and shakes her head.

"I…can't leave…my babies…"

"We're not going to hurt them," I say, defensively. "There is no point in returning to dinner if the smell is going to make you sick. I would like you to at least be able to keep down what you managed to eat this morning."

Though she is still wary of me, and does not want to leave her sons to eat alone, Teresa knows I am not wrong.

"On that note, I would like to have either Naomi or a specialized doctor examine you once a week, to make certain you and the baby are both healthy. I don't think you've been eating enough," I admit. "Would you be amenable to that?"

Teresa blinks at me, startled.

"That is very generous of you, Captain," she says.

"No, it's not," I correct. "It is basic medical care. But you did not answer my question, Teresa."

"I would appreciate it," she says carefully. "As long as they listen to me. I…I don't have an education, but…whenever I have seen doctors before, they'd make me do what they want without even listening to me."

"No one is going to force you to do anything you don't want to," I swear.

I feel as if, in regards to Teresa's personal health, I can promise that. Of course, given how she felt it necessary to say so, I am tempted to question her about her previous pregnancies, and her experiences, but I do not want to cause her further distress. While I'm not certain Teresa believes me, I can only reassure her so many times. Eventually, it will be entirely up to her whether she wants to trust. Even if Septimus has ill intent for the palace's occupants—which, to myself, I will admit I doubt—I will look after Teresa and her children.

"If you don't mind, I only need a few seconds to sit here," Teresa says. "After, we can go back to dinner."

"If you insist," I say. "Take your time."

Teresa nods, then closes her eyes and begins what I assume are some breathing exercises. As the seconds pass, I realize this is the first time in several days that I have allowed myself to do nothing but sit still and think. I've been doing my best to avoid that and perhaps that has helped keep me from falling ill the way the king has.

Sometimes the emotions creep in, especially when looking or listening to Damen and Aiden. It is easier, with Ayla, since I helped raise her, in a way. I have had the opportunity to meet her many times over again. But I can't even begin to know what Teresa is experiencing. I do not even know what basic relief might help her. I will have to depend on Naomi for that, and I feel she already resents me, somewhat, for giving her the responsibility of the Smiths while the king has not fully recovered.

I know I must converse with Teresa. Otherwise, my own thoughts will drive me mad.

"You are brave," I admit. "You could have ended your pregnancy early on, and your husband would have never known."

She keeps her eyes down and shakes her head.

"No," she says hoarsely. "I could not. This is my daughter. I won't let anything happen to her. Not ever. I need to protect her; I owe at least that much to her. Maybe more. She saved me."

This is the most she has voluntarily said to me, without me inquiring. I've touched upon something important to her, then. Something she must have thought about extensively before making the decision to leave.

"Then let me say instead that your willingness to sacrifice for your children is admirable," I try instead.

"It is what any good mother should do. It is not my sons' fault their father is a monster. It's not my daughter's fault that her mother was unfaithful. I am responsible for my own choices. My children don't deserve punishment for my mistakes."

I cannot argue with that.

"Besides, this life is precious," she says, smiling vaguely at her stomach. "Even if life is hard for her, my daughter deserves the chance to live it. If I didn't believe that, I would be no better than my husband…I will die for my children, if necessary."

"And I will ensure that is never necessary," I say.

Teresa looks surprised by my conviction, but I am sincere. Teresa has been braving enough, on her own. She has no way to make money, no husband, no home, and three children who need mothering. Rian had centers set up for such women in our own country, who decided to bear and raise their children alone, despite the way others might look down at them for it. It is the least I can do, to make sure my cousin receives the same benefits.

"I have promised you that I will look after you and your sons," I remind her. "I will uphold that, even if you don't believe me."

"I don't think you're lying," Teresa says, guilty over her doubts. "It's…"

"Hard to trust. I know. It is something we both need to exercise. You know," I add, having just thought of it. "I think Naomi may have a scented balm you can apply over your upper lip. It should help keep the smell of meat from bothering you."

"That would be appreciated," she says. "Thank you."

She lets me help her stand.

While I have not changed her mind enough to convince her to trust me completely, I think we have made some small progress.

I WAIT TWO days before trying to speak with Septimus again. I tell myself, as I told Korvaan, that I decided to do so because I want to intimidate him, but it is mainly because I don't want to spend all my time in the cellar before I know Rian has fully recovered. Simultaneously, I try to resist always running to his bedside and mainly rely on reports from Qhan or Korvaan.

I only visit him when I know he is sleeping, at which point I usually take Mango out for exercise, and some sunlight. Rian is improving daily, which reassures me in several ways. In fact, every day that passes in which enemies do not attempt to break down our doors makes it easier to trust the Smiths. I begin to wonder if I have been unreasonable to be so suspicious of them.

That said, when I take Qhan down to the wine cellar, I put on a mask for Septimus' sake. I must be harsh with him. If he realizes I am losing my patience with him, he may be more inclined to spill his secrets. As Qhan warned, Septimus knows better than to lie.

The wine cellar has hardly become hospitable in my absence, but Septimus has been provided with the necessary comforts. He notices our approach, and goes to seat himself eagerly at the table while Qhan unlocks the door. Instead of letting his time in the cellar unsettle him, Septimus greets us with a grin and a cheery attitude.

"Back so soon?" he starts as I come to stand across from him.

"Why did you neglect to tell me Teresa was carrying the child of Aiko Shinya?" I snap at him. The mirth suddenly drops from his face.

"Ah. So, you found out about that, then."

For a moment, I am confused, sure that I've heard someone say that exact same thing to me before, but I cannot place it. It does not matter.

"Did you think you could have hidden a pregnancy? Did it even occur to you that your sister should have a doctor?"

"We'd hoped we could put that off for as long as possible," he says with a sigh. "It was a matter of balancing how to protect her health and how to protect her from those who may not want a Smith-Aiko bastard in the world."

I roll my eyes and seat myself in the second chair.

"Well done. As if Fate's Fingers have not already spun our family into chaos. I have brought a doctor for her," I admit. "I will not withhold medical assistance for answers; that is not the way we do things, here. But you should have told me. We might have done something to help her sooner."

Septimus nods. "How far along is she?"

"Twenty-six weeks. Every day that passes simply increases the child's chances of survival. But your sister is much too frail."

"She told me she wants to name the baby Rika," Septimus murmurs. "In case something happens to her and she…"

"Nothing is going to happen to her," I interrupt. "As long as she eats well, she will begin putting on weight and will no longer be at all at risk. We will look after her and the boys."

Septimus does not bother trying to hide his relief.

"While I didn't want to think you'd do otherwise, there's always that small hint of doubt," he admits. "You didn't interrogate her like you threatened you would either, did you?"

"I asked her a few questions," I say. "Obviously. Now I am here to ask you questions. As I said before, I expect answers."

He gives another smile; I suspect to hide whatever he is really feeling.

"We shall see."

"Starting with this," I say, ignoring him. "Who did Teresa marry?"

"No," he says instantly, shaking his head. "Not that one. Try again."

"Septimus, for her safety, your nephews', and for the sake of everyone in this palace, I must know," I demand. "Teresa said he may hunt her."

Septimus snorts. "There is no 'might' about it. He undoubtedly already is."

"Then I need to know how to fight him. What his fluke is. Last time these monsters came to Isaaria, they managed to infiltrate the Pyrian Palace with ease and kill Taris and my sister, so—"

"Korsiko," Septimus says.

"What?" I demand, shocked by what I have heard.

"Korsiko," Septimus says again. "In another time, you knew who he was."

I bristle.

"I know who he is in this time, too," I hiss. "He is the bastard who killed Lune. He took my sister away. He came here with Mercer Ralhan's former bodyguard," I add, remembering that bloody night. "But I doubt Marques is the one who hired them, was he?"

"Marques," he repeats. "Now that's a name I haven't heard in a long time."

"But you heard of him?" I ask, excited to start getting somewhere for once.

"I met him," Septimus admits carefully. "Many times."

"How?"

"The first times, it is because he happened to be in the area," Septimus says, and I let him be evasive because at least he continues talking. "The second time, it is because he was looking to borrow Korsiko for something of a revenge scheme. Korsiko works for a man I used to know."

"Name. Now. Or I leave you down here for a week."

"Kryto…Grey," he whispers. "He is named after the same 'Kryto Grey' from the old stories. The one who began the practice of Dadj'zcha. Teresa's husband is one of the soldiers in this Kryto's army, if you must know."

I feel Qhan look at me unexpectedly and I know.

"What interesting things you choose to lie about, Septimus," I say. "Why lie about the identity of your sister's husband?"

He does not miss a beat.

"Because while I would like to trust you, Soleil, I'm still wary of what might happen if I tell you everything. I've told you before, and it has not ended well. Not at all."

"I am not giving you an option," I warn. "I need to know more about my opponents. I need to know who I may need to outwit, to protect not only my king and people, but also your family. Our family."

He grimaces, but does not refuse again.

"Teresa's husband. He is not a soldier of the Greys, he is a weapon, of a sort," Septimus confesses.

I look to Qhan and he nods. The truth, then.

"I see you have decided to believe me about the Greys, then," Septimus notes. "Or you're humoring me."

"I believe you," I say shortly. "The Greys are real, I am a Magicsmith. Let us not linger, here. Tell me as much as you can. Teresa told me her husband is vengeful. That has become a serious concern. Especially if these people are the ones powerful enough to start wars."

"Unfortunately, you're not being unreasonable," Septimus sighs.

Qhan almost laughs at that, but holds himself back.

"I'll talk," Septimus agrees. "But if I hold details back, you need to let me. I promise that these details will not severely impact your desire to keep everyone in the palace safe."

"Very well," I agree.

"We grew up with the Greys," he confesses. "Right alongside them, their people, their…supporters." He clears his throat. "Teresa's husband is very important, to the Greys. He has a powerful fluke over emotions that allows him manipulate people. Along with Teresa, together, they're…Well. I'll only say we're all lucky Teresa's nature is a gentle one."

He is inadvertently helping to convince me it might be acceptable to allow Teresa and her sons outside in another few days, so long as they promise to keep their hands gloved. I have all but decided there's no threat of Teresa using her fluke against us; I've only been trying to be vigilant.

Septimus is looking down at the table top, only vaguely paying attention to our reactions.

"You cannot possibly imagine what it was like, living in that place for all those years," he says with a cruel laugh at himself. "Your enemies are our enemies, Lady Soleil. I don't think it's possible to say who's suffered more. But if I had to hazard a guess, I would say Teresa has been through the most.

"The Greys are monsters. Complete monsters. And they employ fellow dark creatures for company. My sister's husband is one such monster. I hope he is dead. I mean that."

I frown. "Could he be dead? Teresa has implied otherwise."

He shrugs. "We did not kill him ourselves. But as I have mentioned, anything can happen in war."

I nod and gesture for him to continue.

"As I said, he is manipulative. But he could not hide his habits from her forever. Teresa ran from him on several occasions, but she has no skills for surviving on her own. Eventually, he wrangled her back and married her—in fact, I think he has convinced himself he loves her. But even so, manipulating us both entertained him. He would play us off each other, favoring one whilst hurting the other. He made us so desperate to please him…Yet, somehow, he still made it impossible not to love him."

It is that last sentence of his that makes me jerk my head up. Septimus is gazing absently at the table top, his arms still crossed loosely—he did not say that to shock me. When I look to Qhan, his expression tells me that Septimus is not lying to me: he and Teresa are truly still in love with a man who caused them nothing but abject pain and suffering.

"I do not expect you to understand," Septimus says. "But we grew up together. We were children together. He was, for the longest time, my closest friend. When he was kind, he was incredibly so. Especially after Teresa ran. He was so damned sweet on her. Any little thing Teresa or I wanted, if we were in his favor, we received. He knew us so well…He'd be so sweet to her, I've no doubt the reason their children exist is because Teresa loves him. Despite everything, she loves him."

I still say nothing. I know he is expecting commentary, but my mind is completely flustered. I cannot even begin to imagine how Teresa and Septimus' could fall in love with the man Septimus has described to me.

"I'm sure this sounds mad. An impossibility, to you," he says bitterly. "But we both loved him. I am not so sure we do not still love him."

Qhan and I stare Septimus for a full minute. I can practically hear Qhan attempting to think of something to say, but he cannot compose a full sentence, and continues to stop himself.

Septimus looks from one of us to the other.

"Well, say something," he says with a nervous laugh. "Does it shock you that much?"

I flounder to think of something other than simple curses and fail.

"Fate's Fingers," I say hoarsely.

"Is that all?"

"You love him?" I say, and can't help the disgust in my tone.

Qhan curses in Isaarian. I cannot tell if Septimus knows Isaarian well enough to understand exactly what was said, but I'm sure he can guess. He chooses not to address it and simply sighs.

"I can love him and accept the fact that I know what he's doing is wrong. But I've tried other ways too many times. I've blamed myself, and Teresa, for not being able to change him, though I have since realized we are not to blame, nor are we responsible. It is safer, for us, for my nephews and my niece, to run from him. So, we run."

"You said you hope he's dead," I remind Septimus.

"Because I do. Because it would be far easier to handle that, than to try and reconcile what we may feel when he eventually comes for us."

"Easier for everyone," I challenge. "Or for you?"

"All of us," Septimus claims. "The children included."

"It would be easier for them if they never saw their father again. Never got to say goodbye. I understand having enemies, Septimus, but even with those I would call my enemies, I recognize they may have families," I say, starting to think his emotions are getting the better of him. "I mark them with the Signs of the Dead."

"You don't understand," he claims. "It is not the same. Teresa's children are not stupid. They grew up with their father making no illusions about what he did to their mother. For Damen, I think, it has confused him; his father always doted on him. Always acted lovingly. But he would terrorize my sister. Hurt her. He made her help him do terrible things to his enemies. Then he would turn around and kiss her and stroke her hair."

I'm tempted to ask what sorts of things that man made them do, but I don't think my cousin will ever tell. So, I do not interrupt him.

"It horrified her, and he knew that. But a routine is a routine. Even after Damen came, it was not so bad, because her husband absolutely adored their first-born. In fact, he was so pleased with Damen and Teresa, it made him act civilized, for a time. He would buy Teresa endless gifts and spoil her. Kiss her and hold her close and tell her all sorts of sweet things, regardless of who was around to see. It convinced me and Teresa both, I think, that he had changed. When she was expecting Aiden, he insisted on carrying her around everywhere, so that she could rest. He would not let her lift a finger."

"But then Aiden was born," I say.

"Then Aiden was born," he agrees, and is silent for a moment. "Born less than perfect. After that, I cannot tell you who I worried for more: Teresa or Aiden. Her husband would never kill her on purpose, but Aiden…"

He looks gray with paleness. I doubt he realizes the blood has drained from his face, talking about his brother-in-law murdering his nephew, but I'm glad he is sitting down. He might have passed out at this point, otherwise.

"The only reason Aiden is still alive," Septimus finally continues hoarsely, "is because Teresa always put herself in the way. She would take the blame and the punishment. For everything. Whenever Aiden ever did anything 'wrong', she rushed to protect him."

"What kind of man would harm his own child?" Qhan cannot help but say in disgust and anger. "Or even threaten to do so?"

Septimus swallows. He still looks sick to his stomach.

"He would," he mutters under his breath.

I frown. "But Teresa would do anything to protect them."

"She would," Septimus agrees, sounding admittedly proud of his younger sister's unexpected grit. "And she does. She was always a gentle soul, but strong. For as long as she could be. I watched her get so despondent that she looked too weak to walk. Logically, I should not have cared; her misfortune with her husband was my fortune, the way he played with us. But she is my sister. The only sibling I have left.

"When the idea to escape finally crossed my mind, it took me months to convince Teresa to trust me. After all, how could she know that I wasn't trying to trick her, to make sure I was the favored one? So, I started helping her, to constantly hold her husband's favor. I think I preferred that, anyways; I could always handle the pain. It made it easier to try to hate him. That wasn't enough to convince her, but it helped. Then, I was the one who found that Ronin for her, to get medicine for Aiden, and I'm sure you already know what catalyzed her decision to leave."

"Her pregnancy. From Aiko Shinya," I say.

Septimus sighs. "I knew who he was—I recognized him—but Teresa didn't, and I didn't see a reason to tell her. It wouldn't change anything."

"I'd accuse you of letting her offer what she did, but Teresa told me it was all she had to give," I admit.

"We were kept a close eye on," he agrees. "Almost always. We had one chance, and we knew it. Aiko knew that, too, I'm sure. In times like these, I don't begrudge him for demanding payment, to procure such a rare and expensive medicine. I know Teresa thinks we are all lucky, that he accepted her offer. I do not know why he did; whether it was pity for Teresa or Aiden, or pride that he'd be taking to bed the wife of one of the men who helped destroy his country. Maybe he saw it as a form of conquering. Revenge. Who knows."

He shrugs miserably.

"I told her not to. I told her we could find another way, eventually, but she said we could not afford to wait. Aiden would die, if we did. So, as I said: Teresa will do anything for her children."

I nod. I fully understand, now, why Teresa has been so careful not to leave her sons alone. Even if she believes me when I say we would never hurt the children, these are patterns she has lived with for years. It is what she is accustomed to.

"I'm assuming her husband was away when all this happened?" I say.

"Yes. He was gone. Still, it wasn't easy, getting past Amerson especially."

"Amerson?"

"Amerson Grey. The eldest of the three Grey boys. His brother Kryto's favorite general. A particularly cruel brand of monster. He visited often. He…

enjoyed Teresa. And her husband did appreciate someone keeping a close eye on her while he was away."

I am practically gaping at him. Qhan is more visibly expressive than I have ever seen him before.

"See, this is why I am careful when I tell you these things," Septimus says. "About Teresa. Our lives. Us. In past times, when I revealed these things to you, you were younger and not quite so level-headed. You went off to go and kill all the Greys and their supporters. It did not go well. And it shouldn't matter, now. We did manage to escape, that is what's important. We fled west. Towards you. I knew you would help us, and I knew it was time. Time to finish this cycle, and start the new one."

I don't try to defend my past self; I'm still angry enough to want to skin the Greys, now knowing what kind of people they are. I'd take Teresa's husband apart for good measure. But Septimus is right: I am more level-headed now than I was in my youth, even if only a little. I'll be no help to anyone, now, if I run off to the west on a quest for revenge.

"Then tell me," I demand. "At this point, how do we proceed?"

Septimus is relieved, but only takes a moment before he leans closer across the table and explains.

"First: bring my sister and nephews safely to this summer palace of yours. It is better defended, and therefore a safer place for Teresa and the boys. After, there will be some travel involved for the two of us. There are a few things we need to ensure, before you run the timeline back one last time."

"And this is the last time?" I clarify. "You know that?"

"I cannot know that," he admits. "But let me say this. Soleil: if the next time is not the last, I cannot go through all this again. You can start over again if you like, but I can't help you with that. It has been…too much."

I think the Soleil of even a few days ago would insist otherwise. She'd attempt to prop Septimus up some, threaten or possibly reassure him. Guilt him. Remind him of how much is at stake. But I know Septimus is aware of this, already. Given his past, he's accustomed to being manipulated.

Remembering most of everything nearly killed Rian. I can't imagine what knowing as much as Septimus does has done to him.

"I understand," I say. "Can you tell me what still needs to be done?"

Septimus hesitates. "I could try to explain," he admits. "But it is personal in nature. Rest assured, I'm almost positive I know what must be done for the sake of the world. But our last mission in this timeline will be for the sake of individuals as well."

"Will you swear to reveal everything to me at some point before you ask me to wash the timeline back?" I ask.

"By the end of all this, you will know everything I do," he promises. "And

Soleil: in the final timeline, you will need to remember everything. That is the only way any of this will have been worth it. Fate all but requires it."

"And if I can't trust you, I'll at least have Fate," I say.

For the first time since he started his sordid tale, Septimus gives a genuine smile once more.

"Now you're getting it."

Four

I FINALLY LET Septimus out of the wine cellar. I find him rooms not far from Teresa and her sons', and make certain he is cleaned up and given new clothes before they get the chance to see them. I have them all join me for lunch, where the four make a heartfelt reunion that causes a bitterness to stir at the base of my throat. I try to be happy for them, but even Teresa's tearful gratitude insults me.

Ayla joins us for lunch, of course. Naomi and Valor usually eat with the Smiths as well, but treat their relationship with Teresa as professional. The princess, by contrast, is as bright and cheerful as she can possibly manage, paying particular attention to the two boys and including them in conversation whenever possible. Now that Septimus has joined us, she continues to play hostess well, asking polite questions that the Smiths can answer without complication. The boys' father is never mentioned. Ayla instead inquires after all their personal interests, their experiences living in the west, and how she might better improve their experience in Isaaria.

Septimus plays along. He acts as a good foil to her, and makes very few requests in order to be polite. He asks only for pairs of glasses for both himself and Teresa. Hers, to improve her vision, and his, to preserve. Apparently, eye-sensitivity is common in those with albinism, and Septimus prefers neutral to dim lighting. Darkening glasses help keep him from having to squint or otherwise strain his eyes.

Teresa, of course, asks for nothing.

Her sons are happy with what Ayla guesses they would like, including food items. The boys do love their sweets, but they have healthy appetites for anything Isaarian, really.

Teresa does not eat much in general. I am not sure if she is a picky eater or if her pregnancy is upsetting her stomach in more ways than what she told me, but she will, at least, eat rice. In fact, that woman can consume buckets full of rice and still be hungry. So, while I don't say anything about it either way, I ensure there's always rice at meals for her. A variety, too: sometimes with saffron, sometimes made with coconut milk or broth, or doused in butter or in various sauces. Teresa never says anything either, but if there is rice present, she eats it.

Within a few days, she begins to look healthier. It is astounding what good food, rest, and care can do: she is even prettier than I first thought she might have been. Though her hair is still thin from malnutrition, and her skin looks too pale, there is something enchanting about her, facial scars included. In fact, sometimes, when I catch her out of the corner of my eye, even I am drawn to her the way I might be a siren's sweet song. Now that I consider it, the moment Teresa arrived, though I was suspicious, I still wanted to help her. I wanted to keep her safe and look after her. I imprisoned Septimus, but not her, despite her having told me of her dangerous fluke.

I must wonder if it is a part of her fluke, or if she and Septimus are part Fair folk. Distantly if at all, but while the grime and wear of travel hid them at first, they are both strangely beautiful. There always were stories of the Smiths having an elven ancestor or two; perhaps the stories are true. I used to think nothing of the concept, as I did not believe Magicsmiths were real, but now I have to consider the possibility.

Regardless, I have realized that Teresa's charm is unintentional. She is always so surprised when people offer to do something for her, and sometimes, even embarrassed. It is sweet, in a way, but puzzling. I'm surprised she hasn't learned to be more manipulative, and conniving. I'm left only to suppose that she's the sort of person whose kindness and sweet nature cannot be beaten down by unfortunate circumstances.

She is so selfless, I'll admit, it inspires me to be the same.

The morning I decide to take the Smiths out to the gardens, I have much to see to in terms of business, first. I have put off my duties for too long, over the past few days, and it has postponed our departure for the Summer Palace. Now that Septimus has made his requests clear, though, I know the sooner I escort everyone to the west coast, the better. Septimus has, admittedly, told me much. He has given me something, now he expects something in return before revealing his plans.

It's easier to deal with Septimus via compromise, and this is fair enough.

I have a message sent to Ayla describing the afternoon plans, and while she has packing to do, she is ecstatic to join us as soon as she is able.

As I am still somewhat wary of the Smiths, I decide we will take this outing after an early supper. The sun will be setting, so while they will have enough light to see by, they won't get the full power of the sunlight. Still, I understand the boys are pleased to be allowed out-of-doors, especially considering the recent snowfall. I doubt they're thinking about strengthening their flukes.

After bundling up the children and tucking Teresa into one of the queen's fur-lined cloaks, we meet with Septimus, Valor and Naomi by the door to the back gardens. Aiden is practically jumping up and down with excitement. I cannot tell if he's really babbling in Lusch or if he's simply speaking so quickly that it sounds especially childish, but he is adorable. Damen is more controlled, but keeps looking up at the adults in anticipation.

"You don't need to stay together constantly," I allow. "But I would appreciate it if you were accompanied by either myself, Valor, or Naomi if you decide to go off your own ways."

I give Septimus in particular a stern look, to impress upon him that I expect him to follow the few rules I've put in place.

"If you don't mind, Captain, I may go off my own way for a stroll," he says, instantly relaying his intentions. "I'm due for a bit of strenuous exercise, and I don't think Teresa and the boys could keep up."

"So long as you don't cause trouble and stay in the gardens, I will allow it," I say carefully.

Septimus smiles and holds his hands up to show me his gloves.

"You have my word, Captain Marson," he says. "The gloves stay on, I stay with Valor, here."

We head out. Despite the snow and general lack of sunlight, the weather holds fairly. Inside our coats, I'm sure everyone is a comfortable temperature, and there is no wind to chill our bones.

The boys happily throw themselves out in the snow. Septimus says a few reassuring words to his sister before wandering off into the maze of gardens. He does not attempt a conversation with Valor as they depart, but the two of them seem comfortable enough together. Teresa hurries to follow her sons, making sure they keep their gloves and scarves on.

Naomi and I trail along behind as the children explore the gardens, running out their energy and sometimes falling face-first in the snow only to pop up with glee. Damen is interested in the different types of winter plants and questions everything. He, apparently, previously believed that everything died in winter time, and is amazed to find such an assumption wrong. It's oddly mature of him to be so interested in natural beauty, but I suppose I shouldn't expect anything less from him. He is an odd child.

Aiden is mainly interested in the snow, and is much quieter than his brother, but I think this is mainly because his first language is Lusch and sometimes, he can't be bothered to translate everything to Alarkian and back again in his head. I wonder how that must be for Teresa; Alarkian is her first language, and she stumbles along while speaking Lusch. Did her husband do that on purpose, in an attempt to distance her from her own children, or is it merely the natural consequences of the boys growing up there?

Regardless, I find Damen pulling me along ahead of the others, running along from one spot to the next, all but ignoring Teresa's request for him to wait. Naomi lingers behind, offering Teresa a helping hand if needed. Aiden hovers near his mother, too anxious to be far from her.

"What's this?" Damen asks, running up to a bramble patch covered with deep red flowers.

"Blood-weed," I say, making his face crumple.

"It's a weed?!"

"That is only what we call it," I say. "It would be considered a weed, only the fairies like using them as homes. Their magic keeps the blood-weed from infecting the rest of the garden, and even beautifies it."

"Fairies?" Damen says, brightening. "There are fairies, here?"

"Winter fairies," I say, "yes. They hibernate during the summer, come out during the winter. They like to live inside the blood-weed flowers. See all those petal folds, over and over on top of one another? There is quite a lot of space inside. These blossoms are large ones, after all."

"Can I see one? A winter fairy?" the boy asks.

I get the feeling that Damen's father is the sort of man who does not like his children being around magical creatures. Given his wife's obvious magic-sickness, I suppose that makes some sense, though I suspect Teresa did not contract her illness from creatures of magic. More likely, the corrupted magic came from someone's fluke.

"Let us see if I can coax one out for you," I say, and begin to tickle one of the flower's petals while Damen calls for his mother and brother in Lusch.

With enough encouragement, and the promise of fairies, Aiden finally runs over. It takes his mother longer, even while hanging on Naomi's arm.

I stroke the blood-weed blossom, careful to wake but not irritate the fairy inside. I would like the boys to appreciate and enjoy this experience, not have to run away from irritated fairies. At least blood-weed fairies are not picky about time of day. They will sleep when they like and wake when they like, and tend to be amenable to humans.

Once I have the petals pulled back, I slowly stroke the fairy's side, clicking my tongue at her and whistling softly. I'm careful to use only the tip of my finger; I touch her only enough to brighten her pink skin, but not to turn it an angry red. Eventually, she starts to yawn, sigh, and stretch.

Damen peers in close next to me, and soon Aiden joins him as the first of the fairies emerges from her flower and begins to flutter her delicate wings. As soon as she finds herself staring at a tiny male human child, the fairy's wings begin to flap in earnest. She raises herself up so she's almost brushing Damen's nose.

"Hold your hands out like this, in a cup, if you want her to sit in them," I say, demonstrating. "But you must be very gentle."

Damen immediately mimics me, cupping his hands together and waiting. He seems surprised when the fairy almost immediately lands on his palm, stepping across with delicate footsteps. The fairy then seats herself in his palm and sits there, waiting.

"What do I do?" Damen asks, so seriously one might think he was following instructions on learning to string a crossbow.

"Can you whistle?" I say, but he shakes his head.

At this point, Teresa has joined us, and now kneels in the snow beside Aiden, careful to rest her knees on the cloak as not to wet her dress. She speaks to her younger son gently, helping him to cup his hands in the same way I showed Damen. Aiden is a touch more nervous, understandably, but Teresa continues to coax him and reassure him.

"Well, if you can't whistle, then humming works just as well," I suggest.

"Humming?" Damen repeats.

"Like this, baby, I can do it," Teresa suggests, and begins to hum a lullaby.

Almost immediately, the fairy in Damen's hand sits up straighter, perky and attentive. Then she begins to chirp, copying Teresa in a higher octave, until more fairies begin to emerge from their flowers, happy and curious. They are soon fluttering around about our heads. They are accustomed to me—they've seen me for years and years whenever the king or Ayla walk in the gardens—but they're happy to see new faces in Teresa and her sons. The fairy in Damen's hand takes flight again and relocates to his mother's hair.

The fairies flutter about, singing Teresa's tune, creating their own song out of it. Aiden hesitantly sings a little Lusch, and the fairies go mad for it, landing in his hair and burrowing into his coat. Aiden is hesitant at first, but with reassurances from his mother, begins to enjoy the attention instead.

Naomi kneels on the other side of Aiden and starts to show him how to "trick" the fairies into overlapping songs with one another without starting a quarrel amongst them. Damen, meanwhile, ducks away, his interest waning now that they are paying more attention to Aiden than to him.

"What's that one?" he asks me, pointing to a tree off in the center of the gardens, some distance away in this maze.

It is the most glorious tree we have, and the largest. Even from here, one can tell that its branches extend over several sections of the garden, and from it, currently, bloom pure white blossoms that will soon bear fruit.

"That is the dryad tree," I say.

Somehow, Damen becomes even more intrigued than before.

"Can I see it?" he asks.

"I think your mother and brother would rather linger here for a while."

Before I can finish my sentence, Damen has already turned to ask his mother if we can go ahead, and see the dryad tree. Teresa is reluctant to give her permission, mainly because Aiden is still enjoying himself immensely with the blood-weed fairies, and she doesn't want her sons split apart from her. But even she can see that Damen is excited, and she does not want to disappoint him. She is aware of how much the traveling and separation from their father have taken a toll on the children.

"If you like, darling. We'll be here," she says. "Please don't be long. Just a few minutes, then come straight back."

"We'll be quick, Mama, promise," Damen calls, already running through the snow, as if he is being timed.

I am quick to follow, moving through the snow with ease considering my much longer legs and dependable boots. Damen's excitement gives him speed, but I'm used to matching the king's jaunty strides. My own gait has since accustomed itself to those who otherwise might outpace me.

Once he realizes I can keep up with him, Damen approves of me even more than he did before. I suppose his mother is usually unable to do so, and I have also noticed that, while my rather gruff nature tends to frighten Aiden, Damen almost enjoys it. I try to tell myself that this has nothing at all to do with him missing his father, but I cannot avoid that likelihood.

It is a relief when Damen begins to engage me in conversation.

"You help protect the king of Isaaria, right? That's your job?" he asks me.

"In a way, yes. I am a bodyguard of his," I say.

"Valor said he's a guard of the king, is that the same thing?" he asks, ever intrigued as to what exactly it is I do.

"I am the king's chief of security," I explain. "While Valor is a kings' guard, and does what he can to protect the king and his interests, it is my duty to know what is happening in the palace, at all times. If an attempt is made on the king's life, or the princess's, one such as Valor may be the one to thwart said attempt, but it is my duty to discover who arranged it in the first place. And put safeguards in place to stop all further efforts."

Damen considers this. "Have you killed people, then?"

I decide it's best not to lie to a child. Particularly one like Damen.

"Yes. Though I only do so when necessary. It is not an easy thing, taking a life," I say. I had to learn that lesson myself.

The boy does not respond to that, and I wonder, for a moment, if he is aware of the things Septimus described to me. I already know I must be careful around Damen, when it comes to his father. Like most boys his age, Damen idolizes his father, and perhaps for the sake of his developmental sanity, his mind has come up with a myriad of excuses for his father's behavior. I cannot directly accuse Teresa's husband of anything.

"Is it still hard if it is a bad person, though?" Damen says after thinking about it for some time. "They're trying to kill the king anyways, right? So doesn't that make them bad?"

"It means they're doing something wrong," I confirm. "But no. That does not necessarily make it any easier."

Damen listens to my words with care, practically taking them to heart. He's a highly intelligent boy, as I have already noted, but he's young and naïve. I am happy to give Damen more of an education when it comes to the magic in our world, but I am wary of the responsibility of a moral education as well. I suppose, at least, Ayla managed to turn out well enough.

We reach the center of the gardens, and Damen reveals first in Lusch and then Alarkian that the tree is impressive and even bigger than he expected. He circles around it several times, peering up into the thicket of branches. No doubt, he is searching for the dryad. I chuckle at him, as he hunts without question, and move towards the bushes surrounding the tree. From there, it's easy to acquire a handful of winter berries.

"Where is she?" Damen finally asks me once he's given up.

"We're going to tempt her out," I say, "Come. Hold your hands out."

Damen does so curiously, and I pour berries into his hands to fill them.

"Now step closer to the tree roots, hold your hands up and wait," I instruct. "She will come down. Only, do not make sudden movements. That will frighten her."

I help move Damen closer to the tree, and then start to whistle a bird's trill, several times over. Fairies, dryads and naiads all love music. They can't help but be drawn towards it. Sure enough, the dryad slowly crawls downward towards us, like a tree-frog. Her round, clear eyes blink with frank curiosity as she sees Damen with his little offering. The boy gasps and almost jumps backwards once he gets a good look at her, but stands his ground and waits.

The winter dryad's skin is pale blue, her mouth small and indigo, and her ears pointed. She technically wears no clothes, but an almost indistinguishable layer of bark and soft petals cover her where necessary, like an extension of her skin. Her eyes are white, but hair dark as silt, wild, thick, and long.

She releases the tree with one hand and leans forward towards Damen, plucking some of the berries out of his hands with her long, spindly fingers, with webbing stretched high in between them.

"Her fingers are cold!" Damen whispers to me while the dryad continues to sample from his offered berries.

"That is because she's a winter dryad," I remind him. "When spring arrives, she will crawl back to live in the tree roots, and the spring dryad will emerge. Then summer. Then fall. Then winter, again."

"So, this tree has four dryads living here?" Damen says curiously.

"It is a large tree," I say. "And rare. It could not survive without them. It is the one of the only plants in the world that blossoms and bears a different fruit every season. As it needs much care, it needs many dryads."

The boy considers this. "That makes sense," he decides.

He spends another few minutes waiting while the dryad does as she pleases. He stands still long enough for the dryad to become fully comfortable with him. She comes down to sit amongst the coils of roots, still snacking.

"I didn't know this is what dryads looked like," Damen admits after a little while, still whispering. "Can I talk to her? Do they know any languages?"

"Of their own sort," I say. "Some scholars have tried to decipher and learn the dryad tongue. Some say the Wolffs could speak it; there are tales, that the first Wolff prince learned to speak the language, to charm himself a dryad wife, and so, all their descendants can naturally speak the tongue as well."

Damen appears awed at the concept.

"Can you talk to her for me?" he asks.

"Unfortunately, I cannot. We have no records of the dryad's languages, here in Isaaria. No one has it but the Wolffs, if you believe in them. But, perhaps you might study it on your own in the future."

I say so hesitantly, hoping I have not said the wrong thing, but Damen goes along with my suggestion with relish.

"Mama said I can do whatever I want when I grow older," he says.

"She is a very wise lady," I say.

Once the dryad has finished with the berries, she looks at Damen curiously, opens her mouth, and makes a few singing phrases with a purring in her throat. She is pleased, then, with our little offering, and to meet someone new. She plucks at Damen's coat, which startles him, but then he giggles. The dryad lengthens her spine, curling up towards Damen so she can observe his facial features. She is particularly taken with his locks of blue-black hair, and plays with them, chittering and singing happily.

After another minute, she pulls him closer, kisses both of his cheeks, pats him on the head, and scampers back up her tree.

Damen instantly whirls back to me. "Did I do the wrong thing?"

"Not at all," I say. "She's fond of you, I think. She'd like to see you again."

Damen frowns. "But aren't we moving? Going to the other palace?"

"We are," I confirm. "The dryad tree is to be transported there as well. There are gardeners coming by tomorrow to remove her. She is to be re-planted in the west. You will be able to see her there."

"Won't that hurt her?" he asks worriedly.

"Not at all. That is why we have professionals coming in to look after her," I reassure him. "Some might find it a little gauche, but where the king goes, the dryads like to go, too. They beautify his gardens, yes, but they enjoy seeing him as well. It is for them as well as him."

"Oh. Good, then," Damen says.

I hold a hand out to him. "Right, then: let us get you back to your mother. You've seen your dryad, now; I don't want to worry her."

Damen nods in agreement, and takes my hand so I might help him out of the tree roots. "Mama does worry an awful lot," he admits.

I almost chuckle at that.

I turn to escort him out of the gardens, back to Teresa, when there is suddenly someone here with us.

"Oh," Rian says in slight surprise, but instantly smiles. "Well, hello there."

I stare.

I'd been reassured many times over that Rian was recovering, but I didn't realize he was doing so well. Here he is, dressed in both the clothing and aura of a proper Isaarian king, wearing one of his grandest coats, Mango perched on a shoulder. Qhan is trailing behind him dutifully, and nods when he sees me. Korvaan is further behind, near the entrance to this section of the gardens.

"Your majesty," I finally say, finding my tongue. "I didn't realize you… That you would be in the gardens today."

Rian smiles as if he knows something I do not. "Of course, you wouldn't. You have been avoiding me, Captain Marson."

Before I can think of something else to say, he is crouching down before Damen, giving a great sigh as his knees creak.

"Ah. Well, then. You must be Damen, am I right?" he says, and offers a hand. "Pleased to meet you. I am the king of Isaaria. But you may call me Rian, if you like."

Damen hesitates, but then shakes Rian's hand in the Alarkian fashion.

"How do you know my name?"

Rian laughs. "I am king, here, boy. Naturally, I know the names of my guests. Even if this palace were full to bursting will folk beyond my count, I at least would make sure to know our lovely Captain Marson's cousins."

I clear my throat pointedly. "Is there a reason you are outside today, your majesty? I was under the impression you weren't feeling your best, lately."

And so, you should not be outside in the cold, you hapless fool.

Rian merely shrugs and smiles. "I wanted to say a brief farewell to our winter dryad before she moves tomorrow. But I see you've already taken care of that for me. Did you like the winter dryad, Damen?" he adds to the boy.

Damen nods. "She is the first one I've ever met. And we got to meet *fairies* earlier, too."

"Fairies and dryads, well, well. What a day," Rian says, and removes the dragon from his shoulders. "Here, I shall complete the trio. Say hello to my most steadfast companion: Mango."

He shows Damen how to hold his arm up, as if waiting for a falcon to land on it, and gingerly places Mango down on top.

"Won't he jump off?" Damen asks.

"Unlikely. He might have done, in years past, but Mango used to be a lot spryer when he was, aha, younger," Rian admits. "And to tell you the truth, I'm feeling that myself, lately."

Any other child his age would not find this funny, but Damen smiles.

Mango has since grown used to being passed around and held by different intrigued folks. Though Rian only has Ayla, and never had any children with Asmer, he still often returns to visit the University he was educated at and brings Mango with, to the pleasure and awe of the children there. They run after Mango, play catch with him, pet him until he purrs happily, and feed him no end of unnecessary snacks.

Now, the dragon settles himself on Damen's arm with impeccable balance and resigns himself to the usual pampering. He would likely fall asleep while Damen tentatively pats his head, only, Rian reaches into a pocket of his coat to dig out a handful of dried papaya.

"Here, give him one of those. He loves them," the king says, pouring the dried fruit into one of Damen's hands not unlike how I'd shared the berries with him earlier.

"Will he bite?" Damen asks, but doesn't sound afraid of the possibility.

"He ought to know better than that. See…? There you go. Look at him smacking away. He loves that, doesn't he?"

Damen is grinning ear-to-ear. The fairies might have intrigued him, and the dryad was mystifying, but meeting Mango is an improvement on both. The dragon is a creature of magic, yes, but tamed. A friendly companion. For all their openness to humans, fairies are not the sort amenable to taming. A human's relationship with a dragon, meanwhile, is more symbiotic in nature. Rian fed, raised, and cared for Mango; Mango brings endless joy to almost everyone who chances to meet him.

"Is he a miniature sunblood dragon?" Damen asks after a moment.

Rian is surprised, but pleased. "Yes, exactly right. How did you know?"

Damen shrugs.

"I read about them. My father got me a book about dragons. It's my second favorite. Or, it's my first favorite right now. Because I miss it so much. I wanted to bring more books, but Mama said we couldn't, because they're heavy."

"What a shame," Rian says. "But you've seen our library, I'm sure. You'll find plenty of books in there about dragons, if you like."

Damen nods, petting Mango's back for a few seconds before speaking again. "Does he have a family? Baby dragons?"

Again, such a question from a child startles Rian somewhat, but he adjusts appropriately. "Oh. No. No, I'm afraid Mango never found his match. He is too much of an individual, I suppose."

"That's too bad," Damen says, and frowns as he continues to offer Mango pieces of papaya. "Sunblood dragons don't like being lonely. They like other dragons lots."

"It's all right," Rian says. "He's got me. Just a pair of old bachelors, us."

"'Bachelor' means you never got married?" Damen deduces.

"Ah, well. Hmm. I suppose that is not accurate, then," Rian admits. "You've caught me there: I did marry, but my wife passed away some time ago. I guess I grew so accustomed her not being here anymore that I..."

He stops himself, a puzzled frown showing up on his face. Damen looks up at him, too, away from Mango while offering some papaya, and almost immediately there's an accident.

It's neither Damen nor Mango's fault, exactly. Mango is happily eating out of Damen's hand and has never bitten anyone before. But I guess Damen moved his hand to the wrong spot inadvertently, or got his finger stuck in with the dried papaya, because the next thing I know, Mango's nipped him.

To his credit, Damen does not allow for tears, only gives a little, startled cry of pain and yanks his hand away. In an instant, Rian has bent down again to Damen's level, to see what the damage is.

"Any blood?" he asks, taking Damen's hand and looking it over.

"No. It was just an accident," Damen reassures. "He's a good dragon."

"That's a sure relief," Rian says with a laugh.

He pats the boy's hand before snapping his fingers and letting Mango crawl up his arm and back onto his shoulders.

"Can I—" Damen starts, but is interrupted in an untimely and unfortunate fashion.

"Damen!" Teresa screams, somewhere far off. "Damen!"

"Oh, Fate's Fingers," I sigh.

First off, we certainly took our time with the dryad, and beyond that, I'm sure Teresa heard Damen's yelp echo, followed by silence. She is worried that the security of the palace may have been compromised.

It does not take long before we find Teresa running up to us as best she can in the snow, holding her skirts up, her cloak flipped back. Naomi is following quickly, carrying Aiden, but Teresa reaches us first. She grabs Damen by the shoulders the minute she stops and pulls him back, panting, and looking at each of us, clearly overwhelmed. The moment she puts together the fact that Rian is the king of Isaaria, she pales, and looks ill.

"I am so terribly sorry for the disturbance, your majesty, so very sorry. Please forgive him," she begs, falling to her knees and dropping her head down as if in prayerful supplication. After a moment, she tugs on Damen's little coat sleeve until he mimics her. "Please, please forgive him."

Rian's brow furrows. He frowns.

"What…? Oh. No. I think there has been a misunderstanding," he says, and then goes to take Teresa's arms and draw her back to her feet. "Your son wasn't interrupting anything. And I wouldn't mind it if he were, truly. I quite like children. I always wish I'd had more."

I feel my face flush. Rian is talking to Teresa, not even glancing at me, but I still feel as if he said so because he wanted me to hear.

Teresa is confused, however. She is wary of Rian but is too physically weak, and encumbered by her pregnancy, not to except his help in standing.

"But I'm sure you're very busy," she says. "There's much you need to see to, as a king. Many responsibilities. You can't have children underfoot. Especially when they are not even your own children."

"Not so many responsibilities that I can't enjoy a nice walk outdoors from time to time," Rian says. "And when I'm out here, there's a rule. No working allowed."

"That's a smart rule," Damen quips.

"My daughter Ayla made it up. Have you met my Ayla yet?"

"Oh, we like Ayla!" Damen says, as Naomi and Aiden join us.

"Most excellent," Rian says. "I hope I can meet the same approval rating."

He offers a hand to Teresa while Naomi places Aiden back on the ground. Teresa is hesitant, and confused, but gives Rian her hand. He promptly bends to kiss the back of her knuckles, like a proper gentleman.

"It is lovely to finally meet you, Miss Teresa," he claims. "I'd heard you were settling in comfortably, and apologize for not coming to address you sooner. I'm afraid the palace is a hub of activity, lately. I'm sure you've heard about the move ahead of us."

"Oh. No, that's quite alright," Teresa says haltingly.

But Rian has already deftly moved on.

"I was boring myself to death with work when I realized it was a lovely day for a walk. I suppose you all thought the same, because who should I meet but Damen and Captain Marson out here by the dryad tree! ...I'll admit, they took me a little by surprise, but I'm glad for their company. As is Mango."

Mango gives a satisfied growl when he hears his name, settles himself into the comfort of Rian's coat, and closes his eyes.

Damen pulls on his mother's skirts, and switches back to Lusch in order to jabber at her, presumably about the king's dragon. It's odd, because I have only heard Aiden talk like that before. Damen has used Lusch, of course, but usually he is more careful about choosing his words. Slow to speak, and cautious. I suppose it took a presence like Mango's to remind him of his own childish whimsy again.

"Yes, I see," Teresa replies, her discomfort starting to fade as logic catches up to panic. "You're right, Damen, he does look mango-colored. An apt title."

"I thought so," Rian says, clearly proud of his naming prowess.

Teresa has bent down as best she can with her pregnancy, trying to bring Aiden forward, away from where he is hiding under her cloak.

"Do you want to see the dragon, baby? He's like the dragons from your storybooks, only smaller."

Rian notices the boy's shyness and crouches down again, this time without a quip about his aching old man body.

"Are you Aiden, then?"

Aiden scrunches close to Teresa's leg and nods.

"And how old are you, Aiden?"

Aiden holds up the appropriate number of fingers.

"Four!" Rian repeats.

"And a half," Aiden whispers.

Rian whistles. "Impressive. You and your brother must do an excellent job looking after your mother. Especially coming all the way from the west! You must be very strong. And brave."

"They are," Teresa says, putting a hand on Aiden's head.

"Then I bet someone as brave as you would be perfectly fine meeting a dragon, huh?" Rian says.

He waits until Aiden nods before pulling Mango back off his shoulders again. Damen joins them, reassuring his brother in Lusch and showing him how to pet Mango, and feed him dried fruit.

"Look at that: both of you, expert dragon handlers already," Rian claims. "If you like, and if your mother approves, you can even let Mango sleep at the foot of your bed. He loves children."

Both the boys are pleased with that idea.

"What an opportunity. Say thank you, Aiden," Teresa says, and the child echoes her quietly, but clearly.

His endearing little voice causes Rian's face to break into a wide grin. His eyes seem a touch brighter. I think, over the past few years and everything we have been through, he partially forgot just how much he loves children. He'll always love Ayla, of course, but she is a full-grown woman, lingering in her father's household mainly out of concern for his well-being.

They have already experienced that natural reversal, when child begins looking after parent. Rian still wants someone who he can dote on, who will not lecture him on looking after himself better.

"Hello, all!" a voice calls from the entrance to this clearing.

Ayla has come to join us, waving as she huffs and puffs in the cold air, slogging through the snow that comes up to her shins. Behind her are a pair of staff members carrying baskets and trays of who-knows what.

"I was told I might find some of you out here," she continues, "but look at this: the perfect makings of a party!"

As she joins us, Ayla stands up on her tiptoes to kiss her father on the cheek, and looks to me to wink: she was right. Rian has recovered after all.

"I'm not too late, am I? Going back inside already?" she adds, sensing a strange mood about us.

Teresa's sons instantly look to her and plead otherwise: they have been trapped inside for days, and want to appreciate the fresh air as long as they can.

"Not at all," she tells Ayla. "I think the boys would like to stay out a while longer. If that is acceptable."

She flicks her eyes sideways at me, as if recalling my ever-changing rules about whether the Smiths can remain out-of-doors.

"I say, if they want to stay out and play, let them run until they drop," Rian proclaims before I can open my mouth.

As his chief of security, I would be irritated with him, but I'm tired of being the one to always make the hard decisions. If Rian is not worried about letting the Smiths outside, and neither is Qhan or Valor or Naomi, then I shall try my best to continue stiffing my usual paranoia.

"Excellent!" Ayla says, and steps over to loop an arm with one of Teresa's. "The boys can play while we ladies have a tea party. This way!"

She leads a surprised Teresa off to the side of the clearing, where a metal set of table and chairs await. The two ladies are a funny sight, with Teresa standing at nearly a hand and a half taller than the princess.

I look to Qhan, give him a nod, then follow just as Ayla is having the snow dusted clear, and cushions placed on the seats.

"Here: sit," Ayla directs. Once Teresa does so, Ayla gestures for her maid to arrange blankets on Teresa's lap and about her shoulders.

I glance back, sure Aiden, at least, will soon run after his mother, but Rian has quickly captured both boy's attentions well. They are not clinging to their mother, nor are they especially wary of the king. For right or wrong, it is impressive Ayla and her father can ease folk to their presences so effortlessly. One could call it the charm of royalty, but I would not attribute the same skill to the grand princes and princess. Not all of them.

Within minutes, Ayla has been brought the items she's desired: warm tea with honey, cinnamon apple tarts, miniature cakes with delicate pastel frosting and edible flowers, coffee, and a small assortment of flaky pastries, some made into sandwiches. Teresa is shocked by how casually she is being given such treats, and for no specific occasion, even. This is a common tea taking for Ayla, but a lavish spread of delicacy for Teresa.

She waits for Ayla to start picking out things to eat first, and then chooses a single item and puts it on the center of her plate. Ayla notices, and without wait fills the rest of Teresa's plate until it matches her own. She does not say anything, doesn't make teasing quips about Teresa needing to eat for two. She simply keeps talking about how she enjoys taking tea. She explains how she's partaken in the custom since Asmer married Rian, informing Teresa of the seasonal changes one might make to the offered menu.

Teresa is overwhelmed but blinks away grateful tears. She is learning she is safe to expect this form of simple kindness from us.

I stand by Teresa as Ayla directs their impromptu tea conversation with grace and welcoming congeniality. She is a sweet young woman, and seeks a friendship with Teresa. She is already acting the elder in their relationship despite Teresa's six-year advantage on her.

While I vaguely listen to them, I watch Rian play with Mango and the boys. They spend several hours in the snow, too active and filled with laughter to feel the cold. In fact, it is the first day I've seen where Damen smiles more than not. It transforms him into a completely different child. He runs about with Aiden, fleeing from Rian, throwing snow at him, and pretending as if they are knights on an adventure. Damen always makes certain Aiden can keep up with him, and keeps his brother from falling or hurting himself. It's instinctive. It reminds me that Teresa and her husband must have done some good in raising their boys.

Or perhaps it is all from Teresa. Who is to know.

Either way, how Rian acts with the boys makes me somehow love him even more than I already did.

Eventually, Ayla notices that Teresa is more invested in watching Rian and the boys than holding a proper conversation. Teresa smiles as she sees them running about through the snow, but it is a sad smile.

Ayla is hesitant to broach a personal topic with Teresa, knowing the poor woman fainted when I tried last time. But she decides it is different, chatting with someone who might be a friend versus facing an interrogation, and tries regardless.

"Oh, yes. They are adorable, aren't they?" Ayla says, as if she just noticed the way the children interact with her father.

"They always did like playing outdoors, but I couldn't take them out on my own," Teresa admits distractedly. "I wasn't allowed to."

She trails off, remembering, and Ayla frowns.

"Something on your mind?" she prompts.

"It's only…My husband used to play with Damen," Teresa says haltingly. "He was always so good with Damen. It is hard to explain. Or describe. But he was…A good father. To at least one of our children."

Ayla looks horrified. She has been properly filled in on the gossip, at this point, or at least knows enough to be uncomfortable to hear that.

"Oh," she says.

Teresa continues.

"I know how it sounds. But it was hard not to fall in love with him all over again, watching him play games with Damen. Make believe, with sticks for swords and fishing rods and such. We could have afforded to give Damen any number of fancy toys, but no matter what we bought, he always liked simpler play-things. His imagination."

She quiets, thinking. Ayla glances up at me, helpless. I think she genuinely wants to be friends with Teresa but does not know what to do when faced with this topic. She is no counselor, and, her own life's struggles have been in an entirely different field.

I step in to help. It might not be much, but I cannot leave Ayla to manage this on her own.

"If you are feeling guilt for taking the boys away from their father, you ought not," I say. "Septimus told me enough. You have done your sons a service."

"I tell myself that," Teresa says. "But some days, I don't know. He is their father. He loves Damen. And if he'd managed to love Aiden the same way…I don't know if I would have had the strength to leave him."

I struggle to know how to answer that. Teresa's selflessness is inspiring, but also, I've realized, potentially damaging. We can never know for certain, but at least by her own testimony, Teresa would have stayed in her marriage for the rest of her life if not for Rika. I know I can't convince her she did the right thing for her own sake. I can only appeal to her through her sons.

"No child should have to be raised under the roof of a man who abuses their mother," I say.

"He never touched them, though," Teresa whispers. "He would never hurt Damen. And I don't think he'd hurt Aiden, either. It was all just talk."

"And do you think seeing that, or hearing that, did not affect them?" I say.

Teresa is silent. She picks at the threads of the blanket around her shoulders and looks down at her lap. I don't want to depend on guilting her to validate her choices, but it may be the only way to help her understand. Her husband has made her into this pitiful, apologetic little thing who is scared of offending anyone lest they lash out at her.

"I don't know," she whispers. "I only want them to have good lives."

Ayla reaches across the table to put a hand on Teresa's hand, making her look up again.

"You're doing that," she says. "Trust me, you are a wonderful mother."

Teresa's eyes water. I'm worried she will cry, but Septimus and Valor arrive in time to keep her from it. She sniffs and wipes at her eyes before forcing a smile. It is curious that she would hide her emotions from her own brother, but I must remind myself that even a year ago, Teresa might have seen Septimus as the enemy; someone her husband might send to manipulate her. Septimus has centuries of memories to turn him from the Greys' side, but Teresa has almost no proof of that, only trust.

"Sorry to interrupt, but I think it would be best if we went back inside, Teresa," Septimus says, going to put his hands on his sister's shoulders and help her up. "I'm sure they are looking after you, but it is winter, still. And you have never done well with the cold."

Teresa's sons, having noticed their uncle, run over, puffing. Their faces are red enough to convince me it is time to send all the Smiths inside. I do not want them getting sick. They have been through enough.

Rian is apparently in agreement.

"Right, then, boys: time for bed," Rian says, and surprisingly, neither of the children argue. He has an authority over them that I've no doubt comes from them missing their father-figure.

It helps that the sun has set, and the children have exhausted themselves by playing in the snow. Aiden lets his uncle swing him up onto his shoulders, practically already falling asleep. Damen offers his hand to his mother so she can walk him back into the palace. Ayla's staff start to clean up the impromptu tea party while the rest of everyone head towards the palace.

I take Valor aside for a moment.

"Did he do anything suspicious?" I ask.

"Septimus?" he repeats, with such shock the question is practically already answered. "No. We walked. Made casual talk."

"Casual?" I repeat. "Did he say anything about their past in the west? Or his sister's husband?"

"Not at all," Valor admits. "We didn't speak constantly, but when we did talk, it was simple things about his family. His nephews, specifically."

"But nothing of import?"

"He made significant efforts to avoid anything you might use to extrapolate more about their pasts."

I sigh but wave his dismissal. I catch Septimus looking back at him, and ignore his smirk as best I can. He knows exactly what he's doing, but I'll admit, I'd prefer to have him on our side enough that I'll excuse this obvious mockery. For now.

I am about to head after them when Rian steps up next to me. A quick glance in his direction tells me he is still grinning ear-to-ear.

"Those boys," he says, shaking his head. He pats Mango's snout. "One would think they'd never been allowed outside, the way they enjoyed today."

Though I've seen first-hand how protective Teresa can be over her sons, I know it's not that. Rian is the reason Damen and Aiden enjoyed today. Well, Mango assisted, undoubtedly, but Rian is the one who essentially taught them how to be children again. I worry that, in their flight from the west and the ensuing travels, they may have started to forget that.

"You are a good man, Rian Yakarami," I tell him.

Rian turns his grin on me. "Well, that is a relief. Here I was, all worried I was secretly a horrible, horrible person."

"You know, it is a good thing for you that I appreciate your confidence," I warn him.

"Delicate egos cannot survive in this world."

He tentatively wraps an arm around me. I don't pull away.

We slowly follow the others back into the palace, Qhan walking a respectable distance behind us. I don't know what to say to Rian, considering everything that has happened this past week. I have so many questions for him, but cannot bring myself to ask them. I want to know what he's thinking, and how he's feeling, but at the same time, I am terrified by it. He was right in saying I've been avoiding him.

He has been my principal, my crown prince, my king, my husband, and the father to my children. There are so many aspects to our relationship, now, I do not know where to start.

I suppose this is as good a place as any.

Mango crawls across Rian's shoulders and onto mine.

"Traitor," Rian scowls, but in good fun.

"He likes the smell of the soap I use," I claim.

"Anyone with a modicum of common sense would," he says, so smooth and casual about it that I have to give him a look. Rian is grinning, as always.

"Too soon?"

"I don't think I can be the judge of that, at this point," I admit.

If anything, it is too late.

We walk a while longer, our feet crunching down the snow. The others have already vanished up ahead of us, save for Qhan and Korvaan, who linger to protect their king. Mango's purring in my ear is strangely soothing. I always did have a soft spot for the little sunblood, despite myself. I find I'm saddened by what Damen pointed out, considering dragons and their loneliness. I suppose neither Rian or Mango found their match in time.

"Sorry to surprise you," Rian says after a minute. "But you have been avoiding me. I figured if I gave you fair warning of where I'd be, and when, you'd continue to dodge me until we left for the Summer Palace."

"Possibly," I admit.

"Why?"

"Because much has happened, Rian," I say. "Beyond what Septimus allowed us to remember. I have a sister. Cousins. A family. I'm supposed to have you. I cannot stop thinking about what you said, about, perhaps, what we should do if we don't go back for Taris and Lune. Septimus told me he has some plan, to fix things, and I want to trust him. I'm trying to. But it is… difficult. I am at war with myself and I don't need further complications."

To my relief, Rian does not speak straight away. Nor does he attempt to counter my argument directly when he finally gathers his thoughts.

"If you need distance for now, you could always say so," he says. "But I would prefer some form of communication between us. Even if it is only for professional means."

I consider this and give a slow nod.

"That said," Rian continues, his tone brighter. "There are always other options. What if I wasn't around to complicate, but simply to support? If ever you need a partner for discussion...I could be that person."

For a moment, I must stop walking and allow myself to think. Rian removes his arm from around my waist and stands a few steps away.

"It is a confusing time for us both, is all," I say. "I don't want us to acknowledge one another out of mere formality, given the past. But I worry that anything more might compromise my current duties and your safety."

"Oh, Vilaneau is set to replace you, soon, anyways. Besides, we could start slow. Build from where we are to wherever you think we ought to be."

"You'd be content letting me control everything that way?"

"Soleil, I have been content just seeing you today after so much time without you. I figured, if today is day 'one', then by day fifty you might let me kiss you again."

I scoff and then lunge forward to grab his hand and begin dragging him back towards the palace. That ought to show him.

Rian laughs, and when I glance up at him, I realize he's smiling like an idiot. For some time, I focus solely on the crunching of snow beneath us and the darkening blue sky around us. But every time I check our surroundings for threats, and inevitably catch sight of Rian, he's still grinning like this is the single greatest moment of his life. I glance at Qhan and Korvaan, but they are pointedly looking elsewhere. This is as much privacy as can be afforded a king, I suppose.

"What?" I ask, unable to ignore Rian's expression any longer.

"You cannot understand how happy you're making me right now."

"I'm only holding your hand," I point out.

"I know."

I slow my pace some. I'd meant to call his bluff, but I suppose Rian's been nothing if not honest with me this entire time. Embarrassing though it is, I think back to previous times when the king has paid more attention to me than his own wife. At the time, I thought nothing of it, figuring it was merely because we had a respectable, platonic relationship that lent itself to friendly banter more easily than his exchanges with Asmer. I had thought it was because the king was not much one for romance.

It must have been hard for him to be with Asmer when he was smitten with his own bodyguard.

Idiot.

If I'd discovered this before Septimus revealed the truth of our pasts to me, I do not know how I would react. Currently, I am both horrified and smug. Horrified I inadvertently destroyed any possibility of a successful marriage for the king without my involvement.

Smug for admittedly similar reasons.

"Have you said anything to the princess, yet?" I ask, hoping for a distraction.

"Not much," Rian says, "but Ayla is no fool. I'm sure she knows. Not about your fluke, but at least about us."

I hold back a groan, wondering who else in the palace has known all along. How I could have been so stupid and blind not to realize it before? It is not as if Rian is subtle.

"We should not confirm anything, now," I warn him.

"Agreed."

"But if you are willing to let me control the pace and keep it from public knowledge," I consider out loud, "I think it may be best to still do what we can to cultivate the relationship we know we once had. See what we can make of it, now."

I wait for a few seconds for his answer. But then Rian gives me a strange look. Almost an uncharacteristic grimace.

"...I am truly sorry, and I in no way want you to think I am not taking this seriously," Rian warns me. "But you said 'cultivate' and that made me think of cheese. And then I stopped listening."

It takes me a moment to realize he is teasing me, but afterwards, I cannot help but laugh. Some part of my mind tells me, *"This. This is why you love this man."*

I almost say an iteration of it out loud, but stop myself in time. It would be too confusing a thing for Rian to hear, now, given all that I've said. It isn't that I have somehow magically stopped loving him. I am only trying to reconcile how many different times and ways I have.

"I can't fault you for that," I say. "My mistake. I shall expand my vocabulary and make certain I use non-cheese-related verbs from now on."

We both laugh. Out of the corner of my eye, I think I catch Qhan smiling. Instead of saying anything about it, I continue walking with Rian, holding his hand, and attempting to keep my mind focused on one thought at a time.

"I do believe we have lost the Smiths," I note.

"Ah, more like they have lost us," Rian agrees. "...Do you not think of yourself as one of them?"

I raise an eyebrow at him. "The Smiths? Why would I?"

"Are you not also a 'Smith'?"

"Technically, no. My father's surname was 'Marson'."

"Yet the Smith blood from your mother clearly impacted you and Lune's flukes more powerfully than anything your father's line might hope to contribute," Rian notes. "Historically speaking, female Smiths have still considered themselves 'Smiths' even after marriage. It's the bloodline."

I wisely keep myself from asking if I should be considered a Smith or a Yakarami.

"I suppose, then, it is because it takes some getting used to," I say. "I know they are my cousins. I know my mother was a powerful Smith and so was my uncle, but...It is a strange revelation. They do not even look like me."

Rian scoffs.

"What?"

"Don't look like you?" he repeats.

"Well, they don't. They are delicate. And Septimus has albinism. Besides, you wouldn't be able to guess we were cousins by sight alone if you didn't already know."

"Oh, yes I would."

"How, exactly?" I challenge.

Rian stops and faces me. We are nearly out of the gardens, at this point, very close to the castle. We are perhaps standing too close together for it to be reasonably appropriate, were we truly concerned with maintaining the illusory relationship of mere bodyguard and principal.

"Your eyes," he says. "I could tell you and Teresa were related the first time I saw her. She shares your eyes."

"It is not the same," I say, realizing the effect Teresa's eyes have on me must be the same one they have on everyone. "I find I can barely refuse her anything."

"If you asked me for something, I couldn't refuse you," Rian claims.

I hope that the chill disguises what feels like a reddening of my face. Admittedly, now and in the past, Rian's compliments occasionally make me angry. I hate to be embarrassed, and he is so good pretending to be casual while saying such things.

He's waiting, looking directly at me as I stubbornly refuse to meet his eyes.

"It's not wise for a ruler to let anyone have such a hold over him," I say.

"Probably," he says.

He is so close I can feel the heat of him.

"But for some reason, I think you have Isaaria's best interests at heart," he adds.

I try to scoff and brush his statement off, but his closeness and tone of voice still sends a shiver through me. Before I can stop him, Rian opens his coat and wraps it around both of us so I have to glare up at him from practically under his nose.

"What?" he says innocently. "I don't want you to be cold."

"You are treading dangerous ground, your majesty," I warn him. But that imprudent smile of his, and his closeness, and the memories, are winning me over all the same. "Yet, I think I'll allow it. Just do not press your luck."

"How am I to know where the boundaries are if you're so unclear?" Rian complains playfully. "Is this pressing my luck?" he adds.

His arms were already around me, holding the coat about us both, but then they constrict. We are scandalously close together.

"No," I say, without truly thinking about it.

I am the most contradictory, weak-willed woman alive.

"What about this?" he says, and suddenly leans down to lightly kiss my forehead.

"You're getting close," I warn him.

However, I have become equally teasing. I find I don't actually want him to stop this playful progression.

"What about this?" he asks.

I already know what he plans to do, and I tilt my head up to meet his kiss. I don't know why I even bother pretending as if I have self-control when it comes to this man. I don't know why I bother putting rules in place when I plan to break them instantly. I tell myself stupid things, like how I want us to keep our distance for Ayla's sake. Or Isaaria's sake. Or our own sakes. But given what I remember, and what Ayla's said, is this a surprise to anyone?

We kiss for much too long, but I have forgotten that Qhan and Korvaan are still here, keeping their distance in an attempt at privacy. I snake my arms around Rian. The shared warmth is not unappreciated, and can almost be practical given the weather. But it does give me such terrible, terrible ideas.

"Did you not hear what I said about taking things slowly?" I mutter when we finally make ourselves stop.

"I'm sorry," Rian says. "But I have missed you more than you could ever know. And you kissed back," he muses.

Oddly, I am now no longer embarrassed but somewhat smug. If memory serves correct, this is not unusual for me.

"You know, I think my hands are cold," I say.

Rian grins. He unwraps his arms from around me and pulls off my gloves, letting them fall so he can kiss my fingers.

"We are going to need to be proper about this," I warn him.

Rian raises an eyebrow. "Kissing passionately in the middle of the gardens is counted as 'proper'?"

"It is when there is no one around to see."

"Qhan and Korvaan are here," he reminds me.

I glance about. Qhan is further off, with his back to us. Korvaan is closer, facing to the side.

"Not one word, Korvaan," I warn.

"I'm not even looking," Korvaan promises, making a show of keeping his eyes averted.

"I think we can trust them to be discreet," I say.

"Because she will kill us if we are not!" Korvaan calls over his shoulder, still looking anywhere but at us.

"What did I just say?" I call back.

Rian chuckles. "You have such a way with words."

"Mock me and you'll regret it," I warn.

"Maybe I will enjoy regretting it."

I smack his arm and he laughs at me.

"You are a—"

"Dirty old man, yes, you've told me," he says. "Not that you're any pure spring chicken yourself."

"At least I'm subtle," I sniff.

"Oh, Soleil. There was nothing at all subtle about that kiss," he claims. "Trust me on that."

I scrunch my nose, groan, and flop my forehead against his chest. "We are...the absolute worst people."

"At consistency? No, sweetheart, that is just you," Rian says, and pats the top of my head. Mango, who I had honestly forgotten about, climbs up to the top of my head and jumps back onto Rian's shoulders.

"Now, come along," the king adds cheerfully. "I'm sure we're missed inside the palace."

I free myself from his coat and hastily snatch up my gloves from where he dropped them on the ground. Rian has already started back by the time I've straightened, Mango along for the ride and his bodyguards in tow. I catch up with him, the snow crunching under my feet as I run.

"Where are we going, exactly? And what are we doing?"

"I'd say it's about time for those boys to be going to bed, wouldn't you?" he says, so bright and happy that I almost forget about how muddled things are in our world. "And it's been ages since Ayla listened to bedtime stories!"

His excitement is enough to keep me smiling all the way back inside.

Five

NAOMI, VALOR, AYLA and my cousins have found themselves in Teresa and the boys' suite, preparing the children for the evening. By the time Rian drags me there with Korvaan and Qhan in tow, the boys have washed up and dressed for bed. All that is left is for them to let their mother brush through their hair, still damp from the snow. Teresa's eyes widen when she sees me enter with Rian, but she quickly calms herself with reminders of his gentle nature. He may be a king, but he is a kind, congenial one who has treated her sons admirably.

I understand why she may be wary of authority figures, particularly male ones, but I truly hope that Teresa manages to overcome this with Rian as an example.

He is a good man. If anyone deserves her trust, it is him.

Still, she sounds uneasy and hesitant when she asks him if there is anything she can help him with. Rian is all cheer, but I don't miss the subtle twitches of his facial features. He does not like how generous Teresa is with herself, at least in respect to him. He has noticed how much she believes she is expected to serve in exchange for kindness or even attention. While that is not surprising, given what I have been told, that does not make it any less uncomfortable for the rest of us.

"I've only come to see you all off to bed," he insists, his previous buoyancy now somewhat forced. "And to offer my services as a story-teller to your sons. I'm sure if Ayla has only told you one thing about me, it's—"

"Oh, he tells the most marvelous stories!" Ayla cannot help but interrupt, as if she'd forgotten over the years.

She is sitting beside Teresa's own chair, with an open book on her lap and a pair of shears nearby. I can guess at their purpose and don't bother to ask. Teresa's impromptu self-haircut was not poorly done, and her hair's natural waviness helps hide uneven ends, but Ayla is the sort to want things done properly, especially if it means she can try something new.

"I suppose if they're interested…" Teresa starts, glancing at her sons.

They are practically bouncing up and down in front of her. She has only gotten to comb through Aiden's hair with her fingers, but Damen pats his own hair down hastily, and does not bother acting the elder when it comes to begging his mother for the king's stories. I am certain Mango's presence has contributed in their excitement as well.

The next few phrases are exchanged in Lusch, but I can guess at what is being said by tone, and Septimus' expressions. From the gist of it, Teresa has struck a bargain with her sons, because Damen waits while his mother finishes getting the snarls out of his and his brother's hair. After, the two of them leap up into the large bed and flip down the covers expectantly.

I suppose the novelty of the cupboard beds may have worn off a little, or else they are simply wanting some extra attention from their mother lately.

"I'm assuming that's a yes," Rian jokes.

Teresa gives him a somewhat forced smile. "I'm sure we'd all be appreciative of you taking up your time to entertain my children."

"To be honest, this is more for me than them," he says.

He is playful, but it is undoubtedly the truth, and that turns Teresa's smile a little more genuine.

Rian tells the boys a tale that is not at all related to their own heritage, which I appreciate. It is completely Isaarian, with no Smiths or Greys or even Wolffs, about one of his so-lauded scholars forced to leave his books and lonely tower and take up a sword to slay a dragon. In classic Isaarian fashion, the tale does not go quite as expected, and because he is telling it in Alarkian and not Isaarian, some of Rian's usual phrases get changed around. Nevertheless, both boys enjoy it greatly, and I believe the rest of the room does, too. Rian always could hold an audience captive with his tales.

I don't need Septimus to remember that.

The children are sufficiently drowsy once he is nearing the end. Ayla has long-since finished trimming Teresa's hair and has tucked her legs up under her skirt, nearly asleep herself. The rest of us are waiting to see what Rian intends to do once he is finished.

I glance at Teresa. She is sitting there, crying quietly, but I cannot tell if her tears are strictly from sadness. It's when she goes to dry her eyes with a hand that a small smile appears, and I'm relieved. My cousin may be a melancholy woman, filled with doubts and fears, but seeing her sons listening to a bedtime story, safe in an Isaarian palace, is good for her.

Naturally, Fate had no intentions of letting us go for even a minute without further testing.

When she glances back up at her sons again, Teresa's expression turns. I watch the blood drain out of her face, and as no one else is watching directly, none of us act before she does. Even Rian is so caught up in his own story that he hasn't noticed what's horrified Teresa so.

"Damen!" she suddenly shrieks.

We all snap to attention and look over just in time to see a series of shadowy figures, which had previously been surrounding both Teresa's sons like a smoke cloud, suddenly flee. Disappearing back whence they came; back into Damen.

For a moment, the rest of us cannot do anything other than stare. I have leapt to my feet, from where I'd taken up a perch on an empty chest, but while I recognize a potential threat to Rian, I cannot bring myself to act. Not when I realize that said potential threat is a child.

Korvaan is in a similar predicament. Ayla, startled awake, is rooted to the spot in her chair, and neither Valor nor Naomi dare move. Teresa and Qhan are the only ones who can make themselves act at first: Teresa flies to the bed instantly, to her children, who are quick to throw themselves at her. Qhan is there to take Rian by the arm and pull him off the bed, away from whatever those shadows were. We have quickly split the room again, between us and them. Septimus is cautious, but pointedly moves himself between us Isaarians and where his sister is allowing her crying sons to cling to her on the bed.

Aiden, I think, is crying because his mother's scream frightened him. But for Damen, there is something much different bothering him.

"I'm sorry, Mama. I'm sorry, I'm sorry," he sobs.

She holds him and Aiden both against her, but Damen is obviously her more pressing concern.

"It's not your fault, baby," she soothes, and shushes him. "It's all right. It's my fault. I'm sorry. I scared you. You didn't do anything wrong."

Still, she flicks her eyes past her brother, at me, as if she is not confident in her own words. To her, Damen did nothing wrong. She is not sure how I will react.

Neither is Septimus. While my cousin is not a large man, and has no weapon for me to worry about, I can tell from the look on his face that he will not stand by idly if I take a single step closer to his sister or nephews.

All eyes are on me, in fact. Before a king and his retinue, I am in control of what happens next, which is both a blessing and curse. While I have the opportunity to deescalate the situation, the fact that so many around me have assumed I will react violently instead does not speak well to my reputation. So, when I pose my first question, I force myself not to sound cool and calculating, but merely cautious. Intrigued.

I cannot tell from reaction alone if this is successful.

"What were those?"

I direct this at Teresa, who is still holding her sons tightly against her though at least they have both resorted to sniffling instead of bawling.

"It is Damen's aptitude. His fluke," she admits.

I frown and look to Rian. "But the boys wore their boots and gloves outside, at all times. They never made direct contact with the earth."

Teresa is hesitant, and holds her boys close to her, but explains. "Damen is…That is, sometimes he can pull energy directly from the sun. Without touching the earth. Not much, but…"

She trails off and scrunches herself even closer to the headboard, keeping both her sons pressed against her.

"If he did anything wrong, it was only an accident," she whispers. "He does not know how to control his fluke much yet. I doubt he even knew he was absorbing any energy at all."

"I have never heard of such a thing before," Naomi admits with a frown.

"Nor I," Valor admits quietly with some discomfort.

It is Qhan that proves there was no subterfuge about, with his commentary of, "That does not mean it is not possible."

So, Teresa believes that Damen did not know what he was doing. She is not lying. He activated his own fluke by accident, only reflexively, likely due to an emotional input. From what I can guess, this means his fluke must be a powerful one.

Septimus guesses my thoughts and speaks up on his family's behalf.

"Yes, Damen has a powerful fluke," he says, almost coldly. "It's what one would expect, considering his parentage. He cannot do much with what little energy he has, without touching the earth, but even the presence of the sun alone can keep his Shadows alive."

"Shadows?" Rian repeats.

Septimus shrugs. "They are not true shadows; I suppose. But they look like ones. They are a part of him, reacting on his emotional behalf, usually without his knowing about it consciously."

"His entire fluke is subconscious?" Naomi says dubiously, unconvinced.

Septimus sighs. "Look: likely not. It is only that, because he is untrained as of yet, he has little purposeful control over it. But he is not ***dangerous***."

I cannot help but share a look with Qhan. If the child's fluke is entirely subconsciously activated, he is dangerous. Perhaps not dangerous enough to kill or even seriously injure someone, but he is just a child, still learning how to maturely handle emotional outbursts. I cannot help but think how quickly he and Aiden escalated in arguing about their father.

There could be accidents.

Naomi looks to me, struggling to make a decision. "Perhaps...for the sake of the king's safety, and the princess..."

We don't learn what she planned to say, because Teresa allows her worst fears to guess, first, and is quick to speak up.

"Please don't," she stammers, trying to hold back tears again. "I promise, they would never hurt anyone! They aren't dangerous! We don't even know Aiden's fluke yet! We don't know if he will develop one; they couldn't tell!"

She sounds so desperate, and scared, it is as if Rian's kindness and Ayla's budding friendship means nothing, now.

I notice that, as much as he has attempted to act adult thus far, Damen has not hesitated in scrunching close to his brother and mother, and hiding in the latter's arms. So, he is frightened, then. Yet: no shadows flailing about causing trouble. He must have some small level of control, even if it is unintentional. Regardless, it may be safe to allay any previous fears about accidents, or at least to begin gathering evidence in Damen's favor.

Rian hesitates. He makes no effort to hide the fact that Teresa's fear of us pains him. He is trying so hard to be a gracious host. His frustration is not necessarily directed at her, but at the fact he must imagine what the Smiths have been through to make her so distrustful of a man who has shown her nothing but kindness thus far.

If this happened a week ago, I would be frustrated with my cousins: they knew the rules. They knew I was allowing them out at dusk to avoid the sun and moon as much as possible. They knew I wanted their gloves and boots on at all times. If Damen can draw power so easily with such little presence of the earth and sun, they should have said something.

The only thing that stops me from a lecture is the clear realization this was not done surreptitiously, with ill intent. I have no doubt the only reason Teresa did not say anything is the same reason she is crying, now. She is terrified that if we knew what her son could do, we might lock him away, hurt him, or separate him from her. While I may still seek answers any way I can from Septimus, he has proven to me that most of his motivations when it comes to Teresa and his nephews is merely to keep them safe.

"Please, do not worry yourselves over it," Rian insists, trying to take control of the situation. "Damen did nothing wrong. He is young. I wouldn't expect him to have mastered his fluke already. That would be unreasonable."

He smiles at her. Septimus still looks from the king to me and back with some suspicion; he does not trust me to keep the promises Rian makes. But he makes no move to start trouble.

Teresa sniffs and wipes at the tears in her eyes aggressively with one hand. She does not unwrap her other arm from her children.

"Ayla, why don't you finish the story? I'm sure you remember the rest," Rian says with forced cheer. "Let us see if we can't get the boys back to sleep. I think I'll take Miss Teresa to get a warm drink; calm her, some."

"I won't leave them alone," Teresa insists, fear creeping in once more.

"They won't be alone. They'll be with Ayla and Korvaan," Rian reassures, but it's the second half of his statement that makes Teresa's shoulders lower. "Septimus can stay as well. Is that an acceptable compromise?"

Teresa takes her time in answering, and first looks to Septimus for his approval, but then nods. She allows Rian to offer a hand in helping her back off the bed again. Aiden asks her something innocently in Lusch and though she struggles to respond haltingly, Teresa must have given a satisfactory answer to both boys because they settle in and are no longer worried.

At least, Aiden isn't.

Damen watches his mother when she leaves with the king, Qhan, Naomi, Valor and I. I cannot know what the child is thinking, but the situation with his own fluke frightened him. Whether it was his own lack of control, or his mother's reaction, I am certain Damen will follow his mother's example with her reluctance to trust others.

I can tell the moment we are halfway down the hall that Teresa is already regretting leaving her sons. Either that, or it has occurred to her that she made certain they were with people she trusts but that she has now placed herself alone with relative strangers after revealing a potentially dangerous secret.

I wish there was something I could say to reassure her, but I cannot think of anything. If everything we've done thus far has not helped, my words won't. Maybe our actions will have more of an effect.

The kitchens are empty at this hour. If the palace were at full capacity, it would never sleep. As it is, the place is quiet. Qhan turns on several of the electric lights when we enter, but not all, so that the island of light forces our group into one small area.

"I'll make some tea," Valor says, recalling Rian's offer of hot drinks upstairs. "Any preferences, Miss Teresa?"

She shakes her head.

He goes about putting a kettle on. The rest of us trust him to choose the appropriate flavor; I don't think any of us are too picky at a time like this.

"I'm sorry we frightened you at all. That was not our intent," Rian tells her as Qhan finds a kitchen stool for her so Teresa does not need to stand.

Teresa hesitates. She must know as well as the rest of us that most of the fear was self-generated. Yet, she doesn't know how to acknowledge that.

"I know it is important, here, for you all to be safe," she says. "I didn't want any of you to think that we…That we intended to harm anyone. Damen doesn't mean anything by it. Really, he doesn't. His shadows aren't dangerous. I don't think."

"Does he take after his father, then? In terms of fluke?" Naomi asks.

I'm glad she thinks to pose the question, because if I were to do so, Teresa would never answer.

Teresa takes her time, but it's for a moment of thought for once, not because she's considering lying to us or begging off an answer.

"Not exactly. His father's side of the family, yes. But not his father. Unless you count in terms of strength. My husband…He is very difficult to resist."

If Septimus were here, he would likely have warned her against answering that. But because he didn't, I can now extrapolate from her words and from her body language that her husband has used his fluke on her before.

Septimus wasn't wrong when he called the man a bastard.

I share a look with Qhan, and I'm sure he's thinking along similar lines as me. We know Teresa's husband will come after her and the boys. We need to be ready for him. If we can coax details of his capabilities from his wife, it could save lives. The only question is whether now is the right time to attempt such a thing, with Teresa in this fragile state.

Thankfully, even Rian is not so obtuse that he tries to jump in. We leave this line of questioning to Naomi. She is nurturing enough that it seems as if she seeks answers only for the children's sakes and for no other reason.

"Did your husband have Damen start taking lessons? On how to control his fluke? Nurture it, in any way?"

Teresa looks conflicted.

"I don't know," she says. "He never let me do anything in regards to Damen's schooling. Only Aiden. He had other people teaching Damen. And Damen never mentioned anything about that type of practice. Only what other things he was learning about, that he enjoyed. He has already had more schooling than I ever have."

"I'll ask him, then, if that's acceptable," Naomi says, and quickly continues. "Not tonight, of course. I think the poor children are too tired for any more excitement, now. But if you don't mind, once we're in the Summer Palace, I'm certain we could find someone to help teach Damen about his fluke. And how to use it."

"You would have the final say, in approving the teacher," Rian adds. "You could sit in on the classes, if you like."

Teresa nods as Valor returns to hand her a steaming mug of tea. There is a brief respite as those of us who intend to partake receive mugs of their own. Naomi fetches honey, to satisfy any sweet-tooths.

"Do you mind telling us anything you do know about Damen's fluke?" Naomi asks as she returns. "And, you said you don't know if Aiden has one?"

"Oh. Well. My husband had fluke readers at each of my sons' births, and for every birthday after," Teresa explains. "They knew right away Damen was capable, and by the time he was three, he was showing. Aiden, they couldn't tell anything. So, he may still develop a fluke. He's only little, still, and I read that most commonly flukes show on average between ages six and ten…"

"Ayla was about six or seven, I think, when she showed hers," Rian says thoughtfully. Reminding Teresa that he, too, is a parent with concerns for his own child. "And while Naomi showed hers early, you didn't even begin to master it until you were…what, twelve, Naomi?"

"Something like that," Naomi says. "It sounds as if Damen is a little ahead of the rest. Nothing wrong with that."

"Isn't there, though?" Teresa says. She sounds more aggressive than usual, and I realize she'd rather her voice shake from frustration than fear. "Do you think I don't know what they could turn Damen into, if…If they trained him to do what they wanted? His fluke could be used for monstrous reasons."

"Not here," Rian says shortly. "Your sons will never be taken advantage of so long as they are in Isaaria. I will make sure of it. They will be safe."

Teresa simply nods again.

"That is appreciated. But even so," she says. "I don't know how powerful Damen will become. I don't know how to properly parent around that fear. I truly do think his shadows are harmless. For now. They are not sentient, as far as I can tell. They are a part of him. I do not know which part of his subconscious, but I've always thought of them as a sort of physical entity for the way we sometimes talk to ourselves. Only, he can also affect the physical world. Always peacefully! Damen's a sweet boy, I swear. I suppose…I am worried that by taking him away from his home, he will grow up bitter. Missing his father, because he only ever saw my husband as an idol."

I cannot reassure against these fears of hers, but I do know Damen isn't stupid. He may be conflicted about being caught between his parents, but based on what I saw from him, he is at least aware of the fact that his father did less than pleasant things to his mother. While it must be confusing for a child to try and reconcile his parents' supposed love for one another despite obvious abuses involved, I believe Damen will eventually come to understand his mother's decision. And he will know it was the right one.

"Well, we cannot know the future," Rian says. "So, we will all simply have to do our best to ensure the boys are not missing home. In fact, what do you think they'd like for Holrith? We have twelve days to celebrate, after all, and it will be upon us soon," Rian points out, his cheer genuine again.

Teresa glances at him, questioning what she heard.

"What?"

"Well, I figure, if the rest of us are going to celebrate—which we are in a matter of weeks—we should include your sons. I noticed they both like the outdoors. And Damen likes dragons? Yes?"

Qhan already has a handkerchief to hand her when Teresa starts crying.

Rian looks to me.

"What did I do," he says in Isaarian, sounding as if he has given up on managing to speak to Teresa without making her burst into tears.

I shrug. At least this time no one can blame me. But then, Teresa speaks and gives Rian the opportunity to explain his motives to her in a way that makes sense.

"You've been so good to them," she sobs. "So kind, to the sons of a monster. I don't understand why…"

"She is distressed," Naomi says to Rian, also in Isaarian. "This is not necessarily because you have upset her. It may simply be her reaction to being overwhelmed."

That makes more sense to Rian. He crouches down next to where Teresa is sitting, not unlike how he would to talk to her children. He switches back to Alarkian so she can understand. Naomi, though, is still muttering in Isaarian to her husband about how she wants to find someone to needle Teresa once we arrive at the Summer Palace. Valor offers to start looking for a professional we can trust. I can't help but overhear, and can't help but note how Naomi's mouth tightens and how her eyes flick at the far end of the room, into the dark, as if it's the light that's making her eyes water.

She didn't cry at Taris' funeral. I wonder if she wishes she did, now.

"I think you're being hard on yourself, Miss Teresa. I wouldn't call you a monster. You're much too pretty," Rian says.

Resa sniffs and frowns, clearing her tears. "What?"

"Well, they're your sons, Teresa. That's the only thing that matters to us."

Teresa bites her lip and almost looks at me, but stops herself. I have sabotaged Rian, in a way, because Teresa and Septimus both know how badly I want to know the exact identity of her husband.

Theresa does not mention that and simply finishes wiping her tears away, then folds the handkerchief into a square that Qhan insists she keep.

"Then…Damen does like dragons. Yes," she sniffs. "Aiden…Aiden likes fairy tales. And drawing, some. They didn't get to go outside very much at all back in Lusch, so…so a lot of nature they have only seen in books."

I consider how enamored Aiden was with the fish tiles. It's strange to me to think that they've likely never seen a living fish before, in a pond or otherwise.

I remember the small stuffed octopus.

"Aiden likes sea creatures?" I guess, and Teresa nods.

"And books. Actually, if…if you wouldn't mind…when we arrive in your Summer Palace, could I have…something to draw with? And some paints?" she asks. "I…enjoy art. I've been teaching Aiden, some, and he likes that, but I'd like to make something for him. He had many of my pictures hanging in his room, but we had to leave most of it behind."

"Of course!" Rian promises. I can tell he is excited she's finally willing to ask for something for herself. "I shall call ahead. Have it in your rooms when we arrive. Just be sure to give me a list at some point and I'll pass it along to Soren Carsans."

"Oh. I wouldn't want to bother someone else," she starts.

"You are a sweet, sweet girl, Teresa Smith," Rian laughs. "But Soren wouldn't mind. Honestly. It's his job."

She looks as if she's going to protest that but then nods instead. Progress.

"I'm sorry," she says. "I don't know why I've been so emotional these past few days. I promise, I'm not usually like this…"

"Nothing to apologize for," Naomi insists before Rian can. "Drink your tea, dear, before it gets cold. And you," she says, giving the king a stern look, "the point of coming down here was to calm her. Stop gifting her things."

"I'm trying to be a courteous host!" Rian insists.

"Stop trying," Naomi says.

Teresa smiles weakly into her tea.

"I am not—oh!" Rian says, realizing something. "What would Septimus like? Do you think? Oh, so much shopping to do…"

Naomi groans, but only to make Teresa smile again. The conversation distracts Teresa from the more distressing parts of her life, after all. I doubt she has ever celebrated Holrith before. While she is still shy around us, the more Naomi and Rian discuss the possibilities of wintertime celebrations, the more open to conversation Teresa becomes. I learn considerably generic, almost unimportant things about her and Septimus that will do nothing to help me with their past but does give me insight into them as people.

Teresa is defined by more than just her children. Septimus seems less like someone for me to punish and more like someone I could have been friends with in another life.

Time passes. The conversation devolves into descriptions of Holriths past. Valor joins in, and Korvaan later brings Ayla down to say goodnight, allowing her to become distracted and determined to tell a story of her own. Qhan and I stand by, but do not have much to offer by means of conversation. Qhan occasionally corrects something or fills in a missing detail but I do not bother adding anything. I can't think of what to say that would be of any use.

Eventually Teresa falls asleep, exhausted. There is a short, whispered debate over whether we should wake her or not. Qhan elects to ignore the talk and instead picks her up to carry her. I send the others off to sleep and follow Qhan and Teresa upstairs.

As predicted, Septimus is still awake, though both Teresa's boys are fast asleep in the big bed. No one says anything while I help Qhan tuck her in, but we can both feel Septimus watching us. I know he wants to know what we spoke of downstairs, but he can't bring himself to ask. He sits in the corner of the room and waits for us to leave. For a few moments, I think Septimus will follow us out and speak with me.

But when Qhan and I leave, he is still sitting there alone in the dark. It is as if he believes there is still enough of a threat here that he needs to sit up all night, keeping watch.

I DON'T SEE the Smiths at all the next day. After that, for another two days, I see them only at dinner, where Rian and Ayla join to explain to everyone the plans for moving to the Summer Palace. I know the Smiths are still weary from travel and cannot be looking forward to traveling back the way they came, even partially. However, they will be much safer in our western palace, and there will be more opportunities for them there as well. Perhaps socially, for Teresa, as I am certain Irina Lundan and Yvette Pike would be happy to keep her company.

After dinner that third night, Rian takes Damen and Aiden back out to play in the snow with Mango, and the four of them have a merry time while Ayla insists on teaching Septimus and Teresa how to play *yi-chong*. They seem to enjoy themselves, able to forget the rest of the world and their troubles for a good while. Even Teresa manages to play a full game without apologizing or worrying or continually checking on Rian and her sons.

It is a small victory, but still decent progress. I know that Ayla has insisted on meeting with her father, Naomi, Korvaan, Valor and even Qhan to discuss how she plans to help the Smiths adapt to their new lives. I wish I could partake fully in these discussions, but my duties keep me busy.

Yet, from what I understand, or at least from what I've pieced together on my own, Teresa is managing to flourish in Isaaria more than Septimus would have thought possible. She has asked Ayla to teach her some Isaarian, quite enjoys our customs of wearing veils and gloves, and has improved at accepting Rian's offered gifts since the night we shared tea.

I am hoping she will trust us enough that, when it comes time for her to have her child, she will no longer be crippled with fear.

We are nearly ready to leave for the Summer Palace. Though we are somewhat behind schedule, it is not by enough to worry me. The Pyrian Palace is all but emptied, and most of Ayla and Rian's things have long since been packed and sent away. Rian has, cleverly he believes, had some fittings done for the Smiths so that seamstresses may set to work immediately while we travel and my cousins may enjoy new clothing when we arrive.

The night before we are set to depart, I surprise myself by how calm I am. The plan is to finalize packing in the morning, take our things, and leave by carriage for the train station. Rian plans on having the Smiths with him and Ayla in their cars, so they can help with the boys. Qhan and I will be close by, while Korvaan patrols the train. We've all agreed to allow Naomi and Valor some well-deserved privacy as they barely ever take time off from their work, and since Valor is a part of the guard keeping watch tonight.

I am meant to be sleeping, but I find I am not at all tired. I have been able to keep myself distracted, these past days, but when left with my own thoughts in the quiet of the night, I can't help but think of Taris and Lune. I do not want to, but I do, consistently. Out of love or guilt, I cannot say.

I am trying to make sense of old cycles, particularly this past one, when there comes a knock at the door and I bid them entry before considering who it might be. To my surprise, the king lets himself in, and without hesitation, takes a seat on the bed.

"Oh, good," he says as I'm still trying to find my tongue. "I knew you would be awake, Soleil. I wanted a moment alone."

"I am not in the mood for anything other than talking," I warn him, though I try not to sound too sharp about it.

"I only wanted your company," he promises. "I have missed you, these past days. I was beginning to worry you were avoiding me again."

"Not purposefully," I say. "But honestly, Rian, we have a long journey west ahead of us. You should be sleeping. We can always find some time to talk on the train tomorrow."

Rian sighs and flops down back on my bed. I snort but allow him to stay there while I take a seat in the desk chair, crossing my arms and legs.

"Very well," I say. "What is it that can't possibly wait until tomorrow."

"I don't know," he says, staring at my ceiling. "Nothing. I'm tired but I cannot sleep. As I said, I've missed you...Tell me about something."

"Why? And what?" I say.

"Anything. Because I want to hear you," he says, and looks up to give me a smile that he knows I cannot refuse.

"At least give me a topic," I insist. "Otherwise, I'll do nothing but bore you with the details of cycles past that I can't get out of my head."

"That's fine. What in particular?"

He is getting rather comfortable on my bed. If he starts drifting off, I'm ejecting him from the room. I would like to think I am better than most at controlling myself but having Rian in my bed is a tempting prospect.

"For one, I know for a fact Septimus has kept certain memories from me," I say. "And I'm starting to think that I've met some of the Greys before."

Rian sits up. "Soleil, don't joke."

"I'm not," I insist. "When Septimus said the name 'Amerson' to me, I knew I'd met someone by that name. Only, I can't remember when, where, or why. There are gaps in the last cycle alone that I'm sure he's blocked out. I can recall holding you while you died from some type of poison from a bullet that clipped your temple. But I also think I tracked down the man who fired the bullet. I could have sworn I did."

"I remember you leaving and coming back," Rian offers. "But most of my memories of dying are fuzzy. I don't know if Septimus did that on purpose to protect me or if that's merely a natural reaction to death."

"I'm tempted to ask Korvaan, but I don't think he'd know, either," I say. "And the more I've been going through my timelines, there are gaps. Or small things Septimus has edited. Blurred faces and forgotten names. But I would rather not accuse him of anything. He'll react…poorly."

Rian considers this, but we both know there's little chance of us discovering new information by comparing memories. If Septimus was thorough enough to omit certain parts of my memories, I'm sure he did the same for Rian.

My cousin's control over his fluke is admirable if nothing else.

"But you can't never ask," Rian insists. "Soleil: you said Septimus wants you to leave someplace with him after we arrive at the Summer Palace. I don't want you going anywhere with him if he's keeping things from us."

"I think I could take him in a fight," I say. "He didn't even bring any weapons with him here."

"Yes, but…Even if he doesn't mean us any harm, that does not mean this 'plan' of his is going to have an outcome we approve of," Rian warns.

I sigh. He is right, naturally, but I'm tired of this. Trusting Septimus, not trusting him. Teresa trusting us, not trusting us. I am tempted to gather everyone around a table and made us each explain ourselves fully.

"Let us reach the Summer Palace first," I say. "If nothing else, the grand princes and their families are there. The company might help Teresa feel as if she is in a safer place, and if I can get her to trust me, it will influence Septimus to do the same."

Rian considers this. "That is possible. But Soleil, we do need to consider what we are going to do if Septimus has no intentions of telling us anything more than he already has."

"He has promised to tell me everything. Qhan verified it was the truth."

"But you're still suspicious of him, now, are you not?"

I give him a look.

"That's what I thought," Rian says.

"I feel horrible," I admit, "but Septimus has made no illusions that he does not trust *us,* which in turn…"

I do not need to finish.

"Tomorrow," Rian starts. "On the train, I think we should carve out some time to talk. Just the two of us."

"About this?" I ask.

"About many things. But partially about us," Rian says.

There are several quiet moments as I pick a loose string from my sleeve. Rian fiddles with his own fingers.

"Can I ask you something?" he says.

"I thought we were saving this for tomorrow."

"Just one question," he says in defense, "and then I'll go and we'll leave the rest until tomorrow."

"Fair. One question."

We'd started to tease, but now Rian sobers.

"Would you marry me again?"

He throws that at me so quickly that it is a struggle not to instantly respond with a one-word answer.

"A bit curt for a proposal, wouldn't you say?" I make myself laugh. "We've completely abandoned 'taking things slow', then?"

"I know, I know. Not my most romantic," Rian admits. "But I would rather know, one way or another. Besides, we could be secret about it. Tell no one except perhaps Qhan. Maybe Ayla, if that's all right. But I, at least, want to marry you. Again. This time around. I don't know if that's what you want, so I decided I needed to ask."

He sits there on my bed, his fingers laced together, waiting expectantly.

I know I should have considered an answer to such a proposition over the last few days, but I've been busy. It is always my excuse these days, it seems. Busy, busy Soleil. Too busy for personal matters.

But Rian does not become impatient. He merely continues to sit still, not moving, looking at me and waiting.

"If we had time, then yes," I finally say. "I would. I would marry you again and within a matter of weeks I probably wouldn't even care who knew."

"But?" Rian prompts.

"Nothing," I say. "That's all. I don't think we have the time, Rian. Otherwise, yes. I would marry you again. And again. And again. But, to tell you the truth, part of me still struggles with how to describe my feelings. For you. In general. It sounds ridiculous, I know, but it was easiest the first time. Saying 'I love you', saying 'yes, I'll marry you', saying 'til death do us part' as if…As if I haven't seen you die so many times over, now."

He seems to understand that because he nods and allows me to take a moment longer in thought.

"It is more complicated," I add. "Over time. Especially now that I remember. Not in a bad way, I do not think. It is harder. But still worth doing. If we did have the time, I would do it."

"Whereas, it gets easier and easier for me," Rian says with the hint of a laugh about him. "I was so nervous, that first time, marrying. Even though we'd been betrothed for *years*. Stupid, I know."

"I don't think it's unrealistic to feel nervous about a wedding."

Rian snorts at his own expense. “Yes, well. About every time we get around to walking down that aisle, my legs feel close to jelly. I swear, you are usually guiding me to the front of the alter.”

I must smile at that. “I remember that first time, you gave yourself the hiccups and could barely withhold them through our vows.”

“…Do you remember our time on the island together? That once?”

I narrow my eyes at him while I think. “That was before the wedding.”

“Hence why you know I’m not talking about a dirty story,” he claims. “Now: do you remember?”

“I remember you collecting shells and making the mistake of putting a hermit crab in your pocket. Which made things exceptionally fun for me when I got my finger pinched sorting through them.”

“You remember watching the sunset on the beach?” he asks, still smiling.

“I remember Taris having a conniption there was no good vantage point for him to watch for potential dangers from,” I admit. “He didn’t want us spending more than half an hour on that beach at most. But yes. I remember the sunset. I also remember you getting your hand somewhere it probably should not have been and Taris wasn’t happy about that, either.”

“Well, I don’t blame him. You are practically siblings…I thought we agreed this was not going to be a dirty story?”

“I also thought we agreed one more question,” I say, standing and taking one of his arms to escort him out. “Time for you to get some sleep.”

“But Soleil…”

“Bed,” I order, pulling him out of my room and escorting him part of the way down the hall. “And before you say anything: yes, I will attempt some sleep as well. I want to check on the Smiths first.”

Rian gives me a side-eyed look. “That best be the truth, young lady,” he says, with the same tone he used to take with Ayla when he suspected her of telling him fibs. “I want you asleep within the next half-hour. If I’m to be forced out of your bed, you might as well make good use of it.”

I smile at that, but refrain from kissing him goodnight. That, I think, would be overstepping. He goes along his way, to his room, and I go off to the Smith’s rooms, a floor away.

Once arrived, I open the door a crack as not to disturb them and allow my eyes to adjust to the dark. Septimus has decided not to stay in his own room, but sleeps on the couch in the room his sister shares with the boys. He is fast asleep, now, flat on his back with an arm up over his eyes and one leg off the couch, his heel on the floor. For a man so slight, he can certainly sprawl himself over a good amount of real estate while he sleeps.

His sister is practically his opposite. Teresa sleeps curled on her side, her legs folded over one another and her arms wrapped around her younger son. From what I can tell from the mussed bedsheets, Aiden must have gotten scared, or perhaps had a nightmare, and crawled up onto his mother's bed. They both look as if they are trying their best to be as small as possible, and I suppose that makes sense for Teresa, given what I've been told about the man she used to share a bed with.

I smile to see Mango nestled by Aiden's feet.

But I see no Damen.

I'm not suspicious, merely concerned and somewhat annoyed. It seems as if Damen cannot sleep either and has decided to wander about the Pyrian Palace looking for a way to amuse himself. So long as he is still on this floor, it technically is not a breach of the rules I set down in front of them.

I find him sitting in the mirror hall. The hall does not work so well in the nighttime, but I suppose the place still made an effect on him whenever Ayla took him and Aiden here.

"Damen?" I say, as I approach, as not to startle him.

He turns his head, but remains seated in front of one of the mirrors, his knees pulled in to his chest. I think I can see hints of his shadows around, but they are not as mobile as last I saw them.

"Why aren't you in bed?" I ask, trying to sound somewhat gentle as I join him. As Rian has mentioned, I'm not as young as either of us once were, but I can still sit cross-legged on the ground with only a mild ache in my low back.

"Mama finally fell asleep. I'm not tired, but I didn't want to wake her up, being in the room, so I came out here," he says.

"Oh. Does she not sleep well? Naomi can make her a tonic if she—"

"That won't help," Damen interrupts me.

If Teresa were here, she would scold him on his lack of manners.

"Mama doesn't sleep because she can't. She has bad dreams, I guess."

"Oh," I say again, a little uncomfortable. "How did you know about them? That is, has she discussed them with you?"

He shrugs. "She cries about them. She tries to be quiet. She doesn't want us to know, and I don't know if Aiden does or not. We don't talk about it."

"Does she often have bad dreams?" I venture. I try to mimic the way Ayla speaks with the boys. She is so good and caring with them.

He shrugs again. "Whenever she did at home, Father made them go away."

"With his fluke?"

"No," Damen says to my disappointment. "He'd just make Mama less scared. Every time he went away, she'd get sad and the nightmares would come back. When he came home, she would be happier. Sometimes."

Sometimes.

"Damen," I start. "Your father—"

"He's not a bad person!" the boy snaps, interrupting and looking up at me with a glare. "He's not! Mama's bad dreams…They're about other things! Not our father! Aiden and I wouldn't exist if he didn't love her!"

I sigh. Who knew children could be so difficult? I'd always thought of them as smaller adults, but I realize now that there are things that I'd tell an adult-Damen about his father that I know I cannot say to a child. I am curious as to why Damen seems to think children only come about if love is a factor. I don't think Teresa would have told him that, and from what I've gathered of his father, from those letters, the man probably would give Damen an entire biological explanation if the boy formally asked how children are made.

It makes me wonder what he was exposed to, while living with the Greys. If he was not lied to, he may have seen things that forced him to come to that conclusion on his own.

I decide to take a different approach. I do not intend to upset Damen, but someone needs to explain in a way that makes sense to him that his father is not the man he so idolizes.

"Well, I can't say one way or another," I admit, and that surprises him a little. "I don't know your father. But I do know some things about love. For example, you love your mama, don't you, Damen?"

He frowns. "Yes? Aiden and I both love Mama. Lots."

"And you know your father has hurt her," I go on carefully.

"Only when they argue," he protests. "It's not as if he does it for nothing."

"I see. Do you and Aiden argue?"

He shrugs. "Sometimes."

"And would you ever hit him?"

Damen whips his head around to look at me, horrified. "No! Never!"

"Why not?"

He frowns and thinks, perplexed. "Because…He's…It's *Aiden.* He's my little brother. I have to protect him. Mama said so."

"So, what's the difference with your parents?" I point out.

"Because they're adults," Damen claims, though I can tell he is struggling to make sense of it and I feel mildly guilty over this. "Things are different for grown-ups. And...and Father loves Mama. He's said so. A lot. And he doesn't lie. So, it's fine because he says he's sorry. Sometimes they just have fights."

"Do you think your mama feels like he loves her when he hurts her?"

Damen shrugs, but this time its hesitant.

"So why would it be acceptable? You wouldn't hit your brother. You wouldn't hit your mother. Why do you think your father can?"

Damen frowns, growing frustrated. "It's different. Besides. Mama has problems in her head. Father told me about it. So sometimes she does things that 'aren't reasonable'. A-An-An-And even if he didn't love Mama and Aiden, he still loves me! I know that!"

Now he has started to cry.

Excellent work, Soleil. You certainly have a way with children.

"Damen, I never said he didn't love you," I say quickly. "Perhaps he truly believes he loves you all. You and your mother and Aiden."

Though given what Septimus has told me, I doubt Damen's father cares much at all for his younger son and made no effort to hide that fact.

I press on.

"But sometimes, if a person says they love you, yet they hurt you, what they say doesn't matter. Your mother made the right choice, in leaving."

"Do you have any kids?" he asks me innocently, sniffling and wiping messily at his eyes. Aggressive in his childish frustration.

He doesn't mean to hurt me—he's a boy. But I have to swallow a lump in my throat before I can answer.

"No," I say.

Perhaps I should have said yes. Perhaps I should have said I have Ayla.

But I didn't want to cause confusion.

"Then you don't know," Damen insists. "Father must miss us a whole lot. Mama, too. Because we're his. And he loves us. He must be very sad. He needs us. He says it all the time."

It occurs to me that if Damen believes adults must love each other in order to have a child, it's likely distressing for him to know he has a half-sibling that came from a man not his father. No boy wants to grow up in a broken-apart family. No person does.

He is only a child, part of me tries to soothe.

But I was only a child when I was given the responsibility of an entire kingdom. Ayla was only a child when she was starved in that rotting orphanage. Rian was only a child when he was chosen as future king. Lune was only a child when she was told she would be spending the rest of her life as a bodyguard for me. Taris was only a child when his father said he would never be allowed to marry, have children, have a family, know his siblings, or even know what happened to his mother.

I was only a child. Being only a child means nothing. It did not save me or the ones I love. It does not give Damen protection.

Nor does your past give you an excuse to force similar pains on him.

I partially hate that thought. I am caught between bitterness and mercy and I do not understand which is better, for me or for him.

"Perhaps," I begin, trying to think of the right way to say this. "Perhaps you are right, and I cannot understand. And yes, Damen, if your father has said he loves you, I believe he does. I believe he loves your mother, too, in a way. But maybe that's the wrong kind of love."

I have confused him even more.

"How can there be more than one?"

"There are many kinds," I say. "So, your father loves you. But maybe it's a selfish love. Maybe, if he can learn to be less selfish, things will be better."

"And then we can go home," he says stoutly.

I cannot tell him that, if it's left to me, I am never letting Teresa near her husband again. I cannot sit here and tell Damen that I would happily keep him from ever seeing his father, so long as it meant he and his mother and siblings were safe.

"Or you could move here," I try suggesting. "You like Isaaria, don't you?"

He considers this idea.

"Father would like Mango," he says. "And the dryad tree, I think."

"So, there's that," I say, standing and brushing some stray dust off my trouser legs before offering him my hand. "Come along. Let us get you some warm milk and then back into bed."

Damen hesitates, then takes my hand. He surprises me by not letting go when I start to walk for the kitchen. So long as I have begun to cultivate even a minor relationship of trust with him, I need to do my best to maintain it. I do not know what will happen in the future, but if I can somehow help show Damen what real love should look like—though I've no idea why Fate would choose me to do so—then I'll try my best.

"Now, you said you like dragons, didn't you?" I say, and he nods, brightening. "I say let's get you that milk, then stop by the library and find a book about dragons."

"I can read in bed?" he asks excitedly.

"So long as you don't wake up your mother and brother, I see no reason why you can't," I say. "At least it's educational."

He smiles, which makes me instantly feel better about everything.

I realize that, between myself and Rian, we might end up spoiling our younger children a little, once we are finally allowed to have them.

Six

I KNOW SOMETHING is wrong. I have barely managed an hour asleep before I somehow, almost subconsciously detect something is wrong. I throw myself out of bed and into my clothes. I am a disorganized mess, still attempting to grapple with what weaponry I manage to grab whilst stumbling out into the hall. I run, first, to Rian, but he is not in his chambers. Korvaan is nowhere to be found, either.

I can feel my heart racing. Something is wrong. The palace is too quiet. It is too empty.

When I come across the first body, I know my instincts were correct. It is one of the guards I assigned to watch Ayla for the night. I do not know why he is so far from her rooms, but I assume he tried to come and find me or Qhan; someone who could help. He left a trail of blood behind whilst succumbing to his injuries. I follow it.

Despite my mental exhaustion and lack of sleep, the sight of blood has me riled like a wild animal. While I know I should be anxious for my cousins, my main concern is finding the king and Ayla, to protect them. I cannot begin to imagine where Rian has gone at this hour or why he wasn't in his rooms, but at least there were no bodies to be found there. So, either he left of his own free will, or he happened to be elsewhere when our enemies decided to strike.

I do not know how they managed to bypass all our security, but for now, I do not care. Seeing that guard has made me terrified for Ayla, and before puzzling out the how, I need to uncover the who and where.

We end up coming upon one another.

The invaders are foreign, but I don't care enough for any of them to make an impression on me. They are about to round the corner down the hall from me when the first of them spots me and pushes the rest back. I have a reputation, then, and they know it. I'd have dashed down the hall immediately, sword drawn, only I find I can't risk it.

It was only for a second, but it was long enough: before they hid themselves again, I saw two of the men hauling Ayla around, still dressed in her nightgown, her hands tied behind her back. She screams for help the moment she sees me, but is yanked back around the corner before I can make a move.

For a few moments, nothing happens, but I can detect whispers. I have heard the Smiths use Lusch enough to know that is the language these intruders are speaking. It does not take much thought to guess at who these people are and why they are here.

Septimus and Teresa, both, warned me her husband would come after them. I suppose I thought we had more time.

I suppose Septimus thought so, too.

"Captain Marson," one of the men finally addresses me, his Lusch accent much thicker than the mild one I have detected in Teresa's sons.

Time, I decide, to go back a few minutes and see if I can make my way around them. Since I know which direction they are headed, I can sneak up behind them, attack, and free Ayla before they know what is happening.

I have not been meditating under the sun at all lately, nor have I been outside much, and the sun is not a lengthy visitor during these wintry months. Yet I hope I still have enough reserves to buy myself a minute or two. Just enough to make certain this encounter happens in a way I can manipulate. There is definitely some form of energy there, when I reach for it. I can feel it, vaguely, like a tickling in the back of my mind. But for some reason, I cannot use it. I can't begin to conceive of what use this secret store may be to me, even though it was only a mere moment before that I knew precisely what I intended to do.

And then I remember: in many previous timelines, Clanaugh or Septimus himself helped me recover the use of my fluke: dozens and dozens of years of practice, precision, and mastery.

Neither of them has done that, this timeline.

I have a fluke. But I cannot use it.

Fate's Fingers.

Before I can think of how to manipulate the situation without my fluke, I am once again being addressed. This time, I'm being ordered:

"Captain. Put down your weapons and surrender yourself. If not..."

Ayla screams again. I can't see what is happening, but that sound, and her choked sob that follows soon after, is enough to convince me to let them win this round. I can form a contingency plan once I know what I'm dealing with, but I refuse to act foolishly in a way that may result in Ayla's death.

I am aware that the Greys want me alive. They have no use for an Isaarian princess. While I have no guarantee they will not hurt Ayla once I surrender, I don't believe they will. They have been dragging her around thus far for another reason; they won't kill her now just to spite me. If this will buy Ayla time and ensure her safety, I will comply. I've gotten out of worse situations.

"Very well," I say loudly, making a show of keeping my arms up and visibly. "I'm putting my weapons down."

They wait until they are certain I'm not about to cause trouble before coming at me. They move quickly, still wary of me, but at least somewhat sure that their hostage situation holds significant sway over me. I won't hide from the truth in that. This will give me more time to gather information on who these people are. I assume they want the Smiths and they work for the Greys, but I will need more details than that if I want to fight back effectively.

For one, if any of them have flukes to be wary of.

I can still hear Ayla crying, though now her sobs are muffled by either a gag or a hand. I want to reassure her that this is not the end for us. That this is somewhat of a calculated decision. I am unable to do so. She is likely too terrified, now, to trust me, but I swear to myself that I will keep her safe no matter the cost.

They tie my hands in the front, which means I cannot work on picking knots discreetly behind my back, but it does give me more mobility than they probably should have allowed. The reason why becomes clear in a moment when one of them presses a cloth against my mouth and nose. I'm at least smart enough to realize what's happening: I hold my breath and allow myself to go slack prematurely. It is not enough to prevent my head from spinning, but at least, hopefully, I won't be completely incapacitated.

They exchange a few words in Lusch. My head swims and I cannot think straight enough to even guess at what they are saying, but moments after, I am hauled around by the arms. They are taking me downstairs, away from Ayla, who is still screaming for me whilst being dragged elsewhere. I would take the opportunity to fight my way back to her, but I cannot organize my thoughts well enough for form a plan. I need a few moments, first. I need to focus on my breathing and regain control of myself.

I tell myself that, if they have Ayla and are using her as a hostage, this is likely because they have not yet found Rian. They still will not hurt her, then, so long as he is free. Not yet. If I can escape with their assumption of my incapacitation, that will give me the upper hand, in freeing the princess. A clear head is the priority.

Though I have always been trained in resiliency to most poisons and gasses, I am not completely immune to their effects. Likely someone else may have passed out completely at this point. I am merely disoriented and dazed.

I will take this as a boon from Fate despite our circumstances. So long as one of the intruders doesn't get it into their head to drug me more effectively, and still want my conscious enough to shuffle along so they don't need to carry me, I know I am still a viable threat.

We are headed towards the throne room, where I first met Septimus and Teresa. For a moment, I think we're about to halt, there, and wait. But no. We're still moving, with great haste. They drag me beyond to the hall, with its marble pillars and carefully carved furniture placed against the walls to entertain court gossipers that have long since moved to the Summer Palace.

There are only three men that remain with me, now that the rest left with Ayla. I am not at my peak by far, but I am starting to clear my head. Exhaustion begins to set in its place, but I suppose I can only press my luck so far. I work at the knots as discreetly as I can; slowly, so as not to draw notice.

Only three men. I think I can take them with the element of surprise. They relieved me of some of my weapons, of course, but I know they did not find all of them. The only question is, while they want me alive, how much are the Greys and their people willing to damage me?

If I'm even a moment too slow, I risk injury to myself. If one of them escapes, they may alert their comrades, and injure Ayla. Is now the time to take that chance? Or should I wait, hoping for more information first?

In the end, the choice is made for me. Previously hidden behind one of the pillars, as we draw near, Teresa appears. She swings a knife and by chance makes contact with the leader of the pack.

I have no idea where Teresa got that knife. It would worry me to see it in her hands, appearing so suddenly, but in this case, I am glad for it. I would never have expected this from her, yet she clearly is not helpless.

There is blood. Teresa shrieks, staggering back as her unsuspecting victim collapses. She is wide-eyed, hands shaking, as the other two draw their weapons. As she refuses to look at the man she stabbed, I am sure she has never attacked someone before in such a manner. I cannot expect her to be capable of more. But I don't need Teresa to do more.

I have my poisoned needle knives in my boot, and I've slipped my hands out of their bonds. Years of loosening Asmer's necklaces, tying sashes and practicing knots on my own have made me a quick study of them.

I do my best to make fast work of the remaining two men, but I'm not as swift as I've come to expect of myself, and they are younger than I am. One of them manages to cut one of my arms—not deep, but enough to bleed—before I get the needle knife stuck.

Still, I have achieved the desired effect. That is three opponents taken care of, and at least another half dozen ahead. Likely more, if Teresa knew there was danger about and left her rooms.

Like Ayla, she is still in her night clothes, with a dressing gown over the top, but found the time to stuff her feet into proper slippers. Not outdoor shoes, no, not in this weather, but still something. Given that, and the knife she is carrying, I know I have underestimated her in many ways. She is no killer, but she will do what is necessary to protect herself.

I was right to begin trusting the Smiths, then. There is a good chance Teresa's actions tonight may lead to my saving Ayla.

Still, the exhaustion in my bones makes me loathe the idea of a fight ahead. I slump against a pillar and try to keep my legs under me. I have never known exactly why I am so resilient to toxins, but while I surely will have a clear head soon, it is not without consequence.

The fight ahead is for a younger woman, with better weaponry. I am going to need help, and Teresa cannot provide that. So, we need to find Rian, recover Ayla, and find a place to hide until I can alert the remainder of our security to this threat.

"Children?" I ask.

Teresa whispers to me breathlessly, as if she is afraid that we will be overheard: "I hid them. For now. In the bottom panels of the bookcase."

My eyes flicker over to the wooden case, now. The bottom panels she mentioned could be seen as merely decorative, but they are secret cupboards meant for extra storage space. If I peer, I can see that Teresa has crammed what was previously in those cupboards underneath the bookcase itself, but I doubt anyone else will notice.

Again, she is more resourceful than I'd previously given her credit for. I'd have never thought to hide the boys, there, and I doubt anyone else will think to look. It will be a small fit, and likely a claustrophobic one, but her children know to stay put.

"Lock the door," I rasp at her. For a moment, she blinks at me in confusion until I begin to repeat myself. "Lock the door. The far door."

Finally understanding, Teresa staggers to her feet, despite her unbalanced figure, and hastens across the room. Before she reaches her destination, however, the door opens, and a man enters, not wearing the proper uniform to be an ally. Behind him, pushing to enter after they spot Teresa, are others.

Teresa screams, and slashes at the man's face before running back towards me. It does not occur to her to kill or incapacitate him the way I would have. But the mistake does not matter. We are too late.

A dark figure drops down before her from the high ceiling, his descent slowed by a pair of large, black wings that he clearly cannot use properly. His dark hair is peppered with gray, but is still thick and worn slicked back. He is impressively, terrifyingly large. Teresa looks like a scrawny child before him, with him only kneeling.

She whirls, to see if she can run back the way she came, but there is no chance of that. What I assume is the rest of the invasion party fills into the room. I am grabbed and dragged back behind the pillars where someone decides to retie my arms behind my back and truss up my ankles as well before unceremoniously dropping me to the ground.

I can't help Teresa until I receive a perfect opportunity, and I certainly can't do it with my hands bound. This situation is slipping further and further from my control.

Given how she attempts to at least stumble back and gain some distance, I know Teresa recognizes the winged man in the uniform. I think I should, too, but I cannot put my finger on who he is. He is a quick one, though. Before she can put more than a step between them, he grabs her arms and holds her there while she struggles to break free again.

"Ah. Our sweet little Teresa," he mocks.

He stands, and kisses her briefly on the cheek in a familial manner before he leans back, grinning. He needs only one hand to wriggle the knife out of her grip.

"You have no idea how happy we are to find you and the children safe. It has been several long months, little Dove."

Teresa's face is white. She is shaking, but doesn't dare look away from him. Nor does she chance a look at her sons' hiding place.

"Do you like the wings?" the man asks. A new development, then. "They aren't much use, I'll admit. But I've found women go mad for them. I picked up a grafter and took the wings from a stupid Kachin boy out east...Oh, don't worry. *He won't miss them."*

Teresa doesn't care about the wings. She has other concerns.

"How did you find me?" she gasps.

He ignores her and releases one of her arms to finger her shorn locks.

"You cut your hair," he notes. "It's curlier now that it's short. I would never have guessed that."

My cousin is breathing so erratically, I'm surprised she retains a grip on consciousness. She flinches away from him, and manages to wrench herself free of his grip on her arm.

"How did you find me?" she asks again. "You—You're dead! Septimus killed you!"

"Ah, yes. Our dear, dear Septimus with his clever, lying tongue," the man hisses, advancing on her as she attempts to put distance between them. "Where is he, now? I think I'd like to cut that tongue of his out and make him swallow it. That ought to teach him, wouldn't you say?"

"H-He's not here," she lies. "He went to the apothecary for me. For medicine. I've had a headache. I don't know when he'll be back."

"Oh? So late at night?" he challenges her.

"He insisted," she whispers.

"Well, that gives us a few hours to make up for lost time, doesn't it?"

He grabs for her and catches her around the waist. For a moment, he is puzzled, but then realizes something that should have been obvious before, were he not so intent on terrorizing her.

"Aha," he says, and grins at her. "So it's true."

"Don't touch me," Teresa snaps.

She slaps him with the sort of ferocity I would never have expected from her if I had not just watched her stab someone. Her voice trembles, but she still stands her ground before the winged man.

"Oh-so charming, isn't she?" he sighs as he rubs at the side of his face.

Then he hits her back, hard enough to knock her to the ground where she barely keeps her head from smacking against the marble. While she struggles to rise, he pushes her back down and pins her, then takes the arm she hit him with and twists it the wrong way until she cries. Teresa hits at him with her free arm, but her efforts are futile.

"Let us try once more," he says. "Where are the boys? Where's Septimus? Your sons?"

Teresa shakes her head and he smacks her across the face. When she still refuses, he hits her again and she screams something I cannot recognize. Whatever it is, it makes them all laugh at her. I let my anger help lend me further energy against my malaise.

"Oh, there is no one here to protect you, now," the winged man mocks her. "I can do whatever I want to you. No one is going to stop me. I'll carve that child out of your belly, if I have to."

"Y-You wouldn't," she stammers through her tears. "He would—"

He leans in close and grabs her face.

"Stupid girl. *He knows about the Tourrannese, Dove. He found out."*

Teresa has nothing to say. She is horrified.

He laughs. "He was not pleased. Not pleased at all. But while I said to simply kill the child, and Jarrod said to kill you…My little brother had a better idea in mind. He said I can bring you home. He's going to let you have the baby, dear girl. And then you get to choose: this one, or your son. The little one. The useless one. A more fitting punishment, I think."

Teresa begs him to let her go. She begs him for a lot of things: to leave her alone, not to hurt her sons, not to hurt her baby. I beg my mind to clear and for my fingers, stiff and fat with blocked blood, to work better at picking knots. Every word he says makes me want to beat his face in even more. Not a pure and forgiving thought, I know. But I've never been the charitable sort.

"But, of course, we must get home before anyone can choose anything, won't we?" he says. "So. Where did you hide the children? Where are those darling boys?"

She is crying, but stubbornly shakes her head. He pulls out a knife.

I can't move fast enough to save her. I can't get the knots untied, can't force my bound feet up from under me, can't decide what to do to help.

Regardless, I know I will look back on this night many times, wondering what might have happened differently if I'd acted first.

"Mama!" Damen cries, bursting from his hiding place before the knife can be put to her.

Everything stops. I can see hints of Damen's shadows, weak but portraying his fear in how they cling to him. He knows he should not have drawn attention to himself, but he only takes a few small steps back when the winged man sheathes his knife, stands to release Teresa, and approaches her son instead.

"I knew someone would see reason," he says.

Teresa rolls over and tries to push herself off the ground on arms that shake from wracking sobs.

Damen looks so small, standing his ground before the man smiling at him.

"Do you remember me, boy?" he is asked. "It's only been a few months, but children have short memories, don't you?"

I can see Damen clench his fists and swallow. He is pretending to be brave, but his flickering shadows and his stammering when he answers betray his fear.

"Uncle A-A-Amerson," he says.

I stare and stare. My head hurts. Because I *do* know Amerson. Not well, as I suspect Septimus has muddle my memories of that in past timelines on purpose. Even if I do not recall meeting him, though, I certainly know the name. Septimus himself said that Amerson is one of Kryto Grey's two brothers.

Kryto. Amerson. Jarrod.

Uncle.

Either I am a complete fool or, more likely, any time I've discovered it, Septimus has made me forget. Forget that his sister is married to Kryto Grey so that I won't immediately run half-way across the world to murder the man they both claim to love. They are both liars, and I believed them. While the fact that Septimus has refused to let me put the pieces together before makes me suspect he has more than one reason for hiding this information, I am too angry about the obvious nature of Kryto Grey's identity to care.

"That's right, boy," Amerson says, smiling and crouching before Damen.

Teresa manages to stand but keeps her distance. Her body shakes as she watches, terrified, but unsure of what she could possibly do against a man twice her size. Her previous efforts have proven already: not much.

"Your father sent me to fetch you and bring you home. I'm sure you know he misses you all so very much..." Amerson says.

"I-I-Is he angry with Mama?" I hear Damen whisper.

His shadows are clinging to his shoulders like a second skin.

"Oh, if he is, he won't be for long," Amerson reassures. "After all, who could stay angry at such a pretty girl?"

Teresa shudders.

"My Mama is the prettiest in the world," Damen agrees stubbornly. As if he thinks that should help the logical conclusion that the prettier his mother is, the quicker his father will forgive her.

"That she is," Amerson agrees, musing. He glances back at Teresa. "Perhaps that is why your father simply couldn't keep his hands off her. Not that any man here would blame him."

Damen is clearly confused.

"That is enough," Teresa snaps, crossing her arms over herself.

Her words predictably have little effect on Amerson.

"It turns out your mother is an easy woman to woo, boy," he says to Damen. "It only takes a few sweet words from your father to get her where he likes. Makes one wonder…what, if anything, the Tourrannese had to say?"

"Amerson," Teresa snaps, her face pink with anger and embarrassment as she guesses at what he might say next. "Leave him alone. He's too young—"

"I'm only trying to educate the poor boy," Amerson says innocently. "I've no doubt you've spent the last few months telling lies about his father. I think it's only fair he understands a few truths about you. In fact," he adds, "they should both enjoy furthering their education, shouldn't they?"

He turns to the bookcase again and reaches for Aiden, still hiding behind the panel. Teresa runs over as Amerson yanks Aiden out by his prosthetic so hard that, if it were a real arm, he would have dislocated it. Naturally, Aiden starts to cry. Teresa throws herself at Amerson, trying to force him to let go however she can.

"Don't you dare touch my sons!" she screeches.

She beats at Amerson until he lets go of Aiden to grab her throat and drag her around in front of him. Damen and Aiden both begin to cry and reach for their mother. Amerson pulls her away. Two of his men approach to take the children.

"Your sons? *Your* sons?" he snarls, tightening his grip on her throat.

Teresa struggles. She kicks one of her slippers off. She scratches at his hand, but his gloves are too thick for it to do her any good. Her children are confused and terrified. Aiden sobs loudly, flailing about in the arms of one of Amerson's men. Damen continues to scream for his mother, struggling to reach her. His shadows are whipping around him, weak, but frenzied and completely out of control.

Amerson snarls something at Teresa in Lusch that I have no hope of understanding, and the children are too panicked for me to take cues from them. She responds by trying to kick him in the expected place.

She doesn't get a clean shot, but it's still enough for him to release her.

Teresa scrambles to her feet. Before she can take but a few steps away, Amerson grabs her wrist. He yanks her back, and throws her over a shoulder to carry her in a way that I imagine must be uncomfortable whilst expectant.

"Amerson!" she rasps. "Put. Me. Down!"

"I liked it better when you couldn't speak," he mutters.

There is a crackling, and a booming noise, like thunder. Everyone freezes, and looks up. Storm clouds are brewing in the high ceiling. There is a crackling in the air.

"Aha. Is this the work of our little Isaarian king, then?" Amerson calls.

I know it is not. Valor is the storm-summoner. It must be exhausting for him to try and do so inside, but if he can create rain, then Rian will have enough water for his fluke. That means there are at least two of them, now, trying to stage a rescue. While I'm certain they can't do it alone, Rian knows me well. He knows I need to incapacitate Amerson first. He is attempting to give me an opportunity.

I'm working on it.

Amerson hoists Teresa on his shoulder again as the storm clouds roll in.

"Come out, little king!" he calls, and laughs as a light spattering of rain drops fall. "Play hero for this pretty damsel in distress and her mewling pups! Or are you afraid I'll—?"

There's a tremendous, terrifying sizzle in the air the almost immediately follows by the strike of lightening. It cracks the marble floor where it lands, and blackens it, only a mere foot away from one of Amerson's men. Valor missed, then, but I do not think he will again.

Neither does Amerson.

His mirth fades, and he calculates his odds. He knows he cannot seriously hurt Teresa, or me. Or Damen. That still gives him one hostage left.

"Very well," Amerson says, and gives a hand signal. "Kill the younger one."

"No!" Teresa screams.

Damen screams at his uncle as well, in Lusch, understanding the threat against his little brother. They should know, as Amerson clearly does, that Rian would never allow that to happen.

A knife is barely pulled before Rian steps out, from the still-open passage to the throne room. Valor has stopped the storm, allowing the crackling to fade and the clouds to slowly disperse, but he remains hidden. Rian appears with his hands up, accepting this temporary defeat.

While seeing Rian here and allowing his hands to be bound frightens me, I know he and Valor could not have walked into this blindly. If they are here, they have evaded Amerson's men so far. They must have a plan. I only hope it will coincide with my own.

Amerson all but throws Teresa off to one of his peons, grinning as he approaches Rian. He purposefully takes the few steps up to tower over him. The king is not a small man, though at times he has tried to disguise that fact; as his wife, I recall appreciating the breadth of his shoulders and the strength of his arms. Yet Amerson overshadows him just as he appears to everyone else. He truly is a monster of a man. Knowing what I do, I'm sure he is immensely pleased to be the one to apprehend the elusive Isaarian king.

"Well," he says, "you are not at all what I expected. Perhaps you'll do me the favor of making your last words the location of our mutual friend Septimus Smith. It seems even her children's lives aren't enough leverage to loosen Teresa's tongue. Cruel of her, wouldn't you agree?"

I glance at Teresa, who is obviously horrified he'd say so. Not because it is true, but because she knows her sons can hear and understand their uncle perfectly. She is frightened they may believe it.

"Oh," Rian says casually. "I don't know. I doubt you gave Miss Teresa an opportunity to say much before threatening her son. But if it is what will keep you from indulging the worst of yourself, I'm happy to tell you anything you need to know."

"Coward, aren't you?" Amerson says, as he looks Rian over.

I'm going to gouge his eyes out.

"Quite the opposite," Rian says. "I'm not afraid of handing myself over to my enemies for the sake of others. One might think *you* a coward, though, sir. For using the death of a one-armed child to threaten me in the first place."

He is truly not frightened of Amerson. In fact, if I did not know him so well, I would believe that Rian is not scared of anyone or anything. At least, he does not react to fear the same way I do. My fear turns to anger; it must, or else I could not function.

But I have maneuvered myself into a position I can use, now. I'm too far from Amerson, though. I need him closer and I have one last thing to reach, at my boot.

I'm thinking of how precisely to do this without appearing suspicious when Rian says something so casually, and almost cheerfully till the end, that I've no doubt he is being inflammatory on purpose. I want the attention on me, but he's trying to keep the attention off of Teresa. He promised he'd protect her and her children. All eyes are undoubtedly on him as he says what he does:

"Forgive me if I've misunderstood—I don't know much about Lusch so perhaps this is merely a cultural difference. But at least here in Isaaria, *we don't terrorize our brother's wives.* I think that's the very mildest word one might choose for what we both know you enjoy; don't you think?"

Rian knows what he's done, and he's seen how easy it is to rile Amerson. The smack across the face he gets for his trouble is predictable and it gives me enough time to do what I must. There is another needle knife hidden in my boot tip that I can use, now that the guard is released. I merely need close range and the right angle; Amerson is too tall.

"Ah," Rian says, wincing as he licks his split lip. "That is going to swell."

Amerson grabs him by the front of his robe and drags him up so Rian's toes barely touch the ground. Rian is shockingly unperturbed by this.

"You have precisely ten seconds, and then I gut you," Amerson snarls.

But in the supercilious manner only he can maintain in such conditions, Rian continues to smile.

"I'd likely be more intimidated, only, you couldn't even manage Soleil without drugging her and she's over a head shorter than you," he says.

He purposefully looks in my direction and gives me a wink.

Amerson looks, too. His eyes narrow. He visibly considers something, then drops Rian.

"Captain," he says. "I've been told some interesting things about you."

I try to sound my most offended, most infuriated.

"If you touch him again, I will—"

"Not do much of anything, I expect," Amerson interrupts.

I bristle, but force myself to wait a moment, as if thinking, and then say. "If you promise not to harm anyone else and let the boys return to their mother, I will tell you where Septimus is. Or how to find him. I'm sure you could track him, but that would be harder."

Amerson raises an eyebrow. "So, he truly is not here?"

"He went looking for something. Something he said would thwart your brother's plans," I lie. "I'll tell you what it is and where he is, but give me what I want first."

Amerson appraises me suspiciously, but then flicks his fingers back at his men. They release Damen then Aiden and the boys flee to their mother. She drops to her knees, pulling them tightly against her. Just like all others in the room, she is watching me and Amerson, now. I can see she is confused, but she and I both know Septimus has not left the palace. So, Teresa trusts I am clever enough to get the better of Amerson.

It is strange how pleased I am to know that, even at a time like this.

"And now?" Amerson says.

"Untie me, get me some water, smelling salts, and a map," I say.

He laughs. "That was not part of the deal. *Captain.*"

But he is approaching, now. I cannot guess at what he's thinking, but I know I have caught his attention properly. Amerson enjoys terrorizing people, but Rian and I are not afraid of him. He knows that. It must feel like a challenge, to him.

"Your men drugged me," I snap. "I'm not giving out information of any kind without having a clear head."

"Didn't drug you enough, I suppose," he muses.

He stops just an arm's length away from my feet. I need him closer.

"I'm captain of the king's guard. We learn to be resilient to such things," I say. "If you'd prepared sufficiently for this invasion, you would have known that about me."

There; that is enough bait for him to take it. Amerson enjoys mockery and pain, and now he thinks there is something he can use against me.

"Oh, I know more than most: would-be queen of Isaaria. Not much of a queen if you ask me," Amerson adds, leaning down so his face is close to mine. Too close. "You know, I always thought you'd be prettier."

I glare at him.

"I've never bitten a man's nose off before," I say, and despite himself, he leans back slightly, into perfect position. "And no one asked."

He glances at Rian but remains crouched close by to me, now. "I would not have guessed you had a taste for wild cats, your majesty."

Rian shrugs.

I ignore them both.

"Now here's the thing, *Amerson Grey,"* I say. "You might think that you have this all wrapped up neatly, and, yes, I suppose, that's a nice thought: to be the man to sneak in and take down Isaaria from the inside. But that's all it is; a nice thought."

I see suspicion flash in his eyes, but he is enjoying himself too much to imagine a scenario where he does not win tonight.

"You may want to take a look around you," he laughs, and pushes me onto my back, coming close to me, to intimidate me. "I don't think you're getting out of this one."

I shrug. "I'm only saying," I claim. "You've forgotten something."

"And what's that?"

"There's probably a very good reason why the king of Isaaria's still alive."

I enjoy the confusion in his eyes.

"What?"

I look around behind him, where Teresa is staring at us, horrified and confused, but perhaps a little hopeful.

"Cover their eyes," I warn her.

Teresa's own eyes widen as she realizes what I'm about to do not a second too soon.

Amerson is not quite as lucky.

Teresa turns her children away.

I kick my ankles out of the bonds I've spent the past few minutes untying whilst on my knees, and swing my leg up, using the needle knife the pops from the toe of my boot to stab Amerson in the neck.

He grabs my ankle, now furious and prepared to exact revenge. It is already too late. I pull my leg free and use the needle knife to cut out the rest of my bindings as Amerson stands and staggers backwards. For a moment, his men are shocked at what they have witnessed.

I know we have seconds to act with us vastly outnumbered. Valor and Rian know this, too. Rian clicks at a lighter hidden in his palm. The storm clouds once again crackle overhead. I glimpse Qhan and Korvaan rushing into the throne room as well, having lain quietly in wait with Valor. I do not know how the five of us together can win this fight, but I know this is our only chance.

Only, it does not matter. Because before any further violence can break out, a strange aura darts through the room. Before anyone can raise a hand to hurt any of us further, every single one of Amerson Grey's men collapse to the floor and don't move again.

Seven

THE CARNAGE AROUND US is shocking in how simple it is. Every one of Amerson Grey's men is dead, yet there is no trace of blood and neither Rian nor I have lifted a finger. We all stare in wonder at what has happened. No one moves for several long moments. Slowly, I turn to look at Damen Grey, realizing that whatever happened to kill all these men, it must have come from him. I am not the only one looking, either—practically everyone has turned to either Damen or Teresa. The later has pulled herself upright and is hiding Aiden behind her while she grips Damen's shoulders, ready to pull him back as well.

"Don't look, baby. Turn around. Look at me," she insists, trying to turn Damen with one hand and keep Aiden pushed back with the other.

Damen is barely listening, speaking over the top of her in Lusch. He is understandably scared, but what is strange is that I can see that fear is not directed at the men laying across the marble. Damen glances at me, at Qhan, and he fears us.

Once it is clear that the deadly presence has left, Qhan pays the Smiths no mind. His attention is focused on his king, whose self-endangerment was worrisome for all of us to watch. Rian insists he is unharmed, but Qhan, Korvaan, and Valor still encircle him, claiming he must sit and rest. I am certain Qhan understands as well as I do why Rian acted so, but still. It must have been horrid, staying back as ordered for the sake of a ruse.

I am less concerned about Rian at the moment. While his face will bruise, it is a minor injury, and I exacted my revenge on Amerson for that. The king's guards will see to him.

When she sees me approach her and her sons, Teresa grabs Damen by the shoulders and shrinks back. I pretend not to notice.

"How is everyone?" I ask. "No lasting injuries? That essence did not touch of any of you, did it?"

I already know it did not. Whatever happened, whatever that presence was, it only harmed our enemies. It is undoubtedly a dangerous thing, considering what it did and how easily, but I am of two minds regarding it. I want to understand exactly what it is first before I make any decisions.

"It's Damen's Ghost," Aiden whispers.

Teresa's eyes widen. "Aiden, don't—"

"Let him speak," I say, and crouch down to his level with aching bones. "What did you say?"

"Damen's Ghost," the child repeats innocently. "He follows us around and, sometimes, he looks after us."

I look to Teresa, who is still shaking her head.

"I swear," she says. "I *promise,* that wasn't him. It…It…I don't know what it is. It follows him and Aiden around but that *was not my son."*

I can tell she is still terrified that, if we think Damen is a threat, we might hurt him. However, I don't think Damen, a mere child, could channel his fluke that expertly, targeting only our enemies, and have the strength to kill them all and still remain standing and conscious.

So, I believe them. Whatever that was, it wasn't him.

I glance back at the men. They have gotten Rian to sit on the steps and are attending to his injuries. Rian is trying to wave them away but they are most insistent.

"How many times has this thing come to your aid?" I ask. "This creature?"

Teresa hesitates. Aiden babbles something in Lusch that I think refers to some instance in which Damen's Ghost has saved them before. He is trying to help his mother, speaking more than I have ever heard from him before. Usually, Damen would take up the responsibilities of aiding his mother, acting much older than his years. Now, he shrinks back, distressed, and silent.

"Several times," Teresa whispers. "Six in total. Since…since Damen was a baby. Never in front of…of my husband. Only on rare occasion, and then I all but forget again until the next moment it arrives."

I narrow my eyes, feeling her nervousness, but do not accuse her of anything. "So, your husband has no idea at all."

"No. He does not. I have kept it that way as much as I can. But not because of Damen!" she insists, hoping for no misunderstanding. "Because…I do not know what it is. I am frightened that things would not go well if…"

She trails off. I can see she is flustered and can barely follow her own train of thought. She has endured much in the past few minutes alone and she can hardly be expected to answer my inquiries now. I suspect Septimus will be more reliable and forthcoming.

"Teresa," I say. She flinches as I touch her elbow. "I understand your concerns. But I am not a fool. You and your sons are not a danger, and I will not treat you as if you are."

She glances at her children and I feel the muscles in her arm tighten. But she nods.

"Come," I say, steering her. "Sit a while and recover yourself. The boys should as well."

She allows me to ferry her to the steps and seat her on them. Her boys scamper after her, talking so quickly in Lusch that Teresa struggles to respond. The children clamber over her the moment she sits, staying close. Even if he does not understand why she left his father, Damen still loves his mother dearly, and at least he had no illusions about his uncle.

Exhausted though I am, I force myself to stand up straight.

"I want to know immediately how this invasion was possible," Rian is instructing. "Valor, find Naomi. Bring her here. Korvaan: find Vilaneau. See what may have possibly happened in matters of security. Given his and Captain Marson's best attempts, something like this should not have been possible."

Something stirs in my memory. That is not entirely true. We faced an invasion like this once before, nearly two decades ago, the night Rian married Asmer. The night I watched Taris and my sister die.

I would correct him, only there is something I must see to first.

I pick my way carefully across the room again to where Amerson lays, unmoving. I retrieve Teresa's knife on my way, along with my own bolt shooter and darts from the men who took them. I cannot find my other needle knives. I strap my weapons back in place and look over Teresa's knife. It isn't from the kitchens, nor does it look like anything she would have picked up at random. It is of high quality, and custom. Beautiful, and well suited to her small hands.

In my examination of Amerson, I find very little new information. He carries a few weapons on him, but nothing specialized or overly impressive. So, either he did not expect a fight here, or he is a secret coward who lets others do his work for him while he terrorizes scrawny women like Teresa.

His clothes are finely tailored, made of expensive material, but are not the sort someone who considers himself a king would wear. I manage to remember details from what I have learned in the past; enough to remember that Amerson is merely one of his brother's generals, and Kryto was chosen as their father's heir, and the heir of Lusch.

This would not be peculiar, except I am certain Amerson is, or was, Kryto's older brother.

I flip back his lapel. Firebird pin. I remember that.

I rip the pin off his jacket and tuck it away.

"I'm almost certain I've killed him before," I mutter to myself.

"Oh, you have," Septimus announces from behind me.

We all whirl to see him enter the room, Ayla leaning on his arm. The moment Rian notices them, he stops mid-sentence and rushes over. I, too, want to hurry to Ayla, but manage to hang back and give them space. I remember Ayla as my daughter; she does not. As close as she may be to me, she will appreciate her father's embrace more, now.

"Did they touch you? Ayla? Did they hurt you?" Rian demands after finally letting her go.

His eyes flick all over her for signs she is hurt, though she is currently wearing Septimus' coat to cover her.

Ayla's still sobbing, but she shakes her head pointedly so her hair swishes over her shoulders. Trying to reassure her father she's well, though I think it's clear that, emotionally at least, she's not. She has no blood spatters on her that I can see, and no bruises, yet. There is no telling what might be beneath the coat, though.

I try not to think about it, and examine Septimus instead. He has discreetly moved towards his sister and nephews during this reunion. He appears uninjured, and is still dressed in sleep-ware. So, he at least did not expect the invasion. I can trust him on that account.

There is blood stained on his right sleeve and hand, and in that hand, he still holds a sword. It looks to be taken from the guards' barracks.

Septimus reaches into his pocket and pulls out the pair of glasses Teresa has been using to see properly. He hands them to her without a word and she dons them, but it occurs to me that I have not seen her wear them often. I suppose she must have gone for so long with poor vision, living with the Greys, that it takes some getting used it.

It explains even more how terrifying everything must seem to her. So blurry and impersonal.

"Captain," Septimus says, noticing me.

He approaches, bows before me, and offers me the hilt of the sword.

"Keep it," I decide. "I think if you were to use it against us, you would have found a way by now."

Septimus straightens and raises an eyebrow at me.

"Are you certain? Not still worried I might kill you? Perhaps I only rescued the princess to further gain your trust before later betraying you for some assorted reason only your paranoid mind can think up."

"And maybe you're saying all this to make me second-guess myself while honestly still planning a double-cross," I snap.

Septimus smiles. "Ask Qhan, I suppose."

I glare at him. I will concede: he saved Ayla. In another life, I adopt her, which means Septimus saved my daughter. I feel as if I have an obligation to stop doubting him. But perhaps not at the expense of the secrets he has kept.

Given the greatest of those secrets, now revealed, I do not think we can proceed further before setting the facts straight.

"You said I killed Amerson before," I accuse.

My words catch even Ayla and Rian's attentions again.

Septimus nods. "You have. In many, many timelines. He enjoys what he does, and so, he is often allowed to indulge himself."

"Allowed," I repeat. "By his brother. Kryto. *Teresa's husband.*"

Qhan takes a step closer. He does not draw a weapon, but the threat is clear enough. Septimus hesitates, but then speaks.

"Yes. My sister married Kryto Grey. Has always married Kryto Grey. I'm sorry," he concludes.

I feel my blood boil. It's not enough.

"You lied," I say.

"I think if I lied, Qhan would have picked up on it," he says irritably. "I did not lie. I misled you because I thought it was the right thing to do at the time. I had no way of knowing how you would react to Damen and Aiden being Greys; I needed to be certain you would not hurt them."

"You did not have the right to make that decision."

"Every time I have revealed it in the past, you have not responded well, and the subsequent events have been disastrous. I can only do what makes the most logical sense each time, to try and avoid the necessity of another loop, so—"

"You led me to believe Teresa's husband was but a tool for the Greys, not *one* of them!" I accuse him.

"Yes, well, I thought it truth enough!" Septimus snaps.

"Evidently so! You cannot treat us like your pawns, Septimus! We have minds! Perhaps if you let us use them in conjunction from the beginning things would turn out better!"

"You think we didn't try that at least once already?! I'm doing whatever I can to try and keep my nephews alive! Did you ever consider that?"

I scoff. "Out of everyone here, they are the safest."

"They are not," Septimus hisses. "You know it. I'm sure you do. And if your foolish actions have led to Aiden dying before, why would I tell you anything again that could repeat that possibility?"

At an intellectual level, I understand Septimus does not necessarily mean to imply I would kill Aiden. There are many who might attempt to harm the children, should they learn they are Greys and understand what that means. In this moment, however, I am still greatly offended. I take it personally.

"You—!"

"Would you stop!? You're frightening my children!" Teresa interrupts loudly, and we quiet. We can hear, then, that both boys are upset and crying, trying not to be heard.

I suppose I didn't realize they were old enough to comprehend what their uncle implied. Either that, or merely our argument has brought them to tears.

"Hush. Don't cry, darlings," Teresa says, ignoring the rest of us and pulling her boys both to her and kissing them on their foreheads. Ruffling their hair and wiping their tears away. "We're going on a short trip, now. We're going to live someplace new, where we'll be safer."

"You said we were safe *here!*" Damen accuses, the harshness of the statement softened only by his tears.

Still, I watch Teresa grimace; the declaration hurts her, and I'm sure she feels as if she's failed her children by allowing them to fall into danger once more. I am reassured somewhat by Damen's words only because it means some part of him must recognize that it was not safe for any of them, back home with his father.

I hope that, eventually, he will be able to realize that none of this is his mother's fault.

I can feel the others all looking at me, but despite the children crying and Teresa's request, I refuse to leave Septimus be. Besides, now that I've already reduced the children to tears, why stop now?

"She married Kryto Grey, the man responsible for killing my sister. Killing Taris. Breaking the world. Having my husband and son killed over and over, every time I relive the same damned events, and you decided to lie to me about that?" I hiss.

Septimus looks down.

"Again, I wouldn't say lying, I would say occasionally lying, occasionally, conveniently, making you…forget. That I'd told you."

"Why? Why in the world wouldn't you let me kill him?" **I demand.**

In fact, the question I should be asking is why shouldn't I turn back time, find this man wherever he is in the world, and kill him as a child, but that is not what comes out of my mouth.

Septimus does not bother to defend himself or his sister much. He merely looks up at me, hopelessly, and shrugs, a small, sad smile on his face.

"What can I say," he says hoarsely. "We love him."

Teresa chokes on a sob. She covers her mouth with a hand, her head bowed, shoulders shaking, and she begins to cry.

I have nothing else to say. I give Septimus a disgusted look, but when I catch sight of Rian out of the corner of my eyes, I can feel he is disappointed in me. Whether this is because he is merely naïve, or a better person than I am, I cannot decide, now.

Qhan steps up to be diplomatic with me. "Captain, we have much to do to secure the palace."

"I know," I say. "The king sent Valor to find Naomi, and Korvaan after Vilaneau."

"Leaving only you and me to protect him," Qhan says.

I take his point.

"We need to bring him and the princess to a known safe place immediately," Qhan says.

"I agree," I say. "But so long as we have control of this room, we shouldn't move them until at least Korvaan or Valor return. Close and lock the far door in the meantime. I'll get the main doors."

I don't need to tell him to keep his wits about him and his eyes open.

Rian has been watching me and Qhan both carefully. I nod to him and gesture towards the still-open towering doors. "Help me," I order, and between the two of us, we manage to close them. There is no way to lock them, but the doors are heavy, and take at least two people to open and close each. No one will come through with ease. Even if we are only bought seconds, they are seconds that count.

Qhan stays by the far door, to unlock it again if Korvaan or Valor return.

Rian hovers by my shoulder for some time after. I know he wants to say something to me about my argument with Septimus, but does not know how to broach the subject. It makes me generally irritated. In my opinion, Septimus and I were both out of hand. But I know that Rian is not the sort to lecture a still relative stranger.

I do not feel like letting anyone tell me what to do anymore.

To avoid this eventuality, I brush past Rian muttering something about necessary security. There are still several matters to take care of.

I find a place on the steps to sit near Teresa and ignore the way she flinches. It is not personal; it was likely a bad idea to approach Teresa from behind after such distressing events.

She is brushing Aiden's hair gently, murmuring to him in Lusch. Damen sits nearby, sniffling and glaring at the floor, refusing his mother's comforting.

"I wanted to apologize for the shouting," I say. "Upsetting them was not my intent."

I'm glad Teresa does not ask what my intent was, because I'm not sure what I'd say. She only nods. I suppose that is all the forgiveness I deserve. I take out her knife and offer it. So long as I'm letting Septimus keep a sword, I won't begrudge Teresa some small form of protection.

Still, there are some things I must know.

"Where did you get this knife? Did you have this all along?" I ask.

Teresa will not look up at me, but pulls up her nightgown skirt until I can see a knife's sheath on her thigh. I recall the position she took in the shower, turned to the side, so her right leg faced the wall, so I could not see she wore it. She had more than one thing she wanted to hide from me that day.

Something tells me I should have had her searched as thoroughly as I'd had Septimus. But at the same time, Teresa has had this weapon all along, and has not once used it against us.

That, and how Septimus saved Ayla without needing to, tells me they truly did come here seeking allies, and refuge. If Septimus and Teresa intended to betray us to the Greys, they disregarded a spectacular opportunity. Teresa did not even try to bargain away Rian or her brother to save her son's life.

Septimus was right on that, too; Amerson had no qualms about killing Aiden.

"You hid it cleverly," I note.

"I'm sorry," Teresa whispers, "but I needed a way to protect my children."

I do not refute that. "Where did you get it?"

I doubt it was a gift from her husband.

"Our father Janos was a Smith, like us. He could make magical weapons. Things that defy description," Teresa says. "He made this knife for me. Before he died. It cannot break, and it does what I need."

"Did your husband know?" I ask.

Teresa nods. "It is a pretty plaything. That is what he said. So, he let me keep it. And the Kachin hair pin. To protect myself. From 'our' enemies."

I watch her hand freeze while combing Aiden's hair. She shudders. A memory has crossed her mind she would rather soon forget, then. It must be difficult for her and her children to live as they do, trapped between potential allies and enemies.

"Take it," I tell her, offering the knife. "And keep the hairpin. You ought to have some small way to protect yourself."

For some reason, Teresa hesitates before taking it. But the knife finds its way back strapped against her thigh, and her skirts are resettled into place.

We sit in silence for some time longer. It occurs to me I should draw the Marks of the Dead on the fallen intruders, but it is an effort to even think of standing. Every muscle in my body is overly aware of itself and displeased to be so. I suppose I could hand off the paints to someone else for the task, but I do not want to distract Qhan at a time like this. That leaves Septimus as a reasonable possibility.

I decide not to say anything. Someone else can do it.

Korvaan returns, banging on the door. He runs to us, still gasping when he meets us in the middle of the room. Far enough away from the Smiths and Ayla that they will not hear us so long as we speak in low voices. I've no doubt he has been running the past ten minutes. I give him a wave, acknowledging it may be best for him to take a moment to breathe first. But the king is more demanding.

"What happened?" Rian says, approaching. "Did Vilaneau explain how this could have possibly happened on his watch?"

"Your majesty," Korvaan pants. "Vilaneau claims the perimeter of the palace was never breached. Wherever they entered, it was not from any known portion of the palace. Inside the palace is another story. Patrols found several of the palace guards…immobile," he says, faltering.

I frown at his wording; certain this has something to do with an unknown fluke. Or two flukes, more likely. One used to enter the palace, another to restrain our men. But Rian focuses on something else entirely, and understandably so. His daughter and guests were attacked and nearly killed. Even with the bodies before us, someone must be blamed.

"The palace has been infiltrated, all our lives put into severe risk, and my own security has no idea how this could have happened?" he demands.

Korvaan has nothing to say to that. He glances at me, helpless and wishing I would handle the king for him. No luck. Even I am too exhausted to try and manage Rian at a time like this.

"Go back to Vilaneau," he orders. "Tell him that unless he can tell me precisely what happened in the next hour, he can consider himself dismissed. Then dispatch teams to search every inch of this palace. If there are more intruders, I want them found and dealt with."

"Of course, sir," Korvaan says.

"And send a team back to escort his majesty and the princess someplace safe," Qhan adds.

Korvaan agrees and begins to leave once more. I motion him aside while the king is distracted with his daughter again. Ayla is sitting, curled against a pillar, huddled in Septimus' coat. She does not say anything when her father crouches near her again, but I know his presence must be at least somewhat soothing to her.

That is more than anything I could offer at a time like this. At least in this timeline, I am a better bodyguard than mother.

"Whatever happens, do not dismiss Vilaneau," I murmur to Korvaan. "This happened on my watch, yours, and Qhan's as well as his. I suspect our answers will reveal themselves soon enough."

Korvaan gives me an uneasy nod, but runs off again with my orders annulling the king's.

After he has departed, I walk back towards the steps. I make eye-contact with Septimus and crook a finger. He sighs, but heaves himself up and joins me. I would prefer Rian and Qhan to also be present for this exchange, but I need Qhan watching the far door, and Rian is clearly not in the right state of mind. I know it is possible he will join Septimus and I soon, anyway, but I hope to prolong that eventuality.

Ayla's needs rightfully dominate his attention.

"I know you know how they got in the Pyrian Palace," I tell Septimus without wasting time. "Your coyness stopped being an endearing trait quite some time ago."

To my surprise, I find Septimus nodding. "In my defense, before you make accusations, I did not know they could use the orb again so soon."

I narrow my eyes. "This is not a fluke, then?"

"Perhaps it is better for us that it is not. There are certain *anomalies* the Greys use that defy imagination, even in a world like ours," Septimus says. "Ten that I know of. The orb is one of them."

Ignoring the wave of dizziness that comes with the action, I nod my understanding. I should have anticipated such a thing, given how Septimus told me the Greys used Magicsmiths as pets for centuries.

"And can another of these items induce stasis?" I say.

"Stasis?" Septimus repeats.

"Korvaan told me some of our men were found in a state," I explain. "I want to know what we are working against. If they used merely objects, then it may indicate our may threat has been neutralized. If it is a fluke, there is at least one more intruder to worry about. Assuming you killed all those who took Ayla, which I realize I should have clarified with you."

But Septimus has stopped listening to me.

"Oh, Fate's Fingers," Septimus curses in a hush. "They brought Phoebus."

I'm about to ask, but I hear a small gasp first that stops me. Teresa has been listening in to our discussion, and that name means something to her. She has turned so white, I can see it in her face down to her fingertips. Despite Damen's irritation with her, she stands and pulls him closer, hoisting Aiden in her shaky arms.

"I-I-If Kryto's here," Teresa stammers. "If he's here—"

"He won't be," Septimus insists, ignoring me. "I promise you, he's not here."

"If he is, though, I-I-I…"

"Go with the king," her brother says. "You'll be safe with him. Go, now."

Teresa nods, then pulls Damen along with her as she rushes over to Rian and Ayla. I'm, again, about to speak when Septimus interrupts me.

"We need to get your royals, my sister, and my nephews someplace else. Someplace safe," he insists.

"We are in the process—"

"It can't wait," Septimus insists. "Please, Soleil. I know what a pain I am, and how little I have done to help you trust me. Realistically. But it would be better if we had as few people present as possible for this."

"For what?" I demand.

I watch Septimus argue with himself over what he wishes to explain. But I am not so stupid that I cannot put together a few basic facts: there is another intruder in the palace. One that Teresa is as scared of as she was Amerson, and one who has the ability to place people into stasis if he so chooses.

"Can you fight against a powerful fluke? Now?" Septimus asks quickly.

"I think I can take him, with what I have left in me, but I need your help. I cannot do this by myself."

"I'd help you, but—"

"Excellent," he interrupts.

He begins to turn, to explain things to a confused Rian. Teresa's frightened babbling likely isn't helping much at all. I grab his wrist.

"Septimus," I warn. "I can't. I'm too weak, from whatever they gave me…"

He looks me over. "Not as weak as you should be, actually. Let's have you sit for a moment. Sit, Soleil. I'll be back momentarily."

I frown, confused. "What?"

Septimus has levered me to the ground, to sit up against a pillar. I almost force myself to stand again, and start up after him, but it is a relief to allow myself to rest, to let someone else take the lead.

"Qhan!" he calls, motioning for everyone to gather.

I close my eyes for a few moments and let them speak in the background. We cannot wait for Korvaan to return. The king and princess must be taken to a secure location immediately. Captain Marson agrees; such a thing cannot wait. They must try to meet Korvaan along the way. If possible, send someone to search for Valor and Naomi Ondra, as well.

It vaguely surprises me that Septimus would think to have someone search for them, to ensure they are safe, but perhaps it should not. By his own admission, he knows us all better than we understand.

Rian and I mean something to him. Perhaps Taris, Korvaan and Naomi do, too. It has never occurred to me to ask.

I am starting to drift off when I feel Septimus return to me.

"Wake up, now, Soleil," he says, jolting my side. "I need you to help me with this. Please."

"You're not powerful enough to do it on your own?" I mock.

He sighs. "Soleil."

"I'm tired."

"Naturally. Now wake up," he says, and smacks my cheek lightly.

By the time he goes in for the second one, I'm much more awake, and catch his wrist. For some reason, I still feel as if he has won that encounter.

"Good. Now, I left some portions of your abilities intact to protect you and the timelines, just in case," Septimus said. "For one, if you were ever in danger of dying, you would automatically go back. Not a full reset. Just to keep yourself safe. But in case of non-lethal poisons, that was the tricky portion. So, I left another ability with you, for protection."

"Congratulations. Leaving a woman with a form of self-defense: you're less of a miserable excuse for a god than you were before," I mutter.

"Yes, you're very funny, Soleil. You'll have noticed you are exceptionally resilient," he says, speaking so quickly I'm having trouble keeping up with him. "It's not merely resilience, Soleil. You've been turning back your body's state of being while still moving forward in time. It's tiring, which is why you're exhausted now, and have been after using it in the past. But it purges your body of toxins."

"Why haven't I done it automatically, this time?" I demand.

I cannot think of another reason to feel so weak.

"You likely already have," Septimus says. "But that means using your fluke without properly giving yourself the energy to do so. And," he added, with some hesitation, "you are older, now, than you were twenty years ago."

I grumble at him, but will relent, there. I am no longer young, and these are curious monsters we find ourselves facing. At least Septimus appears to have some idea of what he is doing.

"Soleil, I'm going to fully release the rest of your abilities to you, now," he warns me. "Because I want you to use them to help me."

"Against 'Phoebus'?" I say. "Who is this; another Grey you conveniently forgot to warn me about?"

"Phoebus Kagen works for them. He knows me, and he knows Teresa and the boys. If they sent Amerson looking for Teresa, though, they will have sent him looking for me. So, are you going to help me, or not?"

I give him a nod. Regardless of personal opinions, and potential grudges, Septimus and I need one another, now. Neither of us can do this on our own. Not to mention, the men who work for the Grey family and the members therein are the sort who have allowed their power to turn them psychotic. Amerson is the perfect example of that.

Septimus takes a deep breath. "Steel your mind, then," he warns me. "You are about to feel more power in your fingertips than you have in decades."

Though I'd grown used to feeling comfortable in myself, body and mind, when Septimus releases the recollections and capabilities my past selves have mastered in regards to my fluke, something changes. There is a rushing in my head, like the releasing of a damn. There is no liquid to fill in, but it feels as if there should be. My mind is an egg cracked open inside a bowl of milk. The yolk splits and spreads.

I am powerful, and weak. Perhaps there is much truth in what Rian said in his fever, about no one having the power I have. I am powerful, but delicate. My body is a vessel for a gift a supernatural being deemed me worthy to receive when I am anything but.

This is both everything and nothing like I expected. Septimus cannot possibly hope to understand, yet he watches me carefully with knowing eyes.

"How do you feel?" he poses when my eyes lose their glossiness.

"Awake," I say. I lever myself to my feet.

The exhaustion is still there, beneath, but that is the only way I know to describe this. I am acutely aware of my capabilities. What I could do, and what we intend to do. There is not much energy left to draw on anymore, but I still intend to push myself as far as I can.

"Good," he says.

"How do you intend to go about this?" I ask, allowing him to lead the way.

Each step feels more certain than before. I am aware this is temporary, and the price I will pay for it in a matter of minutes will be great, but recoverable.

"We will need to hunt him," Septimus whispers. "And keep him from knowing our whereabouts for as long as possible. He can place people in stasis," he adds before I can ask. "Temporarily, but if he incapacitates the two of us, I don't think Kryto wants me back alive."

"So, what's your plan?"

"We take him out as quickly as possible. The moment he attempts to use his fluke on either of us, you go back," Septimus says. "As far as you have to, though I'd prefer you at least keep Amerson dead. I'm sorry if it means some form of trauma for those we care about, but I'd rather not try to manage two of them at once."

"Fine," I say. "For the record, I am displeased with the order in which you've decided to disclose this information."

"Your complaint has been officially noted," Septimus says.

But I can hear in his tone, and see in the vague smile playing at his mouth, that he is relieved. Some part of him is positive he and I can manage whoever this Phoebus is. I wonder if that says something in Septimus' confidence in me, or simply to the massive power I have been gifted. More likely the latter, if I'm being honest with myself.

We exit through the throne room and into back passages meant for servants but often utilized by myself and other members of the king's guard. Septimus is quiet, a hand steading his sword, and I keep my footsteps unusually light. I'd forgotten how much my weight began to make itself known as the years pass. I am still fit, but less spry. With the return of my missing pieces, there is a temporary return to youth. Septimus and I both will depend on that, now.

We exit the inner passages back to opulent hallways with marble and chandeliers. The glamour of the Pyrian Palace does not belong to the two of us, skulking about, looking for a monster to penalize. We clear rooms, and hallways, checking them over, finding nothing. I listen carefully, but the palace has either been abandoned naturally, or cleared by the king's men.

I note the echo of footsteps and gesture for Septimus to stay close and follow me. I track the sound of sure, heavy steps and a weaker second, dragging, stumbling pair. That cannot be natural. Either someone is injured or someone is a hostage, or both.

It is a relief we find him before he notices us, this Phoebus Kagen person Teresa is so afraid of. We hide ourselves behind the marble pillars, assessing, both prepared to enact Septimus' plan. As usual, nothing goes as expected. It is the one thing in my life I suppose I should expect, at this point.

Between the two of them, I decide Amerson Grey is more a terrifying, impressive creature. Phoebus is tall, but much less a monster. From what I can tell, he appears to be Alarkian, but I know that means nothing in terms of the Greys' allegiances in the western wars. I can tell that Phoebus should look older than he does; there is a strangeness to his physical youth that does not extend to his bearing, or the way he looks around his surroundings. This is an older man, in a younger man's body. I don't think it's the recurring timelines that have accomplished this.

This man practices *Dadj'zcha,* in a way that Amerson did not.

The unexpected portion is who he has taken prisoner. He drags Naomi with him, an arm around her neck, and she stumbles to keep up and breathe at the same time. She looks as if she attempted to put up a fight against him, but could not manage on her own.

Septimus did not anticipate a hostage. When I glance at him, behind his pillar, I can tell this is a surprise, and he is rapidly attempting to recalculate.

I let the sudden trill of energy run through me, waking my mind and flooding it with ideas on Naomi's behalf. Some small part of me practically insists it should not matter if I allow Naomi to die as a hostage so long as Phoebus is stopped. I know we will need to reset this timeline at some point anyways. But I cannot be that person.

For better or worse, regardless of what even Septimus would say, each timeline does mean something to me. Each death does.

Even if she does not remember it, Naomi is my sister. I love her, Valor loves her, Korvaan loves her. Taris and Nusk did.

I will not let Phoebus hurt her more than he already has. But I don't know if Septimus feels the same.

I look Phoebus over for weaknesses. There is a small silver ring glinting off one of his fingers. It matches jewelry Septimus and I both know far too well.

If I go back, even if he is disoriented, he will remember. This is to be a battle of wits and skill, then. Unfortunately, with his own agenda, I am not positive if Septimus will be a hinderance or a help.

I quickly take stock of my weapons and choices. I've my needle knife, but that is imbedded in my boot, and I cannot risk a prolonged close-range fight. It will give him too much of an advantage; especially considering his fluke and Naomi as a hostage. That leaves the darts and their wrist shooter.

Looking across to make eye-contact with Septimus, I raise my arm and gesture to the bolt shooter. I am only good for a distraction with the wrist shooter. The poison in them would take too long, and Phoebus could harm Naomi, or either of us. If he managed to put me in stasis after long enough to kill Septimus, for example, I don't know what I would do next.

I count down on my fingers for Septimus and then duck out from behind the pillar, raising my bolt shooter. I only have one chance, one shot, and I need the best visual field possible.

With the full view of the intruder, my aim is impeccable. Firing the bolt, I hit Phoebus directly in a shoulder. He and Naomi both look startled to see me, and neither move until after I've made my mark. Naomi is quick witted; she strikes Phoebus in the ribs and staggers away, attempting to flee him.

This Phoebus Kagen is quick-witted, too. He snags her by the hair and, the moment Septimus moves out from behind his pillar, he flings an arm out in that direction. He's gotten Septimus frozen, then. Put into stasis. Then that hand goes back down again to find the gun at his belt. There's always the chance a weapon like that could misfire, but I don't want to take it. I know it's too late.

I draw on every part of my capabilities and I stop. Everything.

I have no time to think, but I need to outsmart Phoebus without putting anyone else I care about in jeopardy. That includes Septimus, now, I realize.

I feel my grip over time like it's a measuring tape. I hold myself still and pull the tape backwards. Septimus told me not to try moving forward, or perhaps it was Rian. But I'm not. Everyone else slides backwards. I'm the one who stays still; still one bolt less. Still standing in the same spot.

This buys me time to get a better shot at Phoebus, and buy Septimus a few extra seconds as well. Ideally. But Phoebus is thinking on his feet. I do not even have time to fire the shot.

He blocks me by freezing Septimus in stasis the moment I release time again, despite his being moved all the way back to the doorway in this past version. I need Septimus to take Phoebus out for me; I don't have any realistic way of doing it on my own. But I know I can't go too far back. If I give him the opportunity, Phoebus will hurt Naomi and there will be nothing I can do about it.

He knows he has leverage over me, which means he either took an accurate shot in the dark or he's using information the Greys have on me.

I freeze us again. I cannot let this happen eight times over again until one of us is lucky and the other is not.

Perhaps there is a logical, reasonable explanation. A perfect solution that would solve everything without making a mess of things. But I can't think of it. I'm simply not smart enough.

Therefore, I need to use my best skills and assets.

I consider the layout of the palace. We were hunting Phoebus, yes, but based on his trajectory, and our usage of the servant's passages, he was heading towards the throne room and the great hall beyond. That means he knew where to meet Amerson. He was bringing Naomi with him, then likely going back out again for Septimus. That means he understands the palace's layout, and he can likely deduce that we came from that direction.

Considering he was dragging Naomi along, alone, I conclude Phoebus is the last one standing of the Greys' invasion force. Septimus said Phoebus was sent looking for him.

I map out his most reasonable path in my head. So long as we're here, together, with Naomi present—and he has that ring—I haven't a chance.

I drag the tape back again, and this time let myself be pulled along with. It's not long that we move, but I pray it's enough. If not, hopefully I only must do this once, but I'm prepared to adapt if necessary.

We are back in the grand hall.

"I-I-If Kryto's here, I—" Teresa's stammering, her chin wavering, and eyes watering. Septimus puts a hand to her shoulder to reassure her, but then stops and seems to realize what has happened.

I lurch over and grab his arm. Teresa looks dreadfully confused, and we've garnered the attentions of the rest of the room as well. Only Septimus and Korvaan would know I've used my abilities, after all. Only they and Phoebus Kagen would remember.

Septimus frowns at me. "You went back—"

"Yes, and there's no time to wait," I gasp.

I'm feeling dizzy once more but I blink it away. After this, I will rest and someone else can manage the details of the king's traveling plans for me.

"Fate's Fingers, Soleil," Septimus mutters. "You need to be careful you don't create some kind of paradox."

"No time," I pant. "Quick."

If Phoebus is smart, and truly wants to control how I move through time, he will kill Naomi. She will try to fight him off; she'd have no reason to change her actions based on a past she no longer remembers. But I also know that Phoebus will win that fight in the end. So, we haven't much time.

Septimus adjusts to the change in timelines and immediately responds to my orders. He runs behind me, a hand to steady his sword again, calling behind him instructions for Teresa to go with the king somewhere safe and not to worry. She still looks shocked, but manages to start stumbling off towards Rian with Aiden in her arms and Damen pulled behind her.

In my head, I am running back through the palace schematics again and simulating Naomi and Phoebus. I nearly forget entirely to tell Septimus the plan. Or, the new plan, as I'm certain he remembers the old one.

"Cut off his hand," I pant as we run.

"What?"

"Cut off his Fate-damned hand," I tell him. "With the ring. Cut it off."

Septimus appears to understand because he does not fight my logic and simply follows me. He must recall our past few failures, but I've no idea if he remembers precisely the path we took. I'm sure he knows we're running through servant's passages longer this time than we did last.

Septimus has undoubtedly more energy than I do, but I'm faster with the rush of desperation pushing me. I want all of this done and over with, already. Enough of this madness and this danger.

I can hear them as we approach. I duck out of the servant's passage and run through the corridor to turn sharply right down another. I have no exact plans but decide to simply attack and leave the particulars to Septimus. If I manage to get Phoebus hand first, that is fine. But I trust Septimus has skill enough with a sword to use it properly. I would rather not have to cut at someone's wrist with the toe of my boot.

My legs aren't up for such ridiculousness today.

Naomi is struggling with Phoebus when I arrive. He must need at least one hand free to use his fluke, because she has kept him from freezing her by grappling with both. All I know is that I want him far away from her, and that I am meant to be the distraction. No doubt about that.

But I can't let him put me in stasis, either.

So, I improvise. I run straight up and throw myself into Phoebus so that Naomi can scramble away. He uses my momentum against me and twists me so I'm dropped to the ground. I'd usually be back up faster, but it takes me three seconds too long. He opts to play the long game with my powers, and when he gets the opportunity to use his fluke, he freezes Naomi, not me. As I'm getting to my feet, he takes out the gun and shoots her. The stasis he's placed her in drops and she doesn't move.

I didn't come here to save Naomi, now. Just to take his ring so I can save her later.

Phoebus turns to freeze me, next, but by that time, I'm back in the fight, and I am using all remnants of my energy. I save nothing at all for my next loop because I cannot afford to. This man is bigger than me, and I don't have the strength to manage a full fight. I go on the offensive, targeting Phoebus' hands and forcing him to fight me back. He knows what I'm trying to do, but I refuse to give him an opportunity to use his fluke.

I start with kicking the gun out of his hand and quickly drawing my leg back before he can grab it. We're both brutal. He does not care I'm a woman, and I am not looking to take prisoners. Like with Amerson, I'm looking for a specific, opportune moment, and keeping himself hidden and out of sight, so is Septimus.

Keeping myself at a respectable distance when I can, I know I don't want to grapple with a stronger opponent. When possible, I rely on my legs; my arms are stronger than most women's, but certainly not most men's.

He gets a few good hits in, but so do I, and I'm angrier. When he is disoriented enough, I pop the needle knife out of my boot. I get Phoebus off his balance, and then strike. I know it would be near impossible to cut off a man's hand using the needle knife in my boot, but there are other uses for it. Such as stabbing the knife up straight through his hand.

I've used such a tactic before. I remember. Except I think I used a fork.

I've one of his hands occupied, then, but there is always the other, and I'm in no position to stop him unbalanced as I am. It's a good thing I decided to trust Septimus to come in and help me, then. He sweeps in with an elegant slash of his sword that confirms to me he has been training to use such a thing for years.

When Phoebus stumbles and drops, he brings me with him, but I don't care. I fall properly to keep my head from hitting marble, but otherwise allow myself to lay there, panting. I do use my other foot to pin Phoebus' arm so he can't pull the needle tip of my boot out of his hand and try anything. But otherwise, I attempt to stay conscious and useful.

"Not leaving Naomi. Like this," I gasp.

Septimus looks over at her, then Phoebus and me. I watch his mouth twitch unhappily; he knows I'm creating more work for him. But he nods.

"Take a moment, then do it," he sighs.

I prop myself up on my elbows and motion for Septimus to help me sit up. He keeps a wary eye on Phoebus, but does so. This allows me to lean forward enough to reach the ring on Phoebus' remaining hand. With some slick difficulty, I begin to pull it off.

Phoebus ignores me. He laughs and garbles something at Septimus in Lusch, but it sounds more like a reaction to pain than distinct mockery. If he's trying to rattle Septimus, it's not going to work. In fact, before responding in kind, Septimus even rolls his eyes. I don't think I've heard him speak Lusch before, but he is better at it than his sister.

"He wants to know how I got you to trust me this time," Septimus says before I can inquire. "I said by telling you the truth."

"I don't care," I pant, and I realize it is true. I don't.

Whatever Phoebus said to Septimus, it means nothing to me. I've had enough of talk, from Amerson.

Septimus crouches next to me. "Can you make it back, or will you let me convince you to end things here?"

I shake my head. "I'm not going forward. Without Naomi."

"She doesn't remember how close the two of you really are. And you'll get her back the final time around."

"I don't care."

"Be logical, Soleil."

"I am."

I'm not explaining to Valor how I let his wife die because I was too tired to find a solution. I'm not facing Korvaan or whatever guilty conscious I think I deserve. If Septimus wanted me practical enough to let people I care about die simply because they don't have the cosmic significance Rian apparently does, he should never have given me my memories back in the first place.

Besides, if he was as coldly practical as he is pretending, he would have been able to use the same logic months ago. He would have left his sister and nephews in the west.

I know this very reason is why he will not try to argue the point with me.

It is as slippery as handling the bloody ring, with my wavering mental statis, but I find and grasp my tape measure again. There is a small mental groove, where I last left us. I drag it back very slowly, rewinding us a matter of minutes that feel like entire days.

Perhaps I do not return to the exact second, but at least I'm close.

"I-I-If Kryto's here, I—" Teresa's stammering.

Septimus suddenly jolts. The old timelines no longer exist, after all, but he and I still remember them.

Though Teresa is, again, confused, Septimus shushes her, pushes her aside, and turns to me. To all others in the room, I've suddenly, unreasonably become exhausted and dizzy, as if poisoned. I think I hear Rian call for me, and there are footsteps. Septimus reaches me first, and surely, he already knows what to do, but I still manage to speak for anyone else listening.

"Phoebus. Kagen," I pant. "Here. Upstairs. Naomi."

I waver on my feet, staggering until I find a pillar to lean against. Septimus grabs for my arm and I scramble to find his hand.

I manage to push Phoebus' ring into his hand. Then I pass out.

This is someone else's problem, now.

IN A SUITABLE REVERSAL, Rian is sitting on the side of my bed when I wake. It is evening, now; an entire day passed without me, and at least from the king's presence, my primary purpose was not missed. He and presumably the rest of the palace's inhabitants are safe.

I find that, despite this obvious fact, I remain displeased with the situation.

"Why didn't you wake me? Is the palace secure?" I ask, my voice raspy.

"You were indisposed," Rian says, raising an eyebrow. "You overexerted your fluke, Soleil. I couldn't have woken you even if I wanted. Rest assured; order has been restored to the palace in your absence. It can be done."

"Don't dismiss Vilaneau," I croak. "He is not of noble birth and he—"

"I changed my mind in regards to Vilaneau," Rian reassures me. "Given the circumstances, and Septimus' reassurances that this so-called Anomaly of the Greys may only be used sparingly, and likely not again for some time. Years."

"That is a reassurance," I agree, and allow him to help me sit up. "Even so, I would like us to leave for the Summer Palace immediately."

"You are not well, Soleil," Rian says with disapproval.

"Yet, time is as always of the essence," I say.

I try to leave the bed and he forces me back down. I glare at him; this is not very dignified for either of us.

"Rian, whether through peculiar means or not, this palace has been compromised. If there are any more of Amerson's men hidden—"

"We have thoroughly expunged the palace, Soleil," Rian says. "Now, just like any mere mortal, after what you put yourself through, you need to recover."

"What about Valor? And Naomi?" I say.

"Fine," he reassures. "All fine. Septimus said that you, ah, went back using your fluke. To take care of the last of the threats in the palace?"

I nod, and close my eyes.

"You looked suddenly as if you had been struck by lightning, gasped, and staggered over to hand him a ring," he says. "Then he took some of my men and went to take care of this fellow, this…I can't remember his name—"

"Phoebus Kagen," I mutter.

"Precisely him!" Rian says. "Apparently, they took him by surprise. Without the ring, he didn't remember that you'd gone back a number of times at all. I would have preferred we take him prisoner, but Septimus wasn't having it, and I suppose—"

"Septimus gets what he wants," I say, cutting him off again.

Except that is not entirely true. In this case, I got what I wanted. Septimus and I had managed Phoebus Kagen's threat neatly, together, but I made us do it again so I could have Naomi for the rest of this timeline. Septimus had to manage things on his own, then. Even taking his opponent by surprise, that could not have been a pleasant experience. Especially since, if a mistake was made, I would not be available to have us go back again.

Truly, I did not make the most logical, reasonable decisions in that scenario. But it worked out in the end, as far as I can tell. So, I do not care.

"I would like you to sit outside for a few hours while I attend to the necessary businesses that remain," Rian decides. "After, we will pack and leave. But we can hardly travel with you so weakened anyways."

"I am in no way weak," I say.

"Soleil," Rian sighs. He has become exasperated with me. "You are a human. You age, you tire, particularly when you exert yourself. As anyone with a fluke, you must recover after overuse. Simple as that."

"Queens should be above such things," I say bitterly.

He rolls his eyes.

"I think I see, now, why Septimus may have found it wise to prevent you from using your fluke more than necessary," Rian sighs.

I glare at him. I cannot help but be disagreeable.

"So, you agree with his decision to keep something from me he never had the right to in the first place?"

"May I remind you, your majesty, that it was actually your idea, originally."

"Then perhaps it was a very bad idea made by a very foolish and desperate woman," I snap. "Now leave. I'm going to dress then sit out with my feet in the snow and my head basking in sun, if it pleases you."

"It would please me, very much," Rian says, brightly as he can.

As if the news alone is enough to change his mood entirely. He is putting the act on for me, but I am too bitter to appreciate it in my current state.

I do, admittedly, feel better after doing what Rian suggested. It makes sense, after failing to spend any time in nature in the first place then overusing my fluke. I try not to reflect much about the past day and a half, to avoid overthinking the entire scenario. I have decided to be certain in my temporary trust of Septimus and Teresa. It is possible I have made and remade this decision about six times already, but I am determined to keep my convictions this time.

I am going to trust them, on an official basis. If I cannot, at this point, then why even bother pretending as if the world can be fixed.

That settled, I find myself thinking on past timelines instead. Of the little things that I can suddenly remember. Not regarding the Greys, but Nusk, Taris, Lune. My parents. I do not recall my father's name, though I remember what he looked like. While Septimus has told me my mother's name, I do not think I'd have recalled it otherwise.

I must wonder what kind of people they were, particularly for my mother to make Lune my *Khashtani,* and to return west. What decisions of hers were made because it was a calculated choice, and which because she loved us? If she did love us?

I honestly cannot tell if I have been unfair to her or if she made every decision simply because she thought Samioth would benefit. A sacrifice for the greater good. Part of me wants to ask Teresa and Septimus about her, and my father, but I can't even decide which I'd approach, or what I would ask.

Perhaps I do not want to know the answers.

Despite myself, I fall asleep during this meditation. Valor comes to wake me sometime later, informing me that we plan to leave within the hour. Strangely, my feet are not purple from the snow, nor am I at all cold. I decide not to question the matter and leave it to the mysterious nature of the world.

I don't want to think about any potentially supernatural reason why I might have been spared from the cold.

Inside the Pyrian Palace, we pack with quiet haste. One could argue there is no time for it, but it is the dead of winter. We cannot afford to go out in this sort of turbulent weather without protection.

I help Teresa first. She is quick, efficient. Within perhaps five minutes, she has everything she and her sons own, including what I've given them, packed. Their previously deflated bags are stuffed to bursting, but their straps still close securely. She must have practiced many times, gathering all her sons' things while they traveled, making certain she did not leave anything behind, didn't leave a trail. Not that it helped, but she tried.

Naomi is there as well. She insists on helping Teresa strap her knife securely on her leg again, and to twist her hair up with the Kachin pin. From how casually she acts, I know Septimus opted not to inform anyone of precisely why I made us go back even after recovering the ring. I will not have Naomi's gratitude, then, but I can live without it. So can she.

I help Teresa into one of Asmer's fur-lined coats, and stuff her boys into similar wrappings before adding mittens, hats, scarves, and boots. Then it is off to my own chambers, before checking on Rian and Ayla. I do not bring much for myself; only what I must. I want to leave space for travel provisions and canteens.

I meet Rian and Ayla both in the hallway. There's not much to say, but I check over their winter ware, make sure Ayla's boots are sturdy enough for her, despite their fanciness, and check to make sure they have packed extra socks. Cold feet are one of the worst winter afflictions.

Most of Ayla and the king's things have already been shipped over to the Summer Palace, and anything I think might be of vital importance in terms of information is likely amongst Rian's Magicsmith research that went out a few days ago.

It does not take me long to replenish weaponry, finish the distribution of rations, and gather proper winter gear. From there, I rejoin the others in the front of the palace. There are guards everywhere, now, keeping close by and on watch for threats. The only conversations held with me are the necessary, mainly regarding activities over the next few days.

Once I am certain every detail has been seen to, we hurry out of the Pyrian Palace, flanked by bodyguards, determined to make a quick and quiet exit. Qhan stops only to give instructions to the king's coachmen, who he has told to drive about the city for two hours before doing as they please and consider themselves excused from their posts. They may seek other employment or make their way to the Summer Palace if they wish to continue working for the king.

They will act as a decoy for us while we move on foot, planning to meet up with Grand Princess Nissa, who will take us through the Isaarian countryside safely. From there, we will make our way to a different train station than our previously planned arrangements and finish the journey in relative luxury, at least compared to the traveling we will have ahead of us.

While this was not the original plan, we will need to adapt quickly. There is no telling what might happen, now, and I will not have us running from one catastrophe straight into another. To keep our traveling party small, Qhan and I divide the rest of Rian's guards up into several decoy groups. If all goes well, they will meet us eventually in the west. But I do not want to draw unwanted attention. Between us, Nissa, Korvaan, Valor, Qhan and I should be able to keep everyone safe. And as they have proven, the Smiths are not completely helpless.

Neither is Rian.

Eight

I CAN TELL THAT Rian much prefers to travel without the usual pageantry associated with a king. I find myself in agreement with him, there. We can move much quicker without so many attendants and guards, and we are much more discreet.

Even in the brisk cold, I feel revived whilst out in the fresh air.

Qhan has us travel as much as we can before stopping for the night. We encounter no complications. By his estimation, it should only take another day before we meet up with Nissa, and then a handful more to reach the new train station.

We choose a location mostly free of snow and clear the rest away. The dark is a reprieve from the glare of such vast whiteness, and I wonder how Septimus can stand it in the day. I know his eyes are already sensitive. Korvaan lights a fire, and Valor takes it upon himself to find dry wood for us to keep it burning. The rest of us set up camp. Qhan keeps watch.

Teresa's boys are fussier than usual, but that is to be expected. She does her best to help with the camp at first, but Septimus insists she sit, and Naomi is never one to pass up on the chance to mother someone. So, Teresa rests while the rest of us finish our work and settle in for the long night.

"I don't like it," I overhear Aiden whispering to his mother as I finally find a place to sit. "It's dark. Scary."

"Think of it as an adventure," Teresa offers.

"It's cold," Aiden says.

It is more of a dismayed comment than a complaint.

"Here. Snuggle close to me by the fire," his mother says, pulling him into her lap and wrapping him up tightly. "When I'm a little stronger, I'll make a coat for you that will keep you from ever being cold," she promises.

She gives me a quick glance as she says so, but I'm not concerned with whether the Smiths use their flukes or not anymore. If Teresa could use her fluke, she might have stood a better chance against Amerson. Besides, I won't begrudge her the chance to keep her children from falling ill.

Septimus throws himself down not far from me and begins to help Valor tend the fire.

"I feel as if we have done this before," I admit to Septimus as we eat. "Running from the Pyrian Palace into the forest, but I cannot tell for certain. We have done this before, haven't we? It was…It was last time?"

"You get used to it," Septimus says with a massive yawn. "Or you don't. Once you're around long enough, you start seeing patterns you fully believe are there, but aren't. Everything feels as if it is repeating, when it isn't, and before you know it, you're twisting things to fit that pattern."

"So, there is no pattern? Or it merely eludes you?" I challenge.

"How would I know? I'm a Memorysmith, not a god," he mutters.

"I recall you saying something different, once."

"Don't hold me accountable for what past iterations of me may or may not have said," Septimus says. "They're all idiots. Every one."

I cannot help but smile vaguely. Sometimes, with all the knowledge he returned to me, it is difficult to remember that the version of Septimus I met last cycle, while Rian was dying from poison, is technically about forty years younger than this one. He has grown, in that time. He is a completely different version of himself every time we meet.

"After they are settled in the Summer Palace, we go east," Septimus murmurs. "You and I."

"I know," I say. "You said already."

"I'm reiterating because it seems you need to get your affairs in order first," he claims. "Whatever you want done, however you want to indulge yourself, whatever you want to say: do it all before we leave. Because I do not know what's going to happen, east. We may have to re-set the timeline before you can return to Isaaria."

I have many questions for him, but glancing around at the rest of our party, I decide to save them for later. Ayla, for one, could not handle listening in to this discussion. Probably Teresa's sons should not, either.

They are currently sitting close to their mother, accepting warm tins of tea from Valor that Teresa insists they drink. Valor even helps cajole them into it, telling a little story to them of how unique and perhaps even magical Isaarian tea is. It is all fiction, of course, but he knows how to appeal to the children's fanciful interests.

I understand why Teresa feels most comfortable around Valor out of all the men. He is soft-spoken and gentle. Rian is a kind man, but he has a level of authority she has told herself not to trust. It will be some time before she can push past such a thing, despite all he has done to help her. Korvaan, then, is much louder and more dramatic; I have noticed her flinch at the sound of his voice on several occasions. Qhan can be terrifyingly intimidating.

Meanwhile, I can still remember Valor buying Naomi flowers when they courted. He is the sort of man who reads poetry for its own sake, and can find beauty in every sunrise. I decide to assign him to the Smiths while Septimus and I travel east. Rian will still have Korvaan, Qhan, and any number of other protectors. Naomi and Valor, I trust to look after my cousins well, especially considering the identity of the boys' father. Many would not be so charitable to the sons of a monster.

A few minutes pass in silence.

While Damen drinks his tea slowly, Aiden has his head pressed against his mother's stomach. For a moment, I assume he has fallen asleep with the warm tea in his belly, and positioned himself there by chance. But then I realize that it was purposeful, and probably not the first time he has done this.

"Baby's still well," he finally says, looking up at his mother. His seriousness is so childish it is endearing. "I can hear her."

Teresa strokes his hair.

"That's good, Aiden, thank you for checking," she says, and he smiles.

"I'll keep checking," he reassures his mother. "To make sure she is well the whole time. Until she comes out."

"I'm sure she'll appreciate having big brothers who take good care of her," Teresa says. "Try to sleep, now. We have a few long days ahead of us."

To my surprise, the boys do not question this, though Damen is still quiet and temperamental. I know this will have to be addressed eventually, but personally want no part in it. It is too complex an issue for me, as I think I have already proven to myself.

Aiden falls asleep the quickest, his arms wrapped around his mother, his head still pressed against her stomach. Damen is next, though he purposefully yanks himself away from his mother when she tries to pull him into their circle. He eventually drifts off and leans against her, but I'm sure his anger with her remains, beneath the surface.

I cannot tell if that anger is for being weak against Amerson, for taking him away from his father in the first place, or if it is merely misplaced frustration. I just hope it does not become a problem for us later.

Rian sits with Ayla for a long time, stroking her hair and speaking to her quietly until she manages to drift off. Naomi promises to stay close by, in case Ayla wakes with nightmares, and says she will call Rian over if this is the case. Valor is gracious about the situation, and does not complain about his wife's attention being elsewhere. Once Teresa and her boys have fallen asleep, he and Qhan set up a perimeter and speak with me about keeping watch through the night. Both Rian's bodyguards are insistent that Septimus should get some sleep, and that they will split the remaining responsibility between the two of them. I know better than to interfere and try to interject myself into the rotation beyond my first watch.

I am honestly too tired to do anyone much good, but my mind refuses to relax enough to allow me rest.

Naomi still has not said anything to me. Not about Phoebus Kagen, my cousins, or the timelines. I wonder if she will ever willingly speak to me again, or if we will only cross paths when necessary.

I remember how frustrated she has been in times past, about being a part of my *khashak,* when I was a *Khashtani,* about not being allowed to have her own life, and marry. She has had that chance, now. She and Korvaan have both had that chance. But this is no longer just about giving them the lives they deserve; the entire world is at stake. Their brother, as one example, deserves better. My sister does. My children.

Fate-dammit, poor Asmer does.

I have more people to think about than Naomi and Korvaan Qurvo.

As our companions take the opportunity to rest with me on watch, Rian leaves Ayla to seat himself next to me. He draws a cloak around both of us and we sit still for several long moments. I'm not certain where we stand with one another. There was much that required discussion before Amerson's invasion. Now, it seems as if the issues have been magnified tenfold.

I decide to start with something simple.

"I believe it may be appropriate for me to apologize for my shortness with you earlier," I say.

Rian waves it off. "Think nothing of it. These are stressful times."

"Still, it does not excuse my behavior. I'm sorry."

"Apology accepted."

An arm finds its way around my shoulders and I snort at him.

"What can I say? What you did in the grand hall, against Amerson? That was very impressive, Captain Marson," the king says.

"Thank you."

"What I mean by that is: I'd be doing a lot more than sitting casually next to you right now if I thought I could get away with it and keep my life. I thought the arm around the shoulders was a decent compromise"

"Oh, stop it," I chide, but I smile privately. "You are being rather forward for a man who has already had a wife to bed, this timeline."

I hear Rian make a little shocked noise in his throat. Even in the dark, I am sure he is turning red.

"What? She was your wife. I'm not bothered by it, Rian—"

"No, not that. It's…Ah, so…Asmer and I…never actually…Aha, that is…So. We did not. Do. Anything."

"What?"

He defends himself. "Neither of us wanted to! It felt so awkward on our wedding night, we both decided to put it off, but then…We never… did it. I suppose we got used to not doing it, and thought we had more time. Though now, I realize for me it was because I did not love her, and for poor Asmer, she remembered everything. So that would have been uncomfortable for her."

I cannot help it: I laugh. Loud and barking.

"Something amusing?" Septimus asks, sitting up and brushing away the siren call of sweet slumber.

Rian squeezes my shoulders in warning.

"Nothing," I say as Septimus rubs his eyes and inches closer to us, by the fire. "Rian somehow continually surprises me. I would have thought it impossible at this point."

"I've been in a similar place," he says. "Though, I think you're likely to learn not to make that assumption much faster than I did."

"Possibly," I say. "Now, so long as you are awake, I would like a sufficient explanation. No more secrets, Septimus. Tell me everything, and leave nothing out. Or this trip east will not happen at all."

He frowns at me and Rian both. "You will not like all of it."

I give him a look. "Have I done anything you disapprove of thus far?"

He must admit, particularly given how I handled things in the Pyrian Palace, I have not.

"Then prove to me you are different than the pompous versions of you I've met before," I challenge. "Believe that I am not the same head-strong woman you first met when changing sides. I will be reasonable, if you will be. I will do things your way, because you have all the information and a plan with which to use it. But let me know what I'm doing first, and why."

"You have become more diplomatic than I remember," he says.

"My point precisely," I agree. "Now, if you please."

I raise an eyebrow. Septimus turns to Rian.

"I apologize in advance for inadvertently making her this way," he says. "A warning: you are never going to win another argument against her again."

"Oh, I never could anyway," Rian claims, though I know for a fact that is not true. "Now, I suppose we should probably start somewhere simple, don't you think? Why don't you at least tell us what it is the Greys are attempting to *do*. That is probably simple enough."

"Oh, I wish…" Septimus mutters. "The Greys...Well. They believe they can kill the Dark. The evil essence from old stories and the Theebin religion alike. So, that is what they're trying their best to do."

I stare at him. Rian starts laughing.

Septimus remains grim and dead-eyed.

"Oh, you were serious," Rian realizes. "Well. Fate's Fingers."

"Exactly," Septimus sighs. "It is pure madness, but they think it possible.

So, obviously, they believe they are doing the right thing for all mankind; anyone who falls victim in the process, then, is necessary collateral damage."

"How exactly do they think they can kill it? The Dark does not have a physical form in our plane of existence," Rian points out.

"Precisely," my cousin says. "They believe they must prime the world and allow the Dark into our reality so that they can kill it. Usually, it can only seep in here and there: corrupting, manipulating, what have you. So, likewise, they could not kill it so long as the Dark is in the Otherworld."

"But that's the entire point of him being imprisoned in the depths of the Otherworld's darkest caverns in the first place!" Rian insists. "He can attempt to influence humanity, but he cannot force us to do anything or harm us. I doubt they'd be able to kill the Dark anyways; he'd be far too powerful in physical form in our realm! We are more protected if they left him alone."

"See, I know that," Septimus says, "and you know that. But the Greys? They oh-so-nobly want to liberate humanity from all its ills. They do not realize their goal is fully stepped in hubris: doomed to fail regardless of what they try."

"It doesn't appear noble at all, merely foolish," Rian mutters. He has nearly thrown our cloak off in exasperation. "They must realize that even what they refer to as 'collateral damage for the greater good' is not worth permitting for a mere chance at destroying the Dark! They are practically doing his work for him, even using *Dadj'zcha* as they do! Do they not understand that?!"

"Evidently not," I sigh, and turn back to Septimus. "So, the Dark thrives on pain and entropy; I'm supposing that's why the Greys are manipulating countries into toppling over into wars, famine, disease and chaos?"

Septimus nods. "Undoubtedly there have been bad times through history before, and there will be again. That, we cannot stop. But never as disastrous and desolate as now. Never as hopeless. The state of the world must be such, in order for the Dark to enter our world. Such depravity strengthens it."

Rian scoffs. "See? They're even puffing it up with power before attempting to fight it. Stupid."

"Hush," I say, understanding his frustration but wanting answers.

"They don't see it that way," Septimus says. "They believe that they are the ones leading the Dark on. Making promises to it and deals with it they don't intend to keep. The Greys believe that they can make themselves powerful enough to 'double-cross' the Dark once they free it. And destroy it."

"Could they?" I ask. "Is it possible to break a deal with the Dark?"

Septimus shrugs. "Honestly, Soleil, I do not know. At this point, I'm just glad you believe me. But from my point of view, even considering the hypothetical is pointless. It's a fool's gamble, wagering the fate of the world against the smallest of chances that persons as powerful as even the Families

Three could survive a fight with the Dark: an Otherworldly creature of unimaginable evils. It would be better to deal with the worst of mankind as it comes. At least then, our odds of survival and prosperity are far greater."

For a moment, I consider his opening line. I do believe him, I realize. Though the me of even months ago would insist I have no religious beliefs and only hold a mild respect for Rian's in most timelines, past versions of me have been much more devout. Given all I have seen and all that has happened, I now believe Septimus utterly. Not only that, but I know there is validity to what he says.

"But the Dark itself must know their intentions," I point out. "Why would it deign to forge a contract with them?"

Septimus winces.

"The only reason I can come up with is it knows for a fact we could not possibly defeat it, and wants as many fools as possible to forge contracts with it in exchange for power. At the end of the day, even if the Almighty's angels swooped down to take pity on us, the Dark takes the souls of the fallen."

"Cheery," I mutter. "Right, then: so, if we're doomed if they free the Dark, how do we stop them from doing that?"

"To understand that, you'll first need to understand how they plan to free it," Septimus says. "First off, the state of the world must be in chaos. So long as we can keep countries from falling into war and panic, then even if the 'Gateway' for the Dark was opened, it wouldn't be strong enough to leave."

"Gateway?" I repeat.

"For lack of a better term," Septimus says.

"So, we keep the world peaceful and all's well," Rian says, and then continues before Septimus and I can open our mouths to chide him. "I know, I know: we can try, but it is impossible to sustain world-wide peace. It's safer to keep this 'Gate' closed. Proceed."

"Thank you. Now, there are several different ways for them to free the Dark into our plane by opening this 'Gate'," Septimus says. "And, of course, several 'tasks' that each method requires so that the Greys can accomplish their goal."

"Sounds complex," Rian notes, somehow able to maintain a touch of humor about him at a time like this.

Septimus merely rolls his eyes. "It is witchcraft: of course, it's complex. *Dadj'zcha* has always required a number of ingredients and blood sacrifice of some kind to perform. This is just a mass scale version."

"Very well: what's method one?" I pose.

"Method One, if that's what we're calling it, is simple in theory, difficult in practice," Septimus says. "It requires the inter-marrying of the Families Three: Smiths, Greys, Wolffs. That way, the Darks' contract with the Greys infects all three families that were otherwise chosen by Faith, Hope, and the

Death to protect the world. The divine protection the angels were allowed to bestow on the world would be, essentially...gone."

Rian and I exchange a look.

"That does sound simple," Rian says. "Why haven't they gone that route?"

Septimus sighs. "Oh, they have tried. Hence Kryto and Teresa's unfortunate union. But the trick of it is that it cannot be a forced marriage and must be consummated with the possibility of a child coming about from it to continue the line: again, not by force."

"So…" I start.

There is Septimus' typical eye roll.

"Yes, yes: true love must swoop in and muddle the waters. Granted, the Greys had a serious advantage with my sister and Kryto. They raised the two together, and once Teresa was old enough, let Kryto be his charming adult self while she was still a poor, stupid, naïve girl. When she married him, she willingly gave herself away to him and to the Grey family, thinking she understood what she was doing when she really didn't.

"But those Wolffs. Ah, the Wolffs," he says, and smiles. "The Greys have a saying. 'Beware of Wolffs—they are feral creatures', they claim. And there's good reason for that."

Something dawns on Rian and he perks up, sitting straighter.

"Aldrich Wolff!" he exclaims, only for me to shush him quickly.

"Sorry," he whispers. "But Aldrich Wolff. He is the last of the family. Married into the line and killed his own sons rather than, I assume, let the Greys get their hooks into them."

Septimus nods. "So they say, at least. There is no confirmation of the Wolff boys' deaths, but they certainly appear to be gone. At that point, there was no wooing Anna Wolff, so: Method Two. Naturally, the Greys never fully give up on Method One, but they know there is not much of a chance. Which is why they've decided to kill the Seven Eyes of the Death instead."

Rian and I both wait expectantly. I look to him.

"What?"

"You had notes on that," I say. "You know something about them?"

Rian blinks. "I don't recall. It's been years since I touched any of my research. Though that does sound familiar."

"Then I suppose we'll see, now, how good you are with your religion and history," Septimus muses. "As I'm certain you know, from the stories: the Wolff family was chosen by the Death to help protect the crossings between the Otherworld and our world. To guard it. Once upon a time, they strengthened the barrier surrounding the Dark's prison by placing a wardship into seven mortals with powerful flukes, chosen by the Death himself. Every generation, he picks seven new ones. They are his chosen wards on Samioth. Their very existence protects the barrier from all witchcraft attempts to weaken it, save for the one previously mentioned ritual. Otherwise…"

"The only way to get the Dark out is to kill the Seven," I say.

"And collect their blood and bones," Septimus adds. "But yes. Precisely. This is, in some ways, an easier method for them. Killing is easier than getting a Wolff to fall in love with a Grey."

I consider this. "So, are you and I going east to find some of these Seven Eyes of Death?" I guess. "I suppose if we knew who all of them were, and where, we could always protect them. If the Greys can't get to them it would solve everything, wouldn't it?"

"That's assuming you could keep the Greys from them," Septimus says. "Which we know for a fact you can't."

"Why not?" I bristle.

"Because as of right now...Rian is the only one left."

I come to the realization of what this means before Rian does. Then he gives this absurd little laugh.

"I must say, Septimus: not an enthusiast of this new development," he says.

"It explains much of your remaining questions, though, does it not?" Septimus says. "Searching all over the world takes time. If the Greys cannot share information across timelines anymore, they will have to start from scratch. That is good. That buys us plenty of time."

"But?" I say, sensing there is a catch. Isn't there always?

"But I don't want to chance things by doing the work for them and finding the Seven Eyes."

"So, you haven't bothered? To find a way to save the lives of six other people who could keep the Dark at bay just as well as Rian?" I challenge.

I feel Rian glance at me and can practically read his thoughts. He knows he is not replaceable to me; I have more than proven that. But he swallows the dry joke waiting to write itself. He knows now is not the time.

"Look, no matter how many times we do this, Rian is always one of the last they reach," Septimus says. "We have Soleil to thank for that, in many ways. But that does mean that, every time he dies, we were forced to start again. Either that, or risk the Greys managing to free the Dark, and I could not do that. I decided to let those I'd call my allies focus on protecting only Rian, then, as you already were doing. Then, I could focus on a more reasonable way to stop the Greys."

"What's all this about our son, then?" I demand. "Why don't the Greys want him alive? He has nothing to do with any of this."

"As far as I know, your son has nothing to do with the methods required to open the Dark's prison," Septimus agrees. "But I think he could stop it from happening. Or reverse it. Close it again?"

"Well, which is it?" Rian asks, clearly anxious.

That doesn't stop Septimus from being annoyed.

"Well, I don't know," he snaps. "It's not as if I can write this all down; I have to memorize it. The Greys hardly left a book lying around labeled 'Our Dastardly Plan and All It's Foils' for some light reading I could entertain myself with."

I'm sure Rian and I both have a number of other criticisms and suggestions we could make. But we could spend all night telling Septimus lists and lists of things we think he has done a poor job of handling only to see he has a rebuttal ready. If he has a plan he believes will work, now, and we are still alive to see it through, he can't have made too big a mess of things.

But we have set him off, now, with our constant questioning and criticism. He is exasperated, and prepared to rant.

"Look, all I know for certain is that the Greys know that your son could stop them regardless of their successes, and since Rian is an Eye of Death anyway, it suits their purposes nicely to kill him and take him out of the picture before you two manage to procreate!"

"It's a strategy game we're playing against one another, then," I muse. "They have decided to optimize their best chances by subverting the Carsans' prophecy regarding our son, killing Rian along the way because they know they must do that eventually anyway. And as far as leaving me alive? Trying to take me?"

"Well, you are a Smith," Septimus says. "The Greys are possessive people. We've belonged to them for centuries. It must infuriate them that one of us slipped away and birthed a pair of spectacularly talented daughters they can't get their hands on no matter how hard they try."

It takes me a moment to realize he is talking about my mother.

"What about Lune?" I point out. "Why do they not want *her?"*

Why do they kill my sister?

"Probably because, to them, you are more useful. She is more dangerous. They could use your fluke to their great benefit, if they found a way to control you. But Lune?" He chuckles.

"I don't understand," I say.

"You could be a useful tool. I suppose they think if their fight against the Dark goes poorly, you could wind back time and let them try another way. But Lune could take your or Teresa's or *Kryto's* power, even, and throw it back in their faces. They would never risk that."

"Are the two of them that powerful?" I say.

Septimus grimaces. "Unfortunately. That is not even counting the Grey's

Dadj'zcha, or the Anomalies. Which I suppose you will be wanting an explanation for as well?"

The way he speaks, I know he's aware of how Rian and I are struggling to keep up with this new information. Septimus did warn me, after all, that this would be difficult to understand. I'm not certain how the Soleil of a few days ago would have responded, particularly if he told me everything at once.

I groan. I know Septimus said the Anomalies were what the Greys must have used to enter the Pyrian Palace, or they used one of them, anyway. One out of the ten he casually mentioned. But I do not feel like stretching my memory.

"We'll save it for later," he placates. "Suffice to say, that is how they've been corrupting the world, inciting wars and the like. But I suppose it's not the mission I want to task you with, so there's no point in trying to explain."

"Can't you give me a short version?" I say. "I don't need all the details, but I'd rather not be playing this game without vital information."

"Fair enough," he says. "There are ten Anomalies: magical items created by Smiths and Greys, using Smith's flukes and the Grey's witchcraft. They are corrupt magic, and can accomplish incredible feats. But also, can be used to corrupt the people they are given to by their owners. In this case, the Greys."

"Incredible feats such as bypassing our security to infiltrate the Pyrian Palace. Twice," I say.

"The orb," Septimus says. "Yes. It can bring any number of people any place in the world within seconds. But it needs at least a decade to charge."

"Which is a relief, though I'm curious as to why none of us found said orb on any of the intruders," Rian admits.

"It stays put. The people around it move," Septimus says. "Of the other nine, I believe the Greys maintain three of them for their own purposes. The rest they spread around the world. They are presented as gifts, to be sure, but they easily twist the mind in dark ways."

"Which explains some things," I mutter.

Rian frowns, less satisfied with the explanation thus far.

"But why do the Greys keep succeeding?" he asks. "Statistically, we ought to have gotten the better of them once or twice, even if they are using corrupt magic."

I am surprised but pleased to find Septimus, yet again, has the answer.

"Well, at least one problem I know of is this: we need Lune, Taris, and Mercer. We quite literally cannot succeed without them, and they keep getting themselves killed."

"Mercer?!" I repeat, unable to completely mask my snarl.

Rian is quiet, plucking at blades of frozen grass.

Mercer and Taris were his closest friends in the world and they've both been sacrificed for him, in different ways.

"Here's what I know," Septimus says. "People we need, without question, are obviously your husband at the very least, yourself, Soleil, your son would be a nice safeguard in case things go wrong, Lune, Taris, and Mercer. They all do something significant to foil the Greys or the Dark in one way or another, and they all keep getting killed in different timelines. I have confirmed this through numerous individuals with various precognitive abilities."

"So, we keep us all alive and protected, why would that be so hard?" I say.

"Because, for one thing, Lune and Taris are raised as *Khashtani,*" Septimus reminds me. "You try being the child to explain to all the adults why that's a bad idea. They would assume you were trying to protect your sister. It wouldn't make any sense to them. Even Nusk: I've tried using him multiple times, and for the most part, he listens. But he almost always will choose to protect you over making the correct decision. Even if it's only emotional protection. Regardless of whether I prove I have the knowledge of ten men, I suppose it is hard to trust that, coming from the mouth of a boy."

He does have a point, and I see that; we cannot all be safeguarded, all the time. Convincing Nusk alone would be difficult.

"But we cannot let them be *Khashtani,*" I argue. "It will kill them."

Septimus drums his fingers on a knee.

"Perhaps. Perhaps not. It is a curious equation," he continues. "As far as I can tell, Lune and Taris have died in nearly every single timeline since the first time you decided to go back and be a *Khashtani* yourself. The only times they have not died is after Rian has."

I can feel Rian looking at me. Inside my coat, I can feel my body so uncomfortable with heat, I have started to sweat. It feels like I've suddenly taken ill.

I shake my head, already refusing this. "No. No. I won't accept that it has to be Rian or them. You said it yourself; we need Rian, too. No. I—"

"Technically, we wouldn't," Rian says quietly. "Not if I live long enough for us to have our son. All Lune and Taris would have to do is stay alive until after I die."

I turn on him, about to snap, when Septimus interrupts.

"Would you two shut up? I wasn't even half finished. Stop jumping to conclusions: it's not one or the other, Soleil, because if you recall, there have been many times when Lune and Taris have died and *so has Rian.* And you," he adds, giving Rian an oddly parental look, "stop acting as if you're disposable; you're not. You're an Eye of Death. Even if you weren't, you've been absorbed into the Smith family, now. I'm not going to let you die."

Rian scrunches his nose. "Still not enjoying that title," he admits. "Besides, how can you know for certain? Is there a test?"

"Not a test, exactly. But your second fluke."

Rian sighs. "My second fluke is a weak aura sensing. It's rather useless; I don't use it much at all."

"Not so useless after all, actually," Septimus claims. "As an angel gave it to you. Clearly, they thought you would have need of it. The Seven Eyes of Death all have dual flukes. That is not to say everyone who has dual flukes is an Eye, but, if you are an Eye, you'll have two. At least two."

"At least?" I say skeptically. "I have never heard of someone having *three* flukes."

"Some of the stories I found about Aldrich Wolff said the Death loved him so much, it gifted him a third fluke," Rian says quietly. "But I didn't think it possible."

"Nor is he one of the Seven, I'll admit," Septimus says. "But I'd say the greatest trap we humans continually fall for is putting a cap on what is and is not possible in the world we live in. The Death thought you would have use of a second fluke, and so he gave you a specific one, tailored to your fate."

"My fate of apparently, occasionally making good decisions based on auras?"

Rian is skeptical, but I am admittedly more open minded now than I have been in all my life. Somehow, what Septimus says makes sense to me. It feels as if he is filling in the blanks while simultaneously creating more questions, and yet, it feels good. It feels right.

"It's more than that, really," he says. "You must cultivate and practice it, just as you do your elemental skills. Now, Rian, you don't remember this, but you've told me before and I'm sure you do remember the feeling: when Mercer, Lune and Taris die, it causes a physical reaction. You feel pain."

"You almost fell down a staircase," I say, recalling what he told me. "The night of your wedding to Asmer. And Mercer, you couldn't give the order to execute him even for treason. The Carsans had to do it by proxy!"

Rian sighs and I stare at him. I had always assumed the only reason Rian didn't order Mercer's execution was because they had been such close friends. I assumed he was experiencing emotional pain over the matter, but not physical.

All of a sudden, his illness makes sense to me. To remember feeling that over and over, for every time Mercer, Lune, and Taris died. He did a good job of hiding that pain whenever I was around, but still. Experiencing it all at once is undoubtedly enough to make anyone ill.

"Yes, I could have expected that," Septimus says. "What you do is not 'aura' sensing. You can feel intentions, and fate. You have conveniently never fallen victim to an intimate betrayal before Mercer and when you are allowed to be king long enough, always choose trustworthy allies even in foreign countries. Because you can feel their intentions and know they are good. I'm assuming you've attributed it to instinct, but this is not the case."

"As you said. With the exception of Mercer, apparently," Rian mutters, closing his eyes, remembering all the times he stalwartly defended his friend only to be proven wrong.

"Except not 'with the exception of Mercer'. Though yes, it's the same reason you adamantly were against suspecting Mercer of anything," Septimus continues. "You could feel how good he truly is. You couldn't sense the thing corrupting him because it's an Anomaly."

I guess, "An 'Anomaly' because it changes the way things ought to be."

Septimus considers this. "I suppose. The one Mercer had altered his mind, but it did not change who he is, or who Fate intended him to be. It only manipulated."

"The hairpiece!" Rian guesses, and then corrects himself before Septimus can. "Wait, no, no. Not the hairpiece, he gave it to me...Ah! His necklace! That stupid Alarkian necklace!"

Septimus stares. "As always, your powers of deduction are astounding."

I am too busy letting my mind whir away to grin at the good-natured slight.

"But if you knew Mercer would always betray us, why didn't you…?"

"Why didn't I just say so? Why didn't I let you and Lune and Taris know?" Septimus says. "We tried that. It never worked. I suppose because there are certain things that must happen. That always happen. Mercer always goes west, and we always need him alive. I couldn't have you all locking him up anyplace or executing him for something he hadn't yet done on the off chance I could prevent it! …Lune didn't want him to die, either. She said it would ruin you."

Rian decides not to answer that. Or, perhaps, he is too astounded by the realization Mercer is still his friend that he did not hear Septimus.

"So, I'm not an idiot," Rian says, relieved.

"No, you *are* an idiot, because you have a painful lack of self-worth and awareness and it makes me want to smack you," Septimus admits.

It's a shockingly violent idea for someone of his proven temperament.

"Which brings me to the other reason I think Lune, Taris and Mercer are doomed," Septimus says, reminding me of that point. "And it is because something supernatural is at play. I think the Dark is sabotaging us."

I huff and roll my eyes. Rian groans.

"Why even bother trying, then?" he says in exasperation. "You've just said some things always happen no matter what, including the betrayal of my best friend and potentially my *death*. Who are we to say that this was not meant to happen?!"

"Because I refuse to believe that it's the fate of the world to end now, by the Dark's hand, in fire and blood and suffering," Septimus says. "The angels love humankind, and according to the rest of the doctrine of the Theebins, so does their God. It can't be that the Dark determines the end of the world. Or for him to win over Samioth and torture humankind as much as it likes. I refuse to believe that."

"But Rian has a point. You can't ignore it because you don't like it. What if that is what is meant to happen?" I ask nervously. *The end of the world.*

"Then why would the Almighty give your son such a role?" he challenges. "Why give you your powers? Why give us no chance to fight back against something that is anathema to the Almighty himself? Why give humankind a chance to save itself if we are doomed anyways?"

I suppose he has given Rian's point some thought, then. It is easy to forget, but mentally, Rian and Septimus and I are several hundred years old. It feels distant, for me, but this must feel like one long, continuous life for Septimus.

"The Almighty has promised never to directly interfere with humankind's choices," he says. "His angels must abide by the same rules. But the Almighty still gifted *you,* Soleil, with the power to give us so many chances to save our world. He gave your son similar abilities. I cannot believe that would happen for no reason."

"You can't know for certain," I say. Someone must oppose it. "Even Theebins believe the world will end at some point. We could be dooming the world and ourselves to suffer over and over, even going against the wishes of Fate, simply because we don't want the world to end."

"The only way we could know for certain, I suppose, is to ask Fate," Rian says, making light of the idea.

Septimus is dead serious.

"That is precisely what Soleil and I are going to do. We are going east. We are finding the Wolffs' lantern to the Otherworld. We are going to the Otherworld, and we are asking Fate himself what to do."

Rian and I sit and consider this for a moment. Then he sighs heavily.

"I'm too exhausted to care about any of this anymore," he says. "If you want to go east: go east. But you're not taking my wife with."

"Afraid I must," Septimus says flippantly. "And she agreed she'd come."

I cut them off before they can argue. I can feel Rian's anger rising; irritation, at the least. He may be exhausted and confused, and he may know me to be highly capable of looking after myself, but he is still protective. He has only just gotten me back, after several decades of pinning in this timeline alone.

"The Wolffs are all dead; you said so yourself," I say.

"True," Septimus agrees. "But Anna Wolff was the one chosen to guard the materials a human could use to enter the Otherworld. Now, usually only the Wolffs would do so, but, before she died, Anna Wolff managed to send someone else there. Which means it is possible to go there and survive without Wolff blood in one's veins."

"And survive?!" Rian splutters, indignant.

I shush him.

"I'm not going around the world on a treasure hunt for something that *may* or may not be in the east," I warn him. "I did not know what this journey entailed when I originally agreed to go with you."

"This will not be a treasure hunt. I'm certain I know where to find the Wolffs' lantern. If it is there, it will be with a young man formerly of the Kachin army named Jin Riyong," Septimus says. "If we go to Kacha and meet with him, he can help us."

The name stirs a distant memory.

"Jin Riyong. He is named after Rian," I say. "Why do I know who that is?"

Septimus sighs and closes his eyes. "This is going to be a very long trip if you continually assume I know everything," he says.

"What irony," Rian mutters, still bristling.

He is displeased with learning Septimus' much heralded plan is less certain than he originally hoped.

"This will work," Septimus promises, sensing our unease. "We will find Jin Riyong, have him help us enter the Otherworld, I send Soleil in to have a chat with Fate and figure out what's going wrong and how to fix it."

"And we've...never succeeded in doing that before," I remind him.

Septimus gives me a look; two parts astounded, one part disgusted, a fourth part insulted.

"Soleil: we've never gotten this far before. I couldn't make you do anything with Rian dead, let alone bargain with a holy entity in a void of space and time over the fate of all of humanity. And it would be risky. In other timelines, when Rian dies, it either paves the way for the Greys, or leaves Anna Wolff as the last Eye of the Death. If we went to ask for her help, we'd be leading the Greys right to her. I couldn't risk that."

"But they already know where and how to find Rian," I point out.

"Yes, but he is a king with sufficiently more protection than the Wolff girl. And he has always had you," Septimus says. "Between you, Taris, and Lune: you are formidable. You generally expunge at least a few of the Greys."

"Like Amerson," I say. "Which seems a little pointless given how he keeps coming back."

"Yes, well, he's stubborn that way," Septimus mutters. "Look: don't worry about Amerson. The two of us will travel east as quickly as possible, put an end to all this, and reset the timeline the final loop before the Greys can kill Rian and perform any rituals. This is our best chance, trust me."

I frown at him. "I still don't understand why it has taken so long."

Septimus stares at me, then gives the most expressive, over-wrought eye-roll I have ever seen.

"What, you want me to explain everything that's gone wrong every single time? Because trust me, I can do that. Let us begin with the first half of the timelines you made: I worked for the Greys. Which means they had me to tell them what to do to become more successful each time. I gave Phoebus a charm, the ring. Which means even after I got it through my thick skull that I was on the wrong side, they knew something had been reset. They have always known I'm a Memory Smith. So: not a lot of progress to be had when you must spend time undoing your own mess.

"After that, I was on my own. I had to find a way to reach you all, determine why in the world you were re-setting timelines, and how to balance that with combating the Greys' scheming. It took me *decades* to determine there even *was* a way we might be able to talk to Fate. After that, I had to *find* Anna Wolff without the Greys spying on me or forcing me to tell them or following me, all the while knowing that whatever happened with you and Rian left me a ticking bomb of when you were going to re-set things. So, yes, it has taken me some time, Soleil, because I have been trying to find a way to stop the world from *eating itself*."

He sits back with an almost self-satisfied thump as he leans against his pack, and crosses his arms. He is practically panting from exertion. If I were to guess, I'd say he managed all that with a single breath.

"I'm done with all this," Rian says, shaking his head. He shifts and leaves the cloak around my shoulders. "I, for one, am tired of knowing the answers. I am going to sleep."

"I'm more than willing to give you even more answers," Septimus says.

"I would rather not," Rian grumbles, and settles down on one side, tapping my shoulder. "Don't wake me when you come to bed," he mumbles, as if it would make perfect sense for me to simply curl up next to him and not expect questions all around in the morning.

I don't know how to respond, but it doesn't matter. I'm sure he'll be asleep within minutes, and I have more time to sit in watch.

We allow the fire to crackle between us for a few moments. I'm sure Septimus is aware he has rankled Rian, and his unspoken apology hangs in the air. There is no point in him saying anything, now, of course, but surely, he feels guilt over it. There was no reason to bait him like that and Septimus knows it.

I let my eyes scan the woods around us, but they are as silent as they have been the entire night thus far. I truly believe we are safe from the Greys, for now, but cannot forget the way Teresa sounded when she confirmed her husband would come after her. They will come again. I don't want to imagine not being at Rian's side when they do.

Though I know I promised Septimus I would go with him, and I'm sure it is what I ought to do, the idea of being away from Rian terrifies me. I haven't been away from him for long ever before in my life. Never. There is a temptation to tell Septimus I will give him all the resources he wants but that he should do this all himself. One could argue this is all his fault, anyway.

"What if I were to tell you that I do not believe in any of this?" I challenge. "What would you say to that?"

"That you're a liar," Septimus says with a smirk.

"You can't know that," I accuse.

"I suppose not. But I do know how you think," he admits. "I know you don't want to leave Rian. I didn't want to leave Teresa and the boys, either."

"You had the luxury not to, though, I see," I point out.

"But you could argue I should have. Knowing what I do, how every little decision should change the outcomes of our world, I should have. I know the consequences. I tried different things, learned different things, manipulated different things, large and small…I'm the puppet master of this hell, yet, things always seem to manage to spiral out of my control. Worst of all, usually it is my own fault."

"So, you've given up," I accuse. I don't really mean it, but I can't help it.

Septimus glares at me. "Evidently. Not," he says through gritted teeth. "Your little fixes are like slapping a bandage over the crack in a dam and expecting it to hold the water back forever. I am trying to redirect the flow of water: so a dam will not be needed at all."

I raise an eyebrow. Seems Septimus is as easy to rankle as my husband.

"You needn't take it so personally."

"Why wouldn't I? If this succeeds, we reset, the world will go on and no one will remember I contributed anything. If it fails, either we live half-lives, re-setting them possibly for an eternity in hopes of stalling the end of the world or we experience the end of the world. Which does not appeal to me, for one."

I am admittedly suspicious of this statement; I did not take Septimus for one who would care about getting credit for good deeds. But the emotion behind his words is genuine. Something else bothers him about the possibility of a final timeline, even one with Fate's approval.

"If entertaining the two outcomes doesn't do you any good, I would stop thinking of it for now," I say.

"Suddenly full of wisdom, are we?" he says.

"Wisdom but not knowledge," I say. "Does that offer for more answers still stand? Rian won't take you up on it, but I will."

Septimus is amused. "So, you haven't learned enough for one night."

"You starve me of information for so long and then act surprised I'm ravenous when you give me an opportunity to eat?" I say.

Septimus cannot argue with me for that.

"Fine," he sighs. "Two more questions. Then I'm going to sleep."

I don't need even a moment to think of my two. If Septimus wants me to travel east with him, I will have plenty of time for interrogation. I want information that will do me the most immediate good and give me a more accurate picture of both my enemies and assets.

"Tell me about these 'generals' of the Greys," I say. "Anything will do. I want to know who else Kryto might send after his wife and sons."

Luckily, the topic is serious enough that Septimus simply supplies answers and does not tease.

"There are five total. Phoebus, who you met, and Amerson. Then three more: Alaster T'Chorot, Argo Nox, and Bastien Pike."

"Bastien!" I say, eyes widening, then almost immediately narrowing.

I knew I should have had him killed when the chance arose.

"The Greys didn't put him up to the debaucheries you're aware of," Septimus admits. "Nor is he under their influence. I believe he merely holds an interest for their work and was invited to join."

"Before or after," I say tightly. There is no need to clarify.

"I don't recall. When was Aloysius Pike II born, precisely?"

"Early spring. In 3011."

"...After. Then."

I nod, thinking of the Pikes: Bastien, Vásan. Their mother, whom I know is responsible for at least some of the assassins that have tried to kill Rian in timelines past. Vásan's wife, Yvette. And their heir. Aloysius Pike II. Whose clothes Damen and Aiden are currently still wearing.

"I don't want to hear any more about Bastien Pike," I say tightly.

"How about Alaster and Phoebus, then?"

I'm curious and relieved at his willingness in indulging me to inquire further.

"Why them?"

"Both were both meant to be a member of the Grey family," Septimus adds. "Phoebus was to marry Kryto's Aunt Margo, while Alaster was engaged, for a short period of time, to Kryto's other aunt. Anya."

"Mmm," I say thoughtfully. "What about their flukes?"

"You already saw Phoebus' abilities," Septimus starts.

"Can he come back from the dead, too?" I ask wryly, and he fixes me with a look.

"No. Lucky us, that's an Amerson specialty."

"Yes, lucky us...What are the odds of us avoiding the remaining generals, now?" I ask.

"Not terrible, actually," Septimus says. "If they sent Amerson and Phoebus out, and never heard back from them, they won't risk blinding sending out more. No, I think we're safe from that, at least."

"Who does that leave? Who they might still send?" I ask.

After all, Teresa said her husband would come after her. That means that, while Kryto won't act impulsively with his men, he won't give up, either.

"Maybe Nexa, his cousin," Septimus poses. "Maybe Jarrod. His other brother."

"Mmm."

It does not escape me, then, that Kryto Grey would rather risk the lives of family members than lose any more of his trusted generals. I force myself not to be relieved that Phoebus Kagen is dead. He is, for now, but if I reset time for a final run, he will still be a threat to face.

Septimus takes my thoughtful silence as an opportunity to quit the topic.

"I presume you've another question burning a hole in your tongue?" he asks, teasing over how quickly I jumped on the opportunity to ask the first. But once he knows what the question is, he sobers significantly.

"Who is Damen's Ghost?"

There are several moments I am acutely aware of when Septimus chooses to say nothing, and allows his face to remain blank. Finally, his shoulders lower an inch; the haunches of an animal daring to trust.

"Oh, who knows," he sighs. "If I had to guess? I'd say he's Kryto's cousin. The dead one," he adds, as if that clears everything up. "Anya's son. All I know is that there is a ghost who looks after my sister's sons, and it gets insurmountably angry if anyone tries to hurt them."

I frown. "Can't Damen simply ask the ghost who it is?"

"Ghosts have very limited methods of communication. This one cannot speak at all. Or 'talk' to us through writing or pictures or any other method. I don't know if it's aware of itself enough for that, or there are some 'rules' of the Otherworld that prevent it but…It's definitely cognizant. It was a person."

I nod to myself, thinking. So, Damen's Ghost is as real as the rest of this. It is not a part of his fluke that Teresa has lied about in fear, to protect her child. Aiden's innocent testimony, and now Septimus' admittance, has proven that. There is now a proper family tree for me to fill out on the Greys' side of Rian's chart. I was right; they did connect to the other Families Three. Merely not in a way I suspected.

Though I have more questions, about the Greys and the Wolffs and my own family, I keep my promise in allowing Septimus some rest. There are purple bruises under his eyes. Surely, he needs what sleep he can manage.

I allow him to turn in, and sit up with my own musings. There are plenty of them to choose from, after Septimus' account. I understand why he did not want to tell me everything all at once, in the palace wine cellar.

I kindle the fire, and tend to my thoughts in an equal manner. Instead of allowing things to tumble, overwhelming me, I consider each small piece in turn before turning it over and prodding the next. I am aware of my trust in Septimus and how it has morphed over the past days. I am aware he could have been lying to us about Rian's second fluke, but I do not believe so. Naturally, Rian's generally welcoming attitude towards my cousins implies Fate himself approves of our allying with them.

Further away, Ayla tosses and turns in her sleep. Naomi drowsily finds the princess with an arm and pulls her closer. I envy her acting mother hen to a flustered chick; I should be the one lying next to my daughter after such a distressing event. All I can do is promise myself that I will never allow this to happen to Ayla again. I am certain Rian has made a similar vow.

So, I shall tend to another flock of chicks I've a strange urge to protect. Teresa and her sons sleep close by, curled closely together, now, for warmth. I take the cloak Rian placed around my shoulders and tuck it around them. I take note that the cliché of intensified youth in sleep is particularly true in my mother's side of the family. I listen to the three of them breathe deeply in their sleep, hoping that Rian and I can truly over the sanctuary they fled here to seek. Not only in the immediate future, but perhaps in another future to come.

Nine

WE MEET NISSA relatively early the next morning. The half-Isaarian, half-Hoitsokin grand princess has traits from both sides of her heritage, though she has always looked far more Isaarian to me. She travels lightly, for a woman who refuses to live in the ancestral Sondushki home her father gifted her. I so not know where home is for Nissa, but I would say she carries anything of importance to her on her back or at her belt. Everything else is extraneous. That is her nature.

Fate must have laughed when he saw she was to be born a princess.

She dresses in furs with warm boots and looks pleased to be pink-cheeked in the winter air. Personally, I am miserable during these days of lesser sunlight, and I withheld a groan to wake in the bitterness of this morning. The way it aches my bones.

"You all look terrible," Nissa says, beholding us.

"Thank you, Nissa," Rian replies, without bothering to hide the exhaustion from his voice.

"I heard you had some excitement at the Pyrian Palace, but it looks as if all the usual suspects are accounted for," she says. "And a few extras?"

"My cousins, grand princess," I say. "Septimus, his sister Teresa, and her children. Damen and Aiden. From Alarkia."

Septimus bows. Teresa curtsies.

Nissa is intrigued. "I did not know you had cousins, Captain Marson."

"Apparently, no one did."

We walk on. Nissa and her hyena both fall into step with us. I can see Teresa is nervous, having the beast around her children, but I am not. It has bonded to the grand princess so deeply that it will only ever do what is in her best interest. Teresa's two children are hardly a threat to the grand princess.

Naturally, Damen is fascinated with the hyena and is practically a moment away from petting it. I'm not certain how Nissa managed to fortify the animal against such an unusual climate for it, but I do not care enough to expend energy asking.

The winter landscape is more taxing than romantic, and we trudge through the snow at an agonizingly slow pace. Teresa says nothing, but oozes waves of guilt each time one of her sons stumbles or complains. All the while, she refuses help from anyone other than Septimus.

I ask the obvious question when I can tell Nissa wishes she could move ahead with the king and his bodyguards, leaving my feeble cousins behind.

"Are we keeping the pace acceptably?"

Nissa glances up at me out of the corners of her eyes and then briefly flicks them back at the others trudging along. When she speaks it is quiet enough that only Qhan, the king, and I hear. We are the only ones close enough.

"If we move any slower, Vilaneau will send search parties out all over the country in a matter of days, convinced the king has been lost," she says.

"Is there any way to arrive faster?" Qhan says.

He knows as well as I that Nissa is barely exaggerating. Vilaneau always was mildly paranoid, even before the attack on the Pyrian Palace. This made him an excellent peer for Qhan and I, preparing to one day take over my duties as captain of the king's guard.

This said, it is still a good thing I am not yet readying for retirement.

"We could take a more direct route through the forest," Nissa admits. "But we'll risk being beset by the Fae."

Rian waives that concern.

"I have an agreement with their master," he claims. "We should be fine."

"'Should be' is not exactly comforting," Septimus mutters. "Clanaugh can be a right bastard."

He has snuck up on us, listening in. I note Qhan's irritation, but do not bother telling Septimus off. Part of me believes my cousin thrives on such attention. I am too tired to indulge him and, apparently, so is the king. Rian has no words of lecture prepared, either. He glances at Septimus out of the corners of his eyes.

"You've met him."

It is a statement, not a question.

Septimus sighs. That is a "yes", then.

"You would think they would be amenable to agreements that could save the world they inhabit," he says. "And yet."

"Clanaugh would never make a deal with you," Rian says. "What with you being…who you are. He'd rather keep you all for himself, I'd suspect."

I know he barely refrained from saying the word "Magicsmith" but Nissa is still not privy to that information. She does, however, understand that the

Fae tend to clamor over anyone with a powerful fluke. There is no reason for her to be suspicious.

"The only payment he would accept was my sister," Septimus says.

Everyone glances behind at Teresa and her sons.

"We'll take your new route," Rian decides, and Nissa nods.

"I'll scout ahead in the mornings, and report back if I see anything in regards to the Fae," she suggests.

Rian visibly cannot determine whether this is a good idea, but he finally gives her a single nod. We change courses slightly, but if anyone else in the party notices, they do not ask.

There is little conversation to be had, as we mainly focus on reserving our energy. I cannot help but keep my mind busy to stave off boredom; rerunning through the different loops in my head, trying to sort out true allies from those we can no longer trust. I'm happy knowing I have Korvaan and Naomi's loyalties, even if they are not always pleased with my choices. Qhan, as well, has been nothing but a friend and protector to the king.

However, even among the other royal families, there are threats. The Carsans have attempted to use the unprecedented situations Septimus' creative loops bring to their advantage. After all, in the times Rian has not become king, there is a clear opening for a substitution. We are nearly always at a disadvantage, threatened by both the Greys and enemies from within.

The only consolation is I now have my fluke to once more grant me the power I was always meant to have.

From what I can recall, there are several things I can do using my fluke's powers. The main ability, of course, is the creation of a new timeline, and seemingly the simultaneous destruction of an old one. This is the main abuse of my fluke, given how many times I have forced us to start over or even to go back a matter of minutes.

I believe this will be the most useful ability of mine when it comes to traveling east with Septimus. Surely, he knows this as well; that is why he wants me to accompany him.

Second, I can move only my own body forwards or backwards in time, down to a miniscule level. Mainly backwards, from what my memories tell me. Forwards is more difficult, and dangerous. Regardless, this would explain my seemingly impervious relationship with poisons. I have perfected the art of protecting my own body by retroactively using my fluke. It is an extreme exertion of my energy, yes, but better than unconsciousness or death. This so-called resilience of mine has undoubtedly saved my life on many occasions.

I believe I have used this ability, as well, to save myself when falling from great heights, or suddenly recovering from injuries. I always have been able to heal well with the simple application of sleep and outdoor exercise; now I know why.

I can understand why Septimus has been so wary of me. I am untapped potential. In a way, I control all our lives, and I have not always wielded this power wisely. All I can do, now, is make better choices in the future. Even if I create a new timeline, to change things, my current choices determine what type of person I want to be. The kind of woman that is going to raise my children.

I refuse to become anything like the Greys. My hubris will no longer be my downfall. With the future I want ahead of my family, it cannot be.

Though I try to keep my wits about me, aware of our surroundings, it's difficult not to enter self-reflection with such silence and monotony. Ayla is the one who breaks me from it, nearly on accident. By chance, we have found ourselves walking nearby. Though I am the tallest woman in our party, Ayla always has moved with a quick stride, and she has more energy in her youth.

Considering Naomi's comforting of her last night, I am tempted to coax Ayla into discussion, but the timing feels wrong. If she is willing to walk alongside me in silence, I won't press her.

Regardless of what is happening in Ayla's head, she has not been so damaged from her experience that she cannot recognize when we step into Fae territory. We all notice it, and even the drowsiness of the children fades as their heads pop up and their spines straighten.

It is the smell in the air of fresh grass and sweet summer fruits; the bland monotony of our winter landscape has given way to a pungent crispness that seeps all around us. There are no more birds chirping, and no more scrambling in the underbrush.

"Ayla, stay close to me," I warn.

She nods, her eyes wide and scared, and presses in by my side. I'm glad she does not grab onto my arm, and restrict my movements, but I can tell she'd like to.

Damen reaches to tug on his uncle's coat, and as Septimus turns, he visibly flinches to see the boy there. He manages to recover himself, but not after taking in a sharp breath. I saw it; Damen must have seen it, too. But he says nothing about it and only asks Septimus why it smells like summer.

Nissa does as she suggested and continually scouts ahead of us, looking for signs of meddlesome Fae, but none dare show their face. When night falls, and we are approximately a third finished with our journey, Qhan decides it is time to set camp again. We remain in what the Fae call their land for now, but it technically belongs to the king of Isaaria, and they must bend before his right. Rian is confident even Clanaugh would not dare advance against us.

I am not so certain.

With my nerves as such, I volunteer to take the first watch once more. Nissa will sit up with me, noting this task is one best done in pairs. After a fire is built, the rest of our party settles down to sleep. Nissa perches herself on a tree stump, feeding her hyena bits of dried meat. At least tonight, we are free from the snow; somehow, there is a portion of this wood with only dead grass and a sprinkling of frost. Teresa's sons are most notably pleased about this. Even Damen is in better spirits today, though perhaps he is too exhausted to be bitter.

They are quick to eat their rations and settle down to sleep. Septimus fusses over Teresa as if she is his patient, trying to swaddle her in blankets that she is awkward in receiving.

"Too cold?" Septimus asks his sister sympathetically, clearly prepared to search for more. I recall him mentioning her not doing well in winter, before.

"No," Teresa says, as if equally as shocked by her answer. "Too warm."

Septimus reveals nothing but likely he is as surprised as I am. He helps relieve his sister of her coat and pulls the blankets off her shoulders.

"Keep these, and use them if necessary. Tell me if you need anything," he insists, and she nods.

This move seems more to placate Septimus more than it is a true promise to speak her mind; Teresa rarely says whether she wants anything.

Everyone settles down for the night, and I take a silent first watch with Nissa. After three hours, I wake Qhan for his turn and settle in to sleep. Unfortunately, I only manage a few hours before a particularly loud crackle from the fire wakes me again.

I am startled to see that I am not the only one struggling to sleep. Naomi is propped up, drowsy and with eyes closed, but playing with Valor's hair so it is clear her mind is too busy for rest. Teresa is sitting awake, huddled by the fire, her arms wrapped around her knees. Across from her, Nissa perches on a log, her hyena at her feet, gnawing on a bone while the grand princess herself sharpens a hunting knife. Every now and again, she will glance at Teresa with curious, narrowed eyes, but does not ask anything. I know she is not happy with Rian's terse explanation to her, but I'm not about to break his confidence for her sake.

If Rian thinks it best to keep certain things about the Smiths a secret, at least for now, I shall follow his lead. All Nissa needs know is that Teresa is fleeing an abusive, powerful husband, and that she and Septimus are my cousins. She does not need to know that we are Magicsmiths. Not yet, at least.

Nissa notices I've woken.

"Qhan went to secure a perimeter for us before his watch ends," she says.

I nod and stand with a fur cloak wrapped around me to replant myself closer to the fire, and to my cousin.

"Trouble sleeping?" I ask, crossing my legs to sit next to her.

Teresa nods but does not look at me.

"I suspect everyone will be having that difficulty during this trip," I sigh, and pick up a stick to give our fire a good poke. "Something bothering you?"

"Only nightmares," Teresa admits quietly, as if she has grown quite used to such a thing after years and years of them.

"Anything in particular? Perhaps it would help to reason through it," I say.

I offer this not only because I am curious what things Kryto Grey's wife dreams about, but also because, in my experience, talking does make it easier.

"Amerson," she says, and cannot even say his name without shuddering. "I'm terrified of him. I have **always** been terrified of him."

I feel Nissa frown, watching us, but she does not comment.

"I can understand that," I say, which I think surprises Teresa. "But you were still brave, to face him like you did. Not everyone could do that."

"I couldn't **protect them,**" she says, her voice cracking. "I'm **useless** against men like him. I couldn't protect my own children from their uncle..."

"Did he hurt them?" I challenge her. "Did he hurt them in any lasting way, or did you stop him from that?"

I expect her to answer me, but she does not, or cannot. She shakes her head, uncertain. She is lost in her own thoughts and I must pull her out of them if I ever want my point made.

"Teresa, he is gone, now," I promise her.

"I thought that once before," she whispers. "I thought Septimus killed him, that night we fled the manor, but then he came back."

"Teresa, I promise you, you are safe now."

I stabbed the bastard in the throat. I don't care what Septimus says; no one comes back from that.

She shudders and again says nothing.

There are bruises on her face and arms from where Amerson grabbed and hit her. They make me feel a sting of guilt; I feel as if it is partially my fault that this happened to her. I feel as if, if I were younger and stronger, and more willing to trust, I could have protected her and the children better.

"You should ice your bruises," I tell her. "The snow would help."

"Oh. Don't worry about them. I am accustomed to it," she promises. As if her main concern is that I don't inconvenience myself worrying after her.

"Put some snow on them anyway," I repeat. "It will be cold, yes, but it should keep the swelling down. I can help you, if you like."

"No, thank you," she says, but makes no move to do it on her own.

I will ask Naomi if there is something she can do to help in the morning. Otherwise, I'm not sure Teresa will bother looking after herself at all.

"What happened," Nissa says, so blunt it does not sound like a question.

Teresa makes a small sound, as if she is about to explain, but cannot muster the energy to manage it.

"The events that changed our travel plans were…distressing," I say.

Nissa raises an eyebrow. Teresa's shoulders inch higher.

"I am thankful the boys are not having nightmares," she whispers. "They are all right, for now. I think."

"Children have a certain mental resiliency," I agree. "They were frightened, but so long as we keep them safe and comforted, they should recover easily."

Nissa is still frowning at Teresa. She takes in my cousin's general posturing, the haunted look in her eyes; the gauntness that merely a few minutes with Amerson has returned to her face.

"It was not simply one night," Nissa decides.

Teresa and I both look up to her; the grand princess is nodding to herself.

"You are strong enough to have endured that. But these bruises are the least of your injuries. There is more, there. I can tell."

Teresa bites her lower lip. There is no coy intent in the motion; she is biting until she draws blood. Nissa has given her an opportunity to share her story, but while some may find such a thing cathartic, I think it is clear memories are as painful for my cousin as they are for Rian.

"Teresa?" I say, and put a hand on her shoulder.

She shakes her head. "The sorts of things that happened in Lusch, I...I don't think I could ever tell anyone. I'm so ashamed," she whispers.

I think Nissa is disappointed, her curiosity driving her to look for answers. Strangely, I do not react similarly. While even days ago I was happy to push for answers no matter the cost, I feel a strange empathy for my cousin. Perhaps, it is because my own reaction to pain is to fight harder for what I want. I imagine it would take a lot to break someone the way my cousin has been broken, so that she struggles to find a reason to fight.

I have no doubt that if her sons were not in danger, and she did not have an unborn child to protect, she would not have tried to stand up to Amerson at all.

"I'm sorry," Teresa cries, and buries her head against her knees. "I'm sorry; it is all my fault!"

I find myself wrapping an arm around her shoulders, hushing her. She sits stiffly and does not allow me to pull her closer.

"If I w-w-were stronger…the monsters. The things terrorizing people. I made them. It is my fault," she cries.

Her words are garbled and quiet enough under her crying that I do not think Nissa will put the facts together on her own.

I feel a hand on my shoulder. Naomi has come to lend what assistance she can. Given her general annoyance towards me lately, I expect Naomi to say something accusatory, insinuating Teresa's tears are somehow my fault. Instead, she generously keeps from making such assumptions.

"I can make a little tonic for her," Naomi whispers to me. "So that she might be able to sleep. I made some for Ayla, and it seems to work well."

"That might be a good idea," I acknowledge. I do not bother whispering. I think, mentally, Teresa is not home. "It wouldn't bother her baby, would it?"

She shakes her head. "Besides, it is not that strong. Not that it has to be."

I nod. "Fix it, then. Thank you, N'omi."

There is a moment where Naomi looks shocked to hear that nickname, and I cannot accurately recall if I have used it in this timeline. She must decide, as I have, that it does not matter, because she retreats to find her bag and begin mixing.

I feel a nudge at my left hand and flinch, startled, only to find Mango there. He licks at my fingers and tilts his head to one side, inquisitorially. I blink at him. I cannot remember who thought to take him along with us—either Rian or Ayla, I'm sure—but I had completely forgotten he was here. I suppose he has spent his time curled up with fur cloaks and blankets in someone's satchel; sunblood dragons aren't fond of the cold, after all. Now, he has sensed Teresa's distress and is here to lend his assistance.

Sunblood dragons are often like this. They do not like upset in general.

I pluck him up as I would a cat and place him in Teresa's lap, under her arms. She sniffles and raises her head, startled, but then lets Mango nuzzle into her and gives another few, obligatory sobs.

I pat one of her shoulders slowly, gently. This time, her posturing is more relaxed, and she allows me to touch her without stiffening up. A moment later, Naomi returns to sit close to Teresa, practically holding her like a child to help her drink. Teresa does not even bother asking what is in the flask. She drinks, and sniffles, and continues to hold Mango. Naomi shushes her and strokes her hair.

A soft growl from Nissa's hyena reminds me that the grand princess has been watching all this, inquisitive yet trapped at a distance.

For a moment, I expect her to say something cruel. I know she is a hard, independent woman who likes to rely on only herself and enjoys the fact that she is just as capable of doling violence as someone twice her size.

Instead, she gives a nod towards Teresa and says, "We women are able to endure much. I think she has endured too much."

She sees Naomi and I are both surprised to hear this from her. Teresa does not know the grand princess well enough to know this comment is not like her.

"N-N-No," Teresa says, her voice shaking. "I'm only w-w-weak."

Nissa merely speaks to Teresa instead of addressing either of us.

"When I was a young girl, I watched my mother die," she confesses. "My mother was Hoitsokin. My father, an Isaarian grand prince. The only reason I became his heir is because I happened to be born early, two months before one half-brother, and a good seven years before my second half-brother on my father's side. Would you say this is not enough to qualify as 'much'?"

Teresa frowns. "N-No. I'm s-s-sorry—"

Nissa interrupts her.

"Then, if you have been through worse, it is too much."

Teresa still shakes her head. "They treated me like a princess. Mostly."

"I am a princess, by chance alone," Nissa argues. "That changes nothing about the other half of my life. I do not look fully Native Isaarian to you, do I? No. My full first name is Nissakagh. Which for the Hoitsokin means 'red haired'," she says. "Everyone in the south knew I was the daughter of an Isaarian prince. But that did not matter to them until a messenger arrived to tell my mother I was the next crown princesses for the Sondushki family. Born just before my half-brother."

"Is such a thing truly so arbitrary, here?" Teresa asks.

"No," Nissa admits. "I think it was more a matter of preference. My father was the sort of man who wanted his sons all to himself, not to be burdened with the necessities of being a crown prince of Isaaria. So, he seized the opportunity to make me his heir instead."

Teresa looks distraught by this idea, as if it is somehow personal to her.

"Your brothers do not…resent you for this at all? At least the one? For taking something that so easily could have been his inheritance? Something he might have thought…belonged to him?"

Nissa shrugs. "My brothers and I have always gotten along well together, I think. So, they do not appear to resent me for our father's choices."

"What a rare luxury," I think I hear Teresa murmur.

I cannot tell if she's referring to herself and Septimus, her husband and his brothers, or someone else entirely.

"It was difficult to grow up in the south with my mother's people with such an inheritance awaiting me, regardless," Nissa says. "Some of them resented my mother and me for it, and they continued to, until I proved myself. We were out hunting, you see—it is always tradition for a man to take his son on his first hunt and for a woman to take her daughter. To teach them. We were all alone, out in the southern wilds, and for the first few days, it was peaceful. Beautiful.

"They say that a bear will not attack unless it is protecting its young and otherwise it will leave folk alone," she says, stopping the story directly to muse. "That is not entirely true. We frightened it, tracking a doe into its territory. My mother and I were both too excited to realize it was there. It was too busy eating to notice us, either, until we were upon it. Our presence alone was enough to make it feel threatened.

"We ran, and it chased us. My mother made me climb a tree but did not follow. The bear could have climbed after us, after all. But she correctly figured if she let it catch her, it would forget about me. So, I had to stay completely still and silent in that tree while I watched that bear maul my mother to death."

Naomi makes a sound deep in her chest, horrified. I know she does not remember her own mother; Nusk's second wife died not long after Naomi was born. But she must have imagined her mother's death before, wishing she could have at least been there at her mother's bedside. Maybe she is thinking better of that, now, knowing what Nissa endured.

"That's horrible," Teresa says. "What did you do?"

She is drowsy, now, from Naomi's tonic, and is stroking Mango as she leans against Naomi.

Nissa gives a toothy grin. "I grew. I made myself an expert hunter. Then I hunted that old bear down and killed it. It was quite the accomplishment, in my people's eyes. So, I gained their respect, and I earned my revenge."

"I think that's an accomplishment for anyone," Naomi says, horrified at the idea of the petite Isaarian princess pitting herself against a full-grown bear.

Nissa shrugs. "No one had ever told me it could not be done. All I knew was: that bear killed my mother, and bears are dangerous. But wolves are dangerous. Unicorns and gildhorns are dangerous. I saw no reason why I could not hunt the bear. So, I did. And I made jewelry from its bones."

I swear, the fire flashes in her eyes as she says so. I have always been mildly wary of Nissa, deserved or not. I think it is that bloodthirstiness in her I sense. However, perhaps there is that same trait in me. Perhaps that is why so many are frightened of me, and why Teresa finds it easier to trust Naomi and Valor than me.

Oddly, it's Teresa herself who murmurs drowsily, "That's beautiful."

Nissa appears to approve.

"It's fitting," she agrees. "I used the tenets of my mother's people and still got what I wanted. I believe my little Isaarian half-brother kept the pelt, and gave it to my nephew when he was born. But even using every portion, making every tool I could, using every bit of meat: I can never get back what that bear took from me. I can't change the fact my mother sacrificed herself to a painful death for the sake of her only daughter.

"So, while I do not have the compassion of a mother, and I cannot understand that strength, I know of it. I saw it," Nissa says. "You have that strength, too. Even from what little I know of you, I'm sure of it."

Teresa has already fallen asleep, and does not hear that last affirmation. Naomi's tonic has worked, and while Nissa's story is not the typical sort one would tell to put someone to bed, it has served its purpose.

Naomi shifts, and I help her lever Teresa down to sleep. Qhan returns to the outskirts of our camp and exchanges a look with me, but says nothing about our midnight women's council. He only wakes Korvaan for his shift, then settles back into place for some sleep.

"I didn't know that about you. About the bear. Your mother," I admit to Nissa. "Why haven't you ever let that story spread across the Isaarian elite?"

"Because of exactly how you reacted to it," Nissa says. "You respect me more, now, do you not?"

She does not need an answer. She could hear it in my voice.

She nods to herself. "I never want someone to respect me more for killing an animal that was simply doing what animals do. It hurt me. I killed it. It was a personal vendetta, not something I did for the grand princes to respect me. They should know to do that regardless of the bear."

"It was kind of you to say those things to Teresa, and to share that story with her, then," Naomi admits.

"I meant every word of compliment. I have great respect for women like her," Nissa says, startling me yet again. "I am not suited for parenthood. But she has devoted her life to it. I have seen it in her, over the past day alone, and can infer even more from what she has said. It is impressive."

Naomi nods, agreeing, and sighs. She adjusts herself so that she, too, can lay more comfortably. She has elected to stay here instead of returning to Valor, I note. Apparently, she has decided Teresa might need her more. I do not know if this makes me feel jealousy or not, but I decide to also settle in where I am for the remainder of the night.

Nissa notices us making ourselves comfortable.

"One more thing, Captain," she says.

I sigh. "If it is too personal, I may elect not to answer," I warn her, but Nissa pretends not to have heard me.

"Who is Amerson?" she asks curtly.

I am startled she would remember well enough to ask, and consider the implications that such a question has been sitting in the back of her mind. She correctly assessed that Teresa would not be able to answer properly, and that a change in subject would be good for her. That did not staunch her curiosity.

"He was her brother-in-law," I say carefully.

"Was?" Nissa repeats.

"I killed him."

The fire glints off her eyes. "Good."

She throws a bone to her hyena, slides off her perch, and pulls her coat around herself. It occurs to me that if had my answer been otherwise, the moment we reached the Summer Palace, Nissa may have excused herself to go on a hunt, for the sake of my own cousin.

I'm not sure what it is about Teresa, but she has acquired a pack of loyal allies who would happily kill for her, to protect her and her sons.

The strangest part, perhaps, is that I do not think she's aware of it.

I MANAGE TO SLEEP the rest of the night, close to my cousin and Mango, Naomi, Nissa, and her hyena. There are several strange looks cast our way when morning breathes life into our camp. Teresa's sons are quick to find her to share breakfast, but no one asks, not even Septimus. I think Ayla is too caught in her own head to even notice, and otherwise the menfolk understand there is some things best left to us women to manage.

Mango allows the boys to share their food with him, happily snapping up whatever scraps they offer. When it is time to move on, Rian whistles and makes the dragon clamber up onto his shoulders. No doubt Damen and Aiden would attempt to do the same and slow us down with the effort, if only to be close to the sunblood dragon.

With the camp packed up, we are soon on our way. The monotony of travel is beginning to take its toll on our Alarkian companions, and I can see in Teresa's face that she is not looking forward to another day of carrying extra weight in front of her. Valor must have noticed her exhaustion as well, because he insists on carrying her bag for her and reassures her that our travels by foot are nearly over.

Our party trudges for about an hour assuming today will be much the same as our previous day in Fae territory. It is not so.

We all sense the shift. If we thought the silent forest was eerie before, the feeling of a strange company amongst us is now oppressive. We cannot see or hear them, but each of us are certain the Fae are there, watching us.

Nissa moves ahead with her hyena, looking for traps and clearing the path. No one speaks a word of her intentions, as if we are all secretly afraid that even mentioning distrust of the Fae will invite their mischief.

"We should not have come through here," Septimus mutters unhappily after some time of enduring this pervasiveness.

I think, for a moment, that Rian is about to argue with him, seeing this comment as an attack on his good sense. Instead, he only nods and notes we will be leaving this portion of the forest soon. While I cannot imagine anything going wrong, I wonder if this is because I have assumed the Fae will act with human decency, using human logic. One would think Clanaugh would find it in his best interests not to hinder us, as I am certain he has great knowledge of what ails the world and how it is meant to be fixed.

Yet, they are inherently greedy creatures, as well. Clanaugh has likely desired a Magicsmith in his clutches for years. Why should we assume common sense would stop him from wanting one, now?

We come to a portion of forestry that is thicker than the rest, where there resides no alternative path for safe traversal. Septimus drops back to help

Teresa, escorting her. At least there is less snow to trudge through, so the boys can keep a quicker pace.

I decide to stay near Ayla; while her fluke is generic enough the Fae likely will not take an interest in her, I know they unnerve her. She is not the child she once was, intrigued by her father's stories, unaware of the danger. Rian, too, walks closely by. At first, I assume it is to protect his daughter, same as I might. But Rian has often acknowledged my capabilities as a bodyguard and would not change his mind now.

So then, I realize, he is walking to be near to me.

I suppose I am a Magicsmith, after all. Clanaugh may have sworn to leave all Isaarian citizens be, under the old accords he had with past kings. Rian is not taking a chance with me.

I wonder if I should find this insulting or sweet.

Mango crawls off Rian's shoulders and onto mine, setting my braid swinging like a pendulum.

I decide on the latter.

We can only have walked a quarter hour at most when Naomi suddenly makes a startled noise behind me. It is enough to make me whirl, hand already reaching for a knife. I have brought my bow along with, but Korvaan has been carrying the bow and arrows for me. A knife is the best I have available, and yet, it is still useless considering what we are up against.

Septimus, Teresa, and the children are gone.

I hear Ayla take in a sharp breath beside me. I call for Qhan to stop, ahead of us, and Rian immediately rushes back to where the footprints for our four companions stopped.

"What happened?" he snaps at Naomi. "Did you let them fall behind?"

"Korvaan has been in the back the entire time," Naomi insists, defensive. "He is still here. The Smiths are not. Up until this very moment, I swear, they were walking directly in front of Valor and me."

I join Rian, feeling Qhan hovering behind us.

"Sir?" Qhan says. "Your majesty. Should we wait for Grand Princess Nissa to return before doing anything?"

Rian waves him off, too overwhelmed to answer reasonably, though it is a fair enough question. I know him too well, and I know how much he despises the Fae; he is not going to wait for anyone before acting. He knows too well what Clanaugh will be trying to do in the interim.

"Everyone, gather," he commands, in the stately tone he generally avoids using for the sake of humility. However, when Rian wants to be king of Isaaria instead of a friend, father, or lover, he fills the role spectacularly. "I am going to invoke the right of the Isaarian heir."

"You are taking us directly to the Fae? After they stole Soleil's cousins?" Naomi says, critical only because such a decision makes no sense to her.

"The longer we wait, the more likely it is they will not—or claim they *cannot*–give the Smiths back," Rian warns.

"What if one of us is next?" Naomi demands, crossing her arms.

"They won't come after us," he snaps. "Clanaugh has decided his agreement does not cover members of Soleil's family who are not Isaarian, only mine."

"Korvaan. My bow," I say, and hold a hand out to him.

If I'm going to be surrounded by Fae, I want a long-range weapon on hand. Guns would hurt them more; the metal would kill even if a flesh wound was intended. Yet, I have better aim with my bow, and I do not want to kill, only threaten. The Isaarian heir's truce with the Fae has always been tenuous; I cannot be the one to break it entirely by killing a Fae.

"What will happen to them?" Korvaan asks as he hands me the weapon.

"Because they are Magicsmiths?" I say, and pull an arrow from my quiver. "Clanaugh will convince them to give him their names, then sequester them away in his little hidden kingdom and feed on their magic for as long as he can until they die of natural causes or from neglect. I doubt the latter, though. Fae might tire of regular humans and seek variance, but not Smiths."

From Rian's lack of correction, this is an accurate assessment. I am not the expert, but it does not take one to know the Fae are greedy for magic. I remember that well enough; it is part of how they survive.

Despite cynics like Naomi, our party gathers close together. Ayla wants to curl under Rian's arm like a chick beneath mother hen's wing, but Naomi draws her away towards herself and Valor. They will look after the princess, knowing Rian will not have her best interests in the forefront while negotiating with Fae.

"Clanaugh!" Rian calls.

Unlike times past, that is all it takes. What we could not see or hear, but what was always there, is revealed. Clanaugh cannot refuse Rian's request for such.

I see Septimus first, then Teresa. The two of them are clearly both drunk on Fae kisses, with their eyes glossy and their limbs limp—they are all but incapacitated. Their inhibitions have been lowered severely, so the Fae can try and wring their wills from them.

Septimus sits with his back against a tree, his legs sticking out in front of him, his body slack. There is a Fae woman kneeling next to him, grinning with pointed teeth as she kisses all over his face. He is silent, but his mouth keeps wavering, trying to form a word: his name. Teresa is sprawled on the ground, on her back, her eyes drawing closed sleepily. There is a Fae sitting with her head in its lap, gently stroking her hair. He leans over to kiss her forehead.

"Give me your name, pretty little Magicsmith," he tells her in Alarkian.

There is no sign of Damen and Aiden.

Rian takes a single step away from our group, towards Teresa. The Fae behind her looks up, meets eyes with the king and grins.

They all vanish again. Clanaugh is playing tricks, I see; he must heed Rian's call and request, but no one ever said for how long.

There is a foreign laughter all around us as the Fae mock our human surprise. It is not a sound easily described, but it sets my body on edge and makes me grind my teeth.

"Clanaugh!" Rian all but bellows, and suddenly the laughter quiets. "We had an agreement, Clanaugh!"

I set an arrow against the bow but do not draw it. Qhan and Korvaan stand close by the king.

There are a few more moments of silence, and then there are suddenly Fae, there, in the clearing. No, that is not right; the Fae are not the ones who have suddenly appeared. We have been relocated. Most noticeable is the drastic change in weather. Our chapped lips and cracked skin are greeted by Isaarian humidity. Winter reigns in the realm of the king, but the Fae boast a perpetual summer.

No one dares remove an article of clothing. I can already feel the oppressive heat sending beads of sweat down my spine, but don't wish to bare more of myself to these creatures. Even the removal of a coat is too much.

Theresa and Septimus have not reappeared. No doubt they have been tucked away someplace safe while Clanaugh has his fun with the rest of us.

There is a twisted throne of roots, and on it sits the Fae's ruler. His sister leans against the side the wood, arms crossed, long legs mimicking them. She maintains a smirk at all times, which makes me wonder if that is merely how her mouth naturally curves.

I recognize Clanaugh as the Fae kissing Teresa, and asking for her name. I also have memories of him, from timelines past, but he is not wearing the same skin. I am not positive how it is the Fae change their appearances, though Rian has warned me before that what we see, and what hideousness they hide by taking more human forms, are completely different.

Now, Clanaugh looks like an easterner. Tourrannese, perhaps, with his hawkish eyes, dark hair and lashes, and skin coloring. I wonder how often he changes, and why.

I wonder why he still looks strangely familiar to me.

"We had an agreement, Clanaugh," Rian repeats.

"So we do."

"Return our party members to us, and we will be on our way," the king demands. "There is nothing in said agreement that states I cannot pass through your portion of the forest whenever I wish."

Some of the Fae surrounded the clearing giggle and titter. I think I hear some of them whispering in Isaarian, but the words sound foreign to me. It is as if I have suddenly lost hold of my own native language.

Clanaugh stands and brushes his hands down the front of his clothes in a somehow elegant gesture. Without him needing to move, some of the trees surrounding us bend and part to form an arch. Beyond them is the appearance of a small gathering chamber set for tea, in the throes of summer with the sun directly overhead. All is made of plants and roots, yet it somehow attempts to rival the splendor of New Isaaria's two palaces.

"Come. Parlay with me, little king," Clanaugh says with a pleasant grin.

I feel rather than see Rian narrow his eyes.

"I am not going anywhere without Soleil," he says.

Clanaugh looks surprised for a second, then smirks and waves a hand dismissively. "Very well. Bring dear Captain Marson along. Though what help you imagine she will be is beyond me. The rest of your party is welcome to enjoy our hospitality as they wait."

Rian flicks his eyes at Qhan in warning. His bodyguard gives a small nod. They will stand back and allow Rian and I to parlay with Clanaugh, but Qhan will not let his guard down. I doubt any of the others will either.

"Very well," Rian says, and gestures for Clanaugh to lead the way.

The Fae does so, with a grin, descending steps and sweeping by, towards the archway. Rian and I follow. The moment we pass through, the trees close in again, but I force myself to remain calm. Even Clanaugh knows the strength of ancient promises, particularly made by Fae. They cannot break a promise, only use their natural love of trickery to bend it as best they can. Even the king of the Fae will not want to make an enemy out of Rian, given his fluke.

At the table, I follow Rian's lead and hang my quiver and bow around the back of a chair, but I keep my knives handy. I don't realize where Clanaugh's sister went until we take our seats, and she appears behind me.

"What lovely long hair you have," Kaetscha croons, taking my braid in her hands and stroking it. "Would you sell it to me?" she asks, grinning and bearing her pointed teeth.

"No, thank you," I say, gritting my own teeth.

The sound of her voice is grating. She smiles, and circles around to take her own seat further away, watching us.

"*Clanaugh,*" Rian says again, trying to bring these Fae back to the matter at hand. "We'd like to continue on our way, if it's all the same to you. You have no right to deny me that."

"You can go if you like, little king," Clanaugh croons. "And you can have your entourage. I'd like to keep your Magicsmiths. Except for the bodyguard—you can have her, she's useless."

"Excuse me?" I snap, and glare at him. "Useless?!"

Rian sighs. "Soleil, do you want to be kidnapped by Fae?" he points out.

"Now, Clanaugh. You have no claim to our party, you know that. No one has given you their name, no one's broken your rules, and no one's killed one of your fellows. Now, if you would be so kind, the weather is about to take a nasty turn, and we'd like to be on our way."

Clanaugh considers this, tilting his head to the side.

"Mmm, you aren't entirely correct on that one, little king," he notes. "In fact, you should consider yourself lucky I am willing to let you keep your captain at all. Magicsmith blood is dreadfully useful to a Fae, you understand."

Rian fixes him with an even stare.

"I know you think it possible to keep the Smiths because they are not Isaarian citizens. However, they do have Isaarian blood," he says. "And they are Soleil's cousins. I would return them, if I were you. You may regret it otherwise."

"I never regret keeping a Magicsmith. They keep us alive for eons."

Implying he has stolen some of them before.

"If you keep them, know that you may be instrumental in the end of Samioth as we know it," Rian warns.

"Oh, I very much doubt that," Clanaugh insists. "After all, Septimus has told you his plan at this point, hasn't he? So, he has served his purpose. And poor little Resa will do nothing but slow you down. The boys, too. If you want to stop the Greys from freeing the Dark, you'd likely do better without them."

A realization makes me bristle, and frees my tongue. I talk as if I am Rian's equal, and in some ways, if considered queen of Isaaria, I should be.

"You knew about everything," I accuse. "You met Septimus, before, and you knew about the timelines."

Clanaugh shrugs. I loathe it when he does that. It makes such a human motion turn awkward and dismissively disgusting. As if we were the ones who adopted it from the Fae; worms trying to imitate gods.

"I know much," he says. "I know the Fae have been dying for centuries, and with the continual growth of your world, we grow weaker. I know the Dark has a grudge against you mites, and wants you all to burn for eternity. But it has never had an issue with Fae."

"Perhaps you were always weak," I accuse. "Perhaps your depravities have made you so. After all, other creatures of magic have survived and even thrived in our world."

"Not the Fair," he notes. "Not the Averti on their Floating Islands. Would you say their seeming lack of depravity was their downfall? No, no, no, Captain. It has always been 'you' versus 'us'. Only now, you have provided me with a way to survive the next few dozen centuries. Your Magicsmiths have enough power in them to keep us sustained through whatever the world has to offer."

"That does not give you the right to kidnap them."

"Kidnap? No, let us consider it a gift to me on your behalf. Call it a charitable service on your part, for sustaining the temporary survival of an endangered species," Clanaugh purrs.

"You will still be here long after we are gone," I hiss at him. "You require nothing from us."

Clanaugh laughs and glances at Rian. "What is this, little king; nothing to say? You would let her do all the talking for you?"

Rian shrugs, arms still crossed. "She's managing fine on her own."

"Even if she misrepresents you?" Clanaugh challenges.

"Rian and I are in agreement," I insist. "He won't abandon my cousins."

The Fae king gives me a mocking, pitying look. "Oh, come, now," he says. "Naturally, he considered it. His daughter is poorly, his body and mind are tired; he wants to reach the Summer Palace and find some semblance of true rest, if only for a few moments. Now that Septimus has told you everything, do you need him, keeping you on your toes? Do you need his little sister and the children? No, you do not. So let me keep them, and be on your way."

Rian sighs. "Clanaugh. She is not so stupid that you could turn us against one another with such ease. Flickering thoughts and actions are two different things. Here I am, king of Isaaria, demanding you return the Smiths. Now, I understand you have leverage here, so I am willing to oblige you: what can I do to hasten this process? Because the Smiths are coming with us, no negotiating that. This is but a game to keep you amused. At the least, let us see what you've done with them, and then we'll keep talking. That's fair enough."

"Fair?" Clanaugh chuckles. "Fair? Compared to what humanity has done to the Fae, nothing in the world could be considered proper recompense."

"I'm not seeking to give you reparations. Do not go looking for them."

"Not looking," Clanaugh corrects. "Found."

I hear a familiar clicking noise. So does Clanaugh. It's a lighter being snapped open and shut. Rian does not say anything, doesn't draw attention to the action otherwise, but he is clear enough in his threats. Clanaugh scowls for a moment, opposed to fire as he is. I watch his long fingers clench on the tabletop. For a moment, he is feral.

Then he forces himself to recover, and resume his normal posture, as if he is some debonair gentleman and we truly are sitting in the sun, taking tea.

"Who is the spirit?" he suddenly asks, eyebrows up.

"Spirit?" I repeat, startled by the sudden change in topic.

"The 'ghost' that's attached itself to the children," he says flippantly. "It feels familiar to me, but I cannot quite place it."

A memory sparks out of the many new things I've learned.

"Oh. Damen's Ghost. Septimus said it was a cousin, of Kryto Grey's, I think. 'Anya's Son'?"

Understanding blooms over Clanaugh's face and he gives a sharp-toothed grin. I think I catch a flash of surprise as well.

"Ah," he says, nodding and smiling to himself. "Of course. Anya's son. The most unfortunate of the lot, I'd say. What a sad, sorry story for our little crow king."

He is baiting me, yet I cannot help but bite. Neither can Rian, it seems, what with his family histories of the Magicsmiths, Greys, and Wolffs.

"What happened?" he beats me to asking, leaning forward.

Clanaugh is dismissive in both body language and tone, giving us the most obvious piece of the story: "He dies."

"Clanaugh," Rian says.

The lighter snaps shut.

"Very well. I'll let them go if you tell me how she tricked us," he says.

He is referring to Teresa, I realize.

"What are you talking about?" the king says. "From what you let us see, I sincerely doubt Teresa was capable of doing much, let alone tricking you."

"Yet, she did," Kaetscha snaps from her place on the sidelines. From the way her eyes flare and shoulders raise, I suspect she is not used to being made a fool. "Her children. Their wills are weak; children's always are. They gave us their names. 'Damen' and 'Aiden'. But the binding magic did not work. Which can only mean that *those are not their names*," she spits.

"No games, no deals, no compromises," Rian says. "You've had your fun, I'm sure our human folly has been more than entertaining for you. Now: let us all be on our way. I'm not asking nicely again."

"You cannot have them," Clanaugh says, blasé. "It is not my choice anymore; it was theirs. They gave me their names. Gave themselves to me. So, with me they must stay. Or, I suppose, I only have our little Resa. Septimus gave himself to my sister. It's a shame you didn't bring the eastern half-breed," he adds, in a thoughtful lament. "My sister does so adore him; the magic dances so beautifully on his skin, he may as well be a Magicsmith himself…"

"You really should leave them," he continues, now looking back to me again. "You can still go east, Captain. Go all on your own and look for Jin Riyong. Now that you know what your cousin intended, why bring him along if you can't still trust him? Do you know why he's here, trusting *you,* at all?"

"I believe my king gave you an order," I say, trying to stifle my temper.

"Aren't you curious how it is that sometimes you remember things and sometimes you do not?" Clanaugh asks gleefully. "How some folk appear to have dreams, shades of timelines past? Curious how this all works?"

"No," I snap. Even I don't know if it is a lie or not.

"Not the right answers to tempt you with?" he mocks. "Mmm. I suppose it doesn't mean enough to you, then. Very well. Let's see…"

Then Clanaugh smiles a disturbing, eerie smile. He knows what he plans to say next is going to hurt.

"Don't you want to know if there is a way to save little Asmer al'Yibna's life? I know poor Mercer did. He tried to ask me, knowing there is nothing I want from him. Stupid boy. I think it just about drove him mad. So, does Asmer mean enough to you, Captain? As you do have something I want…"

I hear tittering again. There are Fae all around this clearing, too, watching their king mock us. Finding great amusement in it.

"I won't leave my family here. Not in exchange for anything," I say.

"We're not the nasty Fae you hear about in stories, dear Magicsmith. We're more…ambiguous," Clanaugh claims. "Septimus and little Resa will have a pleasant life serving us. No one will do anything to them that they don't want. They'll be continually dressed prettily, brought to parties with drinking and dancing late into the night…They are safer with us than you. Or anywhere else in the world. If you left them here with us, it would be a mercy. I cannot break the magic, anyways."

"You'd best find a way to break that magic, then, or I'll burn the forest to the ground," Rian threatens, and the Fae around us hiss and yelp as they retreat, while Rian clicks a fire in his palm with the lighter.

Clanaugh does not react, as if challenging Rian. So, Rian sets a tree on fire.

The Fae clinging to it yelp and screech in pain, leaping away. They quickly put the fire out before it can spread, but the king's point is made. He is not handing out idle threats, and he is in no way amused by this situation. He is not the sort of man who finds a thrill in trying to best the Fae with his own wit.

For a moment, I see absolute rage in Clanaugh. It seethes in him. In that moment, I understand what Rian meant when he once told his students that the Fae were truly monstrous creatures. I can see Clanaugh's true form, and it is hideous in its twisted beauty.

But then he settles, again, to his current preferred human form.

"Let's play a game," Clanaugh suggests. "We shall make a deal of our own, with magic, to counteract the magic that bound Septimus and Teresa to us when they freely gave their names."

He continues quickly before Rian can set another tree on fire. I cannot help but smirk to see how Rian can fluster even the king of the Fae.

"If you win, you take your Magicsmiths back. If you lose, you gift the children to me. The ones that call themselves 'Damen' and 'Aiden' but are not."

"I have a better idea," Rian suggests. The flames in his hand flare, and the nearby tree branches catch fire. The Fae scramble to put it out again. "Why don't you give them all back, or I kick off my shoes and have more fun than I've ever had these past two decades?"

"You wouldn't burn down the forest," Clanaugh challenges. "It is ours, but yours as well. Isaaria would suffer."

"No," Rian says. "I'll just burn it until you all wither and die in front of me. And the forest will be better for it. A 'controlled burn', I think they call it."

Clanaugh scowls and curses us in his own tongue. But even his eyes shift warily, continually drawn to Rian's flames.

"Very well," he finally concedes. "You can have the children. And the albino. I'm keeping the girl."

"Ah, but if I can have the children back, that includes the unborn one," Rian points out. "Which, unfortunately, means I need Teresa back as well. So sorry. It is the way of things."

He smiles. I have always seen Rian's smiles as playful, bright, or sometimes even sheepish things. Teasing. Knowing. Now, I can see how one in the Faes' positions may see this one as a sinister smirk.

I can feel Clanaugh is furious. His sister is even more so. But they cannot refuse any longer. Rian has bested them at every turn, one way or another. We have promised them nothing and refused to give into a single trick.

Clanaugh does not admit defeat vocally. It is not in a Fae's nature to do so, I don't think. Yet, it is clear Rian has won, because a mere second later, we have been returned to our party. All of us have been. We are back where we started; Clanaugh's throne and magic is gone. It is winter again, the snow crunching under our weight, the bitter cold nipping at my ears. Septimus, Teresa, and the boys are sprawled in the snow at our feet, looking bewildered and out of sorts.

Ayla is the first to speak, nearly throwing herself on her father with a relieved cry of, "You got them back!"

Naomi crouches down next to Teresa and the boys, checking up on them.

"Hope's Head…?" Septimus says.

Teresa moans and puts a hand to the side of her head. "What happened?"

"You gave the Fae your names," I say. "They had a claim over you, and Rian forced them to give you back."

Teresa frowns, confused. "I remember…someone, there. I know him. But I knew he couldn't be here. He left. So, I never gave anyone my name."

I exchange a look with Rian. It does not take long for several of us to realize this means Clanaugh lied. He had no claim over Septimus and Teresa at all. He merely hoped we would believe he did, and believe that there was therefore a magic bond he could not break.

Septimus scrambles to his feet.

"Clanaugh!" he all but bellows. "Damn you to a thousand hells and may the Almighty have pity on the devil to whom you're charged!"

"You may regret cursing out the Fae like that," Rian warns.

"Oh, he knows he deserves it," Septimus seethes.

I leave the men to talk and crouch next to Teresa and Naomi, seeing the former is struggling to understand what happened much more than her brother. If Clanaugh chose to take that form for her sake, I suspect he resembled a now adult Aiko Shinya.

Her sons are babbling to her in Lusch, grabbing at her arms and no doubt jabbering details of all the incredible things they saw from even a few minutes in the Fae's domain. They are too excited to translate to Alarkian, and I can see Teresa is struggling to keep up.

"The Fae took you; they weren't allowed to keep you," I told her simply. "You didn't give your name, and neither did Septimus."

She notices who I left out and frowns at her sons.

"Damen, darling, did you tell the Fae your name?" she asks nervously.

He must answer truthfully in Lusch because, for a moment, Teresa looks horrified and asks me, "What did your king promise them, to get my sons back?"

"Nothing," I say. "He didn't have to. Clanaugh said…Well, he insisted that while the boys gave the Fae their names, the binding magic did not work. Which means that 'Damen' and 'Aiden' aren't their names."

The boys look confused, so if there was subterfuge involved, they were unaware of their part in it.

"Teresa?" Naomi says gently. "It's all right. You can trust us."

"It's not that. Kryto named our sons, a year after their births. I had different names in mind," Teresa confesses. "I used to whisper their names into their ears, when they were babies, when no one was around to hear. Silly, perhaps, I only…I wanted…I don't know," she says, and sighs. "When they were older, I resigned myself to calling them the names Kryto gave them. I did not want to confuse them."

"What were their other names?" Naomi asks.

"If it's all the same to you, I'd rather not say just now," Teresa says, flicking her eyes around the forest about us.

"They can't take the boys unless they are freely given or unless they freely give their names," I reassure her.

"Even so."

None of us chide her for her caution. In fact, for the rest of our travel on foot—until we are free of the Fae's domain and finally reach the station to board a train for the Summer Palace—our party is hauntingly silent. When Nissa rejoins us, she can tell something is different, but does not ask. Even Teresa's children barely say a word unless it is necessary.

It is as if we have brought Clanaugh's taunts along with us, and are afraid that in some way, he may be right. That it may be better for Samioth, and Smiths ourselves, if we were captive residents of the Fae's domain.

Ten

TRAVEL BY TRAIN is more comfortable, and quicker, but does not allow for us to easily converse as a group. Rian and Ayla have their own cars, as king and princess of Isaaria, which is expected, but I'm sure they are less than pleased with the necessary isolation. Though Rian originally planned to speak to me while on the train, he spends most of his time asleep and I cannot be bothered to wake him.

It is a relief when our train enters the outskirts of the city and heads for the summer palace. Early as it is in the morning, most of our party are asleep. The only two I find awake when I make my rounds are Nissa and Ayla. Nissa is keeping her hyena calm in this metal beast, and she has always been the sort who requires little sleep, but I'm surprised Ayla is awake. I slide open the door to her compartment.

"Princess? Do you need anything?" I say.

She is curled with her feet pulled under her onto the cushioned bench. It looks as if she never had an attendant pull down the bed for her and has sat up all night.

"I want to be alone," Ayla whispers, still looking out the window.

"Are you sure about that?" I ask.

Ayla hesitates, then frowns. "No," she admits. "Yes? I don't know."

"Then I'll sit with you until you do," I say, and take a seat across from her.

Ayla allows the silence to perpetuate for at least a full minute until finally sniffling, then apologizing. I offer her a handkerchief before she can dig out one of her own. A moment later, I hear a cart rattle past; likely coffee being offered to those who have ordered it, but no one disturbs the princess or I. The glass on the cart clinks loudly near our door and sound makes her flinch.

"You are safe, princess," I say. "Let go of your fear. Otherwise, you will never sleep well again."

"I don't know if I can," Ayla confesses. I'm relieved she'll speak with me; I'd expected to give advice to deaf ears. "I was so afraid. All I knew was that… that you could have fought those men, and killed them. If they didn't have me, already."

"Anyone would have been afraid in that situation," I say.

"But you're never scared of anything," Ayla insists, sniffling.

"That's not true," I say. "I was terrified, Ayla. That is why I could not think. It is why I could not save you, and I'm sorry. I was terrified they were going to hurt you."

If my words surprise her, she gives no indication. I suspect she does not believe me. She has assumed I am only saying this for the sake of her comfort. But fear is a familiar visitor for me.

"I have watched you grow from a child to a virtuous young woman, princess," I tell her, whilst choosing my words with utmost care. "And I will admit, I have come to see you as something of a daughter. You are important to me. And it is my sworn duty to protect both you and your father. When I saw you, then, I was afraid. Because I care for you."

I cannot bring myself to say love. I am too much of a coward to risk that this morning, and I do not want to startle Ayla into silence.

"I thought I was going to die," she confesses. "I ran through the likelihood of you managing to rescue me and I realized I was finished. We were dead. I was dead. And who would miss me? I don't mean as princess of Isaaria. Who left alive would truly miss me? Aside from Soren?"

"I would," I say. "The king would. Qhan and Valor and—"

"But the number is so small. I haven't done anything with my life."

"You have made many charitable contributions to Isaaria and its people."

"Is that enough?" she challenges. "Have I done enough that if something happened to me, and I died, would people care? Would they mourn? Would they remember to pray for my soul and its passage in the Otherworld? Or would my death merely be a political nuisance?"

There is an answer, but I fumble mentally in how to organize my sentence, and it makes me look speechless. Ayla is in a state of mind to take things negatively, and I worry she likely will not listen to me regardless of what I say.

"The worst part is, when I ask myself what I would want to do, to change how useless my life is, I can't think of anything," she admits.

"You don't want anything at all?" I say. Dubious of this.

Ayla turns pink. "Not nothing," she says. "But not anything worthwhile—"

"Who says?" I challenge. "Tell me, Ayla. I bet you are wrong on that."

It takes her a while, but she always did treat me more familiar than she should have. Captain Marson would disapprove. But Soleil Yakarami, meant to be Ayla's mother, is glad Ayla finally reveals her dreams to me. Fair or not, it makes me selfishly feel as if I am reclaiming a territory Naomi and Asmer started to invade.

"I want to teach children," she says. "Like how Father did for a short while. At the University."

"That's admirable," I say.

"But it's not only that," she says uneasily, and bites her lip before whispering to me. As if she is afraid someone will overhear. "I want to teach my own children. I want enough of them to have a full class size! I don't even want to be queen, one day!"

I cannot help but laugh. "I would say that is still ambitious, Ayla."

"I'd always thought of it in a vague, dreaming way," she admits, off in her own head. "But then, looking after Damen and Aiden, I thought…I want this. I want it now. I don't want it to be a thing to look forward to any longer."

"Perhaps you should say so to Soren. And your father," I suggest.

Ayla returns to looking out the window. "Maybe so," she says quietly.

While she may consider it, I suspect this confession will not come today.

Though we do not speak further, I sit with Ayla for the last quarter hour of the journey. We admire the view of the city as we approach, and the towers of the Summer Palace perched beyond its skyline. It is beautiful, but the winter morning is grey and dour. It significantly dulls the grandeur.

There is no time to allow the city's people to see their king. From the train station, we gather our party together, meet the guards Soren sent to intercept us, and take carriages to the palace. We would have likely taken Alarkian motorcars now, if our deal for them ever manage to reach completion. But when the war in the west broke out, all halted. We only purchased a small number of the motorcar prototypes beforehand.

We disembark once safely within the palace gates. Ayla is quick to allow Damen and Aiden to find her, and babble to her in their bright-voiced Alarkian. She expertly conceals her inner doubts, forcing a façade of brightness and pitching her voice higher to applaud the boys' second language skills. She trails behind our party with them as we mount the first of the many steps ahead, while I walk close to my cousins, prepared to introduce them.

At the top of the steps, seated in a wheeled chair, is a young man with golden hair dressed in a flattering suit of soft dove gray. There are rings on his fingers, the representative circlet of the Carsans family perched amidst his curls, and both an embroidered sash and a broach boasting their crest of gold peonies and griffins to further cement his status.

Even at a distance, it is easy to recognize Grand Prince Soren Carsans.

In any other circumstances, Ayla would have broken into a smile and run to him immediately, prepared to tell him her many adventures since they last saw one another. Instead, she allows Damen and Aiden to hold her hands and takes the steps slowly, almost ill at ease. It is as if she thinks her ordeal during the invasion of the Pyrian Palace will make him think less of her.

Beside Soren stands an Isaarian woman about my own age, but with dark hair and softer facial features. Kaoli Qurvo has acted as Soren's aid since he was a child, and though she plans to pass her position to a worthy successor soon, she is still physically capable of looking after him despite her growing age. I'm sure she and Korvaan will be pleased to see one another again, though neither of them is the sort to run into the other's arms without being properly dismissed from service first. They think alike in the ways you would expect a married couple to.

The stairs are difficult for Teresa, but she hangs on her brother's and Naomi's arms and continually glances back as Ayla dawdles with the boys behind us. We make it to the top of the steps ahead of them: the king, Valor and Qhan and I, with Korvaan and the rest of Rian's bodyguards.

Nissa does not accompany us to meet with the custodian of the Summer Palace and has already vanished. I doubt we will see her again until necessary.

"Your majesty. It is good to see you've made it here safely," Soren says, and tilts himself forward into a bow. "Vilaneau was becoming concerned."

"Thank you, Soren," Rian says. "Safe, yes. But also, exhausted."

"I expected as much, sir, which is why I had your rooms and a meal made up in advanced."

Rian cannot help but smile. "As ever, Soren, you are indispensable. Now, might I introduce the spare guests I telephoned ahead to warn you about?"

"It would be my honor to meet them, your majesty."

"Naturally! I forgot to say when I told you of them, but they are Captain Marson's cousins; they have sought refuge with us, from the wars in the west. Septimus and Teresa Smith, and Teresa's dear sons, Damen and Aiden," Rian introduces.

Teresa gives a wobbly curtsey and Septimus, a more distinguished bow. Damen and Aiden are still taking their time on the steps with Ayla.

"I do hope the rooms I had prepared are suitable," Soren says. "A suite, interconnected: how does that sound?"

"Whatever you had available is much appreciated," Septimus says. "But yes, it will be good to keep us all close together. Thank you."

Soren smiles, but looks at Septimus with curious eyes. I am certain he has many questions, and unlike Nissa, is not content to attempt piecing the facts together on his own through mere observation. Least of all, I'd imagine this is the first time Soren has met someone as fair as Septimus is with his albinism.

Rian interrupts before curiosity can get the better of the young man, forcing attention away from the Smiths.

"I know I shouldn't have expected a welcoming party from your peers, but still," the king notes with a laugh. "Where are the other grand princes?"

Soren gives a small nod; keeping track of the grand princes is a full-time occupation on his part. Regardless of the decision to move the king's entourage permanently to the Summer Palace, they would be required to gather wherever Rian's household resides for the coming yearly counsel, made around Holrith routinely. They have reports to make, and decisions to parse out in regards to the Isaarian lands they are expected to oversee on Rian's behalf.

From the speech Soren gives, describing, it sounds as if all the grand princes have arrived before us, if only just, for some:

"Vásan is here, in a spat with his wife, again, so they are occupying separate spaces. He is being quite cold about it all, refuses to acknowledge Yvette's existence. Poor Alo has given up on trying to bridge the gap between them, or so he says. Yuugo is out of the city, but not far. Just went to a hot springs site with his lover—the one we are meant to pretend he is merely in a platonic relationship with. Detrus and Irina are waiting inside. I think they look forward to seeing their king is safe, but their children keep them busy. Patrice finally showed a fluke; they are ecstatic."

"And Grand Prince Oram?"

"Magnus is out, for the day. Still within the city limits, looking after refugees. Seeing what they might need to make them more comfortable. His parents are here as well, though, to offer their support. Grand Princess Nissa, I assume, came with you."

"Mmm," Rian says thoughtfully. "As always, Soren, you know precisely what you ought to. Do we not have that formal dinner tomorrow evening?"

"Yes, your majesty," Soren says. "They will all attend, as they're meant to. They may not all be happy about it, but they will do what's expected of them."

"Mmm," Rian says again, thinking, nodding. "I hope they will be on their best behavior for our Alarkian guests."

I am startled as a hand suddenly clenches on my shoulder.

Though I'm tempted to fly into combat, the fingers soon loosen and slip off. I turn to see Teresa slide to the ground, not unconscious, but unbalanced and woozy. She blinks, trying to clear her no doubt fuzzy vision. Naomi is quick to go to her, fussing over her and insisting Valor come to help prop Teresa up so she can drink some water.

It takes Septimus a moment to notice, but then, he is quite concerned.

"Teresa!"

He practically throws me to the side so he can reach his sister, which seems to startle Teresa herself even more than it does the rest of us. Given my conversations with him, I know Septimus cares for his sister, but I suppose it is difficult for her to trust him after being manipulated for years by the person they thought loved them.

"Is she quite alright?" Soren asks, leaning forward in his chair while Rian crouches besides Teresa.

"Damen and Aiden," she starts.

She's worried they'll be scared, like when she fainted in the Pyrian Palace.

"You are safe. So are the boys. Do not exert yourself with worries," Septimus is reassuring her.

I cannot help but sigh as I crouch down beside them. Though I know it is not charitable to think so, Teresa's delicate health is becoming exhausting to manage. It is the deep shame I see in her face, and the way her eyes dart around nervously, that reminds me this is likely even more exhausting, and humiliating, for her.

Ayla and the boys have reached the top step. I notice Soren glance over at them, attempting and expecting to catch Ayla's eye, but she ignores him. She cheerfully insists Damen and Aiden sit down on the top step and gaze out over the view of the city, as if this is a holiday for them, and they are sight-seeing.

Damen frowns. Even Aiden takes more to be fooled.

"Why are we sitting down?" he asks innocently.

Ayla smiles at him and ruffles his hair. "Your mama is resting her legs. She is tired after carrying your little sister all over the place. So, we shall take a rest, too."

Aiden considers this for a moment, then nods, Ayla's logic making perfect sense to him.

"I'm all right," Teresa insists, though she is mumbling. "Only dizzy."

"Perhaps it would be best to reconvene inside the palace. We can bring a doctor immediately, if necessary," Soren says.

I glance at him to see he is visibly concerned. He may only have met Teresa moments ago, but he wants to look after our guests' health as best he can, I'm sure. That is in Soren's nature.

"I do not need any doctor," Teresa insists; I have noticed she is not fond of those in the medical profession, save for Naomi. However, Naomi is no specialist, for expectant women. Her skills lay in other fields.

"I think perhaps, Miss, you do. With all respect," Soren says, and turns to Kaoli. "Please have a doctor summoned."

Kaoli bows and disappears inside the Summer Palace, disregarding Teresa's meagre protests. Once Kaoli has vanished, my cousin gives in to our insistences and finally allows herself to relax. The cogs are turning and she cannot stop them at this point.

"I—" she starts, and I can hear the apology coming.

"Is it possible that we could have someone help stabilize Miss Teresa while we walk her inside?" Naomi interrupts, anticipating this.

"I'll happily carry the lady, if his majesty will excuse it," Qhan says.

"But of course," Rian insists. "Valor can escort me to my own rooms. We could all do with a bit of cleaning up before the rest of the day commands our attention, I should think. Miss Teresa: no need to dress for dinner tonight. I'll have something sent up. You and the children should rest."

Teresa cringes, but accepts their invitations without further fuss. Qhan picks her up before she can insist otherwise, anyway. She is stiff in his arms for a few moments, but then allows her spine to relax and sighs. She is too tired to care.

"I'll bring the boys after a little more exploration," Ayla offers. "I'm certain they will want to look around some, first. We will come upstairs after."

She will wait until after the doctor has looked at Teresa, then. Ayla is smart to know the boys should not be present for such a thing, just in case there is bad news to share.

"I will accompany them," Septimus promises his sister, as if knowing she would not like leaving her children without a family member.

However, Teresa does not look particularly panicked. I believe she has grown to trust Ayla with the boys.

Soren agrees to this plan and wheels his chair around expertly before leading the way. I feel mildly slighted in how Rian does not once glance my way before heading inside with Valor at one shoulder. I force myself to brush it off; I am sure his mind is preoccupied with matters of the kingdom. He wishes to wash, redress, and likely speak to Magnus Oram at once about the refugee crisis and the portents of looming war.

I, too, have my duties to see to in regards to his security, though I would rather allow personal matters to take priority.

"I'm dreadfully sorry about this," Teresa mumbles, still sounding dazed.

"Don't be sorry," I hear Taris say as he carries her through the doors. "Don't ever apologize, Miss Resa. For anything."

My head jerks up. For a moment, just a moment, it is Taris I see, turning to bring Teresa through the doors and into the Summer Palace. I don't see his face, but I don't have to. It is Taris, most certainly. That black, curly hair of his is unmistakable. The sound of his voice, with the slight, southern Isaarian lilt he has had since he was a child, has always remained as a permanent memory in my head. Locked away, old, and dusty: but there.

I'm not sure how it happens, but suddenly I've walked into one of the stone columns that frames the platform at the top of the steps. I force myself to blink, to breathe. I demand my ears stop ringing.

I snap my head back in the direction of where I saw Taris.

No. No, it is Qhan carrying Teresa. I'd imagined it. I imagined it, because Taris Qurvo is dead, and has been for nearly two decades.

"Captain, are you quite alright? Soleil?" Korvaan asks, a hand hovering at my shoulder.

His voice shakes away the remains of ghosts.

I clear my throat.

"Perfectly well. You can dismiss yourself for now," I add, sure to distract him before he can get another question out. "Rian should be safe with the security of the Summer Palace, and I'm sure you want to visit with Kaoli."

Korvaan hesitates.

"Soleil, not to be a man who disregards my wife, but I think you may need me more than Kaoli right now. You look white as a sheet!"

"I said I am fine, Korvaan," I say, glaring at him. "Now go greet your wife. I know she has missed you. I'll make it an order if I have to."

I can tell he is displeased with the curt way I'm speaking, but the concept of being forced to greet his wife via Captain's orders is enough to guilt him.

"We do need to speak, Soleil," he says. "About all this. This journey of yours to the east. Your cousins. The timelines. Everything."

"Of course," I say. "I will summon you when it is amenable for all of us."

"Including your cousins?" he says. There is something critical in his tone. He goes on before I can reprimand him. "All I want, Soleil, is some time with you alone. Well, Naomi and I would like that."

I agree to give them whatever privacy they desire, but their assumed opportunity to berate me, I place last on my list of responsibilities.

I follow Qhan inside, hurrying to catch him as he reaches the top of the grand staircase with Teresa. Soren has beaten us to the top of the stairs, having taken a lift that he can operate on his own using only a lever and electricity. Such devices have been around for centuries using hydraulic pressure, but are refined, now, for use within a building instead of in mines or canyons.

"Genius, these lifts," Soren says approvingly as he rolls himself out. "Next time, Qhan, you should have accompanied me instead of taking all these dreadful stairs."

"Miss Teresa is not so heavy that I found it necessary," Qhan said plainly.

It is true; for an expectant woman, especially, my cousin is far too thin. I'm sure even without being an expect, Soren has noted this.

Knowing her, Teresa surely would have continued to protest Qhan's carrying her, only we are off again before she can start. Soren wheels ahead of us to lead the way. A flurry of maids who are still finishing their work on the Smiths' suite are holding their grey skirts up as best they can as they rush up and down the hall, veils almost slipping and flying off behind them.

Many of them slide to a stop as Soren passes to hastily bow to him, murmuring respectful greetings, before running off again the moment he has moved on. It is an effort not to snort at their panic; they should know by now that Soren is as reasonable a person as a prince could possibly be. Perhaps it is because someone like Soren, and even Rian, is so sensible and fair that the staff wants to impress even more.

"Ah, here we are," Soren announces as we reach the entry point for the scurrying maids.

He rolls himself inside, expecting us to follow.

"You will be quite comfortable here, I think," I hear him say to Teresa as I enter, the last in line.

The maids still inside begin begging for forgiveness that they somehow have not managed to prepare the rooms in the ten minutes they have had since Soren confirmed the suite was acceptable to my cousins. Soren laughs and promises them it is no trouble. Teresa does not appear to hear them.

She is captivated by the room, which is airy and fair, more delicate, and more fitting a place for her than even her richly grand rooms in the Pyrian Palace. The curtains are lightweight, gauzy things that allow the sun in no matter their status across the glazed windows. There are no steps for Teresa to worry over, and there is a nursing chair and bassinet already brought up. A wardrobe is waiting to be filled with fine dresses, and a nightstand and vanity hold pretty glass bottles, their contents in dyed pinks and yellows, white creams. The pencils, paints, and papers she requested sit on a fine white-wood drawing desk.

Even in the palace staff's haste to prepare something, personalization was taken into account here. I've no doubt the boys' and Septimus' rooms are likewise decorated with care.

"This is so very lovely," Teresa whispers.

"The boys' room will be just through the second washroom," Soren tells her. "The first will be only for you. So, you can have some privacy during your laying in period. Your brother's room is conjoined to theirs, on the other side. All three have doors out to a main gathering space, for private dinners and such, if you cannot or do not wish to prepare for anything formal."

Teresa looks shocked as she counts the number of rooms.

"I have one…all for myself?" she says, confused.

However, I do not hear who answers her, or what they say. There is a gleeful laugh, back from near the bed. A sound I know well. It sends a chill down my spine. I know it is impossible, and yet, I hear it.

I turn and see my sister, my little sister, with her hair in loose, wild waves, dressed in the most beautiful gown she is likely to ever wear. It is glorious, delicate, and thick with skirts. She throws herself onto the bed with its white furs so she can stare up at the ceiling. She is giddy, and all smiles. Though she has yet to apply the usual cosmetics that I know she prefers, particularly to darken her light eyelashes, she is more beautiful now than I have ever seen her before.

"Oh, how much more spoiled can a girl be than when throwing herself down in a bed of furs to rumple a perfectly good party dress," Lune announces, giggling.

"Only, that is no party dress, Lady of Leitfeld, it is your wedding gown," Asmer insists, appearing in her own fine gown, my sister's long veil folded over an arm. "Now get up and let me fix your hair. Unless you want to greet your husband and all of Isaaria like a wild dryad."

Lune giggles again, ecstatic, and kicks her legs like a little girl before flipping over onto her stomach. I can see in her excitement how much she loves Taris; how much she cannot wait to call herself his wife.

"When is Soleil coming?" she asks. "She promised."

I'm startled to hear my own name in this context, and to hear Lune so happily anticipating my arrival.

"Soon," Asmer reassures.

Then, I realize Soren has tried addressing me several times over, already. The ghosts are gone, and I am here with Soren, Qhan, and Teresa.

"Captain?" Soren says again.

"If you don't mind, Captain, I said I'll return to look after the king, now," Qhan says slowly.

"Yes, yes," I say. "Let us get Teresa to the bed, first, and then we will be having a doctor in for her. I'll see to that."

Qhan and Soren both look at me with mild concern, but I ignore them. Teresa says she would rather not be laid in bed all day, like an invalid, so Qhan compromises and sets her up in a comfortable armchair, a blanket over her legs. I dismiss him but walk out of the suite with him, stopping him for a moment to ask a question. Something mildly personal I do not want to say in front of Soren and Teresa.

"We should see about having guards specifically for your cousins," Qhan says, thinking this is what I mean to suggest. "After the Pyrian Palace, I think it might be a good idea."

"I'll see to it," I say. "But Qhan. Did you say something? To Teresa? When you brought her inside?"

Qhan frowns at me. "No, Captain. I don't believe so. Should I have?"

I shake my head and wave him off. "No, no. It's fine. I thought I heard someone say something, that is all. You may go. I'm sure the king will need you."

Qhan looks suspicious of me again, concerned, but he obeys and heads off down the hall to the king's rooms. I return to Teresa, so that Soren can see to the rest of his day as planned. I'm sure, as professional as he may appear, the needs of four extra guests are not things he wanted to worry about today. The next days will be filled with work for him already.

"The doctor should be here shortly," he says. "I'll send him in directly."

"Thank you, grand prince," I say, and we trade places, him wheeling out and me going to sit at Teresa's side.

There are a few moments of silence between us, as Teresa is still embarrassed and is not entirely at ease alone with me. She trusts me more than she once did, but it is difficult to be sequestered with a person of my temperament. I'll be the first to say I'm not the most emotionally available of people, and often do not express my thoughts accurately in speech.

"I think I'll ask Prince Soren to ensure there is always a doctor readily available for you," I finally say, to break the silence. "Given your habit of collapsing on us, this is likely necessary."

It was meant to be somewhat of a joke, but she does not hear it.

"It is not unusual for me," she claims. "I had dreadful vertigo with Damen and Aiden, too. Apparently, it is quite common for women expecting."

"Even so, I would like the doctor to examine you again on a regular basis," I tell her. "Through the rest of your laying-in."

Teresa looks uncomfortable at the insistence of future appointments with a doctor, but quickly hides her expression and merely nods her consent. I am tempted to inquire, only I suspect her reluctance is related to the many things that happened in Lusch that she said she is too ashamed to ever speak of. The next thing I say instead, then, is not without hesitance, but I cannot help but ask. I know it is unlikely I will ever get a full story out of Teresa in regards to her past and Septimus'. But I like to know my enemy.

"How did your husband look after you? When expecting the boys?" I ask, and am quick to add, "If there is something in particular you need, or usually have, I'm sure we could acquire it with ease."

Teresa shakes her head. "There have been some similarities, but overall, each one has been completely different," she claims. "There is no one thing I need. Even between Damen and Aiden, it was different. With Aiden, they barely allowed me to leave my bed."

I notice how well she dodged that first question, almost innocently.

"So, there's nothing at all you want?" I challenge, doubting this.

"You could not give it. I only wish my daughter could meet her father," she adds with a sigh.

"Her father?" I repeat, startled by this. "You barely knew him."

Teresa shrugs, her smile remaining. "Yet: this is his daughter, who he does not even know exists. He might like to; how would I know?"

I cannot help but scoff. "You are too kind-hearted," I say, expecting her to flush and look down in that mild-mannered, innocent way of hers.

But while Teresa does look down, it is with a pensiveness I did not expect.

"I must confess something to you," she says after a moment. "I did not lie, precisely, but I did purposefully mislead you."

This startles me, particularly because of the topic at hand. I cannot imagine what she may have mislead me about, knowing their story so well, but I urge her on regardless.

"I...I am not so innocent as you have imagined," she murmurs. "When

Aiko Shinya appeared, and I knew he was my only hope at saving Aiden, I was relieved and grateful. But I was also angry. No; I was furious."

I cannot picture my little cousin angry. She goes on, lifting her head so I can see the bitterness in her eyes.

"You cannot imagine how much I hated him, in those moments. Not Aiko. My husband. Kryto," she says, nearly spitting his name. But then she pauses, and when she begins again, her voice has become gentle once more. "Here came a stranger, asking for whatever I could pay for his services, willing to take anything, and willing to help save my son. The son my own husband was going to let die. When I offered what I did, I knew precisely what I was doing. It is true, I did not dare give him anything I owned, no jewelry, nothing of significant expense. Kryto would have noticed. He kept such a close eye on my belongings. But Septimus was right; we could have found another way. Knowing what I later learned of him, it is possible Aiko would have done it for much less..."

That sounds more like the young Aiko Shinya I once knew. Though, to be completely accurate, the boy he used to be would have saved Aiden for nothing at all.

"But I did not care," she continues. "I knew it was foolish, I knew there were other ways. I hated Kryto. I wanted revenge against him. A humiliating secret that I could hold over him, even if he never found out. But I...I think part of me did hope he would learn of my infidelity. Because I knew it would kill him, inside. It would pain Kryto more than anything else I could ever do, and I wanted that. I wanted it to *hurt.*"

I cannot think of anything to say, so when she falls silent for a few moments, the quiet remains just where she has laid it until she picks the story up once more.

"I knew it was foolish," she says, and gives a light little laugh. "Oh, I did. I understood the stupidity in it. I knew Kryto would be so pained, so angry, so hurt, he might kill me in his rage, but I did not care. I was willing to die knowing how much pain he would have to live with, knowing I was unfaithful. Knowing he had killed me because of it. I admit, I was almost gleefully awaiting his return, and the inevitable discovery. As Aiden recovered, I pictured sending him and Damen safely away with Septimus, to you, but staying until Kryto returned so that I could see for myself what my betrayal did to their father."

"...But then you learned you had Rika," I say.

I recall what Septimus himself said, about watching his sister grow so weak and hopeless he did not think she would last. But I had not imagined this: this near suicidal determination to hurt her husband no matter the cost.

Despite her mild deception, and her insistences she is no innocent girl, I cannot bring myself to be angry with Teresa. All I can think of was how much Lune hurt inside, to cut herself the way she did with those scissors.

Teresa sighs.

"Then I learned I had Rika," she repeats. "And I knew I had to go with Septimus, for my daughter's sake. A realization came upon me. Suddenly, I was glad for my brother's refusal to leave me behind. I was glad I had this child, because it occurred to me, when it never had before, that in my pursuit to hurt Kryto the most, I would also hurt my sons."

There is great regret and sorrow in her voice as she says this.

"So, do not hold the circumstances of this child's conception against her father," she says quietly. "I am the guilty party."

I frown, still uncomfortable. "He used you."

"And I used him," she says. "Don't make me into a saint, Soleil; I've been married for a decade, *I know how to seduce a man.* I was scared of him when I first offered, because I didn't know if he would accept such a dreadful, cheap price, but I won't pretend as if I was naïve and innocent. I know it was wrong, knew it was wrong, but I…"

She shrugs helplessly.

"At the time, nothing else mattered," I finish for her. "It was both a way to take revenge on your husband, and the only way you could think of to save your son's life."

"Yet, you insist on painting me in such a noble light, for an adulterer," she says. "Soleil: if Aiko Shinya had asked me for more than he did, I would have continued to give it. I was prepared to let him hurt me, if he wanted, but he did not. And then, there being such a difference between him and Kryto…I wanted him to stay with me, I wanted…to stay with him. I wanted…Oh."

She grimaces at her own words and then sighs.

"I suppose I didn't know what I wanted, then. I understand how all this makes me look, but I don't care. I know my feelings for Aiko Shinya aren't real, and are only because I was desperate for someone, anyone, to help me, but…He was so kind to me. So attentive to me. It was as if he was truly concerned for me, and for Aiden, in a way Kryto never was that…I suppose, at the time, that was enough."

"At least you are trying to do the right thing now," I say.

Teresa looks down at her stomach and sighs, wrapping her arms around herself. "But I can't think of my daughter as a mistake. I can't think of it as a mistake to do whatever I could to save my son."

"Do you think," I start, but then stop myself, realizing the implications of what I am about to ask.

Teresa is too smart not to guess.

"Do I think this will all happen the same way, again, when you clean our slates and start all over one last time?...No. I don't. But do I think, somehow, someway, I will have Damen, Aiden, and Rika to love and care for? Yes. I believe so. I think some things are simply meant to be. Their lives are their own. Not mine, not their fathers', not anyone else's. They will be conceived and born, and they will do great things with their lives. Just not in this time, and not in this way."

"It means no matter what, you are agreeing to marry a monster," I remind her, warning her. "For you to have Damen and Aiden, you must marry Kryto Grey. Or at least be intimate with him."

"If it means getting my sons, then so be it," she claims.

I'm too shocked to respond, but a knocking at the door saves me from needing to conjure words. My own confusion swirls in my head as I answer the door; I have known for some time that I am meant to be a mother, yet, I cannot fathom how Teresa would agree to such misery simply to ensure she have her sons. I can't imagine being with a monster like Kryto Grey, especially when I have Rian for comparison.

I offer to stay with Teresa while the doctor looks after her, but she surprises me by declining. So, I take my leave of the room and hover outside the door, leaning up against the wall so I can shut my eyes and pretend I am not exhausted. By the time the doctor emerges, I am nearly asleep on my feet, and need to clear the grogginess from my throat before speaking.

There is no emergency to speak of. The diagnosis is much the same as before: Teresa is fine. She needs rest and plenty of good food. Exercise is encouraged, but not so strenuous as she has been managing. Her anxiety also needs to be kept at bay. Dragging her across a country, even if most of the journey is by train, is not an option.

It is not as if we had a choice, but the doctor's stern point is taken.

Before I can decide whether Teresa would want me to return, I hear a pitter-patter of little feet and am sure I know who is about to appear. The boys must have run ahead of Septimus or Ayla because they are alone when they stumble to a halt in front of me and the door. Damen is much faster than Aiden, whose little legs and unbalanced figure can hardly be expected to keep up with his brother. However, Damen has not sped ahead completely, and has tugged his younger brother along by the wrist.

"Is this going to be our room?" Damen asks me uneasily.

"Your mother's room," I correct. "You and your brother's will be attached."

"Is Mama feeling well?" he asks, sounding very young.

"She is perfectly healthy. She merely needs rest."

"Oh."

I feel someone tug on my sleeve on the other side of me. Aiden.

"Is the baby well?" he asks, quiet and worried.

"The baby is also perfectly healthy," I reassure him. "She is growing a little more every day. Just like you. Now, there is no need to worry. Settle in here. In fact, when Naomi comes to watch after you, ask her to take you to the library. The one here is different than the one in the Pyrian Palace. I think you will enjoy exploring it."

"Can't we see Mama now?" Aiden says, completely ignoring my comments about the library. I wonder if his Alarkian is good enough to have understood.

"Of course," I allow after a moment. "Where are Ayla and your uncle?"

Damen gestures back. "Miss Ayla went somewhere. She has something to do. Uncle Septimus is back there with that man with the chair."

I blink. "Prince Soren?"

"Yes," Damen says dismissively. "Can we see Mama, now, please?"

I step aside and let them throw the door open, calling for and running to their mother to fling themselves up on the chair with her. A smile tempts my expression, but I'm also moments away from insisting the boys leave their mother be. Still, she sounds happy to have their active company, and listens to them jabber about how much they are enjoying the Summer Palace.

I hear Soren before I see him, along with the clacking of a maid's heeled shoes. Septimus is not with them when they appear, the maid carrying a tray of drinks, but Soren anticipates my question.

"I showed your cousin to his room. He will have access to the entire suite," he says. "I think he wanted the opportunity to clean up first."

The maid has moved past me, balancing her tray with one hand so she can knock on Teresa's door before entering. She closes the door behind her.

"I ordered some warm tea for her. And there is hot chocolate, for the boys," Soren explains.

"Thank you, Soren, that was very thoughtful."

It's the first sentence he's let me get out, anticipating what else I may say and beating me to saying it. But there's something that's bothering me about how he is here, bringing Teresa and her children whatever they could possibly need, and has yet to find time with Ayla. I am not sure if this is because they want to be as discreet as possible, or if there is another explanation.

"Soren, you don't have to answer. I know it is an odd question," I start.

He smiles and speaks before I can finish. "I'm no stranger to odd questions, Captain Marson. I'm sure I won't take offense."

Still, I consider my words carefully before saying anything.

"Did you stay to help with Teresa because it is something you would have done for anyone, or because of *her.*"

Soren looks uneasy for a moment. "What do you mean? Was I not meant to do anything?"

"All I want to know is if you felt unnaturally obligated to take care of her," I try to explain. "Beyond what you would reasonably do for anyone else."

"Captain, as far as I'm concerned, I'm still the steward of the Summer

Palace even with the king in residence, until he revokes that. It is naturally my responsibility to take care of my guests, especially when one collapses on the front steps!" Soren says.

I do not think he fully understands the question, and yet, that answer is enough to tell me what I need to know. Whatever it is that I've noticed about Teresa's eyes and their effect, they do not influence everyone. They did not do anything to make Amerson spare her.

"I'm sorry," I sigh. "I'm sure I am being overly familiar, and confrontational. There are many questions regarding my cousins, that may relate to me and my family history."

"I will not pry," Soren says. "But Captain, please: whatever you experienced in the past weeks, you are all safe here. Unless there is a legitimate reason otherwise, allow me to take care of my guests."

"Just don't let her pull you in with those eyes of hers," I warn him, trying to both say something of that regard and make it sound like a tease.

Soren laughs. "Oh, don't worry. I already know the one for me..."

He surely must know that I am aware of him and Ayla. However, because of the norms of social protocol, he will not say so blatantly before asking Rian's permission to marry her.

"Your majesty?" I hear.

This surprises me mostly because Soren does not react in the slightest.

I am shocked to realize what I feel is fear when I turn to the side and see who has joined us. I know the voice, and I do not want to see.

It is Lord Aiko Shinya, older than when I last saw him, but younger than he would be, now. He is standing in the hallway, facing someone who isn't there. He is dressed in Isaarian clothes, but his hair is longer than he'd usually wear it, as if he hasn't had the chance to see a barber in some time.

"I am so very grateful. For all you have done for her," he says. "For looking after her in a way I never could."

I catch my breath and force myself to close my eyes. In the hall below, the grand clock chimes the hour loudly, echoing in my ears. I find myself sway, but my hand automatically finds the wood of the banister and grips it tightly. When the last of the chimes fade, I force myself to open my eyes once more.

There is no Aiko Shinya, there, just as there was no Taris.

There is only Soren, who looks up at me with great concern.

"Captain?" he says. "I think this journey of yours has taken a toll on everyone. Perhaps you should rest for a spell."

"No, no. I have work to do," I insist. "Where did the king go?"

"He is looked after well, Captain Marson," Soren insists. "But I won't take you to him until you at least make yourself presentable. In two hours, after you've taken care of yourself, I will take you to the king."

I narrow my eyes at him, fully aware of how much authority he has over me. I am only the captain of the king's guard, and Soren is a prince. Whatever he says is precisely what he has the authority to make happen. I suppose Soren could order worse than my recuperation.

"Two hours," I warn. "No more."

Soren smiles. "Of course, Captain Marson. Of course."

I swear, one might think he was up to something.

I cannot force myself to sleep, even for a short time, but I do clean up and change into a proper uniform for the Summer Palace. This one has been modified, as we are in residence during the winter, but still holds enough appropriate embellishment for me to meet the weight my title carries. Qhan will have to appear the same way, given his notoriety, though Korvaan and Valor have more flexibility. They are less well-known to the public.

For me to travel the palace and potentially the city with Soren, however, some prestige is necessary. Anything else may be seen as an insult. Fate knows the last thing Rian and I need is to slight the Carsans. Soren may be reasonable, but his parents are not.

The young grand prince arrives just as I am pulling on my gloves. He surprises me by walking with his canes instead of using his chair. He has excused Kaoli as well, leaving him without an aid. I am tempted to offer him my arm, but am unsure whether he would find the gesture insulting. He is not a child anymore, and he outranks me.

My conundrum is only made worse when he acknowledges, "The king went into the city to meet with Magnus. And, I suspect, to let the people see him. They need something to believe in, now."

I frown. "You'd have us go out to meet them?"

I try to remain as unspecific as possible so it is unclear why I see this as an issue, but Soren is too smart for that.

"Don't worry. You can walk," Soren says. "It isn't far. I'll take Bludcawl, as not to slow us down."

"If you please, grand prince," I say slowly.

It is a solution, yes, but it means we will not be traveling discreetly.

Soren's griffon, Bludcawl, is highly affectionate towards her master and is almost always prowling about him protectively. I'm sure the only reason I haven't seen her yet is because Soren didn't want to scare Teresa's children, as griffons are not easy to tame, but he has a natural talent with animals of any nature, including magical.

I still remember the first time Bludcawl met Mango, which we all assumed would have disastrous results. Much to everyone's surprise, though the two at first had no idea what to do with one another, Bludcawl eventually realized what an idiot Mango can be and unofficially adopted him like he was one of her own. Even now, while Mango is considered relatively middle-aged for a sunblood dragon, Bludcawl has the tendency to treat him like a pup.

We don't speak as Soren and I make our way to the pen where Bludcawl is comfortably kept when Soren doesn't need her. I do my best not to be obvious in how I curb my usually quick stride.

I'm not sure what continually pushes Soren to overexert himself, whether it be his parents, public reaction, or personal frustration. All I know is Ayla, at least, would be furious. If there's pressure being put on him, it isn't from her.

Soren is breathing hard by the time we reach Bludcawl but I don't say anything. There is an attendant holding the griffon's reins at the ready, and a saddle has already been strapped on, so I do not need to worry about Soren doing it himself. I do not offer to help him climb onto her back, either, as Soren has been doing this on his own for years. I would help only if he begins to struggle, and otherwise let him keep his dignity.

The griffon herself nudges him up with her nose, like he is considered one of her fledglings along with Mango. While I'm not sure if this is the right way for me to handle the situation, at least I haven't insulted him.

I should probably be striving for something better than that.

I'm admittedly uncomfortable with the amount of people around as Soren takes me out of the Summer Palace and into the city. Even if I had not grown used to the solitude of the Pyrian Palace over the past few weeks, the city here feels more bloated than usual. The weather is less than ideal, yet the streets are packed with people scuttering from task to task, faces drawn, heads covered. It makes my general sense of irritation grow with every accidental brush and hastily squeaked apology. I wish it was not so easy to recognize me and Soren on sight.

It is strange, and yet still telling, that I'm certain we are close to Magnus and Rian simply based on the reactions of those around. They walk straighter, with brighter faces and eyes. It is incredible what that a single man can do without a fluke relating to emotions: he can still spread his lightheartedness to anyone he meets. Even if it has put on, and he does not feel it, he'll do his best for the sake of what others need.

We find Magnus and the king outside of the city's great cathedral, near the top of the steps. They are off to the side near the railing of an extended portico, so that they are not obstructing the entry way to the cathedral, but it does not matter. Given their blockade of guards at the bottom of the steps and surrounding the area, no one is getting into the cathedral at this time. Rian is facing out and away from the steps with Magnus by his side. They are obviously deep in serious discussion, yet Rian maintains a smile and waves cheerfully to anyone who calls up to him.

Having Soren take Bludcawl at least makes it clear we are approaching, and Magnus's extensive guard let us pass readily. Rian is facing away, and does not see us, though I receive many nods of respect from his guards. For Soren, they bow. Qhan and Griffith Reach, Magnus' most stalwart bodyguard, stand back so we can approach.

Magnus ignores us completely. Rian flicks his eyes at us, and I see a flash there that tells me he is glad I've come. But he holds a finger up for us to wait.

"As you can see, the refugee crisis is at its capacity," Magnus says.

I can see Rian thinking. "Are there people waiting for placement?"

"Not currently, but there will be soon," Magnus says. "Isaaria cannot possibly support the people fleeing to our borders. They are coming from all over Samioth, because they know there is no war here."

"Is there nowhere else left in the world for them to go?" Rian asks, horrified by the idea.

"No place as free and safe as Isaaria," Magnus admits. "The church has helped look after many of the refugees, but again, your majesty. It is only a matter of time before this becomes a problem."

Rian nods. "I need to see as many foreign ambassadors as possible," he says. "The world cannot be left to simply smolder. Let us see what we can do about our former allies and rebuilding economies. Magnus, I'd look through the refugees and see if any of them want to assist. I'm sure there are more than a few of them who want to rebuild their homes, not settle permanently here. Ask around and tell me what you find."

I know this is unlikely to happen, at least before Septimus and I turn our timeline back again. But I appreciate that Rian is still determined to make a change in our current world.

"There aren't many foreign ambassadors left to speak to," Magnus warns.

"Then make a public statement on my behalf," Rian instructs. "Have it broadcasted that I would like to revive the positions. Not in person; not at a time like this. But we need to establish communication."

"I doubt we'll get any response from Tourran or Kacha."

"Leave that to me," Rian says. "Captain Marson and her cousin plan to head east on a mission for me. If they can, they will be interacting with the remnants of state in both countries. See if we can't salvage them."

This is news to me, but it is clear Rian has not been sitting idle after Septimus' revelation. He will need an excuse, at least for the grand princes, as to why he is sending his own Captain Marson to the east. But with an important mission, one that requires absolute trust and professionalism, no one will think twice as to why Rian is sending me.

Magnus raises an eyebrow. "Her cousin? The albino?"

Word travels fast. I suppose if Rian was going to trust any of the grand princes with his plans, Magnus is the obvious choice. Nissa already knows much as well, after all. Soren, too.

"Septimus knows people in the east," I lie, stepping up and bowing. "Your majesty. Prince Soren agreed to escort me. I believe you wanted to see me?"

This is not entirely true. I wanted to see Rian. Besides, I'm sure he's tired of handling Magnus' temperament for over an hour. Magnus means well, but he can be blunt, and somewhat disagreeable.

I see a corner of Magnus' mouth twitch in a smirk. I'm not sure what he thinks I'm here for.

"I see I'm out of time," he says cryptically, and bows. "Your majesty. I will take my leave. That announcement will be sent out directly after Holrith."

"A good idea. Thank you," Rian says.

Magnus leaves, giving me a strange, sideways look that I do not appreciate. Half the guard and Griffith go with him. The other half stay, presumably to protect both the king and Soren.

"Your majesty," I greet, and bow to Rian as anyone would expect me to.

Rian lets his lip curl up. "Oh, don't," he complains. "I'm going to be bombarded with such mockery every quarter hour for the next few days."

"I believe it is a sign of respect," I correct, but straighten. "Now, shall we escort you back to the Summer Palace?"

"Actually, Captain, there's something else that requires your attention," Soren interrupts. "Yours and his majesty's. If you would come with me?"

I would be suspicious if it were anyone but Soren, and I can tell from Rian's general aura, and the smile successfully fighting its way across his face, that this is not something entirely unplanned. The king is aware of this mysterious business, and possibly planned it. I am not naïve enough not to realize this is some surprise on my behalf, though I'm curious what it is.

Soren dismounts from Bludcawl, this time accepting assistance from Qhan. Allowing Soren to lead us means knowing our destination before we enter, and I am ashamed to admit it takes me the entire time outside the cathedral to realize what business Rian and I might have there.

Inside the cathedral is completely empty, which is unusual. There is almost always a handful of folks inside, praying or adoring, even when there is no mass at the time. I suppose it would make sense to clear the area with the king so close by, but we Isaarians are rather hesitant to interfere with the spiritual for our fellow citizens. There is even an old joke about hiring an Isaarian assassin and their refusal to eliminate targets on a holy day which, dependent on how serious the hypothetical assassin is about the Theebin religion, could honestly account for the majority of days in a year.

A moment later and I realize I was incorrect in my original assessment; the cathedral is not completely empty. Waiting inside for us, hovering near the doorway in one of her prettiest dresses and holding a crown she has made from winter flowers, is Ayla. Most of our guards we have left outside, but we've Qhan and Soren and one of Soren's bodyguards. I'm sure there are men of the church around close by as well.

"Oh, good," Ayla says. "You are perfectly on-time. You could not have convinced her to wear something prettier, though, could you?"

"Sorry, princess," Soren says, and takes Ayla's hand to kiss it. "But you should know how Captain Marson is. At least she is wearing the sash."

I narrow my eyes.

"What's this about?"

I already know, but I have to ask.

Rian's smiling. "Soleil. Would you marry me?"

I'm shocked. It's one thing to ask me in private, with all that has happened between us. It's another to do so now; it makes everything feel more real.

"Well. Well, yes," I manage to say. "I already told you that."

"Good," Rian says, and takes the flower crown from Ayla to slip it on my head. "Because we're doing it now."

"Surprise," Ayla says.

It is with less enthusiasm than I know she could usually muster, but I can still see a genuineness in her smile. She and Soren had undoubtedly planned this with Rian, though I'm not sure how; as far as I've seen, the three of them have all kept busy and in separate spheres.

Rian is still grinning when I look at him.

"You told Magnus," I accuse.

He shrugs. "Well, I had to. At least two of the grand princes need to know, for legal purposes. So, he and Soren are aware, but the rest of the grand princes do not. I figured that was the best way to go about things."

"I would have preferred Nissa," I claim.

It is not entirely truthful. I could not care less which of the grand princes Rian chose, I am simply trying to find something to complain about.

"You said we didn't have time," Rian says somewhat smugly, "and that was the only restriction. And so: I made some time."

"Funny, I thought that was my wheelhouse."

"Ha. Get over here, wife. We are getting married."

"Technically, this is elopement."

But I don't refuse to take his arm, so we may walk up together.

Our wedding party is small, and the ceremony is without a mass, so it is not long, but it is legitimate. Rian and I are both given certain sacraments to ensure we enter into our marriage in a state of grace, to fulfill the church's requirements. Afterwards, Soren has us sign the necessary papers to confirm the marriage legally, for the state's requirements. With his knowledge and Magnus', and our small number of witnesses, I become queen of Isaaria once more by the laws of man and God.

It is not an especially memorable ceremony in terms of function: we have done this before many times, now, with larger audiences and grander style. Perhaps it is the simplicity instead that makes our actions and words mean more to me. There is nothing to distract me or Rian from one another. Even if we are wed again, more formally, in a final timeline, Septimus has suggested we may, this will be the time I look back on:

When I am forty-sixth—no, forty-seventh year, as of today, actually—and no longer as young or as pretty as I've ever managed to be.

When I am well aware of the hundreds of years Rian and I have spent together.

When we marry both knowing that perhaps it means nothing, and we will need to do it all over again, but do it anyway.

We do not allow ourselves to exchange signs of physical affection once we have left the cathedral, particularly after we have gathered the rest of the guard and begun the trek back up to the palace. However, given my position, I stay close to Rian's side. Now and again, he will flick his eyes over at me and smile. Ayla hangs back to where Soren is, on Bludcawl. She is not particularly talkative, compared to how she was before Amerson's arrival, but she seems happier than this morning. Despite having been friends with Soren since childhood, she is shy around him, now.

There is an unspoken agreement between us all to walk slowly. It is twilight, with most folk bundled inside as the temperatures drop and a chilly wind whispers through the streets. Neither Rian nor I are cold enough to hurry past such a moment, though. Regardless of what happens over the next few days, in our walk back to the Summer Palace is when we are married in the word's purest definition.

We shed most of the guard once we have reached the palace, climbing back up the steps to the top entrance. I almost miss Magnus waiting just inside the doorway, with Griffith. The moment he sees the king safe, he peels off to disappear inside, as if dreading an interaction. We hover there, for a moment, as Soren is helped down and gives Bludcawl a pat on the nose.

"I suppose no one would find it particularly unusual if my captain helped escort me to the royal suite," Rian says, pretending to think hard on it.

"I'm sure I have no idea what you mean, your majesty," I say.

Rian grins.

"By chance," Qhan says, "it appears neither of you will be needed much tomorrow morning."

"A fortuitous coincidence, I'm sure," I say.

"I'll look after the Smiths, especially the boys, in case they need anything for the rest of today and tomorrow morning," Ayla reassures. "Soren is taking care of everything else."

"You will have your wedding dinner in the king's suite," Soren rattles off, "I've arranged it discreetly, so it is not traditional fare, but allowed the king to choose what he thought the two of you would most enjoy. Qurvo and Khaleem know, and have agreed to manage the rest of the guard in your absence, as well as keep the information from spreading. Prince Magnus likewise will handle things politically. And I will manage the household."

"You sound a little too pleased about this scenario, Prince Carsans," I say.

Soren smiles. "It will be good to have a queen again."

I force myself to smile back, and ignore the cynicism that insists it does not matter; not in the way Soren believes it will. Still, I decide to allow myself tonight, to pretend as if I am still ignorant of my own abilities, and of Septimus' plan. Free from the knowledge of eventualities, I will spend one night as if I am queen of Isaaria, and then I will do what I know I must.

I tell myself it will not be a burden. After all, Rian is not the only one I love.

Qhan and I escort Rian upstairs. Despite evidence to the contrary in how ordinarily we are treated, I'm sure our actions are somehow spelled across my face. I suppose even I do not know if I'm blushing. Any rosiness could be excused by the frosty air outside.

We are utterly unceremonious: outside the door, Qhan bows, bides us good night, and leaves us, noting the usual guard will be on rotation. Rian enters first, and I follow into the king's suite, feeling a strange light-headedness at the many memories I have.

The antechamber has a fire lit for us already in the hearth, with fur rugs and two cushioned chairs awaiting, but that is standard fare. Those chairs have always been here, and there are always a number of furs, not particularly chosen for a pair of people instead of one. Beyond that, there is a second fire lit in the bedroom. I can hear Mango making small snuffling noises as he eats his supper.

This feels strangely of home.

"Ugh," Rian says and sniffles, "I almost forgot how cold it was until I had true warmth to compare it to."

He unlaces his boots, sheds his outer coat, and wanders off to find his closet, and a mannequin to hang it on. There would be attendants to assist him, traditionally, but Rian has always been known to dismiss them in the evenings, particularly when something has kept him up late. The hour is not unreasonable, now, but as king, I don't suppose he needs a reason.

I perch in one of the chairs to take off my own boots and catch a glimpse of myself in the glass covering the picture above the fireplace. It is a highly detailed mural, depicting the founding of New Isaaria, the Theebin religion, notable Isaarian figures and saints. It is equal parts beautiful, gruesome, and famous, and my red-tipped-nose visage is a laughable addition.

I pull faces in the reflection and watch my scar rearrange itself. When Rian slips back into the room, his outer coat and boots stowed away, it startles me.

"Amusing yourself?" he asks.

I find a pillow to throw at him. "Shut up. I've caught you doing the same."

"True, true," he allows. "Now, why don't you take off your coat and stay a while. And let us see about some dinner, shall we?"

While I undo the buttons of my surcoat, he rolls up his sleeves before crossing behind me to the sideboard. There is a tray waiting there, with dinner for the both of us. A metal dome keeps it warm, though it can't have been waiting long. There is enough heat in the food for the spice to hit the roof of my mouth from across the room: excellent.

I make him let me test the food for poison first. I catch him rolling his eyes when he thinks I'm not looking, but he doesn't complain. He does not say anything, either, when it turns out the food is all clean.

Soren was right to say this would not be a traditional Isaarian wedding dinner, but it is delicious all the same. The vegetables are cooked Isaarian style despite the recipe's Kachin flavors, which is to say they are cut very small and barely heated to maintain a pleasant crunch. I taste chili, garlic, and green onions in the broth; an excellent choice on Rian's part, as I'm quite fond of garlic and beef, and I know he likes his noodles. It's yet another reminder that he really does know me inside and out.

There is wine as well. We indulge in that significantly.

We sit on the floor in front of the fire, wrap ourselves in the furs and take our time with dinner. For the first half of the meal, there is nothing to say, until Rian begins an innocent game of "do you remember" that slowly grows less and less innocent over time. I overeat, especially considering the poor diet we experienced while traveling, but the dish is too pleasant to resist.

"Today was long," I admit while finishing the last of the food. "Yet it feels as if not much has happened."

"That's rather expected for weddings, I think," Rian says, and deftly slides himself over so he can sit with an arm around my shoulders.

"…I can't tell if my memories of us doing this are truly memories, or the worst parts of my imagination," I admit.

Rian laughs. "Worst? Should I be insulted?"

"You know what I mean," I say.

For a few moments, we let the fire speak. We lean against one another. My head fits well against his shoulder, and it is a familiar resting place. Rian plays with my hair with one hand. I think there is a certain intimacy in near-stillness, and silence, and we have found it. We could spend hours sitting like that, and I would not notice the time passing. At some point, I close my eyes, and though I do not fall asleep, I am able to think of nothing at all. I believe that is something Nusk would be proud of me for finally achieving.

"Soleil," Rian whispers after a long time. "Soleil, Soleil, Soleil."

"Mmm." I open my eyes. "What?"

"Nothing. I love your name, Soleil. 'Soleil' is sufficiently sensual."

His last two 's' sounds whistle in my ear and nearly send me into a fit of youthful giggles that normally would not suit me. It's been a long time since I've heard him purposefully use alliteration. I forgot how much I enjoy it.

He silences me with a kiss. I prop myself back up on a hand and kiss him back, until we wordlessly agree to stop.

"I want to do everything for the rest of my life with you," he says. "You are my best friend. You understand me. You curb my more stupid decisions. And I think we can face the dangers of the world together."

"Mmm, those are good reasons," I say.

"Yes, they are."

He kisses the tip of my nose, which is still cold. Then, surprising me, he stands, stretches, and yawns.

"Right, then," he says. "Sleep. We'll sort out breakfast in the morning."

"That's all?" I say, and refuse his offered hand.

"What's what."

"We're not going to fool around?" I say, raising an eyebrow.

Rian blinks. "I thought we'd both be tired. It's been a long day, you said."

"Is that a no, then?"

He considers this. For long enough that I am able to take in his expression and remember how much I've enjoyed watching him think; in his study, pouring over books, muttering to himself and Mango. It is only a matter of seconds, of course, before Rian grins and breaks the spell. Before I can stop him, he pulls me up to my feet and then straight over a shoulder to walk into the bedroom.

"You are going to injure your back," I chide him.

"You're not *that* heavy."

I hit his shoulder. He smacks me back.

The bed is high up enough and large enough that even after he's thrown me down and climbed up himself, Rian and I are hardly in the middle of it.

"This thing is ridiculous," I say as we move.

"I know. Sleeping alone in it feels like a waste," he agrees.

We settle down in a spot with the best pillows and return to our previously scheduled activity. It turns out that wine, kissing, and laughing are well-suited companions. Our sashes get flung over the side of the bed without a care. Rian works his own stockings off with only his toes and then gets to work on mine—again, using only his own feet. It is a very laughable experience. I remember how much I love the feel of his hair as I gently pick the ornaments out and let them get lost on the mattress.

At some point, I realize his hands are on the tie that laces the entire front of my jacket together, closed up from waist to collar.

He takes a moment for us both to consider everything. It's strange, but I think my heart is pounding faster than it ever has before in my life. I can hear every single sound as the bedcovers crinkle and rustle beneath us. I wonder if Rian is taking note of my breathing the same way I'm so intently listening to his.

"May I?" he says.

"Yes," I say. But then instantly think of something better and catch his hands before he can start. "Yours off first."

Rian grins, and obliges me. He always obliges me, I realize.

There are times I think he is too good for me, yet I agree with precisely what he said earlier. I, too, feel as if I can face the rest of the world with Rian. I believe we will do well raising our children together and I want that future.

We are kissing again. As always, there is much happening in my mind.

"You were very impressive with the Fae," I say between kisses.

"Mmm. I know."

"I love how gentle you always are. Until you know not to be."

"I know that, too."

"It makes me feel safe with you," I admit haltingly.

There is some embarrassment in admitting it, but Rian is the only person I could say it to. As confident as I am, there is a part of me that wants someone else looking after me, as much as I have vowed to look after my king.

"Good," Rian simply says.

And he leans down to kiss the scar on my face. My ability to admit such a thing is one benefit to come out of everything this timeline has put us through.

"Fate's! ...Fingers!" Rian suddenly yelps.

"What?"

"That's Mango," he says, scrunching his nose. "Mango has crawled on my calf and scared me half to death."

I must laugh, because I suspect we both completely forgot about poor Mango. Intelligent though the little dragon may be, I doubt he understands what Rian and I were getting up to. Or, he does not understand why his company on the bed would not be appreciated at this time. After all, he has curled up on Rian's pillow for years.

"I think we'll have to shut him in the king's washroom," Rian whispers.

"Bit rude."

"Yes, but so was his intrusion."

"Will he be all right in there?"

"He's an old man. He'll complain for a minute, then curl up on the bathmat and take a nap."

I consider this.

"It seems there is no other reasonable option. Take the interloper out," I say seriously.

"Right, then: dragon extraction."

Rian rolls off the bed, deftly scooping Mango up and striding towards the washroom almost ceremoniously. Mango is pleased at first, but then seems to realize he has not been picked up for cuddling and starts to wriggle. Outside the washroom door, Rian brings the little dragon close up to his face, as if to stare him down and get a point across.

"You are not invited to this party," he warns Mango gravely.

Mango whines and licks Rian's nose. I laugh.

"Nice try. Get in, you pervert," Rian says, and deposits Mango unceremoniously in the washroom, quickly closing the door behind him.

True to form, instead of whining and scratching at the door like a younger Mango might, the dragon only patters around the tiled floor for a moment before finding the bathmat and settling in.

Rian takes a few jogging steps back to the bed, jumps up near the foot of it, and somersaults over before flopping himself back next to me.

"I am as graceful as a youth," he claims triumphantly.

"You are going to hurt your back," I warn him again.

"Even Fate knows wedding nights are holy exceptions; nothing bad is allowed to happen, and nothing is allowed to interrupt."

"Someone forgot to tell Mango, then."

"I suppose that might have been me. Now, come here: that jacket has been annoying me," he says.

He finally manages to get all the buttons undone without interruption aside from that of his own kissing and then goes directly to untuck my blouse. I almost let him, too, before an idea occurs to me.

"Ah," I say, grabbing his hands to stop him. "Yours first."

Eleven

RIAN AND I skip breakfast and sleep until about noon. We do make sure Mango's comfortable, at some point, but he spends the night in a corner of the king's washroom to give us some privacy, and we use the queen's washroom for our own purposes. As well as allowing him to manage household matters, Rian has delegated his authority to Soren for the morning, which Soren is delighted about, seeing it as a proper challenge.

I think he is pleasantly surprised that Rian has not revoked his title as steward to the Summer Palace. With the king in residence, the title means less than it would otherwise, but the ceremonial importance of it remains.

The Carsans still have not formally named Soren their heir, despite him being their only living child. Rian honors him more than his own parents, and I cannot be the only person to notice this.

Soren's ambition and sense of duty allows Rian and I to spend many lazy hours together, even beyond when we have fully woken and should have risen from bed. Rian enjoys playing with my fingers, and I amuse myself with his hair. It is not quite as silky as it was in his more youthful years, but I am pleased to find he is in no way yet balding.

It makes me smug on his behalf.

What is more difficult for me, but just as necessary, is when Rian asks me to join him in Theebin meditation. I am hesitant, and uncomfortable with the idea mainly because I believe I will be dreadful at it. After all, I could barely manage the clearing of mind that Nusk asked me to do, from a non-Theebin standpoint, let alone enter a prayerful meditation to a god I hope is real. I worry privately we will go east only to find there is no Otherworld, no Almighty, no seven angels to praise him and look after us.

I do join Rian all the same. I do try. Rian is much better at it, and does not pry into what I am thinking, though he does give advice. He tells me to try things slowly. To give myself only a quarter hour, to start. He uses a passage from a Theebin Bible, reads some to himself, then sits and contemplates.

I try to list things I am grateful for. I do not feel particularly inspired by anything, which does make me feel some guilt, but I suppose I must accept the fact I am not going to be good at everything.

Meditation, Theebin or otherwise, was always a struggle for me.

"I think you should have Teresa accompany you to dinner this evening," I say suddenly, once Rian has put his book away and comes back to sit on the bed with me. "Escort her in, that is. And we'll have Septimus escort Ayla. To be proper about it."

"I think I'll escort *you*," Rian says, in that tone of his that tells me he expects to get exactly what he wants.

I roll my eyes at him. "Don't be ridiculous."

"I'm not," he insists, and kisses my shoulder. "I'm Rian."

"You're impossible."

"No," he grins. "Still Rian."

I break his grip on me to climb out of the bed and start retrieving pieces of my uniform. I will need to change into a different version for tonight's dinner, with the finest of trappings and ceremonial décor, but we unfortunately did not have the foresight to move any more of my clothes into Rian's rooms last night. Hopefully I can casually make my way to my own room and change without garnering suspicion. My hair has dried after washing late in the night, at least, so that will help my subterfuge.

It is a mild relief to remind myself I've been in the king's chambers many times in the past without talk circulating. So long as I play my part, and Rian does not give us away, no one should have reason to question my presence.

"Are you sure you can't stay longer?" Rian asks.

"Not if I want to avoid your attendants when they come looking to prepare their king for the evening's events," I remind him.

He groans and rolls onto his side to watch me without rising himself.

I pull on my gloves and fasten the clasps on my uniform's front. I can feel Rian looking at it disdainfully, but we agreed to keep our union a secret, for now. No use in upsetting the public at such a time. I know he wants me dressed to suit my new position all the same, and yet, he must know people would ask questions if Captain Marson suddenly appeared at dinner in a queen's gown. Besides, I'm convinced that I would look ridiculous.

Though I'd rather not leave yet, I know one of us has to be responsible about this. We've indulged ourselves; now we've duties to see to.

Or, more accurately, I've duties I would like to see to. Rian has finally climbed out of bed to trap me in his arms and refuse to let me go despite a gentle nudge and chiding.

"I have something for you. A gift," he says before I can start in on a lecture. "If you won't wear the proper trappings of a queen, I hope you at least will wear this."

He lets me turn around, my interest clearly piqued, and he knows he's got me. Rian lets go to rummage around in a desk drawer.

"What kind of gift?" I ask suspiciously.

I can feel his grin across the room, even with his back turned away. I know him so well, and he knows me, which is why I am curious. Surely Rian knows there is no piece of jewelry I could wear as his captain that would not draw suspicion.

He finds the desired item and keeps it hidden away in a small blue velvet box until he has returned to me. I reach for the box and he whisks it back for a second, teasing, before finally allowing me to take it. Upon opening, I find nestled inside a golden pocket watch, with the sun etched beautifully amidst Yakarami climbing jasmine. Its chain will clip to my jacket securely, practically, and it will fit inside a pocket snugly.

"This is beautiful," I say, turning it over in my hands.

"It is to keep track of the time, of course," he says. "Which is something that holds a certain significance for us, doesn't it?"

I smile. "Time for us, a sun for me, the jasmine for you."

"A sun for 'Soleil'," he agrees, making his "s" sounds whistle again.

I gather the chain and watch up together and keep them held tightly in my hand. Rian knows to step closer to me so I can stretch up and kiss him.

"Thank you," I say, and let him wrap his arms around me again for a moment. "I shall carry it with me the entirety of my journeying."

"...Soleil," he whispers. "Please be careful."

"I always am," I start, but he interrupts.

"No. You are careful with your job, protecting me. Protecting Ayla. You are rarely careful with yourself."

I do not know what to say to this, because based on the memories I have, he is not wrong. Often, I am prepared to throw myself into great danger, foolishly and impulsively even, with the confidence no harm could possibly come to me. Many times, I have fretted over Rian or Ayla, but always assumed my own well-being and survival.

A sigh escapes; as Nusk would say, this reaction is likely some sort of flaw in my manner of thinking. Ironically, perhaps in a real *Khashtani* it would be a virtue, but not in a surrogate daughter, and not in a queen.

"I promise, then," I swear. "I will be careful."

Rian still looks displeased. He leans back to perch on the side of the bed and I step forward so we can see eye-to-eye. His hands feel cold in mine.

"I don't want you to leave and go east," he says, quieter. "I know, I know: I don't get a say in the matter. I don't get a choice. I just don't want you leaping off to the ends of the earth while I..."

"Sit back on your hands and do nothing?"

"Well, yes."

"I know it must be maddening," I say. I brush a strand of his hair back. "But you're wrong: you're my husband, you should get a say in the matter."

Rian's brow is furrowed. It exacerbates the wrinkles I could otherwise ignore in his face, and I wish I could smooth them away.

"Then I'm saying it: I don't want you going with Septimus east while I stay here and worry and pace and do nothing useful at all. I know you can protect yourself, Soleil, I've seen you. You're more than capable. But I want to be there for you. I want to be the one to watch out for you because I don't know enough about Septimus to trust he can do it. I hate the idea of staying here and doing nothing while my wife risks her life. Again."

"You're not doing nothing," I insist. "You'll be king of Isaaria."

"And so on, and so on. I know you could counter my every argument and make sense of things, so I suppose I'm saying I don't care. I still don't want you to leave. I don't want to lose you," he admits. "I love you, Soleil."

"I love you, too," I admit. "And I do not want to lose *you*. That is why I must do this. I have to trust Septimus, and venture out on this quest of his. I may not like it, either, but it is only way."

He reaches for my free hand again to tug me forward. He gives me another kiss, but on the forehead, as if granting a blessing. His permission to go forth and do as Fate would will on this quest. Though, he still holds on to me for a few more moments, and I let him. I want to tell him that I don't want to leave, either; that I would rather stay here and see what the future holds with him. After all, we have gotten this far, and the Greys cannot win without killing him.

Why not live the rest of our lives, here, together, for as long as we can?

It is knowing the guilt I will live with over Lune and Taris that convinces me I would be happy for only a matter of days. Even the briefest of glimpses ahead is enough to predict a refugee crisis, wars, and who knows what else.

If that is the world we'd live in, I don't want that anyway.

"I'm going to go manage the assignments for your guard, while I'm away," I say. "After, I'm going to see to the Smiths. Make certain they are ready for dinner."

"You're not dining with us," Rian says in disappointment.

"You know I cannot. But I will stand at my post."

I can feel his displeasure. He sulks the same way Mango does.

"I'll eat a late supper in here later tonight with your company, before bed," I offer, and that at least brightens his spirits some. "If you promise to escort Teresa and don't complain."

"You make me sound so whiny," he complains. Irony.

"You are. Now, be nice to my cousins. Teresa is nervous enough around you."

"Oh, ah, wait: Septimus and Teresa," he remembers as I reach the door.

"What about them."

"They know, too."

I throw my gaze up to the hand-painted silver gilt paper on the ceiling.

"Of course, they do. Who doesn't know?" I complain.

Rian chooses to defend himself, not answer. "I thought I should speak with the only known blood family of yours around before I stole you away for the Yakarami clan. For the record, Septimus granted his permission."

"He had no right to give it," I sniff imperiously.

Yet secretly, I am pleased. It feels culturally significant and traditional; a real wedding for us. We have had several them before in other lives, yes, but it is different. Those feel like watery dreams, now, but this time, it is real. This time, after so many tests and trials, there can never be a doubt in my mind again that Rian loves me, and I love him.

We will endure, because we were meant to, and because we can.

"For the record, Ayla gave her permission for me to marry you as well," Rian adds, teasing.

"Of that I was aware," I say.

I leave Rian's rooms and walk as properly as possible on my way back to my own rooms. The palace staff acknowledge me with respect, as do Rian's guards, but no one is surprised to see me. In fact, when I alert his attendants to his rising, I am thanked, as if it has been assumed Rian slept late and I entered only to rouse him as it is known only I can.

Part of me nearly deviates early from my path, to see Ayla, but I decide to refrain. Excited as we may both be to find ourselves in a family, it likely would be uncomfortable if she realizes I'm in the same clothing as yesterday.

In my own rooms, I wash my face, discard yesterday's clothes, and pull together the components of my most ceremonial uniform: underclothes, blouse, trousers with the two gold stripes, double breasted jacket with a flare at the hips and the delicate gold ornaments, sash stitched with the jasmine and dragon of the Yakarami's crest. I secure a broach at my throat and re-braid my hair before pinning it back professionally. I am tempted to have it sheared, as it would likely be more practical in the coming weeks, but I am pleased with my hair's length.

I take the time to sit and lace up my boots—these are formal boots, with a higher heel, rarely worn and still stiff, so they require a boot hook to assist. I have actually begun to overheat by the time I've finished and need to tuck a few stray hairs into place before I leave.

My afternoon is not exceptional; I meet with Korvaan, Qhan, Valor, and Vilaneau separately to arrange matters of security while I'm away. I keep to

Rian's excuse about a diplomatic mission east when asked, and remind myself to tell Septimus the same. I allow Vilaneau to try his hand at scheduling the king's guard rotation for a number of days in the coming week and check it over, pinpointing to him any errors and acknowledging correct choices.

I also take the opportunity to study several maps and the last diplomatic messages we received from the Aiko family before Tourran and Kacha erupted into war, and we heard no more from them. It is still peculiar, trying to reconcile my image of a young Aiko Shinya with what I know of him from Teresa. I could even, possibly, convince myself it was merely a wandering ronin using Shinya's name, except he also showed Teresa his fluke.

Despite my general stubbornness when it comes to all things spiritual, and feeling somewhat embarrassed, I offer a silent prayer that I might somehow find Shinya in the east. It is impossible, I know, but I pray all the same.

Ayla is not in her rooms when I stop by, which is surprising considering the hour. I'm told when I inquire that she dressed for the evening early and then went on a walk in the winter gardens. At first, I assume she took Damen and Aiden out with her, to give Teresa some time alone, but I am informed otherwise.

So, I make my way to my cousins' suite instead, as time ticks down to their dinner with the grand princes and princesses of Isaaria.

Teresa bids me to enter immediately after my knock. As I do, two maids who must have helped her into her dress exit, curtsying. Inside, Damen is sitting curled on the window seat with a large book open in his lap. Aiden clamors around his mother. Both boys are wearing new clothes suited to the fancy occasion, though I can see these as well have been modified from some of Alo Pike's old clothes.

Teresa stands before the full-length mirror wearing one of the dresses Rian had made for her, with puff sleeves falling off her shoulders and beautiful pale blue fabric. The dress is cut under her breasts with a thick ribbon, and has enough skirts puffed outward away from her to not entirely conceal her pregnancy, but flatter her changing figure.

Though they are merely cousins, she looks startlingly like a young Lune. Lune always did like to wear blue. Though her costumes were usually of a darker hue and spangled with galaxies, there is still an unquestionable resemblance. Teresa shares Lune's hair color and the family blue eyes, her cool-toned skin and slim frame.

"What do you think, your majesty?" Teresa asks, curtsying to me when she notices my presence.

She twirls in the dress much to Aiden's delight. He likes seeing the skirts flare out spectacularly. Even after she has stopped to stand and look at herself in the mirror again, Aiden sits on the floor and plays with the fabric.

"You look lovely," I say.

"Please remind me to thank the king for such fine dresses," she says in that quiet voice of hers, smoothing down the front of her skirt.

"Surely you are accustomed to such a thing," I note.

"Yet, this is both beautiful and comfortable. And I owe him nothing for it," she adds. That second point is clearly more significant to her.

A light knock comes at the side door and Septimus is bid to enter just as Teresa sits before the vanity. She immediately begins to see to the pinning of her own hair and rouging of her cheeks. She has already applied a powder to help hide her bruising. The glasses Rian acquired for her sit on the vanity and, occasionally, she will don them only to see herself better, fuss with her appearance, and take them off again. She must squint without them, but the lenses make her eyes look smaller.

I wonder if it is habit not to wear them, or her vanity at play. I'd previously assumed the former but now I'm not so sure.

"Captain," Septimus says, and gives me a short bow that I believe is of genuine nature for once.

He bends to ruffle Aiden's hair as he passes to stand behind his sister. Teresa catches sight of him in the mirror and looks him over.

"Isaarian fashion suits you," she says.

"And you. Though your cheeks are pale. Are you certain you are up to this?" Septimus asks, rubbing his sister's shoulders nervously. "You can always say you were not feeling well. No one would mind. We are hardly important figures, here, anyways; the princes might be disappointed they couldn't meet you, but they'll forget quickly I'm sure—"

"Sep, it's fine," Teresa interrupts him, and puts a hand up to still one of his. "I'm feeling well, I promise. Besides, it would be best for us to go, confront them all, and put our story together properly. So that we know the lies we are keeping to."

Septimus looks shocked to hear her say so, for a moment, but then nods to himself and removes his hands. He steps back.

"Of course," he says. "Of course."

She slips a pair of earrings in her ears that Rian must have gifted her.

"You lead the way," she says, tilting her head just so. "And I'll endeavor to keep up with the general idea of it. Perhaps sticking to the truth as much as possible would be best."

"I would agree," Septimus murmurs.

"Though I think we should not mention Kryto by name," she says. "And be careful of what we say in front of the boys. As always."

"Actually, Teresa, the boys will be eating with the other children. The young sons and daughters, nieces, and nephews of the grand princes," I say.

"Oh?" she says, and her hands stay for a moment in fixing a wayward curl of hair. "Well. I suppose they may take the opportunity to make new… friends."

There is a lingering question in her voice; she is unsure if such a thing is possible or not. But there is hope, too, in the fact that she would say so at all.

"I'm sure they will settle in. For one, their mother looks right at home, here," I say.

She twists a hairpin into her hair and arranges the loose strands elegantly against her neck. I cannot help but imagine her having to do so for one of her husband's revelries. Apparently, she is thinking similarly.

"I've prepared for fanciful dinner parties before, Captain," Teresa admits. "Though usually I had attendants to help me, I still remember how to make myself presentable before royalty. Or, before those who would consider themselves as such."

I clear my throat and check my pocket-watch gift from Rian.

"The king would like to escort you in to dinner," I tell Teresa, changing the subject abruptly.

"That's fine," she says. "And appropriate, I believe."

She is startling calm about this. It occurs to me that we are finally playing on her ground. Kryto Grey is the leader of a country as well as my enemy, and she was his endearing, sweet little wife who no doubt was embroiled in politics as much as he allowed her to be. I'm certain she has had to resort to manipulation no small number of times to keep herself in good health and her sons both alive. While she may be trapped by her love of Kryto Grey, she has also managed to convince a madman that he is equally in love with her. Enough so that, as Septimus claims, he would be willing to give her anything she wanted.

While she has always seemed meek and helpless to me, I need to remind myself Teresa is not entirely so. Physically, perhaps, she is frail, but she is not a fool. Even from the beginning, she concealed a weapon from me. She made herself appear as innocent and weak as possible. She may not have purposefully fainted, I'm sure, but while I was assessing her and Septimus, she apparently was assessing me back.

"Wait," Damen says, finally looking up and frowning. His book lowers. "We don't get to eat with you?"

"You'll be fine, baby; you'll be with little people your own age, or thereabouts," Teresa reassures. "You can make friends."

Damen slams the book shut. "I don't want to make friends," he complains. "Aiden doesn't either. We want to stay with you. Like in the other Palace."

"Not tonight, darling," Teresa says, keeping her tone light. "After, I promise, we can eat dinner together again whenever you like."

"We never got to eat dinner together at home!" he says. "You said because we left, things would be different! That we got to all the time, now!"

Teresa sighs. "Damen, please," she says. This time it does not work.

"If it's going to be the same as home anyway, why can't we go back?!" he argues. "Uncle Amerson's not even there anymore, so it would be fine!"

"Damen—" she starts.

But he leaps up and runs off, slamming the door behind him as he escapes to the room he shares with Aiden. Teresa sighs again but forces herself to stand and offers a hand to her younger son.

"Come along, Aiden," she says. "I think we need to have a family talk. Captain, please excuse me," she adds for my benefit.

"Do you want me to come?" Septimus offers.

But she declines and leads Aiden out after his brother. Whatever she plans to say to them, I know there will be no exceptions made tonight. Teresa may be a gentle, patient mother, but she will not coddle her sons perpetually. Damen may be frustrated by their situation, but he will not get away with yelling at his mother. If Teresa herself did not decide to do something about it, I know I would.

That leaves me with Septimus, who is in strangely high spirits.

"You can't possibly be this happy over a fanciful dinner," I say.

"She called me 'Sep'," he says, practically beaming.

"Does that mean something?"

"Not necessarily," he admits. "But it is what our parents called me. Our other siblings. In past years, I've only ever heard it from...Well. From Kryto. Or his brothers."

He falls silent for a few moments.

I put a hand on his shoulder. "She trusts you," I say. "You have proven you will look after her, and her children. And she loves you. You are her brother."

"I still have much to atone for," he says, shaking his head. "But it's a sign we're moving in the right direction."

AGAINST RIAN'S WISHES, but in keeping with to his promise, he does not escort me downstairs to dinner. I enter alone and with no fanfare, slipping in to watch and listen at the back of his entourage. The king himself enters after most of the royals have, with Teresa on an arm, her boys off with the rest of the royal children, and Septimus trailing behind. Ayla is tardy in appearing for drinks and aperitifs, but Rian makes her excuses. He privately admits to me she is waiting until after the rest of the royals have arrived, so she can better disguise speaking with Soren as merely making the rounds.

I don't mind Soren and Ayla's interest in one another, but I can't imagine his parents would be pleased.

Grand Prince and Princess Carsans look as unapproachable and cold as ever tonight, possibly more so in their most formal ware. They do not intimidate me anymore, compared to thirty years ago when I'd sweat to feel their eyes on me. Though I had almost no association with their family, I always felt as if they were judging me harshly, and given their status, their judgement mattered.

Perhaps things would be different, if Septimus had not restored most of my memory. Or maybe I'd still have grown out of that nervousness at this point. Who is to know? All I do know is that, in times past, Grand Prince Alion Carsans has conspired to manipulate his own prophecy so he might place Crispin on the throne. He was willing to use both Lune and Soren as tools to accomplish that as well as manipulate Vásan Pike, who I have known in enough timelines to understand was, in fact, in love with my sister.

Layering my realities, I'm now starting to think that Soren is the only good thing to come out of the Carsans family for the last century. Harsh, perhaps, but possibly accurate.

The Carsans are practically dismissive of Septimus and Teresa when Rian takes the time to introduce them. Anyone else in the room would be honored to entertain the king first while the rest wait their turns. Not the Carsans. Poor Soren does his best to rescue the situation, asking politely after Teresa's health and insisting how pleased he is to know everyone is settling in.

There is an awkwardness to the hospitality now, however, because his parents occasionally make commentary in Isaarian that my cousins cannot understand, but the king, Soren and I do.

They are not especially welcoming comments. I think everyone is relieved when we part ways from the Carsans.

"I don't usually smoke, but perhaps I'll start tonight," Septimus says.

"They are right to be wary of us," Teresa says, more understanding, prepared to make herself an ideal guest this evening.

"Then I think I will fetch a drink," Septimus says, straightening his dinner jacket. "Teresa, would you like anything?"

"Oh, something sweet," she says. "Thank you."

"Your majesty?"

"Better not," Rian admits. "I'll be introducing your sister to the grand princes in the meantime."

"Don't hurry back," Teresa insists. "If you find yourself in conversation, feel free to stay. Enjoy yourself?"

There is a question in her words as she and Septimus are still attempting to understand their relationship to one another. As someone who barely knew her own sister, I know siblings are more complicated than most would assume.

"Let's see about getting you some friends while you're here," Rian tells Teresa once Septimus has left. "Yvette and Irina ought to be up to it; they've been hounding me forever to remarry so they'll have someone new to talk to. If I offer you up in the meantime, they might leave me alone for a few weeks."

He glances back at me and winks. I roll my eyes.

"Aha, and there's Yvette," he says.

He gestures to where Yvette Pike stands in her pale lilac gown with her skinny arms crossed over herself, hovering a few paces back while her husband speaks with princes Magnus and Yuugo. She looks uncomfortable, but that is as natural to her features as it is for me to be intimidating.

Grand Princess Yvette Pike is approximately eight years younger than Vásan, having only recently turned forty, I believe. There is still not a touch of gray in her caramel-blond hair, and few wrinkles visible on her face. She is of average height for an Isaarian woman, but looks petite because of her slight shoulders, breasts, and waist. Her hips are her shapelier portion, but her skirts hide them entirely.

If taken by vague description alone, Yvette could look somewhat similar to Lune, but she doesn't. She is softer, meeker, quieter, and her personality shows through her features. I have always pitied her, for the difficulties she has endured, though I've never gotten much of a chance to speak with her.

Yvette sweeps over with only a touch of hesitation after the king gestures for her to join us. She doesn't want to be, but she's curious about our guests.

"Your majesty," she says, curtseying and addressing him first, as she has yet to properly be introduced. "It is good to see you again."

"And you," Rian says. "You look lovely. I expect your family is well?"

"Certainly. I'm sure you've read my husband's reports. And Alo…Oh," Yvette says, remembering she's alone.

She looks around the room to find her son.

I spot him first. He is hovering on the side of the room with two of his peers and friends. His neutral expression and closed off personality may be mistaken for aloofness, but I know from watching him grow up it is a matter of shyness and uncertainty. Alo Pike strives to be like his father, but even he cannot obtain a shade of Vásan's impressive reputation.

As they are all young adults, now, Alo Pike and Sacha and Elodie Lundan have been invited to dinner with the king, though the rest of the grand princes' children and heirs have not been permitted such an honor, including little Patrice Lundan. They will all be dining with Damen and Aiden in a separate room, to accommodate their youth.

In contrast to Alo Pike, the royal Lundan children are more confident and louder. Elodie looks much like her mother, Sacha like their father, and their younger brother Patrice is a perfect in-between. The only break in the pattern is that all three children have Detrus' curly hair, even if Elodie and Patrice adopted their mother's sandy blond coloring. The Lundans could not have done better if they'd planned this.

Sacha leans over to the other two with a grin and whispers something that is likely an inappropriate joke based on how his sister smacks his arm and glares in warning. Alo gives no reaction, but that is what is expected of him, as Vásan's son. Or, Vásan's son as far as most know.

I am aware of the fact that Aloysius Pike II is not his father's child, but am not sure who else is privy to that information. Alo looks almost like a replica of a young Vásan, and that helps hide the family's torrid secret. The fact that Vásan acts a proper father to the young man instead of an uncle certainly helps. It is his mother who occasionally slips up, but I suppose no one blames Yvette for that.

There is hardly a proper way to respond to bearing the child of your husband's brother. The affair had not been her fault, either. Not at all.

It is a simple equation: Yvette loved Vásan, he did not love her, but they were wed anyway. Vásan's brother Bastien loved Yvette. She did not love him back and rejected his advances.

The Pike's have mind flukes. Bastien got what he wanted.

As soon as Vásan realized his wife was with child, and knew he at least had barely touched her, it did not take long for Bastien to be found out. Vásan nearly killed him, but their mother convinced her elder son to have mercy. She asked Rian to banish her youngest from Isaaria instead.

If it was left up to me, I'd have had Bastien killed anyways. But this was shortly after Mercer's betrayal. I suppose it was difficult for Rian to order another execution of a high noble and expect Isaarian citizens to still trust their rulers.

"Alo!" Yvette calls, somehow managing to carry her light little voice across the room while barely raising it.

I think she and Teresa will get along well.

Alo hears his mother, politely excuses himself from the Lundans, and makes his way over to us so the king can make proper introductions.

"Princess Pike. Please meet Captain Marson's dear little cousin, Teresa Smith," Rian says, still holding up Teresa's hand, guiding her. "She and her brother fled here from the war in Alarkia. Her sons are enjoying themselves with the other children this evening."

The grand princess falls into a graceful, trained curtsy. "We welcome her with open arms, your majesty," she claims in Alarkian. "I'm certain her company will help pass the rest of this long winter."

"Thank you, your grace," Teresa says, stumbling over how to address the grand princess but still managing to maintain her composure.

Yvette rises, and brings her son forward. He bends to kiss Teresa's hand.

"Miss Teresa. May I present my son. Aloysius Pike the Second," Yvette says. "Though most everyone calls him Alo."

"Oh," Teresa says, looking over the familiar pattern of the silver Tochia ice bird and the northern blue poppies on his sash. I realize, possibly at the same time as everyone else, that Yvette's sash bears only the poppies. "I think we borrowed some old items of yours when we arrived in the Pyrian Palace. For my sons. I hope you don't mind. I don't think anyone asked."

"Not at all, Miss Teresa," Alo says plainly. "I am glad they could be of service."

"Alo!" a childish voice cries happily, startling me.

But Aloysius does not react. In fact, no one else does at all, because once again, I am the only one to have heard anything.

There are children in this room, now. Young ones, of perhaps eleven or twelve years. Both look wiry and stretched-out with too-big heads, the way children tend to when they are between stages of development.

I recognize a younger version of Alo straight away, being half-tackled in a hearty embrace. The second boy, I realize after a moment, I also know, but for different reasons.

I catch my breath. Of all the ghosts I have seen, this is by far the most painful. I can see it in his eyes and the shape of his face, his nose, his brow, most especially that smile: this is my son, my son with Rian. Or he would be, should be.

"Alo's my best friend," my son claims. By chance, he is looking up at Teresa when he talks, but she has no idea he is there. In another time, he is likely speaking to someone else. "We've been together practically since birth."

"We can't have been. I'm two months older," the young version of Alo Pike says bluntly, in that formal manner I have come to associate with Vásan.

My son laughs. He laughs and it hurts my heart.

"That's why I said practically, you knob," he teases.

The young version of Alo Pike smiles. I don't think I have ever seen him smile before. Then, in a blink, they are gone.

Aloysius Pike and my son are meant to be as close of friends as Rian and Mercer once were, I realize.

The idea startles me.

Here we all are, continuing to live our lives with most none-the-wiser. But Alo becomes a different person, when raised next to my son. At least, seeing the ghosts of them, he looked much happier.

The world may supposedly suffer my son's absence, but individuals do, too. Alo Pike leads a much better life alongside my son. I won't forget that.

"Grand prince," I hear Yvette calling to her husband, jolting me back to the present moment. I do not know what has been said in my mental absence. "Please, come meet Captain Marson's little cousin."

Vásan does not ignore her, precisely, but finishes the last few comments necessary with his companions first. He is practically a professional representation of what people think a prince ought to be, and remains that way nearly always. In fact, I believe I have never even seen him break character before the moment he lays eyes on my cousin.

From there, he looks both shocked and horrified. It escapes no one's notice.

"Teresa Smith, grand prince," I offer, breaking the spell when all others are too startled to make proper introductions. "From Alarkia. My uncle's daughter."

"You," Vásan starts, and then must clear his throat uncharacteristically. "You have beautiful eyes, Miss Teresa. Like your cousin."

He glances at me gratefully and nods, as he lifts Teresa's hand to kiss her fingers just as his son did. He is doing his best to hasten their greeting through so he can make his escape from this woman, who reminds him of the ghost he loves. The remnants of Lune Marson, Lune Carsans, Lune. Whom Vásan somehow has dreams of that distance him from his wife.

Septimus has been delayed by Clair and Absolum Oram, former king and queen of Isaaria. They are curious about him, no doubt, but as he has been retrieving a drink for his sister, it is clear to them they can't keep him for long and they save most of their questions for dinner. Clair Oram's pora'bola fairy does not appear to like Septimus much, given his fluke, and wants its distance from him.

His return rescues Vásan from the situation, as it means new introductions to pass around. Vásan recovers himself enough that he and his son are stoic mirrors of one another once more. He asks several polite, generic questions. Septimus reveals they grew up traveling all over Alarkia, but generally places in the north. Teresa gratefully thanks them again, considering her sons have been allowed to borrow Pike clothing.

Natural conversation slowly descends, but with a nervous overlay. There is great relief when Ayla makes her appearance. Instead of allowing her and the king to finish addressing everyone, Soren approaches to suggest a transition to the dining room. It is technically a break in protocol, though not enough to create a stir.

We all know this has been done in an attempt to smooth over Vásan's uncharacteristic reaction to Teresa.

The seats at dinner are arranged with great care. Soren is nothing if not attentive and observant. He takes one end of the table, while Rian is seated at the other, Ayla to his left, and my cousins both to his right. Teresa is thankfully between Rian and her own brother, and Soren has kept his parents close by him. Seated beside Ayla are the Lundans, starting with Elodie, then Sacha and their parents; on Septimus' other side, the Orams. In between, then, is Nissa and her brother Chance Sondushki, the Pikes, the Idos, and a smattering of representatives for the highest noble families in Isaaria, such as the al'Yibnas.

These nobles' seats rotate, to keep a certain balance, but the al'Yibnas are highly relevant, now, as wardens of the southern border. We have not had ideal relations with the Ishtak Empire and Milash, of late. The rest of the nobles are seated at separate tables, through a short corridor, in a larger room, while the youngest members of noble society are beyond even that.

For some occasions—particularly weddings, holidays, or feast days—all are seating in one large chamber, to share in merriment. There will be grand, celebratory dinners in this manner to celebrate Holrith. However, most other nights, when the eight royal families gather, there is an expectation of privacy, so that more intimate conversations may arise, and no time is wasted.

I take up my position behind Rian's chair, standing back at the right-hand side of the doorway that frames his seat. Vilaneau stands to the left side. Qhan is across the way. With all at their places, after a blessing for the meal, most of the awkwardness dissipates. So long as the dinner manages to pass without any of the guests mentioning the perpetual absence of a representative for the Ralhans, the meal should go smoothly.

Rian makes several general, gracious comments, thanking them all for their attendance and inviting his guests to enjoy themselves. He announces introductions for my cousins, for all those who did not get a chance to greet them beforehand. Teresa plays her part well, with her practiced smile and bright eyes; Septimus, now, is the uneasy one. He fiddles with a tablecloth tassel brushing his left thigh, and his smile is uncomfortable.

A light first course is served for a traditionally Isaarian meal; olive spread, cheese bread, onion tarts. I notice throughout the evening that Teresa's meal is somewhat modified, so either Soren noticed or Naomi informed the kitchen staff of my little cousin's condition and nausea.

"How are you finding Isaaria, Miss Teresa? And you, Septimus?" Irina Lundan says as soon as conversation naturally takes its course.

I was not surprised to learn that she is taking the lead in conversation. The Lundans have acted as the royal families' unofficial liaison to the public; many people see themselves in the family of five, regardless of differing social standings. The Lundans rise to that challenge as well, and enjoy the benefits of the unofficial position. Irina is nosy and conversational, and Detrus is a jolly giant who enjoys social activities and listening more than speaking.

"Yes," Septimus confirms and glances at his sister. "I'd say we're enjoying our time so far."

Teresa expands, smiling. "We honestly did not expect such hospitality when we decided to leave our home and come here," she admits. "All we knew about our cousin Soleil is what our Aunt Olivia told us; we were hoping to rely on that connection, but it truly only was by hope alone."

"Curious," Magnus says, "we did not even know Captain Marson had parents, let alone cousins."

I don't appreciate the sudden scrutiny on me, but I knew to expect it. All eyes will be on Septimus and Teresa tonight, and that will extend to me as well. I know it is not my time to speak, so I allow Teresa and Septimus to build their own defense, and weave their own story. They are the ones who will need to keep to it, Teresa most especially.

"Our cousin is a private person," she says casually. "But the situation is less complicated than you may think. Our parents were struggling, and Soleil's mother came west to help. Later, complications arose that made it difficult for her to return, and when war broke out, it was impossible. We never met before, but Aunt Olivia did still tell us about Isaaria and her daughter, here. It became a desperate option, but our only one."

"How are things in the west, then?" Detrus asks, attempting to be congenial about it while moving away from traditional scrutiny.

"There are still some safe places, but it is all still bad enough that I wanted to take my sister and her sons away from it all," Septimus says evasively. "I'm sure you've heard stories."

There are nods around the table, but I cannot accurately say if they truly have heard the stories. Mercer was unofficially our ambassador to the west; he was the one who cared about the war there while most of his peers were, and are, more interested in keeping house in Isaaria.

"It must have been dreadful, traveling in winter, though," Clair Lundan notes sympathetically using her pora'bola fairy. She faces Teresa despite her sight challenges, for decorum. "Especially in your delicate condition."

It is not the Isaarian way to ignore a woman's becoming with child the way many other countries in Samioth might. The way Teresa reddens reminds me of how quiet most cultures tend to be about the matter, particularly Alarkians. But she recovers herself and places a hand over her abdomen, beneath the table. She is doing well to adjust and act casually about situations that are not normal to her at all, while Septimus is driven to distraction by the pora'bola and Clair's cloudy eyes, both.

"Actually, my terms with my sons were more strenuous. Comparatively, this one has not been so bad," Teresa says, and raises her glass to drink.

"Are you married, then, Miss Teresa?" Irina asks politely.

She and Clair have taken control of the dinner conversation, directing it at Teresa, which Detrus and Absolum are pleased about, while Septimus is relieved. Other reactions around the table range from neutral, to mildly interested, to irritated. The Carsans do not like my cousins.

To her credit, Teresa does not choke on her drink. She simply swallows, puts her water glass back down, and answers plain as day. As if she were not married to an absolute maniac who'd recently sent his equally psychotic brother after her.

"I was. I'm afraid we were separated, by the war. It has been some time since I've seen him. I'm not sure if he's still alive, in fact."

The women are instantly sympathetic. But Magnus never has been skillful with minute social cues, or else, he never cared enough about them to let them get in his way.

"Not too long ago, though, could it have been?" he says.

It is as if he intends for this to be an interrogation. He could not be more pointed if he tried.

"Oh. Aha, this one is not his," Teresa says candidly.

She surprises me, by not sounding at all meek and embarrassed by it. My cousin is a better actress than she has led me to believe, it seems, so long as she has enough time to prepare herself for the role.

"I took a lover, I'm afraid. I grew lonely, and as my husband is a cruel man, it was difficult to maintain a relationship with him. He did not love me, even if he promised he did. So, I sought that affection in someone else."

Nissa smirks. "Hear, hear," she says, and raises her wine glass to Teresa in recognition. *"Kandanga co'tchok."*

I don't know much of the Hoitsokin language, but I recognize the phrase as one Nissa has used sarcastically many times in the past. Now, she means it genuinely, if a bit humorously, congratulating Teresa.

This startles some of the other royals, particularly the ones already critical of my cousins' presence, but they do not know the whole story. There is actually some relief from Irina; now she knows Teresa's husband is not necessarily too painful a topic for discussion. At least, Teresa will not succumb to tears at any reminder of his absence, and this opens Irina's game of social balance. Nissa does not have the entire story either; however, she is aware my cousins fled a dire situation. Only, I forgot we had not told her that Teresa had an affair.

Teresa is still too modest not to flush. She clears her throat.

"It is what it is," she says dismissively. "It is safer for all my children in the east, now. So, to the east we've come."

"We do not consider ourselves eastern, so much," Irina corrected gently. "But yes, many have fled to Isaaria these past years. It is safe, here."

For now.

"So, then, where is this lover of yours?" Magnus challenges, his mother gives him a warning touch on the arm, but he does not stop. "He would leave you to wander across Samioth without him, and with his child?"

I can see that visibly hurts Teresa. It takes her too long to respond.

"He is further east," Septimus says easily, saving her. "Captain Marson and I hope to connect with him when we travel that way in the coming weeks. But you understand how it is in the world, these days."

He shares a look with Teresa. She smiles.

From there, my cousins together craft a story that is believable, but does not betray the most clandestine facts. The conversation throughout the next five courses of the meal does not exclusively center on them, but there is enough interest to keep my cousins involved.

There is another pair to watch, however, much less obvious to most, and that is Ayla and Soren. They sit at opposite ends of the table and barely look at one another. Ayla is much quieter tonight than she usually would be on other occasions. Soren does not say much either; he lets others direct the conversation where he might otherwise be dominant. The pair never directly speak to or about one another, though I'm sure Rian and I are both looking for every interaction between them.

When the main components of the meal have finished, and the royals prepare to move on away from the table for free socialization, Ayla and I both decide to act. I have a house to set in order before I leave, and she is thinking similarly.

I discussed such an opportunity with Vilaneau before dinner, so he is aware I am about to leave the king's side. Rian, of course, knows me so well, I've no doubt he will be able to make correct assumptions. As company begins to mingle with the lesser nobles in the adjoining room, I exchange a nod with Vilaneau and leave to make my move.

As soon as there is an opportunity, I approach Soren. Most allow him a grace in taking his time to transition from a seat at the dinner table to his mobile chair. Only Kaoli is there, to help him, while others pretend not to notice politely. This will give me the chance to take him aside privately without anyone making a fuss socially.

"Thank you, Kaoli," Soren says dismissively, but appreciative, when he notices me. He knows I would not approach him at this time unless it was for a matter of extreme importance.

"Join me on the veranda for a spell, Prince Carsans?" I offer.

"Thank you, Captain, I would love to," he says, turning his chair towards the glass doors of the dining room veranda behind him.

I notice Ayla hurrying over before he does, but her heels make a clicking that is unavoidable even beneath the noise of the evening. She pretends to be headed this direction by chance, overhearing us also by chance, but there is careful calculation involved that Soren and I cannot ignore.

"Oh, the veranda?" she repeats. "Just a moment. Prince Carsans, allow me to lend you my cloak. It is cold this evening."

She takes her fur-lined cloak from an attendant to drape it over the back of Soren's chair, and over his shoulders. He reaches to clasp it around his neck at the same time as her, so their gloved hands touch as if by accident. Ayla does not immediately pull her hand away.

"Many thanks, princess," Soren says. "Your thoughtfulness is appreciated."

She smiles at him. "Happy to be of service, grand prince."

"I'll be sure to find you later, to return it," he adds.

"Be certain you do," she says.

It is not exactly secret code, but Soren will conveniently forget to give her cloak back at a reasonable time during the social hour, giving him the excuse to seek her out later. I suspect, if she had not seen me approaching, she would have found some other excuse to manufacture a private meeting with Soren. I'd worry for her honor's sake, only, I trust Soren with Ayla's well-being, and I am sure he will have Kaoli present as chaperone.

I offer to push Soren but he declines. I open the doors and let him roll out first before following. With his chair, he cannot roll down the veranda steps, but surprises me by levering himself out of it to sit at the top of the steps. He takes Ayla's cloak with him. I sit beside him carefully.

"I'm stronger than I look," he jokes. "But if Kaoli offers to help, I take it. She has looked after me for so long, I cannot push her out now."

"Understandable," I say. "It is humble of you to do that."

"Well, it is good for people to look after one another. It's the gesture that matters. Lovely night," he adds after a beat.

"It is," I agree. "Despite the cold."

The small tease makes him smile; he fingers the fringe on Ayla's cloak.

"Tonight was difficult for you," I note. "Usually, you are a much more attentive host. It is not a criticism," I add. "But it is unlike you not to steer the conversation to appropriate topics."

Soren sighs and reveals the cause of his distraction. "I made the mistake of mentioning Crispin to my father before dinner. It did not go as planned."

"I'm sorry," I say.

I understand enough about the Carsans to imagine, but he expands anyway.

"My parents never hid which of us was their favorite, though I do not think they are aware of this fact. It does make sense, to me. For the longest time, he was their only, perfect child. They did not expect me. His early death is a sore point even without my…being different."

"Because you have dual flukes and he had none?" I say.

My feigned ignorance makes him laugh, which was my intent.

"It's strange to think of how few people know Crispin never had a fluke," Soren says. "My father decided not to have it known publicly, because he thought it would damage our family's reputation, should anyone discover the truth of it."

He does not have to explain further for me to understand. His father thought it would reflect poorly on their family if citizens learned that

Soren—the crippled, younger son who almost was never even born—was the one who bore the responsibility of the Carsans' Prophecy fluke.

I feel myself growing irritated on Soren's behalf. He has always handled the public's reactions to him maturely, even as a child, yet he should not have to. Most are completely accepting of him, and whatever he can or cannot do. Others go out of their way to be cruel, and others still masquerade as having Isaaria's best intentions at heart when they criticize Soren being his father's potential heir. It is, perhaps, part of what pushes Soren so hard to attempt walking even when he shouldn't; even when his body fights against him.

No doubt Soren has hesitated in asking for Ayla's hand out of concern for her own reputation. The Isaarian people adore Ayla. Some preferred Soren as a child, when it was assumed that he would not live past the age of fifteen.

"It has been so long, now, since Crispin died, I keep expecting my father to formally name me his heir. I think everyone is waiting for that, whether to approve or criticize..." Soren continues.

"You have more than proven yourself capable," I promise. "You accepted Crispin's role as steward of the Summer Palace when you were twelve, Soren. Twelve. When Crispin was twelve, I think he was still getting into trouble in school for refusing to wear shoes in class."

"Yet, ironically, despite being less physically able as my brother, what I do will never be enough," he sighs.

There is painful truth to that.

"Well. Even if your parents never formally recognize your right, the king will," I say. "He likes you. Quite a lot, Soren. He will make certain you are given what you deserve. What you've more than earned."

The subtext between us is both painful to ignore and acknowledge.

"The odd thing is, until others comment on it, I do not think of myself as lesser than anyone else," Soren admits.

"Have you considered developing your second fluke?" I offer.

Perhaps the acknowledgement of Soren's having not only one but two flukes would help soften the blow of any other publicized rumors.

"Unfortunately, I'm not sure if that's an option. My parents are concerned. Because I have two flukes, they are worried that if I ever have children, they might take after that second fluke instead of inheriting the prophecy fluke and effectively put an end to the Carsans' line and our form of government."

"That would be a problem," I admit. "But one that Isaaria could adapt to."

"I think I'm enough of a problem without maybe being blamed for tearing our government down," Soren says.

I resist a sigh. Soren has always been too hard on himself, even as a child. I wish my words could be enough to convince him that he has value equal to anyone else's. He claims he does not think of himself as lesser, but his derogatory statements tell me this is not entirely true.

"You won't be," I say. "In fact, Soren, I think if you show your strength, there may be more support for you than you can imagine. Not just from the king and his daughter."

"I'm not so sure about the daughter," Soren says, lightly, joking at himself. He knows Ayla is fond of him, but she has been in a peculiar mood of late, ever since Amerson's invasion. "Hopefully that changes."

"I'd say so," I say. Yet I cannot help but pry, for my own sake. The knowledge that Ayla is my daughter demands it. "Has Ayla spoken to you at all, yet? About what happened at the Pyrian Palace?"

Soren hesitates, but I know the two of them have spoken. They must have, in order to plan my wedding to Rian.

"Some," he confesses. "I do not think she wants to tell everything, yet. I think it makes her uncomfortable, even talking about it."

All I can do is nod. That is partially what I feared; I know Teresa's children are young enough to quickly recover from their experience with their uncle's men, but it is different for Ayla. She was isolated, used as a hostage against me, and injured. Teresa's boys were at least with their mother, and she did not let Amerson put a hand on them. For the most part.

"If she ever does tell you," I start slowly, "I don't need to know the details. All I want to know is that she told you. That she has spoken to someone. That would be a relief, as someone who cares for her greatly."

"Of course," he reassures. "I understand."

"Thank you, Soren. Ayla…cares for you," I say slowly. "More than in mere friendship. She has confided in me as much."

"I see," Soren says.

"I'm sure she has made her own implications in those letters you two tried so hard to keep secret," I add wryly. "Should you decide to finally make your intentions known to the king, I can't imagine he will be surprised, either."

"I…ah, see. Yes. Thank you," Soren repeats, this time reddening.

I smile and take a deep breath. Sorren would make a good son-in-law.

There are a few moments of peace, knowing that no one has come looking for us yet, and we have the moon for our company. It reminds me of a common Theebin prayer: *Most high, all-powerful, all-good Almighty, all praise is yours, all honor and all blessings. Praise be you and all your creatures, including Sir Brother Sun and Lady Sister Moon. Brother Sun, with his beauty, radiance, strength, and splendor. Sister Moon with her stars, precious, gentle, and fair. Praise be to all your creations on this earth and sky.*

They were only ever words before. With the moon and Soren's company and the threat of mortality, however, the prayer feels more reverent.

"You have grown into a good man, Soren Carsans," I tell him. "Please look after Ayla. Do what is best for her. And look after the king as well."

Soren hesitates. "You say that as if you do not expect to come back."

"I don't know if I will," I say. "But if you are tired of waiting to ask…At least know you have my blessing. And though you should still ask him, the king's, as well. So long as you promise to do what is best for her, no matter what."

I say this in case I do not come back. Regardless of what my best hopes and faiths may dictate, there is a possibility we may fail. If that is the case, I need to be prepared to leave some semblance of a life behind for Rian, Ayla, Teresa, and her sons.

Soren is troubled, but nods. I have more I need to tell him. There is too much to say and not enough time.

"Make a place for Teresa in the Summer Palace," I say thoughtfully. "Nothing in the nobility, nothing so drastic. But keep her and her children comfortable. Rian will do his best to look after them, but if I do not return, you will need to take the lead for him. He will be distracted. Coordinate with Irina Lundan. She will help. Be good to Alo Pike; you always have been, but it will be good to have the Pikes' support. Argue with Rian on this if you must, but invite Mercer's nephew back to court. Adrian. We need our country to appear as unified as possible."

I stop to think, but in doing so, I lose my momentum. That is all I can think of, though I am certain there is more.

"Unity," I repeat. "That's what the country will need."

Something in what I have said has bothered Soren. He has been absorbing everything I say thus far, but he hesitates before giving me more confirmation.

"Captain, I…I found something," he admits.

I am immediately no longer Rian Yakarami's new wife or Soleil Marson, Magicsmith, but Captain Marson again. If there is a threat to Rian that Soren has uncovered, I can't leave him until I know for certain the household is safe.

"I debated with myself, whether I should tell you. Only because I was not sure if it would be any help," Soren admits.

"Soren," I say sternly. "Do not draw it out. What is it?"

"I found Grand Prince Mercer's travel journal. One of them, anyways. I thought…you would want to have it. I considered giving it to the king, but I realized it may be painful for him to read it. Or even know it exists."

His words are a relief, and a weight lifts from my chest. This is no real threat against Rian, but new information instead.

"No, that was a good thought," I tell him between deep breaths. "That was wise of you, Soren. Thank you."

"Do you want it instead, then?" he offers. "I don't know what good will come of it, now, but when you mentioned Adrian Ralhan, I thought…"

"No, I'll take it, Soren, thank you," I say.

Knowing what I do of what happened between Mercer and the Greys in the west, there may be more information in that journal for me. This gift is more than Soren understands, and more than I can explain at this time.

"I have taken up enough of your time, for now," I decide, standing and brushing the frost from my clothes. "Thank you, Grand Prince Carsans."

"Thank you. My queen," he says with a small smile. "For trusting me."

I hesitate before saying what I do next, but I gift him this. I know he needs it; I know that it will mean much to him:

"If I had a son, I would want him to be like you."

Soren is stunned enough by that he allows me to assist him into his chair without a word. He blinks many times, but does not know what to say. I allow my words the silence they need after to fortify them, and hope that he will take away from them all I intended.

Back inside, we are quick to lose ourselves amongst those gathered. I do not know if Soren would like to have said something more, because neither of us get a chance. He is noticed and pulled away into conversation with Ayla, Elodie and Sacha, who are enamored with Damen now that the children have been allowed to join us. Damen is visibly thrilled with the attention.

His little brother, meanwhile, is falling asleep on his uncle's shoulder while Septimus shifts his weight back and forth. I can tell, as I make my way towards him, that he is pleased Teresa trusts him enough to allow this. She stands a small matter of paces away, so while Septimus can listen to her conversation, he is not participating.

Despite their facial expressions at Teresa's extramarital confession, Irina and Yvette have struck up a conversation with her, and all appear to be getting along swimmingly. There is no awkward air about them, and Yvette has even graciously put aside Vásan's uncomfortable reaction to my cousin.

"Oh. No, I am in my thirty-second year," Teresa says in answer to an obvious question, and Irina looks absolutely thrilled to hear it.

"You look so young! I thought you could be my own daughter's age!" she laughs. "Though, I suppose I should have known better, given your sons."

This is a playful exaggeration, as Elodie Lundan is only nineteen.

Teresa takes the jest as she is meant to and smiles genuinely. Mothering is something of an unspoken Isaarian trait in our women, and Teresa must have noticed as much in Ayla and Naomi, let alone actual mothers like Irina.

Teresa watches me out of the corners of her eyes as I approach, but lets me pass by to reach Septimus without stop. She is testing the waters of friendship with the noblewomen and wants that opportunity without me pulling her away. Despite her concerns, I am more than willing to allow Teresa to cement herself as a permanent fixture in the upper echelons of Isaaria. I think she more than deserves those luxuries, and I do not intend to complicate matters for her.

Septimus, meanwhile, has much to answer for, as he himself has admitted. I feel less guilty about cutting him off from the social scene with my presence.

"Enjoy your chat with the Carsans' heir?" he mutters as I stand beside him.

"He is not their heir, and you know that," I say a little bitterly.

"I did not, actually," he muses. "Peculiar. It is not as if they have any other options. But I suppose Soren always has been the sort to have a long road ahead of him."

I narrow my eyes, having started suspecting something as soon as I put the pieces together. "Is Soren Carsans an Eye of the Death?"

"No," Septimus says honestly. He adjusts Aiden in his arms, propping him up higher. Aiden remains solidly asleep. "Soleil, I told you: Rian is the only one left. The rest are dead."

Another relief for the evening. I have been wobbling between caution and paranoia and I believe it is starting to take a toll. There is no reason for Septimus to lie about this, so I will take the reprieve as it is, at face value.

"I want us to prepare for our journey tomorrow, and for us to leave within a day or two," he says.

I should not be surprised; I know timing is important, and the appearance of Amerson and Phoebus has lit a fire under him. I even prepared myself for such a situation in my meet with Soren. However, there is a comfort in my new marriage with Rian. I want to be with him and regret the fact that I will be leaving him behind.

"Very well," I force myself to agree. "But you must give me proper information. Once we leave the Summer Palace, where are we headed?"

Septimus rubs at his eyes. Out of respect, he did not wear his darkening glasses tonight, but the lights were not dimmed on his behalf. Somewhere, that fact slipped through. His eyes must hurt.

"I assume we can travel by train to the southern border. I have some allies waiting there; they should have a ship prepared to take us east."

"Allies?" I repeat. "Who did not come with you?"

"In case something went wrong with you, I wanted them to be able to make the trip without us. I would not want to risk it, preferably, but I figured it was necessary to put precautions in place."

I am not angry, but understanding. Allowing my memories of times past to sink in has allowed me to understand my own nature. Septimus and I have been dancing around each other, wanting to trust, but wary. If there are allies whom he trusts waiting for him on the southern border, ones securing passage for us east, I will take their involvement as a boon.

That said, tonight in privacy, I will be discussing with Rian who we can afford to spare here, so that they may take the trip east with me. I will be a reasonable piece in the puzzle, but I will not be naïve.

Twelve

OUR FINAL PARTY for the trip east took some time to develop, not only for the obvious reasons. First, Rian decided I must bring Nissa and her hyena, claiming they would be able to help protect myself and Septimus, who admittedly does not look like much of a fighter. That I agreed with readily enough. Nissa is loyal to Rian and has been helpful thus far in multiple ways.

I was much less pleased with the attempted addition of Grand Prince Vásan Pike and his son.

"Please take them with you, Soleil," Rian said as I paced in his bedroom, having just been given this news. "It will bring some reassurance and comfort to me, knowing they're with you."

"Vásan is a grand prince; do you have any idea what would happen if I let him get himself killed? Or, even worse, if his son got himself killed?" I hissed.

"Nissa is a grand princess," he pointed out.

"Nissa has lived in the wild for years!" I insisted. "She knows exactly how to handle herself and how to avoid dangers. If she is with us, I do not need to be looking out for her because I know she can look out for herself. Vásan and Alo are liabilities."

"Fine, maybe Alo is," Rian allowed. "But Vásan is not helpless, and it would make sense for me to send him at least to keep up the illusion of a diplomatic mission as we've claimed this is."

"Nissa can fulfill that roll. There is *no* reason for **Vásan to come**—"

"If I can't be there to protect you, I want Vásan there to do it for me!" he insisted, proving me wrong.

That halted the argument. I realized it did not matter how many logical arguments I presented: Rian made the decision to send Vásan with me out of an emotional place. I tried to probe regardless, perhaps so I could understand his thinking better, while knowing he would likely get his way.

"Because you think I need protecting?" I ventured, not particularly offended by the concept, though I had a good argument against it.

"Because I'm scared, Soleil!" he said. "…I do not want to lose you. Vásan may not be a good man, but he is a fair one. He cares for our country. I trust him. If he knew you were my wife, Isaaria's new queen, then I know he would do anything he possibly could bring you home again. Whereas with Nissa… Sometimes I think she is only doing what is best for her."

I stopped pacing to sit next to him.

"Rian, I will come back," I promised him.

"Then why are you making plans as if it may be otherwise?" he challenged. "Why did you tell Soren what you did?"

I had no idea how he found out about that, but in the end, we compromised: Vásan would accompany us.

Alo would not.

Of course, this meant telling Nissa and Vásan the story of the Smiths, the Greys, the Anomalies, the Dark and the quest ahead, as well as the truth about me and Lune and Taris, and Mercer. Nissa kept an eyebrow raised in doubt the entire time, while Vásan kept his expression blank. I do not think they'd have believed us, except we had Qhan to back us up, and they both respect him. Then, thankfully, Teresa was there to tell part of the story.

Nissa and Vásan both believed her instantly, even if they doubted my words seconds before. I suppose that suspicious effect Teresa has on people is finally paying me dividends.

The morning of our departure, we do our best to appear more like a diplomatic envoy than weary travelers prepared to fight and crawl our way to a finish line that may not exist. We plan to take a train to the southern border, to travel by ship through the straight and eastward, past the Ishtak Empire's waters, beneath Tourran, and to Kacha. Though most of the journey will be done on some form of physical transportation instead of hiking across the land, we still do our best to pack lightly, and do not withhold means of protection.

Ayla is still asleep when we leave, early in the morning, but Rian comes to see me off, and I leave a letter for her with him. It is a pitiful offering, but if I wake her, I suspect Naomi and Korvaan would manage to make appearances as well. I can't imagine them being pleased that I'm leaving without managing to make an appointment with them. After all, I did promise they could have their private conversation with me. Now, at best, they will have to wait. At worst, they will never get it.

It is a cruel thing I am doing, I know, and I am ashamed of it. However, I selfishly push the guilt away, making excuses for myself. I am no saint.

Yvette Pike even appears to bid her husband farewell, along with his son. Vásan and Alo are businesslike, though I'm sure Alo is nervous about the possibility of taking up his father's mantle. Yvette is displeased with the idea of her husband traveling without proper protection, but she is not the sort to raise complaints. She says goodbye formally then hovers while Teresa fusses over Septimus, holding us all from our departure.

"Do you have your glasses? For bright days? So it doesn't hurt your eyes?"

"Yes, yes, Teresa, don't be such a worrier over it," Septimus insists. "And I'll have the spares as well."

"And promise you will take Soleil's advice and won't try to make all the decisions on your own?" she says. "You know you overthink scenarios if you haven't encountered a version of them before, and this is all new territory."

He smirks. "Yes, yes. I will listen to what Soleil says once every six days or so. Or whenever she is not making things difficult."

I know he is only needling me in good fun, but I cannot help but bristle. As I said, I'm no saint. After all, between the two of us, I am more physically able than Septimus and I am doing my best to be relatively understanding, patient and trusting.

"You know you need me. I am a sun, *flower,*" I insist. "You would not survive without me."

Beside me, Rian barks a laugh. We all look at him; even I am not sure what was particularly funny. I only said it because I determined it is true.

"Flour…because…he's white," Rian says, disappointed in our stoicism.

"I think she meant 'flower' as in 'delicate', your majesty," Septimus admits.

"What would 'flour' have to do with the sun anyways?" I say.

Rian blinks at me. As if he did not think he'd have to explain this to us.

"…Wheat."

Only Nissa laughs.

When it comes time for final farewells, I embrace him even in front of all those present. While I pretend that this is done only for his sake, I know that I need this as well. I feel Rian's arms wrap around me and enjoy the feel of them, the comfort and safety of them. Voluntarily leaving this safety, even if it is only an illusion, is dangerous, necessary, and painful.

"Stay safe," Rian says in my ear.

I snort because cockiness is better than allowing a single tear.

"I am usually the one to tell you that," I lecture him.

"Ha. Well. Now it is the other way around, I suppose," he says. "…Soleil, do promise you will try to contemplate, meditate, for just a few moments. If you are to enter the Otherworld…I think the Almighty is trying to tell you something."

"I don't know how to listen," I say stubbornly.

"What, and you think I'm an expert?" he laughs. "…I'm not a saint, Soleil. But I think, in some ways, with the right directing…You could be."

Considering the justifications of my own poor actions in the past few minutes alone, I almost hate his saying so. If that is a direct message from the Almighty, it is more than received, and I do not like that.

I don't know what to say. Rian has always appeared more reverent than I, more holy, more dedicated to his faith. I suppose it is our faith, truly, in that I attended the same masses he did that first time around. I was Theebin, once. I stopped being so much with the Qurvos.

But is that so much an excuse? Taris was Theebin. He meditated in the Theebin tradition. He prayed. He kept it private, but we all did know, and he did pray. I wonder if he ever prayed with Lune. I wonder if, all those times he meditated, he was asking for grace for her.

"I will…Try my best," I say, though I do not know if that's true.

I force my way from Rian's embrace and look to Qhan sternly.

"Keep him alive," I order, pointing at Rian. "And do not let Vilaneau's paranoia get the better of him. He is ready enough."

"Yes, my captain," Qhan says, and then corrects himself. "My queen."

I consider whether this is enough before my departure—enough of a farewell—and decide there is no good way to say goodbye to those I may never see again. I give a single nod, straighten my jacket with a final jerk, and turn my back on them. Facing Vásan and Nissa, knowing what they expect of me, makes it easier to keep my face plain and professional. When I am alone, and in privacy, maybe I will give myself a moment of emotion. Otherwise, I must keep myself on task.

Magnus arranges transport for us, though he does not bother coming to bid us farewell. He permits us use of a rare Alarkian motorcar that rumbles and rattles through the streets with us packed onto the two benches, men in the front, women in the back. Septimus drives, which does not surprise me, and takes us to the train station with Vásan's direction.

Citizens make way for us to move through the streets, but are too caught up in their own survival to watch us properly. Their concerns and fears are too many to care much about the possibility of a prince, a princess, an albino man, and the king's *Khashtani* driving a foreign motorcar through the streets. Perhaps a child or two notices, given their propensity for observation and the possibility for dreaming still in their minds. By the time they manage to tug on their mother's sleeves, however, insisting on what they have seen, we are gone. Moved on. Disappeared with motorcar smoke.

The train station is not as busy as one might think, but only because it is organized well. Many folks are coming in to the city, for the refugee shelters or to fetch family members and bring them to the countryside west and north. A considerably smaller number of people are leaving, daring to move south or east. North is a safer destination, if one wishes to leave the west coast at all. The train we will board for the south, then, is not completely empty, but passengers stay clumped together in their small parties, unwilling to fraternize with other groups.

Isaaria may still be free of war, but fear has choked this land.

While the others manage our luggage, I find the stationmaster and relay Magnus' message in regards to the motorcar and what is to be done with it. By the time I have returned, I spot Septimus hanging in the doorway to one of the coaches, leaning back and waiting for me. He is not looking my way, but I appreciate his being there all the same.

The train whistle blows, signaling a last call prior to departure. The platform is emptying of those that were there to begin with. Perhaps this is why I notice the peculiar pair standing downwind of me, far to my right. Alternatively, perhaps it is a divine warning, or merely instinct. Whatever the case, I feel the hairs stand up on the back of my neck.

I pause in my walk to the train and glance down the platform. There is a woman watching me, smiling. She looks directly at me and offers me a small nod, her eyes dipping beneath the brim of her western-style hat as she does so. Her companion happens to not be looking in my direction, but stands out as much as she does: a tall fellow in a dashing off-white Alarkian walking suit, visible beneath his open coat. In fact, I must stare hard and blink several times at the later: he looks so much, startlingly like Rian that it shocks me. For a few moments, I am convinced this is another one of my ghosts, as I know Rian could not possibly be here.

As I peer closer, I realize that though the resemblance is startling, it is not Rian. It is merely as if someone took all the physical traits that I find pleasing to look at in my husband and borrowed them for a moment. There is an awkwardness to it the longer I look, similar to the strange beauty of the Fae.

The train whistle blows again, startling me. I hasten to the coach and nearly push Septimus out of my way in hopping aboard. An electric current is run to close the doors on a timer as we prepare for departure; the rest of the train still runs on coal. A cabin attendant should be by soon to ensure we are in our seats, with the doors closed properly, but I do not move from the door immediately, so neither does Septimus.

"Something spook you?" he suggests.

There is an attempted tease, but also legitimate wariness. He has experienced too much not to expect mischief.

"I think that woman knew me," I say.

Septimus frowns. "What woman? What did she look like?"

"Business attire. Dark brown hair. I was too far away to see her features well. She was maybe Alarkian? She had a broad smile, and a pinkish birthmark just here," I say, pointing to a corner of one eye. "Like a splotch, all the way to her ear. The way a Magic-blind might."

He is uncharacteristically jumpy when I mention that.

"Did she board the train?" he demands.

"I don't think so. Not that I saw. But if she did, it would be in the back half," I say. "Why? What's troubling you?"

He ignores my question in favor of his own interrogation. "Did you see anyone with her? A terrifyingly tall man, perhaps? Or a boy with bright red hair, eighteen or so? A Hoitsokin? A blond woman?"

"There was a man who looked startlingly like Rian," I confirm. "I was too shocked by that, and how that woman was looking at me, to notice anyone else. Why? Septimus? Do they work for the Greys?"

He draws a hand over his face, looking tired. We have Vásan and Nissa's attention as well, now. They are standing by the door of the coach, moving no further into the train yet. I wonder if we will need to depart from the train immediately and make separate travel plans. I pray not.

"Who were they?" Nissa asks, prompting him again. "Trouble?"

"That would be Camilla and Lure. Of the Mitaurus," Septimus sighs.

"The Mitaurus?" Nissa repeats, startled.

Unlike the tales of the Families Three, legends of the Mitaurus are recognized as being likely exaggerated, but still true. For a long time, they have been the name to fear when it comes to those who are known practitioners of *Dadj'zcha.* They tend to avoid Isaaria, however; we have too many churches and holy sites, and they abhor such places. If they have traversed my country before, they have been quiet about it.

I'm not familiar with all of the lore their troupe tends to carry about with them, only a few rumors here and there, or bedtime stories meant to frighten small children into being good. I know they are witches, and I know—or always assumed, up to now—that their private agendas and devil worshipping at least had nothing to do with toppling countries or killing kings. With Rian's protection as my main priority, they barely registered as threats. I merely considered them as disgusting people who existed, somewhere else in the world, causing trouble for others, but not for me.

"What exactly do they want?" I ask.

Septimus snorts. "Damen and Aiden. Teresa would be a nice addition."

"That does not answer why they are *here,* though," Nissa points out.

She is uncomfortable without her hyena close by, I am sure, but it was necessary to pack the animal in a crate for the sake of travel. It is not far, relatively, though it would be of no use if we suddenly found ourselves in the midst of combat.

Septimus sighs and gestures for us to move away from the door.

"If they aren't on the train, I wouldn't worry. If they wanted to do anything more than unnerve us, they would have made their move. They have not."

"So, they only want to frighten us," I say, uneasy by their presence but willing to manage enemies that only hover and do not attack.

"That seems likely for now, at least," Septimus says. "Let us find our seats. If anything peculiar crops up, we'll reassess. But I suspect that pair was merely tasked with following us, or to follow anyone who may be connected to Teresa and the boys. They cannot know what we are attempting to do, yet, and so, I would not worry."

That implies there may be a time to worry coming, perhaps relatively soon, but I agree with Septimus for now. I am loathe to abandon the comfort and speed of travel by locomotive simply out of panic, and we will travel significantly faster this way than we would on foot. I think I would rather risk an encounter with the Mitaurus than the Greys, but I do not know enough about them to be sure. It is concerning that both parties have an interest in the Smith bloodline, enough to have followed Septimus and Teresa here.

I stay close behind Septimus as we travel further into the train and find our cabin, so we can continue the conversation without a moment wasted.

"Between the Mitaurus and the Greys, which should I be more concerned about?" I ask. "Which of them is worse?"

"Worse?" Septimus repeats without turning around. "Fate's Fingers, Soleil, what a question...I suppose it depends. Which do *you* find worse: a group intent on spreading horror through the world because they worship the Dark, or a group intent on spreading horror around the world with the foolish goal of *freeing* the Dark, believing they can kill it?"

"I can see how they might equate," I admit. "At least they haven't joined forces, I suppose."

Septimus sighs. "Yes. The good news is that Charrion absolutely despises the Greys and would never help them. Well, for the most part," he amends. "Since Kryto and Teresa were promised to the Dark, the Mitaurus treat them like their captive prince and princess...Or they'd like to, if they could get their hands on them and the children."

He swings himself down into a seat on a cushioned bench inside our cabin. There is enough room in the cabin to comfortably seat six, which leaves the four of us with plenty of space. There is not much to look at out the frost-glazed windows, but Septimus takes one of the far-seats anyway while Nissa curls herself into the other. Vásan and I both prefer to be close to the cabin door, which I slide shut with a foot.

"Why Damen and Aiden?" I ask when I cannot think of a good reason on my own.

I suppose Damen does have a powerful fluke, but Aiden is only a one-armed boy who loves his mother and has no real knowledge of the workings of the world, even if he has seen much of it for his age.

Septimus remains relatively relaxed in his answer, despite the words said, so I suppose that unofficially answers my question about which group I should worry over more.

"Because the Greys decided it would be a brilliant idea to ritualistically, ah, donate Kryto, Teresa and their children to the Dark, to 'prove' their loyalty to it, which is the second-worst idea they have ever had. Possibly third worst."

Nissa is bemused. "Wouldn't someone need to freely agree to that?"

"Well, technically Teresa did. It was built into her wedding vows. The Greys explained it all to her, but they implied it was a cultural tradition. So, she went through with it of her own free will. Unfortunately. If you can count agreeing to a marriage while drugged 'free will'."

Isaarians would tend not to; and so, from my perspective, Teresa would not have agreed. It does explain how Kryto convinced her to marry him, though. I cannot imagine Teresa was prime to make good decisions in such a state.

"What about the children?" Vásan demands shortly.

Septimus thinks and scratches his chin. "I mean, I'm no expert on how to sell people to the Dark, but I think they have more flexibility. They were promised by someone else, after all. Not their fault. But if they happen to, well, choose that lifestyle, which is how their father was angling to raise them, then, ah..."

He shrugs.

I get the feeling that he is not at all comfortable with this topic. I am tempted to ask why he did not try to stop his sister, if he knew what her marrying Kryto meant. However, I assume Septimus has already tried a variety of methods to keep Teresa away from Kryto; nothing has worked. I cannot expect him to avoid every unfortunate circumstance on behalf of those he cares about. Despite what his past iteration insisted to me, his knowledge of what has happened in past cycles does not make him a god.

"Is there any way to break that bond?" I ask instead.

To my surprise, Septimus shrugs again.

"If there is, I have not the slightest idea. All I know is that it happened, Teresa is now closely bonded to both Kryto, and that when she and Kryto are far away from each other, *both* suffer, physically and mentally. At least when one of them is doing 'better', the other is 'worse', which means Kryto has probably been miserable for months now. Not that Teresa is doing spectacularly, but she has been through worse."

Nissa frowns. She shakes her head and mutters something in Hoitsokin. I only know a small portion of the language but understand Nissa herself enough to know that she finds the entire family structure of the Smiths and

Greys deplorable and confusing. Why anyone would think it a good idea to bond themselves to the Dark in any fashion is beyond her comprehension.

I do not know **Vásan's opinion on the matter**.

Septimus goes on, speaking mainly for the sake of hearing his own thoughts aloud. It us likely tiring, needing to constantly assess and plan around groups with unreasonable motives.

"I suppose we have found ourselves trapped between two troupes of witches," he says. "Both will do their best to stop us if they learn of our intentions, but they should hinder one another as well. It is possible the Mitaurus are only following me out of habit, knowing I am, or was, once close to Kryto."

"Do we have to worry about them attacking?" Nissa asks.

"Likely. I doubt they will target Teresa so long as she is in the Summer Palace—Charrion is not fond of full-scale invasions unless necessary, and he knows he does not have the numbers. But they may could try to use Soleil here and trade her for Teresa if they think Rian would go for that."

"He wouldn't," I reassure.

I do not miss Vásan's skeptical expression. Nissa, as well, is likely assessing how to best protect me should anything happen. I am not accustomed to being in such a position, at least not in this lifetime, and I do not like it.

For the next hour or so, tension runs high in our little cabin, for three of us. Septimus betrays no obvious concern regarding the Mitaurus aside from his initial reaction, but this may be because he is trying to predict the future with the assumption that things will go smoothly here on out.

As time passes, and nothing in the train explodes, no commotions erupt, and no one attempts to shoot one of us, even I begin to relax.

It will take us two days to reach the south as intended, counting this one. I am not sure how much of that time I can willingly spend in this tiny cabin, but I am determined to push myself as far as possible. As Rian indicated, meditation is a good practice to delve deeper into now that I have a fluke to balance, and I do not want to appear restless and hot-headed before Vásan. Nissa and I are similar enough to understand one another, but Vásan is here to keep an eye on me, sent by Rian. He is aware of that.

If I ever want his respect, I must earn it.

Time passes, and I attempt to think of anything but how I already miss Rian, and how I hope Ayla is not upset I did not say goodbye. Nissa braids a leather thong into something to properly hold her hair back from her face. She occasionally asks Septimus a sporadic question about Lusch, about the Greys, about his life there. Most of it I already know, from my own inquiries, and Nissa's reactions are about as expected. I think, if Amerson Grey does manage to come back a third time, she would be more than happy to engage in combat with him.

I fiddle with my new pocket watch, recall Amerson striking both Teresa and Rian, and pretend I do not have emotions.

At noon and later in the evening we have food brought, but otherwise receive no visitors. It is not until after the sun has long-since set when Vásan bothers to say a word to any of us, and this is only because Nissa has left to stretch her legs and Septimus has closed himself into the corner tightly with his arms crossed and eyes closed. With only each other for company, I suppose it occurs to Vásan that I am an option for conversation.

Not that much is said.

He digs in his bag and produces a well-worn journal before offering it to me without fanfare. It takes me a moment to realize what it could be, and I am surprised that there is some relief in knowing it wasn't forgotten. At least, I hope, it will distract me from how pitifully I am succumbing to emotions, and so early on in our travels.

"I nearly forgot. Grand Prince Soren Carsans requested you receive this," Vásan says simply. "Perhaps it will be decent late-night company."

He says this without a spark of irony about him, though I have no doubt he knows precisely what is written in that journal, and who its owner was.

I decide to tuck the journal away, not wanting to crack the cover in Vásan's presence. If I read Mercer's last travel journal, it needs to be with relative privacy. I do not know what I might find in the pages, and I do not want to risk my expressions becoming someone's entertainment, particularly not if that person is Vásan.

I manage to nod off for perhaps a quarter hour. When I wake, Nissa is still gone, and Septimus is sprawled in a new position in an attempt to stretch out. Vásan, meanwhile, looks as if he has not moved once this entire time. This is ironic as he is the tallest of us and has the most cause to be uncomfortable in these relatively cramped quarters.

Septimus and Vásan appear to be in the middle of a conversation when I crack an eye open, though neither of them notices me. I quickly catch up on the topic and am not surprised by it. After all, I suppose Nissa and Vásan both have plenty to think about, **Vásan in particular.**

"One has to wonder..." he mutters.

"What?" Septimus asks, curiosity in no way hidden.

"When we do all this again, the 'proper' way. The way the world is allegedly meant to be...Will I still have Alo?"

"That is the question, isn't it?" Septimus says. "From what I have seen, likely, yes. Though, when you learn of his conception and the reactions to certain circumstances have varied."

"But he is always...my son," Vásan says uneasily.

"As far as I know, you always raise him as your son, yes," my cousin says, somewhat evasively. "Regardless of whether Yvette is already your wife when he is born or not. But he is always Yvette's, biologically."

Vásan nods slowly, considering this information. I know that on occasional timelines, Lune has been promised to Vásan, though he has always married Yvette instead. So, should Vásan marry Lune, Septimus is confirming that Alo would no longer be his son. Yvette would have no reason to allow Vásan to adopt her child; not when it means giving him away when she loves Alo so.

I could have predicted Vásan's next question. I already know the answer to it as well, and I would not need Septimus to tell me.

"I know you do not know everything," Vásan says. "But I must ask: the woman who died on the king's wedding night. Captain Marson's sister…"

He struggles to choose his words, but Septimus guesses at them.

"You know her, yes. At least, you have known her, most cycles."

Vásan sucks in a breath. This is confirmation of a thing that has tortured him for years.

"Does she ever choose me?"

"No," Septimus admits. "I'm sorry."

His tone is genuine. He knows what it is like to love a person and have them choose someone else over you.

"And Bastien. My…brother. Did he ever have contact with one of these so-called Anomalies?" Vásan asks. "Those items you claim corrupt a person and their good intentions, altering them?"

This one Septimus hesitates to answer. He knows what Bastien did to be banished from Isaaria.

"No," he finally says. "And I am even sorrier for that."

Vásan nods, sits back, and thinks. He does not betray his emotions with physical cues, and appears to accept Septimus' words as mere fact, nothing to be sensitive over. Yet, it is the most vulnerable I've seen him, in any timeline.

Perhaps in the silence that follows one of them realizes that I am awake. It hardly matters; all three of us are lost to our own thoughts. The possibilities that we are left to consider, in this single example alone, are the sort that would boggle the best of scholars.

It is torturous. If we do restart our lives one last time, as Septimus and I discussed, I will have to keep my memories for our efforts to be worthwhile. I will have to know about everything. It is one thing for Septimus to ask me not to interfere with himself and Teresa, as they will be half-way around the world anyways. However, for Alo Pike to exist, I will have to let Bastien Pike take advantage of a young woman right under my nose. As Septimus has suggested, Bastien does not need an excuse to be capable of such evil. He has always assaulted Yvette, when given the opportunity.

So, could I allow that? Could I let Yvette Pike be raped by her brother-in-law if stopping it ensures Alo—a child Vásan and Yvette both love—never exists?

Similarly, what if, in this final, new universe, with Lune and Taris publicly married, Vásan stops pining over my sister? What if he lets her go and does fall in love with Yvette and they have Alo, together? What if, in our final, new world, Bastien Pike never thinks to do something so evil in the first place? What if he is somehow a better man?

If I sat down with Vásan and Yvette directly and asked them what they would want, I cannot begin to guess at their answers. I cannot speak for Yvette Pike. So, perhaps the right thing to do, in the end is nothing. Realistically, I could never, ever stop every rape, murder, abuse, injustice. Even if we prevent a war between Alarkia and Lijimata, we will not be able to prevent every war in the world. We will not be able to fix everything. We can only maintain the most peaceful world possible for mankind. Or so I hope.

I wish Rian were here for me to discuss this with. He is smarter than me, particularly in the field of morals, and I worry that I am not capable of making the correct, moral choice, but merely neutral ones. The correct outcome for the world does not necessarily mean that every event that happens has been morally dictated by the Theebin religion. After all, for me to control or even attempt to control all outcomes implies a hubris even worse than the Greys, considering the concept of humanity's free will.

At this point, I have no idea if my actions are morally justified or if all this self-philosophizing is a way to justify what I want to do, even if it is wrong. I suppose if I do meet with Fate, I will learn the truth regardless. I no longer live under the illusion that I am a good person. It will be a relief to have a divine being telling me precisely what to do without me needing to constantly assess their motives and trustworthiness.

"You are looking perturbed, dear cousin," Septimus notes after perhaps an hour of thought.

We are the only two still awake, or so I assume. Nissa has crawled back into one of the bunks set into the wall above and behind our heads. Vásan has insisted on sleeping sitting up, still by the door. I think by the morning, he will likely regret that decision.

"I am starting to think that, in forcing everyone in the world to relive their lives according to my whim, I am the worst of villains," I say.

Septimus raises an eyebrow. "That may be something of an exaggeration. Technically speaking, without your rewound timelines, its possibly our world as we know it may have ended already."

"But I did not do this for the world," I press. "I did it for selfish reasons. For my family. For myself."

He shrugs. "Who cares about motives? So what if you had a more powerful personal connection? At least it has forced you to do the right thing. Eventually, even, for the right reasons."

"That's my point," I say. "What if it is actually the wrong thing?"

Naomi, in particular, comes to mind. I am already beginning to regret leaving without saying goodbye to her, Korvaan, and Ayla first. Despite going off on what sounds like a hero's quest, I do not often make the heroic, noble choice when left to my own devices. I relay as much to Septimus.

"In regards to your foster family, they cared enough about you to promise to help you in the first place," he says. "They agreed to do this."

"I don't think I should have asked at all," I admit.

"That is beside the point. If we are speaking entirely on the basis of right and wrong, innocent or guilty, for what you have done, there is a specific question to ask. Should those around you be allowed to hold you accountable for things your past selves have done while insisting they cannot be held accountable for the promises of their past selves?"

I consider this, stumped for a moment.

"I don't care who's right or wrong anymore at this point," Septimus admits with a sigh. "I only don't want the world to end and I don't want the Dark unleashed. Everything else is flexible as far as I'm concerned. Perhaps you would be less miserable if you adapted a similar viewpoint."

I believe he says this if only in an attempt to help me quiet my mind, and get some rest as we rumble along. Whatever peace Septimus appears to have made with himself after decades of introspection, I fear my journey in the same vein is only beginning. Regardless, I must remember that while I have sought out and appreciate Septimus' advise, he is not exactly a moral authority on such topics. If either of us are the best the world has as its heroes, I must wonder what kind of humor the Almighty subscribes to.

Later that night, I can't help myself any longer, nor do I feel too sickened to talk myself out of it. I crack open the journal that Soren Carsans sent and read what notes and scribbles Mercer Ralhan left behind: his memoirs of his last journey to the west. I suppose, so long as I already cannot sleep, this is unlikely to make my insomnia worse. Perhaps the reading will even calm my mind enough to let drowsiness take over.

The first few dozen pages are filled with consistent entries whilst aboard a ship. Mercer relates the events of each day as if planning to re-tell his story hour by hour when he returns to Isaaria. This is hardly surprising to me; Mercer was always good entertainment at parties and gatherings, regaling folks with the tales of his travels. I believe the meticulous nature of his detailing is what draws people in to every word he says, not unlike how they are easily enthralled by Rian telling his fairy tales.

Rian was always the better story-teller, but Mercer's worldliness made him an easy target for conversation. He seemed to know about every issue a person could possibly mention and had an anecdote for everything.

Then, there is a startling gap in journal dates, just before Mercer was meant to arrive in Alarkia. There is an accidental page skip before his first, official entry whilst in Alarkia. I can see evidence in the pages themselves, in the crinkled corners, warped surfaces and occasional dark smears, that this is not a passage meant for future storytelling. No, this entry was necessary for Mercer to keep his thoughts in order; to have something to share the pain with, even if it was only ink and paper. His bodyguard, Marques, was not exactly known for having a sympathetic ear, though I have no doubt Mercer needed one:

> *I am sick of the smell of blood and rot. It is unimaginable until you live it.*
>
> *I am not permitted to remain with the so-called common folk after nightfall, for my own safety. I am, according to the Alarkian authorities, much too precious an Isaarian prince for anyone to risk my blood being spilt on their soil. The truth is, they are terrified of anything happening to me, and risking the wrath of my closest friend, the* <u>*king*</u> *of Isaaria. I cannot blame them for that, I suppose. One war is enough.*
>
> *Yet, soon as dawn breaks, I return to see who has lasted the night, and who will never breathe again. I would rather be there to watch them die; it is worse, showing up in the morning to see bodies carted away. It feels as if, for every one person I save, three more die. The Death does not even spare the little ones in his collection. I can only hope he treats them kindly, escorting them to the Otherworld.*
>
> *Marques has not said so explicitly, but I know he would rather I return home by the next boat available. He does not understand why I torture myself like this, or so he has told me in his own way. But I cannot imagine returning to Isaaria. I haven't decided how I'll be able to stand facing Rian and Asmer and the Carsans again. Rian most especially.*
>
> *Having to smile. Having to pretend as if life can go on, when every soul I've lost weighs heavily on me.*
>
> *I am expected to return and act the grand prince I am meant to be. I am not sure who that man is anymore. I only know that he was an optimistic fool who believed that he could take a simple trip out west, do what he could to help the poor victims of war, and return unscathed.*
>
> *I should have known better. I should not have allowed myself such an ego as to think that I, one man, whose own country has no money or political interest in this affair, could make a substantial difference here.*
>
> *Since my arrival, I have treated many wounded by these past seven years. Widows and bruised children. Those who have suffered the brutalities of war.*

Orphans missing limbs who watched their own parents be butchered in front of them. Men who have returned from the front lines with dead, haunted eyes. Wailing girls who cannot quite reconcile the fact they've been raped.

Today, I watched an infant die while her mother held her and sobbed and sobbed. They had traveled northernly as quickly as they could to escape the war's worst ravages, but it was not fast enough. The child was dreadfully malnourished by the time she was under my care. Her chances of survival were all but imaginary. This Fate-damned war has seen to that. She is not the only infant to die, and will not be the last by far.

This can never happen again.

Never.

I stop reading but place a finger against the page to mark my spot. My eyes have begun to water, and I need to tilt my head back. Reading the journal is not helping; it only poses more moral quandaries instead of the placation I'd hoped it might offer. Is this all a matter of trading one suffering for another? Excusing some, if it stops this terrible war in the west, that has so clearly ruined thousands of lives and ended thousands of others?

"Is he lamenting the tragic loss of life in the west?" Septimus asks from his position, sprawled across the seat as a make-shift bed.

I pray my sniffling is not what woke him. That would be beyond mortifying. How is it that I have become so moved to tears so easily, now?

"You have never read this," I say, a question and accusation both.

"He mentioned such things often when he stayed in the Grey household," he mumbles, closing his eyes again.

"You met him over and over," I say.

We may do what we can to affect the circumstances, but Mercer will always visit Alarkia at some point, so long as there is a war and people he desires to help. Whether we can keep him from running into the Greys or not whilst he is there, I suppose, remains to be seen.

"Mmm. Let me know when he mentions me," Septimus says. He sighs as he rolls onto his side away from me, resting his head on his arms.

I doubt he has fallen back asleep so easily, assuming he was asleep at all in the first place, but he is in no mood for conversation. I turn my attention back to Mercer's travel journal, noting that more than a week has passed from the previous entry to this next one. At least his tone is less dismal as he records:

I met the most extraordinary young woman today, who, for a moment, allowed me to forget all other things that have been weighing on me.

Now that I am even further north than before, the direct effects of the war on Alarkia have diminished. They are still present, but it is easier to pretend, for both myself and the Alarkian citizens, that life might go on as normal. Shops are still open. Luxuries are still possible for those with enough money to sustain them. There are refugees from the south aplenty, yes, but at least there is housing for them. There are no bodies in the streets.

After the assistance I was able to lend the women in the refugee house last night, I honestly felt buoyed. Their gratitude made it possible to forget, for a short while, what my nightmares would surely remind me of. One of the girls, when I inquired, insisted I visit the Creative's Corner, to see about picking up gifts for my noble friends. Whatever Alarkian culture has survived, I am likely to find it optioned for purchase there.

Naturally, when I found the book printer's shop, I immediately thought of Rian and entered. There was no proprietor about that I could see, only a girl sitting behind the counter, keeping watch over the shop while burying her nose in a book. I approached, to ask about a shopkeeper, but found words evaded me the moment she looked up from her book.

The girl had small scars across her face that I recognized as facial sores of magic-sickness. Yet she appeared in perfectly good health, her mental faculties intact. Astonishing. Extraordinary. In my travels, I have accidentally found a girl who has survived magic-sickness, something I did not think possible.

She apologized for startling me, and once I recovered myself, I apologized in turn for my staring. She said her name was Teresa Smith, and that she indeed had contracted magic-sickness as a child, but miraculously endured it. The fluke of a family friend of hers ensured her survival. Intrigued though I was, I decided to first focus on my primary quest.

Despite my initial assumptions, after explaining briefly who I was and why I had entered the shop, the girl proved more than capable in helping me with my quest. In fact, I learned she worked here as an apprentice to the printer. She drew illustrated lettering as well as full-page illustrations of astounding skill, examples of which she showed me when I expressed interested.

I suppose the Almighty works in peculiar ways when parceling out innate gifts. I said as much, in compliment, and the girl laughed. She claimed it was no innate talent, but hundreds of hours of practice. I maintain that, practice or no, something must have blessed her to have such skill at such a young age.

What was meant to be a brief stop at the printer's stretched on, though I admit I barely noticed time passing, I was so entranced. I must have stayed past closing time, though the girl did not notice, either. It was only when she rang me up for my purchase–a rare book I know Rian will be thrilled to receive, not only for the beauty in its illustration work–that I was reminded of the time. Even Marques had not bothered to lecture me on staying late.

But I suppose it is different: a foreign grand prince being escorted back to his lodgings by a bodyguard and a girl being expected to walk herself home in the dark. From the back room of the store, leading directly behind the counter where she worked, came a pair of men, the younger perhaps a year older than Teresa herself, the elder in his twenties. Her escorts home, I later learned. They immediately came over to her, making themselves at home and teasing her. The elder, Amerson, pulled out her hairpin and held it high above her head, I believe in good fun, while his younger brother Jarrod collected her things. Their teasing made her act her age, which is to say much younger than I was used to given her previous maturity.

I would have merely collected the book, paid my dues, and left them to their evening, except the younger boy, Jarrod, recognized me. He inquired about my being in Alarkia, and my interest in these books. I answered honestly, admittedly intrigued by them just as much as they were me, as they had introduced themselves as Jarrod and Amerson Grey. Two Greys and a Smith, I thought, was a strange accident given Rian's studies. When I mentioned this to them, Amerson laughed. He said he was well-aware of such coincidences, and further said that Teresa was their future sister-in-law, as she was betrothed to their middle brother, Kryto Grey. Named after the same Kryto Grey as the stories.

The poor girl did not look entirely comfortable when mention was made of her fiancé. But she was smiling heartily later when it came time to see me off, so I suppose I may have misread the situation. Or else, it was a simple bout of nervousness or embarrassment. I'm certain she could read in my face that I was shocked to learn she had a betrothed, considering how young she was. Perhaps I am the reason she was uncomfortable.

Amerson noticed as well. He explained to me that Teresa and her fiancé would not marry for at least another six years. Teresa is only fourteen, after all. But Kryto is the heir to the Grey's wealthy estate. Teresa marrying him will secure a future for her and her family in their war-torn world.

This appeared to give his brother Jarrod an idea, and they mentioned that they should invite me to dinner at their estate with the rest of the Grey family. If it was rare and curious tomes I was after, they had plenty more to look through, and it would be an honor to host an Isaarian prince. I did my best to receive this invitation graciously, and humbly, but the idea of being offered hospitality was tempting. Especially considering the trials of the past days.

I agreed to come up to visit what they called their 'Northern Alarkian Estate'. Wealthy indeed, I suppose. Jarrod, gregarious and pleasant young fellow, drew me a comprehensive map and relayed further verbal instructions to a stunned Marques regarding what trains to take and which places to tell a driver to bring us. They are so excited at the prospect at having guests, a reason to properly celebrate and host a dinner, that I do not know how I could possibly refuse.

When we parted ways, I'd promised to take the trip up north to visit in two days, giving them enough time to prepare and to alert the other members of their family that they had invited guests. Jarrod insisted over and over that no one would mind, and that Kryto would definitely be pleased. They look forward to seeing me again soon, they promised. Even Teresa appeared pleased at the idea.

I plan to see to my own business and put everything in order, including stopping by the postal office to ship off Rian's birthday gift before I head up north.

I HAVE FALLEN asleep whilst in the middle of Mercer's next entry, explaining the complications of posting a package from a war-torn country to Isaaria. Movement about the cabin is what stirs me. One of my companions getting up in the middle of the night restlessly, I first assume. However, when I crack my eyes open out of drowsy curiosity, that is not what I see.

Though I'm not pleased to admit it, I am too terrified to move. In our cabin, standing directly in front of me and watching me, is a woman in a white dress, her long, unkempt blond hair dangling loosely to her elbows. Her eyes are wide and some shade of burgundy red with long, pale lashes, like Septimus'. Only, unlike my cousin, I get the distinct impression from this creature that she is not alive.

Her teeth are too sharp.

"Oh, to sleep. To dream," she says in a sighing, musical voice. "It has been such a long time since I visited that realm. Would you let me into your dreams? Would your grand prince, here? I would say his is a tortured mind."

I try to speak, to call and wake Septimus, but my voice is a croak in my throat. She does not acknowledge my attempts.

"How delicious would those dreams be?" she says. "So much agony."

I shut my eyes tight, like a child attempting to prove to themselves their nightmares are naught but their own imagination. Of the many magical creatures in Samioth, I cannot think of one that could get into this train and act as this thing has. She is not a Fae, decidedly not what I picture a Fair would be, and is too corporeal to be a ghost. Yet something stinks of dark magic about her. Something is not right.

A hand is on my shoulder. I nearly shriek but manage to open my eyes in time and see it is only Septimus. In fact, there is no sign of my haunted visitor at all, and there is even the dim cabin light turned on, offering us a pale-yellow light to see by.

"Get up," Septimus says, shaking my shoulder again.

"What?" I croak, rubbing at my eyes.

There is a sore crick in my neck that I roll out as best I can. Nissa and Vásan are awake as well. Nissa has acquired her hyena and is putting away what little requires repacking while Vásan buttons his coat. He has yet to put his gloves back on, and it startles me to see his bare hands. I do not think I ever have before; **Vásan has always been so careful.**

"Someone isn't going to be pleased about that," I tell Nissa, gesturing to where her hyena sits gnawing on a bone.

She shrugs, nonplussed, but does not try to justify why the hyena is here. Septimus answers for her regardless.

"Something isn't right. We're jumping off and walking the rest of the way," he says hastily, and goes on before I can open my mouth. As if he expected a complaint or accusation. "Consider us lucky we got this far already."

It does not take me long to prepare to brave the cold and secure my belongings about my person. The concept of jumping from a moving train is not pleasant in the first place let alone with so much gear, but at least a snowbank ought to soften our landing.

Septimus shoves the door to our cabin aside and checks the darkened hall in both directions before letting us spill out of it after him. I wonder if he is looking for signs of the Mitaurus. Whatever mischief is afoot, I suppose their hand could be directing it. Still, we all keep our wits about us as we follow Septimus down towards the nearest exit. I suppose it is not the exit that we have interest in, but the coupling between train cars. The outer doors should be locked securely, so that passengers do not experience unfortunate accidents, but movement between the cars is necessary for crew members and staff, so these doors remain unlocked.

A blast of cold air and biting snow snaps at my face the moment Septimus shoves the door aside. On the other end of this car is a covered passage for movement to a dining car, but this direction leads only to the back half of the passenger cars, and is not meant for folk such as ourselves to move about.

The rush of wind makes it so that Septimus must shout over the wind, but I resort mainly to reading his lips anyway. We cannot all jump together, given the small opening in the railing, so he will go first. The rest of us will need to follow as quickly as possible, so we are generally in the same place, given the train's speed.

I am directly behind him, and keep myself as close as possible while Septimus waits to time his jump. I can feel behind me that Nissa's hyena is not pleased with this situation, but it is bonded to her, and will obey her. Vásan, then, is behind her, still in the train car.

Even if he said nothing, I am looking ahead enough to predict when Septimus will jump. A long snow drift approaches, tall enough and soft enough that it will break our falls. His words barely matter to me, as instinct and common sense are enough to instruct me. The moment he flings himself forward off the train, I am close behind him and jump but a few seconds after him. With the weight I'm carrying, I'm not flung too far from the train. Its noisy rattling, enough to shake me, does perk one's senses in a terrifying way. I think it is only because I have faced much worse that I am able to overcome the primal urge to not jump.

The snow does soften my landing, which happens both quicker and less gracefully than I would imagine, but it still hurts. I somehow land on my back, head pointed down towards the tracks, face up at the blizzard in the sky. My body aches. I force myself to struggle upwards to sit just as Nissa lands in the snow perhaps two meters to my left, hyena yowling in displeasure. The two pop up in the snow and Nissa gives me a pointed-toothed grin.

I think she enjoyed that.

Vásan, on her other side, is also struggling slightly to force himself up out of the snow and to his feet. By the time the caboose has rattled past us, and the cacophony begins to fade as the train continues its journey without us, we have all managed to stand. We begin the process of dusting the snow from ourselves, searching for lost items, and adjusting articles of clothing.

Nissa, as the smallest and most compacted of us, has managed the best. Vásan, as the tallest, then has understandably predictable results.

"This is probably the most undignified thing you have ever done, isn't it?" Nissa smirks. When Vásan corrects her, it is clear she did not expect more than a grunt or perhaps a glare in answer.

"No. I think beating my brother within an inch of his life and mentally torturing him with my fluke until our mother begged me to stop likely takes that award," he says.

It is the most he has said at one time since we left. Nissa understandably has nothing to say after that, and focuses her eyes on the ground in front of her until it is time to move on again.

We do our best to struggle up the snow drift to reach the other side, and I note that the sun will be rising soon. So, we have at least covered most of the journey by train and saved as much time as we possibly can.

I have just reassured myself with this good news when a strange, terrifying noise splits the air, cutting through the howl of the wind. It is a strange sound, nearly impossible to describe. If it is a scream, it is not a human one. It is a hunting cry, the likes of which I have never heard before. It reverberates for some time and is followed by the distant tearing of metal and a mechanical screech. Nissa's hyena immediately cows, becoming jittery and snappish in obvious fear. Even Nissa instinctually moves closer to the rest of us, and has drawn one of her knives instinctually.

She reverts to Hoitsokin in a question or perhaps a curse as we all look to Septimus. I suppose he was right in knowing something was wrong.

"Fate's Fingers," I murmur. "What is that?"

"One of Kryto and Teresa's worst so-called 'demons'," Septimus says. "A big one. Stay close, and follow me. There is nothing we can do about it, now. The closer we get to the border, the more you can expect them to crop up."

"We're going to leave?" I say.

I look back to where the train disappeared, the same direction those noises came from. It does not take an imagination to guess at what will happen, but it is still too dark out to see anything. The blizzard does not help.

"The other people on the train—" I start.

Septimus grabs my arm to stop me, but I was not about to trudge through the snow merely to satisfy curiosity. Even before he says it, we all know what has happened, and how close we came to disaster if Septimus' instincts had not saved us. Perhaps something divine stepped in to save us; who can know.

"We can't do anything about it," he says. "Not now. Just tell yourself that the quest we're embarking on may make it so that these events never occur, and keep moving."

I am too shocked to argue. I force myself to nod, so that he will release me, and let him lead the way due south as best as we can whilst avoiding the train tracks. Still, I am certain I am not the only one who feels a chill not only from the cold.

Thirteen

WE WALK ALL DAY once the sun rises, sticking to country roads and continuing due south, having left the train tracks far behind. The blizzard stops around the same time as the sunrise, making travel conditions mildly more bearable. Occasionally, we stop to rest and allow Septimus to check our progress as best he can. Nissa is incredibly helpful in such instances, as she knows southern Isaaria better than anyone else present, and perhaps anyone I know. She also is not one to shy from an argument with Septimus if she disagrees with him about the quickest path to Mouloix, the southern hub for most Isaarian foreign trade by sea. It is there that Septimus' allies should await us, having secured passage east.

Most of these arguments, Nissa wins, and we set off again on aching legs with little to distract us from the journey. After all, Nissa is a mostly solitary traveler and is not accustomed to keeping up conversation. Vásan has apparently no questions that need answering enough for him to deign to ask. This leaves me and Septimus, and while I would rather not be left alone with my thoughts more than necessary, it takes some time to conjure a decent topic that will promote conversation instead of a question-and-answer session.

I cannot imagine Septimus would be thrilled about another of those, particularly not if it has anything to do with the Greys.

Around noon, we stop by a river. Nissa breaks through a thin layer of ice with the heel of her boot and catches a trio of fat fish for us to cook when we stop for the night. Vásan and I do not interfere with this process, though Septimus apparently has some interest in ice fishing the way Nissa insists on performing it: crouched over her hole in the ice with her long knife as a spear.

It is admittedly more effective than one might expect, but this is probably due to practice and skill. When Nissa allows Septimus to attempt it, he only ends up wet, and she ends up laughing.

Septimus insists we do not have time to stop long enough for his clothes to dry, and lucky for him the weather is warming significantly the further south we travel. The sun is high in the sky, a cloudless day, and he requires the use of his shaded glasses as well as a hood and scarf. Otherwise, he claims, the sun will reflect off the snow that remains and he will burn.

I walk next to him as we head downhill, a long slope leading to a road below. Vásan walks more carefully behind us and Nissa allows her hyena to run up and down the hill ahead of us while she takes her time carrying the precious fish. She was right in her directions, and we are well on our way towards Mouloix. We should be able to reach it by midday tomorrow, so long as we don't oversleep.

With his clothes still wet, the fabric clings and hangs on Septimus' frame in a way that reminds me: though it was more obvious to see in Teresa, in her skinny arms and gaunt face, her brother is hardly the picture of health, either. As tired and aching as I am, I suppose stubborn persistence is what has kept Septimus going, and not much else.

"You and Teresa are both quite thin," I say, noting that my arms are bigger than his, and possibly my legs, too.

Septimus scoffs. "Oh, yes. That."

"'That'?" I repeat. "I thought it was from the travel. I wanted to make sure it does not happen again, now."

I must sound apologetic, because he brushes it off, trying to be blasé.

"If you feed me, I'll eat," he promises. "But sometimes, when it came to treading carefully around Kryto, when one was not certain what kind of mood he had taken to, you felt as if you should not breathe. No—it was more than that. You felt as if you could not make a sound. Even the sorts your body makes without your consent. Your heart pounding. Your guts squirming. Your eyelashes when you blink."

As I essentially crave Rian's attention whenever possible, even when I was meant to be invisible to him, I cannot imagine having that reaction to a person and still managing to love them. In many ways, no matter how hard I try, Septimus and Teresa's love for her monster of a husband is unbelievable.

"I think Teresa came to dread dining with him," Septimus says. "She only ate things she could consume without making a sound, which was not much. It was all useless, of course. He is obsessed with her. There was nothing Teresa could do to keep his attention off her. But still. Any little thing."

Nissa, listening in and knowing what she does, makes no attempt to hide her utter disgust the way I might.

"How is it that you have not killed these men a long, long time ago," she criticizes. She is thinking not only of Kryto but of how terrified Teresa was of her own brother-in-law, too. "How did you not kill them in their sleep the second you saw or heard…*anything?* How did your *parents* not kill them?"

She is angry with him, and my aunt and uncle, for not defending Teresa the way a good brother should, for not defending their daughter like good parents. Nissa's own brothers are only her half-siblings, and still, they are better siblings to one another in her eyes. Nissa even named her nephew and niece as her own heirs, one after another, the moment they were born. Even if she had her own children in the future, as addressed at the time, she insisted nothing be changed, no extra clause written in, just in case.

How strange it is, the way we are seen as people, and the way we see ourselves as members of our own families.

Septimus needs to think on this. He has no defense, I am sure. After all, he spent decades siding with the Greys before it occurred to him that he was wrong for doing so. He did not allow these things to happen only once, but many times over again. Even I cannot pretend to be in Septimus' situation and come up with a decent excuse.

Vásan is the only one of us three not visibly disgusted, but that could be only because I cannot read his expression. Nissa and I, though I admit having Septimus on our side is helpful, are more judgmental.

"I'd like to be honest with you all," Septimus finally says.

It is an effort not to snort and roll my eyes at him. Honesty, I think, is somewhat of a joke with Septimus.

"There have been cycles when I've grown to know you, Soleil, and Rian very well," he says. "Well enough that I now love him like a brother. But I need you to know...that when I have spoken of loving Kryto...It was not a brotherly love. It was much needier than that; filled with more blind adulation than that."

"I inferred as much," I say, though I had hoped otherwise for Septimus' sake.

This is not much of a surprise to Nissa or Vásan, either. Though they do not know Septimus as well, and only recently learned the truth of things, I suppose they have heard enough already to draw their own conclusions. Perhaps it is the only way they can imagine giving Septimus an excuse.

"I tell you this because I need you to understand," he presses. "Imagine if Rian had married Lune instead of you, Soleil. You still loved him, but he loved her more. Then imagine further, if you can, that you realized one day that he was a *monster* who terrorized people, most especially your own sister and her children. Imagine knowing the world would be better if Rian were dead. Would you be able to bring yourself to kill him?"

"But Rian would not ever do those things. Never. Rian is a good person," I press. "Especially to Lune? No. He could never—"

"There," Septimus says, stopping me. His expression is one of self-effacement. "That's precisely my point. That's exactly what it was like for me."

There is a moment of silence as we each try to put things in perspective, with our own examples. Septimus used me and Rian, but I suppose the analogy could work in several ways, though for some of us better than others.

"That still makes no sense," Nissa decides. "No sense at all."

"It makes perfect sense to me," Vásan says.

For the second time in less than a day, he has managed to shut her up with ease. Nissa shoots him a glare, and huffs, but has no defense. It takes her a few moments to think of something else to say, leaving me with my thoughts in the meantime.

The more I think about it, I suppose it would make the most sense to Vásan, out of the three of us. Rearrange things a touch and, did Vásan not love his own brother, before what Bastien did to Yvette? Did he ever, for one second, imagine his own little brother capable of something so evil?

In fact, no one did. There was a time, nearly two decades ago now, when someone might have called Bastien Pike a good man. There was a time when many even preferred him as Aloysius Pike the First's heir over his so-called cold-hearted elder brother.

"Still," Nissa huffs, settling her ruffled feathers. "Even if you love him, how could you not love your sister more? Enough to help her?"

Septimus is prepared for this accusation, too. While he is explaining himself, he is not making excuses. He has a comprehensive catalogue of the sins he has committed.

"Because at first, I blamed Teresa," he admits. "I recognized what Kryto was doing as wrong, but could not bring myself to blame him. It had to be her fault. She made him...violent."

"You must have known that wasn't true," I say.

Septimus is too smart to fall for that, even if it was his own trick.

"Of course I did. Once I realized the fault for Kryto's actions could only lay with him, and once I was able to see my sister similarly to how I had begun to see myself, it got easier. From there, it was a matter of finding new allies. People I could trust."

"And your own cousins did not occur to you?" Nissa points out.

After all, as a Memorysmith, having alerted the Greys so many times of what I was doing, one would think Lune and I would be the first ones Septimus considered. Especially since he had the luxury of knowing my own mother better than I ever did.

"Honestly, no," Septimus says. "At first, I did not know what to do. How could I? I had the knowledge of a full-grown adult, but every time we went back, I was placed in the body of a young child, at best. An infant, usually."

I am seven years older than Septimus. If I kept rewinding things to about the time I was seven or eight years old, he really would have been only an infant. How infuriating that must have been. If I went back further, he would not have even been born yet. I wonder if that was a fear of his, or if Septimus manipulated me to ensure this never happened, but I do not ask.

"It did, at least, give me time to think," he admits. "And scheme. The Greys had a fluke reader come for each birth, so everyone knew from my birth that I was a Memorysmith. My mother was not a Smith except in marriage, but she and my father knew how to use me, to make gifts for you and your sister Lune."

"You were a child," I say, somewhat aghast as I realize this.

Septimus shrugs. "My father was what you might call a 'classic' Magicsmith. Anything he physically crafted himself, he could imbue with magic. I suppose he chose to make jewelry for you and your sister imbued with *my* magic. So that you might use your fluke without much consequence."

"...My mother said the gifts were from you and your father," I remember. "But you didn't have any choice in the matter. Did you?"

Septimus shrugs again.

"Perhaps that is for the best. We accidentally created something that can traverse time itself, Soleil. Do you understand how nearly impossible that is? If I was cognizant of helping my father make such things...It might have given me an even bigger ego than I already have."

He is trying to make a joke out of it, but I am still appalled.

My uncle was doing it for what he thought were the right reasons, I am sure. He wanted to help his sister—my mother—keep Lune and me secret and safe. He was willing to use his own son to do that. It must have been taxing on Septimus' small, young body.

"Besides," he continues, "I think it was an attempt on my father's part to try and make amends, for the weapons he had made. The Greys owned him and my mother as much as Kryto has come to own Teresa and I. But they still, I think, desperately wanted better lives for their children. I think their greatest regret is not being able to give us that."

Vásan and I contemplate this, or at least I do. Nissa does not bother. She does not understand this on an emotional level and has no desire to.

She snorts and shakes her head. "You would make an excuse for anyone. Even Mercer Ralhan, you would—"

"It wasn't his fault," Septimus snaps, interrupting her.

He turns back to give her a look.

"You can disagree with me on the rest of them, maybe I am making excuses, even for myself," he says. "But not Mercer. Not him."

Even I am startled by Septimus' conviction in saying this. I understood perfectly well when he claimed Mercer had been manipulated, but even Rian, who loved Mercer, would be unlikely to claim such a thing. I certainly wouldn't.

"Regardless of his former friendships, or who manipulated him, he still chose to betray our king," Nissa insists.

"It was not entirely by choice," Septimus argues.

"Because of the necklace?" Nissa says. "The Anomaly?"

Septimus does not need to confirm it so plainly. "I thought I explained this well enough, but perhaps not. It takes whatever good intentions you have and twists them. Makes things jumbled up in one's head, so it is nearly impossible for you to think straight, or think like yourself."

I can see in the glance Nissa attempts to give me that she is not convinced. Perhaps she thinks she could withstand the corruption of the Anomalies Septimus claims the Greys keep. Maybe there is truth to this; maybe she is not pure-hearted enough for them to work on her. I doubt the Greys would try to use them on me.

"Think back some time," Septimus urges us, like a disgruntled tutor managing exceptionally poor students. "What is Mercer like, before he sees death? Before he sees it and thinks, because of his schooling in the sciences, that he is somehow responsible for those deaths?"

I reflect for a moment.

"He's good-humored," I admit. "Light-hearted. He cares about changing things, in the world. About finding a cure for magic-sickness…Children," I remember. "He loves helping children. He is not so much a womanizer, before he sees such violent deaths. He drinks less, too. He still entertains with Rian but it does not have such a destructive nature to it."

"He wanted to save Asmer al'Yibna," Vásan mutters under his breath.

I think I am the only one to hear him, and am somewhat startled that he, of all people, would know that and remember it. He never was close to Mercer or Asmer after all. I cannot recall a single conversation he had with either of them.

I know for a fact Septimus does not hear, as he soldiers on. He might be the only person in the world, but he is solidly in Mercer's corner.

"Mercer saw tragedy. Dead children. War-torn countries," he says. "He encountered the Greys who convinced him that in causing a great catastrophe in the world, the last great catastrophe in the world, that they will be able to alleviate it of the Dark and all man-made evils entirely. They gave Mercer that Anomaly, that necklace, to make him more compliant. To make their plan seem logical. As if it coincided with his own moral code perfectly."

"He must have been weak-willed for it to work, though," Nissa says.

"Not necessarily. The necklace works on people with good intentions," Septimus says. "Or, I suppose it works best on people with good intentions, who want to change the world. Idealists. Like Mercer apparently used to be."

He is not entirely wrong. For a doctor, Mercer was an extreme idealist. He had always thought he could cure Asmer. Cure magic-sickness. Cure anything if he tried hard enough. He thought it was his fate, his purpose in this world, to do so.

"But Mercer loves Rian," I say with a frown, remembering as much. "Why would he ever agree to hurt him? How could he possibly justify that?"

"People do silly things for love," Septimus warns me. "I wouldn't dare use it as an excuse. After all, Mercer cares for Rian as his best friend, and knows him better than anyone. So, possibly, his Grey-addled brain concluded that someone as generous and kind as Rian would of course allow himself to be sacrificed for the greater good."

"And that would make sense to him," I say dubiously.

Septimus shrugs. "I've seen people, incredibly good people, convinced to do worse under the Grey's influence. Their brand of moral corruption is particularly detrimental to the mind."

"But that wouldn't affect you, at least," I note.

Septimus gives me a bland look.

"You...I thought you would be immune to mind-flukes," I remind him.

"I am," Septimus confirms. "But while no one can use their Almighty-given gifts of magic to addle my head or read my mind, that doesn't mean they cannot control me in other ways. My mind can't be manipulated, but Kryto doesn't use the mind. He uses the heart."

"Is that not, in some ways, the same thing?" I challenge.

I'm not the most scientifically-learned of people, but I know a little, from Mercer. He has spoken of the things that happen in the body when one falls in love. How most reactions for a person are simply chemical. That in no way lessens that reaction, that emotion, or the outcome, but the idea of it fascinates him.

Fascinated him.

Septimus does not rise to the debate. He looks ahead of us, his eyes unseeing and glossy. His expression ashen.

"No," he says hoarsely. "It really isn't."

We have reached the bottom of the hill. Septimus takes the time to straighten himself out, pulling the damp clothes away from his skin, adjusting his pack.

"Keep reading the journal," he says specifically to me, clearing his throat. "Maybe by the end of it, you'll understand."

With that as proper enticement, I endeavor to do so. That evening, we stop to prepare an evening camp, planning to sleep in shifts with only a small fire and minor usage of victuals. Septimus, surprisingly though thankfully, happens to be a better than decent cook, and manages to make a stew for us using Nissa's fish. It is not a cheerful campsite we keep, to be sure, but at least the fire gives me enough light to read by, if I sit close. I am wrapped up well enough that I do not feel cold, even without my gloves.

Septimus is keeping watch with me, for which I am somewhat relieved. If I have questions, it is good to have him awake, irritably poking at the fire, ready to answer. He must have anticipated such a thing as he flicks his eyes in my direction now and again, waiting for my questions.

I finish Mercer's passage about posting a package for Rian, written from aboard the comfort of a private car in an Alarkian passenger train. After meeting Teresa, Amerson and Jarrod Grey, he is admittedly in better spirits. He does not believe they are the descendants of myths, no, but he is ecstatic at the coincidence he believes it is.

It is a struggle not to rush through the entry, knowing what is to come next. It partially does not feel real, knowing that the Teresa and Amerson who Mercer writes about are the same people I have already met. Teresa could tell me the exact story, from her perspective, and so could Septimus. The Kryto Grey that Mercer will meet is merely a younger version of the man who married my cousin and gave her both her sons.

This man Mercer met is Damen and Aiden's father, whom the former loves and the latter fears. I suppose the very first sentence Mercer wrote about him is fitting, then:

> *Kryto Grey is not quite what I expected.*
>
> *I believe even the most difficult person to please would admit that he is quite charming, though I doubt I could get Marques to say so out loud. Kryto is a handsome man with the most disarming of smiles, and though he does not bother to hide how he uses that to his advantage, it somehow does not feel manipulative. When Marques and I arrived, he came out to meet us with open arms, welcoming us to the estate, instead of waiting for a steward to show us inside.*
>
> *He is a young man, too; younger than his brother Amerson, at perhaps only twenty years of age. He somehow has not allowed his obvious wealth to influence him despite his inexperience, and to be clear: obvious it is. I cannot fathom why his little fiancée would need to work at a printer's shop, as they certainly are not suffering monetarily, even in the middle of a devastating war.*
>
> *When I asked, Kryto laughed, and said he arranged the job for Teresa because she enjoys such things. She loves books, and has a talent for art, so why shouldn't she be allowed to practice it? He did say he manages the wages for her, as she has no head for numbers and unfortunately never learned even basic arithmetic.*
>
> *Such a thing is inconceivable to me; any working woman in Isaaria, even at Teresa's age, would be able to manage their money and work with numbers. I suppose, engaged to a wealthy man, a career-making talent could be a mere hobby to her. Something worth passing the time with. Astonishing.*
>
> *Teresa was there to greet us at the door when we entered, dressed much finer than she was in the shop. She is a bright-eyed little lady, but shy initially, despite*

her conversation with me. It is only after some light teasing from her future husband that she warms to me again.

It is impossible not to see that he dotes on her, in an admittedly innocent fashion. Though I was originally concerned with their prominent gap in age, particularly considering their difference in development, I am reassured by the gentle care he attends to her with and the promise that they plan to wait to wed for quite some time, yet.

Additionally, despite that nervousness I thought I noted in her yesterday, Teresa appears to enjoy Kryto's attention. She becomes quite giggly and bashful, and though Kryto keeps things proper between them, I am sure Teresa has developed feelings for him already. Oh, they are likely only of the innocent variety girls her age are capable of, but still: she enjoys his companionship.

What I <u>have</u> realized instead through the evening, however, is that Teresa's occasional discomfort stems from Amerson. Their interactions worry me, I will admit. He sometimes acts in a questionable way, as if he feels that Teresa should belong to him.

But I must remember, while Teresa may remind me of my own younger sisters, this family's dynamic is not my concern, nor should it be. They have been gracious in inviting me here to supper, and in fact have extended their offer of hospitality for several days, so I might meet the rest of the family, due to arrive tomorrow. I have accepted, if only to be polite, though I will say I privately hope to convince this wealthy family that they could do quite a lot of good in helping me with my own endeavors. I know it is impossible to purchase relief for this entire country, but still. It must have simply never occurred to them; how much good they could do.

And then, in the next entry, dated a day later:

I can barely write my hand is trembling so! But I must record this, if not for myself and for Rian, then for history! <u>For the entire world.</u>

Let me make sense of this concept for my own sake. I always knew my words were historical record, merely by my being a prince traveling in a foreign land. However, sometimes it is easy to forget that one day, there may be copies of this journal read not only by scholars, but the layman and any curious proprietor of libraries. It is a strange honor I have found myself with.

I will endeavor to record it properly:

I spent the night in one of the Grey's estates, of the apparent several they own. Despite myself, in such comforts of a soft bed and feather pillows, I slept longer than intended, missing breakfast entirely. Once I managed to wash and dress properly, in the clothes of a prince that they lent me, I hurried to find my hosts and apologize. It was late enough in the day for them to be taking early afternoon tea, out in their gardens, dressed like kings and queens: these three Grey brothers, their cousins, Nexa and Lysandra, sweet little Teresa, and a young man with albinism introduced as her elder brother, Septimus. Of this company, Teresa was the youngest by a considerable margarin.

Kryto was exceptionally gracious about the matter of my tardiness. He claimed there was no harm done. The rest of the family (his parents, Aunt Margo, Uncle Whitt as well as the Smiths' parents and the youngest of their brood) would not arrive until suppertime, and no one was at all offended. I thanked him for this, and accepted his offer to join them, taking breakfast for myself as they had their tea, and engaging in several discussions about matters of the world.

I will add here for my own sake, so long as I have already mentioned him, that I did take a liking to Teresa's brother. He is a quiet one, some years older than her, about Kryto's age, but when he does open his mouth, he is quick-witted. A smart lad, with a scholarly air about him. I intend to seek him out for conversation some time again later. He is close to Kryto and seems to think in similar channels to me. He will work best with me, I think, in humanitarian efforts for Alarkia. Though the Greys do not look particularly Alarkian, Septimus and Teresa do, and I suspect they will both care for the well-being of their countrymen.

I will expand on that later when there is time to sit down and discuss the matter properly. For now, I must record all I can on the most pertinent conversation of the afternoon.

Once I had eaten plenty, and we had spoken at great length on many matters political and otherwise, it somehow came up, almost in jest, and I could not help but remark again on the supposedly coincidental nature of Kryto Grey being named so, and being engaged to a girl surnamed "Smith". Like from the stories, I believe I said. I expected laughs, and did receive them, but I did not expect what came along with it.

"Yes, like 'Kryto Grey' from the stories. Just like, in fact," young Kryto said. "As the Kryto Grey scholars make note of is in fact some-great-great-grandfather of my own father. It is he whom I am named after directly."

As anyone could imagine, this was hardly enough to convince me. I was certain this boy was speaking merely in jest, and that this was some kind of game. It did not help in the slightest when he additionally claimed that, of course, Teresa and Septimus were Magicsmiths, and it should be no surprise, given that the Greys and Magicsmiths were so tightly woven in Fate's loom.

I will not bother to relay the precise repartee between us all, as not a one of them around the table broke from what I then assumed was an act. Even Septimus, who I would have thought not the sort to play that type of game based on his personality thus far, engaged in the conversation. They were, all these young people, either utterly convinced they really were Greys and Smiths of old stories, or attempting to dupe an Isaarian prince for their own amusement. Some part of me, I think, most affected by Rian's insistences, wanted to believe, too.

"Let us see if we can't convince Prince Ralhan, here, that I'm telling the truth," Kryto said playfully, to the amusement of them all, and he looked to Teresa. "Go on, my dear. Why don't you show him? After all, there is no avoiding what Magicsmiths are said to be able to do if there's proof in front of one's face, is there?"

I acknowledged that, yes, if there was physical proof, it would be difficult to talk myself out of believing. Half of me was starting to believe that this was certainly real already, while the other half insisted on skepticism, as if out of propriety.

Teresa was nervous, and shyly asked Kryto what he thought she should do, or if he expected anything in particular. If this was an act, at that point, I decided they were exceptional performers, this young girl especially.

"Make anything you like, precious," he told her. "Anything at all."

She took a moment to think of it, biting her lip, brow furrowed, and then began to gather materials as if inspiration had struck. She stood up, moving items around the table, making a little workspace for herself.

I watched, amazed. I had my eyes fixed on her the entire time, and yet, I struggle now to describe it. If only I were some type of wordsmith to do the sight justice. All I can do is speak factually, in truth: from a delicate golden spoon and a tiny teacup painted with flowers, she reshaped it as easy as wet clay, and made for us a living china bird with a golden beak and gold tipped wings. This china bird fluttered about and sang as if it were real. And it was. Real. Somehow, someway.

I had seen automaton birds before, with tiny cogs moving their wings in clicks and tinny music-box notes to imitate song. But no, no, no–this! This was real! A real, living bird made of dishware, born from the imagination of a fourteen-year-old girl!

When I was allowed to hold the bird, and stroke it, I felt a beating heart underneath a strange combination of cool china that softened the same as any bird's breast beneath my fingertips.

"What would happen if you made more than one?" I could not help but ask. "Could they breed?"

It was said half in jest, but Teresa replied quite seriously and honestly that they could. She has made an entirely new species out of her imagination and her dinnerware and only looked a touch pale from it. There was a little tremoring in her hands. That was all.

This girl is incredible. What she can do could change the course of our world, and in short, I hope that she will.

Kryto was greatly pleased with this result and praised her mightily, until it brought a pinkness back into her face, though I suspect the kiss he planted on the top of her head may have helped with this. He insisted on unlacing her boots for her, so she could walk barefoot in the gardens under the sun and regain her strength. We all rose from the table at their leaving, and Kryto invited me with a flick of his fingers to join him. I walked behind the pair of them, Teresa on his arm, too stunned to speak.

I can still barely believe it, though I saw it with my own eyes. This girl took life from herself and gave it to a china bird. She is a Magicsmith, no doubt! These incredible people of story and myth, who I convinced myself did not exist the same as so many others. They are real, and I have somehow stumbled onto them!

Rian is going to be shocked, amazed beyond belief, terrified, and thrilled. I wonder if I might convince Kryto and his estate to pose for a photograph, so that I can show it to Rian. A keepsake for him that may prove exceptionally valuable in the future, depending on how things go.

The Greys and Smiths have been hidden away from the world for centuries, now, and I have somehow stumbled upon them. Incredible. Unthinkable. Perhaps this really will be the end of all wars to come. With this power, we will be able to do all that I have imagined in my most optimistic hopes. Perhaps this girl could create something to cure magic-sickness, perhaps even cure Asmer's disease! It is almost too good to wish for, yet, here it is: the chance of a lifetime! This is all precisely what I prayed my life was meant to accomplish, though these past few years, I will admit, I was beginning to think it all a foolish dream born of naïveté.

This evening, with the heads of their families present, I will appeal to Kryto's father. Here, I will do my best to record the outcomes of that.

This will be more than a minor footnote in history.

The entry over, I glance up at Septimus. He had told me to say when Mercer mentioned him, but their meet was unavoidably eclipsed by what Teresa proved she could do with household items. I can hardly believe that the bright, pretty girl who made the china bird for her betrothed's pleasure, and the young woman who dragged herself to our Pyrian Palace with two starving children and another swelling her belly, is the same person.

However, Septimus is different. Brief though Mercer's description may be, Septimus was, and is, still, undoubtedly Septimus. How funny that his knowledge of the future might keep him the same while Teresa's ignorance has allowed her to change so much.

"Yes?" Septimus sighs when he notices my watching him.

"I had hoped Mercer's journal would make things clear to me," I say.

"It is not so, then?" he guesses.

"No. It's all worse," I say.

He sighs. "You don't understand why my sister and I could still be in love with a horrible, disgusting, obnoxious, murdering monster like—"

"I don't understand how he became a monster," I interrupt him, which is not what he expected to hear. "The way Mercer describes him is different than I thought it would be. Less sinister. More…like any Isaarian noble I know. Notably flawed, but not…evil."

Now that I have presented a new commentary, compared to my usual criticism, Septimus has relaxed his guard, and is more inclined to speak with me. If only I had known that would happen; I would have been more open-minded in the first place.

"Kryto is just as Teresa likes to describe him," he says. "A complicated man. I prefer 'monster', honestly, even in my own head. It makes things simpler. And I do my best to forget the good things he has done."

"Debatably good, from a certain perspective good, or in its purest sense?"

"Kryto saved Teresa's life," he admits to me quietly, and allows me to judge that for myself. "Or saves her life. Every single timeline. He saves her. I will forever owe him for that. So will she, and she knows it. His particular brand of magic—his fluke, his casting, whatever you want to call it—it saved her. He was just a child when he did it. That should impress upon you just how powerful he is."

I consider this. If Kryto Grey really was a child when he saved Teresa's life, it is possible the only reason he managed to save her at all was because he believed he could, and hadn't yet been tainted by the foolish adult notion that there are some things that cannot be changed. Some things with unavoidable consequences.

He saw no reason why he could not save Teresa's life, so he did. He used his fluke in a way no one else would have thought. So, it is not simply power that allowed Kryto to stop magic-sickness in its path; it is a form of pride, too. Entitlement.

"No one else could have done it," Septimus continues, poking at the fire with a stick. "No one else dared. She was magic-sick, after all. No one lives through that. It is such a wide-spread notion that to contract it and be eaten away by corrupt magic is essentially a death sentence."

"Magic-sick can potentially live for a long time so long as there is someone to care for them," I remind him.

Septimus gives me a sad, bitter look. "Do you really think the Greys would have bothered? She would be a compliant puppet, yes, but they were convinced they could make her so, anyways, while allowing her to maintain some semblance of her own agency. Without having someone care for her every second of the day."

"They could have, though," I say. "They have the numbers. The funds."

"The Greys have an interesting idea of 'mercy'," Septimus mutters. An involuntary shudder runs through his body and he looks away.

I turn the page. Whatever summit Mercer imagined having with the Grey patriarch, he does not record it. In fact, I doubt it ever happened at all.

It is strange to think it so clearly, but I have found that I am enjoying myself immensely. I cannot remember the last time I so honestly and strongly felt such peace, such pleasantness. Somehow, being here feels more like home than Isaaria did. I have no idea how, or why, but it does.

Not a day goes by that I am not given attention to. It is as if each morning is my first one here, and I am as interesting a guest as always. Everyone here wants to know so much about Isaaria: about Isaarian custom, our traditions, our lives. They are especially interested in the people I know back home, like my best friend the king and his fiancée and his infamous Captain Marson. Qhan Khaleem. Qurvo. Even Vásan Pike, of all people.

The only unfortunate thing is that I have not seen Teresa's brother much since our first interaction. Septimus. The albino boy. When I thought to ask after him at supper today, Kryto took it upon himself to explain. Septimus is, apparently, his closest friend and ever the loyal companion. However, his health is less than stellar. I, of course, offered to perform an examination, to see what might be done for him, but my proposition was oddly refused.

They have their own doctor, apparently. I did meet with him briefly: a Doctor Daseem Alik, who I would guess is from some portion of the Ishtak Empire, or his parents were. I must say, of those I have met here, I felt most uncomfortable around him. Though, I suppose so long as the Greys and the Smiths enjoy the company of their family doctor, I should not make complaints. It would be rude.

It is a shame. Though my time with him was brief, first impressions alone led me to believe I'd quite like Septimus.

Here, strangely, the entry stops. There are several blank pages I must flip through before Mercer's narrative continues, and even then, the passage has no date. I have no way of knowing how much time passed between entries, but it likely was more than a week given how familiar Mercer seems with the Greys. He does not, however, appear to notice their influence on him:

I have such dreadful migraines. The Greys know much but I feel they know almost too much. I have not the heart to tell my hosts I cannot bear the daily conversations about the world; I thought knowing of the destruction and violence in Alarkia was bad enough, but the Greys know of horrors happening all over Samioth.

My hosts routinely inform me of these things. Politely, to seek my opinion.

I can no longer sleep despite my luxuries here or, if I do manage sleep, it is only by the earliest hours of morning, so that I do not wake until afternoon. I wish I could sleep entire days away, now; it would be better to do so than to be left with my own thoughts.

What is the point of what I do–of living in this world at all–when mankind insists on perpetuating such horrors? Even if this war ends, there will always be another war. A mother who would purposefully harm her own children. A husband who beats his wife. Children who disparage and abuse their elderly parents. Rape, murder, disease, suffering, coercion, and greed.

Is there not a single, truly good person left in the world at all?

Then, a much shorter passage:

I am terrified to admit that I am starting to feel as if coming here was the worst mistake of my life. Yet there is some other part of me that knows this is exactly where I should be. I am meant to be here.

There is a gap in the paper before:

I can't remember where they said Marques went. I should find him.

The idea chills me, because I know that Marques was a good bodyguard to his prince, and rarely left Mercer alone. Whoever went with Mercer to the west, Marques is not what came back, at least not mentally.

The final passage in the travel journal is perhaps the vaguest, and the most chilling. The implications are not beyond me. I cannot help but shudder when I consider what accompanied Mercer this final day:

We went on a stroll today after supper, again. Conversations with him are always scintillating. Intriguing. Filled with questions and answers I could never think of myself. What a fool I was to ever think I was an intellectual.

Ended up catching Kryto kissing Teresa in the garden, on the fountain. Pretended as if we did not see and left them to it.

They will be married at some point anyways.

This is perhaps the last thing Mercer wrote in his life, and that is both terrifying and sobering. It is a grim reminder of the individual lives at stake, and how different all these people were twenty years ago.

I glance across the fire at Septimus again, but do not say anything to interrupt his thoughts. I have no desire for conversation anymore, and neither does he, though he surely can tell I have finished the journal.

In retrospect, I no longer know what I expected to find in Mercer's travel journal. I only know that, learning what I have through the words of others, I have no desire to ever meet Kryto Grey face-to-face. Regardless of the simplest solution, to kill him for his wrongs and be done with it, I do not know what I would do.

Fourteen

"THAT," SEPTIMUS SAYS, "is not a good sign."

He lowers the spyglass Vásan lent him, though even without one it is not difficult to come to such a conclusion. Ahead of us, Mouloix has several unwanted fires that surely should be put out by now. While we can see no flames licking the sky or engulfing buildings, thick plumes of smoke pollute the air. Not a sound comes from the once industrious city, its port the largest in Isaaria.

"Would your allies still be here, despite that?" Nissa says dubiously, arms crossed, expression dour.

She is not accustomed to being around other people much and I suspect our continual company is beginning to make her tetchy.

"They will be there, for certain," Septimus promises, and then surprises me by drawing the sword he has been carrying. "But I suspect we'll be needing to go through unwanted company, first."

"Do you really think that will be necessary?" I say.

He shrugs and walks ahead. Nissa yanks out a knife and orders her hyena something in Hoitsokin. Vásan sighs, but draws his pistol. So, I suppose we all know whose lead we are following, now.

We each take care in our approach of Mouloix, Nissa with a practiced hunter's step, me with all my training. There is a great stench in the city that is not quite death, not quite rot, but somewhere in-between. It has not been long enough for the buildings to have fallen into disarray, but there are small indicators there is no more life in Mouloix: unwashed windows, overflowing water barrels with stale contents, rats scrambling in the streets unhurried, unafraid of us. Curtains are drawn, most doors locked up tight, but some ajar or kicked down by the raiders that would unapologetically take advantage of abandoned homes. These raiders are not always of the expected sort: no distinguished bandits or dastardly villains, only starving children and lost refugees taking what they can before fleeing.

The wind whistles through the streets, banging loose shutters that no one is here to secure. We are lucky we are here in winter-time, or else I suspect the stench would be worse.

"I don't understand," I say. "Surely someone would have been informed by now that Mouloix has been completely abandoned!"

"I wouldn't be too sure of that," Septimus says. "I doubt any family fleeing for their lives is too concerned about the prosperity of the country as a whole."

Nissa snorts. I would glare at her, only, she is not looking in my direction.

A certain eeriness settles over us. Despite my initial doubt, I can feel in the air that something is about to happen, here. We are being watched, and if it is not by other human beings hiding in the apartments, or simple creatures that have moved in to make this place their new home, then something more sinister has us in its sights.

We follow Septimus, who knows best which way to go. The further we move into the city, the hollower the place feels; despite all evidence to the contrary, a part of my mind, and perhaps all of ours', expects to see someone, anyone, appear. We have learned through our own experiences that cities are lively, boisterous places. Mouloix, then, is a dead zone, an Otherworld. Every creak of my own boots sounds out of place.

"I suspect," Vásan says lowly, startlingly me, "that it would be imperative to keep quiet, in which case the use of my pistol would be discouraged."

"It would be best for us to avoid drawing attention to ourselves, if at all possible, particularly if there are dark creatures afoot," Septimus confirms without turning to look at him. "We wouldn't want them to find us."

"Ah. So, this would be for the better, then," Vásan says.

I turn just as he raises and fires the pistol at the abomination that has been following behind us. It shrieks an earsplitting masterpiece of a death-song that mingles with the ringing shot from the gun as Vásan's marksmanship proves true. Everything erupts around us after that.

There is no doubt that the things that come out to attack are what would be referred to as demons, though that classification has never been sorted one way or another. They are at least the dark monsters we have been warned about many times over, now, implicitly and otherwise. I am glad not only of Septimus' initial caution before entering the city, but of the weapons we had thought to bring with.

The creatures leapt from places above and below: metal balconies leading over this alleyway into fire escape stairs, sewers, rooftops. Anywhere they could have been lurking and watching, waiting to potentially corner and devour us.

At least these things are significantly smaller than whatever made that monstrous bellowing on the train tracks.

Nissa snaps at her hyena in Hoitsokin and it rushes into an attack. She draws both her hunting knives. I would be concerned, but this woman has killed a bear; no doubt she can manage herself. I stick by Vásan instead, with my captain's sword and knives of my own, my pistol tucked away for now. As Vásan's flintlock pistol can manage six rounds at a time, he will need someone to cover for him when he reloads. He may carry a saber as well, but I'm not certain how good he is with it aside from the ceremonial fencing all the royal heirs are trained in, whether a crown prince or a grand prince.

Septimus is on his own.

Of the creatures attacking, four of them turn their attention on Vásan and me. This alleyway we have found ourselves down, on our way back to a main road, would be a cutthroat's dream, but here, it works somewhat to our advantage. Given their size and general haphazardness, there is not much space for the monsters to attack us all at once. Still, out of the four, one has wings, another can hover, and still another can obviously climb up walls given its current position near the roof of a building, stuck to one side. So, we must be vigilant in the direction of attack.

All of them maintain some level of familiarity to me, not unlike the china bird Mercer described, yet remain alien all the same. They are like nothing I have ever seen before, but are products of Teresa's imagination and are likely breeding themselves at an alarming rate.

Two are leathery, one like a lizard with millions of tiny legs and whip-like appendages that end in spike-toothed orifices, the other like a flying red splitjack from the jungles, but with a feathered hood, a pair of wings, and has no arms or legs but a gigantic maw that opens vertically the way a splitjack's would. Of the remaining two, one has matted fur, fangs, and claws like some feral version of Nissa's hyena, but larger, and with a strangely humanoid face marred by a protruding snout and a disturbing scampering in how it moves. The last is the biggest, with great, protruding ridges along its back and a strange nakedness in its lack of fur, scales, or anything protective. It looks like deep-sea slug that somehow crawled from the grossest levels of a cavernous abyss and found its way up here to torment us.

The furred beast is the quickest; moving on too-long legs in its hasty scampering, it leaps our way. My sword is the best defense in this case and I raise it in a grand sweep, stepping in front of Vásan to do so. I manage to slash the monster, surprising all of us, I think, as its hot blood splashes both Vásan and me.

At first, I am panicked at the thought of poisonous or acidic blood—something a young and gruesome Teresa might have come up with.

Thankfully, it is only sticky, thick, and blueish, cementing the need for a good wash after this.

The beast yowls, but lives, still. Behind me, Vásan rattles off two shots at the splitjack-mimic. One hits it in one of the bulbous rounded spots on its head that I believe are its eyes, so that it lets out a thrumming that shakes the ground under our feet. The other bullet strikes a fleshy portion of the mimic and, to all appearances, is absorbed, no damage done.

One of the appendaged mouths on the lizard shoots between both of us, sending us dodging to either side of the alley. The mouth snaps at us before being whipped about, striking my arm as I raise it in defense. It stings, but my clothing has protected me somewhat. The worst injury from that, at least, will be red welts tomorrow morning.

With my left hand, I pluck out one of my daggers and send it spinning at the retreating whip, severing it from the lizard. What spurts out from it is not blood, I do not think, but some pulpy, gelatinous liquid of a purple hue. It spatters Vásan's white-blond hair and I gag for him at the stench of it. Now, at least, I suppose we know some of the reason why this city reeks.

"These are Miss Teresa's monsters?" Vásan confirms.

"I believe so."

"Perhaps your cousin ought to see a priest."

I would be offended on Teresa's behalf, only, he might be right about that.

So long as three of these creatures are injured, Vásan takes the opportunity to use up his remaining shots: one after another in a perfect cluster, he hits the splitjack-mimic in the largest of its red bulbs, shooting it down in a massive squelching. At least it is courteous enough to careen forward in its death-throws, blocking the alley.

I step forward to stab it through its head so that it, too, shrieks and spasms. I have little time to celebrate a victory, though, before the furred beast is back up, attempting to leap at me a second time. Vásan is reloading, and I cannot bring my sword up in time.

I use my arms to block it as best I can, and luckily the puff in the sleeves of my winter coat takes the brunt of the damage. I still feel the pain of its jaws trying to clench, teeth trying to sink into my skin deeper, but it is not painful enough by far to paralyze me.

While I may not be as quick and lithe as when I was younger, I am still strong. With the beast still gripping on as tightly as it can, I swing my arm out and use its weight against it, slamming it into the wall of the closest building. When it does not let go, I give it no time for reprieve, either, and swing it in the other direction, so that when it does release, it is slammed into the metal fire escape.

Something crunches. It does not rise, but whimpers. Vásan, having dropped to a knee to reload, puts it out of its misery before rolling to a side to avoid another of those whipped-jaws. He uses another five shots to bring the lizard tumbling down from where it clung to the wall, leaving me with that strange sea-creature.

It ungulates as it moves, as if there is viscosity in our air only it can feel. I fear my sword likely will not reach it with enough force to do decent damage, leaving me with my pistol—though I've never been a particularly good marksman, at least compared to one such as Vásan—and my knives. The latter will suffice.

I hurl a dagger at the creature as it approaches, simply to test what will do the most damage, and where. Vásan was lucky with the modified splitjack, as it was at least obvious in where its weak points may be. With this pale, flapping creature, there is no telling how to hurt it, or how it might hurt us.

Unfortunately for me, while my dagger tears through the thing like it is made of butter, its fleshiness is quick to reassemble, as if sewing itself back together from the inside-out.

It retaliates by the front of it opening completely so that it is almost nothing more than a gigantic, ridged maw with teeth along the top so long they could pass for one of my leg bones, only thinner, and sharper. There must be hundreds of them. Apparently, they are also projectile.

Several of them pass by Vásan and me so quickly, the air whistles. We both evade them, and given the distinct lack of screaming, they likely evade our companions engaged in their own combat as well.

"Fate's Fingers," I hiss.

That earns me another projectile zooming so close to my face it nearly modifies my scar. This thing is blind, I realize. It must be hunting us by sound. Given our luck, those projectile teeth likely grow back. So, unless Vásan and I want to be fish-food, we should need to make quick work of this creature.

He comes up with the idea first, but I'm faster. The moment I see him begin to reload, I realize what Vásan's about. I pull my own pistol and fire off all the shots, not bothering to be particularly accurate in regards to hitting the creature at all, just ensuring they vary in direction. One ricochets off a pipe, making a spectacular pinging. Another lodges itself into the brick of a building.

They make the creature go wild, spinning about, shooting its projectiles angrily, rather bothered by the sound. I suppose that at least explains why it kept some distance before; it is smart enough to have learned by sound that Vásan's gun is not to be reckoned with.

By now, Vásan has reloaded and takes up the task of firing in distraction while I make sure to move, before this thing can pinpoint my position to know where I might have fired from. Vásan is better in his targeting than I was, and precisely aims to make loud noises, even louder than the shots themselves: shattered windows, that pipe again, a metal rail.

We have well and truly angered and confused this monster.

I am just about to pluck up my sword again and do what damage I possibly can when Septimus is there.

He moves faster than any of us, and startles Vásan and me. Continually moving, maneuvering himself beneath the creature so it cannot pin-point him either, Septimus slashes and dices at the thing so that it cannot possibly restore itself quickly enough. It makes horrific sounds of pain that I am certain make my ears bleed and it flaps and twists so its ridges slam against the buildings on either side of us, scraping off bricks.

It is too miserable to do anything but let Septimus continue to hack it to pieces, chopping off bits of it so that they splat to the paving beneath our feet in large, heavy flaps. When the biggest remnant of it comes down, slopping into the rest of its pieces, trying its best to sluggishly pull itself back together, I am sure Vásan, Nissa and me have been doing nothing but staring at Septimus in shock. Even when he whirls on us, a hand out, it takes me a moment to process his words.

"Light!" he demands from us, and then reiterates when no one moves in the next half-second. "Fire!"

Nissa tosses him a lighter. With a flick, Septimus clicks the lighter into action, and the creature is set ablaze. Even without fuel, the flames easily devour such an opponent; Rian would have made quick work of it. The fire spreads as if licking down a puddle of fuel and sets the creature completely ablaze, burning it so it crisps, curling like dried seaweed dropped into hot soup until it scatters into ash.

The fire burns itself out in a minute at most, and with it goes the monster.

We are left with the remnants of the creatures we have dispatched of: four on this end, with me and Vásan, another three handled by Nissa, her hyena, and Septimus. Regardless of differing traits, these things must know well-enough to hunt in packs. Otherwise, they were merely each searching for the nearest humans to prey on and happened upon us at the same time.

Whatever the case, two things are clear: that the monsters Teresa created were made with the purpose of seeking out and harming humans as much as possible, and Septimus, of all people, is the most prepared to kill them. Either he knows his sister and her imagination well, or he has had plenty of experience.

"...Well," I say.

I cough and pretend I need water so I can take a long drink and consider what to say before going to collect my weapons. I can see that Vásan is impressed as well to see Septimus so skilled, but he does not acknowledge it.

"You're good with that sword," Nissa says in approval. She is the only one of us humble enough to say so aloud.

"Thank you," Septimus says, giving it a few more swings before sheathing it. "I ought to be. I've years and years of practice, at this point. Ironically, all thanks to the Greys." He nods at Vásan's gun. "I'm assuming this is one of those modern versions that have seen a noise-muffler's fluke to kill the worst of the blast or else we'd all be quite deaf at this point."

"It is standard manufacturing practice in Isaaria. For safety," Vásan says.

"Still. So long as we are going to do it, we may as well do it better," Nissa says, Fluke or no, it must have startled her poor hyena and made it more difficult for her to control.

Septimus looks about at each of us, assessing. "I suppose there are no injuries bad enough to keep us from moving on?"

"I think I took the worst of things," I admit, from what I can tell visually. "I'm fine enough."

"Good," he says, already moving to walk out of the alley, as if·nothing ever happened. "The others will be expecting us, and we ought to reach them before dark."

Us three Isaarians are still stunned by the turn of events and our first fight with the dark creatures tormenting our world. One thing is for certain: these are not demons, but that does not mean Teresa has not made demon-like creatures. On the contrary, from what I've seen in many timelines and this one as well, I suspect she has been greatly inspired by artistic renditions of demons in her past works. This is more of a sampling of what I suspect she sees in her nightmares.

It is no wonder she struggles to sleep.

Nissa moves ahead first, whistling for her hyena before stomping through the entrails of the things we have killed, so she can catch up to Septimus. I go next, letting Vásan walk behind me. While I was concerned about his well-being initially, he noticed that first creature well ahead of the rest of us, so perhaps I might prefer having him at my back.

We knit ourselves back together as we reach a main road and continue down it through the city. For once, I am not the one filled with inquiries for Septimus, or at least am not the first to bother him.

"Do you mind if I ask you a personal question?" Nissa inquires.

"Go on," Septimus says.

He is not as brisk with her as he usually is with me.

"How is it like. Having albinism? I would not ask," she goes on, "only, I did meet a man with albinism, once. He was a trader, from the Juja islands, so his skin should be black, but it was not. And he was nearly blind."

"My eyesight is not as keen as the average man's," Septimus admits. "As I am sure you have noticed with my need for darkening glasses. I am quite used to it. I burn easily, my skin is delicate, my eyes are sensitive, and it is often difficult to concentrate when looking at anything small. Yet compared to many others with albinism, I am quite fortunate."

"Yet you move well. I hate to use the word 'normal', but—" Nissa says, and cuts herself off.

"Then do not use it. The choice is yours," Septimus says. "For my own part, I am used to who I am; someone simply taking note of my physical features is not insulting. It is unavoidable. I am more concerned with those who practice witchcraft who would happily kill someone like me."

Nissa looks disgusted. "Why?"

"In some countries, generally where the majority of folks have naturally darker skin, they believe albinos host rarities in their blood that makes their bodies good use in witchcraft. It is an archaic practice, and I am certain it will slowly fade away with time."

Nissa frowns.

"We will not be going to any of these places, will we?" she asks gravely.

Septimus laughs at her concern. "No, not in the slightest. Even if we were, I would be more worried about the Mitaurus and the Greys than any other fool who thinks himself a witch.

"Quick, now," he adds, having recognized something in our surroundings. A land mark given to him, perhaps. "We should be nearly there."

He picks up the pace again, forcing Nissa into a jog with her shorter legs. Vásan and I follow.

The buildings are beginning to look cleaner the closer we are to the coast. We are not headed directly for the docks, but the wealthiest district of the city where those who can afford such things might stay in grand hotels with seaside views. These are the sort of establishments that enforce strict dress codes and have ballrooms in use every weeknight. The street deposits us to a walking path safeguarded by a delicate metal rail; beyond that, it is a two meter drop directly into the water. The view of sunrises and sunsets are no doubt spectacular.

The walkway is wide enough for bicyclists and seasonal street vendors, though there is no one out now. Cafés have abandoned the sets of their outdoor seating and hotel fronts have their doors shut tight. There are stacks of cargo crates and barrels here and there, as if someone attempted to build barricades against the invading creatures. There is a suspicious lack of blood, but perhaps that is a good thing. Perhaps I can convince myself, then, that somehow, these monsters have not killed any Isaarians.

The further we traverse down the walkway, careful with our footsteps now, the better I can hear several voices ahead. They must be beyond one of the barricades, set up directly in front of a once-glorious hotel with flowered balconies and iron gates in front of the entrance. It is as good a place as any to set up camp, I suppose, and much better than sleeping on the ground as we have been.

"Xerian, what part of 'less-unhealthy' means 'healthy' to you?" a woman's deep voice says. Her accent is startlingly like Damen's.

The person who replies is much younger, lighter in tone. I am surprised to hear a northern accent, indicating some part of the Rumshtaman Empire. "The… 'un' part? No, wait, the 'less' part!"

"He will make himself sick," mutters a man; his accent is Lijimi.

The woman sighs.

"Let it be noted we have both warned you, now," she says dryly to the youngest of the group, though there is playfulness between those two from what I can hear.

I notice Septimus give a quiet snort and look over in time to catch a smile. I cannot remember seeing such a look from him before; these must be more than merely allies to him. He quickens his pace.

"Well, come along, then," the Lijimi man sighs. "I suppose we will need to spend the remaining daylight flushing the rest of those beasts out or I won't get a wink of decent sleep."

"I would not be too sure about that," Septimus says, announcing our presence as he slips between some crates and hops down a step to the hotel's veranda. "It seems we have managed your infestation problem for you, at least in part."

I exchange a look with Nissa and we move slowly in following him. I would like to think we can trust Septimus' allies, but I do not know them.

"You made it!" the young man cheers, quite pleased to see Septimus here.

I inch into view to see the woman standing up from her spot crouched before a tiny fire.

She is older than myself, with hair once white-blond, now merely white, and olive skin etched with sharp wrinkles. She has done well to keep herself in fair shape, and still makes quite the striking figure in her traveling clothes, despite her age. As we come closer, I find her exceptionally tall; about as tall as Rian, and her shoulders match her frame. At her hip is coiled a peculiar weapon that looks like neither a bladed piece nor a whip but something in between; a preposterous but curious item.

"Not very sporting of you, Sep. You've taken our fun," she chides lightly.

"And your money," he quips, and goes on to answer her frown. "Ruskin didn't make it. I'm afraid, unless Margo manages to die another two times, you lose the bet."

She scowls and tisks. "The scoundrel…Fate's Fingers!"

She kicks the crate she'd been sitting on. The young man's face brightens and he whoops. The older man sighs, shoulders slumping.

I'm sure he is my age, if not older. There is not a touch of gray to his hair yet, though his face bears wrinkles prominently at his eyes and mouth. From smiling, if I had to guess, though it does not look as if he has smiled much for a long time, now. He shivers and scrunches in his winter coat, half-hiding his Lijimi features of tan skin, dark hair, angular features, and wide mouth. He wears a goatee, but the hints of a full beard are starting to catch up, given recent traveling.

The last person is a young man perhaps in his late twenties or early thirties. While the other two are impressive in a physical manner, he is much more average in size, but unique otherwise. His coloring is lighter than either of his companions, though not as chalky as Septimus', and his hair is dark by contrast. While the rest of us are bundled to endure the wintery weather, he seems not to feel the cold, and has left his coat draped over a nearby post. He is definitely Rumshtaman, then. No one else reacts so blasé to such chilly temperatures.

He also happens to be eating an entire loaf of cinnamon bread, uncut; his less-than-healthy supper, I suspect. Although, it is likely a good idea to take advantage of scavenging from bakeries while the bread is still edible.

"I'm sorry, what's this?" Nissa inquires.

She, Vásan and I are content to hover by the unofficial entrance to this make-shift camp. At the sound of her voice, two of the three stand straight and face us. The Lijimi man is still slouched on a crate and makes no move to rise, only glancing our way. I flick my eyes over their expressions and am surprised to see that each one of them appears to know of us. Vásan and Nissa, I suppose, are somewhat recognizable internationally, but it is clear that I am the object of interest. Septimus must be generous, with them, in terms of information.

"Introductions, of course," he says. "Soleil, grand prince, princess: this is Margo, and that's Castel Voskoss over there, formerly prince of Lijimata. And our young fellow here is Xerian Vicell. Ruskin, sadly, is no longer with us."

Vásan raises an eyebrow. "Vicell? As in the former royal family in the Rumshtama Empire's latest conquest, Vicell?"

Xerian smiles brightly. "You know your history!" he acknowledges.

He appears surprised Vásan would pick up on that first, instead of the fact that we have the missing heir of Lijimata slouched before us, drinking something out of a flask that I assume is not water.

Vásan's own expression does not change. Something occurs to Xerian and he takes his hat off, clutching it in both hands as he gives a sweeping bow.

"Very pleased to meet your acquaintances, Grand Prince. Princess."

Nissa gestures to me sharply.

"Your majesty," she adds. "Our king married her."

Xerian smiles. He straightens only to drop into a deeper bow, with an unabashed "Your majesty!". Castel Voskoss rolls his eyes. Margo smiles at the antics and steps forward, offering her hand; a decidedly Alarkian style of greeting, where they have no king.

"Glad you all made it safely," she says. "We expected you a little sooner, but I promised the lads you'd make it."

The name Margo sounds familiar to me. In a moment, I remember Septimus having mentioned a Margo to me before. A Margo and an Anya. While I am certain it is a common enough name, I do not believe in coincidences. Especially not considering Margo's appearance. Her hair may be blond instead of dark, but otherwise, there are familial similarities.

"You are a Grey," I realize, all but recoiling from her.

My hand automatically goes to one of my knives, but I have no idea if I plan to use it or not. Septimus moves to stop me, yet Margo waves him off. She does not seem to see me as a threat.

"Yes. Amerson, Kryto, and Jarrod are my nephews. Nexa is my niece," she confesses. "But I do not condone their actions. I apologize for any suffering they may have caused you."

I bristle. Her nephews are the reason my sister is dead. They are the reason Rian has died so many times over again. Nevertheless, I hold my tongue and simply nod.

Vásan predictably takes the diplomatic approach. Margo offered her hand to me, but he steps forward with his own to take it with both his own in a two-handed clasp. He has met Alarkian diplomats before, and while Margo is Lusch, not Alarkian, I suppose her decision to choose this form of greeting is a subtle way of claiming no king.

"We appreciate any assistance, regardless of who offers it," he says.

He does not bother to sound appreciative, but the gesture is not lost on Margo Grey.

"You all look like you could do with a good washing-up," she says, and gestures to the hotel front. She talks like an Alarkian, too, in that easy, casual way of theirs. "We have set up shop here, for the past few days, scavenging food from the kitchens to conserve our own supply for the trip east. The water still works, at least for now. Cas can take you up, if you like. We shall spend one last night here and get an early start tomorrow."

After spending several days on the road, but especially after our gritty encounter with those creatures, none of us refuse the offer to wash. Castel Voskoss does not bother pretending he wants to escort us anywhere, but still heaves himself to his feet with some effort and gestures for us to follow him without looking our way.

"Sleeping alright, there, Cas?" Septimus poses.

He gets a muttered Lijimi curse for his trouble.

Castel leads us all inside the hotel and takes us directly up the stairs.

"Second and third floors have the best working water, still," he says, explaining the trek, "but the third floor gets hot water. I suspect you will be wanting that luxury."

Vásan claims not to care, leaving us on the second floor immediately, and I do not doubt his words. Out of all of us, he is covered with the most filth. Septimus leaves as well to accompany him; best not to leave any one person completely on their own, but especially not a grand prince.

Castel leads Nissa, her hyena, and me down the hall to another staircase; the main one has been blocked further up. His decidedly poor temper and contradictory former reputation make me curious. He worked with Septimus, or for Septimus, more accurately. Lune was one he could call comrade, as well. While it is not the wisest option, I cannot help but open my mouth.

"I believe we have met on occasion before," I say in Alarkian, trying to be congenial in how I go about this, knowing Nissa is listening to everything.

"We have," he mutters, and does not expand.

"You have worked with my cousin for a long time," I say. "Through many of the timelines. And, with my sister, too? Lune?"

And Taris?

"I recall," he sighs.

He is exasperated with me already, I think. I take a moment to think of how to steer the conversation properly the way I want it to go. If only Rian were here; he would be so much better at this.

"I suppose it must have been strange, having to trust Septimus. He was not much more than a boy when he must have helped steal you away, after all."

Castel doesn't say anything, so I go on.

"I know I, for one, sometimes wonder how it is he comes up with these schemes of his. After all, would you not be of more use back in Lijimata?" I say. "You are their prince. Likely, you could do something about the war with Septimus' help."

Castel scoffs.

"Oh, certainly," he says, mockery dripping from every word as if intending to poison me out of spite. "Yes, how could that go wrong: my turning up and insisting our government is being controlled by Dark-worshiping witches. People would definitely believe that."

I almost flinch as he stomps ahead up the stairs. For a moment, I am violently reminded of Taris.

"Perhaps steer clear of 'could-have-beens'," Nissa suggests.

I agree and follow Prince Castel more cautiously up the staircase.

Nissa and I take conjoined apartments, and Castel waits outside while we wash. I clean myself and my clothes, planning to let this set dry while changing into spare items. I strangely miss the comfort of my uniform, but know it is far better to travel in casual clothing, with no clear identification of who I am. If Vásan can manage it, I can, as well. However, I do keep handy

Rian's gifted pocket watch. It has already become a great comfort to me, as if, somehow, my holding it will tell Rian that I am safe and well.

I finish before Nissa, no doubt because she is taking the time to scrub clean her hyena. This leaves me to wait in the hallway with Castel, who I can tell does not appreciate my company. I do not expect an apology for his harshness, but he does not scoff or glare or purposefully turn away from me. So, I suppose that is progress.

It is always an effort for me to swallow my pride, but if I want to work well with Castel Voskoss, I suspect such a thing will be necessary on a regular basis.

"I should offer you an apology," I begin.

"Yes, you should," he interrupts.

I take a deep breath, and force myself to go on.

"I am sorry, then," I say, trying to be as genuine as possible. "I understand this has been hard for everyone. I should have been more careful before saying anything."

He does not soften his posture or acknowledge my attempts in a traditional sense, but at least he gives me a short nod. So perhaps my willingness to say so has won me points with this disagreeable man.

"If you would not mind it," I continue, "please consider allowing us to start again. I believe I made a poor first impression."

That is not to say he or Margo are the sorts I would spend holiday afternoons with, but we are on the same side, trying to achieve the same goals.

"I suppose that is possible," he acknowledges.

I consider what times I have encountered him before, and do my best to pick the most flattering version. It will do me no good to acknowledge he used to have a brighter personality, and I know now he will not appreciate me making any direct inquiries. But if I am willing to make my best attempts with him, it is at least statistically likely he will be feeling guilty he did not offer first. He knows well who I am, and all that has been done. I think he braced himself to meet someone who expects all others to sacrifice simply because it appears she is the most necessary linchpin in Fate's record.

I will do my best not to be that person, particularly around a man who has lost his entire country and family both.

"I know I should not have been eavesdropping," I go on, "but in our last cycle, if you remember it?"

"I do."

"You met with my sister, Lune. You were…kind to her. Knowing what she had suffered, and how she had suffered alone."

Knowing that she had just lost her child and needed to press on pretending as if it had never happened, without Taris close by to comfort her.

"I always did like Lune," Castel says, and takes another swig of his flask.

"I think you may have saved her life, too," I admit. "The night Amerson Grey and his men came. The Greys are wary of Lune. I think he would have killed her, if you had not...whisked her away."

He laughs bitterly, but I do not think it is directed at me.

"Ah, my wormholes. I would not depend on them now, if I were you."

I frown. "I'm sorry?"

He turns up his arm to show me his bare hand. Lijimi do not have a culture that necessitates they stay gloved, after all; that is strictly Isaarian. I suppose I ought to grow accustomed to seeing him, Xerian and Margo without gloves. In fact, my aversion to looking might be why I did not notice in the first place, but it is unavoidable now with Castel showing me so bluntly. The skin across his palms is marred by thin, twisted scars. I have never seen it done before, but I still recognize the marks; he cannot use his fluke if he tried. It looks like whoever did this did not cut with care. These scars must ache in the damp and the cold. He must not be able to even use his hands as normally as he once could, fluke or no.

"I was forced to give up my casting. Fluke, you call it," he claims. So, he did this to himself. "Trust me, if I had a choice, I would have kept it, but I was not given one. It was this for the life of the woman I loved, and then they killed her anyways. I watched her die. Choking on her own blood."

"I'm sorry," I offer.

He merely shrugs. "You're sorry, Margo's sorry, Septimus is sorry—everyone's sorry about it, and yet, dead is dead. She is dead, my parents are dead, my cousins are dead, my half-sister Falisia is dead. My uncle and my sister Emmelina are the older ones left, and Emmelina has gone mad."

I consider carefully my words before speaking again.

"I know it at least helps, for me, to think of this as a mere stopping point in a long journey," I say. "I have lost people I care about, too. I know it is not the same," I add quickly, "but..."

"Oh, no: I'm aware that this is technically some new cycle of life," Castel Voskoss claims. "I know that, for you, dead is not always dead. Septimus has made it more than clear that he supposedly believes we non-Smiths are all but expendable so long as we do our jobs. But for the rest of us, it is different. It does not matter if you go back in time like Septimus says we will by the end of this. You cannot save everyone. I know there is a possibility that some of us are going to die no matter what, and you would not restart the universe for them. For us."

I consider how quickly Septimus decided not to risk ourselves trying to save anyone aboard that train. I allowed that, too. Surely, I could have rewound time, even for a few hours, warned someone else on the train of the oncoming danger, or even prepared for the fight ahead and stayed onboard. I am struck by the fact that the thought never occurred to me.

However, it did occur to me immediately to use my power to save Naomi. She is not even necessary for our quest, yet I insisted on going back not only as a tactic to defeat Phoebus, but because I did not want to live through Naomi dying. It was less a moral decision, and more an excuse, perhaps. Even Septimus cannot keep his ideologies consistent: choosing to sacrifice others, if necessary, but insisting on rescuing Teresa and her children. He wants to make his decisions out of pure logic, and even I assumed he did. It is clear to me, now, emotions are involved. For us, perhaps they are impossible to be rid of entirely.

"You are right," I tell Prince Castel. "I cannot save everyone. I do not even know how I would begin to. I am sorry you have had to come to that conclusion yourself by witnessing such awful things. That said, I do appreciate your presence. Your assistance. I hope that, at least, with all the knowledge we have accumulated through timelines, perhaps you will be able to prevent some of these tragedies yourself."

Castel shakes his head. "If we receive confirmation of a final timeline, I do not want to remember any of this. I have already decided."

"You would give up all this experience?" I say. "Even if having it might save the woman you love?"

"I do not wish upon myself the tragedy of learning her death was always inevitable. And, if that is the case, having to watch her throat cut even once is more than enough. I'm certain Qurvo would agree."

I think of every time I have watched Rian die. Castel and Taris, then, have been forced to endure the same heartbreak. Only, there is no guarantee of a new timeline for them; no messenger from heaven to tell them that they and their loved one are meant to be together.

It is a great gift I have received, in both my fluke and my fate. The man I love was chosen for a great purpose, and I was given a power to protect him.

I can see why Rian would think, so many times over, that perhaps no one should have that power. It is a privilege that I have seen mainly as a duty. I have assumed I am the one who must sacrifice, while ignoring how lucky I am to be placed in such a situation to begin with.

"I understand," I say quietly. "I know, I know: it is not the same, because of who I am. But I do, at least in some part, understand."

Castel considers this, then gives a short nod again, and goes back to staring at the wall across the way. It is hardly a victory, but I have made progress.

When Nissa finishes washing, her hyena shaking itself dry, we return downstairs to the others. Vásan and Septimus have predictably finished before us and are sitting around the small fire with Xerian and Margo.

"Are we sleeping out of doors?" Nissa says, not necessarily critical of the idea.

"We shall move inside," Margo promises, "though the heating and lighting no longer work consistently. The rooms have fireplaces, at least. During the day, we have been out where the sun is as much as possible."

"Are there gardens around here?" it occurs to Septimus to ask.

"This is Isaaria," Castel mutters. "There is one in the back of the hotel."

"Then, tomorrow morning we meet with the captain?" I say.

They all exchange looks before Septimus says, "Oh, right. So, there is not going to be a captain, exactly. Margo will be sailing for us."

"Do not worry. I am an excellent sailor," Margo says, grinning at me like a mad woman.

I am not comforted much by this.

"How big is this ship you've acquired, then?" I ask dubiously.

"Big enough for me to work with," Margo promises. "A former fishing vessel, but not local. Steam-powered. It will be big enough to house the seven of us, just don't expect much personal space and comfort. It should get us to Kacha, at least, though I cannot vouch for the return trip."

No one says anything to that. I can tell Septimus is not convinced there will be a return trip, and at this point, neither am I.

We manage a simple supper around the fire while the sun finishes setting and a night chill sets in. Everyone packs their things up whilst still outside, with the light of the fire to assist, as, once we move indoors, it will be merely to sleep. Septimus and Margo patch together a new watch rotation, which thankfully results in more sleep for everyone, and Xerian pleasantly notes that there should be coffee in the morning. Nothing delicious, but serviceable.

Instead of taking the penthouse, our new companions have decided upon a medium-sized suite on the fifth floor. There is not much of a view from its windows, but nothing will be able to ambush us with ease, and there is a wide enough gathering space that we can spread out and sleep before the fireplace.

Septimus and I are assigned the first shift. At first, I assume this was done by chance alone, but I later decide it is likely we were partnered on purpose. Septimus is jabbing at the fire with an iron poker, which I believe he has made a point of doing every time we have one lit. The act also is an excellent representation of him as a person.

The fire started in this room is not roaring like the fire of a great king's hall, but it crackles enough that I hope it will cover our whispers so as not to keep the others awake. Something has occurred to me recently; a memory brought on by my own reaction to Margo Grey.

"Why does Damen think you don't like him?" I ask bluntly.

The worst part is, Septimus is not shocked, nor does he deny it. He only sighs. He knows precisely what I'm talking about.

"It's difficult to explain," he claims. "It is not even the boy's fault, it—"

"So, you don't," I interrupt. "That is what you're saying."

"No, I…" He cuts himself off and sighs again, wearily, before going about taking off his boots. "I know you look at those boys and see nothing but my sister, Soleil, but Damen…Damen looks just like his father. He sounds like his father. Acts like Kryto did at that age, a little. It is surreal, to be transported back in time, that way, to when we were all children. It is difficult, for me to look at Damen and not see Kryto."

"Your sister has managed it. And I'd wager her husband has done worse to her than he did to you," I say.

"Teresa does not struggle that way," he agrees. "She loves her children so much; I don't think she can see their father in them. For her, they are hers and hers alone. But they are not my children, Soleil. I do not love them the same way she does. I cannot. **Vásan—"**

He cuts himself off just before I glare at him. We both know what he was about to say, in regards to the grand prince's own experiences. It is probably a good thing Vásan is asleep, or I think he would be furious enough to do something I would disapprove of. I do not think he'd regret it, though.

"It is not those boys' fault their fathers are monsters," I say.

I am not being specific, but I am including Alo Pike in that.

"I know that."

"So why can't you treat them that way?"

"I'm trying."

"You don't try enough," I snap. "Or else Damen wouldn't have realized you favor his brother over him for something he has no control over."

He jabs at the fire violently with the poker.

"Would you treat Rika differently?" I challenge him. "For being a bastard? Because of who her father is?"

He snorts. "Aiko is a far cry from Kryto Grey."

"Still. Whoever Aiko Shinya used to be, I think it is clear he is not that man anymore."

Septimus shrugs. "These years have changed all of us. Whatever Aiko is, whatever monster he hoped he could be, he wasn't when I met him. At least not to Teresa."

I suppose I cannot know any different.

"It's strange," Septimus says, like he is confessing something dark and secret. "But I think some part of him managed to fall in love with her, even in that short a time. The way he mentioned her to me, even briefly…I think he slipped out while she was asleep because he knew if he waited any longer, he would not leave her."

"You cannot know that," I say, but more because I want to hear more about the interaction than argue against the possibility.

"You did not see the way he looked at her," my cousin claims. "He was so apathetic, at first. So cold. Bitter-angry. Feral, maybe. It was as if he wanted to be a monster. All I know is that, by the time he left, he had to try and force himself to resume that persona once more, after my sister ruined it, simply by being herself."

I feel as if we are talking about two different men. Regardless of the excuses Teresa has made for Shinya, or the further descriptions I get of him from Septimus, I cannot imagine him becoming what he is now. Given how many lifetimes I have met him, I would like to think I know him better than my cousins do.

While I am somewhat angry at the man who left my cousin with a bastard child, I also want to speak with the boy I knew. I want to give him a chance to defend himself.

"I remember, once," I say suddenly as I recall. "I spoke to him when he was young. He was at a celebration. Before Comus Day. He could only have been eighteen or so, and he said…he was waiting. Waiting for the girl he dreamed about."

I turn to look at Septimus, and he purposefully avoids my eye. He is tired of all my supposing and hypotheticals.

"Septimus, can people have urges, and perhaps even dreams and memories, based on our past cycles? Is the reason Aiko Shinya always, *always* manages to fall in love with Teresa because he has fallen in love with her so many times before?"

He snorts. "Ha, Soleil. You already know my opinion on love. I don't think it matters what it was, love or lust or revenge or anything. We are hardly going to ever see the man again. All I can do, at this point, is hope that in our true lifetimes, Aiko Shinya is the person you remember him being, and my nephews never even know who their father is."

I ignore that last part, partially for my own sake.

"But that makes sense," I press. "The reason why he, now, still becomes gentle and kind despite himself: it is because he really *does* love her. Or, at least, he must have these ghosts of emotions telling him he does. If he had dreams of Teresa, before, in a past cycle, perhaps he has had them again, all his life. Perhaps that is why he agreed to it. Out of love."

Septimus does not look convinced, but he thinks about it.

"I do not—" he starts.

"Do you two ever shut up?" Castel groans.

"They do not, in fact," Vásan answers for us, not asleep after all.

I am mildly offended out of habit. Septimus merely smirks, shrugs his shoulders, and settles in.

"Let us see this watch through, and then get some sleep," he tells me. "Stop theorizing. It is not going to do anyone any good, now. Tomorrow, we will head down to the docks. Within a matter of weeks, this will all be over with. One way, or another."

I nod, and lean back against my pack. I am facing the door, which we have locked, and two of the windows, shut tight and barricaded. But given that we have already killed several monsters today, I don't think we need to worry about more swarming in so quickly. Septimus must think similarly, because while his sword is nearby, it is sheathed.

"Oh, before I forget: the moment the sun rises, you will all be up, barefoot, spending an hour before we depart," he says. "Everyone must be ready."

"Are you expecting trouble?" I ask.

"Not especially," Septimus says. "But I have lived long enough at this point that I can recognize opportunity for it."

All I can do is agree. At this point, I do not think I have the right to ignore Septimus' instincts. However, I am not so sure I can take his advice about the theorizing; now that he has given me a taste for answers, I want to know everything I possibly can.

Perhaps, knowing me as well as he does, Septimus' solution to simply send me to the Otherworld to ask Fate himself is inspired.

Fifteen

THE SUN RISES LATE and sets early in winter months, so we take advantage of it while we can. Of our party, I now know Castel's fluke will be no good to us, so he refrains from bothering, but the rest of us spend at least an hour with the sun or the moon. Out of the five of us with flukes, then, I note Margo, Nissa, Xerian and I prefer the sun. Vásan and Septimus, the moon. No one says so explicitly, but that somehow makes sense to all of us.

While no one bothers wasting water with a full wash in the morning, we still clean up, put ourselves in order, and manage a meager breakfast before heading out to the docks. Xerian rustles up coffee, as promised, but I decline his offer while most of the others partake. Even the smell of it warming reminds me too much of waking up in Nusk's hut, on the edges of campus, Korvaan brewing coffee, Taris oiling his curls in front of the mirror.

I wonder if Rian and Ayla are up early, now, perhaps breakfasting together. I wonder if Soren has yet to ask if he may court Ayla properly, and how Teresa is getting along with the Isaarian noblewomen. These cursed thoughts embroil me in a homesickness I do not deserve to enjoy the torment of; after all, we are only in the south of my own country.

"Before I board a ship for several weeks with any of you, I would like to know your flukes," Vásan says as Xerian distributes the coffee in the hotel's scavenged dishware. It is tonally clear this is not a request.

"Fine," Castel says, and holds up his hands so all can see his scars. "Useless. Your turn, kid."

"I'm good at things," Xerian says vaguely.

Nissa sighs.

"No, that is it, I swear!" the young man insists. "Margo calls it my 'master of none' fluke. I can adapt skills from other people, and although I will not be a master at it if they are, I will be proficient. I can only do one at a time, though, at least for now. I need more practice, if I want to stack them."

"So, say the boy has never picked up a gun before in his life and adapts from a sharpshooter," Margo explains, and blows on her coffee. "He will be a better than decent shot, then, without needing to practice a day in his life."

"Handy," Nissa admits.

"I can't use it with someone else's fluke, though," Xerian admits. "Only learned traits and skills."

"Still," Nissa says. "It seems as though you could save yourself plenty of time."

Xerian shrugs. He is too young, I think, to understand fully. However, Nissa spent most of her childhood and young adult years perfecting herself as a huntress. She knows how much time, effort, and training is needed to become a master at one's craft.

"And you, then, Lady Grey?" Vásan poses.

Margo laughs. "Oh, I am hardly a lady," she says, "and barely a Grey. But I do benefit from the family trait of hosting powerful flukes." She holds her arms out dramatically and nearly sloshes hot coffee on Castel. He scowls, but she does not notice, as she is too busy proclaiming, "I am unkillable."

"By anyone with a fluke," Septimus corrects her.

"Well, yes, there is that caveat," Margo says. "My family thought I had no fluke, at birth. My parents had a reader brought but they found nothing. Until I was quite a lot older, that is, and had an unfortunate attempted assassination prove successful. Only, I do not think the assassin counted on my coming back to life. He certainly did not expect me to come back to life hosting a copy of his own fluke."

"How many other flukes do you have, then?" Nissa asks, awed and somewhat horrified by the concept.

Margo shrugs. "A few dozen, at this point. It varies depending on how many people have tried to kill me, in different timelines, now. But my freshest one is always the most powerful. I cannot even remember what the first fluke I acquired this time around, is. Unfortunately, my nieces and nephews are well-aware of my abilities. They have been careful to delegate their attempts to kill me."

She says this in a disturbingly casual way. I cannot imagine being in her position, and having Lune and Taris' hypothetical children wanting me dead. Though I am well-aware by facts alone, at this point, that the Grey family is all kinds of twisted, it seems they manage to outdo themselves with every new anecdote.

Her fluke and Xerian's both remind me of Lune's, but I do not say so. While I am curious if Margo Grey and Xerian have met my sister and Taris the same way Castel has, I am also wary of what they might reveal should I ask. After all, they know me as the woman their party has sacrificed over and over again for, and Lune was one of them. Perhaps a reminder of her at this time would go about as poorly as reminding Castel of his dying nation and murdered love.

So, I wisely hold my tongue.

"We will need to head to the boat house, first," Margo says, once we have gathered our things, prepared to leave Isaaria. "There should be permits, there, for traveling as far east as we intend to."

"Is that entirely necessary?" Nissa says.

"I do not want to be the one to explain to a Tourrannese patrol why we might be headed to Kacha, do you?" Margo says. "Particularly not carrying the king of Isaaria's own bodyguard, and grand prince, and grand princess."

Nissa withdraws her complaint. Tourran may be in ruins politically, but warring factions of their once noble families have devoured what power they can, paranoid and primed for a fight. Were we to trespass in territory they consider their own, we would be lucky to experience mere detainment. Even then, we cannot afford to waste time when we know for certain Kryto Grey is prowling about.

The boat house Margo mentioned is the Mouloix Pieze: affectionally named the feet of Mouloix. It is not so much a house as it is an impressively large storage unit, trading post, ship repair and commons area all in one. In fact, it should not be referred to as a "house" at all, but that is the Alarkian word Margo chose. It is far too finely built, and too pretty. After all, for travelers visiting our country for the first time, there is a chance the inside of this building is the first taste of Isaaria they will get after disembarking from their ship. Passengers can find a washroom, food, maps, and rest their legs before purchasing train tickets and a carriage to the station, if they like. As many Isaarian craftsmen and merchants often sail out to the neutral southern isles to hock their wares or trade with passing-by ships, the Pieze usually would be a bustling hub.

Now, it is uncomfortably silent, abandoned like the rest of the city from the looks. Somewhere down the docks there is a haunted clanging, as the wind raps the rope pulley on a number of discarded ships against their masts, and a snapping, as metaphorical ghosts flap at limp sails.

Our trade with Milash dried up first. They claimed a Hoitsokin assassin killed their king, which is all but the same as accusing Nissa herself of treachery. Knowing what I do now, I sense the Greys' hand in such tragedy, though I doubt having this information earlier would have changed anything. All alliances fell through. Milash did not declare war, though it is known to all the former king's brash, young daughter, Queen Taikawa, would like to.

Her advisors held her back as a child, but she has long-since left that season of her life. War looms. The abandoned trade ships here are a physical reminder; mere portents of the death and despair to come.

It seems such situations with brazen matriarchs are common-place, lately. As far as I know, Queen Emmelina Voskoss of Lijimata is still alive, but the long-drawn war with the Alarkians devastated both countries involved. The prosperity of the west has dried up and with it, some of Isaaria's most vital trade agreements.

That leaves Tourran and Kacha, but a conflict between them followed by an uprising and civil war in Tourran ended those prospects, too.

The only ones left to trade with now are the pirates. I suppose there is not enough demand, these days, to justify keeping up the expenses of a ship, for most.

While Mouloix is near forsaken, as far as we can tell, no one dares speak as we quietly make our way to the boat house. Every sound, from boots clacking beneath us to the shift of fabric and occasional deep breath, is amplified by the emptiness around us. A flag snaps in the wind, close and loud. Nissa's hyena growls and she shushes it.

We all head inside the boat house, and stagger ourselves to keep watch while Margo takes Vásan to the offices, as he is the most likely person to be of use considering her quarry. I climb the metal stairs with them, to the second floor that opens to the main level below. Septimus accompanies me, and keeps one hand on his sword hilt the entire time. Nissa hovers near our place of entry below, with her hyena prowling about. Xerian flops down on the dusty, cushioned seat surrounding a marble pillar. Castel walks all the way down out of the visitor's portion of the building and through a large pair of open glass doors to ship maintenance. He plants himself facing a second pair of double doors, now closed, but wide enough to bring a boat in from the docks for repairs, when necessary.

A sense of uneasiness pulls at me to see him alone, and so far away from the rest of us, but I suppose someone ought to keep watch at the far doors. The last thing we need is to be pinned inside this building with enemies between us and the docks.

After several minutes pass, and nothing happens, I feel my shoulders relax some. I lean against the metal rail behind me, so I can still look out the glass windows to the main portion of the docks below. Occasionally, I glance to my right as well to see how Vásan and Margo are faring, but despite the mess they are making in one of the offices, I cannot tell.

It is after one of these checks that I turn back to the window and see people coming into the building from the docks, as if they have just disembarked from a ship. I am stunned, but whirl around to watch them enter below me. They are so casual that, at first, I cannot believe they are real. A moment later, I determine they cannot be.

I am shocked to recognize my own mother. She is wearing practical Alarkian clothes in a common shirtwaist and wide-banded skirt with a high waist, sensible low-heeled shoes, and capelet buttoned at the neck. A hat is pinned in place over hair turned lank from travel. She is carrying a pair of travel cases despite being obviously with child. This is most likely because her companion, a man in a brown coat whom I recognize as my father, is carrying a little girl. Is carrying me, I realize. It must be. My parents only had two children, me and Lune, and I am the elder. The two-year-old girl with wispy brown hair and plump, ivory hands sticking out of her little blue-wool coat as she sucks on a stick of maple candy, is me.

I was unaware I could see a ghost of myself.

"Liv," my father says, and holds me balanced on one arm while gesturing to something that exists only in their world.

They tuck themselves close to one of the pillars. To them, it appears Mouloix Pieze is still a busy place, with travelers bustling all over.

"Oh, good," Mother sighs, setting down one of the cases so she might stretch her back. "I could take a moment. When does the train leave?"

"Quarter past two," he says. "Rest for a spell. I shall see if I can get Soleil to walk off the sweets before she is forced to sit again. It's a long trip for her."

"For all of us," Mother agrees. "I'm glad Janos got to meet her, but I do not think we can risk going again. At least, we cannot take the children. It's not safe. Severin has eyes everywhere."

"What if Janos and Leah came here? Would that be possible? Ever?"

"We will discuss it later," she sighs after some thought.

My mother gestures for us to step closer, and my father does. She reaches up to kiss my head, then kiss him. "Don't be long," she says.

I watch her sit, for several minutes, trying to memorize every inch of her as she takes out a fan to cool herself. I look to find every feature in myself that I may have received from her. After some time, she stands again, stretches out her back, and picks up her case again to leave the same way she came in, to the boardwalk and the docks. Perhaps to stretch her own legs, perhaps to look for my father and me.

All I can do is follow her with my eyes, and then turn to the window to press my nose up against it and watch. I have somehow forgotten about why I am here, and who I have come with. All I want is another look at my mother. When I do not see her, I find I have run down the stairs, boots clanking, and out onto the docks after her.

But she never left the building. She disappeared somewhere in-between.

That is when I see him: Rian, out there, on the docks. For a moment, I am furious. I prepare a tirade, a lecture; I need to know why he would be so stupid as to follow us. A second later, and the words are gone. I have noticed enough to make them irrelevant. These are only more ghosts.

Rian looks younger by nearly a decade. His face is brighter. He still dyes his hair. The lines on his face are less severe. Staggering beside him, beneath his coat and clutching a bundle, is Teresa. The youth in her is even more prevalent. Though there is still some gauntness in her face, she looks less like a ghost of herself. Her hair is thicker, skin less sallow, eyes less haunted.

There comes a scoff beside me and I nearly jump. Taris. But to him, I am not here. It is only him and Rian and a shivering Teresa, clutching her bundle.

"About time," Taris says in his usual gruff manner. "If you'd drowned, Soleil would have my head."

"No chance of that," Rian says cheerfully. "Besides, look: I caught a pair of pretty fish."

Teresa smiles weakly, but there is trust in how she lets Rian wrap an arm around her shoulders to guide her as her legs shake. My cousin is still sick in this vision, then, but she is not at her worst. She is rescued, and relieved.

I try to suppress a shiver, but it takes me more violently than I expected, making my reaction unavoidable.

"Soleil!" someone demands, and I feel myself being shook by the arms.

Taris and Rian and Teresa are gone. They were never there, just like my mother and father. I never even left my position staring out the window.

I blink many times over again, to see Septimus standing before me, peering at me with concern. For some reason, my cheeks are wet.

"Sorry," I say, wiping at my face. "Do not worry over me; it is nothing."

Septimus sighs, and rolls his eyes. He is relaxed for but a moment until I thoughtlessly add: "It was only the ghosts again."

"What?" he demands, his head snapping towards me.

I frown. "I said I see ghosts, on occasion. Or, I have been. It is a relatively recent development. I think they may have been ghosts of timelines past."

Though, I will admit even to myself that based on the specifics, it is possible I am merely imagining things. After all, I do not recall ever meeting my son before, let alone seeing him at the age of twelve. Nor has Lune been married in the Summer Palace, and Taris has never met Teresa.

However, while I assumed this was some side-effect to Septimus' mind tricks, his eyes widen, and he curses under his breath.

"What?" I ask.

"Fate-damned Mitaurus. Mar-go!" Septimus calls.

She and Vásan immerge from the offices immediately, and our companions below take note of our commotion. Nissa stands up straighter and draws a knife. Even far down the warehouse, the echo has reached Castel, and he pulls a pepperbox with a sigh. Vásan notices this and mimics him.

Margo narrows her eyes.

"Forget the papers; we must be off. Immediately," Septimus says. "Soleil here's been seeing 'ghosts', apparently."

"...Widow?" Margo says, understanding him.

"Undoubtedly. I'm supposing Charrion has put together what we intend to do and has decided he would rather not let us succeed," Septimus says. "Either that, or...You know what, I don't care what they're doing here. I don't want to wait around and find out."

"How many of them are there?" Nissa calls up, stepping closer to where we stand above her on the metal parapet.

"If they brought all of them, thirteen," Septimus says, as Margo uncoils that whip-like weapon from the notch at her waist.

"There are seven of us," Nissa says, "I'll take those odds."

"I won't," Septimus snaps at her. "I'm not fighting *Charrion.* Cas! Stay put!" he calls ahead. "And get those doors open. We are coming to you."

"I'll cover us," Margo starts to offer.

"No," Septimus interrupts, "we need to get you and Soleil to the boat. Out of all of us, it matters most to get her to Kacha, and you are the only one who can sail. Nissa, Xerian: watch the—"

He is interrupted by a smattering of bullets as they shatter the windows and imbed in the walls. Most of us have the training or mere common sense to drop down immediately and find whatever cover we can, whether that be due to our experience with combat or being on the receiving end of an assassination attempt. The clang of metal under my body is a dull noise in comparison to the shots; I do not dare move and merely keep my head covered from glass until the firing stops. I do not have a good vantage point to see much anyway.

I am shocked when I am not the first to act.

The next thing I know, the moment the shots stop, someone has grabbed my arm and pulled me up to my feet. Margo. We are stumbling along before I can fully get my weight under me. Vásan is behind me. I cannot see Septimus, but I can hear him yelling something. My ringing ears refuse to process his words.

Some part of me notices, when glancing far ahead towards the ship entry, that I can no longer see Castel. The doors are only partially opened, as if he started to do as Septimus said, then stopped.

Below us, Nissa and Xerian have decided to return fire, out the doorway. Margo keeps me closely caught between herself and Vásan as we hastily descend the stairs. We keep as low as we can, to avoid further gunfire.

The moment my feet are on the marble floor, I feel Margo pull me, and then shove between my shoulder blades, shouting at me to run ahead of her. My legs are moving, then, but it is difficult to process. I must continually fight the desire to turn back and face our enemies directly. There is movement behind us; Nissa, Vásan and Xerian attempting to lay down cover-fire, keeping our enemies at bay. Septimus is at my shoulder, the desperate feel from him doing nothing to settle my own nerves.

Someone is zipping about closer and closer behind us; I catch a glimpse of red hair and a lanky, youthful figure dressed in tactical traveling clothes, gear slung over shoulders and strapped on belts. He startles me by looking so young, perhaps only eighteen.

It takes me a moment to understand how he is sliding around so fast, avoiding any attacks from my companions, and coming so startlingly close to me that I cannot help but take a swipe with my knife. The lad is grinning as he slips away again, arms outstretched with insulting gloves: Isaarian style, but with the fingers and most of the palms cut out in mockery of our traditions. On top of their witchcraft, the Mitaurus members must have flukes as well.

A pillar suddenly appears in front of me, like one of the ones I saw in the past with my parents. I halt so suddenly to try and avoid it that I slip and nearly fall back onto the floor, pulling Margo with me. There are suddenly many people around, milling about, seeing to their own business, acting so casual and calm. I blink about at them, wide-eyed.

The noise is overwhelming, overstimulating. Then, suddenly, it is all gone again, and I'm back where I was before. Margo is trying to pull me up and move. Xerian is there with her, a bloody-headed Castel leaning his weight on the younger man with an arm around his shoulders.

I could only have been incapacitated for a moment before we are moving again, but I have no time to warn Septimus of what has happened. We have left Vásan and Nissa behind to fend off the other members of our attackers. The rest of our party are doing their best to pull me along, to bring me to the boat.

I catch sight of the young Mitaurus member out of the corner of my eye, quickly drawing near. Septimus, several steps behind us, stops running to whirl on him, drawing his sword and slashing. But the young witch suddenly reverses, changing course to somehow slide backwards instead. I should not be surprised to witness such a thing, but it is still quite strange.

It appears he is somehow attracting himself to large objects—perhaps they must be things heavier than he is—to pull himself hastily away from us without needing to worry about footwork.

Septimus lunges after him, keeping the boy at bay. It is clear Margo means to leave him behind, despite any attempted protests on my part. I understand that, now that I know Septimus' plan, his presence is not entirely essential. Clanaugh was technically correct in saying so. But it has occurred to me that I appreciate my cousin for more than his knowledge; he is the best companion I could have for this trip, and I do not want to see him hurt.

I curse at my own emotions; I do not know if it is noble, my desire to risk myself for the sake of my companions, or merely foolish. However, the idea of allowing them to sacrifice for me, perhaps in a fatal manner, torments me.

Someone shoots at us, from back beyond where we left Nissa and Vásan. The bullet barely misses Xerian, pinging off the metal of a ship still sitting pretty for repairs that will never come. I know to run even before Margo insists. She shouts at Xerian in what I assume is his native language, taking Castel from him so the boy can run with me. No doubt he is faster, and perhaps Margo has some former fluke that could heal the injury slowing the prince down. She is hiding the two of them behind some temporary cover, down to the ground, when we leave them behind.

Then it is just me and the boy.

We burst out of the Mouloix, out of the narrow gap; Castel managed to start rolling the doors open before being caught by a stray bullet. I stumble as I find myself at a ramp leading down to the sea, for boats to be sent out. Managing to steady myself in time, I grab Xerian's arm and yank him back before he runs himself directly into the water. We are both quick to hop up onto the wooden boardwalk running along the coast and all the way down the docks. It arches high so passersby may stop and watch a ship being repaired, or even see one passing beneath them out to the water again.

But as we exit onto the ship's ramp, we simply cut to the left and then we are up on the docks. It is not exactly a direct path down to the ship Margo procured, but we are close to the straightaway.

Xerian is young, and I am still relatively fast. We could probably make it to the ship in time, if not for what happens next.

Out of the corner of my eye, I catch sight of that woman from the train again. Not the one with the birthmark; the strange blond woman in the white dress. The inhuman one. Before I can think, or even consider if I want to leave the rest of our party behind to only escape with some strange Rumshtaman boy, she flings a hand out toward me, fingers spread. She says a few strange, foreign words in haste, like a curse. Our surroundings immediately change.

The city is suddenly populated and young again, thriving. Xerian and I are surrounded by people giving us strange looks, and widening their eyes at our weaponry, our rugged state. They begin to give us a wide berth, whispering and herding small children away. I can tell that some of them recognize me.

Despite Septimus implying this is all but illusion, it feels startlingly real to me. The sharp change in smells, the sudden bright, clean sounds. I realize that lately, in comparison, the sun has not been shining as brightly as it used to. The sky is so blue, with beautifully crafted puffs of clouds. Even as someone who does not usually romanticize nature, all I want to do is stand and stare at the skyline, perhaps with Rian to accompany me. There is a natural romance to a clear winter's day and I want nothing more, now, than to share it with him.

At least, until the very subconscious Widow has drawn on to torture me proves me wrong.

"Soleil!"

I hear and recognize Lune's voice. Perhaps I would not have, if I had not seen her so recently, in the Summer Palace. Regardless, I know that is my little sister, and for the second time in recent days, I have heard her sound happy to see me. It occurs to me that perhaps Lune always sounded happy to see me, and I simply never noticed.

She is so genuine, with the bounce in her step that sends her hair swishing back and forth. Her breath creates small puffs in the winter air, but she does not appear at all cold as she approaches me to grab hold of my hand with both of hers. Behind her, walking slower, comes Taris. He looks so calm compared to what I have grown used to; I think this is happiness for him.

He has one small, bundled figure propped up on each arm with only their eyes and noses poking out of their winter ware. These children are perhaps two or three, and I know who they are though I have never met them before.

"I'd swear, you have your head up in the clouds!" Lune laughs, tugging me gently behind her, as if we have plans to head in the opposite direction.

"I…Don't…" The words come out with no intention of expansion. I cannot form a proper sentence in my head and am not sure what I would say anyway.

"Oh, I knew it," Lune tisks. "Yeong-jun's got you exhausted, hasn't he? Not to mention, planning Ayla's wedding for the spring. I told you that you didn't have to come and meet us. Where's Rian? I know he won't have let you come alone."

I take a few steps forward with her towards Taris, and their children. I do not know what to say, and I'm not sure where I'm going. All I'm certain of is that I prefer this reality to the one I am living.

It's a shock and horror, then, when it all vanishes. Lune is gone, and so is the sun. She is not holding onto my wrist, but instead, Rian.

"Soleil?" he says, and smiles at me. "Something the matter?"

"I…" I say, confused and dizzy.

It finally occurs to me that this man only looks somewhat like Rian, but is not him, when Xerian shoots him. I stifle the surprising temptation to scream before mentally reassuring myself several times over that this man dropping to the ground is not Rian. I force myself to blink and breathe, taking in the surroundings of the real world. It seems I missed a good three minutes in illusion.

Xerian's nose is bleeding, and there is an injury running the length of his arm, his sleeve ripped open. On the ground are the Rian look-alike and a second man who appears to have come with as many new Alarkian weapons he could possibly carry. The boy is already crouching down to pick through the weapons, choosing a compact machine gun that looks as if it would only ever be used in a war zone.

I frown at the man I thought was Rian. I was able to discern he was a fake so much faster at the train station; why the delay, now? How could I have come even close to walking off with him, thinking he was first my sister, then my husband?

"He—" I begin.

"That is not going to keep him down for long," Xerian warns me. "If Widow gets close, she will bring him back again. Why didn't you knife him the second her illusion broke?!"

"I couldn't. He…He looks like Rian," I stammer.

"He doesn't," Xerian says, picking up the gun and looking it over. "He just does to you. Trust me," he adds, "it's easier to take Lure down when he looks like someone you already know is dead."

He is fiddling with the Alarkian machine gun in a way that does not inspire confidence.

"Do you even know how to use that thing?" I demand.

Xerian blinks. He turns to look at the weapons-man. His eyes are blank for a moment, and then he is back. He breaks the gun open, reloads it, and snaps it back into place again so quickly one would think him a veteran.

"Do now," he says.

We move down the boardwalk again, Xerian holding the gun tightly with both hands. The sounds here and the world around me are so chaotic compared to the peace of my illusionary vision; I cannot deny the desire to return to it. It is Xerian who does not allow me to slow down to even see how our allies are faring.

No one has emerged from the Mouloix Pieze.

We reach the final straightaway of the docks; one long stretch down to the end. Though we have both been careful, nearly overly alert, there are no signs of further members of the Mitaurus. Given that we have incapacitated two of the thirteen, that leaves eleven for Septimus, Margo, Vásan, Nissa, and an already-injured Prince Castel. I am especially wary of Widow, certain I saw her close by before my vision. I worry where she may be, now.

"There's the boat," Xerian says, panting. "Let's go."

I hesitate. "Wait. Septimus—"

"I'm supposed to get you to the boat. I must. After, I will return and see if I can help the others," he interrupts.

He does not sound impatient, but is undeniably worried. I realize what I must represent to someone like Xerian, who has taken the opposite approach to Castel. This boy is likely the last remaining member of his family, and so long as I exist, so too exists the potential for that to change. For Xerian, I am proof of a reason to keep hoping.

As much as I want to be a part of this fight, it is not the role I should play, now.

I nod, agreeing to do things his way, and we move again, prepared to run down the boardwalk. Boots clattering on the wood planks, breath puffing in the winter air in front of us.

We feel and hear it before we see it: the unbalance as the ground shakes under us, the cracking of wood. Then, the screeching roar. I have heard that sound before, not too long ago considering how many hundreds of years I have lived and remembered. I know, even before I manage to get a good look at it, that the Mitaurus are no longer the only party interested in stopping us at the docks. The brightback that once killed Crispin Carsans and its owner have arrived.

Xerian curses in a foreign language before throwing himself sideways against me. I fall off the boardwalk and onto a lower deck, where smaller boats are tied up. He does not. Stuck on his back, he manages to shoot up at the brightback, which appears to injure it somewhat, but in only a minor fashion. When it spits fire back at him, Xerian does manage to roll off the platform to land next to me to avoid being roasted alive, but his hair is singed, and we need to put out a fire started on his sleeve.

The boardwalk is burning.

I watch Xerian glance up at the dragon, and the woman riding on its back. We have seconds to make a decision, and neither of us know how we can possibly arrive down at the other end of the platform to reach our boat. Not without swimming, with our gear hindering us significantly. Even then, it will leave us vulnerable and completely in the open.

This will not work. This will not work at all.

We cannot win this.

I make the decision, knowing Septimus likely will be annoyed with me, but I do not care.

"I'm going back," I decide, pulling off my gloves.

"What?" Xerian says.

He is too late to try and stop me, though I do not think he would try, anyway. After a few deep breaths, I close my eyes and focus. Press my fingertips together and imagine the movement of time around us, how the wind moves, ruffling a strand of hair across my forehead. How each breath of mine and Xerian's fall rapidly, how the chill in the air fills my lungs differently than summer's.

When my eyes snap open again, we go back. I drag us back, knowing the weight of it, the power in it. I push the brightback away. I restore the number of our enemies, yes, but I give us the advantage as well.

It had been my desire to drag us all the way back to the morning. We could rise early, all go at once, and avoid this catastrophe by several hours.

But I can feel the drain this is taking on me, and while I have managed much longer gaps in time before, it is different now. For one thing, I am physically much older than I have been before when playing with time, ever. I have also usually been able to land myself in a time where I can be safe, at least long enough to restore my energy. With the possibility that the Mitaurus have been waiting here for us longer than even this morning, I cannot exhaust myself only to be utterly useless in a fight.

Given how long they have been following us—since I first arrived at the Summer Palace considering the first appearance of Widow's ghosts—it is possible there is no way to avoid this fight and still take Margo's boat.

I land us back inside the Mouloix, as Vásan and Margo are first going to search the upper offices. Snapping back inside myself, I do feel some energy returning to me as I give up a more ambitious shift in time.

Septimus suddenly catches his breath and blinks several times. His eyes narrow, and then he snaps, calling Margo and Vásan back immediately. He draws his sword.

"What?" Margo sighs as she cancels the search. "What is it this time?"

"The Mitaurus are here," I say, and go on, immediately telling them as much as possible. "I saw some of them: the ones from the train station, and a woman in white, a boy with red hair, and more. And there is one of the Greys here as well. The woman with the brightback."

Vásan looks taken aback, but Septimus remembers what happened as well, which is a boon to be sure. He begins pulling off his gloves. I do the same. The others follow; our flukes will be much needed in the minutes to come.

"Nexa, damn her. We don't have much time," Septimus says. "Margo, I need you to hold the majority of the Mitaurus off. Use your clamp fluke. At least one of them has heavy artillery, I'd guess Ritter; do not let him use it. Some of them will slip through, but let us minimize it for now. The moment you feel you cannot keep the barrier up any longer, stun them, and run."

Margo nods; he has requested another of her fluke variety, apparently.

"Vásan—there is a woman who wears white with blond hair and red eyes," Septimus tells the prince. "Widow. She practices a vampiric mind-magic and she has latched onto Soleil. I need you to incapacitate her. Do whatever you need to, and then run. Out of here, down the docks, get yourself to the ship and don't look back. Don't wait for Margo and me. Understand?"

Vásan does not question being told to kill a woman. "Could she influence me as well?" he simply asks.

"Yes, but not as strongly as her main target," Septimus says. "Your fluke will be a hinderance to her. Get in her head and keep her out of Soleil's."

Vásan nods.

"Xerian, get over here," Septimus demands. "Take Margo's skill for sailing, then you escort Soleil. You and Castel, get her to the ship and manage anyone who tries to stop you, understand?"

Xerian agrees, and I see him for what he is: a boy who never fully grew up, simply following Septimus' orders because it is all he knows to do. He has been promised a new life and a return to his dead family. He will not question abandoning half our party so long as Septimus is the one telling him to do it.

However, this may be how Septimus handles things, cutting his losses when necessary, telling himself I can always rewind things again, bringing people back to life. But it is not how I do things. It cannot be. Not anymore.

The idea alone sparks a panic in me: I cannot imagine traveling to Kacha on my own. I understand I will not be alone, fully, as I will have Castel and Xerian. How can I manage this without Septimus? If I do manage to return to Isaaria, how am I going to explain to everyone there what happened to Septimus? Vásan? Nissa?

I grab onto Septimus' arm. "No," I insist. "I can't do that."

"What?"

"I cannot do this alone, Septimus. Please."

He looks disgusted and exasperated with me. "Soleil, do not be emotional. Our lives don't really matter. Don't make me—" he starts in warning.

"No," I say. "Septimus, please. Don't."

If there were enough time for a proper stand-off between us, I'm certain I would win. Not because I have the better argument, but because I am more willing to put my life on the line than Septimus is. As it is, the Mitaurus force him to agree with me.

The shots begin, forcing us to duck down and find whatever cover we can. I suppose I did not save myself as many minutes as I thought for discussion. Hopefully that works in my favor.

"We are out of time—go! Go!" Septimus orders.

"Your majesty," Vásan says, taking me by the elbow and gesturing for me to move on ahead of him, so that he might lay down suppressing fire while protecting me bodily.

Margo flings out both arms towards the direction of the shots. What appears is some strangely opaque but decidedly forceful barrier that somehow repulses the bullets and makes a horrible scraping sound as it pushes, grinding against the doors and ground. The more I see of what Margo can do, I realize it is not a barrier, precisely, but a clamp as Septimus mentioned, keeping whatever precisely she wants from moving.

We reach the floor, no longer in danger from gunfire. With Margo's strange clamp up, she has kept the grand majority of the thirteen Mitaurus at bay, but exceptions have managed to slip through.

I catch a glimpse of a white dress. Vásan does, too, and before I know it, he has left to keep Widow away from me as promised. Septimus calls for Castel to come up closer and join the rest of us while he guides Margo down the stairs, so that she might keep the clamp up and the majority of the Mitaurus away from us. This leaves Vásan, Nissa, Castel, Xerian and I to handle those who did slip through.

This is actually a more desirable position for me than the one our previous tactics demanded.

In addition to Widow, I count three Mitaurus: the shape-shifter called Lure who Nissa and Castel have taken on together, the red-haired boy who Xerian appears to think he can manage on his own, and a second woman. This one dresses in black, and is older than Widow, at least physically. Given their use of witchcraft, it is possible the members of the Mitaurus are dozens of years older than they appear to be.

What startles me most is that I recognize her. I know this woman. Not personally, but I have seen her before, in a small apothecary that Rian once frequented for Asmer's rare medicine.

She wore no gloves, then. She still does not, now.

I take out my pistol to shoot at her, but she is quick. She whips something at me, almost too fast for me to comprehend. It takes a moment, confused as I am, to understand what she has done, mainly because it looks as if she has done nothing at all. Nothing came my direction that I could see. Nothing hits me. Then, I feel my arm go slack, my hand unclenching so my gun clatters to the ground.

My arm is useless.

She moves again, like striking a whip. It is difficult for me to dodge her, mainly because there is essentially nothing to see. I must do my best, then, to make assumptions based on imagination alone. I suppose she does not hit me, mainly because I still have the use of one arm.

I take refuge behind a pillar, ducking behind it while planning my next move. I think it may be best to recover my gun.

Luckily for me, I do still have my bolt shooter, which I have not often used while acting as the king's captain. But my days of sneaking about in the dark and shooting at assassins have paid off.

I fire several shots in the direction of the Mitaurus witch.

It is when I'm desperately trying to think of how to retrieve my gun that I realize I don't have to. Not like this, at least.

I feel time wobble even considering it. I think of the little pocket watch Rian gave me and imagine that thin needle of a second hand, tick-tick-ticking away. Does it make the same sound ticking backwards? I suppose it hardly matters; I couldn't hear it anyway with the gunfire and my ears ringing. And still, I tick it backwards. Second by second, ticked back, and we tick with it until I can feel my arm again, and the pistol clenched in it.

This time, I do get a shot off at her before she throws that whip at me. This time I see it, too.

The lines are very thin, and do not appear to be corporeal. I can only see flashes of them, like light glinting. I am certain this is not a fluke, but some kind of witch's spell. Though I have not seen the Mitaurus using blood in their magic, it is possible they have already made blood sacrifices in preparation for this meeting.

However, this knowledge does not frighten me. In fact, I realize that I can match her. It will not be without effort, but I know I have the skills.

I still do my best to avoid her to begin with; this time I manage to get off a decent shot at her and clip her arm. But she hits me, too, and I lose one arm, then the second in immediate succession. Useless and limp. She manages to get another one shot out at Vásan, too, but instead of simply numbing him, I catch a stripe of red. Stoic though he is, I can see it hurts more than it should.

I know I ought to consider myself lucky that no one in this world appears to want me dead. While this Mitaurus witch must be careful not to damage me too much, I have no such compunctions about her well-being.

I drive back time again, knowing Septimus will likely be the only person here to even realize I've done it. Vásan won't know he was ever injured. The witch will have no idea I'm working several steps ahead of her; from her perspective, she and her companions have surprised us, and I should have no knowledge regarding her capabilities.

This time, I force myself to move even faster.

She is prepared to face me at a distance, with what weapons she has at her disposal, and me with my gun. If she moves those strings fast enough, I don't know if they could stop a bullet, but I understand they can either numb or cut according to her whim. Possibly, they have further uses.

As she has made it clear, the witch has no issue changing targets if I am not readily available. This means I cannot merely turn back a few seconds and expect to receive the outcome I desire most. If I want everyone to come out of this alive, I cannot let her target Vásan or Margo.

If she manages to hit me, I need to isolate and turn back time only for myself, physically. I know I'm capable; I have done it before to rid my body of poison, after all. Although, that was done mainly subconsciously, almost like second nature. I need to make myself do it purposefully, now.

My first move, this time, is to dodge. I throw myself sideways and roll up into a suitable position to fire at her. She does take the bait, to begin with, leaving me with a temporary opening. After missing me, she is quick to pull those strings back. She whips them into a frenzy to keep me from getting close to her while her other arm raises, folding to protect her head. Any bullets that do hit their mark ping off her clothes as if they are somehow resistant to such a thing.

Still, she cannot look at me and keep her head covered at the same time, so her attacks are to only keep me at bay, and are not precise.

I don't bother to reload the gun, despite it being a more efficient weapon. There is a strange thrill in me as I flick out a knife, spinning it around in my hand before springing forward to charge her. This is a familiar motion; this is a fighting technique that puts me in more danger, yes, but I am good at it.

When one of those strings manages to strike me, before a part of me can even begin to feel numb, I isolate it, and pull it back. It is disorienting, like being suddenly overly aware of one's own body, every portion of it and how it connects. But I can move past that.

I am still in control.

Even once she can see me, and aim more precisely, it does not take long for her to realize she cannot stop me. I am more susceptible to mind tricks than physical restrictions. This is where I excel. When I reach her, slashing with my knife, she needs to leap back, attempting to circle around me. I keep on her, willing to attack again, again, and again until I hit her.

I hear her begin to mutter words in some foreign tongue, arranging and twisting her fingers with the string to form symbols.

The long strings grow taunt around me for a moment, forming a shield for her and a prison for me, not unlike Margo's clamp. I pulse time back just two seconds, and before she can complete her spell, throw a smaller knife at her hands, and the silvery strings woven around her fingers. I cut only the string, not her hands, but the knife does slice her cheek as it travels past.

The second throwing knife I send her way does manage to strike one of her hands. Not a clean cut off like I managed with Phoebus Kagen, but I suspect even with *Dadj'zcha*, one's hands are a necessity.

I note surprise in her eyes. She did not anticipate my being able to resist her traps like this. While she must be intelligent enough to understand by now what I'm doing, given their knowledge of my capabilities, it is clear she thought it would be much easier to incapacitate me.

It is difficult to decide whether I should be insulted or grateful that the Mitaurus have clearly underestimated me.

She dodges behind me again, trying to readjust and come up with a new tactic. This time, I turn back all of time again, a few seconds. When she makes the same move, unaware of what I've done, I can anticipate it. I spin the opposite direction and meet her there. It is as if she has thrown herself directly in my path, or as if I could predict the future.

My knife finds its mark. That is at least one member of the Mitaurus down.

I hear an ear-piercing scream and turn. Widow has dropped to her knees, tearing at her own hair and clothes. Vásan stands by, practically nonchalant, hand outstretched towards her. He is tired from his match against her, breathing hard, but clearly the victor between them. I do not know what he has made her see, but this once imposing, looming enemy who tortured me is now just a screaming woman who believes something that does not exist is killing her.

It is moments like these that make me glad Vásan is an ally. Whatever illusions they threw at one another, it is clear his were superior.

Septimus is there, pushing at me, still steering Margo backwards as she holds up her clamp behind us. She cannot project far, I see; if she moves back, it allows the remaining Mitaurus to move forward within the clamp. But they still cannot reach us so long as she maintains it.

"Run!" Septimus shouts, pushing at me again.

Xerian and Nissa fall in, the latter whistling for her hyena. They and Castel have been managing Lure and the Mitaurus boy as best they can, but while none of them are seriously injured, it is clear they are exhausted.

Margo releases her clamp for but a moment, then readjusts it, trapping the remaining free Mitaurus members: an incapacitated Widow, Lure, and the boy with the red hair. The last of the three looks immediately annoyed, and disappointed, to find himself trapped. But Lure only looks at us all and smiles, relaxing his arms, willing to follow the barrier of Margo's clamp and wait for her to faulter. He looks completely uninjured, perhaps only a little flushed. He is so casual in his mannerisms; I worry that he knows something I do not about how long she can keep this up.

I glance at Margo as we run. Sweat has broken out on her forehead.

The further we hurry through the Mouloix, the more Margo's clamp moves in after us, keeping the thirteen members of the Mitaurus between it. I glance back just twice to try and catch a glimpse at the rest of the members. They are so calm, from what I can see, that it worries me. I was the only one able to defeat a member of them without calling it a temporary draw. Perhaps my opponent simply was not a good match for me, but she could have defeated someone like Vásan easily. Widow could have had me trailing along behind her like a child, in my dream world. We were lucky, that is all.

Castel notices me looking behind more often than he would like. While Margo and Septimus linger at the tail of our train, by necessity, the Lijimi prince grabs my arm and keeps me in the middle of everyone, by Vásan. Nissa and Xerian run ahead to open the doors.

They do not wait for the rest of us, but hurry ahead onto the docks, to clear the way ahead of potential dangers.

To be honest, until we are out on the docks as well, I'd forgotten about the dragon.

Nissa and Xerian are far ahead us down the docks—halfway to the boat, considering their speed—when it appears. Nexa Grey lands the brightback by our two companions so that it shakes the ground startles them both, screeching at them. Nissa barely manages to roll out of the way as it snaps for her. Xerian pulls out a pistol to shoot at it, to give Nissa some time to move back, if nothing else.

He has to jump down to the lower docks, not unlike our first time facing the beast, when it tries to snap at him instead.

"Septimus!" screams Nexa Grey, and her brightback bellows in chorus.

"Fate's Fingers," Septimus sighs, still acting as Margo's support.

Castel says something similarly, though I think Vásan is too shocked by the sight of a dragon to register what we shall have to do to escape it.

We move onto the lower docks ourselves, while Xerian and Nissa do their best to keep the brightback distracted. They are careful to keep some distance from it, both, and keep it from noticing the rest of us through constant antagonization. Unfortunately, the one thing Nissa forgot to do was call off her hyena from attacking any enemies on her behalf.

The moment it perceives the hyena as a threat, or perhaps just an annoyance to be rid of, the brightback lunges for it. In a second, it has caught the hyena between its jaws, throws it up, and snaps it out of the air again with a terrible crunch.

Nissa screams and curls forward, arms clutched up against her body as if experiencing a sudden pain in her chest. She drops to her knees.

Xerian vaults back onto the upper deck to try and reach her but loses his balance and falls again when the brightback tries to grab him next, instead taking a bite of wood from the docks.

Beside me, Vásan has reloaded his gun and stands to fire at the brightback, to give Xerian time to try and reach Nissa again. I suppose the Grey woman has thought ahead and in no way wants to risk us escaping to reach the east, because she lets Vásan get away with this.

Instead of trying to gobble up an Isaarian grand prince, she has the brightback spit fire, starting at the far end of the dock, at our own ship. Castel grabs Vásan to pull him back down again, and we cower as best we can as the dragon burns all the ships, leaving us no methods of escaping via water, no means by which to reach the east.

There are a number of explosions from the steamships as the tremendous fire reaches them. Debris rains down over the docks. Wooden beams crackle, snap, and fall. There is a high-pitched screeching sound, and the world around us all is suddenly orange and blistering hot. Someone is yelling, near me. Perhaps it is more than one person. I cannot tell who or hear what they are saying over the cacophony. For a moment, there is nothing to feel but panic as the dragon's stream of fire reaches us and blasts overhead, singing the wood of the upper docks.

All I can do is hope that Nissa was low down enough, collapsed as she was, not to suffer severe burns.

Margo has been jostled by the explosions; her balance upset as she has thrown down against the wood of the lower docks. Her clamp is gone. Luckily, with the brightback breathing fire, I think the Mitaurus have a bigger issue to deal with than myself and my companions. If they want Teresa and her children, they must see the Grey family as competition. Assuming Septimus' words were accurate, there is little love lost between the two groups.

Even if they dare the fire and heat, there is going to be a brightback waiting for them if they want to reach me.

Once I manage to push the panic aside, my mind races, realizing: I can use the Mitaurus and Nexa Grey against one another. It is a risky gamble, but one I must take. I need the brightback to keep the witches away, as I am certain there is not a chance that we could defeat all thirteen, especially since my previous opponent has likely been resurrected by Widow.

However, I also need the boat. We need to escape, and attempting anything on foot will not do. There are long ways around this issue—ways to still reach Kacha, if we had months to spare, and luck on our side, but we do not, and I never seem to.

This leaves me with the understanding that I need to finesse my powers some way to benefit us, to get us on the boat. But I cannot think of how to turn back the clock while still avoiding the Mitaurus and the brightback, while giving us time to reach the boat. Not before that blast of fire.

Being roasted alive does not sound like a pleasant way to end things.

The realization is sudden and sure: we need the brightback's fire behind us, moving backward. There is no other way to ensure our safety from it.

Nexa Grey is having her brightback burn the Mouloix, now, but I'm sure most of the Mitaurus will survive the experience, if not all of them. This gives me enough time to put my plan together.

I try to calculate, quickly and without error, all that would rely on me for this potential plan to work. There will be extraordinary precision involved, so that I know I will need to use all my concentration, and likely the majority of my energy as well. If a single mistake is made, we are over. But I have moved time around an object before. Granted, that object was myself, but why should I not be able to do it again, simply with more individuals isolated?

There is no time to fully construct the scenario. The last time my party engaged a bright-back, it ended with Crispin Carsans becoming the lizard's snack. I'm not sure I want to add the Mitaurus to that challenge and expect a better outcome.

It's time to move.

I grab Septimus by the arm, which it turn gets the attention of all our close by companions. I raise my voice as much as I can over the din to be sure they can hear me, and am pleased to see small confirmations in body language afterwards.

"When I tell you to, run as fast and hard as you can to the end of the dock by the boat and jump into the water above it. The water above it, understand?" I repeat.

Septimus' brow knits before he realizes what I am attempting to do. Likely he does not know it all; not in all its details, all its complexity. But he is smart enough, and knows my ambitious nature well enough, to have a general idea.

"Soleil, don't—" he starts.

I do not give him the chance to say anything else.

There are several things to be done, and I manage to initiate them all so closely together, it must appear simultaneous.

Time begins to tick backwards as slowly as I can manage it, grain by grain in the hourglass, falling up so that seconds are decimated. Only, ahead of us, I hold the remains of our burned boat down. Nexa's brightback did its best work on that boat, after all; most of it is in pieces, sinking.

There is a thrumming in the air, and in my head. A strange, pulsing distortion of sounds casts itself over all us, and from the flinching and bewilderment of my companions, I can tell they hear it, too. For, while I've the rest of time moving minuscule backwards around us, we are immune. We exist in a temporary limbo, and can move as we please. When time resumes, it will be as if we have teleported.

This is the only way the Mitaurus and the brightback will exhaust one another to give us enough time. The only way we will be able to reach our boat safely before it burns. The only solution I can think of in the time I have.

"Run!" I order.

Margo is quick not to question, and pulls herself back onto the upper docks; the world is still a flaming hellscape before us, but there is enough of the docks left to make it. Down the way, Xerian sees us and copies us, only going to pick up Nissa first. Castel is back on the upper decks, too, almost before I can notice he has moved. Septimus and Vásan help pull me up while I concentrate. I need to run, with the others; I know that. I need to move. My legs pump mechanically as my mind keeps time moving at my whim.

It is not easy, and I know my stamina will not last. It is difficult to keep things moving backwards slower than it is meant to, even with my powers, and I can feel the desire to speed up, to save my energy. I will not be able to keep my precision for long. I'm sure Septimus knows this as well.

So, with the brightback's fire creeping its way back in time behind us, Vásan and Septimus stay by my side and we run.

I feel my heart pounding in my chest. The heat rises behind us, fire licking the docks. I see Margo far ahead of us, sprinting, Castel helping Xerian with Nissa.

My body is screaming at me from the effort. My lungs suck in smoke that soon will not be there, and flames disappear from the docks back into the brightback.

Some part of my mind almost thinks we will not make it. I can feel time moving faster, backwards. I am strong, I know this, but such control and ambition is going to bring me to the brink of collapse. The brightback's fire gets ever closer to us.

I am tempted to release time for a moment, to just give us a few more seconds, before starting up again, but I don't want to risk it. I don't know if I'll be strong enough to begin again once I let go.

The end of the dock grows closer. So does the fire. Every time I think I have pushed myself to the brink, I find some other kernel of reserved energy beneath it to pull forth. To force myself on, one more step, each time. Just one more. More. More. One more second, then two.

Margo is in the water. Now Castel and Xerian, carrying Nissa with them.

We are not too far behind them.

I can force myself to do this. I have faced worse.

Somehow, telling myself this helps. Perhaps I am deluding myself, and I have never strained my body to this point—have never experimented with all the confines of my fluke, tested expanded multiple uses of my abilities at once. But whether the Almighty is humoring my ambition or not, it works.

We reach where the boat once was and jump. For a moment, the feeling of weightlessness nearly makes me fall unconscious, my vision swimming. Then my body crashes into the ocean, and I taste salt as I sink beneath water now warm from the fire.

Water encompasses us as flames, moving backwards, flare overhead. The additional heat is almost enough to convince me winter is gone.

Accustomed to running, my body immediately wants to suck in a gasp, so that salt stings my nose and the back of my throat. Natural panic is triggered; in such circumstances, one ought to immediately push themselves up to the surface, coughing and spluttering. But I do not have time for my own body to imagine it is drowning. I still have work to do.

I hold the boat down, and myself underwater, and I let the reel of time play. Time progresses. Nexa Grey's brightback spits flame, but the boat it sank in a previous timeline is not there to be caught in the blast. This boat is in limbo as we once were, sunk from events that should not take place because it is not there to be targeted; it does not exist. Not until I want it to.

Once the flames have passed us by, I release time like a snap. The boat sunk beneath us suddenly whirls backwards, knitting itself together in mere seconds to avoid a paradox: it was never sunk.

The boat forms beneath us, popping up above the water as we collapse to its deck—a deck dry, from having never sunk underwater. I hear Margo shouting something, and already leaping to her feet to move below decks. The others are moving, too, save for Nissa. I want to rise to my own feet and help; I know this is not over. We only have a minute or two before our ruse is noticed, and the brightback can fly.

But I cannot.

My body refuses to obey me. In fact, it barely allows me to gasp in air as my chest shudders and my head pounds. I realize I likely will not be of much use to anyone like this before I allow myself to fall unconscious.

Sixteen

"YOU ARE A FOOL. A halfwit. A madwoman," I hear Septimus say before I have even opened my eyes. He must have seen me stir and prepared that greeting just in time. I would expect nothing less. He even continues: "An idiot who takes risks and nearly got herself killed just to keep *us* alive—*which,* might I remind you Soleil, would be the worst possible outcome for the entire *world.*"

"Duly noted," I manage to mumble.

Or, I believe I have mumbled it. I am not entirely sure if what has come out of my mouth is words or a musical groan.

I can smell the ocean and feel a light spray across my face. When I manage to peel my eyes open, I see they have propped me up in a deck chair that some rich woman likely once used for sunbathing. I cannot, however, imagine how such an object found its way onto a fishing vessel. I find I do not care enough to expend the energy asking.

Having the sun on my face does help, even if I cannot connect to the earth out at sea. We are clipping along at a decent pace, chugging through the water, powered by steam. The sound of the ocean waves is peaceful, and the sky is so bright and blue out here; it is almost too easy to forget what terror the rest of the world is currently experiencing.

Septimus is sitting on a crate, frowning at me. I can feel irritation oozing off him, though I suspect he'd find a way to be cross with me regardless of what happened. I have saved our lives, and he still wishes I'd let someone else take the risks, for someone else to find a solution.

This is how he shows his concern, which makes his reaction endearing. Now that I am starting to understand Septimus, I find him less aggravating than I once did. There is almost a hilarity to him and his exaggerated mannerisms. His insistence on knowing and doing everything himself, I think, has less to do with him thinking himself better than me and more to do with keeping me alive and well.

Rian would appreciate that.

"Ah, the lady wakes!" I hear a cheerful voice and Xerian leans into view. "That was a fine trick you pulled. I don't know how you did it—it hurt my brain when Septimus tried to explain. But it worked. So."

"It mostly worked," Septimus snaps, and then glances at me. "You managed to get the grand prince shot by one of the Mitaurus on our way out, I'll have you know. Most of them were kept busy by the brightback but not all of them. And I would wager they aren't far behind us."

I stopped listening after that first admission and bolt up straighter only to wince at the pain lacing through my muscles.

"Vásan's been shot?!"

"He's fine," Margo drawls. "He's sitting out, getting some sun just the same as you. Though I doubt his skin will thank him for it."

I manage to crane my neck around and see Margo at the front of the boat, steering. Vásan is sitting up against the boat's rail, eyes closed, arms and legs both crossed. He looks well enough; considering his usual fair skin, it is hard to tell whether he's white from loss of blood, or only looks paler because of the direct sun exposure. One of his arms is bandaged, though it looks as if he will recover.

I turn back to Septimus. He wanted me to feel guilty, and I do. I wish I had been strong enough to stay awake and help everyone else escape the docks after manipulating time. But I suppose I am grateful Septimus has such competent allies, with relatively useful flukes.

"Where is Nissa?"

"Below decks," Septimus says. "She'll be fine, too. By her own admission, for the record. She will merely experience a sickness for a few days."

I nod. "How long was I out?"

"Not that long. You woke up several times, mostly to get sick up all over things," he says judgmentally.

"That sounds right. I do not feel well," I groan as I sit back again against the chair, my guts clenching.

Septimus is naturally unsympathetic.

"That's what you get for being so reckless. I thought I made it clear already that, if anyone needs to survive, it ought to be you. The rest of us can die so long as the overall goal is accomplished," he says snootily.

"Why bother giving me the fluke I have at all, then," I croak. "If not to turn back time for the sake of others?"

He sighs and looks at me in disgust. "Why-oh-why—"

"You look gray," Xerian interrupts helpfully.

I grunt. I never want to eat again, and the skin on my legs is tingling. My muscles scream at me with every small attempt at movement.

"How long have we been at sea—" I start.

"Not long," Septimus says. "But you are lucky. Lucky Margo had a prior fluke that could give us a head-start. You should have let the rest of us act as bait and a distraction, while you slipped away with a smaller party. Otherwise, are you aware how long it could have taken us to get the ship away from the docks? Away from the range of a *dragon?"*

"Not all dragons fly," I croak, though I know from prior experience the brightback does.

Septimus scoffs. I can tell he is furious with me, but the plan did work. We are closer to our goal, now, than we were hours ago.

"I hope you realize you won't have enough energy left in you to act in reserves in case they catch up with us out here," he warns me. "And without the earth, there is no way for you to get more. Your fluke is useless."

"I've worked without a fluke before."

He snorts and rolls his eyes. Xerian pokes my shoulder before handing me a bladder of water. I didn't even realize he'd left to fetch one for me. The water is not fresh, and there is a musty taste in my mouth I wish wasn't there to color the flavor further, but it's still water. My body is immediately grateful for hydration, and I suspect I should take care to drink as much as my stomach can handle through the rest of the day.

I take a few sips at a time, trying to think of what I could have done better at the docks, at the Mouloix.

"Have you ever killed one of the Mitaurus before?" I ask Septimus.

He sighs. "It doesn't really matter. They don't stay down for long, and they heal unnaturally well."

"But have you?"

He shrugs. I suppose I'm not getting an answer, then.

"If you're thinking about how we could have taken them, don't bother," he says. "I think we got lucky. Lucky your powers are what they are," he admits. "Otherwise, we'd have been done for."

"No one is invincible," I say. "Xerian killed that Lure fellow that first time around. And another one of them, if I recall correctly."

"I *did?"* Xerian says, shocked. He does not remember.

"You shot him. I think."

Septimus laughs.

"What?" I say, insistent. "If the kid can do it, I'm certain someone as experienced as myself or Margo could have fared better than you're predicting. We are hardly helpless. I'm not saying we should have fought them—the odds weren't good. But probably not as bad as you think."

Even Xerian looks dubious. Septimus' disagreement, I expected, but having the kid doubtful makes me wonder if the Mitaurus are purposefully careless with themselves physically. Widow can always resurrect them, or so I have been told. Witchcraft at its best.

"That is because you are thinking of them as human," Septimus says. "They are not. They gave that up to be unnatural, to use *Dadj'zcha* the way they do. To be what they are, now. Even if Xerian did shoot one or two of them, I'm sure they were on their way back again. Particularly one like Lure; he is rather high up in their ranks."

"Are the Greys the same, then?" I challenge. "Inhuman, for using *Dadj'zcha?*"

His nephews have Grey blood, after all.

He must give that some thought. "Even they are careful with how they use *Dadj'zcha*, in comparison. Trust me; we were lucky, and we should be thankful for that. That is all. There is likely nothing else we could have done."

That is as close to an apology for his condescension as I'm going to get.

"I should have killed Margo," I say, realizing it. "Then she would come back having a semblance of my fluke."

Septimus barks a laugh. "Ah…I'm very glad it did not occur to you to do that before," he says, shaking his head. He stands and walks away without giving me a proper explanation further.

It has begun to occur to me that Septimus is not especially consistent.

I spend most of that first day laying in the sun, napping, and taking sips of water. Septimus helps Margo with the boat, and I see Castel on occasion—with streaks of charcoal on his forehead—though he spends most of his time below decks. He is not one prone to conversation, I've found; it oddly bothers me, that he dislikes us all so. He only appears to care for Xerian, and even then, it is a strained, almost wary interest in the boy's well-being.

Xerian, then, has been unofficially put in charge of looking after us Isaarians. He rotates spending his time with Vásan, Nissa, and me. As I'm hardly injured, only exhausted from overusing my fluke, I suspect I am the best patient he has. Vásan is likely second, though I think this is mainly because Xerian is fascinated with him. So long as Nissa and I don't need anything, the northerner spends most of his time hovering about Vásan, as if he wants to attempt a conversation with him and simply does not know how. Alternatively, perhaps it is because Vásan is the only one with an open wound for Xerian to look after, but the short exchange between them after lunch makes me suspect the former is a more accurate assessment.

Xerian watches Vásan sit completely motionless with his eyes closed, arms and legs crossed, for a long time. By my reckoning, it was a full half an hour. When he reaches out with a toe to nudge Vásan's leg, the grand prince does not bother open his eyes but gives a single warning: "Don't."

Xerian laughs. "I thought for certain you were dead!"

Vásan cracks an eye to look up at him. "I'm fine."

"Sure, sure," the kid says, nodding. "So long as you're awake, though, mind if I check your arm?"

Vásan uncrosses his arms. "Enjoy."

I allow myself a private smile and spend most of the evening watching every minute interaction between the two of them. It is clear to me, even if Vásan would rather it was not, that he is also fond of Xerian. The young man is older and perkier in temperament than Alo, but something in the kid must remind Vásan of his own son. Maybe it is only the fact that Xerian has no father figure in his life, and has not for some time. Without Vásan taking him in as his own son, Alo would not have had a father, either.

Once night has fallen, and Vásan has disappeared below decks to try to get some sleep, I decide I need to speak with my fellow Isaarians. I owe them an apology for what has happened so far, I think. So, I ask Xerian to help me down, as it is probably a good idea to turn in for the night anyway.

Below, Vásan and Nissa have both been situated on wooden bunks. Nissa is a little gray in the face, not unlike myself I would wager, but she is clearly on the mend. The pair acknowledge my presence, but I wait until Xerian leaves again before speaking. We don't need anything from him, at the moment, and so long as he has energy, I'm sure Margo and Septimus will find work for him.

"How are you?" I ask the both of them.

"I'll live," Vásan grunts.

Nissa flicks her eyes up to reveal furious eyes. "I have found a new bear."

I know she is not exaggerating, or attempting to be metaphorical. Nissa fully intends to kill that brightback if she sees it again. Somehow, I am not surprised. I suppose if anyone was going to take down a dragon, it may as well be her. I do not tell her that I doubt she will get that opportunity, not in this cycle. But perhaps this is one of those moments that is unchangeable. Perhaps Nissa and the bear and Nissa and the brightback are known things.

"I apologize profusely," I say. "To both of you. If I'd had time to properly think, and to do so, I would have argued with the king and myself about your coming on this trip. If he'd still insisted on companions, I would have—"

"Brought someone more expendable?" Vásan interrupts.

Nissa raises her head at that, also shocked to hear him say so. I do not know how to respond to that.

"Offense mildly intended, your majesty, but I don't particularly give a care," he says, then closes his eyes and leans back again.

There is an awkward beat, then Nissa laughs. She still sounds terrible, but she does laugh.

"I dislike you a touch less, now, *notr'u konig*," she says.

I think *notr'u* means something like "cold" or "chill" in Hoitsokin, not "ice", but it's still close enough for the moniker to work. She is teasing him.

Vásan grunts and says nothing else.

I should have let Xerian stay while making my apologies. At least Vásan appears to tolerate the boy. I'm still mostly convinced the grand prince is only here out of a sense of duty, not because he cares about what happens to me.

However, as that first evening passes, I realize that, like with Septimus, it is possible I need to try harder to see how it is Vásan and Nissa show affection. Nissa, at least, does not blame me for what happened to her animal familiar, and while Vásan's company is not the most pleasant, he does not go out of his way to say anything cruel to me. In fact, after giving it some thought, I believe his attempted dismissal of my apology was meant to be a kindness.

Perhaps I am too hopeful; Vásan is an odd one.

Over the next days, we fall into a vigilante monotony. While Margo is an excellent sailor as promised, nearly all of us are positive that at least one of our enemies is on our trail. With dedication like theirs, a little water is hardly going to stop them. Nissa, Vásan and I recover and grow used to taking up daily tasks aboard the boat to help.

After a week, despite Margo and Septimus' constant insistence we are not particularly safe, I allow my mind to calm itself enough to practice meditation. It is not as if there is much to do on a steam boat in the middle of the ocean, after all, though Xerian does attempt some fishing and occasionally finds luck. Nissa sometimes even joins him.

I do not think the seven of us will ever be completely comfortable with one another, but there is a level of trust that develops over the time we are forced to spend with one another in close quarters. Margo is surprisingly pleasant, for anyone let alone a member of the Grey family. Xerian would have Nissa tell him stories of the Hoitsokin all day if Margo let him sit still that long. He'd listen to Vásan's stories, too, if the grand prince was willing to share many.

The only surly one is Castel. No matter how much time passes, and no matter how close I think I'm getting to forming a relationship with him, he purposefully pushes people away. I suppose I should not be surprised. Still, I hope that, in the final timeline, it is not in Fate's loom for him to end up like this. There is a melancholy about him that makes him difficult to be around.

I must wonder if there are some who would have said the same about me, once. Perhaps even still.

Its these sorts of thoughts I ponder for days at a time, during our voyage. We slowly and steadily journey further east, towards Kacha. It is almost enough to convince me we have found good fortune; that the worst is behind us. Only, of course such a thing is too good to be true.

It is in the middle of the night when there is a sudden jolting that throws me out of my bunk, and Xerian and Nissa, too. The moment he has his feet under him, Xerian is dashing up the steps, taking them two at a time. Nissa and I glance at one another, then follow him. Up top, the sky is a ferocious, sick color. The temperature has visibly dropped, and there is a prickling on my skin. I feel a raindrop or two on my nose and in my hair.

We convene with Margo and Septimus in the wheelhouse where it appears Margo is allowing Septimus to hold us steady. I can feel from the air and from her mild exhaustion that she has used another one of her variety of flukes.

"We have some distance, now," she tells Septimus. "But I will not be able to jump us a third time."

"That's fine," he says. "Just so long as we have time before the storm catches us. That came upon us fast. Too fast, I think."

"Are we safe?" Xerian asks.

"Safe? No," Margo says.

She glances over at Septimus.

"If this is a supernatural storm, we cannot allow the Mitaurus to follow us to Kacha," she says. "Especially not if we leave a clear trail for Nexa and the brightback to follow along behind them."

"You don't say," Septimus snaps. "Let me think on this. A detour may be in order. You keep to the course for now. Tell me if they're getting close."

He disappears. Margo puts Nissa in charge of steering, temporarily, while she conscripts me into shoveling coal into the furnace with her, below decks.

We could only be below decks for a matter of minutes before the boat's rocking worsens significantly. At one point, I'm terrified we may capsize, though Margo acts as if it is natural to have the floor under her moving so much. It is practically rolling and she still manages to keep her balance.

"Storm's getting worse," Margo says with a frown. "I'd say, at this point, it is definitely not the natural sort. Unfortunate."

"A fluke?" I guess.

"Mmm, I don't think so," she says and shovels in more coal. "Nexa is probably on that damned dragon, looking for us. We injured it, but not much, I think. So, it'll be the Mitaurus using their witchcraft."

"Hoping to stall us and bring Nex down in one swoop, I'd wager," Septimus says as he drops down to join us.

He takes the coal shovel from Margo.

"Make the kid do this," he says. "I need you steering. We have a tricky bit coming up."

Margo raises an eyebrow. "Got this all figured out, then?"

"I'm a schemer, but I'm good at what I do. Up top," he says again. "If we bungle this, we're likely to all drown."

He stomps up the stairs with quick feet, into the whipping wind that snaps his coat about his whippet frame. The rain is beginning to pick up, blown sideways. Margo follows him, and I, her.

At my conquering of the last step, my new sea legs fail me as the ship rolls beneath my feet. I stagger to catch my balance and Prince Castel is suddenly there, snagging the back of my coat collar. He straightens me and continues walking before I can thank him, joining Septimus and Margo to determine next moves.

Before I can ask after what I might do to help, Septimus turns and shoves a coil of rope into my arms. Castel receives a similar gift.

"Stay above decks, but get everyone tied up to something," Septimus says. "We don't want any of you getting washed overboard. Have Xerian shovel as much coal in the furnace as possible, then bind him up as well."

"What if we capsize?" I ask.

"If we don't do this right, we're dead in the water anyway," he says. "Now move. We've minutes, at the most."

I'm about to inquire further—I'd like to know what, precisely, Septimus' plan is. No doubt it is even more hare-brained than mine at the docks. But Septimus notices this and gives me a shove back, commanding me again to tie myself up in the next few minutes or he'll throw me overboard himself.

I go. I'm getting frighteningly good at following orders, for a queen.

Xerian pops around to help with the rope and knots, acquiring the skill from Margo to make certain we will be safe. I have him tie me as close to the wheelhouse as possible, so I can see what is currently happening. Nissa chooses to be tied near me, while Vásan and Castel are across from us. Septimus is lashing himself and Margo inside the wheelhouse, so they cannot be washed away.

The storm picks up with worrisome speed, rocking the boat back and forth so much it is a wonder we are managing to move in any certain direction at all. The boat tips so far to the sides that water sloshes onto the deck, often giving one of us a mouthful of icy salt-water.

I can hear Margo shouting something at Septimus, and I do not think she is using Alarkian. Lusch, if my ear for it is getting any better.

We crash forward directly into a wave, and for a full second, I swear, the boat is entirely underwater. When we pop back up again, Nissa is green in the face and coughing. I do not say so, but I think it might be a good thing, at this point, that her hyena is no longer with us. I do not think it would do well in such conditions. She is barely managing, herself.

I push down the fear starting to rise in me and try to ignore the irrational thoughts that insist this may be the end for us. The fear fights back, however, insisting we are sure drown in the middle of the ocean, where no one will find our corpses. Rian would never know what happened to me.

How long would he wait, expecting me to one day still come home? How long before he stopped hoping?

I'm fighting to quash these fears when I hear the very last thing a person wants to in such a situation:

"Margo, sail directly into the storm!" Septimus calls to her over the screaming of the wind.

"Are you out of your mind?" I yell.

Margo nods and turns the wheel, so that the icy rain slaps me in the face instead of the side of the head. The boat crashes directly through another rolling wave again, soaking us all. When Nissa comes up spluttering again, I grab the rope around her waist and yank her closer to me, wrapping my arm in what slack remains. I am at least a hand taller than her, after all, perhaps a touch more; if we start taking on more water, I want to get her above the waves as much as possible.

Nissa groans something in Hoitsokin that sounds like an admittance of defeat.

"Don't worry," I tell her. "If you don't make it through this, I'll kill him."

I do not need to specify who.

The next few minutes are some of the most terrifying of my life, even while considering how many times I have brushed against death, how many enemies I've encountered. There is almost nothing to compare with the brute, cruel indifference of nature. Even if this storm was brought down on us through witch-craft, I doubt anyone is controlling every roll of the waves, every billowing storm-cloud. The ocean is a beast that hunts for sport.

Margo does not appear at all concerned. She follows Septimus' bellowed instructions with casual ease, knowing precisely what to do to keep us moving the direction she wants. She is not worried about the storm overtaking us. It is not merely skill at hiding her fear either, from what I can see. I suppose she has died and come back to life enough times that she is no longer afraid of dying, even if drowning means she would not be able to come back.

The sky is so devoid of light that it takes until we are practically on top of them for me to see the rocks. I would shout a warning, only it looks as if that is precisely where Septimus wants Margo to go.

Something scrapes against the side of the boat, perhaps even gouging a hole in it, and jostling us so the rope around me cuts painfully into my ribs. Nissa is practically clinging to me like a cat, her fingernails digging into me.

It is difficult to see through the lashing rain, but if I did not know any better, there is something dark and looming directly ahead of us. A mountain, it looks like, at least from silhouette. It does not look at all as if Margo and Septimus intend to stop. Nissa notices and starts screaming curses at Septimus interspersed with, I believe, an attempted warning. I do not bother. At this point, I pray he and Margo know precisely what they are doing.

The tumultuous waves throw us about, making our course a less-than-linear one, but it is clear we are headed directly for the dark landmass ahead.

Given the storm, it is difficult to tell precisely when we will hit it, but I know shipwreck is coming.

I keep one hand still in Nissa's ropes, grab the rail with the other, and pull us both up against it to brace for the impact. I tell myself if we live through this, I will not slap Septimus. If we perish, it is the first thing I'm going to do upon entering the Otherworld.

The impact is jarring. My teeth gnash against one another as the boat rams straight into land, scraping the bottom open against rock as we tilt, sliding upwards. The sound is horrific as the metal scrapes; I swear I can feel the boat being torn apart. I barely manage to keep a hold of Nissa. I find myself keeping my eyes squeezed tight, expecting broken bones, scraped flesh and possibly even a few cases of pneumonia, assuming we live that long.

The first thing that startles me into opening my eyes, even more than the lack of pain and the fact we have stopped, is there is no more rain. No crashing waves or storm clouds. I can hear birds chirping in the distance, and feel sun on my back. It is warm, practically tropical.

I straighten and crack an eye open, wondering if it is possible we died so quickly that we are already in the Otherworld. It was startlingly quick and painless.

Then I see that we are still on the boat, tied up with soaking ropes, water dripping off us. The sun is bright above us, as if it is late in the day instead of the dead of night. It also is not visibly winter. I cannot tell if this is because we are in a different portion of the world or because there is some magic at work.

I do know for a fact that the sun should not be out at this time of night.

Nissa mumbles something in Hoitsokin and starts to dry heave over the side of the boat. In the wheelhouse, however, Septimus looks mightily pleased with himself. He is already working to untie his ropes. Margo pulls out a knife to cut herself free and offers it to him. I can see they are talking about something, but my ears are still a touch sensitive after the storm and the change in atmosphere.

I stare at them, blinking at the suddenness of the sunlight. I think I would like a few minutes to think about what happened, or otherwise a full, long explanation.

Next thing I know, Castel is there to cut Nissa and I free.

"Don't thank me," he says before I can open my mouth.

Across the way from us, Vásan is also getting sick. Xerian appears in good health, though. I suppose it is possible they have encountered similar escapades before and have grown accustomed to the outcomes.

"You appear to be doing well enough," Septimus says, coming over to help Nissa stand up straight. "You will feel much better after you get on dry land."

"I hate you," Nissa says, and coughs up more water.

"It's what I expect," Septimus says.

He leaps down from the boat onto soft sand below. The island we have landed on looks as if its highest point is a small cluster of mountain peaks surrounded by a forest that grows thicker the further it stretches back over the expanse of the land. It is a fertile paradise.

I climb down after Septimus and attempt to tie back my mess of ratty hair while I take a good look around. I have no idea how we got here or how this is going to help us in the future. I am nearly happy enough to kiss the sand.

Margo climbs down beside me, leaving Castel and Xerian to try and help my sea-sick companions. I, too, feel a touch ill, but I am forcing myself onwards by insisting over and over that it is unqueenly to be sick up in front of these people.

I pray my children do not give me morning sickness.

"You absolutely destroyed the boat," Margo sighs. She stands back with her hands on her hips, looking visibly pained as she appraises the vessel. I think she was starting to grow attached to it.

"It was necessary," Septimus claims. "Shipwrecking is the only way to reach the island, by water. At least we will be safe, here. No risk of being found out. If our enemies want to find us, now, they will have to search every single country in the east."

"You seem to have forgotten that we still need to *reach Kacha,*" I say, glaring at him. I have decided I hate boats.

"Not to worry, I have that sorted. Nex's brightback gave me an idea; we are going to visit a dragon," Septimus says casually without turning around.

He is already starting up a path with the apparent full intent of climbing the nearest peak.

"A dragon?" I repeat, glancing at Castel as he reaches the sandy beach with a still ill Nissa. "Has Septimus lost his mind?"

Castel grimaces, his mouth scrunched up in displeasure. "Unfortunately, no. Though I would have preferred if he had, to be honest..."

He glances at Nissa and Vásan.

"I change my mind," Vásan tells Nissa. "This is the most undignified thing I've done in my life."

"High bar," she croaks.

"Let's start moving, ladies and gentlemen!" Septimus calls from ahead. "The faster we get to the top, the faster we'll get to wash up."

"Dragons have baths?" I say.

"This one does," Castel says. He glances at Nissa. "You're walking," he decides for her, as if anything else was an option.

"As if your legs could survive carrying me," she sneers.

We follow Septimus up the path. The mountain is not a dreadfully tall one—I'm not entirely sure it qualifies as a mountain or not—but the climb will still take the better part of an hour. After a matter of minutes, the enveloping heat becomes more of a detriment than a luxury, with our still-wet clothes sticking against our skin, likely to chafe uncomfortably the higher we climb. I would complain aloud, only I suspect I'd only earn myself a snarky response from one of my companions. I'd bet on either Septimus or Castel; everyone else would likely sympathize.

After perhaps half an hour of climbing up the twisting path, the terrain begins to change. Not drastically, and not all at once, but after the monotony of uneven climbing conditions, one tends to notice when the surface under their feet changes even minutely.

I glance down, something I would not naturally do whilst hiking; I have been busy glaring at the back of Septimus' head. The dirt path we have been trudging up has started to morph into a stone staircase made of mainly flat, unpolished rocks. It is not highly structured or ostentatious in the manner I am accustomed to, but has careful craftmanship. Someone put effort into this.

"Are these…stairs?" Nissa says from a few paces behind me, realizing what I have about a moment after.

"It seems so. Though I would not have suspected dragons needed stairs," I say. Although, once I think about it, Mango did go through a phase in his youth when he thought he was a cat and had no idea what to do with the flappy appendages we call wings.

Still, the higher we climb, the more it becomes clear this must be a man-made structure. Wooden logs have been added to make the steps clearer, more separate from one another, and there are several branching paths that lead off into the forest covering the mountain, to dirt trails. These are not hunter's paths, I don't believe. They are more for recreational purposes, or even berry picking, if one was feeling whimsical. The island certainly appears bountiful enough to entertain such a pastime.

It is near the top of this miniature mountain that our situation becomes clearer. Still a good way from the peak, we come across a large, flat platform, as if someone has shaved away a portion of the land itself to make a front porch for themselves. Moving back, there is a wide, rounded entrance to what looks like a cave system inside the land, with large double doors made of wood and iron. It is there we find our unwitting host.

Seated, lounging at the entrance as if he is sunning himself, is an impressive-looking man with golden skin, dark hair, and oddly intimidating fingernails. The more I look, I realize it is because they resemble claws much more than they do actual nails. He is wearing loose, comfortable trousers, but no shoes and no shirt. His eyes are closed, but almond shaped, and his nose is quite prominent and pointed. It's odd because his features themselves stand out, but looking at him, I cannot tell his ethnicity in the slightest. He could be eastern, or Alarkian, or even part Bhantan. Yet, somehow, I know he is none of those things.

At our approach, one of his pointy ears twitches like an animal's might. He frowns and suspiciously cracks open an eye.

The other eye immediately follows. The color does not drain from his face the way it would for a normal person, but he certainly looks horrified. In fact, it is funny, because his eyes are a bright yellow-orange, but instead of making him look more intimidating, his reaction to seeing Septimus reminds me more of a dragon pup than Nexa Grey's brightback.

He scrambles out of his lounging chair, all but knocking it over in his haste to rise and escape.

"Kang, Kang, Kang, dear Kang," Septimus says as he continues climbing up the last few steps. "How are you? How's the wife? Have any children yet?"

"N-ooOO!" Kang bellows as he hastily disappears into the cave at a run, nearly throwing a door off its hinges and not bothering to close it behind him. "Aisling!! He's *ba-ack!"* I hear him call in distress.

Septimus forges on ahead, but not before glancing back at us. "Kang has mixed feelings about me."

"Truly? I had not noticed," Nissa says.

I frown, recognizing something. "Did you...call him..."

"Kang?" Septimus interrupts. "Yes. And yes, he is that 'Kang'."

I blink. "You have a wide variety of friends."

"I don't think 'Kang' would consider him a friend," Castel mutters.

I am skeptical of invading the home of this cursed dragon man—a figure I still believed was a fictional character up until minutes ago—but I suppose Septimus' logic has not failed us yet today. We are still alive, and apparently safe for now. Even if Kang does not appear to want us here, it's clear the two know one another. It is not as if he attacked us.

So, I follow Septimus into the cave, surprised to find that though the inside is carved out of rock as expected, it is quite lovely. No jagged edges or rough-hewn attempts at furniture, no: there are real amenities, probably imported, a proper rug thrown across the ground of the main chamber, and little flickering lantern lights hanging from the ceiling.

For the home of a dragon, it is deceptively cozy.

In this initial greeting rooms, set up about the tasseled rug, are a number of comfortable cushioned chairs, a low table, and no small number of pillows. The man Septimus named as Kang is currently shielding himself behind one of these chairs and practically hisses to see Septimus again.

"Aisling, keep him out of my sight!" he says, ducking behind the chair and presumedly speaking to the woman occupying its seat as she knits.

She is perhaps from Picland, given her features. She is smaller than myself, with long, straight black hair, an elegant though simple appearance, angular features with a smattering of brown freckles, and bright blue eyes. They are the most noticeable feature on her face, though they are a darker blue than mine or Teresa's. This woman—Aisling—is not jaded like me or weary but innocent like Teresa. Her demeanor is sweet, knowing, welcoming, and warm. She is also, most obviously, heavily pregnant.

"Ah, so you have started in on those kids, then! Congratulations," Septimus says.

Aisling gives him a wry smile as she puts aside her knitting. "Hello again, Septimus. Welcome back. I hope you do not take too much offense, but Kang had rather hoped we would never see you again. Particularly not in such a manner as this."

Kang snaps something in a peculiar foreign language from behind the chair. Aisling responds in the same language, though she manages to make the harsh tongue sound much sweeter. Whatever she says, it must be enough to calm her companion, because while he continues to sulk, he at least is willing to negotiate.

"Fine!" he says in Alarkian. "But *not* the Grey Woman."

Aisling sighs. "Kang…"

"No. I smell *Grey.* And I refuse to smell it all evening. She cannot come in. The rest can stay," he insists.

Aisling looks as if she is willing to argue on Margo's behalf, but Margo steps in first. Graciously, I would say.

"It's fine, Aisling," she says. "I'll head back down and stay with the boat. See if I can't pick out our remaining supplies."

She is gone before poor Aisling can reply, headed back out the way we'd come. I'm wondering if one of us should go after Margo, especially after such a rude ejection, but none of her closer companions appear concerned. By the time I decide to say anything about it, it is already too late. Septimus has wandered off down some passage, calling back to Aisling that he is going to wash up. Kang has gone to sneak away further into the cave, as if to escape us, and Aisling frowns after him, hands on her hips.

"Now look what you've done," she chides. "Before this evening is over, I'm sending you down there to make a proper apology and invite Margo back up for dinner."

Kang makes an irritated noise and continues to slink back into yet another portion of this cave-home. Aisling, who I'm assuming at this point is his wife, sighs, then turns to the rest of us with a welcoming smile.

"I am sorry about him. May I welcome you to our humble home, on behalf of both of us," she says. "Were you planning to stay the night, then?"

As Nissa, Vásan, and I have no idea what the plan is, I'm glad Castel decides to answer her instead of remaining sullen and silent as usual.

"Likely. We need to reach Kacha and have…wrecked our boat," he says.

Aisling's smile remains. "I assumed so. If this is Septimus calling in a favor, Kang can take you all in the morning. In the meantime, would you like to clean up, some while I prepare dinner?"

I'm still startled by meeting these new, strange people living in a cave, on an island I have never heard of before. I can at least put things together enough to understand Kang and Aisling are married and, apparently, they have met Septimus and Margo before.

Kang hates the Greys.

I feel like that is reason enough for me to feel at ease here.

"I would like to indulge in that 'washing up' option," Xerian says.

"If we're going to stay here, we all should," Castel says. "And I will fetch Margo in an hour or so," he adds for Aisling.

She sighs. "Again, I do apologize. He is in one of his moods."

"I'm sorry," I say, refusing to stand by a second longer. "Do you all know one another? What is this place? And…Kang? *Kang?"*

Aisling merely smiles. "I know Septimus and Margo. But Sep talks about all of you every time he comes. You must be Soleil."

"So, you can remember the timelines, then," I say.

"Oh, no," she laughs. "Not on our own, anyway, but Sep gave us some jewelry that helps. Or, does not help, I suppose. Kang grows mightily sullen every time you go back to make a new timeline. Now, there are some hot springs back that way, if you would like to wash up as well," she adds, pointing down the way Septimus disappeared. "I shall hunt down some new clothing for everyone while you do."

Nissa mutters something in Hoitsokin under her breath.

"Don't worry," Aisling laughs. "We keep everything. I'm sure I will be able to find a little something to suit everyone."

Nissa turns appropriately pink, furious with embarrassment. I can guess at what she said, and so can Vásan, who smirks privately.

"Nicely done," he tells Nissa before turning to Aisling. "I trust the men will be separated from the women?"

Aisling points again.

"Head down that way," she says with the same smile. "I'll escort the ladies, and have those clothes delivered before you have finished."

Vásan is gone with Castel and Xerian before I have the chance to question this course of action even mildly. Granted, I feel safer here than anywhere Septimus had brought me so far, but I still feel largely naïve. I suppose it may be easier for Nissa and Vásan, who are being thrown headfirst into this chaos all at once with multiple revelations of myth, as opposed to myself. I am privileged enough to experience the shock in independent situations several times over again.

"Come along, then, this way," Aisling says, already off down the same hall.

Nissa and I have practically no choice but to follow her. Aisling leads us through the cave passages, past branching halls and doorways, towards the sound of running water. I figure we are near the back half of the mountain, facing the flora of the island. When we come to a branch, Ailsing takes us off to the right, where Nissa and I will have some privacy. I suppose if Septimus and Margo have been here before, Septimus knows where the men ought to be to wash.

The hot springs, as Aisling mentioned, keep the little carved room we enter steamy, and fresh. I can feel my muscles starting to relax despite my attempts at meager wariness. Any person willing to feed and bathe us and who hates the Greys is probably a friend. Before Nissa and I can fully take in the sight of the hot springs set into the ground, Aisling has already opened a small cabinet. She pulls out startlingly fine, embroidered towels and gestures to hooks pounded into the wall, as well as a bench, chattering all this time.

"There is a third 'room' we made with these springs, that Kang and I usually share," she says, "and the other two we split, men and women, for when we have guests. Most people find that amenable. Towels should be nice and clean; throw them in the hamper when you have finished. Soaps are in the cupboard; please use whatever you like, and I shall leave those clothes for you at the bend of the entry. We ought to have bathrobes," she adds thoughtfully, "but honestly, I always forget until guests arrive!"

"We are grateful for whatever you have for us to use," I reassure.

"Oh, we're indebted to the Smiths," she says. "Doubly so, truly. The entire family line, from way back when, and I suppose more 'recently', Kang owes your cousin Septimus a little favor. Now, feel free to take however long you like. If I manage to fix up dinner before you have finished, I shall come and fetch you."

She is gone again before Nissa or I can say anything else. It is impressive, how speedy a woman Aisling is, while so expectant. I wish I had her energy.

Nissa and I go about the process of stripping off ruined clothes and trying to comb through the tangled knots of our hair. Aisling did not mention what to do with our things, so we leave them in a somewhat-neat pile at the end of the bench and slip into the hot springs to wash up. Once the work is done, with our hair clean and skin free of salt, we both soak in the hot water, taking our time as suggested.

"I do not understand what is happening anymore. I can only go along with it, I find," Nissa sighs after a minute.

"Believe it or not, that makes two of us," I mutter.

"Why is this 'Kang' someone you know but don't know?" she adds.

"Oh," I say, and think for a moment. "He is a character, from storybooks, mainly. I suppose you would not have read them, growing up how you did. I suppose I did not read them, either, but Ayla did. He is used rather liberally by those who pen fiction, I would say, as if he is some sort of shared character. A myth. Someone everyone agrees is not real."

"So, the same as Magicsmiths," she says.

"Well, no. Not exactly. With Magicsmiths…there is at least debate about it. Kang's fictional. He is made up. He is…"

"Apparently not," Nissa says. "Made up."

I take a moment to think about that. "I'm afraid, now, with all that's been 'revealed', I will never be able to read my children a storybook without wondering if those characters are somehow 'real', too."

Nissa glances at me. "So, you are determined to have children."

I sigh. "I know: I do not appear the motherly sort."

"Actually, you remind me of my own mother," Nissa says, startling me. "I do not understand why all you *nonitrauk* seem to think women must make this choice between being mothering and being fierce. I think Isaarians are the least egregious offenders, but still. When you live like the Hoitsokin do, you understand women are fully capable of being both simultaneously. They must be, in order to protect their children from the world. So few remember that is their duty, as a mother, these days: to protect."

I blink. Nissa cannot know how much I appreciate her saying that. It is so simple a thing, but it does help, having someone else's perspective take away some of my own concerns. The idea that has been bothering me since I first met Damen, Aiden, and Teresa is so simply brushed off by Nissa and her culture. It helps.

"Thank you," I say after a few moments.

Nissa shrugs.

After that, I decide I have soaked enough and climb out of the springs. Nissa decides to stay longer; I'm sure having her animal familiar killed has exhausted her even more than she has let on. I find the clothing Aisling promised to leave for us, outside the entrance to this chamber, and easily determine which are meant to be mine given the size difference in me and Nissa. The clothes are simple trousers and a blouse. I cannot determine the fabric or style, but note the needlework: small, careful white stitches at the hems portray matching rose patterns. I wonder who these belonged to, before, and how old they are. Regardless, the clothes are clean and comfortable, and I appreciate how close they are to fitting me.

With the intention of helping Aisling with her chores, I try to wander my way back to the front rooms, through the halls, and almost immediately find myself lost. I thought Aisling had taken us a straight path to the springs, but apparently am wrong on that account. Eventually, I, distressingly, find myself in what I quickly realize must be our hosts' bedchambers. Though, instead of a bed, there is a truly colossal mass of tangled sheets, counterpanes, quilts, and an assortment of pillows, gathered from all over Samioth.

It takes me a moment to realize, but Kang is buried in them. Glaring.

"Oh," I say. "My apologies. I got turned around."

"Then get yourself un-turned around," he mutters.

"Yes, of course. My apologies," I say again, but still cannot help but linger. "You really are Kang? Like, the storybook character, Kang?"

"As far as I'm aware. Yes. Why—do I owe you something?"

"Oh. No. It's only...My husband has books on you. He bought children's tales about you for his—*our* daughter. When she was little. He would have absolutely loved to meet you. I admittedly feel somewhat guilty it is me here instead of him."

"Well, you can tell him he did not miss much," Kang grunts miserably.

He sinks down into the mountain of blankets, his entire posturing and being reminding me of a put-out Mango. There is even a little smoke as he huffs, glaring.

I would insist that meeting the man cursed to be part dragon would have thrilled Rian regardless of Kang's less-than-desirable personality, but I do not think he would believe that. I wonder if there is an expected self-loathing in a dragon's nature not unlike their penchant for collecting things.

"...Did Septimus do something to displease you?" I ask instead, curious.

"Every time he appears, it means trouble," Kang mutters, just the top of his head poking out of the mound. "I'm enjoying my peaceful retirement up in the mountains with my wife. We do not need trouble. We did not ask for trouble. I do not want trouble. And I do not want those *Dadj'zcha*-practicing, Dark-worshiping bastards anywhere near *my wife*."

"The Greys aren't going to find us, if that's what you're worrying over," I tell him. "Septimus has never told them about this place, so they shouldn't know."

Kang grumbles under his breath and sinks lower into his nest as smoke immerges. He is probably cursing Septimus in his native tongue, but I cannot identify the language. Not that I would fully blame Kang if that is what he is doing. I have no doubt that *Dadj'zcha*-practitioners **would have plenty of uses for dragon scales, dragon blood, dragon teeth**, bone and saliva. It does not matter if Kang is only part dragon, or that his children might not even inherit the curse.

There comes a gentle knock at the door and I turn to see Aisling there. I begin to apologize again, but she ignores it.

"Don't mind me," she says. "I just came to check up on him before finishing the rest of the dinner preparations."

"I could help you, if you'd like?" I say.

I have few culinary talents, but I could chop vegetables. I do feel guilty about having her do all this work while expecting a child. She should be allowed to continue her knitting, relaxed, not looking after seven guests, five of whom she does not even know.

"That would be much appreciated, thank you. Kang, dear heart, do you plan on joining us for dinner?" Aisling asks.

A snort of smoke emerges from deep within the mound of blankets.

"He is being childish, but by the time dinner is well on its way, his stomach will get the better of him. He will climb out before the food is finished," she whispers to me.

"Is he normally like this?" I cannot help but ask.

Aisling considers this. "Childish? Always a little. But it is part of why I love him. That said, I do think Septimus tends to bring this sort of behavior out of him. He was very proud of what a good day he was having before you all arrived. Now, if you do not mind lending me a hand, I planned on stew and fresh bread. I have a good recipe for a loaf with cheese baked in, and that will lift my husband's spirits significantly."

She deftly leads me back through the cave systems, clearly at ease with the labyrinthine nature of her home, until we arrive at a kitchen. It is impressively furnished and well-stocked, so that Aisling could easily host a dinner party if she wished. I suppose, in a way, that is what she is doing now.

She immediately resumes her work, mid-dinner preparations. She has pots simmering on a stove, and bread rising under a hot towel.

"How do you get things you need up here?" I ask.

"Kang has friends," Aisling says evasively. "They are my friends too, I suppose, but they would do anything for *him.* So, whatever we need, we receive. It is to pay us back, for debts we are owed. If there is anything I think we should pay for, I hand it over and they bring back what I need. It is a system that works well, for us."

"And where does that money come from? Does he keep a hoard like a dragon might?" I ask.

I am half-joking but at the same time, given how Kang seems to hoard other things like a dragon, I would not be surprised.

"Oh. I write," Aisling says offhandedly, moving her spoon to stir the nearer of her two pots. "Our stories, mostly. I do take some liberties, but minor ones, so that the story will flow nicer. Otherwise—"

"Wait. You. You are K. A. Manna. You write your story and pass them off as fiction for monetary gain instead of simply printing history books which would get you considerably less revenue," I interrupt. "That is brilliant."

Aisling smiles. "Thank you, dear. Would you mind kneading that bread for me?" she adds. "It should be ready for it. Five minutes."

I go to work, thinking all the while. "Are all the characters in your books real, then?" I cannot help but ask. I know Rian has read them all.

She shrugs. "For the most part, yes. Sometimes I give people larger roles than they really had, or exaggerate conversations and small actions. For the drama of it all. But it really is, for the most part, all true. Ancient history, though."

"But that means you met the Fair," I note. "Royal Fair."

"Oh, yes. Phina and her brother. Seraphina, that is. She was human. He was half Fair-folk, half-Dohremi. He ended up marrying a human woman, though. And Phina married a human, too, instead of a member of the Fair-folk. The two of them brought Fair-human relations together properly for the first time...That was a long, long time ago, though. Back when the race of Averti were still around, causing trouble for everyone from above in their Floating Islands," she says, rolling her eyes. "To think, that was once the biggest problem in my life..."

I'm back still trying to calculate what this means in terms of Kang and Aisling's ages. Eventually, I give up, and must ask exactly how old Aisling is.

"Oh, quite old, I should say," she muses. "I would need to do some calculation to figure the exact number. But when I was a girl, my husband's country, Dohram, was still a full nation with many citizens. Alarkia as it is today did not exist. The Floating Islands had lands beneath them that have long since sunk into the sea. Lusch was most certainly a full country. And entire races of folk now gone from Samioth went about their lives."

I'm shocked by this, mainly because this means Aisling is even older than I first imagined. Older than the events of the Dragon's Tooth.

"You could live forever," I say in awe. She laughs at that and tells me to cover the dough again before continuing.

"We are not immortal," Aisling says. "But we do have long lives, thanks to Phina and her brother. Lives longer than theirs, even. Fair can live for a long time. They do not age in years, I was told, but in terms of 'fate'. It is a difficult concept for a human, but they appear quite at ease with it. They gifted me that. It was Phina's brother's idea."

"Seraphina's brother. The king of the Fair," I say.

"He was, yes, until he died. Of natural causes, nothing sinister. Kang and I have kept in touch with the family," she explains, and then riffles around in her spice drawer, pulling out multiple bags and glass bottles. "Here, hold these for me," she says, shoving some towards me.

It all smells delicious, but I cannot identify all the scents. I think, possibly, some of her ingredients are of a magical nature.

"Why won't you say the Fair king's name?" I wonder, noticing how careful Aisling is to never mention it. To talk around it.

"I swore I never would," Aisling says. "Fairs' names are sensitive. The names they choose and their true names, both. Even in my writing, I chose two different names when referring to him. I promised him I would. Eliath was the human name we agreed upon for him. But Phina was fully human, and did not mind me using her real name. In fact, I think the idea excited her. She was an avid reader of my early drafts, back when it was more of a passing fancy, my writing…"

She smiles and shakes her head. "It was all such a long time ago," she insists. "But I'm glad to remember it. I do miss the Fair. They are not completely gone, no, but I miss their society. Kang and I still visit, when we can, but not as frequently as we once could."

"What do you mean?"

"The Fair folk have decided to take a step back from the world. They determined it was their time to do so. But you can still see traces of them here and there, even within your own bloodline," she says.

I blink. "My...?"

"You are a Smith, are you not?" she says, raising an eyebrow at me. "You may be mostly human, but there is a small portion of Fair blood in you. I can see it in the eyes, and I am certain you have seen it in yourself as well. Even without your powers, I wager you and your sister both react well to poisons, have large appetites, and are noticeably stronger and quicker than most human women. I suspect you as well have noticed some Fair tendencies in your cousin Teresa?"

"I. Oh. Yes," I manage, shocked she has read into me so easily. "In the eyes, at least. Otherwise, she is…rather delicate."

Aisling nods and tastes the broth before adding more ingredients.

"The dual nature of the Fair is strong in the Smiths, I suppose. Strong and delicate, both. And I am certain your cousin has hardly received the training you or your sister have."

"No," I agree, and consider Teresa's Fair nature. "She does have other abilities, however. I can only assume it is from having Fair blood. Those eyes of hers; they appear to have some power of people. Even myself."

I feel foolish saying so, but this makes sense to Aisling. She nods. "It is in the embodiment of a Fair that if they ask for assistance with well-meaning intentions and a pure heart, most will find it difficult to refuse them anything. No doubt this fact shows itself most prominently in your little cousin's blood."

I barely hold back a snort. I suppose that explains why no one has reacted to my hints of Fair blood the same they have to Teresa's. Whatever my intentions, I doubt anyone would describe me as having a pure heart.

"Can you see it in Septimus too, then?" I say instead of noting this.

Aisling takes a moment to think.

"Septimus is...different. I think he has walked the line of the veil too much, between our world and the Otherworld. It has changed him."

"Do you know a lot about our bloodlines, then? The Greys, the Smiths, and the Wolffs?"

"Some," she says off-handedly. "But mostly in olden times. Nothing in the modern sense, I'm afraid, or at least not much. If you happen to read my books, you will see your own ancestors crop up now again. The Wolffs and Greys, too."

This is around the time Kang wanders into the kitchen, still somewhat drowsy and sniffling.

"Have a nice nap, dear heart?" Aisling says sweetly.

Kang grumbles, slouches past her, and starts hunting around for a mug.

"Dinner will be ready in a matter of minutes," his wife says. "Margo should be back by then to join us. Prince Castel went to retrieve her. I hope you apologize."

He nods and mumbles something to her in *Dohremi* that makes Aisling smile. I still cannot figure how this odd couple works together, as Kang is so gruff and his wife decidedly sweet. However, it occurs to me that some may see Rian and me in a similar light.

"Apologize," Aisling repeats. "Soon, please, so that she can have time to wash up before dinner."

"Yes, yes, yes! But she knows I didn't mean it!" Kang says, and leaves his mug on the counter to return to the front room, muttering to himself.

Speaking to Aisling has made him less intimidating though, and I cannot help but share a smile with her.

Regardless of our friendly conversation, however, dinner is an awkward affair in that almost no one knows quite what to say. Vásan says nothing at all, if he can help it. Castel is much the same. Nissa is curious, but still embarrassed from her previous commentary being understood. That leaves: Xerian—who you would think we we'd been starving given how intent his is on shoveling in as much food as possible, Margo—who likely does not want to annoy our hosts given her displeasing bloodline, and Septimus—who, as always, appears to be the only person in our party entirely aware of what is going on. Naturally, he is still of no help.

I've had an entire conversation with Aisling and I am still not entirely convinced she and Kang are real. I would assume this is somehow Widow's doing, only it is too surreal. Despite being illusions, Widow's dreams had a clear touch of plausibility about them.

After we have finished eating, Margo insists on cleaning up and enlists Castel to help. I would not have imagined a Lijimi royal ever cleaning a thing in their life, but Castel does not mutter a single word of complaint and simply gets to work with rolled-up sleeves. Aisling and Kang return to the main sitting space in the entrance, her with her knitting, him holding her yarn while laying with his head in what remains of her lap. He entertains himself by blowing smoke rings at the ceiling. Septimus finds a chair not far from them and makes himself at home. The rest of us are forced to follow.

"Excellent meal, as always, Aisling," Septimus says.

She smiles and continues to knit.

"You are not staying another day," Kang grumbles with eyes closed.

"That has been made perfectly clear," Septimus says. "We'll be gone in the morning."

Kang grunts. "If that bastard *cha'Kudagh* you're so in love with happens to show up here in the next week, I'm disemboweling you."

His Dohremi must have been quite rude because Aisling looks aghast and clocks him lightly on the head. Septimus laughs, to show her no harm has been done, but there is a mild bitterness to it.

Vásan, Nissa, Xerian and I are surely all wondering what insult Kang could have directed at Kryto Grey that would be an insult to Septimus, too. We have a few minutes to think on it, because Aisling and Kang are having a brief, snappish exchange in Dohremi in which he is likely defending his behavior and she, chiding him for it.

"Fine!" he finally concedes in Alarkian. "You are right, Charrion is worse, I don't hate Septimus, he'd never put us in danger…But I'm not taking anything else about Kryto back. I hope everyone in the family fries in the depths of the Otherworld. Serves them right."

There comes an *ahem* from the kitchen space. Kang gives a great big sigh.

"You excepting, Margo," he admits.

"And?"

"…Your younger sister…"

"And!?"

"…Her sad, little prince-son."

"Thank you," Margo says, and apparently returns to her cleaning.

I suppose I have misread precisely what kind of relationship she and Kang have, as they seem fonder of one another than I first assumed. Perhaps I am misreading everything, here.

I'm confused.

"Why do you loathe the Greys so much?" I feel the need to ask, curious.

I previously assumed it was simply due to their practices, but there are others who practice *Dadj'zcha* and the ones Kang consistently complains about are the Greys.

"Well, they're partially descended from my line, aren't they, now?" Kang says in obvious annoyance.

"I thought the Greys originated even before you," I say in surprise.

He gives a very deep sigh.

"I had a Grey wife before Aisling. She was terrible. I never should have married her. I was young and desperate and thought no one else would ever love me. But all she wanted was the dragon's blood, to strengthen the magic in their line. Once I gave her three children, she left me, and kept them from me as much as possible. The modern line is from my twin sons and I want nothing to do with any of them thank you very much."

Kang twirls a strand of his wife's hair around thoughtfully. Aisling says something gentle to him that settles his irritability some, and reminds him of better things.

"The twins were not the worst sort as children. And Ilenna was a darling girl," he admits. "They all married well. I always did like Sorcha; she could have been another of my own daughters. But the rest of the Greys did not let me see them much. Things became more complicated once they had grown, and had children of their own. Ambition can be the worst enemy of any family when it comes to inheritances. I'm afraid it all went wrong, after that."

There is just enough sadness in his voice to tell me he laments the fates of his own past children. His bitterness towards the Greys, now, is no doubt in part due to his own regrets. I cannot imagine outliving my own children.

"So, this would technically make Teresa Smith your some-great-grand-daughter-in-law," Nissa says thoughtfully. "Since she married Kryto Grey. Well, Kryto the Second, I suppose."

Kang scowls and Aisling rubs one of his shoulders in comfort. He has no fondness for either Kryto the First or Second, I believe.

"Don't worry over it, love," she says. "They are not your family anymore."

He is still grumbly, and displeased by Nissa's comment, but at least Kang doesn't snap at anyone. I'm starting to think he's purposefully disagreeable to drive a point home more than he actually cares about deciding if he likes or dislikes people individually.

"You met Aisling afterwards, then?" I prompt, hoping mentioning his current wife will put Kang in a better state.

Aisling laughs before he can say anything.

"Oh, no. Most of our 'written' adventures happened before, actually. But I didn't even consider marrying him until after Eliath and Phina were both dead and buried, actually, and that was a long time after we'd first met. We were mostly companions. Friends, when he was not being too stubborn to admit it."

This light teasing makes Kang almost smile.

From what I can tell, according to her own books, Aisling would have had to re-meet her husband about one hundred years after his unfortunate dalliance with the Greys. After meeting the Fair and being gifted a long life, Aisling did not even consider marrying him for at least another century.

How peculiar. I cannot imagine knowing Rian for so long and never considering him a romantic interest until more than a century passed. Then again, we were betrothed at a young age, so perhaps we only ever fell in love because we were meant to.

Kang mutters something tiredly in Dohremi and mentions "Phina's" name.

"I know, darling," Aisling says. "We will have plenty of time to chat with her in the Otherworld, I'm sure. She will be pleased to have predicted our eventual union."

"She knew it," Kang says. "Smart little mite. She'll hold that one over both our heads for at least half of eternity."

Aisling smiles.

There is not much else conversation to be had, at least not serious conversation. No one wants to discuss our plans, or the future. Kang is not the sociable sort, but is getting drowsy and less snappish after our late dinner. When Nissa asks to be filled in on some of Kang and Aisling's story, Aisling obliges. This is much to Xerian's delight: he apparently is an avid reader of her books, and enjoys excitedly adding in his own bits and pieces. He is beyond himself with glee when Aisling notes his first name is a Fair word, with some difference in pronunciation.

Nissa takes everything in, nodding and occasionally posing questions or making comments. When Margo and Castel join us, the former seems happy to listen. Castel and Vásan at least keep us company, either because they, too, are secretly interested, or they have nowhere else to go.

I make eye-contact with Septimus at one point, when Aisling alludes to our Fair blood. He smiles, but it is half-hearted. I must wonder if Kang's comment to him was even crueler than I imagined, or perhaps he is merely in a pensive mood. He walks off at some point, while the rest of us stay longer. I do not know where he goes, but I do not see him again for the rest of the evening, even when Aisling decides it is time to put everyone to bed.

There are bedrooms that she shows to us, apparently for guests. I am curious what sorts of guests Aisling and Kang entertain, and who their friends are. I would like to learn how it is Septimus came to meet them, at some point in time. But I know better than to ask, now. Perhaps I'll see it in print, one day, if Aisling ever decides to add us to her stories. What a peculiar thought.

"Please make yourselves comfortable," Aisling invites warmly, displaying the bedrooms. "We have plenty of beds. Kang and I prefer..."

"The nest?" I say.

She laughs. "I suppose that is an accurate title for it."

"Thank you for everything," I say. "We appreciate it. Truly. I'm sure Septimus would...Actually, I do not know where he's gone, but he'll probably thank you at some point, as well."

She smiles. "Think nothing of it," she says. "We do owe him, after all. And do not worry; I shall send him to bed before I turn in, myself."

I hesitate, knowing there may be further conversation to be had among the three of them, and wanting to be there. But I tell myself I should not.

Wanting answers cannot be used as an excuse for everything. At some point, I need to recognize boundaries.

Septimus might be prone to keeping secrets, a habit I am not fond of, but even he deserves some privacy.

Seventeen

SEPTIMUS HAS US rise early, which appears to suit Margo and Castel well enough, though Xerian is bleary-eyed and drowsy. When Septimus went to bed, I cannot say, but he is chipper and wide-awake, now. Nissa clearly slept like the dead, and Vásan is his usual quiet and reserved self. The air about him feels awkward and uncertain; I feel as if he has lapsed, somehow, from whatever development he may have managed over the past few weeks.

Though I feel uncomfortable wandering about Kang and Aisling's home while they sleep on obliviously, Septimus wastes no time in boiling water for coffee in the kitchen, and pulling tea bags for those of us who still refuse it. He truly has been here many times before, then. He and Margo help themselves to some breakfast as well, though my stomach is squeamish, and most everyone else is satisfied with coffee alone.

From there, it is a matter of repacking the supplies Margo scavenged from our boat. My bow is gone, unfortunately, though she has retrieved all my knives, and my standard-issued firearm is in one piece. Between the two of us, Vásan and I have a good number of rounds left as well. There is a spare pair of my own clothes that have been scrounged up, that somehow appear to be clean. I'm shocked Aisling would have time to do that—I'm continually surprised by all she seems to get done in a day—but Septimus offhandedly says it was likely "one of the brownies" that help the pair out with chores.

Apparently, so long as Aisling leaves out fresh cream for them in the entrances to hallways, the brownies do absolutely everything she needs finished and does not have time to work on, from churning fresh butter, to laundry, and delivering clean clothes. I wonder if Rian would be amenable to finding some of these creatures, when I'm in charge of running the palace household one day. I think I could use such assistance.

Once we have dressed and put our equipment in order, it is time to leave. And that means waking Kang.

Septimus goes to do so, letting Margo and I accompany him while everyone else stays near the front of the cave. Apparently, it would be best not to overwhelm our hosts in the morning. If I thought Kang was foul-tempered last night, Margo claims that is nothing compared to waking him early.

Kang and Aisling's bedroom is humid, and pleasantly warm. The main source of heat appears to be Kang himself, and I can hear his deep breathing buried beneath the nest he and Aisling have created for themselves. Septimus gives a knock at the door, and Kang's breathing interrupts as he stirs.

"Morning," Septimus says, at least hovering in the door politely. "We're all set and ready to get out of your way."

"You may take what you wish. Then leave," Kang mumbles sleepily from beneath the coils of blankets. I trust Aisling is toasty in there with him; even his speaking creates a puff of warm air.

"Unless you have a boat, I'm afraid that's going to be difficult," Margo says.

Kang growls and smoke rises. I try my own hand at persuasion.

"I believe part of the deal was for you to assist us in—"

Kang lets out a loud, annoyed groan. There is shifting beneath the blankets.

"Darling, you promised," Aisling says dozily. "Besides, while you are there, you can pick up a few things for me. I will make a list."

Kang mumbles in *Dohremi.* Cursing us extensively, if I had to guess. But he is moving beneath the blankets and eventually, essentially, slithers out of the stack, complaining and squinting.

"You're lucky my wife likes Kachin pears," he mutters.

I feel sorry for waking them, but Kang turns away again before I can apologize. He helps his wife climb out of the nest as she rubs at her eyes, half-tripping on her long nightgown. She mumbles insistences she is fine, telling him to be polite.

Kang still grumbles all the way to the kitchen, Aisling basically pushing him onwards, yawning something or another in *Dohremi* the entire time. Moments afterwards, with them both receiving coffee from Xerian, it becomes clear what Kang is complaining about, and it is not actually us, thankfully.

"What if you need me while I'm away?" Kang complains in Alarkian.

"I'm sure I'll manage," Aisling reassures him. "I'll have someone come over to keep me company."

"But 'someone' isn't 'me'..." Kang moans.

"What's this?" Margo asks.

"Kang doesn't want to leave me," Aisling says, indicating her stomach. "He worries."

Kang gives his wife a certain look that I believe I have received from Rian at least once or twice, times past. He does not appreciate her downplaying his concerns, even if Aisling is justified in being jaded over his continual worries.

"A lady should not have to go through such things alone," he huffs. I do not imagine his face turning a little pink.

"I'll stay," Xerian offers. "I'm good at anything, in a pinch."

Kang narrows his eyes at the young man. Vásan sighs and goes ahead to get himself another cup of coffee, expecting this to take some time.

"What. Could you possibly do. To help," Kang says.

"Well," Xerian says thoughtfully. "Do you know how to deliver a baby?"

"Of course I do!" Kang snaps. "I know absolutely everything to do and all the things that could go wrong and how to fix them. Do you think I would not have learned, knowing my wife's—!"

"Perfect," Xerian interrupts, and turns to Septimus. "Then, if it is fine with you, I'll stay. Just in case Miss Aisling needs help."

Septimus shrugs. "If that is what you want. We will manage."

"How very gentlemanly of you," Aisling says.

Xerian blushes. "It's the least we could do, ma'am."

Aisling claps her hands together. "Then that is settled! If everyone is all—"

"Hold on, now!" Kang interrupts. "Whoever said I approved of this? Letting some strange boy stay at my home while I am forced to take a pack of unfortunates across the sea to Kacha?"

"And to pick up my pears," Aisling adds. "Besides, it is not some strange boy, dear, it is Xerian Vicell. He can adapt a serious skill from any person he encounters, and I would say at this point you are more than prepared to assist. He can adapt your skills, and if they are needed, here he is. If not, no harm done."

"If they are *needed! Aisling!*" Kang repeats, horrified. He goes on in Dohremi, sounding like he's giving a rant about still wanting to be here for his child's birth. The rest of us are his captive audience.

The way Kang frets over his wife—this man with terrifying, unique abilities—makes me think about all the people I have met. All the stories they keep. I have always justified my rewinding time and saving Rian by telling myself it was necessary. Fate's own will.

Yet, would Kang not find some similar justification, if he had my abilities, and someone hurt his wife? I am sure Castel would do anything to save the woman he loved, and watched die. Margo would try to keep her niece and nephews from turning to their darker selves, Xerian would save his family, Nissa might save her mother from the bear that killed her. Taris would undoubtedly do whatever necessary for Lune.

Even Vásan, I realize, might save Yvette from her suffering, even if it means not having Alo one day. So perhaps he does love her, in a way. Perhaps his refusal to acknowledge it is more a reflection of how he feels about himself, not her.

There are so many people in the world besides me and Rian, and so many stories. I may have justified doing what I have for the sake of the world in the past, but now I know what that means. Now I know what another chance means to all the people who have sacrificed to help me and Rian.

They deserve a better world, and better lives, than what they've been given.

Kang gives a long sigh, throwing his head back, and Aisling is smiling. Apparently, she has won their argument.

"Just promise me you won't have the children before I come back?" Kang whines, making his wife's smile widen.

She stretches up to kiss him, but even then, Kang needs to bend down for her. Aisling is petite, and his is quite the lanky figure. Without contest, he is the tallest person here.

"I shall do my very best," she promises.

Kang grimaces, but still turns to Xerian, resigned.

"How do we do this, then?" he grumbles.

Xerian is all smiles, same as Aisling. I'm sure they will get along just fine in our absence. They appear to be cut from the same cloth.

"You don't need to do a thing," he says. "Please stand there, and…"

He duplicates the same process I saw him use on the docks, when he learned how to use that Alarkian weapon. Xerian's eyes go unfocused, practically with a glaze coating them. His expression is uncharacteristically blank. Then, suddenly, he snaps back to attention, a little shudder running through him. A smile instantly blooms across his features.

"There!" he says stoutly, pleased with himself. "Now that I know absolutely everything of what to do if something bad did happen, it's almost guaranteed not to!"

Kang looks pained. He says something in Dohremi that I believe is akin to "I hope so". Ailsing laughs at the comment, a hand rubbing over her swollen stomach. I think she is not quite due to deliver yet, if this is a multiple pregnancy as Kang has implied. There is nothing Kang can complain about more, now, though, and while he takes up another ten minutes in a lengthy goodbye with his wife, Aisling eventually pushes him out the front door.

It is not as warm as yesterday outside as we all gather, and I wonder if the weather changes depending on Kang's mood. In fact, it occurs to me that it completely slipped my mind to inquire as to how this island operates. Was it a gift, somehow, of a magical nature? If one does not shipwreck here, how else would they arrive? Aisling said they had other visitors, after all…

"Right, so, I figure we have two options," Septimus starts, interrupting my thoughts as he addresses Kang.

"You are not riding me," Kang growls.

Septimus shrugs. "Fine, fine. How do you want to do this, then?"

Aisling steps in to mediate, offering a solution before any real trouble can arise. "We have a dinghy. You can all sit safely in it, and Kang can carry it in his claws," she suggests. "Though I would tie yourselves in. It would be rather unfortunate, falling from that height."

Nissa looks green at the prospect of traveling through the air, but Vásan raises an eyebrow. I assume that is his way of expressing this is something he thinks he may enjoy. Castel, as always, does not appear to care about anything at all. Margo is blasé, as if she has ridden a dragon before and by comparison, this is nothing to be concerned about.

We begin to make our way down the long steps of the cliff, letting Kang lead the way to where this dinghy is kept. He insists on carrying his wife after about the third step, and Aisling lets him with only a little fuss. As Kang no doubt has supernatural abilities without even having a fluke to host, I doubt she is much weight to him. He will soon be carrying a large number of us in his dragon form, after all.

Margo and Xerian are in the back of our group, just behind me. This means I am treated to her giving him a long laundry list of things to do in looking after both himself and Aisling. Xerian laughingly insists that he can more than take after himself. I believe, from what I have grown to know about Margo, that this lecture is more for her sake than his.

She does not appear to have any children of her own, from what I've been able to extrapolate from her and Septimus' hints. Xerian has filled that role rather neatly, and she is reluctant to leave him behind, now. I, too, will admit that things will be different without the young man's cheer. Naïve he may be, and I would say he puts far too much trust in my cousin. But Xerian is an undoubted bright light. A little beacon of hope for both himself and others. Without him, I am worried the rest of us will soon have demons of doubt and fear trailing behind us, ready to latch onto our backs.

I force this thought away with a shudder, and focus on listening to Margo and Xerian. Her parental banter. His unwavering confidence in himself and his own abilities. In Septimus, and Septimus' abilities. His plan.

What surprises me, however, is that when Margo finally runs out of advice to give Xerian, Vásan is there to add his own. He immediately picks up her thread of conversation, though much more seriously and sternly, pretending as if this is perfectly natural and within his realm of usual behavior.

"...And you mustn't panic no matter the circumstances," he tells Xerian, who is incredibly receptive and ecstatic to have Vásan's attention. "If you panic, she will panic, and that would not be good for her or the children. Certainly, do not raise your voice at her, even out of excitement. I never understood why some people think it best to scream at a woman in such events, even out of encouragement. It's barbaric. It is not a sporting event."

"Right," Xerian says. "I shall be highly solemn and professional."

"...As best you can be," Vásan adds, almost as if he doubts Xerian can be anything less than his usual bright self. "And do make certain she can hold them as soon as possible. She is going to want to, anyway. Kang as well. If they are born before he returns. Get the children to him as soon as possible."

I cannot help but glance back Vásan with an eyebrow raised. I catch sight of Margo as well, who is doing her best not to smile or snort.

"What," Vásan demands.

"Nothing, nothing," I say.

"I have a wife, your majesty," Vásan says defensively.

I insist again it is nothing, biting my tongue against the fact that Vásan and Yvette only have one child. Not to mention, from what I heard, Yvette's birthing experience with Alo was an easy one. I am curious why Vásan knows so much and has so much of an opinion on the subject. The idea of him doing his own research for Yvette's sake is almost endearing.

"I don't know why you're all so worried," Xerian says, somehow both oblivious and highly knowledgeable, given his fluke's usage. "She'd have to be fairly early to have those children before Kang comes back. Most likely, I will just be spending time up here in paradise for the next few weeks, while the rest of you put in all the dangerous and exciting work."

"You have already endured plenty of danger," Margo chides.

"It is not a competition," Vásan says shortly at the same time.

I make certain to keep my face forward. My smile is a puzzled one, to some extent, but despite how peculiarly Vásan is acting, the scenario does strike a humorous tone. I cannot tell if that is Xerian's doing or not. Regardless, by the time Kang has led us to the dinghy, and finally let Aisling stand on her own feet again, I feel as if I will somehow miss Xerian just as much as Margo and Vásan will.

Castel and Margo help pull the dinghy down the beach, close to the water as instructed, while Kang half undresses before taking a rather grandly embroidered Lijimi-style robe Aisling has been carrying for him. With that wrapped around him, he finishes the process. Septimus does not say anything, but folds the clothes for him, tucking them under the front bench in the little boat.

I cannot help but watch Kang carefully, curious. He notices and is less than pleased, though he strangely glares at the rest of the party in general, and not directly at me.

"Do not say anything," he says in advance. "And if you stare, I will bite heads off. Do not test me on that."

"We have been warned," I barely hear Castel mutter.

Kang mutters something in Dohremi again, and does not look at us. But I notice that there is a pinkness to his face that was not there before; it occurs to me that he might be embarrassed about all this.

A shudder runs through his body, and he arches his back slightly, bending forward. How precisely the rest of it happens, I cannot say. There is an absolutely blinding light, so quick, it can only take three seconds at the most. I'm forced to close my eyes, and when I open them again, there is a golden dragon before us, his long serpentine body hosts no visible wings, though he is still capable of flight. His horns look like that of a stag, his two whiskers long and delicate like ribbons.

He is not quite a Kourn feather dragon, but certainly nothing like the brightback. There is something more regal, more majestic, about him.

Kang seems strangely more pleasant, in this form. I would have thought it would be terrifying to stand in the presence of a dragon again, but instead I find this form of his more endearing. He does not look anything like Mango, yet his mannerisms remind me of my husband's little pet. I find I want to scratch Kang behind his ears, between the horns, just as Mango likes.

Vásan and Nissa are both staring, failing to heed Kang's warning. But despite what he said, I think he likes their awe.

Aisling is smiling as she takes in our reactions. Even Margo cannot help but continually glance at the dragon now padding around the beach before us, and I would have thought someone like Margo Grey has seen all there is to see in this world.

"I'd pile you all into the dinghy, then," Ailsing says, prepared to herd us like a gaggle of goslings back into our pen. "Off you get. Xerian, dear, shut your mouth. I am sure you'll get the chance to see him in this form again, when he returns."

Vásan manages to regain his usual decorum and before I know it, he is taking my things from me, helping Septimus stow everything away beneath the seats. Xerian shakes himself free, as well, so he can help Castel tie us in place, just as we'd done on the boat.

Nissa is driven to distraction to the point where I find I must take her by the arm and practically pull her into the dinghy. She breaths awed Hoitsokin oaths and rubs at her eyes, as if she thought we were all lying when we said Kang is a man cursed with dragon's blood.

Once we are seated, and arranged properly, I find Aisling standing close by, with that folded robe. She meets my eye, and gestures.

"You wouldn't mind, would you?" she asks, before adding in a whisper, "He is a rather modest one, and it will embarrass him dreadfully to have anyone see him change. It is a rather personal thing, after all."

"Oh. No, I do not mind," I say, accepting the robe and the responsibility of helping Kang keep his modesty. How very proper of him.

There is a sudden gust of wind that pushes at my back and blows my hair forward. Nissa is similarly assaulted, though Margo's hair is tied back tightly enough that it is not an issue for her, and she manages to stand tall against the blast. The men are not so bothered. When I manage to push my hair out of the way again and look back, I see that Kang has flown off, back over the mountain, his serpent body whipping to and fro in graceful sweeps.

"He's left!" Nissa cannot help but exclaim. I do not think she even necessarily means it as a criticism of Kang, she simply cannot believe that she's seen a dragon, and that he's taken off so easily.

He is a creature of flight, and a magnificent one.

"He'll circle around, then grab you and be on his way," Aisling reassures us. "He only wants to build some momentum, first. And he may be enjoying himself. It has been some time since he has had an excuse to fly."

Nissa stares after Kang, watching him as much as possible. Even Vásan takes a few moments to pointedly watch, to see what he can. But Castel and Septimus are not at all amused and do not bother. Instead, they work on getting our party all tied down to the dinghy, safe as can be. Only Xerian and Aisling remain standing, Aisling pulling him by the arm to make him back away from the dinghy.

Nissa keeps turning around, eyes wide and waiting, but I find myself facing forward, staring at a particular whisp of Vásan's otherwise impeccable hair that has been brushed the wrong way. I do not know why, but I want things to be as much of a surprise as possible.

It is not quite as quick as I expected, yet, I have no discernable thoughts when Kang swoops down to pick us up. His claws clamp onto the sides of the dinghy, two to each, so that we are evenly balanced. Then we are jostled, jolted, lifted forward and up into the air with no small amount of bumping into one another.

I find that I have caught my breath, and that my head feels even higher in the clouds than we are currently traveling. Below us, Xerian and Aisling are becoming smaller, and smaller. Above us, is the golden belly of a dragon, and the blue sky surrounding it.

"Goodbye! Have a safe trip!" Aisling calls, waving to us as we fly further away. Xerian runs all the way to the edge of the water, waving and calling his own farewells to us along with Aisling's.

"Good luck!" and "Don't forget about me!" and "See you next time around!"

The last of these, I suppose may be directed specifically at Septimus, indicating that Xerian, at least, believes that we will find success in Kacha.

Kang flies us out further over the sea, and then, the island and Aisling and Xerian are gone. We are back in the known world again, where there is only ocean and sky and not much else to see at all. It is much colder out here, again, and Kang brings us higher into the sky, where the air is thinner. Everything is much too blue.

The flight is intoxicating, in a terrifying way. I am keenly aware of there being naught but a small layer of wood between myself and my companions and the ocean, so far below us. I can remember, mainly through the feeling of it, being once thrown high into the air by Mercer's fluke, forcing me to be a victim of gravity. I am forced to think on the science of mortality that we often so forget, in our world.

Despite her own worries, Nissa fares much better with this method of transportation than the ship. She is as excitable as a pup, and it makes her face look much younger. She loves this flight, and no doubt will be on the hunt for a dragon of her own to raise, when this is all over. Perhaps she could form a bond with one as her animal companion, next.

Kang is undoubtedly faster than any ship would be. Castel offers me his coat, to drape over my head to keep my hair from being tangled this way and that as the wind blasts against us. I realize that Margo, Nissa and I have been placed in the middle, with the men on the outside, to block most of the wind. But I do not refuse Castel's offer, even if it deprives him of some extra warmth.

I do not think his pride could manage it otherwise.

It takes us the better part of the day and another night, but eventually, I do see land far below us: Kacha. The sky is dark despite the sun rising, and a strange though vague gray cloud appears to hang over the entire country. Kang must know his way around the place, at least somewhat, because he decides to land on a beach, some distance away where I spotted a dock and shipyard. Not that there are many ships here, anymore. I do not see any people.

This entire country, though I have barely seen any of it, feels as abandoned as the city of Mouloix. I know there are citizens, still, living here, but it does not feel as if there are. This country is lost, and I can feel it. No doubt my companions can, as well. I notice even Vásan is markedly uncomfortable.

My legs are shaky and nearly numb when Kang lands our dinghy on the beach in the south-east region of the country before whipping away to transform behind some rocks. I force myself to be the first to climb from the boat, nearly falling flat on my face. But I still have Kang's robe, and I made a promise to his wife. So, I shuffle over to the rocks and clear my throat pointedly so as not to startle him.

Kang's arm appears, and I drape his robe over it. The rest of his clothes are still packed under the dinghy bench, but this will allow him to rejoin us. I stand by and wait for him, watching the rest of my companions force themselves out of the dinghy on shaking legs. We are all sleep-deprived, sore, and well-aware of the long day ahead of us, still.

After a few moments, Kang steps out again, wearing the robe and tying it closed. He stops and stands a few paces from me, watching until someone else notices. Septimus looks back and raises a hand in acknowledgement. Kang, less grudgingly than I'd have expected, returns the gesture. Then Septimus goes back to helping, and Kang continues to hover near the rocks. He is waiting for us to leave, I realize, before retrieving his own things.

"You're not going to come say goodbye to everyone?" I ask.

He hesitates. "I'd rather not," he admits. "I…Don't want to hear about how…" he struggles to find a way to say it. "I am cursed."

Somehow, I understand. Kang is pleased with our party's reaction to him as a dragon, I think. He saw how awed Nissa and Xerian were, especially, and he liked that attention. But there is an almost adorably modest side to him that means he would rather not manage their reactions in human form, where he might be expected to say something back to them.

He is not a social creature. Clearly.

"Then thank you, on all our behalf. Truly, we appreciate your help," I say.

Kang nods. He seems less grouchy to me, now.

"I have one more favor to ask of you," I admit, and go on before he can react. "As I mentioned, my husband quite enjoys your wife's books. You are one of his favorite characters…Do I have your permission to tell him that you are real? I know it would be unreasonable to ask if he could meet you, but—"

"You may tell him," Kang blurts, suddenly.

There is that light pinkness again, and he avoids my eyes.

"…I would…not mind it," he adds in a mutter. "…I know from Septimus, he is a scholar, your husband. The respectable sort. I suppose he may appreciate it…"

He sounds mildly dubious, but I am quick to reassure him.

"Oh, you have no idea what it would mean to him," I say. "Rian would think of it as a travel gift. Rare knowledge is intoxicating, to him. I understand meeting you would be impossible, but just knowing you and Aisling are real would be quite the treat for him."

But at my mention of their never meeting, Kang hesitates. He is clearly thinking of saying something, and cannot properly word it. I imagine he is not quite accustomed to speaking to anyone other than Aisling much, who already knows him better than he knows himself.

"Perhaps…Aisling and I could visit. Sometime. And, if the world truly does need us one day, in dire circumstances, you may call on me," Kang says, his offering and implication Rian may yet meet him one day. "But otherwise, please leave my family be. And tell no one else that we exist."

"I will respect your privacy," I agree. "And won't bother you unless the world is under such a threat that it would endanger your family if I did not ask for your aid."

Kang snorts. "If it comes to that, I'll find you."

I suppose that means Kang's definition of "dire" is a little more flexible, and less focused on the end of the world, than mine. But I approve; it means I am more likely than not to see him again someday. Perhaps every decade or so, he will allow a visit.

"Well," I say. "I...suppose this is goodbye."

"You're looking for a young man named 'Jin Riyong', are you not?" Kang says suddenly, startling me.

"Yes?"

Kang nods. "He is not far. If you walk inward, north-west, I believe, you ought to run into him."

I blink. "Do...do you have a fluke?"

Kang smiles. I think it is the first time I've seen him do something like that without Aisling's prompting.

"Ah. No. This man has gone to the Otherworld, I think someone mentioned." He points to his own nose. "I can smell it on him."

"Thank you," I say genuinely. "I appreciate it. And I am sorry, but we probably will be going back at least once more. I know that means you will have to wait longer to meet your children. And...I understand completely why that is painful."

Kang sighs, but seems more accepting of this than he was before.

"It is not your fault," he mutters. "I know Aisling and I will have them one day, obviously. But it is different for us. Fair age in terms of 'fate'. That was a part of the gift given to Aisling. For many of them, that means they certainly will live long enough for them to look after their children, and usually begin to age afterwards. But that means the process of having children is not as easy for us as it is for you. My curse...does not help."

"At least you will have even more time to prepare yourself for it," I try to tease him. "How many little pups do you think there will be?"

He rolls his eyes. "Oh, at least two. To five. They will be very small, starting out—smaller than human children—and grow quicker after they are born. At least, that is how it was before."

"I'm sure they will be absolutely lovely. I hope to see you all again, someday, in some other time," I say.

"...I...might...agree," Kang forces himself to say.

"You can introduce me to your children, and I will have you meet my son. And my husband and Ayla, of course."

"That would be. Nice."

I leave Kang there by the rocks to rejoin the others, slinging my pack over a shoulder before relaying to Septimus what I was told, about Jin Riyong.

"Is Kang not coming to say goodbye?" Nissa asks, disappointed.

I share a look with Septimus.

"Kang is like that," Septimus says for the both of us. "He is not one for farewells. I'm sure he wishes us luck all the same."

While I can see Castel is dubious of this, I think I understand Kang, now, and know this is likely. Kang has quite the prickly outer layer to him, but I saw how much he loves Aisling, and how he did not refuse helping us even when he could have. He might not have acted like a gracious host, but he still let us into his home, along with Aisling, fed us well, gave us a good night's rest, and brought us all the way to Kacha himself.

Given how easily they seem to have everything else they may need in their little mountain, I think Aisling wanting Kachin pears is a weak excuse, but one Kang needed.

We set off, down the beach, moving up a slope towards where tall grass begins to spring up in the sand before giving way to more shrubbery and deadened plant life that must have once painted a pretty picture of Kacha's fertile land. Even here, I can see distant mountains, as the country is all but covered in rolling landscape, interspersed only by flat lands of farms and dusty roads. Per Kang's instructions, we will not be headed towards the city and port I thought I saw, but around it. The more we walk, the taller the grass becomes, scratching at my upper thighs. The dirt is dry, and cracked, beneath my feet, betraying the potential for drought.

It is winter here, as well, but there is no snow, only ash from the sky.

"This place feels dead," Nissa says, after a long while of silent travel.

There is an oppressive melancholy, here. I feel as if we should not be here. I am certain everyone else can feel it, too.

"It is dead," Septimus says.

He does not elaborate.

The grass is over my head by nearly an arm's length when it suddenly begins to lower again, in a slow progression. We find ourselves approaching what I realize is a graveyard, appearing out of nowhere in this field. We are on its outskirts before we know it, practically stumbling into the rows and rows of graves, too many too count. So many, in fact, it is horrifying. Beyond, I can see distantly the remnants of what must be the once great city of Bonxhui: its broken skyline, its ruins. It is a devastating backdrop, with these graves covering the foreground.

It is there I see Jin Riyong long before he can see me. But this comes as no surprise; the more I watch him move amongst the graves, the more I am certain that he is completely blind.

He is a startlingly tall man, with broad shoulders, like my own husband. Only, unlike Rian, there is a military bearing to Jin Riyong, and I could guess at a fluke related to physical strength with ease. The way he manages to move so carefully despite his blindness and bulk implies a great many things about him that go against general stereotypes. Either he knows this graveyard extraordinarily well from being here many times over again, or he has astonishing self-awareness. Perhaps both.

When he comes close, he appears to feel us there, and turns his head. His eyes are a cloudy white—different than the former queen Clair Oram's blind but colored eyes. Still, there is a feeling of recognition here.

No one knows quite what to do. Septimus clears his throat and gingerly steps forward, onto the land claimed by this gravesite.

"Excuse me," he says, polite as can be, "are you…Jin Riyong?"

"I am."

At least he appears to know Alarkian. That is a relief.

"We were told we might find you here," Septimus says, and I realize my cousin has no idea how to explain this situation. "We…I believe we may have need of something left in your possession. A certain…lantern?"

Anyone else, I would assume, should be suspicious, and wary. Confused, even, given the state of the world and present circumstances. Surely, from Septimus' accent alone, it is obvious we are a pack of foreigners who do not belong here at all. But these words, instead, appear to make more sense to Jin Riyong than they even do to me. I watch his guard drop.

"Septimus. Smith," Jin Riyong says slowly, nodding as if he expected us. "Yunman said you would come one day. I barely listened to his precognitive mutterings usually—we all had grown used to ignoring them. However, he mentioned you several times. He said you would come to help."

"I do hope so," Septimus says, cautious, but allowing this to happen.

I can see he is tempted to ask who Yunman is, but holds himself back.

"Who are your companions?" Jin Riyong asks.

He allows his arms to rest, having put a hand to the sword tied at his left side. I am not sure what damage a blind swordsman might accomplish, but I realize my hypothesis was correct: Jin Riyong is wearing the tattered remnants of Kacha's Bonxhui military uniform. I suppose he may wear it out of familiar comfort, if nothing else, but have no doubt he has acquired the usual skills of one in his position.

Septimus steps back again, as if to present us.

"This is Soleil…Yakarami," he says, stumbling slightly. "Queen of Isaaria. She is my cousin. And therefore also…a Smith."

He speaks slowly, questioningly, but somehow, Jin Riyong has been expecting us, and it appears he was told precisely whom to expect as well. There is no doubt in his mind that Magicsmiths are real. There is nothing to prove, to this man, who has already seen horrors beyond our imagining.

"She is the one going to the Otherworld?" Jin Riyong says shortly.

"I…Yes," Septimus confesses, startled.

He nods again. "And the others?"

"Oh, ah. Grand Princess Nissa Sondushki, and Grand Prince Vásan Pike. Former prince of Lijimata, Castel Voskoss. And Margo…Grey."

There is a moment of tension, knowing what we all do. The Greys are the reason Kacha is a husk of a country, after all. However, Jin Riyong simply continues to nod without any sign of aggression. I do not know who Yunman is, and what he might have said about us, but I know that Anna Wolff was in this portion of the world as well. Perhaps the Wolffs told Jin Riyong much. He has already come to an understanding of how this world works, and what supernatural forces may be in play beyond what mankind presumed to understand before now.

"I see. Well. Follow me," Jin Riyong says. "I will take you to the queen."

I hesitate in saying anything, but Nissa does not. "Your government has crumbled. There is no Kacha."

He sighs, knowing this. "Then she is queen of what is left."

We follow Riyong out of the haunting graveyard, and down the overgrown path leading further into the countryside. Somehow, we all know better than to attempt to speak much, here, out of reverence for the dead we are leaving behind us. Jin Riyong himself offers no further conversation. He moves slowly, with a limp, but surely, knowing every portion of the landscape, every bump and rock, every dying fern. To perhaps no one's surprise, Riyong does not take us down the main road, though we still approach the smoldering remains of Bonxhui's crumbling skyline, and the hills beyond. The smog and grey sky hang over the entire country, it seems, but at least it likely keeps the smoke from any survivor's fire concealed. Our path is old, but new feet have tramped it down lately—it is left from a time before Alarkian industry migrated eastward.

We travel for hours, in near complete silence save for short interruptions. During our entire walk, we pass only one other living soul: an old man bent nearly horizontal from the weight of what he carries on his back, headed to the coast. He eyes us foreigners wearily, giving us a wide berth. But when he poses a query in Kachin to Riyong, recognizing our guide with some comfort and trust, Riyong's answer sends him on his way, reassured and nodding to himself.

"We see one another on the road often," Riyong tells us. "He is going to the coast to fish for the week. I have told him you were ship-wrecked on your way here for a diplomatic meeting with our queen."

"Do foreign ships still come here at all?" I ask skeptically.

"Some," Riyong says. "Not many, but we are limping on. Many folks are willing to travel to do what they can for a little food and money. We will help you find passage home when the time comes," he adds.

"Does the old man not have sons who can do this hard work for him?" Vásan asks, unconcerned with promises of how we may leave Kacha.

Riyong sighs. "No, not anymore. Many of our young men are dead. Bonxhui's population was decimated. When the Grey's army came, our military, our people, the country..." He does not know how to say it in Alarkian, and resorts to Kachin while thinking. "...We were never going to win," he finally says.

I wonder what more he meant to say, now lost in lose translation. I wonder how many trembling young men stood on a Kachin beach, seeing invaders' ships approach, knowing there was no hope. Knowing they would die.

Is there peace to be found such an inevitability, or only despair?

We walk in silence again, then. Wind whistles through the tall grass; a painful cry across an otherwise disturbingly quiet land. While we have long since left the graveyard, I can feel that Kacha is haunted by the dead. No doubt Riyong carries some of those ghosts with him.

When we reach the city, the haunting intensifies. Mouloix was abandoned; Bonxhui is dead. The city has clearly been ravaged intensely, with not a soul left living here. People have either fled, or were destroyed utterly. There are luckily no bodies in the streets—it has been several years since Kacha's decimation, after all—but they are somehow still here: the victims of the great violence the Greys brought with them.

Jin Riyong knows his way through the once great city well, picking his way through the debris-cluttered streets: the broken modern buildings, and burned Kachin-style houses with their roofs caved in. I imagine he may have, many times, patrolled these streets with other members of Bonxhui's military-police. I imagine he had friends, here. Family members.

The idea that they are all dead and gone, along with a large portion of Kacha's populace, is poignantly choking. The idea this could have just as easily happened to Isaaria makes it hard for me to catch my breath.

I feel a hand on my shoulder. Vásan. He does not look at me, watching Riyong ahead of us so we might follow, but he says "breathe, your majesty", and waits until I nod before removing his hand again.

Distantly, I can see the grand, sprawling Seonganbuk Palace, where the king, queen, and crown prince's households reside in separate smaller palaces. I know from historical lessons there are six separate palaces throughout Bonxhui, but Seonganbuk is the grandest. Or, it was.

We appear to be approaching it, and I wonder briefly if, somehow, Queen Park Mi-Sun is still in the city. But then, the street opens into what looks like a town square, and it is here that we change course. Riyong walks leftward, taking a pathway to lead us out of the city again, further into the country. He completely ignores the statue standing in the square's center, but the rest of us cast it suspicious glances, startled and intrigued by it.

The stone statue on her pedestal is, most noticeable two things: firstly, it is new. It cannot be more than a few months old, at best. Second, the woman is western. That is clear enough, in her facial features and the curl to her hair, though she wears Kachin clothing. One of her arms is missing, the sleeve pinned up to clearly show it like how I have seen Aiden wear his sleeves, when without his prosthetic. Beneath it, on her hip, is tied a sword not unlike Riyong's. Her other arm is crossed in front of her body. Gripped tightly in her hand is a lantern.

I hurry to catch Riyong, at the lead of our pack. I am too shocked by what I have seen, and who I am certain it is.

"The statue…The woman without her left arm…" I start.

"That is the Lady Wolff," Riyong says plainly, as if he suspected someone would ask. "We made several statues to honor her sacrifice. No matter how many times the Greys' men destroyed them, the next morning, the statues were restored in full. It is as if something recognizes what she has done for us, as well, and does not allow them to degrade her."

I glance backward at Margo, knowing she must hear us. Everyone must. It is too quiet in the city for Riyong's words not to carry.

"She…gave you the lantern," I say slowly. "The one to the Otherworld, that the Wolffs were charged with protecting. And she gave it to you."

"She sent me there in hopes of helping save my friends," he says quietly.

He bows his head, in shame or sorrow, I cannot tell.

"But I failed," he says. "It was only because of Lady Wolff that I managed to survive at all, myself. She pulled me from the Otherworld, managing to recover all of me except my eyes. I owed her my life…But when Kacha was invaded, and the king was too hopeless over the loss of both his sons to put up much of a fight, I could not repay her."

"She was murdered," I say. This part, I know.

"A few years ago. She was protecting Crown Princess Mi-Sun, who was expecting a son—the heir to Kacha—when the Greys arrived. She stayed, so Mi-Sun could escape with the child. They spent three days debasing and torturing her, and strung her body in the Bonxhui Square when she died, letting the birds peck at it until it rotted away. We sent men to bury her, but that alone was a perilous mission. Not everyone survived it."

I am shocked by the idea that a dying country would risk any number of their survivors to try and bury someone most of them did not even know. They must have truly respected what this foreign woman tried to do for them.

"If failing to do it once resulted in death, it was foolish and pigheaded to try again," Castel says bitterly. "Who cares what's done with a body—she was dead already."

I flash a look at Septimus, wishing he would try to govern Castel's tongue at least a little. Luckily, Riyong is not offended.

"There is something to what you say. But we could not leave her. I could not have. I am personally indebted to Anna Wolff forever: not only for saving my life, but for saving the Crown Princess—now Queen—and…her child. I am even helping you now, in her name, as it is something I believe Lady Wolff would want me to do."

No one has much to say to that.

We leave Bonxhui through a series of side streets, the least damaged from whatever happened here. There is no real path to take, except for one clearly forged by time, and many feet fleeing the burned-out city, headed towards the mountains. I'm not sure where Riyong plans to take us, aside from the mountains themselves. All I can see are long stretches of very tall grass and dust. Even the trees are plain and twisted. Black. Were it not winter, I suspect they still would have nothing to show: no pretty dresses of leaves. I was once told that Kacha was a beautiful, stunningly green place, not unlike Isaaria.

Now, there is nothing to see. Only what looks like a small, old temple that rises out of the tall grass field ahead of us. It is only as we approach the hills directly, and pass the temple across the field from the dead city, that small, crowded shelters begin to appear hidden in the tall grass. They are numerous, and well-crafted despite their cobbled appearances. This is a camp for survivors of the war, for refugees who cannot flee their own country, turned into the bones of a more permanent living space. A village made of scraps.

The most impressive structure at the back of this settlement clearly was built and abandoned centuries ago, left as perhaps a pilgrim's destination, only to be re-used, now. It could have been anything, once, but now it is a meagre palace to host what remains of Kacha's once prestigious royal family: Aiko Shinya's cousins.

We all stop to stare, again. We cannot help ourselves; the structure has a strange, ruinous beauty to it, its architecture in old Kachin style like many of their palaces and temples. It has three squat, interconnected buildings planted close together with one main floor, for the most part. Its roof is a faded red color, and stone steps lead up to its sliding front doors.

"It was an old Munusuan temple, once," Riyong explains when asked. "Adapted by Theebin missionaries when they came here, hundreds of years ago. The Theebin religion spread well, here, in Kacha. We needed something more structured to lay our hopes on, and it did that for us. For a time."

"Do people still believe, now?" I ask.

"Some do," Riyong says. "I feel I must, after what Anna showed me."

He realizes he has called her by her first name and trails off, the rest of what he would have said abandoned forever, now.

There is a wooden bridge stretching over a river that is clean enough, considering. I suspect this is where this new town is getting their water supply from. They are startlingly well-organized. As we move further into town, I see that there is an order to this shambled place, built in the dirt. For one thing, it appears they have created a marketplace. The Kachin people are trading what little they have with one another, and all stop to stare when they see us. I suspect Septimus is their main object of interest, though we are all oddities, here. Kacha was a country that loved foreign visitors, but did not know quite what to do with them once they arrived. Now, that has been compounded.

Riyong calls something to them in Kachin, insisting all is well, likely. Telling them that they should go back to their work. I don't know what else he could have said to them, but while no one stops us, and no one swarms to ask questions, they do keep staring.

I notice that most of the people we pass are either very old or very young. There is a distinctive lack of young men or women, though the former category is the most deficient. Our entire walk, Riyong is the only man his own age I see, up until the end. Even then, there is no one Alo Pike or Sacha Lundan's ages. The oldest boy I see is perhaps twelve.

We survive the stares and whispers of the Kachin people, making our way to the makeshift palace for this country's last noblewoman. There are several small children following us, shocked and staring. Margo plays an unspoken game with them, constantly whipping her head in their direction, and pretending she has not caught them when they duck behind the nearest building, giggling to themselves.

Their mothers catch them and scold them, pulling them away despite protests. These children are too young not to know what world they have been brought into. They are too innocent, lacking the suspicion in the eyes of their elders. Perhaps it is a mercy, that they do not know any better.

At the entrance to that sliding red door, there are two men standing guard, though both are at least ten years my senior. They wear attempted uniforms, but the colors are mismatched. They hold spears, pointed straight up in the air, though I doubt they are here as anything more than a formality.

The door is suddenly flung to the side with a slam, and out runs the second young man we have seen in Kacha so far. He must be Riyong's age, or so, and he, too, wears a cobbled uniform. He is shorter than our guide, but equally fit in form, so I suppose together they are what remains of Bonxhui's once prestigious military. The young man's face is long, accentuated by the fact his mouth is slightly open when he comes to a stop before us. His eyes are narrower than Riyong's, though they are quite widely open, now.

He stares, then mutters what I believe is an oath in Kachin.

"They came," he says, his Alarkian heavily accented. "I did not believe you. But you said they would come, and..."

"They have come to see Mi-Sun," Riyong says. "And for Anna's lantern."

The other man hesitates.

"The queen is indisposed. She will see them in an hour," he says.

Riyong nods. "Yes, of course. Might we come in, in the meantime? The walk was a long one. I'm sure our guests are tired."

"We won't be any trouble," Septimus insists.

"No, no, please. Come, come," the young Kachin man says, leading us inside, expecting us to follow. He appears ready to trip over himself to accommodate us, shocked as he is to see us.

I am beginning to think these people have been waiting for us, based on a promise. I pray we can give them whatever they appear to expect.

Inside these walls, it is clear the Kachin are doing their best to recreate a proper palace, for their queen. It is not necessarily any grander than how anyone else has been living, but there are attempts at making this something familiar to them. Something worthy of this woman. I think it is clear, from what we can see alone, Park Mi-Sun is greatly loved by her countrymen.

She must be. She is all that is left of the world, the government, the stability they used to know. In the place of her father and older brother, she has promised to protect them, as her family failed to do before.

There are two small gardens, to our right and left, immediately, when we enter the compound, but they are not intended for beauty. Though there is not much growing now, in the dead of winter, it is clear by how the gardens are designed they are intended for fruits and vegetables.

Riyong's peer has the doors closed behind us once we have entered, and then gestures around.

"Please, find rest here," he says in careful Alarkian. "I will have someone bring you something to eat and drink."

He bows and is gone before any of us can speak again. I would have liked him to ask where, precisely, we are allowed to wander here, but I suspect the buildings are currently off-limits, until Mi-Sun is ready to see us.

"Nice boy," Margo notes pointedly.

We have not been properly introduced.

"Yu Daeyeon," Riyong says. "He watches after the queen. He has been her bodyguard for many years, now."

This is a mild surprise to me. Compared to how grim and serious I know Qhan to be, with a teasing nature to him only on occasion, with Rian, Yu Daeyeon seems like a much different person.

Riyong bows to us, then, as if Daeyeon doing so made him realize he was yet to do so himself.

"If you do not mind, I have something to do, and must excuse myself. If you wish, you may come with me, or you may stay here, and wait. Daeyeon will be prompt with refreshments, I am sure," he adds.

"Is there that much to spare?" Margo says dubiously, her brow furrowed. She looks uncharacteristically distressed. "I'm sure we could all go a few days cutting out a meal or two."

Aside from Septimus, we are all decently figured. Well-fed. It is clear, I would say, that the Kachin people are not. However, Riyong is insistent.

"It is in the nature of a Kachin host to feed his guests, and feed them much," he says. "It is very much a part of our hospitality. Please. Allow us to do so. It is for us."

We glance about at one another, knowing Riyong cannot see the looks we are exchanging. I can understand what he is saying, but I know that someone like Margo will likely still eat little. She saw those children, in the streets. She cannot justify being treated so well if it means potentially taking away what might be available to them.

Most everyone elects to stay in the front courtyard. Castel leans up against a wall, arms crossed. Septimus asks Vásan if he could please check his wound again, in Xerian's absence, and I'm surprised Vásan agrees to this. Margo goes to crouch by the garden, though I'm not sure why. Nissa has been exhausted, again, by our walk. The death of her animal familiar, so closely linked to her, will take her another few weeks to adjust to before she can start thinking of catching a dragon for herself, I'm sure.

But after making certain Riyong would not mind company, I decide to accompany him. I am somehow not hungry, nor do I feel like allowing stagnation to set it. I do not want my thoughts to catch up with me. Not if we are expected to wait an hour.

"What was it you need to do?" I ask Riyong as we make our way around the buildings, to the back.

"It is not so much a chore as it is a promise," he says.

When I see what is in the back of these buildings, I understand immediately.

I find myself in another graveyard, though this one is significantly smaller, and hosts only a few select people.

Set back a good way away from the buildings, the first of the memorials here, are two stone tombs, standing on platforms. Beyond that, further tombs, less grand. From what I have seen so far, it has been important to the Kachin people to bury the bodies of all those who perished when their country fell, but while the first graveyard Riyong visited was likely done merely out of respect for the dead, this is different. I can tell.

He walks forward, leaving me hovering back by the buildings for a moment. But my curiosity gets the better of me, and I find I must join him at the tombs.

Both tombs are covered with fitted statues: two young men, laying down as if deep in sleep, the elder in a blanket of carved, stone apple blossoms, Kachin roses scattered over the younger. There are live flowers over both, as well, likely placed by Riyong if I had to guess. The flowers are brown at the edges, dying and limp, but I suspect not much grows in Kacha anymore.

It is possible he searched for hours, or even days, to find these. From the significant care put into these statues, and the one of Anna Wolff, I can tell that the Kachin people have a great sense of loss at the passing of these people. They are barely limping on, and yet, they have found the time to honor their dead.

"Princes Park Bogun and Chimhwi," Riyong says, as if he somehow knows what I'm looking at. "The king's dead sons."

"They were your friends," I say.

"…Were. Yes. We were all friends. All of us."

He puts a hand on the nearest tomb, the one with the Kachin roses.

"I do not know what was worse. The ones that were quick, or the ones that were not. Bogun and Hwi…were slow," he says. "I watched them all die, one by one. Horribly. I watched them lose their minds. Anna tried so hard to help me save them, but I…I was not strong enough."

I can feel his distress, at events that have happened nearly two years ago at this point. I can still remember how it felt to hold Lune as she died, that night, the years having passed since nearly ten times that. I understand.

"The Greys did this to them?" I say.

"One of their Anomalies," Riyong says, surprising me, with how much he knows. I suppose Anna Wolff trusted him. "It washed up on a beach. And it tore everyone apart. For those of us that were left, there was Tourran, still, to worry about. Then one day, the Greys were here. And they burnt everything to the ground."

Though I know he cannot see how I'm looking at him, Riyong still turns away, as if he can feel it. He does not speak again, for such a long time, that I know he does not want to acknowledge my presence, now.

I step down and away from the princes' tombs, and walk past them. I am sure Riyong can hear me.

There are other tombs, here, not so majestic as the princes', but still with flowers on top. While I cannot read the Kachin characters written there, I can at least recognize the same surname as the Kachin princes' repeated on several of these tombs.

One of them is very small. For a child.

I believe I knew at some point that Crown Prince Park Bogun had a daughter. Another also bearing his surname, must belong to Bogun's wife. The former king and queen are surely buried here someplace, as well.

I cannot bring myself to try and tell Riyong that we are going back again, and that next time, things will be better. I know I should not, and cannot, promise him that. All I know is that I hope it is true. While I know not every evil in the world will be prevented, I pray that the lives of those I have met can be changed for the better. I want it to be so.

I look forward over the tombs, to the mountains and field wide open beyond. The wind blows the tall grass, bending it, whistling it. The sky is gray, and behind the mountains, the dark of night approaches. How quickly this day has gone, with the sun setting so early in winter, and earlier still, on this side of the world. I have only the aching growing in my legs to remind me of how much has happened.

I am struck by the sudden urge to run, not in fear, but for movements own sake. I push it away and turn back to rejoin Riyong.

"If you would like some time alone, I'm going back to the others," I inform him. I am mildly curious why he would not have asked for me to stay behind in the first place, if he wanted to be alone with the memories of his friends and family.

"I will escort you," he says, though I cannot tell if this is out of propriety, or if he is ready to leave.

I decide not to make a fuss. Something tells me it would do no good.

We return to the front courtyard to discover most of my companions have abandoned us, save for Septimus, who is picking at his nailbeds and yawning whilst leaning up against a wall. More shockingly, however, are the plants that have suddenly sprung up in the garden, fully grown, all of which should be out of season at this time and certainly are not grown together: Kachin apples, pears, peaches, and mandarins hang from the trees, no longer with sickly barren branches, while the vegetable garden bears cabbages, leafy greens such as chives or shepherd's purse and mugwort, radishes, onion, garlic, peppers, and cucumber.

There is bustle in this new palace's grounds, now, as the inhabitants all swarm around the garden, shocked, pleased, and relieved. I see a young woman, perhaps Ayla's age, hastily picking fruit and passing it down to a barefoot boy of eight at most, who manages to happily duplicate the items before placing them with care in a basket. This would explain, at least, why they have not starved, though I imagine a boy so young can only do so much, and can hardly feed them all.

This will help.

Septimus catches my gaze.

"Margo," he says, and rolls his eyes. "She cannot help herself. Guilt of a Grey. At least they can pickle and dry things, I suppose."

Riyong must be able to at least smell some of the produce, because he bows to Septimus gratefully. "Regardless of why, we are appreciative of this. You are our guests. We should be the ones feeding you."

"Oh, don't worry," Septimus interrupts before he can go on, "I stole a pear. Wanted to see what all the fuss was about."

Riyong cannot understand what that means, but I do, and I sigh. I know Margo meant to do that out of the goodness of her heart, but I am beginning to see there is no small amount of pride to be reserved for the Kachin people, and they do not have much left to spare. Whatever else they offer us, I plan to accept. I know how difficult it can be, to receive help and have nothing to give in return.

"Where are the others?" I ask, pointedly changing the topic.

Septimus reaches into his pocket to toss me a mandarin. He knows the prospect of fresh fruit after spending so much time on the open water is too tempting to pass up.

"They have already gone inside. The Kachin saw Vásan's wound and decided something had to be done. About him and poor Nissa, actually. But I stuck around to wait for you," he adds, and levers himself off the wall again.

At least that means they have a way of paying back Margo for this generosity.

"Ah. I know where they will have gone," Riyong says. "Please. Follow me."

He takes us down an attempt at a stone path, though the ground is uneven beneath them, up to the left-most building. The step is so high, I'm concerned for Riyong's ability, at first, but he manages. We climb up onto the wood after him, and allow him to slide open the door to bid us entry. Almost thoughtlessly, Riyong discards his shoes, and I hasten to mimic him before following. Septimus takes a bit longer to do the same, before catching up.

We pad in stocking feet across the wood, to a room on the left, separated by more doors of a sliding fashion. It is clear there have been no industrial changes made, here, compared to the modernity Bonxhui was known for. This return to culture was not a choice, yet here the Kachin are, easily slipping back into roots most of them likely were not even fully aware of having.

Riyong knocks a warning, then slides open another door, and has us step over the lip inside. Margo and Castel are both seated on the floor, before a table. Margo is eating what appears to be soup, rice, and fish while Castel drearily peels and cores an apple with long knife strokes. There are several Kachin citizens, here, likely those who have offered to continue attending to Queen Mi-Sun. There are four, total: two needling physicians and their assistants. Two for Nissa, and two for Vásan.

It is strange to see the grand prince and princess this way, for a multitude of reasons each. Margo is watching with mild amusement, but I find the imagery of the pair of them, both laying on soft mats on the floor, practically a breach of their privacy. I have seen Vásan undressed to the waist before, on the boat, mainly when Xerian saw to his wound, but never laying down, with his back exposed. He appears vulnerable, and clearly does not like it.

A needle goes in at a certain point near the back of his ear, and I see him barely keep from flinching. It is only one of several needles I see sticking up.

Vásan hisses and curses, fists clenching.

"You do not needle often, do you?" Riyong notes, likely half-translating a muttered comment from the Kachin man leaning over Vásan's back.

"Never," Vásan says, gritting his teeth.

"And you are rather resistant to it," Riyong adds, before turning to where Nissa is, sounding rather pleased with her own needling scenario.

She has just about fallen asleep.

I doubt she has been needled before much, either, but whatever points they are targeting, it is rejuvenating her. Vásan's is evidently more painful. I wonder just how deep this therapy intends to go; certainly, there is something obvious to fix, for Vásan, but from what I can see of the targeted points, I am not certain they are all related to his physical injury.

Out of respect for what is clearly an uncomfortable experience for him, I ignore Vásan and let Riyong settle Septimus and I at the table, with Margo and Castel. He bows again before leaving us, claiming he intends to find Daeyeon and see if the queen may summon us presently.

Though I am not particularly hungry, now, I eat, and eat well. The Kachin style used for their culinary offerings, here, are simple, but somehow all the more delicious for that. There is a mild familiarity in it, as I have had similar dishes before, adapted for Kachin-Isaarian citizens of my own country.

It makes me think of Rian, again. I hope he is doing well.

Perhaps a half hour later, the needling physicians are finished, allowing Nissa and Vásan to join us. The former is decidedly loose-limbed, and more relaxed than I have ever seen her before, her shoulders no longer clenched. It changes her figure entirely, and when she slides down to sit cross-legged next to me, she seems mildly intoxicated.

"I like this," Nissa says with a mild smile. "I think I will like to have this done again," she goes on. "This is wonderous."

"You've never been needled before?" I cannot help but ask outright.

She shakes her head. "No reason to, I would say. I am never sick. Never injured. Or, not ever until now. But I do not imagine you have ever been sick much, either," she notes.

I consider this. "My…If you remember Taris Qurvo, he had the talent and knowledge for it. And it does more than simply heal what is most obvious in terms of…physical affliction."

This appears to be enough of an explanation. No one asks much more about it, and luckily, no one prickles Vásan about his experience. Unlike Nissa, he appears miserable, and though he is a difficult man to read, I suspect a mild headache, given his reactions in the following minutes. He is undoubtedly pleased to be properly dressed again, and deigns to join us, but has no appetite.

He does not say much at all to anyone, remaining absent from the light conversation that goes on around him. That is unlike him; I have never seen Vásan so lost in thought before. He is generally so acutely aware of everyone else's comments and opinions.

It startles him uncharacteristically when the door slides open again, though I cannot tell if anyone else has noticed him flinch.

It is not Jin Riyong who has come to retrieve us, but Yu Daeyeon. He bows to us, and after he straightens, he stiffly steps to the side and gestures to the doorway. It is obvious where he plans to take us, but he reiterates all the same, as if for propriety alone:

"The queen will see you now."

Eighteen

THE MAIN BUILDING has what one may consider a throne room, though it evidently has none of the magnificence one should associate with such words. An attempt has been made, and a fair one at that, and similar endeavors have been put into acquiring clothing and accessories worthy of Park Mi-Sun. However, while it is hardly a shoddy effort, no mockery of what once was, and there are clearly numerous Kachin citizens left willing to serve their queen, the absence of true royal adornments is notable for those of us who know what to compare it all to.

So, I suppose, all of us.

It is the stateliness of Park Mi-Sun that carries true weight, here. She makes this room, her clothing, these replacements, what they ought to be. I find I am relieved to notice Riyong standing at the side of her chair, pushed away a pace by the arranged folds of her clothing; for some reason, this queen is intimidating even to me. I realize it is because we have something to ask of her, and I cannot image what Septimus plans to do if she refuses us.

Park Mi-Sun herself is pretty and perhaps a few years older than Riyong, but still seems young to me. I am beginning to wonder, if, after Septimus unlocked what memories of mine he did, everyone will forever seem young.

Most startling about her, however, is her hair. I had heard that Park Mi-Sun was touched by magic in her blood, same as her cousin Shinya, and that her hair was a flaming red, but it is different seeing it for myself. If her fluke had not intervened within the bloodline, she would have had black or dark brown hair like all other Kachin. Instead, just as Shinya's eyes are blue not brown, Mi-Sun's hair is a vibrant red.

Toddling about near Queen Mi-Sun's skirts, playing with some cloth toy, is a small child, perhaps only midway through its second year. A boy.

The child bears a startlingly strong resemblance to Riyong.

I do not say anything. Neither does anyone else.

Once we have mimicked Yu Daeyeon in bowing, he announces us each by name and title—something I suppose Septimus or Riyong must have informed him of, as I do not recall doing so. Afterwards, the Kachin queen speaks first. She wastes no time in looking us over, as if attempting to intimidate us.

"You have come here to ask me to lend you Riyong, and the item Anna Wolff left to his safekeeping," she says openly. "Do you understand, precisely, what it is you are asking?"

Septimus is about to step forward, his mouth already open to parlay, but she goes on, indiscriminately interrupting him. I do not believe my cousin is used to someone not letting him talk his way out of something.

"No, you cannot," she says. "No one could, without seeing the Wolffs' lantern for themselves, and what it does. It is not meant for just any one. Even with Miss Wolff there to use it, it took Riyong's sight. Did you know? Did you guess? Or did he tell you, perhaps," she muses. "He did not happen to say."

There is a pause, then, and Septimus takes quick advantage of it.

"I am certain, though, your majesty, that Jin Riyong did, at least, inform you of why this request happens to be so important. Or, as it was implied, perhaps you had someone else who may have made certain…predictions?"

She allows her face to give nothing away, appraising Septimus thoughtfully.

"You know Anna Wolff died here," she finally says. "Her father made claims, though, before he left us. Claims that coincided with what a friend of ours once said in his precognitive mutterings. I know some of what you intend to do. I do not know how, but I know what claims have been made: that you have a Magicsmith you intend to send to the Otherworld to change everything. To give humanity one more chance. Perhaps the magic in her blood will allow her the safe passage Miss Wolff could not secure for Riyong."

She sounds dubious. I glance at Septimus, but he is looking at her, listening with courteous focus. If he notices my gaze, he is pretending not to.

"I will not deny that Kacha would benefit from this potential…opportunity. We were doomed long before we fell to the appearances of the rest of the world. Our government was weak already after our war with Tourran. My brother Bogun was paranoid. My father, too," Mi-Sun says calmly. "Then, when the military failed to protect the Kachin people, they had no means with which to protect themselves. I knew this was wrong, yet I did nothing to stop them, or to help, because I thought it was not my place. That someone else would manage it all, like my little brother Chimhwi. As if he had not already done enough. Suffered enough."

Mi-Sun does an excellent job playing queen, but her last sentence betrays her. Her voice nearly cracks. She was not raised to hide her emotions, and that is never more evident than when she mentions her brothers.

I have seen Chimhwi and Bogun's tombs, both. Whatever they attempted, and whatever they may have done wrong even without the Greys and their Anomaly's interference, I think it is clear they failed to live up to their sister's grand expectations. She blames herself, now, for not thinking to help them.

"Now, I am queen of a country I do not know how to govern," Mi-Sun continues. "I would like to believe that the goal you wish to obtain is possible, as a redemption for Kacha. And for myself. I know, now, that I will have to work to protect Kacha. That it cannot be left to someone else. I would like one more chance to do things right."

Her tone is too even for it to be a confession, but I realize after a moment that is what this is. She is overcorrecting.

"I will allow Riyong to help you," she says, surprising me. "And I will have a ship prepared, to take you back to your own country when you are finished."

"Thank you," Septimus says. "Your hospitality is greatly appreciated."

"It is not hospitality," Queen Mi-Sun says plainly. "I expect you to fix this world, so that we may even begin to stand a chance against our own mistakes. Consider that the necessary payment required."

She is still severe, still fixing us with a warning. Then she stands, and all those in the room stand with her. Even Riyong bows, and stays bowed, until she leaves. Her long sleeves sweep the floor, as do her skirts. Two attendants, though she surely should have more, follow her with their heads down. Mi-Sun stops only to address her son in Kachin, her tone light and endearing, before she scoops him into her arms. She leaves with him, her final instructions called back to Riyong, in Kachin.

The moment Mi-Sun leaves the room, all others rise and sweep out of various exists, eventually leaving only my own party, and Riyong. Even Daeyeon is gone, so suddenly that I realize our exchange with the Kachin queen was only a matter of minutes long, and none of us did much talking at all. I realize Mi-Sun must never have intended for this to be a negotiation. She was aware we would be here one day, has prepared herself, and said her piece. She decided a long time ago she would allow us to do whatever we thought necessary, perhaps so her son could one day grow up in a world with his uncles still in it. Now, I would not be surprised if she decided to avoid us for the rest of our time here.

We are a means to an end for her. Nothing more than that.

Riyong approaches us again, giving us no visible confirmation whether he knew his queen would react this way. Nissa, most especially, is apprehensive of what has happened, as I am certain she thought our convincing of Queen Mi-Sun went far too easily. I would agree; only, I believe Park Mi-Sun is what she says she is: a young woman who was unprepared to be a queen, let alone one in these circumstances.

I understand wanting redemption for what appear to be crimes of omission.

"I have given this much thought," Riyong says to us. "We cannot do this here; we shall have to do it in the old Munusuan temple."

Margo frowns. "I thought this was the 'old Munusuan temple'? Didn't you say that? It was adapted?"

"Ah, yes," Riyong confirms. "But there is an older one. Smaller. I'm sure you must have seen it. There were many old temples, out this way, back from when Bonxhui was not the capital city of Kacha, and our people lived far apart, mainly all in poverty. They were useful to keep around, for tourism."

"So, we go there to…?" Margo says.

"To send Miss Soleil to the Otherworld," Riyong says. "We will need to be quite some distance from the refugees, you see. I will explain everything. Miss Soleil, for your part, you will need to spend three days in the temple. Sit for these three days, eat nothing, drink nothing but water," Riyong tells me. "I will come by frequently. When it is time…I will send you to the Otherworld."

Vásan appears displeased. "Is this not happening rather quickly, then?" he asks, as suspicious about this as Nissa. Though, admittedly, he sounds tired, nearly to the point of apathy.

Riyong dips his head. "I do not mean any offense, Grand Prince Pike, but I do not think you understand how long we have waited, knowing you would one day arrive. From our perspective, I suppose, there is no reason to wait. What would we do, in the interim?"

"Spend a day in friendly chat, perhaps," Septimus says dryly, and turns to Riyong. "Please, continue. I understand the need for doing things quickly."

Riyong nods.

"We will begin tomorrow, then. On the third day, I will light the lantern over her, and we will send Miss Soleil to the Otherworld. We will need someone to protect her body while she is away, as Anna and her father once did for me. I fear I no longer trust myself to be capable," Riyong says.

"I can do so," Septimus offers gruffly, a hand now on the hilt of his sword. "I have some skill with a blade, and it is sufficient for killing monsters."

I know from experience that he speaks truthfully.

"I will as well," Margo volunteers. "And Cas."

Castel does nothing to indicate whether he agrees to doing this or not, but I suspect he will. Strangely, I trust him and Margo both to help protect me.

Riyong nods again, then turns to Nissa and Vásan's general direction.

"I will need the two of you to help me," he says, before either of them can insist they, too, are willing to fight whatever monsters come our way. "Depending on how long she is in the Otherworld, it will likely become a strain, holding up the lantern. You may need to help me keep my arms raised."

"Oh," Nissa says, shocked by the concept. "Is that all?"

"It is more than it sounds," Riyong reassures us. "In the meantime, I would have you get good rest, if you please," he insists. "I will need you to have all your strength, to help me, when needed."

He summons someone to take us to a room, in Mi-Sun's palace, to share. But I hover back, and when Riyong notices this, I try to keep my voice down as I make my inquiry.

"Is there any reason why I cannot go to the temple tonight?" I ask. "I'm sure that will move things along quicker by at least twelve hours, shouldn't it?"

Riyong hesitates, surprised, but agrees. "It would, yes. Though I do not know if any of your companions could—"

"I will stay with her," Vásan is quick to say. Ears like a bat, him.

"I do not know if that is reasonable," Riyong says. "I will stay with her, sir. But thank you. We will see you in the morning."

"Vásan, go," I insist, when he still hesitates, lingering. "Look after Nissa, please. She has had a difficult time, of late."

He agrees to go with the others, but does not appear entirely pleased with the fact he is leaving me alone with Jin Riyong. Even if Riyong is blind, he is significantly bigger than me.

"I do not see any reason why Vásan couldn't stay with me," I start.

My tone is low enough this time; I am positive Vásan cannot hear me. But Riyong interrupts, insistent.

"They gave him points for trauma, in the needling. Physical and otherwise," he says, with an honesty that reveals more than Vásan would like. "He would like to sleep, I'm sure, and he should need it. If he went to stay with you, it would likely make things difficult for recovery."

I make it clear to my companions where I am going and why, hand over my belongings to Nissa's safe keeping, and then leave, again, with Jin Riyong.

He takes me out of the facility, nodding his reassurances to the guards outside. They have changed shifts, I see. We do not speak as he leads me through the little town, where the streets have emptied and folk have begun to tuck themselves away for the night. From there, it is back to the fields, with the tall grass that the winter wind insists on using to tickle my arms. Instead of angling towards the towering ruins of Bonxhui, Riyong takes me towards that smaller, open temple, where I suppose we will be spending the night.

The temple is mainly open to the elements, given its partial paneling in wall choice. There are stairs first leading up and then, once under the roof, down again to the main floor, which itself is cracked and aged. But there is little dust to speak of, no piles of dead leaves or other debris. So, I suppose someone must clean it, from time to time. There are no monks, here, and no Theebin priests, either, but someone still cares.

Riyong finds a place in the middle of the room and folds his legs beneath him. I do the same, leaning myself up against a pillar. I have many questions, and wish to partake in some conversation, but I suspect Riyong is weary. He traveled twice as far as the rest of us, today, after all. He leans back, closes his eyes, and waits.

I am not certain how long Riyong sits with me, before Margo comes to interrupt us. Perhaps an hour, perhaps more. I wonder if he was meditating, the way Nusk always attempted to make me. Regardless, when Margo arrives, he is not asleep, and appears to hear her approach before I do. His eyes snap open. He rises and he reaches for his sword, before seeing her standing up at the top of the steps. She is carrying a stack of cloth that could be blankets, or coats, and has her own strange weapon swinging from her side.

"I thought you may be cold," she says, descending the steps, "and asked if I might have something to remedy that. Your people have been most accommodating."

Riyong releases the hilt of his blade. I cannot help but want to see how well he may still wield it, without his sight.

"I apologize," he says, and bows to Margo. "For not having thought of that in the first place. I am not cold, but I did not consider Miss Soleil. And now, you have had to come all this way, interrupting your own rest…"

"I'm not tired," Margo reassures. "I will stay up with her, Jin Riyong. You may return to your queen for the night."

Riyong is stunned, for a moment, and then has the good sense to duck his head to try and hide his embarrassment. So, Margo noticed as well, then. At this point, I wonder how common that knowledge is, or if it is merely Kachin politeness keeping people from speaking of it even if most of them know.

"Watching over Soleil is what we will be doing over the next few days, anyway," Margo adds.

This appeases Riyong. I suspect he has little desire to stay now that there is an opportunity for us to ask questions about him and Mi-Sun. He gathers himself, bows, and bids me a good night before departing. There is an awkwardness he leaves in his wake, stemming from him, though it does not take much work to extend it naturally to myself and Margo. While I would say we are used to one another, now, I have not been exceptionally courteous to her, nor have I apologized.

There is a halting nature, in how she offers me a coat to cover myself with and in how I thank her. She seats herself relatively close to me, but far enough away that she is not invading my private sphere.

Riyong had been sitting closer.

Margo truly does not appear tired, as she is content to munch on a bag of nuts she must have taken from Kang and Aisling's. The nuts do not look like anything I have seen before. She cracks them in the palm of her hand eats away at them before dusting the remnants of the shells back into her bag.

"The time will likely pass faster if you try to sleep it away," she says wryly after some time of my absently watching her. "Three days will begin to feel unreasonably lengthy, otherwise."

I shake my head. "I am not tired. I will stay up, for now."

She chuckles and shakes her own head. "Stubborn. Well, I shouldn't be surprised. It is a family trait."

"You knew my father, didn't you?" I guess.

"Mmm, Gabriel, yes," Margo says, cracking another nut. "Good man. I'm sorry he passed away when he did…Unless you meant Khas Qurvo?"

I do not say anything immediately because it occurs to me that I'm not sure who I meant when I said that. Either of them? Both?

"I…" I start, trying to decide on what to say. "I suppose I meant Nusk, yes. I did not know my birth father, much, anyway. I did not have the chance to."

Margo nods to herself, knowing more of the story than I ever could.

"Olivia knew her time in Isaaria was limited. She had struck a bargain with my family, to go there to seek a husband, and to perform reconnaissance for 'the Greys'. But she wanted to find a place to keep her children safe, as well. She had to leave you and Lune, I'm afraid. Or else risk you falling into… ha, well, unsavory hands, I suppose."

Considering what has happened to Septimus and Teresa, I know this is an accurate statement. Yet even if my parents had no choice, it still hurts to know they willingly left me and Lune. After all, even when they chose to have children, my parents knew they would need to abandon us.

I consider how many people close to me were acquainted with one another, with relationships I knew nothing at all about. Septimus, Lune, Nusk, Taris, my own parents. They knew Margo. Lune knew Castel. I think they were friends after a fashion. Even Mercer knew the Greys.

"I get the feeling," I say slowly, "based on what I know of them both, that Nusk and Septimus would not have made good partners."

Margo laughs. "Oh. No, I suppose they did not," she agrees, grinning.

I realize that the awkwardness between us is suddenly gone. In our mutual acquaintances, we share something.

"Nusk loathed taking any sort of order from that pale little brat," she muses. "But Sep was the only one with the power to remember everything. And Nusk wanted what was best for you. In his own way."

"In his own way," I repeat plainly, and the sudden mirth fades. She must think about her words; what they mean, for me.

"Nusk was an interesting man, with ideas of his own," Margo sighs. "I won't say if he was good, or bad, or even 'right' in what he did. But I know he loved you, and his children, and could not stand the idea of you all growing up and leaving him, only to suffer in your own lives. It hurt him, watching you hurt. I think part of him wished he could take on that pain for you."

"Is that why he did…what he did?" I ask.

Now that I have the opportunity to try and understand the man who raised me, I do not want to let it pass me by.

"I'm afraid I couldn't tell you," Margo says. "I don't know why Nusk volunteered his children and trained them in the Milashi Living Shield concept. Why didn't he simply inform the Yakaramis of what he knew, his experience, and leave it to them to find a *Khashtani* for their son? Why did he insist on breaking away from Septimus' plans? Why did he—"

"Why did he love me more than Taris?" I interrupt.

Margo falls silent. I do not know if she would know, how she could, but the idea has been haunting the back of my mind for some time, now.

"He loved me more than Taris," I babble. "The more I think about it, the more I believe it's true."

"I wouldn't know," Margo says slowly, but not dismissively.

"I've done much reflection, in the past weeks," I say. "I'm sure Taris had plenty of time to do the same. If I could put it together, I'm sure he has, too. I do not know if it happened the first time Nusk raised me, or the second, but definitely by the third: he loved me more than Taris. I do not know about Naomi and Korvaan, but more than Taris. Yes. I know that. I do not know how to feel, knowing that he knew that. For potentially hundreds of years, Taris knew that."

Margo listens to this patiently. It occurs to me, briefly, that somehow, she is the only person I could possibly reveal this to, and expect a decent reply. Rian would not know what to say other than reassure me of things he could not know. Septimus is too blasé about feelings for me to trust anything he says when it comes to something so emotionally based.

But Margo is a Grey. She knows.

"It is hard to see the flaws in people we admire," she says sympathetically. "People who we know care about us. And who we care about in turn. I will say this, I suppose: good or bad, Nusk was a man, plain and simple. He will be judged in the Otherworld for the things he has done, same as everyone else, and we will have to let the Almighty decide what was in his heart. We simply cannot know."

"Just as you cannot know what is in the heart of Kryto?" I point out.

Margo is not at all offended.

"I won't make excuses for my family," she says. "I am aware of the deplorable things many of them have done, particularly my brothers, and my nephews and nieces. Amerson. Kryto. Jarrod. Nexa. Lysandra is gone, now, but she was no angel. I know my brothers raised their children in a rather twisted way, and it made them close to monsters. But…" she says, and sighs.

"When they were young, they were full of potential. Amerson was so determined to prove himself to his father, to all of us, to be worthy of the family name. Kryto was so sweet. I cannot describe how he doted on Septimus, and Teresa; I do not think you could believe how innocent it once was. Jarrod always greeting people, even strangers, with a smile, and his… well. I still remember thinking about how much life they had ahead of them. All the things they could do for the world."

I think about how much I want my own son, and have imagined what good he would do for the world. But I suppose that is merely a wish, on my part. I cannot know what sort of person he will become. Once he is grown, he will be his own man. How much, then, are children the products of their parents over society? Over the world they grow up in?

Margo may have tried to be a good influence on her nieces and nephews. It may not have mattered.

"Before Mwakil Rajak, and the curse my family brought down upon itself there, the Grey family usually was a force for good in the world," she reminds me. "With some exception, I know, given Kang's experience. Still: I find myself hoping that, one day, we might be that force for good again."

I do not tell her that I do not know if that's possible. I cannot. If I can hope for redemption for myself and the people I care about, then I cannot deny Margo the same thing. Maybe, in some way, when I return us to our former lives with Fate's influence and wisdom, they could be. So, Margo still clinging to that hope, the way I hope I can save Lune and Taris, is not entirely unreasonable.

From then on, we understand one another better.

THE DAYS PASS AND THE SKY REMAINS GRAY. Riyong brings water regularly but does not stay for conversation. Margo and Castel often stand guard and, occasionally, I hear the murmurs of their distant conversation. Castel refuses to speak to me much, but Margo will, to pass the time. I ask her if she has a way of looking in on Rian and Ayla—some old fluke that could be useful—but she regrettably does not.

Septimus stays close by, but rarely speaks and appears caught up in his own mind. This leaves me with little to do to distract myself from my own thoughts without Margo about to help. I attempt some meditation, but it is difficult, with such a dull, bleak sky.

I never realized how much I enjoyed the sun and moon until now.

It somehow startles me, when the time finally comes for me to leave this world. It is when Riyong arrives with a red silk bag that I realize the three days must be over in their entirety. Despite Margo's warnings about time passing slowly, I find that has only partially been the case, for me. Some part of me is terrified of being sent to the Otherworld, of what I may find there, of what I may be told. I wonder if it is wise, to go where no Smith has gone before, in hopes that Fate will take pity on me and tell me what it is we are meant to do. After all, only the Wolffs were truly meant to traverse the Otherworld while still alive. I do understand why Septimus would think to do this, and why it is our best option. If we are not meant to win this fight, better to know from the mouth of an angel than to simply make assumptions and let the world as we know it perish.

If only it could have been someone else, chosen for this.

If Septimus, Vásan, Nissa and I never made it out of Isaaria, it would be only Margo, Castel, and Xerian here, now. I wonder which of them was meant to be sent in my place, as my surrogate. Margo, I suppose, is the one most likely to survive the process, as a Grey. That is, assuming it worked at all.

When Riyong arrives, it is with Vásan and Nissa, while Septimus and Margo stand official guard around the outside of the temple. I do not see Castel, but likely he is resting, prepared to take his own shift sometime later.

Kneeling close to me, Riyong pulls from his bag a set of three, fat white candles that smell of sweet beeswax. One is housed in a copper lantern. He has me lay down and places the two extra candles on either side of my head, going about fixing them in place and lighting them as he speaks.

"I will tell you, now, what Anna once told me," he says. "There are only a few ways to enter the Otherworld. In Samioth, there are precious gateways, where one might pass between, but they are hidden, secret, and protected. Otherwise, one might enter from anywhere in the world, so long as they have this lantern. The last of its kind. Meant to help the Wolffs protect that veil from wherever they are."

"But all the Wolffs are dead, now," I blurt nervously.

"Yes," Riyong agrees. "Yet I have gone to the Otherworld and back. I survived it. I am certain someone like you, a Smith, will fare even better. So, I will hold the lantern above you, and when you fall asleep, you will wake up in the Otherworld. From there, I'm afraid, I have no advice for you."

I nearly protest: out of everyone, Riyong is the only one who knows what I may encounter. But I suspect his own journey in the Otherworld was quite different. If he was sent there to attempt and save his friends from the Dark, he would have had to venture to its lowest, cruelest depths. I, meanwhile, will be sent to one of its middle tiers, to speak with angels in a realm of light.

"With the lantern lit, monsters of all sorts will try to run to it," Riyong continues, "to widen the opening in the Otherworld they feel. To kill a Wolff or two as well. So, it is necessary that we protect your body, while your spirit is gone from here. If you are away for long, I will need your companions to help me hold my arms up," he reminds me. "The Almighty might have gifted this to the Wolffs, through his angels, but it is still a heavy burden, holding any small portion of God's power."

He hesitates, then lights the last candle, in the lantern, and shuts it. Nissa is watching him intently, awed. Vásan purposefully does not watch.

"When it is time for you to return, you must look for my flame, and follow the light out," Riyong instructs. "Know to look for it—remember to look for it—and you will see it, no matter where you are. Follow the flame back to our world, and do not look back."

The warning in these last words is so strong, I cannot help but inquire.

"What would happen if I do? Even if on accident?"

"You will turn to salt," he warns. "And cease to exist on this plane. I do not know what will happen to your soul."

Riyong lifts the lantern over me.

"If I succeed, you will have another chance to save the ones you love," I remind him.

He does not appear convinced, and his lack of optimism worries me.

"We shall see," he murmurs.

I want to say something more to him, but do not. Instead, I force myself to close my eyes, wondering in practical embarrassment how long it might take me to fall asleep. I am admittedly drowsier than usual, so deprived of nutrients this body is, but I feel too jittery for rest. Undoubtedly, the longer it takes me, the more of an opportunity Riyong's arms will have to grow tired.

To my surprise, there is no effort put into sleep on my part. Before I know it, caught up in these thoughts as I am, I have drifted off. Or, have I? It is not a natural sleep. I never feel as if I truly lose consciousness, though my eyes are closed, and there is a weightless, almost nonsensical feeling to everything that makes me feel as if I am a visitor in someone else's dream.

I am in a dark void, where there is no exact dimensions of a floor or walls or ceiling, yet I feel as if I am in the tunnel of a cave. Underground? Hewn into a mountain? I could not say. If there are rocks, there is a young woman seated on one of them, jutting out from the wall, her back to me. One of her legs is pulled up to her chest, and the other dangles down. She looks as if she is sitting here as sentry, and the moment she feels me arrive, she leaps down.

She is furious. I am shocked by how much of a resemblance the Kachin people managed when they captured the undoubted likeness of Anna Wolff in stone.

"Fate-dammit, Jin Riyong!" she bellows. "I told you not to—!"

She stops upon seeing me and stares, blinking. She stops to brush back a lose strand of wavy hair, to tuck it behind an ear. It immediately swings free again. I am struck by the scars on her face. They are not unlike my own cousin's scars, but I cannot tell, precisely, if they are magic-sickness scars like Teresa's. Her statue did not have them.

"Oh," she finally says. "You are not Riyong..."

"Ah, no. I am not," I admit. "Though I gather from what you were saying that I probably should not be here."

She looks me over and sighs. "Are you a Grey, or a Smith?"

"Smith."

"At least there is that. Are you here on Jin Riyong's behalf to try and resurrect Park Chimhwi and company?"

"No?"

"Then it is just as well," she says. "I didn't want Riyong getting himself or anyone else killed over something that was never his fault in the first place."

I frown. "What wasn't his fault?"

She gestures wildly. "This. All his friends dying. My dying. I know he still blames himself for all that, for me especially, which is damned foolish. I made my own choices. I stayed behind so he could get Mi-Sun and the baby out safely, which was a feat in and of itself, as he was newly blind. What did he think he was going to do to help, hmm?"

I shrug. I do not know what answers she expects from me. She does, I will admit, have the best Alarkian of anyone I have heard, of late. I cannot tell if she is an Alarkian, herself, but she has the accent of one.

"...Well, regardless of what he blames himself for, Riyong still followed your wishes," I say. "He did not use the lantern to attempt a rescue. Only to send me here. I'm Soleil."

"Smith."

"Marson, technically. Actually, technically, Yakarami," I correct.

"Wonderful. I am Anna Wolff," she introduces.

"I thought you lost an arm," I say.

I have noted that, although there is a rather unavoidable stain on the Tourrannese *kundah* she is wearing, presumably from the wound that killed her, she still has both her arms.

"Yes. But now that I am dead, I do not think the Otherworld cares about what happened to my body on that side. With one exception."

I nod absently. I suppose that makes a vague sense. Not to me, but maybe to the rules of the Otherworld. It occurs to me I know only a little of said rules to begin with. After all, Rian always was the more religious one, and even he will freely admit that many of the base tenants of his own religion are things beyond human comprehension, that believers such as himself simply must accept. But there is one rule that I think I know, and Anna Wolff's being here breaks that.

"If you are dead, why aren't you...That is, how can you be...?"

"Here? Instead of the Death having sent me on my way up the mountain to atone before paradise? He can't. We're all stuck," she says bluntly. "I am sure Fate will explain things to you. Come along, now."

"But Riyong said—"

"Riyong only knows what I told him about the Otherworld. Trust me, we all know why you're here. We have been waiting. Fate-knows Septimus has done his best, but even if it is no one's fault, it is damned annoying to have waited so long. Come, now," she says, and gestures for me to follow her before walking off into the nothing.

I am struck speechless by her bluntness and quick manner. It is as if she does not understand that, while this is routine and known to her, I have never been in the Otherworld before. Yet, apparently, she has been sitting in wait here for at least several years, to presumedly keep Riyong out, and escort me in, once I finally arrived. So, whatever is wrong with Fate's loom, his eighty strings at least have recorded my coming here.

I follow Anna Wolff.

I do not know how long we walk, genuinely. Time does not appear to work here the same way it does in Samioth. It occurs to me just how aware of time I usually am, and how I fill it, even with merely my own thoughts. Now, I do not have time to think. We could have walked for the span of an entire day, or it could have been ten seconds.

There is a lightness to me. Though I look like myself, I know that my body is not here. This means we cannot truly be walking, but we are certainly headed someplace. Space, as well, is evidently not the same in the Otherworld as it is in Samioth. I suspect there are concepts presented here merely to help us humans keep our sanity when we arrive in the Otherworld, so we know how to think of it: the concept of the Otherworld's six main levels, its mountain, and so on.

It is not shapeless, but it is not an idea I can fully form.

Anna leads me out of the dark void to a bright one instead, the light adjusting slowly as if we are truly leaving a cave and headed to sunlight. The light is too clean to be from the sun, and once we have exited, and I turn back, there is no cave, no passageway at all. I do not know how to explain where we have come from. Yet here we are, in what appears to suddenly be the courtyard of an ancient civilization. It looks, to me, like an ancient Isaarian civilization, given its architectural style and how nature is interspersed throughout, though I am sure it is not really Isaarian. While there are trees planted in rows and gardens, fountains and waterfalls splashing into aqueducts and open waterways, there is no visible true nature as far as the eye can see. It is all purely civilization. For miles and miles, climbing up all around us.

It is not entirely white, my surroundings, but it is bright, and clean.

This, I realize, must be the void of the angels. I cannot remember its proper name, but it is meant to reside somehow in the same location as Mt.

Poranya, the place we are meant to climb for redemption for ills done in life. It is not above it or below it or beside it, but everywhere all at once.

This is one of the concepts that confused me, when I tried to listen to the classes Rian took on his own religion.

In the courtyard, there are no birds visible, yet there is an illusion, almost, of birds singing, like a ringing in my ears. It makes this place feel peaceful, though I could not identify a tune to it, or even truly hear it.

Most shockingly, though, is the fact I have now found myself in the presence of angels. There are only two, here, now, mainly because even they must know that if there were more, I may lose my mind.

I find I can recognize them almost immediately.

The Death sits balanced on a blackened stone, smooth and atop nothing but air. He wears both black and white at once, his hair changing from one hue to the other and back, as well. I cannot determine the distinct features of his face, but I must subliminally know enough to refer to the Death as a him and not an it. There is a masculine presence to him, and although I know angels do not have a sex the same as humans do, I understand they have chosen to appear to me in these forms as not to terrify me.

He holds a staff across his lap.

Second, there is Fate, just as promised by Anna. His is also a male presence. He is sitting at his loom, which is somehow size-less. It changes. When I first see it, it is huge, enormously so. Then, immediately, I see it is not. It is the normal size of a loom I may have seen at some point in life. I somehow know it has its eighty strings. When Fate notices we are here, or at least appears to notice from a human perspective, he stands and folds his hands into his long sleeves. I suppose his coloring in skin tone, hair, and eyes is somehow clean. It is only later that I realize his coloring mimicked my own. He looked almost like a male version of myself.

"Miss Marson-Smith-Yakarami," he says, as if my surname is something of a joke that I share with him.

"...You are Fate," I manage to say, still taken aback.

"My apologies if Miss Wolff eschewed her manners," he says with a smile. "She had some less-than-pleasant experiences in the course of her death and no doubt would appreciate some retribution."

"I..." I start, and then, looking around, realize that Anna Wolff is gone.

I do not know where she went. I know she could hardly cease to exist, but she has other things to do. I suppose. I am not sure. What would one do, in the Otherworld, if they were forced to sit here in wait? I'm still confused as to how she could be here. I know the Wolffs received special permission in life to traverse the Otherworld, but now that Anna is dead, shouldn't she be climbing the mountain, just like anyone else after death?

"Come sit with me," Fate suggests, and gestures back to his loom where, I see, there are now two seats. One behind it, and one off to the side.

I follow him back to it, feeling like a child next to him. Are he and the Death enormously tall, or am I the size of a child in their presence? I do not know; perhaps it is both. I allow Fate to seat himself back at his loom and perch on the edge of my own seat, wondering why it is I cannot tell what it has made out of. Stone? Wood? It is not comfortable or uncomfortable. I cannot truly feel it. But it does what it ought.

"You knew I was going to come here," I finally say, and watch him continue to weave with an absent deftness. "Are you weaving my being here right *now?"*

Fate laughs. "It does not work quite the way you would think," he says. "But for what I cannot reasonably know, the Almighty does, and I record all that is meant to be recorded. There is much happening in the world at any given point in time, after all. If you think of it in human terms, how could I possibly record it all at my loom, all at the same time? Even if I could, if I ever stood from my loom, then time would be lost, wouldn't it?"

I try to think about this. I am confused.

"But…You know why I'm here?" I say. "You…I do not even need to explain things, do I? Because have you not already woven the conversations I've had, and know them in precise detail?"

"That is correct, in the way it makes sense to you," Fate says. "But yes, I know why you are here. I knew it would be you, coming. It did not have to be. But it is. And it was always going to be."

Which, I suppose, means I am wrong and right at the same time. Regardless, I am relieved I do not need to explain myself. I'm not even sure what I would say, and what I would ask.

"Even as you sit here," Fate continues, "hopeful as can be, deep down you believe that I am going to tell you that there is nothing to be done. That, in fact, the world is meant to end now and that all you have done in so many timelines has been for nothing. A limbo. A stall."

I force myself to swallow out of nervous habit, though I do not actually have anything stuck in my throat.

"That is what I fear," I confess.

"I know. I know your many fears and doubts. At least you still have the courage to think you can hope. But still. Soleil," Fate chides. Yes, I decide, I am a child in his presence. "Do you really think the Almighty would bestow such a gift upon you without already knowing how and why and when you would use it? Could you, Girl of Sun, truly be that foolhardy?"

"We haven't been…winning, so far, I suppose," I say in defense of myself. "From my perspective, and Septimus', we keep losing. Over and over. And from my perspective, in particular, it feels as if we have done it all for nothing.

The Greys have gotten closer to their own goals than we ever have. It is as if we are fighting a losing battle against the Dark and…we cannot win."

At mention of the Dark, Fate's weaving becomes less certain, and he must stop, as the thread has temporarily tangled in a part. I do not know if this is coincidence or not, but somehow, I do not feel as if it is taboo to mention the Dark here. Somehow, where it would feel uncomfortable in Samioth, I know it could not have any power here.

"The Dark in the world does so try to have its way with things," Fate muses, untangling his threads with long, nimble fingers. "It does its best to tangle my threads, thwart and trick the Death—stealing souls, killing Peace and destroying Hope…Banishing Faith and perverting Love. It is a troublesome trickster for humans to face.

"It has pawns of its own, I'm afraid," Fate confirms. "Monsters and demons, temptations and lies. Even the demon on your back, dear Soleil, has gotten the better of you at times."

I cannot help but reach to grab over my own shoulder, and check, but cannot see any demon, there. I wonder, then, if it is gone because I am in the Otherworld, and what, precisely, it focuses on with me. Fear, I realize, must be a factor. Selfishness, another.

"Unfortunately," Fate continues, "the Dark is also good at gathering human souls to do its work for it, getting the better of them. Some of them, because they want to reject what is known to be good. Others, out of a twisted desire to do what they think is right. It is startlingly easy to fool a human being," he adds, though I can tell he does not say so to mock me. He is lamenting souls lost. "You must continually choose to do good, to be selfless, be controlled, and that is a weighty task for anyone to bear over and over, for as long as they have."

"The world is…not doing that well, lately," I say quietly.

"No indeed," Fate says. "And I must tell you, little Soleil, the world will never be at full peace. Not until the end of days. But do not fret. Your fight is not for nothing. Fighting to do what is right, even knowing you may surely fail, never is."

"So, we can win, then?" I ask, hopeful.

Fate smiles and stops his weaving again to look at me.

"In the way that you think of it, yes," he says. "But it is a difficult thing to come to realize, knowing that you could not do it without the help of divinity. Not divine intervention, precisely, but you needed to come and ask for help nonetheless. That has been a difficult ask for you and Septimus both. It is very human, to want to fix things all by yourself."

I have to nod. That does sound like me. I hate having things out of my control. I suppose that, too, is universally human.

"Taris, Mercer, and Lune have all been the same," Fate admits.

I perk up. "Are they here?" I blurt. Anna Wolff was here, after all. "Can I see them?"

Fate sighs. "I am afraid not. They are in the Otherworld, but they are not here. You see, though there will always be good and evil in your world, fighting, until the end of days, something has happened, now, that never has before and was not meant to. It can be undone. But it is meant to be undone by you, little Sunchild. So here you are. To help me fix my loom. And that means you must retrieve your family from the Dark, as it has taken them, though it should not have, and has no right to."

"How did the Dark take them?" I demand, horrified by the idea of my little sister suffering in hell. "If they die, shouldn't the Death take them someplace else? They were good people. Or…or they were good enough!"

I am prepared to argue on that point, but Fate does not fight me. So, I suppose, whenever Lune, Taris, and Mercer are meant to die, in the proper timeline, they will get a chance to climb to paradise.

"They did die," Fate agrees with a frown, looking over his loom. "But they are not meant to so soon. Look here, where the thread is broken," he says, and shows me.

From what I can see, there are many broken parts, the closer we get to what I assume is present time. It keeps snapping, keeps tangling, yet Fate cannot always fix it. He must keep recording. In fact, I realize, if he could fix it, it would negate the free will we have. So, it does make some sense, that it would have to be me to come here if we wanted anything to change.

"It is not their fate to die, when they did die," Fate explains. "It was not Anna's, to die when she did. In fact, there are many here, now, who cannot be sent on. Because of how time works here, and how you are not living the proper lives you were meant to. The Death has done what he can, to collect them all, still, and allow them to wait, here. But things were different, with those three. The Death could not collect them. The Dark took them instead."

I frown. "I do not understand. The Death does not simply collect their souls over and over and then that work is undone when I reset the timeline?"

Fate shakes his head. "The Otherworld does not exist the same way Samioth does. Time is not a forward progression, but exists all at once. For example, we cannot control what mankind does, but I do know everything that will happen, has happened, is happening, all the time. It is both ongoing, started, and completed. When you start over, that is already something meant to happen. Therefore, the Death could not possibly collect souls and begin them on their journey through the Otherworld, or else, when you reset your timeline, they would not exist in Samioth any longer. Those souls would still be journeying up the mountain. So, here they wait, to be released and collected over again, until a final timeline."

"Then how can Lune and Taris and Mercer still exist if the Dark has them?" I ask, frowning.

"Because there is no progression in the Dark's portion of the Otherworld. Nothing but eternal misery. Their souls have nowhere to journey to in the Otherworld, so no progression is made. It is stalled. When the timeline of Samioth exists around it, they are both forever trapped there with the Dark and simultaneously living repetitive lives in which they can only become more miserable. There is no healing for them in Samioth, no matter what they do.

"It is difficult to explain, but in a way, by taking them that first time they died and keeping them when they should not be in its prison with other souls, the Dark has perpetually doomed them. For example, the reason Septimus cannot stop Mercer from betraying and helping attempt to kill Rian no matter what he tries is because that path is now set. Mercer must make himself a traitor so that the Dark can come to collect his soul. This is a flaw in the workings of the world itself; the Dark has subverted free will. Hence, my weaving is broken."

I consider this, applying it to my own memories: how Lune can never heal from her lost children and spirals instead, willing to die for us not merely out of selfless sacrifice, but because she no longer cares much to live. How Taris' anger festers and corrupts all of him, beneath the facade of the man I know he truly is; the good man he is capable of being.

How, in Mercer's travel journal, he cannot feel at all accomplished for the many lives he has saved. He is too burdened by those he could not, and that allows the Greys to trick him into thinking it would be better to live in a world with no suffering at all: accomplished by the most horrific of means.

It makes some sense to me, but it does stretch my intellectual capabilities, considering it.

"Are there other people the Death cannot collect?" I challenge. "People who were not meant to die at the times they did, this timeline?"

"Many," Fate says. "All who have passed on cannot progress because you are meant to turn back time at least once more."

"But the Dark only took Lune and Taris and Mercer. Out of millions of other souls," I say. It is part statement, part bewildered question.

"It would like to take them all," Fate admits. "But you are the only person in the world with your abilities, and Lune, Mercer and Taris are close to you. The Dark stretched its meager faculties in even taking them. The only reason it could take them at all is because we could not interfere. But we have done our best to collect all other souls and at least hold onto them in stasis through every timeline, like Miss Wolff here. It dooms them as well, admittedly, but... We cannot possibly release them and set things back until the Dark releases its hold on the three it stole. Otherwise, your timelines will never act in accordance to my loom. As they ought."

I consider this, chewing on my lip. It had never been a bad habit before, but this entire process has strained me nearly to my breaking point. While I feel as if I am beginning to understand some of what Fate says, this is an entirely new language to learn, and I only know a few words in it.

At least this somewhat explains how others continue to die at the same time, perhaps prematurely, perhaps not. Asmer, Crispin Carsans, Rian's parents and grandmother, and even Nusk all come to mind. Perhaps in our final loop, they will still die at the same times some way or another. Nusk's death, at least according to Rian's experience, has always been set. Or perhaps it is all part of this broken web that has only seemed like Fate's design because Rian and I did not know any better.

"Little Sunchild," Fate says, and places a hand on my head. "You are here because, for your part, you are meant to be. You will fix this, I am certain, though you may not feel as if you can, because the Almighty would like you to. The Dark took who it did to prevent you from success, because it would like you to fail. It loathes humankind. But you can succeed. If you choose to."

I sigh. I wish I could have that confidence in myself, but even hearing it from Fate himself, I cannot. I do not know what to do, despite Fate claiming I apparently do, and can. All I feel is lost.

"What broke things? In the first place? What even gave the Death the ability to interfere so directly at all?" I ask.

I want to put things together in a way that makes sense to me, in a timely fashion. Something I have some small power over.

Fate does not hesitate in telling me. This is a question that it was only a matter of time before I asked.

"The nine deaths of the Alarkian ambassador's daughter. Louisa Erikson. The first of the Seven Eyes of the Death."

I blink. "Nine deaths...? Wait, Rian is one of those. An Eye."

"He is the sixth," Fate agrees. "Louisa Erikson is the first. She has a hidden fluke of nine lives and she died all nine at once by witchcraft. That was not meant to happen. The Greys saw to it so it did."

"First. Sixth. What determines the numbering? Age?" I ask.

"Immortal concepts."

I suppose that means I would not understand, or if I could, it would take much too long to explain it. It is not of significant importance to me.

"But that means we can stop the war," I say. I do not think I can feel lightheaded without a body, but my relief brings something similar. "If Louisa Erikson is not meant to be dead, then there is a chance...We can and are meant to stop the war between Lijimata and Alarkia. We can fix everything..."

He has already said I can. This is reassurance merely for myself.

"No one can fix everything," Fate corrects. "But there are things you can fix, Soleil, with the power given to you. Same as any other soul, with the uniqueness in them. Do not hold yourself to the standard of fixing the world. Of saving it, all, with that responsibility weighing on you. But it starts with saving who you can, when you can. For some, that may mean the lives of ten. For others, the lives of ten thousand. Both are worthy pursuits. So that is the reason you are here. Not for the world. For Taris, and Mercer, and Lune."

This confuses me further. It sounds and feels contradictory. But it also makes my portion in this simpler. It feels manageable.

"So, I…I am here to save them," I say. "And. And that will fix things. To the extent that I can fix them."

The world will hardly be a perfect place, with Taris, Mercer, and Lune back in it, allowed to still live and change and grow and faulter. Perhaps they will still suffer, will still make mistakes, will still experience hardships. However, I would rather they have those experiences than not live at all.

"Yes. You must go and get them back," Fate says. "Bring them here, and the Death will look after them. Once you are ready, re-set your timeline, and the Death will release all the souls back into Samioth, where they will stay until it is truly their time to go. So long as that anomaly is no longer set in stone, things will not be broken in that manner."

"Why can't I just reset the timeline and try to fix things in Samioth?" I ask. "If I just…keep them alive, won't that be enough?"

"I'm afraid not. Because the Dark already took them. As the Otherworld technically exists outside of space and time on Samioth, so long as he has them now, he always has them. I need you to retrieve them and bring them back to me, so that when you reset your timeline on Samioth, you will have freed them. The Dark will win, in some fights, in tempting you to do what is wrong. But you, and many others in Samioth, will not be doomed unrightfully to make the same mistakes, no matter how hard you fight against it. That would not be fair. That is not how things are meant to work. So, this truly will be the last time. You will start over. And things will be correct."

"So, I reset the entire universe?" I ask in horror.

Fate smiles at me as if I am an endearing child.

"I do not expect you to fully understand," he says. "But no, not quite. You simultaneously destroy and create a new timeline for the universe, yes, but you work only with time, not space. There are no multiple, branching timelines with multiple versions of yourselves existing simultaneously, only the one. You can manipulate that one, but things that are meant to exist will exist. Events via the passage of time can be changed. How things happen can be changed. But anything related to space and essence: they do and will and will always exist all at the same time according to the Otherworld. It is only a matter of when they appear on Samioth and when they leave that changes the world you know."

I think that makes some sense, but I cannot be sure. Does this mean that my previous worries regarding Alo Pike are no longer my responsibility? He will always exist one way or another, because I have no effect on that? Does that also, potentially, mean that Damen and Aiden might exist one day, and simply won't be Kryto Grey's sons? I would find the idea reassuring except Fate's explanation has only raised a thousand more questions.

"Ugh. You are even worse than Septimus," I groan.

My head aches from trying to comprehend it all. I felt as if I'd had some grasp on the situation, but now it's gone again.

My commentary brings a mild smile to Fate's façade.

"Septimus is a clever boy," he murmurs. "But even he is only human. In the end, he is the very complication in the equation he is trying to root out."

"What do you mean?"

Fate's smile widens. "Well, without Septimus, you would never have been able to get to this point. That said, in your final 'timeline', Septimus cannot remember all this. That is not the way he is meant to live his life. So, when the time comes, you will rewind things back to as far as you can remember. Your earliest memory. I will make sure Septimus knows he ought not remember any of this, and that he will not. So that things will be right."

This saddens me. It means, then, that it is less likely I will see Septimus again in a timely fashion. But I do not dare stop, now, to try and parcel out facts and fiction regarding my cousins' fates. I need to do what I came here to do; what I can do. While Fate has reassured me time does not work in linear fashion, here, it feels as if it does, for me.

I am anxious to see my little sister. I want to have the opportunity to tell her all the many things I was not able to, before.

I want Lune.

"Right," I say, and I stand, determined. "I'm ready. I will go save them. Right now. What do I have to do?"

Fate stands, too, but laughs at me. It is not cruelly, at least. I would not say he is amused by me, perhaps only touched by my determination. He puts a hand on my head, again, to ruffle my hair. I am struck by a memory of Nusk doing so, once, when I was little.

"Always so determined. A fine quality in you, little Soleil. Let me see you off. We do not dare send you through the Dark's domain itself to reach it," he says as he begins to walk. I follow at his side. I find I've involuntarily grabbed onto his sleeve, like I would one of my parents', and I am vaguely aware of the Death shadowing us in a strangely comforting way. "Jin Riyong attempted that, and it did not end well for him or those he intended to rescue," Fate says.

I frown, remembering Riyong's overbearing melancholy and blindness.

"His friends are there," I remember, and then look up to Fate. "Shouldn't I save them, too? How are they there if the Dark did not take them?"

"The Dark took Lune, Taris and Mercer because it thinks they have done things that deserve its category of punishment, and they agree. Jin Riyong's friends are there because they thought they deserved to be there, but they have done nothing to warrant that. They could leave if they wanted. They simply do not know how."

"So, they were tricked. The Dark does not really have them, but they don't know that," I say. "So, I should save them, too—"

"Because the Dark has no claim on them, when you start again, Jin Riyong and Miss Wolff will get a second chance to save them. You should leave it to those whose destinies are to do so," Fate says, almost gently.

I'm about to argue, but consider that Anna Wolff is meant to be able to traverse the Otherworld. It is part of her birthright, the way being a Magicsmith is mine. If an immortal being is telling me I would stand no chance in the Dark's realm on my own, I should probably listen.

"What about Castel?" I ask.

"What about him?" Fate asks gently.

"He told me he has had to watch the woman he loves…die. I know it was done in a horrible way, by the Greys, I think. Can I do something about that, at least? Fix it?" I ask. "I don't think I can stand by and do nothing."

That applies, I suppose, to the Pikes as well, but it is easier to ask in regards to Castel and his love—people who live far away from me who it would be harder to help—than Yvette.

"Nor am I asking you to, necessarily," Fate says. "If you learn of possible tragedy and find a way to prevent it, by all means, Soleil you should strive to do the right thing. But do not try to insert yourself into situations where you do not belong. It is not your job to solve the problems between Alarkia and Lijimi, Tourran and Kacha, entire empires and world orders. Do what you can. But do not allow your ambitions to make you blind."

I was hoping for a more direct answer, but I suppose Fate wants me to make my own decisions. For now, then, this means saving Taris, Mercer, and Lune. That is something I know is right and just, and something I hope I can accomplish.

"So how am I to do this?" I ask.

"The Death has tunnels within the fabric of the Otherworld," Fate says. "He will allow you to use one so that you may reach the Dark's layer directly. From there, you must find a way to trick it into giving you those souls back. Do not make a deal with it," Fate warns me. "But find a way so it believes it is getting the better end of whatever deal you pretend to propose."

"You will not let me traverse his realm but you'll send me directly to him? It? Whatever the Dark is?" I challenge.

"The Dark has no claim on you, so it cannot keep you there. It is a weak, scuttling little insect compared to true divinity. But, you are only human. Like the friends of Jin Riyong, the longer you are in that realm, the more it will try to convince you that every small sin ever committed in your life is reason enough for you to suffer forever. It has no power, but you and your choices do. We do not intend to give that guilt a chance to work on you."

I want to nod and let these angels send me on my way, but I am already feeling some guilt. Riyong's own guilty conscience and Castel's perpetual mourning were practically oppressive to behold, and I want to do something to help.

"What if...What if in the final timeline, the final time we do everything, Riyong and Anna do not save his friends? And Castel's beloved still dies? What if they cannot save them, the way they could not this past time?" I ask.

"Then there is nothing to be done," Fate says.

I bristle. I feel that this is horribly unjust and unfair. I want to fight against it, if only because I feel guilty. I have been given such an opportunity, when others never will.

"You would let people die and damn a dozen innocent souls to suffer—" I accuse.

"I would not," Fate interrupts. "But we angels cannot influence the minds of men. If they believe they deserve suffering, they will suffer. If they can somehow find a way out of that imaginary obligation...Well, they will have half of eternity to do so."

"Are you telling me that Riyong is destined to fail? Mi-Sun is destined to rule in her brothers' steads after they die?"

Fate nearly smiles again. He knows I am fishing for answers; tempting him to reveal to me what is meant to later be strung across his loom.

"Perhaps. That, it seems, will be up to them and all those involved, when the time is right. You must choose your own fate, same as Riyong and his friends. Would you travel easternly without prompting, leaving your husband and children behind, to insert yourself in a conflict you know little about?"

"Well, it would be wrong not to do something. Wouldn't it?" I say.

"Is it not also wrong to assume you are the only person in the world who could possibly fix all these tragedies?" Fate muses. "You do have a unique fluke, little Sunchild. It is well suited to your destiny. But you are not the only person in the world whose flukes have been given to them for a purpose. The Almighty casts his gaze equally on all of you. Even if that is difficult for you to comprehend."

"Why me, then?" I insist, almost whining. "Why am I the one who has to go and face the Dark?"

"Everyone faces the Dark, if not so directly," Fate chides me. "Besides, Soleil, is it that you must do it, or you are lucky to receive such an opportunity? It seems to me you are succumbing to guilt already, when you have not done anything wrong. Take heart. Even if you are not a perfect person, it seems to me you do strive to atone for your mistakes. You want to be a better person. That is enough."

I realize, at this point, that I am now holding Fate's hand. The feeling of it is the same sort of feeling I have on rare occasion when something makes me want to cry. But I do not let go, and I let Fate walk along with me, leading me. I know he is about to see me off, very soon, and I begin to feel nervous. Perhaps I do not want to go about this so quickly after all.

"What happens if I do accidentally make a deal with the Dark?" I ask, nervous. I try not to think of how all of reality itself rests of my decisions.

"You cannot make a deal on accident," Fate reassures me. "Intent matters. You must willingly trade your soul for something."

I nod to myself. It is a relief to know I cannot accidentally sell myself away, and yet, I am apprehensive about the road ahead of me. I can already feel that I am not meant to be here, and cannot imagine what it will feel like to traverse the Dark's domain. Part of me would like to think that, if Jin Riyong could do it without Wolff blood, I can, too.

Only, Riyong was hardly successful. He lost his sight. He failed to do any of what he set out to accomplish.

"Why can't you go instead?" I ask Fate. That would make all this much easier for me, and likely would have much less risk.

"Well, because, my dear, none of us are meant to do it. You humans must remember to fight for one another. You must remember to do your best to save every soul you can. This is yet another fight for mankind to bear. Angels cannot aid you in this, at least not in physical, obvious ways."

I tighten my grip on Fate's hand. We are leaving the courtyard, now, I think, going to someplace not unlike the tunnel Anna Wolff took me through. We are going to the Dark's realm. Or, I am.

Fate stops walking, so I do, too.

"I'm scared," I say.

"That's all right," he says. "Do you still want to go?"

I consider this, then nod.

"Then do not be afraid. Shall I tell you a secret?"

I nod again, and Fate leans down to my level.

"Do you know why I am called 'Fate', and 'Love' is 'Love', and 'Peace', 'Peace', but the Death and the Dark are so titled? Because the Dark is temporary. It will be destroyed, one day. And the Death is also temporary—for all mortal men die, but they will live again, and eternally. But Fate and Faith, Peace and Hope, Courage, and Love: these things will last forever."

I look at his face and know that I do not need to be afraid. I will feel fear, going into the Dark's domain, as it is a frightening place. But I am not going completely alone. Even if the angels cannot come with me, there is nowhere the Almighty cannot go.

Fate smiles and pats my head one last time.

"Go on, now," he tells me, like he is sending me on my way to play with other children. "I will see you soon. And you can introduce me to Lune."

"I would like that," I say.

"I would, too," Fate agrees.

I'm still afraid, when I decide to go with the Death, but I know that Fate truly believes that I will be back, soon, with my sister. He did not tell me he had woven it, and he did not say that it was predetermined. But I know that, whatever he is in essence, he believes it. So that will be enough to sustain me.

The Death waits for me to join him, and then walks ahead, bringing me with him into a dark tunnel until we leave the light behind.

Nineteen

THE DEATH DOES NOT hold my hand in the reassuring way that Fate does, but I still find some comfort in walking with him. His presence is a different form of relief in his inevitability. I know, walking with him, that one day I will walk with him again. He will come to bring me into the Otherworld, and when that happens, I will remain here in some form or another for the rest of eternity.

Though the concept would undoubtedly terrify me, back on Samioth, here, I find a certain ease in it.

The Death and I walk for a longer stretch than I did with Anna Wolff, and though I still could not say what precisely that length of time was or what it means, I am aware. Eventually, the Death's passage does begin to resemble a place I might find somewhere on Samioth. It is a rock tunnel, though I am unsure whether I see it this way because it was what I first imagined or not. I can feel a chill coming from the dimly lit chamber ahead; there is a blueness to its light, as well, in a harsh manner.

Several paces back from the opening to this new place, the Death stops, turns to me and waits. It is clear that, from here, I must go alone. I realize I am aware of how terrifying the Dark's domain ahead feels. There is something about it that makes me instinctively want to turn and run. For a moment, I almost do. I consider it. All that prevents this is the sudden reminder, from the back of my mind, that I promised Fate he could meet Lune.

I cannot return without her.

So, I take a deep breath, and go forward. I thank the Death for his guidance as I pass him, and though I do not know if he heard me, at first, he gives me a slow nod. He does not reach out to touch me or ruffle my hair like Fate, but even in that nod, I feel a parental approval.

The opening turns into a cave, complete with stalactites and stalagmites, as natural as they might be on Samioth. Otherwise, the place is an impossibility. It looks to be made from ice crystals, or perhaps sort of a mineral variety. I can see my breath in front of me. I am still breathing out of habit even if I do not need to without a body in this world. It is cold. Yet, when I reach out to touch one of the stalactites, it burns my hand, red hot.

I climb down a slope, further into the cave, where the passage becomes narrower. I become aware of distant sounds, of a horrendous variety. Some of the sounds are human, and too distressingly distinct for me not to imagine what they mean, but others are inhuman shrieks and caws and wails, and those make the hair on the back of my neck stand straight up. I shudder, and press onward. My stomach knots. I am becoming aware of a headache pressing painfully at my skull.

I keep my hands out as the passage grows darker, and I struggle to keep my balance down the slope. Though I have never once in my life felt a fear of enclosed spaces, I now understand how those who suffer from it might feel. There is a part of me that screams, still, to turn back. To run away. I try to recite things in my head to keep at bay my imagination, which wants to insist on picturing what is happening above me. First, it is songs, then summaries of Rian's stories at his most whimsical. And then, even prayers.

At this point, I do not think I have the right to say I don't believe anymore.

There is hardly some brilliant flash of light. No visible divine intervention from the Almighty on my behalf. Not even a comforting warmth. But I do continue on without turning back. So perhaps that was something I could not have done on my own.

There is very little light, now, even compared to when I first entered these caves. One of my hands brushes against something gauzy, and sticky, and I pull it back as whatever it was flitters away, like some kind of wraith. It moans, and then gives off a screech, later, behind me. The ground beneath me feels less like rock and more like something too soft. Too pliable.

The passage opens into a chamber, and I somehow know I have reached my destination. Ahead of me, against what should be the far wall of this cave's chamber, is a darkness. It is somehow not an empty void, but something physical. It is not a wall itself, merely; it is a thing. I have no other way to describe it. It is both the Dark and not the Dark, entire, that I sought. When it finally speaks to me, the sound does not come from any one direction. It is ancient and evil and everywhere around me. Though I know I could likely still turn back and run, at this point, I am aware of the oppressing feeling that it is an impossibility. I push it aside as best I can.

It feels as if something, someone's fingers, are constantly brushing lightly against the back of my neck, beneath my braid. It is an effort not to try to slap it away.

"Ahhhhhh," the Dark croaks. "And here is So-laaaaay. Why have you brought no light with you, little Sunchild?"

Its voice is male in its deepness, its rumbling nature. But it does morph, over our conversation, occasionally becoming a higher, more affable, friendly tone.

"I'm not here for a social visit," I make myself say. I clench my fists tight. "I'm sure you know why I've come. Where are they?"

"Ah, and who would that be?"

Though there is no throne before me, and no visible figure of the dark, I somehow still see and know that he has built one for himself, and is levering himself—itself—out of it. It comes to prowl around the chamber floor before me, which is still both the cold cave it has been and the marble of a throne room floor I might have been familiar with in Samioth.

I clench my fists so tightly that my nails dig into my palms. Fate told me I must trick the Dark, but I am not one for immense cleverness. I plan, only, to tempt it as it might me. I will make my demands, and make the Dark believe it may as well humor me; it will believe that I, like Jin Riyong, will fail. Only, unlike Riyong, I may trap myself in this hell, in my failure. The Dark would like nothing more than that.

"Lune!" I snap. "Lune Marson, my sister. Taris Qurvo. Her…her husband. My brother. And Mercer Ralhan. My husband's best friend. Where are they?"

The Dark laughs. It is both decidedly mocking, but also tempting in how friendly it sounds. As if we know one another well enough to share jokes of an intimate variety. That idea, the concept of the Dark knowing me well, does terrify me. Because what does it mean for who I am? And what I've done?

I try to reassure myself: the heart pounding in my chest is an illusion. The fear I feel cannot be real. I have made no promises to the Dark; I can still leave this place.

"I'm afraid you cannot simply waltz into my territory, take what you like, and leave," the Dark chides me. I picture it strolling about the chamber, arms clasped behind its back. "Isn't that…Oh, what would you call it…Stealing?"

I bristle. "You stole them to begin with!" I say, feeling my anger begin to burn brighter than my fear. "You have no right—!"

"Ah, but stealing them back does not somehow negate your thievery. Thieving from a thief does not, truly, make what you are doing any better, does it? I would say not," the Dark goes on, lecturing. It, too, is treating me like a child. But there is nothing comforting in it. "It is only a justification your kind uses because you like to picture yourselves always in the right. You humans all think yourselves as the heroes. Even the child-killers."

I don't want to listen to him, because I know what he's doing. It. This is a tactic, to stall, to try and get me to eventually believe that I, too, deserve to be here in punishment. The Dark wants me to believe that even the power of the Almighty would not be enough to redeem what things I've done wrong in life.

But it has no right to keep them, I remind myself. No right.

"Release my sister!" I demand.

There is a rumbling laugh, starting low, and then growing louder, more mocking, more entertained by itself.

"You cannot make a deal with the Dark," it breathes somehow in my ear, followed by a tickling, scuttling noise that startles me by coming from behind me and around to my left. "Not unless you want to damn yourself."

I tighten my jaw. "I'm not making a deal. I'm giving an order: give me back the souls of my sister, her husband, and Mercer Ralhan, and I will bother you no further."

"You cannot have them, I'm afraid," the Dark warns me, somehow still behind me, strolling in front of me, and still that dark writhing, scuttling mass. "They are traitors. I have claim on them. They belong to me."

I glare in the general direction of the voice. "Mercer didn't know what he was doing. And Taris and Lune are not traitors—"

"Oh? It's amusing you truly believe that," it interrupts. "How have they not betrayed you? They swore they would do whatever it took to keep your family safe, yet, over and over, choose to jeopardize that for selfish reasons. For their own sakes. And they know that. They choose that. Repeatedly."

I tighten my jaw. I am aware that Taris and Lune's motives may be confusing. I cannot fully understand them myself. But I do know some things:

"When they made that promise, they couldn't have known what they were sacrificing," I say. "None of us did. They could not have guessed they were promising to give up their lives not just once, but many lifetimes over again. They were expected to treat every cycle as if it could be the last one, with results they would have to live with forever. If they wanted to have something for themselves amidst all the struggle Rian and I put them through, I cannot begrudge them that."

"That is sickeningly sweet," the Dark says, mocking me. "That you are willing to give them that benefit: the assumption of their best intentions. But here is the truth, little Soleil: if they are here, it is because their intentions evidently were not the best, were they? They were not so good and selfless as you would imagine. And they have not asked for forgiveness, have they? No. They have too much pride for that."

"They didn't have the chance to," I insist.

I realize, then, that I do not even know what Taris or Lune would ask for forgiveness for. Not from me, at least. How could they possibly be here at all, after willingly giving their lives for me? Is that sacrifice, somehow, not enough? What else could they have given?

"And they won't get it," the Dark says casually. As if it entirely controls that. "I'm afraid I've grown tired of seeing you piddly little things go about the world, so easily convinced to commit atrocities, and rarely even receiving the proper punishment for it. Your Almighty, so-called, might care enough for you to be willing to sacrifice for and forgive quite literally the worst parts of humanity. But I will not."

"You don't have that power," I make myself say.

But I do not know that.

"Oh? Don't I?"

I feel the Dark's presence move. I am suddenly imagining it not in some sort of threatening, though at least human, form. It is something larger. Something indescribable and monstrous and scuttling. Huge. Crawling on the walls and the ceiling, prepared to surround me and devour me completely. Easily.

"When I am released, humankind will reach levels of agony previously unknown," the Dark hisses. "You humans will suffer in horrific, distressing ways. Disgusting, torturous ways. And you will deserve it."

I cannot help but feel startled, and uncomfortable. A zing goes through my body from head to toe. I would like to think that I am not frightened by much, but it is difficult to keep calm whilst standing in the utter darkness, with voices whispering around me, unfamiliar things scraping by me, kissing against my skin. The unknown is petrifying, and I am terrified to know that there are things beyond my human reckoning.

"People will tear each other apart in my name and not even realize they've done it," the Dark smiles, and I can feel it all around me, trying to get closer to me. "I'm so-oo close now…"

"Stop it," I snap, and the Dark is back to being further out from me, again. A king in his domain. "I'm not here to play games with you. Give me Taris, Lune, and Mercer. Now. Consider this the last time I will ask."

I do not know, really, if that will work. I have nothing to threaten with, that I am aware of, after all. I do not know what I would have done if that did not work. But, it does. The Dark seems displeased that I did not, somehow, give up or forget what I was here for. But I believe that, while no divine assistance has visibly been lent me, I must have some blessings here with me. I know I could not have done this entirely on my own, otherwise.

"…Very well," the Dark says.

He flings something at me that I barely catch, and even when I do, it is heavy enough to nearly pull me forward to the ground. It is Mercer's Alarkian necklace, I realize. Or, really, a semblance of the Anomaly the Greys gave him. It must weigh almost more than I do.

"And there is your lovely little lady, Lune," the Dark says. I know he uses the alliteration, and my associating it with my own husband, to unnerve me.

There is no human gesture involved, precisely, yet he draws my attention to where Lune is collapsed on the floor, as if she has been there this entire time. I cannot run to her, with the weight of the necklace requiring both my hands to carry it, but I do go to her, and kneel by her. I do not bother shaking her—I know she will not wake. But I cannot help but put a hand to her shoulder. I can feel her. That fact prickles tears at the corners of my eyes.

I put the necklace on to counterbalance Lune's weight, and pick her up over my shoulders. I already do not know how I will manage to walk back up that slope so encumbered, but I know I must.

"And Taris?" I demand.

"He is here," the Dark says casually. "Where the little lady of Leitfeld goes, he will follow. However. You cannot put her down and you cannot look back," the Dark says, so smugly that I am certain there is more to this challenge than what it is claiming.

There must be a caveat. I know I should ask what it is, yet, I know that this is my only chance to save Lune. I'm afraid that if I ask another question, I will reach the Dark's unspoken limit and it will win this game.

"I'll never put her down," I say, accepting the challenge.

Now that I have Lune back, I will not let her down again.

The Dark smiles. I feel it.

"We will see," it says.

And it lets me leave. It has no power to keep me here, but I must remind myself of that, over and over, as I dare turn my back on it and begin to walk out again. It feels as if each step I take is negated by how my feet sink into this fleshy ground. The energy I must expend to successfully move my feet a step further is beyond what I could have imagined.

The idea of how far I walked down here, and how far I still must go, admittedly makes me want to give up already.

I do not. I will not. Time means nothing; I will take as much as I need, but I will escape from this place.

Eventually, I escape the chamber. I am breathing hard, and every particle of the body I do not truly have aches. I must remind myself, constantly, that this is my spirit alone, carrying them. It is not a matter of physicality. Fate entrusted me to this task. Therefore, I must be capable of it, in some way.

And if I am not, dear Almighty, please make it so. Please.

I can feel Taris, walking behind me, a mere shadow slipping in and out of the blackness around. I have no doubt he has managed to retain some semblance of sentience, no matter how small, and I pray that he will follow me out of this hell. As I cannot turn around and look, I may save Lune only to leave the love of her life with the greatest of monsters. But if I do turn around to see him, and therefore somehow trap Taris here forever, I'd be achieving the same effect. Only it would directly be my fault.

So, I do not look, and trust that Taris is still there. Following.

I have made it another hundred paces when I am reminded of the sounds above us, that had been so muted in the Dark's chamber. Those horrific sounds, those things moving in the dark around me, ensuring I know I am not alone. That I know they want me to fail.

I hear a scream, and I know the voice. I have never heard it, but I know what would be the voice of my eldest son, calling for me, a terrified, pleading "Mother!"

I barely catch myself before whirling. I do not know if that makes me a good sister or a terrible mother. Perhaps neither. Perhaps only lucky.

I continue to walk, knowing that the cries I hear, calling out to me, are meant to be the voices of my own children. I do my best to ignore them, until I am sure there are tears streaming down my face. They beg me not to leave them here. I tell myself they are not real; they are only mimics, imaginary. I try to believe that.

I stumble and fall to my knees but do not let Lune touch the ground. I try to block out the sounds around me, and struggle to make it to my feet again. I am already so tired. I cannot imagine how many more steps I have to walk.

So, I tell myself that I will take only a moment. Just a short rest, for a few seconds, so I can convince myself of what I need to believe to make the end of this journey possible. To gather the strength that I need.

I close my eyes.

I AM AWAKE BUT I KEEP MY EYES CLOSED for as long as possible. I am not so tired that I wish to fall back asleep, but it is peaceful to spend the first few minutes of the morning in this manner. I like to think I am doing well to learn meditation and prayer as Nusk has suggested. It will help me grow into my fluke, as it fully manifests and I explore my abilities.

Besides, the palace is quieter at this time of day, before the rest of the nobles have woken. I never did like the way they look at me; I may be betrothed to Rian as the future queen of Isaaria but it is not as if I was born to royalty and they all know that. I think, in the cases of some, they are jealous of my good fortune.

I hear the door open and close quietly. There is movement about the room for a few minutes, then a light figure kneels on the bed to reach me.

"Wake up, Princess; it is time to greet the sun and see to today's business," a friendly, familiar voice soothes as someone shakes my shoulder.

I open my eyes and rub at them as I sit up in bed, trying to recall the fragments of the overly complicated dream I'd just had.

"I wasn't sleeping," I insist as Asmer crawls off the bed and straightens her skirts out with a mild smile. "I was only keeping my eyes closed."

"Of course, Princess," Asmer says as she goes to open the door and bring in the maids to help me dress for the day.

Asmer is younger than me, but somehow acts much older than my twelve and a half. It is almost unfair sometimes; it makes me think, on occasion, that the other nobles would have preferred her to be made a princess over me. I have never said this to her, as I do not wish to ruin our friendship, but it is still a present concern, lingering in the back of my mind. The whispers and disapproving glances that I am sometimes given do nothing to help the fact, nor does my inability to keep my mouth shut when I ought to.

An attendant turns down the bedcovers for me while Asmer picks my clothes for the day. It is considered an honor of sorts, and I have been told that some other young noblewomen are envious of my relationship with Asmer. I suspect they see it as mere favoritism, not friendship.

I will be the first betrothed of Isaaria chosen by the Almighty in over seven-hundred years. Heirs are always chosen by the Almighty via the Carsans' prophecies, yes, but they usually have the luxury of choosing their own spouses. My betrothal to Rian, for the sake of our country, is a rare and historic thing.

Everyone wants to get close to me while they have the opportunity.

Being chosen through divine right ought to be seen merely as a responsibility. For Rian and I, our life's work will be to serve Isaaria to the benefit of her people. But for some members of the nobility, they still cannot escape the wants of the mortal world. They can only think of their worldly futures and how they may benefit from currying favor while they think me young and stupid.

I like Asmer because she sees her assignment to me as an honor, not an opportunity. I know I can trust her to always tell me the truth.

My attendants help me wash, braid my hair and pin it up while Asmer lays out my clothing. She is excellent at choosing items I approve of without me ever saying anything. After I am dressed, Asmer takes a quiet breakfast with me consisting of a warm broth, soft bread, butter and cheese. We discuss the ridiculous difficulty of the assignments my tutors have been giving me lately, as well as all the court gossip Asmer has overheard.

I like to know what opinions about me have been passed around lately.

"Shall we finish your assignments before the tutors arrive this afternoon?" Asmer suggests once we have taken our meal.

"You know I would rather not," I complain.

"They will be disappointed," Asmer says. "But I can always tell them you had a headache this morning and could not complete anything."

I sigh, though I appreciate her willingness to lie on my behalf. "No. I'd best do it and get it over with. I will need to learn it all eventually anyway."

We leave the remnants of breakfast where they are and head off to the study I have been given for my own purposes. It is a lovely nook, and overlooks the gardens of the Pyrian Palace. There is an itch under my skin that makes me long to run outdoors and sit in the morning sunshine, if only for a few minutes, but such luxuries are reserved for after my work is finished. At least Asmer parts the curtains and opens the window for me, so I can feel the fresh air beckon.

Asmer sits across from me with a book, keeping me company. She is borrowing a volume Rian recommended and plans to summarize it for me so I can try and follow his conversation next time we meet. It is not that I would not read it myself, but I haven't the time, and I do not want to disappoint him. He does so love his myths and fairy tales.

I am about half finished when I hear a yelp from outside followed by gales of laughter. I cannot help but glance out the window, over the gardens. Asmer has left to return the book and fetch stationary to write out responses for the many court invitations I have received. They are a formality, really; no one expects me to have the time to attend to all their offers. They only hope that, if a moment in my schedule frees up, I might pick them by chance and give them the opportunity they are so coveting.

Asmer's absence gives me time to take a brief respite. My head is aching, anyway.

I adjourn to the window seat and lean over the sill. I know that laugh. Lune and Taris are meant to be on a run through the gardens during their morning exercises. Only, Lune has decided to trip and let herself go tumbling across the ground. She refuses to rise and Taris has stopped to wait for her.

"Oh, come along, Lune!" he groans in exasperation, and jogs back to crouch before her, trying to pull her to her feet. "Nusk said if Korvaan or Naomi catch us, it's high knees for twenty minutes."

"Leave me," Lune groans dramatically. "I'm tired."

"It's only been half an hour."

"Only?!"

He sighs, but then sits down next to her and waits for someone to come across them to initiate their punishment. After a few seconds, he starts pulling up strands of grass and sprinkling them on Lune's face. She sits up and shoves him. He shoves her back.

Despite this childish behavior from both of them, Taris is the oldest of us, at nearly fourteen. In perhaps a year, he will have to start shaving to keep a clean face. He has started to get tall, too, though he is relatively skinny in youthfulness despite the exercises his father puts him through. I'm certain that will change as time goes on, but for now, he looks too small to be a proper *Khashtani.*

He is fast though, I will admit. His reflexes have kept Rian from accidental injury on enough occasions for people to say the use of a *Khashtani* at all is well-justified. I am not so sure myself. I cannot imagine Taris spending his entire life following Rian and me around.

Another second, and Korvaan runs around the corner, panting as he rushes up and hits Taris on the head as he goes by. Naomi is further back, slower, and utterly exhausted. Even at a distance, I can see in the way her body moves she is relieved to see Taris and Lune both gave in as well.

"You didn't have to smack me," Taris complains as Korvaan continues to slowly jog around them.

Korvaan is too busy basking in the glow of victory to properly lodge the complaint. Soon, Nusk appears rolling around the corner, still on the garden path. I'm sure he could hear them from some distance away, given how easy it is for me to eavesdrop, but he still pretends to be surprised at such a failure.

Taris instantly sobers and rises to his feet, at attention, but Lune remains sprawled in juvenile fashion and merely rolls over at Nusk's approach. Neither of them tries to make excuses. They know Nusk will merely shush them and demand they prove their repentance by doing better, and working harder.

"Up you get, Lune," Nusk croaks, digging for a pocket watch to time them. "Next time, move faster. If Korvaan were an assassin, your principal would be dead already."

Lune groans. "I'm tired! And if Korvaan were an assassin, I'd have turned around and knifed him, then taken a nap."

"Don't be impudent. For a *Khashtani,* exhaustion cannot be a hinderance. You must work through it. Up."

Lune makes a show of dragging herself up, but manages to get into her feet and prepares for twenty minutes of high knees. Naomi and Korvaan meanwhile are both pleased to experience a break while their brother suffers. Cold in a way, perhaps, but Nusk works them all hard. They are to be the best of bodyguards and protectors, after all.

A soft clearing of one's throat alerts me to Asmer's return. As I pull back from the window, she perches on the seat next to me and adjusts her skirts. She knows me too well to call me back to my work immediately; this is not the first time she has caught me watching the future *Khashtani* at practice.

"Perhaps you would enjoy your archery this afternoon if we have a free hour," she suggests. "If we are industrious, I'm certain we can find the time."

It is meant to be a gentle let-down in reminding me I have more to see to through the day first. I do so love my archery, and I am good at it. Many a time, nobles have stopped by to watch me at practice, and politely applaud my efforts. These times are when I am at my most cheerful. Something in me greatly desires activities out-of-doors, with the sun beating down on my head. There is an itch in my bones, and a desire to kick off my shoes to run through the gardens, digging my toes into the dirt with each stride.

"I wish I could learn what Lune does instead of studying politics and such all day," I complain wistfully.

"Miss Lune is meant to be your *Khashtani*, Princess," Asmer reminds me.

She is repeating the words others have lectured me with many times but I cannot bring myself to hate her for it.

"She learns such things out of necessity," Asmer continues, "and it would not be entirely proper for you to take lessons of your own. It might be seen as an insult to Khas Qurvo, as he has given the rest of his life and his children's lives in service to you and the crown prince."

I scrunch up my nose. "Nobody really calls him Khas Qurvo, you know," I say. "His name is Nusk. Even Taris and Naomi and Korvaan call him Nusk."

Asmer shrugs gently. She retrieves her ink pen to continue her writing, but does not lecture me further. She is a dutiful attendant to me, yet bossiness does not suit her, and she knows she cannot force me to do anything I do not want to do. I barely listen to my own tutors let alone someone I consider my friend; someone who is meant to be on my side.

I lever my body back down and lean my arms crossed against the sill, resting my chin on top. Against the floor, my boot toe scuffs the wood as I kick it back and forth. I will watch until Lune and the Qurvos leave, and then I will get back to work. Never mind that there is not much to see, and this is hardly the combat training I would prefer to witness. Anything is better than forcing to stuff my brain full of anymore knowledge: trade routes, treaties, potential diplomatic referrals of the next decade, and the many woes the Isaarian people will expect Rian and I to see to.

I am jealous of Lune; she will never need to memorize all this, nor will she ever have the pressure of the entire world watching her. In fact, she will never need to make any difficult decisions at all. Her life has been mapped out ahead of her entirely. A portion of my maturing brain reminds me that I can hardly know how Lune feels about the matter, but the more childish, selfish side of me insists stubbornly I do not care.

I know Rian is close to his *Khashtani*, but I can barely remember Lune is my birth sister, let alone consider her as such. She, likewise, appears to have no interest in getting to know me better.

Before long, or so it seems to me, Nusk calls time. Taris allows himself to collapse on the grass as if his legs are made of jelly. He pants, his brown cheeks red. Lune leans over, hands on her knees, to catch her breath as well. However, the reprieve lasts only a moment for her before Nusk has her hard at work again.

"Lune, you have got another twenty."

"What?!" she squawks. "But Taris doesn't have to!"

"Taris didn't give Prince Magnus a black eye yesterday," Nusk accuses.

"Oh," Lune grimaces. "That."

"Mmm. So, twenty more minutes. Get started."

Lune gives a pained, somewhat comedic groan of complaint, but starts back into her set: step, step, step in place, knees to her chest as high as she can. Nusk marks the time on his watch, then tosses it to Taris. He orders Naomi and Korvaan back up to follow him as he rolls off to start them on combat practice. They will likely spar their brother and Lune, next.

That leaves only Taris with Lune, to time her and ferry her off to their next portion of training once she has finished her punishment. For some reason, it appears he enjoys keeping her company.

"My feet are going to fall off," she complains.

"Not your legs?" Taris teases.

"No. Just my feet. The bottoms, most especially."

"Well. That is what you deserve for marking up a prince."

"I didn't even leave that much of a bruise," Lune complains. "And Magnus deserved it. It's his own fault, and if Nusk was being fair, he'd know that."

Taris smirks. "What did he do this time?"

Lune huffs and explains breathlessly through her punishment. "He said that I'm so plain, I'd look better as a boy than a girl. I said that's just as well because I could beat him up as good as a boy. And he said I would not dare. So, I did."

"Lune..."

"What! It's his own fault! He deserved it!"

"Yes, he did," Taris says, surprising her by agreeing. "But next time, don't give boys all the credit in defending yourself. It weakens your point, bruises left or no."

Lune considers this.

"I had not thought of that," she admits, which is no surprise. I doubt Lune thinks much of anything.

I sigh. Mention of Prince Magnus is enough of a guilty reminder to force me into retrieving my work and tucking back into it. I see approval flash in Asmer's eyes as she flicks her gaze up from the stationary. Still, I sit back by the window as I continue, affording myself a glimpse at a green summer day and the touch of a light breeze.

Before I know it, Taris' call of time interrupts me. Lune dramatically collapses to the ground. While I do not halt my work completely again, I at least let myself glance over at them between sentences. I watch enough to see Taris stand, give Lune a moment, then nudge her in the side with his toe and order her up.

"Carry me," Lune groans.

Taris sighs, but then bends down and slings Lune over his shoulders like she is a lamb and he, a shepherd. She giggles.

I am jealous of the closeness they share. Once, Taris found it annoying that Lune follows him around everywhere. Now that he is starting to mature, I think he is flattered. He enjoys how much she looks up to him as an example.

Many years later, I still remember that summer day whilst stalking down the halls, angry I am late for my meet with Rian before the evening's ball. It is to be a celebration of our political alliance in the east, with the Kachin and Tourrannese governments. Rian managed the entire affair spectacularly, and I wished to congratulate him privately first. But my lessons and duties as acting crown princess of Isaaria took longer than I thought necessary.

Apparently, my royal tutors think it invaluable for me to learn every precise detail of the Ishtak Empire's trade agreements. Even if those same tutors once instructed me in how every public appearance, ball, and fête can be, and often are, used for great political purposes.

Asmer hustles along behind me, somehow managing to still appear elegant and poised as she does so, despite her shorter legs. She will likely outshine me in her rose dress, as my gold suits me but does not compare to the natural radiance someone like Asmer has. She has been told several times that she should have no trouble finding a man to marry, by those who mean well but have no understanding of what she wants for her life.

She is undoubtedly more beautiful than I am. We could arguably compete in our youths, in the way that children do in their innocence prettiness. However, now that we are much older, she is the flower of Isaarian nobility. Her skin is smooth and soft, her figure ideal, and hair long and luscious. The pointed corners of her inner eyes are longer than most, giving her visage a unique twist.

But it is an illusion, in a way. It is kept a relative secret, but Asmer has a degenerative illness that will take her life early. I, meanwhile, am the peak of health and will likely live even longer than the average woman.

I would never trade my health for her beauty.

We find Rian waiting for us in a wide doorway, hands clasped behind his back, the tails of the ribbons wrapped up his ankles swishing as he fidgets. Qhan Khaleem is with him, a tall, imposing figure newly appointed to Rian's guard. Our *Khashtani* have been asleep for the past few hours, taking their respites at odd times of the day, to always be readily available for public events. They should be joining us soon.

Rian is older than me, at twenty-three, but we have grown up together since I was a small girl. I feel as if I have known him for decades. Mercer has yet another year on him, along with Prince Vásan Pike. Detrus has another year, then, and Magnus is the eldest of the bunch by another six months.

Only Princess Nissa and Prince Yuugo are younger than I am, and I do not see Crispin Carsans enough to care about his status-by-age. He is arrogant and pretends to barely notice me, even if he acts good-humored around Rian. Many of the nobles can be like that; only Mercer appears to genuinely like me and enjoy my company. The rest are polite to Rian, but seem to think I have cheated, somehow, becoming royalty. As if I had any control over what prophecies Crispin's own family divines.

Somehow, even with the fury I stalk about with, Rian finds it in himself to smile when he sees me. I am a bad storm brewing, and he likes dancing in the rain.

"You look ferocious, princess," he says in clear compliment. "And Lady Asmer, beautiful as ever."

"Thank you, your majesty," Asmer says with a curtsey.

"The Carsans will not be pleased about that," I mutter, crossing my arms over myself as we stop before him. "Princesses are not meant to be terrifying and cold. It is too unapproachable."

"But for a queen, it is perfectly suitable," he claims cheerfully. "And a queen is what you shall be, one day."

He always enjoys these charades more than I do. He is talented in making people like him, listen to him, be charmed by him. He can get what he wants with ease because he has made any opposition to him uncomfortable for those who disagree. For my own part, if not for my betrothal to Rian, I have no doubt I would never have a friend as close as Asmer, nor a fiancé at all. I certainly do not get what I want because people like me.

"Are you ready?" he asks.

"Do I look ready?"

"Your necklace is crooked," Rian says. "Here, allow me."

He reaches to straighten it. It is a golden piece with white gemstones to represent the climbing jasmine in the Yakaramis' family crest. At its center dangles a beautiful topaz dragon to finish the crest. It is a clever way around our Isaarian customs, as I cannot rightfully wear the crest official until our marriage, but there is no doubt at all the wedding will take place one day.

Rian smirks at me as the warmth of his ungloved fingers brush against my neck. Asmer notices, narrows her eyes, and clears her throat pointedly.

"Your gloves, your majesty," Qhan says, offering Rian's gloves to him.

Rian smiles. "How could I have possibly forgotten?"

That finally makes me smile, too. He always forgets, I think, so he has an excuse for our skin to touch, if only for a few seconds. It is all rather innocent considering, but still. It feels like a small secret something just for the two of us to share. True intimacy.

"Shall we?" he says, and offers me his arm once he is properly gloved.

"I suppose," I say, and accept.

Asmer trails just behind my elbow with the rest of our escorts, and Qhan walks ahead of us. There is no announcement when we enter the ballroom, though our presentation is still unavoidable. I know Rian understands I hate the concept of heraldry, particularly when it comes to having an entire room stare up at us before we can hide in their mass again. Skipping the process at least allows for fewer immediate stares, and we can descend the staircase to mingle without fanfare.

"How long must we stay?" I ask Rian with gritted teeth and a fake smile.

I cannot abide by how the other Isaarian nobles look at me. The Carsans. The Pikes. The Idos. I suppose Detrus Lundan's future bride, Irina, is somewhat friendly towards me. Otherwise, I have only Asmer.

"Long enough for the easterners to properly enjoy our presence at a party hosted on their behalf," Rian says, almost chiding me.

After all, this party is for the Kachin and Tourrannese nobles, who are both meant to be our allies, jointly. The countries have a close, ripe history with one another, not without its political turmoil and oppressive horrors. However, the marriage of the Kachin king's late sister to the Tourrannese emperor's cousin and their subsequent children were meant to be a symbol of good will and peace moving forward. The Aiko family is here, now, to represent Tourran, while their emperor's family could not be present. The Kachin royal family all came: the king and queen of Kacha along with the three children.

With Rian's prying, I will admit, I do not mind the Aikos or the Parks. I would be amenable to spending more time with the families, if only not in this sort of public setting.

Magnus Oram and his parents have approached to give their respects to Rian, but after I am acknowledged, I let my gaze wander and watch our foreign guests instead. Usually, for Isaarians, we would not have children so young at such a grand event, mingling with the adults. The separation is for their own sake. They would have their own space, where they might engage in conversation with those their own ages, and not feel so intimidated.

Things must be different, for the easterners, because the five Aiko and three Park children are all present. At least, for the Aikos, while the youngest is a boy of eleven, his eldest brother is twelve years his senior; an adult, fully fluent in Alarkian, and able to handle himself.

Meanwhile, the Kachin crown prince, Park Bogun, is but thirteen, and does his best to strike a stately figure. Regardless of his efforts, though, he and his younger siblings still pale in comparison to the Tourrannese ambassador's youngest son, Aiko Shinya, who is two years Bogun's junior. Shinya and his father came here direct from Lijimata, where the Lijimi crown princess was made queen not long ago. The rest of their family met them, here.

While Ambassador Aiko and his four eldest children have found a way to mingle with the crowds, I cannot help but watch Shinya, and how he remains close by his cousins, whose parents have left them to manage on their own. At least, with the Parks, Shinya has familiar faces close by, even if it means allowing Isaarian nobles to stop by them all now and again. They prattle and coo compliments, young and adorable as the children are.

I understand the children, all. As much as they try to act older than their years, I can see that Aiko Shinya, and the three Park siblings would all like to hide. I have felt similarly, at such events. I know what it is like, to be gawked at. To be asked the same, obvious questions repeatedly. At least I have never had to answer in a foreign language. I know Isaarian and Alarkian, but most Isaarians do. At a minimum, the Aikos and Parks all know Kachin and Tourrannese. Isaarian or Alarkian, then, is yet another new expectation.

How taxing.

If only they could hide in the crowd. But even disregarding their small statures, the Kachin princess, Mi-Sun, has red hair, redder than even Nissa Sondushki's. That draws great attention to them even if the Isaarian nobles did not want to pay homage to the young crown prince of Kacha.

Between Mi-Sun and her older brother, it is easy to forget their younger sibling, Chimhwi, the so-called princeling of Kacha. It is a title made up specifically for him. Perhaps that was precisely the point: a verbal reminder. As if we could all somehow forget he is physically half-western with his wider, rounder eyes, smaller face, more pronounced nose bridge and differing skin tone. He is a strangely beautiful child, Otherworldly, but everyone does their best not to say so. His presence is a continual evocation of a disloyalty the Kachin queen likely does not care to recall.

"Want to stop by and relieve them for a moment?" Rian asks me, the Orams having left. My gaze, I suppose, is rather obvious.

"I don't know," I admit. "I would not want to make things worse for them. And given our status, we might."

Rian shrugs. "I like Aiko Shinya. He is a good boy, and rather clever. I think he could manage us."

"I was thinking more of his cousins," I admit. "That youngest one in particular."

I cannot be the only one to have noticed that Park Chimhwi's expression, though on such an adorable little face, has not changed this entire time. I must wonder if there is something wrong with him. I had heard things about him. I simply did not believe them, particularly given how the Kachin phrase their occasionally cruel commentary on the little princeling.

Besides, Chimhwi would not have such a good friend as Jin Riyong if he were entirely the little monster the Kachin public whisper he is.

But then, that confuses me. I do not think I have ever heard of or met someone named Jin Riyong in my life. Nor am I sure how I would know that he might be friends with the bastard prince of Kacha.

How would I know that?

"Ah," Rian says, drawing me back to the present. "Yes, I suppose it might be awkward for them. One little lord-ambassador-to-be, a crown prince, a princess, and…whatever the littlest one is meant to be."

"I think they might be happiest left alone, that's all," I insist. "Otherwise, if we were to approach, they would have to act…different. Even if they would not want to, they'd have to act as if they are on different levels of class. Despite being siblings and cousins…"

I trail off. Why am I so taken with these children, this evening?

There is something strange in this conversation, I think. Something almost wrong and awkward and disjointed about it. I wonder, vaguely, why it is no one else has approached us, yet, when I am standing here, talking with Rian, almost obsessing over the Parks and Aikos. Asmer and Qhan are also strangely quiet. I would expect them both to have an opinion…

"It is rude to speculate," Rian chides, teasing me.

Speculate? Ah. Of course. About Park Chimhwi. Why am I so struck by Park Chimhwi, and his siblings, and his cousin? Do I feel something similar to what I expect he would feel? Me, this fake noblewoman, with no real noble blood. Him, a boy deprived of a proper rank, because he is a bastard child and half-western, whose own father would rather ignore him entirely, even if his siblings love him. I almost feel as if I want to tell him that, dishonored as he is now due to circumstances beyond his control, there are many who would mourn his death. What a morbid, dreadful thought.

I try to push such thoughts away, and find comfort in conversation with my future husband.

"Yet, it is obvious that the second son of Kacha's king is not the queen's," I snort. "Are we truly all going to pretend that a man has not done a disservice to his wife?"

"The Kachin are quite different than we are, culturally speaking. They see their royals in a more forgiving way. They make more allowances."

"Don't excuse it," I say.

"I'm not, I think it's disgusting," Rian says. "But I also know we need an alliance with Kacha. So, perhaps do not be so obvious in staring."

"Yes," comes a new voice. "Staring is so rude, don't you know."

I smile and turn so our newest companion can lean down and kiss my cheek, and then do the same for Asmer.

"Mercer!"

Mercer will fix things. Whatever is wrong with this evening, his being here will put it all right again. I am sure of that.

"What are we gossiping about, then?" he asks me with a grin, despite Rian's eyeroll, and utterance that we are a bad influence on one another.

"The Aiko children, and the Parks," I say.

"Poor little eastern mites," Mercer tisks. "Their lives are going to be Fate-damned for certain. Or, the Aikos and the little Kachin princeling, at least."

"Surely not so bad as to warrant such language," I mutter to him, flashing diplomatic smiles at all nearby who may have caught that statement or whose ears pricked up at the notice of a curse.

Mercer does not heed my attempted deterrent.

"Mmm, worse, likely," he claims. "We Isaarians happen to be quite forward-thinking in this manner, so it is difficult for us to understand, but the concept of *half-breeds* is still strong with our eastern allies. The sins of the father become the sins of the son, and so on."

I cannot help but flick my eyes to the side, considering the half-Kachin Aiko children, and Kacha's half-western princeling. My look of disgust is prevalent enough to color my tone as well as my features.

"You mean, then…that those children…"

"Will be discriminated against all their lives by their own countrymen? Yes," Mercer admits. "But they will be good for foreign alliances because the bloodline is already tainted. Aiko's oldest son is betrothed to a good, well-bred Tourrannese girl, probably for 'family honor' or what have you. But his second-eldest is set to marry some noble girl of the Ishtak Empire to solidify their alliance."

"That is deplorable," I sniff.

Mercer shrugs. "All I'm saying is, I think it is rather telling that any other Kachin bastard would still be considered royal, but not Park Chimhwi. The only thing different about this poor mite they call a 'princeling' is that he is half-western. And he looks it. Never forget that: he is a mixed-blooded half-breed, and it's obvious. They hate that."

"Good thing I'm Isaarian, eh?" Rian jokes lightly, swinging back around into our conversation.

"That's not funny," I say sharply.

I'm offended greatly, and bothered, now. Now that I know how these two prevalent eastern countries treat those of obvious mixed blood, I must reconsider every interaction they have had with my fiancé.

I must wonder if they think less of him because of his mixed blood.

"Evening, Taris," I hear Rian say. We turn again, forgetting the Aikos and the Parks in favor of greeting our *Khashtani*.

"Good evening. Your majesty," Taris says.

He and Lune are here, arrived late, I note. Shouldn't they have been here to escort us in? I suppose, as no one else chides them or makes note of this, it isn't so odd after all. There is still something strange about this evening, though, and I cannot put my finger on it.

Instead, I look my sister up and down, assessing her. I cannot help it.

Lune wears her uniform well. She and Taris are impressive as our *Khashtani*, but she would be more impressive if she were not shorter than her principal and if she did not look so pale, complete with dark circles.

I sigh, but accept her appearance as it is. If she looked as proper a *Khashtani* as Taris did, I imagine our entire entourage would be worth more visually. There is nothing to be done for it, I suppose. At least, once I marry Rian, their uniforms will mirror one another more exactly.

Almost all the Isaarian royals wear their house crests, either in the form of bejeweled pins, embroidered patches, or designed across the sashes that span chests from shoulder to hip. Taris has a patch embroidered for the Yakaramis on his left shoulder, but as I have no crest and no house, Lune's shoulder bears no official crest, only the golden peony of the Carsans, and no griffin to complete it. As the only sure thing among the royals—the only constant—she is employed by them on paper.

They paid the necessary fees for Nusk to raise her, after all. Hardly lavishly, the way one would expect her life to be as my sister, but still. Whatever clothing Lune wears, equipment she uses, and food she eats, it is thanks to the Carsans. The Yakaramis paid for Taris, Naomi, and Korvaan—meeting Nusk gave them the idea of a *Khashtani* and Nusk decided to capitalize on their interest with his own children. But the Carsans, for whatever reason, told our mother they would fund my having a *Khashtani* as well. For my own safety.

My parents agreed, and volunteered their second daughter for the task. After all, I was made royalty, but Lune was not. She had no place in the palace and apparently my parents could not keep her with them. They wanted us together, at least. I suppose they thought that would be a blessing.

"Right then, off we get," Rian says, and begins to make his rounds.

I am pulled with him, my arm still in his, but for some strange reason, I barely speak with anyone. My head feels fuzzy. I feel as if I have been forgetting something. Forgetting it for many, many years, now. That moment, that one thought, about Park Chimhwi, almost made me remember.

What was it?

I feel as if I am reliving something, but with future knowledge.

Lune stifles a tremendous yawn that almost makes her eyes roll back. She pulls at the tight, high collar of her uniform when she thinks no one is looking. Taris must lean down to mutter something to her that makes her snort, smile, and discreetly smack his arm. By the time I turn to better see them, they are both standing straight, expressions impassive, arms clasped tightly behind backs.

I hate that they are both so close and yet so good at hiding it. Only I appear to notice anything at all; others always praise their professionalism.

I'm half tempted to take the matter to Nusk, but he likely will not see the issue the same as I. I would only be a pampered, complaining princess. Perhaps even a jealous one. It is true, after all: I am jealous of Lune. I have been jealous of Lune, and how she's gotten to act a spoiled little lady while I…

While I am a princess? About to be a queen?

Lune isn't a lady. She's my *Khashtani.* Why would I be jealous of her—

"Your majesty," Qhan says to Rian, and I am drawn back into our circle. We have stopped walking. Again, strangely, no one approaches us. "It appears there may be a breach of security. Something strange has been noted."

"I'll take it," Lune says, practically jumping on the opportunity.

No doubt she is hoping the excitement of such an encounter will help keep her awake, assuming there is even any danger to be had. Taris, meanwhile, allows his expression to slip, and he looks worried for her. It is only a moment; by the time Lune has left, he is recovered and looks perfectly bored again. But I did not miss the flash of concern. Neither did Rian.

"Don't worry," he says to his friend, cheerful as can be. "Lune can look after herself, and then some."

"Did I say anything?" Taris challenges.

"You scowled for just a second, there," Rian teases. "And you do not need to pretend with us, Taris. Soleil and I both know," he adds, nudging his elbow into my side and winking at me.

I give him a weak smile back. For some reason, I feel as if I should both be annoyed by this, and guilty. What a strange combination.

"She's smaller than me," Taris says bitterly, forcing me to stop thinking so I can listen. "Younger. She naturally has less strength. *He* should not be making us do the same physical feats and expect her to keep up with me. It is not fair."

Rian frowns. "Lune seems to be doing well enough so far. Is she not?"

Taris shrugs sullenly. "We'd likely be better with more than minimal hours of sleep each night," he mutters. "Honestly, I do not think she should be doing this at all. Does your fiancée not have enough bodyguards already?"

"I think there is a lot of concern, considering the nature of this prophecy," Rian admits. "It puts me and Soleil on the throne, and then our first-born son after us. Not to mention promising a golden age for Isaaria…There are plenty of Isaarians themselves who may not like the Yakarami family sitting in power so long, let alone the empires surrounding us who surely will not be pleased about a so-called Isaarian Golden Age."

Taris rolls his eyes. "Ah, so Lune Marson is going to single-handedly end the bigotry of the Ishtak elite. Centuries worth of hatred and religious oppression, gone because of a single woman. Why didn't anyone say so earlier."

Rian looks him over. "You're right; you are tired," he notes. "You are particularly sour today. Shall I call you 'Lemon' from now on? Or do you prefer 'Lime'?"

"You can call me whatever you please, your majesty."

"Mmm. 'Rhubarb' it is, then."

I find myself drifting away from them, Taris' embarrassed eyerolls and Rian's playful teasing, so I can head to the drinks' table and retrieve myself something. No alcohol. My mind is fuzzy enough as it is.

Mercer drifts with me, though I barely notice him until I am taking a sip of my drink and he leans down to whisper to me, nearly making me choke.

"Someone is jealous," Mercer teases.

I glare at him and smack his arm so that his skips a step away, laughing.

"What? It's true, isn't it?" he says. "You're jealous because Nusk's son and Rian are friends, and you feel out of place around them."

I bristle. This feels familiar. Now I feel as if I am myself again.

"Yes. And? It is not as if I have anyone like that. Asmer, I suppose, is closest, but even she is not to me what Taris and Rian apparently are for each other. It is as if they are brothers more than Lune and I are sisters."

Mercer shrugs and selects a drink of his own. "You could always change that. Who knows, maybe you could make friends."

"Lune doesn't want to be friends," I snap.

"Of course, she does," Mercer claims. "She is your little sister. I am sure she looks up to you: the imposing queen-to-be of Isaaria."

I huff, crossing my arms and holding my drink by circling its rim like a cage. It is not a ladylike grip.

"Fret not," Mercer says, and leans up against the table so we are more level with one another. "You will always have me, Princess."

"Hardly," I grumble. "You're the third brother to their unlikely pairing."

"Ah—but I'm the 'middle child' and therefore the one least likely to do anything with his life. I shall devote myself entirely to your entertainment, your majesty. Lending an ear is my specialty."

I glance at him to find him smiling, and his good mood reassures me further. I do feel better with Mercer, even when talking about things that annoy me. I like gossiping with him and Asmer, both, but it is different with Asmer, as she tends to chide me about it. Mercer indulges me.

"Oh, Merse," I sigh. "What in the world are you going to do with yourself when Rian and I are married?"

"Cure magic-sickness, of course," Mercer says, blasé as can be.

I cannot help but snort. It is something he has claimed he will do since he was a child, and I assume he is now saying so lightly. "Naturally, you will."

But to my surprise, Mercer shrugs. "And why not?" he says. "There must be a cure out there somewhere. So long as I have the time and ability to do my own research, why shouldn't I make an attempt?"

"Good luck," I laugh.

"I have heard that there are some research facilities of interest in Alarkia, doing innovative things," he admits. "Perhaps I will schedule a visit."

"Not before Rian and I wed, you don't," I say. "If you get kidnapped and held ransom by pirates, it will ruin our honeymoon."

Mercer laughs.

I hope he chokes on his blood when he does.

The thought startles me. Horrifies me. For a moment, I was filled with such rage at him, having a precise, accurate memory that I'm sure cannot be real: of Mercer with my knife in his neck, laughing at me while lying on a dusty arena floor. Him telling me he works for a man from one of Rian's Magicsmith stories, Kryto Grey, as he dies. Confessing he has sent an assassin to kill Rian.

I blink several times, the chattering of the thick mob of nobles all through the ballroom suddenly ringing in my ears.

"Are you feeling well, princess?" Mercer teases.

His presence no longer reassures me.

"Excuse me, for a moment," I insist. I barely manage to place my drink back on the table so it will not smash against the ground.

I find a doorway, an exit, and I run to it. No one is there to open the door for me, and I must use my weight to push it open on my own. Its weight pulls it closed behind me, muffling the sounds of the party and shutting out the yellow lights of the ballroom. There is a blue glow to the evening light, in this currently unused hall. That vaguely blue light reminds me of something, but I cannot think of what. I am comparing it—this light is a darker, natural blue, and that other one was an icier, brighter blue—but I do not remember what I'm comparing it to.

I stagger down the hall, gasping, my chest hurting, my ribs heaving beneath the Alarkian-style ribbing to my dress. I find a sideboard to lean over, trying to catch my breath. A curl of my own hair brushes against my neck, making me shudder. I close my eyes and try to relax. I shift through my memories of the past years. Something is not right. But I cannot think of what.

It feels as if I have two minds.

My own flickering thoughts are so confusing. I have an urge to ask someone about Ayla, but I do not know who Ayla is, because Rian and I are not married yet, and so, cannot have adopted a daughter. I want to warn Park Mi-Sun about a war, but there is no war, currently, for Kacha and Tourran.

That is rather the point of all this. I want to tell Aiko Shinya he has a daughter by my cousin. But he is a boy of eleven. And I do not have any cousins.

I feel sick.

"Soleil."

I turn. It is Taris. He has just exited the same door as I did, and is about to make his way down the hallway toward me. I make myself straighten, realizing, for some reason, that when he walks toward me, it feels to me as if I think of him as my brother the same way Rian must.

Taris barely takes a few steps when someone approaches from the hallway perpendicular to this, stopping him.

"What are you doing here?" Nusk demands, rolling his chair towards Taris, making Taris turn back to him. "Why are you not with his majesty?"

Taris hesitates, taken aback. He is startled, firstly to see his father here, and second, to find him so irate.

"His…majesty asked me to see to Soleil," he says slowly. "He is worried. She ran out, looking rather distressed—"

"You are his *Khashtani,"* Nusk interrupts, rolling closer. "You cannot leave his side when you are assigned to be with him. Ever. Could you predict what might happen to him in your absence?"

"No, but—"

"There was a security breach. Did you not hear?" Nusk demands. "You must have. Yet you would leave his majesty's side at a time like this, over something so trivial. Something you should have reminded him that he could ask anyone else to do."

I approach slowly. Nusk must know that I'm here, but he barely glances at me. I can see he is truly furious with Taris, which is a surprise to both of us. Taris is shocked. He does not know what to say for a long time, before he finds his tongue again.

"I…Lune is managing things. And I'm only going to be away from him for a minute or two, to fetch the crown princess back, and then—"

"Then what?" Nusk says. "Do you have any idea what may have happened to him in your absence?"

I watch Taris become exasperated with his father in a matter of seconds.

"This is absurd," he says, and turns to leave, barely remembering me in time. "Soleil, are you coming back inside, or not? If you need some air, that is what I will tell his majesty. Otherwise…"

"I am fine," I say quickly, making myself stand straighter, though my head still hurts, and I now feel dizzy.

"Soleil can see to the crown prince," Nusk says sharply.

For some reason, that makes sense to me. Yet it doesn't. I do not leave the hall, for what happens next, because I do not quite remember who I am supposed to be. I do not remember who Nusk or Taris are to me, either, not because there is a blank space there, but because there is too much to fill it.

Why would Nusk say that to me? Why does it make sense, to me, in some way, that he would?

I slump down into a chair against the wall, trying to understand exactly what it is I am wearing. This is not the dress I had on, before. What am I wearing?

"Remember," Nusk says to his son, "why it is you have never been able to properly act Rian's *Khashtani.*"

"Perhaps because I never wanted to be," Taris says.

"This is your heritage," Nusk argued. "Our heritage. Our traditions. From our country. It is a great and honorable thing to be chosen and trained as a *Khashtani,* and you—"

"I'm only half-Milash," Taris interrupts.

"Who stayed? Your Isaarian mother or your Milashi father?" Nusk challenges. "Who raised you? Who stayed?"

He grabs Taris' arm and Taris pulls away.

"You are from Milash. It is our country. Our customs—!" Nusk insists.

"But it's not hers!"

Taris' shout makes my head ring even more. Something is not right. Two worlds have collided inside my mind, and while the forefront of my thoughts try over and over to convince me it all makes sense, somehow, it still doesn't.

"Ah," Nusk finally says in the silence that follows once the ringing dies down. "So, this is about her, again."

Yes, about Lune, and that makes sense to me, because Taris is in love with Lune. He marries her. Yet I am not entirely certain how I know that Taris and Lune are married.

"Lune is not Milashi. She's nothing like it. She's Isaarian. But you didn't give her a choice. No one did. No one asked either of us," Taris rants.

"Are you in love with her?" Nusk demands.

Taris does not hesitate. "You know I am."

"Do you love Rian? You told me you thought of him as your brother, once. Do you love him?" Nusk says.

It is a challenge that Taris cannot answer. He stumbles in thought, his mouth remaking the shapes for words he decides against over and over.

"If you love him, you will do this and you will not complain," Nusk says. "Lune loves her sister. If she is willing to sacrifice, and do this, for her, then it is not your business to interfere. You will do your job, and she will do hers. You will leave one another be, and will not engage in any type or behavior aside from professional."

"Aside from professional?" Taris finally finds his tongue again. He has found his ammunition. "To follow the rules for the rest of my life?"

"It is not too much to ask for you to sacrifice that for someone you love."

"But you broke the rules! You had me!" Taris shouts.

I stare at him. I have never seen him so furious. I wonder why it is I know this is only partially real. This conversation is real, I know that, but nothing else is. Nusk's shock is real. Taris' was. I know I have never heard them say anything like this to one another before, but I know it is true.

"It is a simple equation," Taris spits. "I'm no fool. I was born when you were still a *Khashtani*. It does not matter if the king was sick, and you knew he would not live much longer; that you were going to be free. You still could not wait. You didn't."

I know I did not know that, but I do know more about Taris and Nusk than I ought to, for someone who grew up as a princess.

Assuming that is still who I am.

Who am I, then? Didn't Rian once hold me on the floor of his bedroom and tell me I am his wife? Didn't he promise to marry me a thousand times over again, only to die in my arms?

"How dare you hold me to a standard that you could not even hold to yourself?" Taris says.

I curl over. I feel sick again, and the dizziness has not dissipated.

"I will not discuss this with you," Nusk says. "You would not understand. You are not mature enough to understand. I think you have made that clear."

He glances at me.

"What are you still doing here, Soleil?" he sighs. "Go. You must protect the crown prince."

"Why would I do that, as a princess?" I blurt.

Nusk looks perplexed, then, and I cannot read Taris' expression.

"You're not a princess, Soleil, you're his *Khashtani,*" Nusk says.

"No, but I…" I start, and then I realize what has happened.

I am not a princess or *Khashtani;* I am both.

With a gasp, I rush back toward the door, stumbling. Taris tries to catch me, as if worried I may faint. I pull the knife from his belt and brush him off before bursting back into the ballroom, leaving them behind. Everyone turns to look at me as I do, everyone. I am too aware of how strange this all is, now: how there is the sound of distant chatter, conversations, and how they are all holding drinks in their hands, but no one's mouth moves. No one is drinking.

I push through people, and they allow it. They do not gossip or titter, because why would they? I know where I am, now. I remember. These people are not real. They are naught but illusions that I came up with on my own. All it took was a little prompting for me to live out years in a world made of memories.

I look for Rian, but I know he will not be here. How absent he has been, even in the years of my own memories, where he should have been extraordinarily present.

Where were the times that he, Mercer, and I climbed over the palace walls and made a nuisance of ourselves? Where was the time that I made Asmer and Mercer help me sneak into Rian's rooms, when he was sick with influenza? Merse and I got sick as well, of course, and I nearly got my hide tanned for it, exposing poor little Asmer to something like that.

Where was the time that I fell off the palace wall, cutting open my upper thigh so that it permanently scarred?

I know that happened. I remember it.

So why is it, here, now, with all these faces around me, that so few of them look properly familiar? They are but mannequins and, now that I am aware of it, poor ones, at that.

I turn in a circle and push back at these faceless people, with those blank eyes and blank expressions. As I move, so quickly, now and again, I catch glimpses of It. I learn to look out of corners of my eyes, and there It is, as if it has always been there, all along.

"Where is everyone, then?" I bellow. "Not so good at mimicking without my memories to use as a base, are you?"

I hear familiar, ghastly sounds. Those sounds I heard when part of the Dark flittered and skulked and stole around me. I wonder if those sounds were always there, just behind me, and I simply refused to notice.

Then I feel it. Behind me. I feel its breath on my neck.

"Aren't I, though?" the Dark hisses.

I cannot help it. I have been startled. It is a reaction. I whirl.

My fist snaps out.

I have struck it; punched it. I have punched the Dark's guise in my own shadowy nightmare, and it reacts, recoiling. The smoke of it disappears, or, it tries to. This is my world it has entered. My mind. And in my mind, I have been a monster in how I've killed. But I also know how to survive.

I grab it before it can escape, near the base of its neck, and it grabs me back, in the same way. I feel the grip burn, but I push that thought aside. It means nothing, because this is not my body.

"You do not frighten me," I laugh at it.

It pulls in closer to me. "Don't I?"

"No."

I find, strangely, this is true. The Dark did frighten me, to my core. But considering all this illusion, all these fake years I have just now lived imagining myself here, such an attempt is laughable. Can the Dark truly do nothing else to stop me but try and convince me to trick myself? I know that it is a more intelligent creature than I could ever hope to be in my human failings. Yet it has no true power over me; nothing that I do not grant it myself.

"You will not take my sister away from me again," I hiss.

The Dark's figure responds in kind, each sound like a snake's tongue flicking the inside of my ear. "Why not? You do not even love her. You did not love her. You never have."

"Maybe not," I agree. "But now is as good a time as any to start."

I drive Taris' knife into it, knowing I cannot kill it, but I do not have to.

I open my eyes, knowing all those years I thought I lived in the blink of an eye were only memories. I am still here, with Lune on my shoulders, Mercer's necklace pulling me forward, kneeling on the floor of the Dark's cave. But I am still facing forward, unturned. I have not given up, yet. While I have tipped forward so that I must use one hand to catch myself, I have yet to put Lune down. She is still balanced across my shoulders. So, I have not lost.

With great effort, I rise. There are still sounds, monstrous things flitting in the dark around me, but I am not scared of them anymore. These are cheap attempts to frighten me. I understand that, now.

I heft Lune on my shoulders, and find the light that Riyong told me to use as my guide. I know Riyong did not know everything, about the Otherworld. I know his own journey was allocated only to the Dark's hells, and that things are not the same. But I also know that if I go towards that candlelight, the lantern will help me escape this place, as it once did for him.

The weight is still unbearably heavy. Of Lune, of Mercer's necklace, of the dragging from Taris pulling me back. But this time, I do not walk. I run.

Twenty

CONTRARY TO WHAT Riyong implied, when I reach the light, I am not brought back to Samioth. I collapse on the ground of the courtyard of the angel's domain, letting Lune slip off my shoulders as I roll to lay flat on my back, gasping. The sky is so beautifully blue, here. I know it is not the same sky as the one we have in Samioth, nor is there much reason for there to be a sky, but it is peaceful, and calming. For a moment, all I do is lay there, panting, trying to chase away the woolliness in my head with reassurances of my victory.

After a moment, I see Fate, leaning down toward me.

"Well done," he says, genuinely proud. "I knew you could succeed. Didn't I tell you so?"

I do not know how to respond.

"What happened?" I finally ask, not yet ready to sit up yet. "Riyong said that if I went toward the light, I would be back in Samioth, but…"

We did not formulate a decent extraction plan, I realize.

"I pulled you here," Fate explains to me simply. "As soon as my power could reach you."

"But you are sending me back. Aren't you?" I demand, almost panicked by the idea of being trapped in this Otherworld forever.

"Of course," Fate reassures.

After being with the Dark for what feels like years of my life, I am almost unreasonably paranoid of these creatures trying to trick me. However, the tone Fate uses, and the mere feeling of his presence, reassures me.

"And, I might add, you always had to return here first," Fate says. "After all, it has been twenty years since Taris, Mercer, and Lune died. There is nothing left for them to go back to, now. So, they will have to wait here, for the next cycle."

I do make myself sit up, then, wanting to see them all. Fate leans back, and for a few moments, I sit there like I would sit sprawled in the grass as a child. There, next to me, where I dropped Lune, are all three of them. They lay there, as if asleep, wearing clothes that appear to fit the ancient ruins around us, mimicking what Fate and the Death wear.

For several seconds, or perhaps many minutes trickling one after another, I do nothing but watch Lune's chest move softly up and down. She looks so young, and delicate. For decades, she risked life and limb to keep me safe; playing a pretty, naïve noblewoman while sacrificing a real life—and her desire for a family—for the sake of my family.

I know that I must protect her. I am her older sister, and for all our lives, I have failed to watch after her as I should. Even in the first iteration, Asmer was much more my sister than Lune ever was, through my fault and my fault alone. I allowed my jealousy to make me hate her.

Lune is still a young woman, here, while I have aged in Samioth. She will forever be this age, in this version of the world. She died too young to ever be anything more. The only difference between this Lune and the last time I saw her, in life, is her hair. Instead of its usual coloring, even lighter than my own, it is white. Down to her roots. It makes her look even fairer.

Then there are Mercer and Taris. Like Lune, their hair is entirely white. It looks even stranger on them, as I am used to seeing them with black hair. They have become inverses of themselves. I feel as if their sleep is not as peaceful, to me, as Lune's appears. I want to shake them awake, and share an embrace, with all of us relieved to see one another again. I want them to know they are free of the Dark's realm.

But Fate puts a hand on my shoulder, reminding me that he is still there.

"Why don't you come with me, for a moment?" he says. "You may safely leave them. Peace will look after them."

I glance to the side, feeling another presence, and see a woman standing at some distance. Or, she looks like a woman, though I know she is another angel. She could be from Picland, like Aisling, I suppose, and, like Aisling, her presence is calming. She takes her hands out from her sleeves to wave at me. I lift a hand to wave back distractedly.

"Up we get," Fate says, picking me up from under my arms.

"I don't want to," I say. "I want to stay with Lune."

Now that I am back here, I feel that all the careful layers built up, from my expectations of self and the pressure of societal standards, are gone. They have been washed away by whatever it is about this part of the Otherworld that makes me more curious and willing to be open and honest. It is complete trust, I realize. I am still myself, but I feel no reason to hold anything back.

"You can see them later," Fate tells me before gently leading me away.

"When?"

"Soon. I merely want to discuss some particulars with you, before you are meant to return," Fate says. "You and our friend the ever-intrepid Septimus Smith. I would like to bring him here."

"He is busy," I say haltingly. "He is protecting my body. From monsters, and things. Riyong said—"

"I am certain the others can manage without him," Fate says, with a smile.

I know he would know best. So, if Septimus is meant to be here, even if only for a few minutes, who am I to argue against that?

"Alright," I agree, and let Fate walk me back to his loom with him.

There are three chairs, there, now.

I watch his fingers intently, yet it still looks to me as if he is not physically weaving on the loom. Things simply move, simultaneously, all at his discretion, but there are no colors for him to draw from except from thin air. To me, it is mesmerizing, but my mind still willingly makes sense of it. I watch him pluck at a few places, and expect Septimus to appear presently, but Fate simply continues to weave peacefully for a time.

Then Anna Wolff walks out of one of the Death's passages, and behind her comes a stumbling, awed Septimus.

He stops walking entirely the moment they are in the courtyard, and then he stares at me and Fate and mutters a few things in, I think, Lusch. Anna Wolff turns back to him, rolls her eyes, then goes back to grab his sleeve and pull him over to Fate. I wonder if she is exasperated with being the Death's errand girl or if she is merely annoyed that she has had to be trapped in the Otherworld so long.

Or, conversely, maybe our awe and disbelief is somewhat of an insult to someone like her, who has lived with and had to live with great, unerring faith and dedication her entire life, including in her own death.

"Here is your Memory Smith," she says, depositing Septimus with us before crossing her arms over her chest. "He has a lot of questions. I told him I could not answer, but he kept asking them anyways."

No, I realize, as I suddenly see her two decades younger than I first did. No, Anna is not annoyed by us, precisely. She simply is a girl, now. She is both herself at her death, and a child again, same as me.

Fate laughs, and reaches over to take Anna's hand.

"That is all right. You have done very well, Anna. Thank you."

She frowns and her lower lip trembles a little.

"Can I go? You let her go down. Will you let me, now? You said I could not let Riyong go again, and I listened, and he listened. But I'm already dead. So, can I go? …I want to see Hwi."

Fate just smiles at her. "Perhaps some other time, Anna."

However, I think we all know he is not about to let her traverse the Dark's domain. She must know that, I'm sure, yet she simply nods, pulls her hand out of his, and walks away.

"I…do not like it here," Septimus confesses before dropping down onto his allocated seat with a thump. When he sits, I see he is, too, a child again.

Fate laughs and continues weaving.

"Naturally, you don't," he acknowledges. "You like to be in control of everything, Sep. Including your own fate. But you do not have control, here."

Septimus grimaces. "I suppose that makes me a bad person, being allowed to step foot in the angel's domain and not liking it, when so few would get such an opportunity as this one."

"Oh, I wouldn't say that," Fate says. "I would say it only makes you human. And that is some of what I would like to discuss with you. You see, Septimus, I cannot have you remembering any of this in our final timeline. You are not meant to. And Soleil, I cannot have you rewinding the timelines any more. So, I will need a promise from both of you."

I am ready and willing to give it. I more than understand, now, to the extent a human can, why I had these powers. I do not need them anymore.

"I will cut my palms and heels and give up using my fluke ever again, as soon as I'm reasonably old enough to do so by Isaarian laws," I promise immediately. "And even before that, I will not use it again. I swear. Not even for little things."

"That would be most helpful, Soleil," Fate says. "Thank you. And you, Septimus?"

My cousin hesitates. There is more being asked of him.

"…If I don't remember, I may never leave the Greys," he says.

"That is correct," Fate agrees.

"I'll hate Teresa."

"You may."

Septimus is quiet.

"I don't know," he finally says. "I don't want to do that. I know that I can, I already have once. But I do not want to hurt her. And you're asking me to."

"No," Fate corrects, "I am asking you to live as if you have not seen a different future, before. You will still be the one making your own choices."

"But I won't have had the opportunity to grow," Septimus protests. "You are not giving me the chance to be a good person!"

"You always have that chance," Fate says. "You always did. What you do with it is up to you. The question is this: do you trust yourself enough to learn what the right thing is, and then do it?"

"I don't know," Septimus insists. "I was raised to think differently, about what is right and not."

"I think, even then, you knew right from wrong in its proper context. You only used excuses to justify doing 'wrong'. As everyone does. But it is premature to condemn yourself entirely," Fate chides. "You have not lived a full life, yet."

"I've lived several," Septimus says.

"No. You have not, really. You have never made it past the age of forty, Septimus. That really is not very long at all, even if you remember it. In the first timeline, you were barely twenty. So how can you know what the original version of yourself would have done five, ten, fifteen years later? You cannot. Regardless of what you remembered, you went back to having the mind of a child, again. And you have never been able to grow up with Jax. He is your friend. That could change you, too."

"Who is Jax?" I ask. I want to know. I feel as if I'm being excluded.

"Jarrod Grey's twin," Septimus says slowly. "But he never lives past the age of ten at most. Because the Greys never wanted him."

"Perhaps he will, this time," Fate says. "Perhaps there is a new variable that should be introduced, but will not be until things are put right in an Otherworldly sense. You cannot know."

Septimus groans and puts his fingers to his temples, leaning his elbows and weight over his knees.

"Now you know what talking to *you* is like," I cannot help but say.

Fate gives me a look of reprimand and Septimus glares, but his expression makes me smile. I wish his parents had run away with him and his siblings, and come to Isaaria. Then I could have kept my mother and father, and so could Lune, and we cousins could have all grown up together.

"Why don't I offer you something," Fate says to him, putting a hand on Septimus' shoulder. "You and I will have Soleil give us some privacy. And I will have the Almighty use me to tell you everything that is meant to happen to you. After, you can decide. But know that as soon as you leave the Otherworld, you will not remember any of what I show you."

Septimus considers this.

"Wait, I want that, too," I insist.

"You already got to, Soleil," Fate tells me patiently.

"I did?"

"Yes. Everyone does. But you do not ever remember. No person is meant to. Now, you can all decide who you think should remember timelines past before going back again, as things will not happen the same way. But Septimus cannot be in that number. He is, ironically, the variable that made your being here possible, but the same one that would ruin the timeline should he remember it."

"Oh," I say, and think about this.

Before I can come up with any more questions, and before Septimus can agree to Fate's proposition or not, we are interrupted. Peace is on her way towards us, for one, but more pressing is the person doing their best to outpace her on their way directly for me.

"Soleil!" Taris cries.

For a moment, I assume he is coming here because he is relieved to be free, and to see me again. A second later, I am glad Peace catches him and holds him back just a few paces away from us, because I see he is not relieved. He is not happy to see me again. He is furious. Despite being a woman in figure, though, Peace is much taller than Taris, and evidently stronger, because she holds him back with relative ease even with his struggling against her.

"How dare you!" he finally snaps at me.

I scramble up and behind Fate's chair, almost hiding behind him. I do not know if I fear Taris or not. But I do not like seeing him so angry. I am used to being the one angry with him.

"I saved you from the Dark," I say, confused.

"We didn't ask you to!"

"But…" I say, and glance down at Fate, who puts a hand back up over mine, without taking his own eyes off Taris. "After everything you and Lune and Mercer have been through…You didn't have to ask."

Taris gives a pained, hateful laugh. The way he looks at me hurts, as if he wishes I'd left him there, with the Dark. But he stops fighting Peace physically.

"You know nothing of what we've been through," he says.

I cannot think of what to say to defend myself, but Septimus steps in on my behalf, almost defensive of me.

"Actually, she does," he says. "She may not know everything, and perhaps she does not understand why you made certain choices, but I have restored most of Soleil's memories. Most, not all. And I have done my best not to let the emotions associated with them overrun her as they almost did Rian. As, I think, it is clear they have you."

Taris glares at Septimus and offers a particular series of curses at him that makes Septimus look down and keep his mouth shut. I suspect what Taris says in Isaarian must not be unlike whatever Kang said about Kryto in Dohremi.

I am embarrassed Taris is being like this in front of divine angels. I glance at Fate, wanting his approval and feeling as if Taris is being rude. Fate only smiles absently, as always.

"Well," he says, "it looks as if you might have something to talk about, Soleil. Taris. Perhaps you should have that opportunity, while I speak with Septimus."

I slowly come around from behind him, knowing I do want to talk to Taris. In fact, I have waited years, now, to talk to Taris again, having so many questions for him. Only, now, I have all the answers to those questions. Septimus gave them to me. Now, I only want to see my brother again.

"I will go. To talk," I clarify.

Taris is still breathing hard, but at least both his feet are on the ground, and are not moving. Peace leans down to his level not unlike how Fate has frequently done to me.

"Are you going to be rude?" she asks him in a motherly way Taris has never experienced before in his life.

"...No," he finally mutters, as his child self instead of as the adult Taris he was when I first recovered him. Peace lets him jerk his arms away from her.

He does not come any closer to me, but at least matches me as I come out from behind Fate. We walk down the large courtyard space. I find a line of tall, uniform trees planted, their roots and branches wild, but still contained within the stones surrounding them. I keep them to my right, using them as a guide, while Taris is vaguely to my left. Peace drifts back, following us, but still allowing us the same privacy I intend to give Septimus and Fate.

Once we are far enough away that I can no longer even see Fate's loom, I stop. Taris stops, too.

"Would it help," I say slowly, after a moment of thought, "if I finally said thank you? For you always being there, for me? You and Lune have been willing to die for me and Rian, and I am grateful. For that."

But my words do not have the intended effect. Taris is still angry with me, I can tell, but he will not meet my eye. He glares at the ground or, if he does raise his eyes, he looks just off behind me, over my shoulder.

"You talk about this like it's an easy choice," he accuses. "As if you assume most people would easily make sacrifices for the world's sake over and over again. Yet, when forced to choose between something vague, distant, and uncertain, and something physical, here and now, most people would choose the latter. So how pious are you all, really? Would you choose to sacrifice a hundred times over again? Or do you merely assume you would because you have never had to face that choice and never will?"

I do not say anything to that. I do not have an answer.

"The first time, it's easy," Taris scoffs. "The second? Fifteenth? Thirtieth? Well, that is quite different. Now isn't it."

"I suppose. Yes," I finally say.

"All this is easy for you, Soleil," he spits. "You have Fate on your side. You can claim to be the just one, the one with the moral high ground, because by Fate's Loom, you are. The world needs Rian. Needs your children. It does not need me or Lune or ours."

I flinch at that, because there might be some truth to it, at least from Taris' perspective. I understand that. I can see how, given the particulars of our circumstances, especially with the repetition, why he might feel as if he and Lune were being punished for something they never did.

"I am sorry," I say. "That you and Lune had to go through that so many times over again."

Yet, another voice in me insists it was not my fault, either.

"When I decided to marry her, I made a promise," Taris says. "All I wanted, all I ever wanted, was to make her happy. And you cannot know how painful it is to have you be the one preventing that."

There is a hidden admittance, in that, and I do not need to hear Taris say it explicitly. I know he loves Lune, but he does care about me, too. And Rian.

"How nice it must be," he says bitterly. "To have an angel itself tell you that you are the hero of the story."

That finally makes me jerk my head up, because he is wrong about that.

"That's not true," I say.

The thought comes to me like my head is an egg cracked open, and out spills everything in an honest mess.

"Fate did not send me to fix things because what I want is what is right for the world," I continue. "But because someone tangled his weaving to begin with. I do not know if I will do the right things, make the right choices—even be a good person—at all times. I suppose I do not even know if the Carsans' prophecy about my son is true. Fate did not tell me that my way is right, or what I want is right. Or good. Or true. He only said that some things are meant to be. Whether those things are good or not."

I think of the Greys, and how Septimus said it was the hubris in their good intentions that has made them how they are now. Their downfall was how willing they are to excuse what they consider minor evils for the greater good.

But have I not done the same thing? I have killed for Rian. For my own desires. Those were lives I destroyed, with families. People who cared for them. For them, I was the villain of their story. For the Greys, too. In some ways, for Naomi, who has been horrified to discover how contrived her life has been and how many choices have been made for her, when she would have liked different ones.

Fate never said that I am the hero of Samioth. In the final timeline, people will still die. Monsters will still exist. The Dark will still do its best to manipulate and destroy. Perhaps if I allow myself to settle with Rian, to have a family, I myself will do less in physically stopping these horrors.

But it also means I will do less damage. I will have children to come after me. Amongst all of us as a family, we will do far more good for the world than I ever could on my own. It is the hope that my children will be better people than I have been that in turn gives me hope for the future of the world.

It is impossible for me to give my children the perfect world they deserve. But if the Greys succeed in freeing the Dark, that world will not exist at all.

"Fate has never called me a hero, Taris," I tell him. "I am not some holy champion. There have been far better saints before me, and will be in our own lifetimes, who deserve greater acclaim. Perhaps you will be one of them. So why don't you give yourself that chance? Why don't we go find out?"

For a moment, I think he will agree. That he will admit there is a purpose to what I'm saying. Then I watch him reject it bitterly.

"Why should I bother with all this again with there being no guarantee. No actual reward for all the suffering of life—"

"What is all this, then! Taris, we are seeing here, now: there is a reward waiting, even if we do not see it on Samioth. And besides that, I'm saying I would help you. Why can't you stop being angry all the time!" I cry, frustrated with him. "Not everyone in the world is against you!"

"Why would you care?" he snaps.

That is what finally pushes me over.

"Because I love you! Fate-damn, Taris! You are so stupid, sometimes!" I cry, and then turn to the sky which flashes angrily when I curse. "Fine, sorry!" I shout at it before turning on Taris again. "You are like my brother. Rian's brother. Even without remembering everything, of course we cared about you! Now that we do remember, we are going to do whatever we can to ensure your happiness, you halfwit! But you must want to be happy, too!"

He stares at me. I can feel Peace watching us, drifting closer. The sky feels overcast, now. It has grown darker, but not in a negative way, necessarily. It is as if the sun is slowly setting on a summer's day, or rain clouds are beginning to drift in.

"You…want me and Lune. To be happy," Taris repeats.

"Of course. You fool," I say again. "Rian does, too. Like I said. We love you. Why do you think I am here in the first place?!"

"Because…you need us," he says slowly.

"Yes," I agree. "But not in the way you think. Yes. We need you. Because I do not want to live a happy life with Rian if it means you and Lune don't get to be there, too. I do not want happiness if it comes at that cost. The world be damned—I could probably convince myself to let it burn down if I had Rian and Ayla, but not without Lune and you."

Taris continues to stare. I think, somehow, he has misread me all this time. I think certain aspects of his life have led him to believe that he is some-how unlovable, and that only Lune is the exception to that rule.

"I'm not the hero of Samioth you think Fate wants me to be," I say. "I'm a selfish person, Taris. That is why I don't want the Dark to have you. Because I want you with me and Rian. Because I love you."

Taris continues to stare at me. Then, I realize, his eyes are rather glassy. At first, I think it is because his mind is no longer here, somehow. But that is not possible in these circumstances. So, I realize, it is because he is crying. I don't know if I've ever seen Taris cry, much. Maybe once, when he and Lune made their original promises to me, and he realized what that would mean for them.

But even those were rather silent tears, in comparison. Once Taris lets himself cry, here, he sobs. He cries freely, as the child he never got to be. Peace sweeps forward readily, with open arms, to pull him against her. I am somehow am not at all embarrassed by witnessing this, though I know I would be, to see Taris cry on Samioth. I am happy he can, here.

He sobs, telling me he is sorry. I tell him that he has nothing to be sorry for, though perhaps he does. I'm glad he can say so, and not be so embittered by it. Besides, Peace can comfort him more, now, than I ever could. I'm glad he is no longer fighting her.

I have said my piece, here, and Taris finally hears me. I think this is the only place he could hear me.

I know what I want to do, now, while waiting for Fate to be finished with Septimus. I look to Peace.

"Where could I find Mercer?"

She strokes Taris' hair as he clings to one of her arms. She does not pull away from him to gesture for me, but says, "Keep walking. You will find him."

I wait a moment longer, while she goes back to soothing Taris. Then I nod to myself and take off at a moderate pace, letting my feet slap the stones of the courtyard. It is such a grand, sprawling place, surrounded by so much architecture, that I know it could conceivably go on forever. I pass under a large, high archway connecting two towering structures, and see the courtyard goes on even further, here. I slow my pace, as Mercer is easy to find.

He is as much both a child and adult, here, as the rest of us. Mercer sits leaning back on his hands, his feet and ankles dangling down into a structured pond. He sits on one of the raised stones around it and smiles when he notices me. I can see it is a strained smile. It is sad. His is a mask of light-heartedness, and we should have all seen it much earlier.

How could any of us expect him to come back from what he saw in the west, and not be changed by it? How is it that no one lent him the ear he needed, wanting to avoid those horrors for our own sakes, not thinking of what he might need after being the one surrounded by it all?

"Afternoon, Soleil," he says, and kicks his feet back and forth in the water. "If it is afternoon, that is. Hard to tell here, isn't it?"

"I suppose," I say, and sit down next to him, finding I have no shoes to take off before joining him. So, I dip my feet into the pond as well, though unlike him, I do not bother to roll up my trouser legs first. The concept of purposefully allowing my clothes to get wet in such a way is strangely freeing.

For a while, we sit there and do not say anything. A duck suddenly floats past, startling me as she quacks, with nine little ducklings following along behind her. I wonder if Mercer manifested them, subconsciously. Curious that he would think first of a mother duck than any fish.

"...You know, for all the times someone has jokingly told me to go to hell, I never thought I'd end up there," Mercer says, and gives a self-deprecating laugh that does not manage to hide the uncertainty in his tone.

I sigh. "Merse. Don't. Please. You know you do not belong there. And you will not. You made a mistake, trusting people who you thought you could ask to help you save lives."

"I think we both know naïveté is not my only sin," Mercer says. "I knew what I was doing was wrong, Soleil. I let them convince me otherwise because... I wanted to feel as if there was something I could do for certain that would change things. Some part of me still chose to believe it would work. And I did not care what it meant sacrificing."

I think about this. I lift my foot out of the water to purposefully throw splashes forward, then watch the intersecting ripples in the water.

"If there is no war, you won't go," I decide. "That is, you at least will not have to see any of what there is, in war. I will not stop you from traveling; I know you like to. But if you see Lijimata and Alarkia without the war, I do not think the Greys would have such an effect on you. I think you will still be you."

"What if I end up there, anyways? I have betrayed Rian—my closest friend—every single time. What if that is simply what I am meant to do?"

I hesitate in answering while I consider this.

We cannot stop Mercer from being Mercer. I know that. But I also know from reading his own words that he is a good person, or he at least has the potential to be. He wants to be. If there are not victims of war to help, Mercer will find others to help, instead. Those others, I'm sure, will have a much better chance of recovering.

He will not need to have someone else tell him what he is doing will matter. He will be able to see so himself.

"You won't," I promise. "Things will be different. You will be able to help people in Isaaria, instead. Because, you know, you do not need to go to some war-torn country for what you're doing to matter. It can matter in Isaaria, too."

"I don't know what I'll do with myself, though," he sighs. "How will I choose what to focus on, what to specialize with, what to use my money for..."

"Don't you remember?" I say, a hint of friendly teasing in it. "You're going to cure magic-sickness."

He almost smiles, then, and it is a real one. Then it disappears again.

"Just another foolish dream. It could never happen," he says.

"And why not?" I say. "Just because no one has found a cure yet does not mean you will not. You could. You could cure Asmer, too."

He is not convinced. "People have tried and failed with all their might to save their loved ones from such illnesses. Why should I be able to succeed when they have failed? I doubt I have Fate's favor."

"Fate will only record your success. He has no hand in it," I say. "And why? Why do I know you will succeed? Because you have more resources at the tips of your fingers than almost anyone else in Isaaria. You are a prince."

"And you do not think Asmer's parents tried everything they possibly could to save their daughter?"

"They never asked you," I point out. "Did they?"

He must think about that, then, because I know it is true. The al'Yibnas never did ask Mercer to try and help Asmer. They asked him to help maintain her where she was, having been told by other physicians there was no possible cure. She would die young, and that was known.

But I know that is not how Mercer thinks of medicine. He does not see it as a stagnant field. If they had asked him, if it had occurred to him that he would not be overstepping his bounds to do so, maybe he could have found something other doctors did not, for Asmer. Not because Fate decided he would be the one chosen to do so, but because he'd be the first person to try.

"It does not matter," he decides. "If I tried and failed, then…what does that mean? Only that I was proud enough to think I could do what others could not."

"So? Who cares? Maybe it will not work. But maybe it will, Mercer. Maybe you will do spectacular things, if you would only allow yourself to."

He bites at one of his nails. Asmer's old bad habit.

"Don't you think you're meant to do something good in the world?" I say. "You are a prince, Mercer. You did not need to learn medical practices, or go offer your help to anyone. But you did. You do. Because you are a good person. So, were there not a war, who is to say you would not put that good heart to different use?"

He does not say anything, merely thinking on this.

"Maybe you will cure Asmer. Maybe you will cure magic-sickness. Or maybe you will not. But you know what I do know? You would make an exceptional role model and a good godfather for my son. And I want you to be there."

He stops biting at his fingernails and looks at me.

"You don't hate me?"

"I did," I admit. "But no. I don't. Not anymore. I'm no angel, either."

Mercer kicks at the water, not unlike how I did, and accidentally splashes the ducks, who are greatly displeased by this.

"I'm going to find Lune," I say. "I must speak to her. But think about it."

I stand up and brush my clothes off, my still-wet trouser ends slapping against my ankles. At about the same time, the irate mother duck swims over to bite Mercer's big toe in retribution for his splashing them.

"Ow! Son of a fuck," Mercer says, pulling his foot in as the ducks quack-quack their way off again.

"Generally speaking, that is how it works," I say. "One would think you'd understand that best of all, with your medical expertise."

It takes him a moment to understand the joke, and then he laughs. He laughs hysterically until he falls backwards, because we both know that is the sort of terrible joke he would make.

I do not know if Mercer will truly think about what I said to him, and I know he will not remember any of this when we go back again. But I know all I need do is make him understand he does not deserve the punishment he thinks he does. Neither does Taris. Neither does Lune. Not because they are perfect people, and not because there should be no punishment for doing wrong, but because if asking for forgiveness does not allow for redemption, then there is no point to anything at all.

I leave him laughing, because that is how I want to think of Mercer forever, now. Not as someone who betrayed us, merely as a friend.

I head off again, not sure where Lune might be, but knowing I likely will not find her back towards Taris, or Fate. I do not know how much time I have left, here, and while I am sure I could find more to say to Mercer, I want to spend some time with my sister, knowing she is my sister.

Besides, I know things may be most difficult, with Lune.

I continue to walk. Whatever serves as a sun, here, sets, until the sky is still lit, but blue and purple. I pass by a tall golden gate that looks as if it extends the courtyard out a separate direction entirely. Ahead of me, the courtyard ends. There are steps leading down, and after that, only the sky. Nothing else, as far as the eye can see, but clouds and stars.

Lune sits on the steps, staring out at the sky and clouds with a distant, almost blank expression. Her arms rest on her scrunched knees. The wind flutters her dress out over the sky, and her white hair over her shoulders. She looks lost. She does not turn her head to look at me when I sit down on the top of the steps with her. There are four more steps, down, and then the air. I partially want to know if we could walk out onto the sky, but I do not want to put that opportunity in front of Lune.

For a few moments, neither of us say anything. I do not know how to begin, so there is some relief, when Lune does. I wonder if she can read my mind and know the context in which I have come to her.

There are so many things I do not know about my own sister.

"It's so…hard," Lune says absently. "I don't know how I can possibly make anyone understand…Why."

Why she and Taris did what they did. So many choices they made, some good, some bad, and Lune does not know how to explain herself. Certainly not to me, I would say, and certainly not to anyone else who would ask, trying to understand, without the comprehension of context. It is no one's fault, either, but how could someone possibly try to understand Lune when they have not lived the way she has, for hundreds of years.

"It's so hard to give up hope," she whispers.

Her voice is quiet. It makes me miss who I know she used to be, or, who she pretended to be.

"It became…confusing. Trying to justify what I was doing," she says. "What I wanted to do. What I knew I was supposed to do. It became a matter of… 'why not'. Why not continue to be with Taris, if there was no changing the outcome anyway? Why not, if everything we did was going to be for nothing?"

I understand that. Didn't I once challenge Rian in the same way?

"Yet, it was always balanced by the fear that…perhaps each time could be the final time. It always 'could' be…Only it never was," Lune whispers.

Though I know she cannot be cold here, she shudders.

"Lune: I will make things better," I promise. "I will find a way…to make certain that the Almighty's intentions for us come true. Just as they are in Fate's Loom."

"Fate's Loom has me bear seven children, all of them dead," Lune whispers. She starts to become angry, as it is the only way she can think to hide her sorrow, same as Taris. "So why, then, would I give a damn about anything's intentions for me?" she demands, her voice quaking. "I am to be the death of my own children. What kind of motherhood is that? What kind of life is that?"

"It is one with some sadness," I agree. "But life will always have that."

"You do not know what it's like," she accuses. "You do not know how it feels. To have a child grow inside you, to feel that life—and then to feel it die."

"You're right," I agree, and do not protest. "I do not know what that feels like. Perhaps I never will."

"You don't know how jealous I was of you," she prattles on, sniffling. "How unfair I thought it was, for you to get to be with Rian while everyone acted as if Taris and I were impossible. Impossible," she repeats, quieter.

She scrunches her body up tighter.

"I don't want to live," she says, "if I cannot be with him. I do not care what anyone else thinks of that. If I must let my children die, if I have to spend my whole life letting other people choose everything else for me, I want Taris. He is the only person who could ever understand. I do not care if we're bad people. I do not even care if we…we suffer forever, after."

I finally realize what Lune thinks she must sacrifice, and what is willing to sacrifice, for happiness. It pains me to know she genuinely thinks she otherwise would never receive it. Not ever.

I turn towards her, take her face in my hands, and make her look at me so I can see the tears in her eyes. How could I have ever looked at her, and not seen myself in her eyes?

I may have rescued her from the Dark's domain, but I need her to understand that there was no reason for her to suffer there in the first place. Not like that.

"Lune: you have never betrayed me."

"I promised to protect you," she sobs. "I promised. Taris promised. We swore to do it. We failed. To do whatever was necessary—"

"It was not a fair thing to ask of you," I say. "Especially not after saying you could retire as my *Khashtani,* and that Taris could from Rian's, to start your own family. I gave you that and then I took it away. It would be enough to make anyone hate me, but you didn't."

"I did," Lune insists through her tears. "I did. I hated you."

I shake my head. "You didn't. You have died for me so many times over again, Lune; you would not do that for a sister you hate."

"But I did! I did! I only died for you because I knew that was the only way I would even deserve a little happiness!"

"Oh, Lune," I say.

I pull her in against my shoulder and am surprised, though pleased, that she allows this. I wonder if anyone other than Taris has ever held my little sister when she cried in her entire life. I comfort her like Peace comforted Taris, and I hope she somehow understands the way he finally did that I do care about her.

"There are others, Lune," I promise her. "Others who can guard my life and Rian's life. Who are paid to do it, and are not expected to spend their entire life looking after us. Letting it consume every waking moment? Your entire life? No one should have ever made that choice for you. Especially not when you were only a child."

"But we owe you," she whispers to me. "Because you let us go."

"That debt is more than paid," I promise her. "If you insist on believing there was ever a debt in the first place, then know that you have paid it back a thousand times over already."

She does not say anything but sniffles.

"Lune, I will sort things," I promise her. "I want you to be allowed to live your own life. In fact, I will make certain you can."

"You won't be able to," she sniffs. "Between Nusk and the Carsans and Mother and Father, they all want me to do different things. And I will be just a child. So will you. They will not listen to us."

"I will make them listen," I promise her. "We are going all the way back, again Lune. Perhaps I will not be able to stop them all from having you start to train as a *Khashtani,* and maybe I won't be able to stop the Carsans from thinking that they are in control of your fate. I know they will want that power, given who you are, and who I am. But I will find a way, in the end, to let you and Taris choose to be together. If you want to be. I swear it."

She considers this for a long time.

"You would do that for me?" she finally asks incredulously.

Her voice is so small. In fact, my sister is so small, I think, compared to me. I am taller than her. As my *Khashtani* self, my shoulders are broader, arms stronger, muscles more capable of doing what she was always expected to do, to begin with. How ironic, that even as my *Khashtani,* Lune has never attained what I have. Even if I know this is all done by chance for the most part, dependent on what traits our parents passed down to us, it is as if fate always had something different intended, for both of us.

"Of course," I soothe her. "I would. That is not too much to ask for. Your life will not be perfect, Lune. I cannot give you that. But it will still be good. I promise. You deserve to have happiness. And you do not have to earn it."

I do not have anything else to say, and can only hope that what I have said is enough. However, since Lune does not let go of me, I do not let go of her. I stroke Lune's hair and keep her pressed close to me. When she quiets more, I hum to her the lullaby she wrote for my son. I do not know the words, but I will never forget that melody. I know she knows it, too.

I watch the clouds out in that deep purple sky and see that they do not move. I suppose they do not need to, but the aesthetic is lovely.

After some time, I realize that Lune has fallen asleep. Looking around for a place to put her, as I do not want to leave her on these steps, I see a low divan behind me and the side, under a copse of trees. I am only partially surprised by the fact I can lift her in my arms and carry her over to lay her down, there. Lune was so heavy, when I carried her from the Dark's domain. She is much lighter, here.

Fate has given me more than enough time, I decide. I would have thought he'd have come to fetch me, by now. So, I start back the way I came, determined to ask him a few more things, if I can, before letting him return me to Samioth.

Before I can pass under the nearest arch again, back towards the pond where Mercer was, I hear someone behind me.

"Excuse me! Pardon me, miss! Wait!"

The voice is not one that would belong to one of the seven angels, I can tell. When I turn, it is to see a girl running towards me, her curly hair a flustered mess, her cheeks lightly pink on an otherwise pale canvas. She smiles, drawing my attention to the scar chipping at the left corner of her upper lip. She is as youthful a child as the rest of us have been made, in this realm, so that I cannot truly tell her age.

"Hello, hello! Are you Miss Soleil Marson?" she asks brightly.

I stare at her, then back at that tall golden gate, where it looks as if at least a dozen people are gathered, some of them hanging on the bars. All of them are watching this young girl, who has obviously has found herself where she probably ought not to be. All I can imagine is that she has climbed over the gate, but I do not know how she could have, given how it is built, and how tall it stands.

"I…Yes," I say.

"Do you know Cas? Castel Voskoss? Oh, and Miss Margo? And Xerian?"

"Again. Yes," I say slowly.

"Oh, wonderful!" she says, clasping her hands together in front of her. She turns back to the others at the gate and waves to them, calling, louder, "She says she knows Prince Castel!"

There are some replies to that, but I cannot quite make them out, because I am distracted again by her.

"Could you tell Cas something for us?" she asks earnestly, innocently.

She speaks as if I would not be bringing a message back from the dead.

I try to imagine who she was, when she was alive. She is Alarkian, not Lijimi, and that alone is curious. I instinctively doubt she was his lover based on how she speaks of him, and I note that the wound that killed this girl is not a slit throat as Castel relayed happened to the girl he loved. Regardless, this girl clearly knows him, and knows him well. I suspect all those hanging about the gates do. They may have considered themselves family.

"Yes, I suppose I can deliver a message," I say, and her smile brightens.

"Oh, thank you! Tell him it is from his Sunguard, and Elena, Farian, Sebastian, and Louisa, and, oh, everyone, really. He will know what that means," she says.

"Tell him he is a fool, and we are all fine," one of the boys calls from behind the gate.

"Tell him not to worry for us; we chose this life, and we knew what might happen," a girl with Margo's accent adds.

"Tell him we put up a good fight, in case he thought otherwise!" another of the boys calls. "Fabian almost killed Charrion!"

"I did not."

"You could have, though."

"I doubt that. It was a fool's errand."

The girl before me whirls back on them, still somehow maintaining her natural ambience of cheer as she shouts back, "Shut up! I snuck through; I get to pick what we say!"

She turns back to me with that bright smile of hers, that pinches her wide eyes into genuine crescents of mirth. She is adorable, I decide. She reminds me of Lune, but without Lune's melancholy.

"Right. Tell him we really are all fine, his Sunguard," she rattles on. "That we are not in any pain, now. Margo understands, I'm sure. She and Ruskin both would. Well, we know Ruskin does, now. Anyway. But Cas always did blame himself for more than he should. Tell him we are all fine. All of us. We are sorry for leaving him behind. Oh! And tell him, in case he does not believe you, 'Wina says "Good morning!"'. He ought to believe you, then."

I am startled by such a simple message.

"That's all?"

She smiles. "That is all! Thank you eternally!"

I try to observe her as best I can, in case I need to try and describe her to Castel once I return to Samioth. It occurs to me I do not know if I will be able to remember most of what I have seen here, let alone in good detail.

I decide to ask after her full name, but before I can, there is a presence beside us. Another of the seven angels, I realize, given her stature and general bearing. This is not Peace, as I suspect she is still with Taris, but she is undoubtedly beautiful, and kind. To me, she looks as if she could be an older version of Asmer, though she does not have Asmer's dark freckles. Her face is the sort that never stops smiling, though hers is a constant, gentle thing, and less deliberate than Fate's insistence on being friendly to me.

"Winifred," she says gently. "I believe you know where you should be."

"I know," Wina says brightly, not bothered by admitting to having broken what may have been a strict rule, or merely a suggestion. It is difficult to know. "But we simply had to be sure Cas knew."

"Of course," the woman says, putting a hand to Wina's shoulder to shepherd her back to the gate. Wrangling the children back together after a long day at the park, to go home.

She glides back toward the gate, with Wina in front of her. Now that she has said her piece to me, Wina is practically skipping back toward the gate. It is as if what pulls the rest of us humans to the ground, even here, is in partial suspension for her. She is so light on her feet.

"Here you are, then, Soleil," I hear Fate's voice behind me.

I turn back to him. I wonder if he somehow knew I was looking for him, or if my timing is simply that ideal, here. I suppose it does not matter.

"Are you ready to go back, now?" he asks me.

"Is Septimus?" I say.

"I already sent him back," Fate says. He is smiling again. "He agreed, if that is what you are wondering. I would not inquire why, when you return. He will not be able to remember."

I nod. That makes sense. I suppose Septimus and I need not return at the same time. It is not as if we arrived here in tandem.

"Before I leave, I…I still have questions," I admit.

"I'm afraid I cannot answer everything for you, Soleil," Fate laughs. "That would rather defeat the purpose of letting you go live it out, don't you think?"

"Well. Yes. I suppose," I say. "But it is not…about the future. It's not that. Exactly. It is other things. Advice, I suppose."

"Go on," Fate prompts me.

"What do I do about Teresa?" I ask, conflicted and tormented by the concepts I've been presented with, and the possibilities. For both Teresa and her life, and Yvette Pike's. "About her and her husband. About her and Shinya. Without these men, the children she loves will never exist. But to let them use her as they have, and to let her marry a man like Kryto Grey… Septimus has told me that I must, but how can I possibly do this and call myself a good woman?"

"Ah. I understand all your concerns for her, Soleil. Like all things, of course, they have been made note of. But as far as the Dark's claim over her: it is invalid," Fate reassures me.

"Invalid?" I repeat.

"Completely. As is her marriage, given how it came about. One cannot choose evil on accident. Even if she consented at one point in time to becoming a part of her husband's family, to being his wife, she was not in the proper state of mind at their alleged wedding. Regardless, she could not know what the Greys meant for that wedding, and her promises, to entail. Nor could she know what she was doing was wrong. They kept her ignorant. Naïve. They tampered with her mind. Therefore: she did not willingly choose the fate they would prescribe to her. I would know."

I suppose I cannot disagree with him on that.

"But what about everything else?" I press. "I'm sure I, at least, will need to remember things, for the final timeline. But how can I let bad things happen? How can I let her marry Kryto, be miserable with him, and then have an affair with Shinya? It is wrong."

"Mmm," Fate says thoughtfully. He surprises me with his next question. "Do you know what Teresa did, the night she spent with Aiko Shinya?"

I hesitate. "Aside from what I assume happened?"

"She cried, while he comforted her, until she fell asleep. She would never have guessed before that night that a man could be so gentle."

This is something worth giving thought to. I knew from their implications that life for my cousins has not been charmed. But I never pictured her night with Shinya being, perhaps, one of the first times Teresa has ever had someone be kind to her, aside from Septimus, who she did not trust.

"You and Septimus believe that it was fear that finally drove Teresa to leave her husband," Fate says. "In some ways, perhaps that is correct. But it was more than that. It was the realization that a man who loved her should treat her the way Aiko Shinya did that night, and not the way she had grown accustomed to, and come to expect. It may be something she cannot recognize without feeling guilt. But being with him made her realize she needed to leave her husband for her own sake, as well as her children's. While betraying her so-called husband was wrong, the outcomes have made her a stronger person. Someone who could do what was necessary, to save a number of lives.

"Would you choose for her, to take that away from her? Without knowing the consequences, for her or for those around her?"

"But it is morally wrong," I point out. "By Theebin belief—which is what all this is—what she did, what they did, was wrong."

"Yet it happened. There is no taking it away, after. Only an opportunity for them to see what they might make right in their lives," Fate muses. "It is better, I think, to allow them the chance for repentance and redemption. But you cannot seek those things for them, Soleil. They must. Besides, most importantly, who is to say things will not be different, when the world is put right? I believe Aiko Shinya once told you he thought Teresa was meant to be his wife. Who is to say she will not be?"

Again, he stumps me. While he does not correct me, agreeing that Shinya and Teresa may have done something wrong in being together with her married to a different man, I did not consider the obvious fact that perhaps, in the final timeline, when things are the way they are meant to be, she might end her union with Kryto before even ever meeting Shinya.

When I saw the ghosts of Rian and Taris rescuing her, after all, she was younger than she is, now. So, perhaps she will learn earlier to leave Kryto on her own. For herself. Then she might meet Shinya in Isaaria, when he is our ambassador to the east. Perhaps she might get the chance to experience his kindness, then, and they might be together.

I sigh. "I only want to make sure, if I'm going to fix things, that I actually fix them. As many things as I can, as best I can."

"Of course," Fate says. "That is noble. But do not forget to live, Soleil. Do not forget that, sometimes, good deeds are not done as pointedly and in obvious charity, as you would expect them to be. After all, when you try to make the world a perfect place, you begin to see humanity as part of the problem. That is part of what has happened to the Greys. Death is a luxury for those they see as less than perfect. Choices are things that cannot be made by those who disagree with their methods or opinions."

I nod. I certainly do not want to make the mistakes the Greys have; the ones they convinced even Mercer into believing.

"You cannot save the world, Soleil. There will still be horrors and deaths and wars. But you can save your husband and the future of your children. Even if they, too, cannot save the world, or make it perfect, they will help the people living in it. They will help the future. No matter what you are told by the flawed logics of reality, that is more than enough," Fate reassures me. "Now. Do you think you can go home, knowing this?"

"I guess," I say. "I suppose if I wait any longer, I will just manage to think up more questions to ask you. Although, I have to say, I do not know if I'm going to be very good at all the things the Almighty wants me to do. Why me? Why not Rian? He is more Theebin than I am. He prays better."

"Oh, Soleil," Fate says. "You cannot compare these things. You have tried on a few occasions, to contemplate the life you ought to live. If you are concerned with what to do next, seek the answers in Theebin meditation."

"But I don't *feel* like anyone is there, listening," I complain.

"Don't seek answers through feelings," he chides. "Feelings are fleeting. If you have faith there is someone listening, and continue to ask for guidance, you will be answered."

I consider this, and sigh. "So, Rian is right again. As always. I suppose, at least, marrying him ought to make me something of a better person."

Fate laughs. "As is only natural and right. So. Let us send you on your way, then, so you might find your way back to him."

"Don't you need Anna?" I ask. "To bring me through the tunnels?"

"Not in sending you back," Fate corrects. "That can be done in but a moment. Just remember that lantern of Jin Riyong's. You do not need to go towards it, not while you are safe, here. But that is where you are going."

Going home. Back to Samioth. How peculiar, that in what I suppose might be hours or days of time, the entire world has become home to me, instead of just one tiny section of Isaaria. I find that I am excited, now, to go back and see Rian one last time, and then to jump back. To start all over again.

It makes me want to cry, knowing that we have come all this way and that it has not been for nothing. There will be troubles ahead of us, Fate has nearly guaranteed that in his reassurances. Yet I do not care. I will accept that.

"Oh," Fate says, as if just remembering something. He laughs. "Just one last thing to keep your mind busy for the next few decades."

"...What?" I say, confused.

"Know that if the clock strikes six at four, your world is doomed, and you have failed," Fate warns me. "No matter what you have promised, you cannot keep that reality. You must find a way out of it."

It is such a vague yet ominous warning that I cannot help but let it strike genuine fear into me.

"What does that mean?" I ask desperately.

It is already too late. Fate does not have the chance to tell me precisely what he means, or precisely how to do what I should to succeed. He does not give himself the opportunity to explain his words to me. So, I will have to move forward in our last timeline with this as a warning, and otherwise be forced to trust my own moral code and good judgement.

As I have already proven to the Otherworld and its denizens that I am no puppet of someone else's good intentions, perhaps that is entirely the point.

Twenty-One

WAKING FINDS ME groggy, bleary eyed and sore-throated. I barely have any time to blink the exhaustion from my eyes when I realize that, as I slept, the world has not been at peace around me. I am not in the old temple, firstly, but have been transported back to Park Mi-Sun's palace. I am laying on a mat with a blanket covering me. As I force myself to sit up, I see Septimus in a similar situation, not far away.

In front of us, sitting on the ground with her legs folded neatly under her, her expression perfectly impassive, is Queen Park Mi-Sun. She is dressed as impeccably as usual, though I note that her overdress is the only thing that has changed. The base is the same dress as the one I saw her wearing initially. Her son, then, has been playing in the corner of the room, his little feet slapping against the wood floor as he learns to move. Currently, he is chasing a paper bird, then throwing it into the air, and going after it again.

I am surprised to see Vásan here as well, leaning up against a corner. He nods to me, noticing I am awake. When the paper bird flutters into his lap, he plucks it up and waits for Mi-Sun's child to toddle over before offering it to him.

"How are you feeling, your majesty?" Vásan asks me, and Mi-Sun's eyes flick up to me as well.

"Dreadful," I say honestly. "How did we get here?"

Mi-Sun answers this.

"You are disoriented," she says factually. "Riyong says that is quite normal, for someone in your condition, after the Otherworld. You and Septimus both went and returned; he first, you after. I had Riyong pack the lantern away and help carry you back here, once he could manage it. You and your cousin were both quite weak. You have been resting, since."

"I see. Thank you," I say.

She flicks a hand dismissively. "We could hardly leave you out there."

The way she says this is telling, and reminds me of what Riyong warned about what sorts of monsters might be attracted, so long as a window to the Otherworld was opened. There is a streak of dark blood against Mi-Sun's cheek that is decidedly not human. There is more on her hands, which she quickly, though calmly, covers under the sleeves of her dress.

"It so happened that there were more creatures drawn than anticipated," she tells me.

"My apologies," I croak.

Park Mi-Sun shrugs her shoulders.

"When Riyong went, he had the Wolffs. They were gifted to manage this life. We have not been. But we have still managed."

"Did they get to the town?" I ask in concern, given her bloody hands.

But Mi-Sun is still calm.

"No," she says. "My people have been safe, though our border has been threatened and still is under what you may call siege. It is not a serious peril anymore. I went out to assist, myself. I have more strength than most would assume, you see. And I have some skill with a bow, besides."

This piques my interest, and I nearly inquire, as I myself am a student of the same discipline. However, something tells me that Mi-Sun would not find this shared trait anything to celebrate over. So, I do not comment on it.

"Margo and Castel managed well, then," I say.

"Ah. Yes," Mi-Sun acknowledges. "They are sufficient. Your Lady Grey has been a surprising asset, I will admit. But we would have managed without them."

I cannot help but give her a curious look. As far as I can see, it does not appear as if there are an exceptionally high number of able-bodied fighters to protect people, here.

"Shinya came," she says plainly, as if I should have guessed on my own. "He is taking care of things."

She must know she has shocked me by saying so, and I'm sure she did it on purpose. But what can I say? Mi-Sun would have no reason to lie to me, nor could she truly know what an impact her saying so would have on me.

Vásan is as shocked as I am, and though he does not show it in the same way, I can tell. He was at that dinner same as I, when Magnus brought up Teresa's lover, and he and Nissa were both made aware of Shinya's identity as the father of Teresa's child. The idea that Aiko Shinya would be here, now, at the exact same time we are, is beyond the statistical likelihood.

But after my time in the Otherworld, speaking with Fate itself, I do not think I can believe in coincidence anymore.

"Aiko Shinya. Is here," I repeat.

"But of course," she says, as if we are fools for not having thought of it ourselves. "He is my cousin. Why would he not come here?"

I do not have an answer to that. I glance at Vásan, again, and he shrugs. I suppose I, at least, have Fate to thank for this. Or, more accurately, the Almighty. There is a point to be made, after all my questioning, and I deserve being taken by surprise considering my doubts.

The door slides open to allow Jin Riyong entry. He sits next to the queen before pulling it closed again. Their son pads over to them, to sit himself on Riyong's knees, and no one comments on it. I realize there is a possibility Riyong is not aware of how much his son looks like him, even at such an early age. But I doubt it. Someone must have told him.

Riyong must know we know.

"Miss Soleil," he says. Perhaps he can feel I am awake, or perhaps someone I did not notice went off to notify him of my change in condition. "I am glad to know you are feeling well."

"Feeling better," I correct. "But yes. And thank you. For everything."

Riyong nods. "Would you say you were…successful?" he asks carefully, trying not to be too obvious in his prying.

I consider the best way to respond. "I would say so. Yes. If possible, though, I would like to return home and discuss a few things with my husband. Then, I plan to turn things back again."

I do not miss his sigh of relief. Mi-Sun's lips tighten for a moment, and then she lets her face resume neutrality again.

"Then that is wonderful news," Riyong says. "I would say, by the queen's own definition, you have fulfilled your portion of this contract. Please, rest for as long as you like. We will be sure a boat is ready for you, when needed."

"We won't stay long," I promise.

I go to braid back my hair when I realize something strange. There is a startlingly thick white streak corrupting my hair, from the roots coiling through my braid to the tip. I stare at it for a moment, then stupidly glance over at Septimus to see if he has one, too. Of course, he does not, or, if he does, I cannot tell. His hair is already white.

"I was just telling our Isaarian guests that my cousin has come to stay with us, for a time," the queen of Kacha says. "They appeared startled to learn he would come to see the only remaining members of his own family, as well as pay his respects to those deceased."

"Oh?" Riyong says. "Well. I suppose Shinya has been wandering about for years, now. He was meant to be our ambassador to Isaaria, if I remember correctly. I suppose they thought he was dead."

"No, it is not that," I say haltingly, and feel Vásan's eyes on me as I decide how best to put this. "It is only, rather recently, we learned that your cousin knew one of my cousins. Septimus' sister, Teresa."

Mi-Sun frowns, her eyes narrowing again.

"You mean 'knows'," she says, correcting my Alarkian. Her own is exceptional. "I assume they are both alive, and so, they 'know' one another."

"Well, yes. They know one another," I admit. "But they also...*knew* each other. I suppose you would say in the Biblical sense."

It takes her a moment. Riyong, with his less pristine Alarkian, does not catch my meaning, but his queen does. I decide it would be best not to draw things out.

"There is a child," I say, and she puts a hand to her forehead, groans, and begins cursing in Kachin.

It does not take Riyong long to put things together, then. He turns to his queen, and the two converse, shortly, exclusively in Kachin. He is stunned, and she is greatly displeased, to say the least. Snappish might be a good description, which feels slightly hypocritical of her, given her and Riyong's positions.

"You cannot tell him," she finally orders to me in Alarkian. "He would loathe to know he had any part in bringing a child into this world."

"It is a bit late for that, now. If that was such a concern, perhaps he should not have bedded her in the first place," Vásan mutters.

The queen glares at him, but cannot disagree.

She looks back to me. "Are you going to tell him?"

"Do you truly not want me to?" I say, and do not give her a direct answer. Even I do not know what I'm going to do about it, yet.

Mi-Sun does not know what to say to that. She sighs again, closes her eyes for a moment, and thinks.

"I do not have any way to stop you," she says. "But do know, now, that this would not be a joyous thing for him. I pray you keep that in mind."

"He is not due back for some time," Riyong warns us.

"I know. He says there are birds on Chimhwi's tomb again," Mi-Sun says. "The black ones."

Riyong sighs. He looks much older than he is.

"There always are," he says.

He heaves himself to his feet again, likely to go and chase the birds off. Mi-Sun takes her son from him, though now that his mother is holding him, he wriggles. He is too young for his words to be much more than babbling, anyway, but even I can tell he is complaining. I'm sure Mi-Sun will be leaving, shortly, to try and see to his needs.

There is one more thing, though, that my own subconscious drudged up and the Dark took advantage of it. I hesitate, only because I know it is a dangerous topic, and it is likely I will get no answers. Bringing it up in the first place may only elicit negative emotions from someone I would rather they not come from.

Unfortunately, I have never been good at keeping my mouth shut when I need to. I take a deep breath.

"Your brothers—"

"I would rather not speak of them," Mi-Sun says, quiet but sharp.

I will not be able to ask her about her older brother, Crown Prince Bogun, whose own wife and daughter are buried outside with him, or her younger half-brother, Chimhwi, whose tomb attracts crows.

"I'm sorry," I offer instead.

She nods, but does not divulge anything more. After several moments of poignant silence, she stands and lifts her son against her shoulder. He still grips his little paper bird.

"If you must see Shinya, I believe he is out beyond the graveyard," she says. "He came to visit my brothers' tombs. But now that he is here, he is managing the pests."

I have never heard of demonic creatures referred to as pests before. Though, I suppose if I had been living the way Park Mi-Sun has been, that might change.

"I will not say anything about his daughter," I promise her.

And I will not. Not now.

"Where can I find this…graveyard?" I add, praying it is not the one we found Riyong in our first day here.

"It is due east. Down the hill," she says. "You will see him."

"Thank you," I say again, but Park Mi-Sun does not answer verbally.

She nods, then leaves, with a swishing of fabric. Someone else closes the door for her. I hear other, muted footsteps following her as she goes, and soft murmuring in Kachin. I should have known the queen would not be left alone entirely. Daeyeon, no doubt, was standing guard for her.

I stand properly, and stretch, my body stiff and sore after spending so much time asleep, likely in one position. I never realized that rest could make a person ache in such a manner, yet my limbs cry in relief for even the simplest of exercises.

I spot my winter clothing and begin to shrug into more layers, taking my time, allowing my body to adjust. If I intend to speak with Aiko Shinya, while he is out slaying monsters, I will need to be on guard, myself. I cannot be taken unawares by any creatures, even if Margo and Castel are also keeping them at bay.

The entire time I dress, I do not keep quiet, hoping to purposefully wake Septimus, but he barely stirs. I wonder if he should have woken before me, as Fate sent him back first, or if it does not matter.

Vásan notices the concerned gaze I give my cousin.

"I will stay with him," he says.

I nod. "…Thank you," I say. "If you see Nissa, please tell her the same."

"She is with the Lijimi prince, and Miss Margo," Vásan says. "I think she is enjoying herself rather immensely, killing monsters with them. I would say this is a game to her, but I doubt even she is that foolhardy."

This makes sense to me, though. "She killed a bear once on her own," I inform him. "I doubt she is scared of anything, much, anymore."

This is news to him, but Vásan does not appear shocked by it.

I consider what things have shocked him, then. At some point, the realization that Lune was furious at the prospect of being made to marry him, and that she was not at all appreciative of his telling her. The idea that his brother could be a complete monster, that is another. He took Septimus telling him Lune was never going to love him in stride, though.

I wonder, briefly, it that will somehow change, now that we have essentially changed the fabric of the universe.

I realize that I hope not.

How in the world am I going to tell Lune any of this, I wonder? In fact, how in the world am I going to manage to hold my tongue about her and Taris when they are both still young and have no romantic inclinations, yet. Will it be acceptable to tease them about it, or could I somehow drive them apart? Do my words even have that kind of power?

"Is something troubling you, then, your majesty," Vásan says.

It is not a question so much as it is a reminder I am still standing there.

"Nothing," I say, and sigh. "I saw Lune, there. I mean, of course I did, but…it was difficult, seeing her like that, and…talking…" It is too much of a bother to explain. "Just, sibling troubles. You understand how it is."

"Yes," Vásan says dryly, "I should say I do."

It takes a moment for me to catch up to myself.

Soleil, you damn fool.

"Right," I say uneasily. I clear my throat. "Well, I'm off, then."

"Take care."

I cannot make myself look at him again when walking out, though at least I truly believe he will take care of Septimus. I contemplate an apology, but do not know how to approach the situation without making things worse. So, I set my mind to finding Aiko Shinya instead, to see if there may be any good that I can do, there.

My shoes are easily found and slipped on, allowing me to escape the building without anyone else stopping me. For a moment, I am tempted to see Jin Riyong, knowing it would be easy to find him, but I suspect he would appreciate being alone at this time. Even if it is only to chase birds off his closest friend's tomb, he deserves privacy in his mourning.

I go eastward, instead, as Mi-Sun instructed, towards the graveyard Aiko Shinya is apparently frequenting.

This will be the third graveyard, then, that I have been exposed to in a small matter of days. I had heard, once, that millions of people lived in Bonxhui city alone. I cannot imagine how many graves there are, now.

Like the first graveyard, when I approach, I find that the tall grass in Kacha—though dead in winter—has helped to hide tombstones and markers. Understandably, there is no placard or gateway announcing the entrance to this graveyard, but it is placed in a specific area with softer soil, set down from a smattering of rocks, which assists the grass in hiding its presence in the first place. A casual passerby could easily fall off the slope and injure themselves greatly, if they were not aware of this graveyard's existence. I doubt there is a single person living in Park Mi-Sun's refugee town that is not aware of where their chosen graveyards are. Each one of them undoubtedly has a loved one or family member they had to bury.

I hear before I see Shinya. As I approach the graveyard, I can feel two other distinct presences: the first being a deep, abiding sadness that likely hosts a few dozen spirits who have not been able to move on yet, like Damen's Ghost. The other is a crueler, more malicious entity. I felt similarly in Mouloix when we fought the creatures, some of which Teresa may have created herself.

There are sounds from this latter category, and I draw one of my daggers in precaution. When I begin to climb down the rocks toward the graveyard, I see the carnage Shinya has wrought from the creatures attempting to haunt this place.

I do not know if he notices my presence immediately, so intent on his work is he. I might have thought, before, that Septimus, Vásan, Nissa and I fared well in Mouloix, but Shinya on his own is a force to be reckoned with. Though I know I should help him, simply to see these monsters done with quicker, I instead stand back and watch.

I decide it is more than likely I would only be in his way.

Last I saw him, Aiko Shinya was only seventeen. Now, nearly twenty years later, he has experienced quite the transformation. I can no longer call him a boy by any stretch of the imagination. His figure has filled out, and he has allowed his hair to grow long enough to tie it back. It has clearly been several days since he has last shaved, given the scruff about his face, and he carries only what is necessary. His travel-worn appearance, along with his tattered Tourrannese clothing and weaponry, somehow makes him look all the more dangerous.

I cannot help but think of what Septimus once called him: feral.

There was always a distinct gracefulness in Shinya, as a younger man, and I cannot say there is not, now, but it is different. It is wilder and more violent. By the time he has finished and whirls even on me, for a moment, I am fearful he may attack me. Luckily, he realizes I am a human person and not a dark creature here to prey on victims of fear.

Shinya straightens, his sword still held before him, though he lowers it. I am sure he is curious why a western woman is standing here, now. I wonder if Mi-Sun even told him there were westerners here, or if she secretly did her best to keep us in our respective spheres. Would that be worth the effort put in, I wonder, considering how likely it is that Margo, Nissa, and Castel are out doing the same work?

It occurs to me too late that, naturally, Shinya recognizes me and cannot place me in his memories. He says something in Tourrannese, first, instinctually. But the sword is continually lowering, which is good news.

"Your cousin Mi-Sun told me you were out here," I say, letting him see both my hands, away from my sides. I have replaced my own weapon, where it belongs. I am sure he has good reason to be paranoid, these days. "I asked her where to find you, so we might talk."

"Why?" he demands, switching to Alarkian as well. "Who are you?"

"You don't remember me?" I say carefully.

He narrows his eyes as he sheathes his weapon. "Should I?"

"I am Soleil Marson," I tell him, still stunned by his sudden appearance, here. If he had not confirmed his identity on accident, and if not for those blue eyes, I'm not sure I would have truly believed this was him.

His hand does not leave the hilt of his blade, but he has not drawn it again.

"I do remember you," he says after a long time. "Years ago. In Isaaria. I was meant to be your king's ambassador. The tensions between Tourran and Kacha disrupted that."

It takes him a few moments longer. We both look much different than we did several decades ago, and I understand that. I doubt he cares at all about Isaaria or our problems while he has been traveling the world, killing monsters and doing his best to conceal the fact he is still alive.

"I do not know why it is I always trust you," he admits, sounding too tired to fully care. "But I do. There is something about you, Captain Marson."

"I'm not asking for that trust," I say, hoping he believes me. "You do not owe me anything. But I would like to talk, if you will accept that."

Shinya does not have a pleased appearance, precisely, as I'm not sure he knows how to express emotions in that way anymore. But his posture changes. He willing takes a few steps closer to me.

"Of course, Captain Marson," he says. "You have come all this way."

"Yes," I say. "Mainly to see Jin Riyong and your cousin the queen. Though, after learning from Mi-Sun you were here, I thought we should speak in regards to Teresa Smith."

That, for a moment, brings him pause. Worlds are colliding for Aiko Shinya, in an undeniably confusing manner. My being here, with Teresa's name on my lips, must be a cause of distress to him.

"How do you know about Resa?" he demands.

"She…Teresa Smith is my cousin," I say, deciding that is the simplest way to put it. "She is living with myself in the Summer Palace, now. In Isaaria."

Shinya is shocked, yet, when I mention Teresa fleeing to Isaaria, there is obvious relief in both his posture and tone.

"She is safe, then."

"She escaped her husband, if that is what you mean," I say, letting him know I'm fully aware of those circumstances.

"And the boys?" he asks, surprising me. "Damen and Aiden—her sons. Are they safe? Are they well?"

"They came with her," I say. "Septimus brought them. They are all very well, safe, and healthy. They are living in the Summer Palace in Isaaria with the king. Being treated like little princes."

"The littler one was sick."

"I know. She told me what you did for her," I note.

"You mean did to her," he mutters.

"You saved her son."

"I am not proud of it. Not of what happened afterwards, in any case."

"But you don't regret it," I guess.

Shinya hesitates before admitting to it. "…No."

For a moment, he moves as if he may draw his sword again, confusing me. But then he relents, sighs, and leans back to sit against a rock.

"You are here for retribution, then?" he says, as if accepting it.

"What?" I say, now doubly confused.

"She is your cousin," he says. "I did wrong by her. You said you came here for other matters, but now that you have learned I am here, I would expect you are seeking a price to pay."

His Alarkian is not exact in its accuracy, but I am starting to understand. It did not occur to me at all, though perhaps it should have, that this is the conclusion Shinya would come to. The idea is one that, in my mind, belongs to the old world. An unbroken place, where a concept such as Teresa's honor would in any way mean more to me than her safety.

In my mind, Shinya saved Aiden's life. Whatever happened between him and Teresa afterwards, that is between them. I only wanted to see if I might convince him to come see her again, not to punish him for spending the night with a married woman.

"I was not going to do it, at first," Shinya admits before I can relay any of this. "When I came back with the medicine, I gave it to her brother for the boy. Then he brought me to where she was, in her bedroom, and left. I had decided, then, I would tell her I did not need anything in repayment. But…"

"But that's not what happened," I say.

I have Teresa's side of the story as well, after all. She is correct; she is not entirely innocent in this.

Shinya shrugs.

"I understand it likely will not sway you one way or another. But I did make up my mind, before stepping foot in her bedroom, not to do it. Things did not go the way I anticipated."

He does not need to say more. I can guess at how Teresa made him feel; they were the kindness, for one another, otherwise absent from the world in their own experience.

"Shinya," I say, making him raise his head to look at me. "I am not here to punish you. I only thought you would like to know she made it to Isaaria, and that she is safe there, with the boys. I thought you, perhaps, may like to come see them."

He stares at me. "Why."

"Why what?"

"Why do you think I would ever want to see her again?"

The question is so cruel, and cold-hearted, that at first, I allow it to make me disgusted with him. I force myself to be patient, trying to understand the man behind these words.

"Because you still dream about her," I say. "I know you do."

He gives me a skeptical, suspicious look that tells me I am correct.

"You might not remember," I say. "But a long time ago, you confided in me that you dreamed about a girl who matched Teresa's description. You have been dreaming about her for a long time. I figured there is no reason why you would not still dream of her."

"I…I think I remember telling you something of the like," he admits, frowning, trying to recall an event that no longer exists. "I think I remember telling you many things I likely should not have…I have trusted you."

His hand is still, almost absently, resting on the hilt of his sword. I suppose either he does not believe that I am here with no ill will against him, or it is mere habit. I could not say. I look him over once more, noting he appears to in no way left his belongings with Mi-Sun, at her palace. He could disappear at a moment's notice, and never tell anyone. Even the flask tied to his sash, I suspect, holds the draught he needs to help him control his fluke without it injuring him. So, he has someone, somewhere, to supply that for him. Even in this world.

"You should come and see her," I insist.

Shinya flicks his eyes at me warily. "She spoke to you about me," he says, more of a conclusive statement than a question.

"I think she would be happy to have you visit," I say carefully.

He makes a noncommittal sound and does not elaborate.

Mi-Sun was right; I do not think it wise to inform Shinya he has a daughter, now. He would not react well.

I slowly, but pointedly, come closer to him, and find a place on a lower rock to perch myself. I know he is still wary of me, and the trust he feels towards me. I understand better, now, that someone like Shinya likely can feel instinctive pulls from past timelines. He is affected by them, and old relationships, even if he cannot remember them. While I change time, as Fate said, there are other factors that my fluke has nothing to do with. I am a Time Smith same as Septimus is a Memory Smith. That is all.

After a few moments of me sitting closer by him, Shinya's shoulders appear less taunt. I decide to return to the topic of Teresa and his seeing her later.

"It is good to see you again. Until Teresa mentioned meeting you, I had thought you were dead," I admit.

Shinya shrugs wordlessly.

"I had heard the rumors, of course, of your survival, but I thought they'd been manufactured merely to give people hope."

"I may as well be dead," Shinya says. "There is no rebuilding the Tourrannese islands, after this. Even if we could, I would never agree to rule there. Never."

My brow furrows. "Shinya. I understand you are angry. But the past is the past. Whatever wrongs were done by who, the Tourrannese are still your people. You cannot eschew half your heritage simply because the government there did terrible things. That does not reflect upon the whole of Tourran."

"You were not there. You could never understand what has happened," he claims.

I slowly work to unbraid and re-pin my hair properly. That new white streak to it is still a surprising development I am not fond of.

"What about the Tourrannese who fought alongside you? What about the ones who tried to do the right thing?" I point out.

"It does not matter. How could you possibly understand?" he demands. I have made him truly angry, now. "How could you know what it is like, living as I have? With a father whose people oppressed the country of his mother for decades?"

"That was long before your birth."

"But it happened afterwards, too. Half of my life has been steeped in war. My family was meant to act as a physical representation of the peace between our countries. But in the end, it all meant nothing."

"It was because of the Greys—" I start.

"You cannot blame them for everything. They are a handy excuse, but people who commit the sorts of atrocities I witnessed knew exactly what they were doing. They chose to do it. No magical corruption can justify that. Mankind is evil."

"You wouldn't say that about Teresa," I challenge him, and am surprised when he has a quick retort.

"But she is not entirely human, is she? She has a least a few drops of Fair blood in her. Her children, too. So do you," he adds.

I'm not sure if I am flattered or horrified by that statement. He has surprised me with his knowledge of that fact. I wonder, then, what he and Teresa may have talked about their night together, before she fell asleep and he left her.

"But Shinya. If you would damn all of mankind, you must know you are including yourself in that," I try again. "You would call yourself evil?"

He barely has to consider it. "Yes."

For a few moments, he allows me to stare at him before adding:

"You do not know the things I have done."

"We have all done things we are not proud of," I say after a moment. "I have killed many, in the defense of Rian."

"I have killed children, Captain. Have you? Can the things you are 'not proud of' even begin to compare to that? If a fifteen-year-old boy came at you with a sword, would you cut him down? Because I did not hesitate. I only regretted it years after," he says, his angry tone quieting at the end.

I take in his profile, considering the innocence he thinks he has lost. He has fought in several wars, now, as a wandering Tourrannese warrior, with no ties to his own government. He must know it is a miracle he is still alive. His father's cousins, the imperial family of Tourran, before their own untimely deaths, disowned him for rebellious notions and actions.

Better than most, particularly after reading Mercer's journals, I understand what sorts of horrors war can bring about. But I also know that much of Shinya's specific rebellion against the Tourrannese government was founded in a fight against religious oppression of the Theebin religion, and the oppression of Kacha. How could anyone believe Shinya would do nothing against the subjugation of his mother's people? His own family?

I understand that he, like Mercer, wants to justify being the villain of this story. However, while Mercer did it in hopes of one day finding justice and peace, Shinya does it because to him, the world is over. His own fight, in hopes of attaining justice and peace, had the worst, most disastrous consequences imaginable. Good cannot win in this world, in his experience. Why bother pretending otherwise.

"Come see Teresa," I urge as I stand, this time more demanding. "If you truly feel as guilty as you say, over things you have done in the past, then come to the Summer Palace. Make things right. At least with her."

Shinya looks up at me, puzzled and unconvinced.

"Are you in love with her?" I ask pointedly.

In a way that reminds me of the boy I had once met, Shinya glances down, his face reddening. It is enough to convince me that the Shinya I knew, who believed in things like honor and justice, and the possibility of goodness, is still there.

"I do not know," he says. "How could I be?"

"Who am I to say what is and is not possible?" I say in response.

The fact he says nothing to this tells me Shinya does suspect he loves her.

"...Perhaps I could be," he finally allows.

"Then come back with me. See her again. Find out," I say. "Otherwise, this will simply be another thing that you look back on one day and regret."

He thinks, then shakes his head quickly.

"Come with us," I urge him again.

"I cannot."

I can feel myself tightening my jaw. I am grinding my teeth again, I realize. How in character for Shinya to be the one to bring back that bad habit. But I suppose I cannot force him to do the right thing, even if I believe it would do him some good. Mi-Sun said he would be horrified to know he brought a child into this world, this place he hates.

Yet he is still here, killing monsters to protect his cousin's settlement. If Shinya truly believed there was no point in living, in trying to persevere, I do not believe he would bother doing that. Nor would he come to see the last living members of his family, to mourn his dead cousins.

If I cannot convince him, I can only hope things are most different for him, in his true fate. Like Lune and Taris, the boy I once knew named Aiko Shinya deserves a better life than this.

"Then at least know that if you change your mind, you are always welcome in Isaaria," I say, knowing full well that in a matter of months at the most, this reality will no longer exist.

What I do here, I would like to believe, still matters. If I can give this version of Shinya any element of peace, I will, even if only for a few days.

Before leaving him, I decide to give him one last thing to consider. I suspect this feral version of Shinya will avoid Mi-Sun's palace and the settlement until we westerners leave, but in his absence, I hope he will consider my words instead of brushing them off stubbornly.

"You are here to see Mi-Sun, and Park Bogun, and Chimhwi. To visit the latter's graves," I say, a reminder I know he does not need.

"Yes," he says.

"They were your cousins," I say.

"...Yes. They were good men. They did not deserve to die."

"And you lament their loss. If they were still here, would you think them as 'evil' as yourself? They do not have Fair blood. They were as human as you. Mi-Sun is as human as you. Riyong is. Their son is. If you do not want to see that, then, that is your choice. But I know you are too intelligent to willingly hold contradictory beliefs, Aiko Shinya."

He does not look up at me again, and I am forced to leave him on the rocks while I return to Mi-Sun's palace. True to my word, I did not tell him about Rika. But I suspect, if he knew he had a daughter—no, if he met his daughter—he may be inclined to change his opinion on the nature of mankind.

Next time, perhaps.

SEPTIMUS AND I take a few more days before departing, so we may properly recover from our time in the Otherworld. Naturally, Septimus is resistant to wasting much time and only insistences from Mi-Sun's physician force him to rest. He wants to return to Isaaria as soon as possible, so we may see to a few final details, and reset the timeline once and for all. The only reason, he claims, that we should not do it immediately is that Rian and I should be the only ones allowed to remember everything, if we so choose. I admit I would like to and, in fact, even Fate implied I should. But I want to properly ask Rian, or to let Septimus ask him, so he might make a final decision one way or another. I suppose Kang and Aisling could also remember, given the gifts Septimus gave them, but I will leave that up to them and Fate. They have lived such long lives, already; while I hope to see them again one day, I accept that is now in Fate's hands.

Besides, after leaving my family behind with so many warnings that I may not return, I want to see them again. I want to give one last goodbye to Ayla, knowing it will be a long time before I can see her again. I do owe Naomi and Korvaan a private discussion, and I intend to keep my promise to them. I may not want to, but I will. Speaking with Taris has convinced me I should, beyond my selfish reservations. There are many things I feel, I have realized, that I have assumed others know and understand. I realize, now, that perhaps actions are not enough after all. Perhaps there are things that need to be said.

When it comes time to depart, we insist that Riyong and Mi-Sun do not need to escort us to the docks once more. It would be too much of a journey for either of them. Particularly the queen, who I am beginning to suspect is in the early stages of producing a second child. Riyong, at least, bids us a polite farewell, and wishes us the best of luck, but there remains a melancholy in it that haunts me on our travels back to the coast. After all, Riyong knows our mission. He knows I may be able to give him another chance to save his friends. Why that would ever mean something negative to him is a mystery to me. For some reason, between him and Mi-Sun's brothers and cousin, I feel as if I have failed more than succeeded for Kacha.

Up until the moment our ship sets sail, I hope to see Aiko Shinya come join us. I begin to pray for it, at the end, sure that returning to Isaaria with us would alleviate some of his grief, and guilt. If he could only see how well Teresa and her sons are, now. If he could, possibly, meet his own daughter...I am certain it would change him for the better. But he does not come.

After an hour at sea, my companions settle in well. We will not, unfortunately, be returning to Kang and Aisling's island, which means we will not see Xerian again this cycle. Margo insists she is at peace with this, having known a long time ago that she may never even meet Xerian in our final time-line. However, I feel a certain sadness for her in that. As Xerian grew up in the Rumshtaman Empire, he is the furthest removed from the rest of us. The odds of us ever seeing him again, without purposefully seeking him out, are slim. Rian and I will not be able to risk angering the empire, inviting ourselves or any of our assets into their territory, particularly to find a remaining member of a formerly royal family.

If I am to ever see Xerian again, he will have to find his way to us. I suppose it is something else I will have to pray for, and trust. Out of all of us, he is the most trusting, the most hopeful. He truly believes in Septimus' plan, and that it will bring him a better life.

Having watched how much Xerian did for Margo and Vásan, simply by being himself, I want that for him.

Margo, meanwhile, is in her best mood yet, having a ship to control once more. It is not as large as the steamship we crashed at the island, but she still knows how to handle it expertly, and has charted a relatively safe course for us back to Isaaria. It will mean several more weeks, for us, at sea, and I intend to spend it learning as much of Margo's craft as I can to keep from boredom. Otherwise, I am so excited to see my family again that I know I will begin to count the hours. It will drive me mad. Learning how to manage a ship will pass the time.

Strangely, or perhaps not given how she has never been rude or unpleasant to me, Margo accepts this suggestion readily. I think going out to slay monsters and beasts of the Otherworld's nether-realm, or whatever we want to call them, has helped her remember what she was made to do as a Grey.

Ironically, aside from Margo and Nissa, everyone else is avoiding me in some way or another. Nissa is more herself, now, though I have heard that she was all but hyperactive the morning after her needling session, and particularly vicious when fighting off monsters. Whenever given the chance, she still insists she is prepared and willing to fight Nexa Grey's brightback for the sake of revenge. If I make the mistake of broaching anything close to the topic, Nissa will launch into a detailed explanation of precisely how she will go about this.

I believe Margo is greatly amused, though not in an indulgent way; she believes Nissa could do it.

All the men, meanwhile, want nothing to do to me, and actively avoid me after my return from the Otherworld. Castel, at least, has never been particularly social with me over the past weeks we have known one another, so that is no surprise. But every time I try to speak to Septimus about what happened in the Otherworld, alone with no one else around to hear, he finds an excuse to escape me, no matter how flimsy.

Vásan has not said more than two words at a time to me after our brief conversation in Park Mi-Sun's palace.

As our first day of sailing comes to a close, with the sun setting and the temperature dropping, I decide to go below-decks and take stock of our inventory. We should have enough to last us until we return to Isaaria—more than enough. Margo's doubling fluke could save us in a pinch, if we did begin to run out. Mine is a therefore pointless, thankless task, I know. The current alternative, however, is to stay above decks and suffer the menfolk's poor tempers. I decide against it.

I am cursing out Septimus in particular, under my breath, for making me think I have done something to offend him, when I see something move out of the corner of my eye. It is not as if they were trying to hide; once I notice them sitting there on a crate, I realize they have simply been still and quiet but otherwise rather obvious. The fact I know everyone else is above decks still makes my heart jump into my throat before I process who it is.

"Fate's Fingers, Aiko Shinya, you scared the life from me!" I insist as I try to catch my breath.

Shinya does nothing but offer a dull shrug of apology, leaving me to cross my arms and observe him while trying to decide what to do next. Of course, this is preferable given what I would have liked to have happen originally. But since I assumed he was not joining us, I will now have to try and recover my abandoned plan for his reunion with Teresa.

"So, you are coming after all?" I say once I have managed to regain control of my breathing patterns.

"Seems so."

"You want to see Teresa again."

He considers the statement, hesitating before speaking. "I do not know if that is the most correct way to say it. But. I will see her," he says, as if both telling me and reminding himself is necessary.

"Well, as there is no changing things, now, I suppose we best get this out of the way," I say, and go on quickly. "Teresa is expecting a child. You are the father. Congratulations. It is a girl."

Shinya stares at me. His face grows pale. Then he rises so suddenly it would startle me if I were not trained otherwise.

"Why did you not tell me this immediately?!" he demands.

He sounds angry, but I am almost certain this is only because he does not know how else to react.

"Because if you were going to return and see Teresa, I wanted it to be for the right reasons. Not because you dragged yourself there out of obligation or honor or what have you. Now I know you are going because you want to see her. So, I thought it best you knew. Sit down before you pass out."

He stands there numbly as he translates my words and makes sense of them. I push down on his shoulders to make him sit and he does not resist, allowing gravity to do most of the work.

He murmurs something in Tourrannese that I believe has to do with the fact that he has a child. Then he adds in Alarkian:

"But it was...only...the once…The one night—"

I sigh. "I don't know why this always seems to astound you young people, but seeing as such intimacy biologically speaking has but one purpose, sometimes the once is all you need."

Shinya runs his hand back over his hair several times, possibly only half-listening to me.

"How do you know it is a girl?" he finally says, his voice still hoarse.

"We had a doctor come in to see her a few days after she and Septimus arrived," I say. "To make certain the baby was healthy. He had a fluke that allowed him to see through any kind of barrier."

His eyes widen at the mention of a fluke.

"Her health!" he realizes, a hand going to the flask he carries. "Me! My drought! The child…She might…Could…!"

He is struggling to string words together in Alarkian, but I understand.

"There is no cause for concern," I reassure him. "As you are an anomaly even in your own family, I doubt the affliction you have will be passed on in such a way. Even if it was, we still have skilled doctors, in Isaaria. I am certain they will take good care of the child and Teresa, both."

That appears to reassure him, though I suspect this may mainly be because he cannot stand to imagine another variable to this situation. Even if I am lying to him, it is a comforting lie to believe in the face of such a revelation. Though, I must say, if Mi-Sun could see her cousin now, I think she would be taken aback. While Shinya is certainly startled by the news, he does not appear horrified.

"I think...I need...to shave," he finally manages to say.

"Likely, yes," I agree. "But perhaps stay seated for now. You look faint."

He nods absently and murmurs something to himself several times over in Tourrannese. I do not need a proper translation to understand he is likely trying to come to terms with the fact he has a daughter.

"Take a few minutes. Come up when you are ready," I tell him. "I think Margo would like to know there is an extra passenger on her ship."

He nods again, still staring off at nothing in particular. I allow myself another moment to take in his expression, his overall reaction. He is understandably shocked by it, but based on Mi-Sun's words, I thought I would need to manage his disgust, and fury. This is not that.

Above decks, predictably, the men still want nothing to do with me. I sigh. If Septimus is annoyed with me for not telling him about Shinya first, it is his own fault. So, I head to the wheelhouse, where Margo is keeping us on course, but otherwise chatting with Nissa about dragons. As one might expect, Nissa wants one as her next familiar, and is already concocting a plan to find one. Oh, she understands she will not remember this in a matter of weeks, and will be a child again at best, but she wants me to influence her if her hyena dies in the final timeline.

Since Septimus is too busy to insist that would be a bad idea, I decide I will probably do it. I do not think hinting to Nissa she might like dragons in our next life is tantamount to changing the course of the universe.

"Where did you disappear to?" Margo asks me as I join them, her tone one I am still adjusting to. I believe she has decided we are friends, with her as a mentor for Nissa and me.

I partially appreciate it, I admit. I have had few female mentors in my life, if any, and Margo is both older than me, more experienced, and capable. I regret allowing my previous assumptions to keep me from interacting with her much before.

"Aiko Shinya is sitting on a crate belowdecks, now aware of the fact he has sired a child by my cousin," I report. "I suggest we give him a few minutes to come to terms with this fact."

Nissa is confused, and requires a full explanation, but Margo merely raises an eyebrow. Everyone on board knows the basics of the story, I am sure, as well as who Aiko Shinya is. To them, it is a miraculous coincidence. I am almost certain, though, that this is the Almighty giving me a nudge behind the shoulder blades for every time I bitterly found reasons why I was positive he could not truly exist. I suppose he has a sense of humor.

Word is passed around, so that within the hour, everyone onboard is aware of our additional guest. I had hoped this will finally get a reaction out of Vásan, who was there for my conversation with Mi-Sun and Riyong, but it does not. I swear, ever since he was needled, that man spends the vast majority of his time in his own head, only vaguely aware of the rest of us.

Additionally, I'd assume that Septimus will want to take advantage of the situation, to sit down with Shinya and discuss a few things. This is the father of Septimus' new niece, after all. But Septimus, too, is lost in thought. I know Fate implied he would not remember all the factual revelations about his true, final life, but I must wonder if somehow a mistake was made. I cannot think of what else about the Otherworld Septimus could be spending so much time in consideration of.

Contrarily, perhaps I am too accustomed to such peculiarities. Perhaps

I should be equally terrified and awed by our experience. When searching deep for some emotional catharsis, all I find is relief. I may not be the hero of Samioth, as I explained to Taris, and I do believe that to be true. I am no saint. But I know I did some good, foiling at least some of the Dark's machinations.

Though, I suppose this means I should probably begin attending mass with Rian on a regular basis. Compared to the rest of Samioth's great populace, I have the no excuse not to, considering.

When it comes time to eat in the evening, I invite Shinya, but he requests respectfully not to join us. I promise to bring him something later, but otherwise let him alone with his thoughts. The rest of us choose to eat above decks in a highly informal, scavenging manner. We keep one another's company mainly because it appears to be mandatory at this point, but Vásan is still removed from the world.

I am starting to think I should be concerned. But who would I tell on his behalf? Yvette? His son? I do not know what either of them could do. Even if Yvette still harbors emotions for her husband, as she once did, he has always ignored her. My telling her or poor Alo would do nothing but worry them, and solve nothing.

I suppose I can ignore the issue at least until we return to Isaaria, and at that point, I do not know if I will bother with it or not. I do not know what meddling in the Pike's already messy family structure would fix.

"I suppose from here on out, things will be easy on the return. Relatively," Septimus says after a long time.

He sounds relieved by this, and gives a tremendous yawn. The rest of us are not so readily convinced.

"What about the Mitaurus?" Nissa points out. "And Nexa Grey? Will they not be waiting for us to return?"

Septimus snorts. "Nex? I doubt it. She is likely flying that poor brightback all over the east, looking for us. I suppose she could cast some sort of tracking ritual, knowing her *Dadj'zcha* capabilities. But, ah, she would need some of our hair for that, and blood. And as she has not found us yet, I would say she has likely run out."

"Run out?" Nissa repeats in disgust.

His words imply there was a store of some to begin with.

"Mmm. Ruskin and I burned down Kryto's manor before we left," he says sleepily, leaning back in his seat. "It was spectacular."

"That explains why she wants to rip your eyeballs out," Margo says dryly. "And here I thought you simply got on everyone's nerves by breathing."

Septimus shrugs. "I figured, the rest of the family already has a grudge against me, I might as well burn bridges with Nex as well, and get things over with. This way, if they finally catch me, there will not be any longsuffering debates about whether to let me live or not."

Castel snorts and I catch the end of him rolling his eyes. He mutters under his breath in Lijimi. I find I wish to simply know all worldly languages, given how helpful that ability would have been over the course of this journey.

Margo looks at both of them, one at a time, thinking.

"That is a concern to consider, though: the Mitaurus," she says. "The Sunguard may be gone, but I think Charrion is at least smart enough to know who came up with the idea, and formed them to begin with."

"No one's going to care about Cas," Septimus says. "As far as the Greys are concerned, he disappeared years ago. Even if he returned to Lijimata now, no one would take him seriously. And Charrion already got the chance to get rid of us all in Mouloix. He did not exactly press hard for it."

I refrain from pointing out that, out of all of us, the Mitaurus did make a point of shooting Castel first.

"Even so. I think we are going to need to split up, Sep," Margo warns. "You should take the Isaarians and Aiko back, to see to your own business and end this timeline. Castel and I will act as decoy for the Mitaurus. At least lead them off, so they will not happen to crop up and ruin things for us at the last possible moment. It would be very like Charrion to do that."

Septimus fixes her with a look, as if he thinks she is being paranoid, but eventually gives in.

"Fine," he sighs. "You and Cas split off when you think it is reasonable, and I will escort the Isaarian nobles home again. Just make sure we know how to manage this damn thing first. I do not want to get blown off course down south, or something of that nature."

Margo seems to think this would never happen, and begins to think aloud as to when she and Cas should split off. She notes it would be easier, in some ways, for us to try and sail northwest, and return to the Summer Palace via Isaaria's east coast. However, considering the trouble we had in Mouloix, and even before that on the train, this option negates the wariness we all feel about heading through the southern strait. If it means avoiding another encounter with Mitaurus members, I think I'll risk dealing with the Milashi coast guard.

Something else is stirring in the back of my memory, though. Something I had forgotten about completely, before I heard Margo mention the Sunguard, and their relation to the leader of the Mitaurus.

"Oh! I nearly forgot!" I realize, and turn to Castel, surprising him and most everyone, truly. "I have something to tell you. I…I do not remember all of it, I'm sorry, but in the Otherworld, I remember there was an Alarkian girl, um…She told me to tell you that they—the Sunguard—were all 'fine'. They are sorry they had to leave you behind. And…And 'Wina says good morning'. She said to say that, specifically."

Castel stares at me, his expression unreadable. I can see Margo out of the corner of my eye, as well, and she keeps glancing at him in concern, then back to me, incredulous. Nissa and Vásan have no context, even less than I do, but Septimus appears to understand who we are speaking about.

"She. She said to say that," Castel finally manages to get out, his tone not as gruff and dismissive as usual. He sounds small, and almost distant. "Wina. Wina was there, and she told you that."

"Well, I do not know who she was," I admit. "From context I assume that is her name. She listed off some other names. Louisa was one, I remember. She said to tell you they were all there. And all fine. They are not hurting. She was rather adamant that she wanted you to know that. That they all wanted you to know that…Some of them also called you stupid," I feel I must add.

I believe Castel has stopped listening to me. He sets his back up against the wheelhouse wall and slides down it until he lands with a thump on the ground. Margo immediately steps out to kneel at his side. Castel starts talking, but only in Lijimi, and I do not understand what he is saying aside from a smattering of names.

"Sep," Margo says in warning.

"Of course," Septimus says, taking her place in the wheelhouse.

Margo also speaks in Lijimi, pulling one of Castel's arms over her shoulders. She helps him up to his feet. She continues speaking to him while pulling him toward the steps below decks. When Castel falls into the wall, she calls for Vásan to come help her, and he obliges without complaint.

I feel guilty, and exchange a look with Nissa, who appears to empathize with me. That leaves me with Septimus, though I suspect that I will get few answers from him given his recent and unprovoked avoidance of me.

At least so long as he is covering Margo's post, he cannot slip off with a poorly-thought-of excuse.

"Should I not have told him?" I ask Septimus.

He gives a heavy sigh, but does not look my way.

"That does not matter. It has already happened," he says. "But if you want things to run smoothly these next few weeks, perhaps stop trying to meddle in other people's lives."

"I was not trying," I snap at him. "I was keeping a promise."

"Stop making promises to ghosts of dead youths Castel feels responsible for, then, how about that?"

I glare at him, then decide it is not worth arguing. How Septimus could have gone from someone whose company I genuinely enjoy back to the insufferable imp I know he can be is beyond me. It is as if he purposefully wants to irritate me, to put the two of us at odds with one another.

For a few minutes, long enough for me to realize I am being childish and not care, I continue to glare at him. Septimus ignores me. I am certain we are both aware of Nissa blatantly eavesdropping, but neither of us care.

"Why are you being like this," I say. "Have I somehow done something to offend you?"

I do not miss Septimus' irritated expression, nor the mild shake of his head. "For once, Soleil, could you conceive of something having nothing to do with you?" he mutters. "Just leave me be, and leave Castel be for, a time, could you? He lost everything. And you…Never mind it."

Nissa gestures for me to leave with her. I decide if Septimus wants me to leave him be completely until he is no longer going to act like a child, I will oblige. Nissa will likely be better company anyway.

We head down below as well, leaving Septimus alone.

"I suppose visiting the afterlife whilst still alive is rather distressing for a person," Nissa offers. "I know I would not want to go."

"I'm fine," I retort.

"Yes," Nissa agrees, "but I am not convinced you have a normal reaction to things, your majesty."

I want to protest, but I suspect that Nissa might not be the only one with that opinion. From the perspective of the others, I went to the afterlife for several days, returned, and waltzed off without a care in the world. It is impossible to explain to anyone else that after conversing with Fate himself, having him reassure me that all will be well, all I want is get back to Rian.

I suppose it is difficult for them to understand why it is easy for me to disregard my experiences in the Otherworld because I miss Rian and Ayla. Vásan certainly cannot comprehend it. The only one who should understand, who has the experience and capacity to understand, is Septimus, ironically.

I wonder why it is he cannot.

Twenty-Two

UNFORTUNATELY, WHATEVER HAS overcome Septimus does not fade with time. He slowly becomes more like himself, but never entirely, and never with me. I thought we had formed an understanding, as cousins, and perhaps potentially as friends. Now, I only see glimpses of that on occasion. Otherwise, he purposefully pulls away from me.

Margo offers no answers on his behalf, insisting Septimus merely is the way he is, and there is no understanding it. When not teaching me how to manage the boat, she spends most of her time conversing with Castel in Lijimi. I still am not sure if I did the right thing, giving him a message from the dead, but I note that Margo and Septimus are careful not to leave him alone. I am not sure if this is because they are concerned about him, or if they do not want to give me the opportunity to try and speak with Castel on the topic again.

Despite having potentially saved the fabric of our universe, I suppose I am somehow still a problem for them to avoid and manage.

This, for better or worse, leaves me with Aiko Shinya often.

It takes a number of weeks, yes. For those first few, Shinya haunts the ship and keeps out of sight unless absolutely necessary. Whenever he does appear, I cannot read him, and he barely speaks. I am tempted to accuse Vásan of spreading some ailment of mutism, simply so someone will acknowledge it. But I manage to hold my tongue.

We have nearly returned to Isaaria by the time anything meaningful happens between Shinya and myself, and I believe it is by accident. I have decided to take Fate and Rian's advice and pray over what to do in regards to the many mistakes I have made. Even without the presence of the sun and moon and nothing to ground me, I decide it is worth an attempt. So, I set aside time to try. This is how Shinya finds me, all but creeping up silently to inquire:

"What are you doing?"

He scares me to the point of potential violence, yes, but once I have settled, I turn to him with a sigh.

"Praying. Or, attempting to."

Shinya considers this. "May I join you?"

"Please. If I knew you wanted to, I would have invited you," I say.

Then he hesitates. "I do not know if I want to. I have not. For a long time. But I do not know what else to do."

"For myself, I am asking the Almighty to let me know what I might do to fix the mistakes I've made," I say. "While simultaneously trying to be grateful for the many things I have received that I think, perhaps, I do not deserve at all. You could do the same, and leave it as such."

"That seems deceptively simple," Shinya says suspiciously.

"I could teach you some recited prayers as well," I offer. "Though, I admit, I may not be the best of teachers. I only know a handful."

"That is fine," Shinya says, and kneels next to me.

His is a much more elegant form. Even the way he sits is somehow more reverent.

Though our first session is awkward and uncertain, mainly caused by my lack of expertise in the very subject I deign to teach, it becomes a habit for Shinya and me. I do not know the details of what he prays for, though I would like to think I can guess. I realize I have no desire to ask, however. I do not care about prying into his privacy.

Despite Margo's concerns, we see no signs of the Mitaurus or Nexa Grey as we draw near Mouloix. We still keep to the previously designated plan, allowing her and Castel to disembark using the ship's one dinghy before we move on, away from the remains of Mouloix, up the west coast of Isaaria. Though there is no way to send warning ahead of time that we are arriving, I am certain having myself, Nissa, and Vásan present will be enough to grant us permission to dock.

It takes us a number of days longer, but they pass quickly, monotonously. I find myself trying to fully understand the concept of perhaps never meeting Margo, Xerian, or Prince Castel again. Some part of me insists that fate will somehow draw us all back together, but I do not know that for certain. In fact, perhaps with some semblance of peace in the world, even if only for our lifetimes, we will never have need to meet.

For some reason, though I know I should be grateful at even the possibility of peace across the world, this disappoints me. I want to know them better. I think, perhaps, Margo and I could have become close friends. I would have liked to keep her in Isaaria, as an advisor. I worry over what kind of queen I will be without good advisors to help restrain my vices.

It is over these few days of mentally torturing myself that I finally can guess at why Septimus may be trying to distance himself from me. Once the concept falls into place, I feel like a fool for not thinking of it before. Fate did imply that, perhaps, so long as he does not remember, Septimus might never decide to betray the Greys. He may never even come to Isaaria. After all, I remind myself, even Widow's ghosts showed Teresa escaping here alone, as a younger woman, whilst expectant with Aiden, not Rika. The next time I see Septimus, it may be with him as an enemy.

He is purposefully trying to make me angry with him again. He is doing this for both of us, in hopes that it will somehow make this easier for us.

So, I let him.

When we dock, there is some surprise from the citizens about, but they are kept back a respectable distance. Before we were allowed to enter Isaarian waters, those patrolling the coast necessitated a statement from us, and identification. The later was hardly necessary once they boarded; Nissa and Vásan are both unmistakable, even if I am out of uniform.

Once word reaches the Summer Palace that we have returned, an appropriate escort is sent. As it is early in the morning, and we are all rather hungry and tired, it is suggested we stay at a nearby inn and continue in the afternoon, to the city and the palace.

With my legs still wobbly after so much time at sea, I agree to this readily. Though there is not much room at the inn chosen, two small rooms are found for us as accommodations. Men to one, women to the other. Many around us are insistent that, considering our royal ties, better rooms could be vacated. We all refuse. I think this is strangest coming from Vásan, as his reputation speaks to a different kind of temperament, but no one questions it.

It is a great relief to be home. I did not realize how much I missed hearing Isaarian spoken around me, instead of always speaking in Alarkian, the most common language in the world. The two languages share equal space in my mind, but Isaarian means more to me. Being surrounded by my own culture gives me a comfort that surpasses even a hot meal and a long bath.

After several hours of sleep, Nissa cannot help but wake me as she rises. I would rather sleep longer, but am anxious to see Rian. I am sure that he feels similarly. I expect a welcome at the palace, when we arrive, though there is some time before that, yet.

Some of my companions accept an offer of coffee, but we all otherwise skip eating again so soon. Magnus Oram has sent a coach to bring us all back to the palace, and insists on us using it. He has also sent ahead proper clothing, that must have arrived some time while we slept. Somehow, this feels so trivial, and yet so much like him in nature, that I know we must oblige him.

I am sure Rian has had to hear no small number of lectures from him over the past weeks about the importance of presentability at a time like this.

I was able to be Soleil, for quite some time, during our travels. Now I must be Captain Marson again. No one else knows otherwise.

Though I did not specify who Aiko Shinya was when initially asked, word must have still gotten back to Magnus that we brought a guest with us, because he has sent something Isaarian in nature for Shinya as well. This helps Shinya look at least somewhat presentable. I can tell it is strange for him to be wearing such nice, clean Isaarian clothes while he has spent years traveling and living off the land, but the look suits him. His hair is still too long but at least he is washed and is clean shaven. Nissa gives him one of her braided leather thongs to tie his hair back, which helps make the look more intentional instead of due to lack of care.

Vásan looks like himself again, in his prince's garb. Surprisingly, or perhaps unsurprisingly after so many years, Magnus did not insist on sending something for Nissa that she would not wear. I suspect he had someone dig a piece of her formal clothing out of the Summer Palace storage.

We are all covered in winter coats, given the still chilly weather and the ankle-deep snow on the ground, but our ranks are still almost hilariously evident with them. I have a winter uniform, after all.

The coach ride is long and unbearably quiet. Nissa insists on sitting in the front with the driver, claiming it is too warm inside with all of us close together. This leaves me with the men. None of them wish to speak, though at least with Shinya I suspect this has nothing to do with me. Septimus, I understand, now. I still am not certain what I may have done to irritate Vásan.

Surely, he could not be holding a grudge over my passing comment back in Kacha, about siblings. But that is the only thing I can think of.

The trip takes several hours, due to the congestion of the city. I admittedly feel jitters when I catch a glimpse of the Summer Palace through the coach window. By the time the coach passes through the gates and pulls around to stop before the steps, one of my legs is shaking, bouncing up and down. Septimus finally cannot stand this; he reaches over and smacks a hand down on my knee so that my foot slams on the coach floor.

I expect Vásan to snort at this, but he does not. He does not appear to even notice the noise. Still not quite himself, he makes sure he is the first person out of the coach, the rest of us following. He almost collides with Nissa, who has jumped off the front seat and is brushing herself down, fixing her clothes.

At the top of the tall steps, I spot Rian first. My heart aches to see him, and I cannot help but smile. Even seeing him at a distance tells me I am home.

Qhan is there with him, and Ayla, who waves fondly when she sees me. Magnus Oram stands slightly behind the two, and I can see Yvette Pike there as well, standing stiffly with her gloved hands folded in front of her, out of her fur lined cloak. I know she once loved Vásan, and his indifference to her broke her heart. She was so innocent and sweet, back then; now, she only looks formal and tired. Aloysius II stands behind her to await his father's return, partially obscured by the angle of the steps from the ground.

I am so pleased to be this close to Rian again that for a few seconds, all I can do is stare up, noting how kingly he looks. Something warm fills my chest. I cannot wait to tell him everything that has happened; about Margo and Xerian and Castel. Kang and Aisling. Kacha. The Otherworld. I want to tell him everything, in exquisite detail. I want to share everything in life with him.

Before I can move, however, someone else does. Vásan, most peculiarly, all but takes the steps two at a time. He does not run, which would be a touch too out of character for him, but I do not think he has ever moved this quickly before while dressed like an Isaarian Grand Prince. Certainly not in public. All I or anyone else can do is watch as he reaches the top of the steps and, before Yvette can curtsey to him formally, pulls her into his arms.

I manage to shake myself free of my shock, enough to take the opportunity to rush up the steps myself. With my aching legs, I slow as I reach the top of the steps. While Rian distractedly reaches out to offer me his hand, he, too, is still watching Yvette and Vásan.

"Forgive me," Vásan says. He holds his wife even tighter against his chest, one hand coming up to cradle the back of her head against his shoulder.

Yvette looks as stunned as everyone else staring at this rather un-Pike-like display. Vásan has never held her like this before. She does not know how to react. Alo Pike's eyes are wide, his mouth slightly open.

Amidst this display, Magnus inches forward to me and Rian. I can tell he does not appreciate how a simple homecoming, which should have taken a minute at most before returning inside the Summer Palace walls, has become a spectacle.

"What happened out there? What is wrong with Pike?" he hisses.

Nissa has appeared at my elbow and offers her opinion with an exceptionally wide grin, though it is done in Hoitsokin, so the specifics are beyond us all.

"I do not think anything is wrong," I say slowly. "Though I am sure he is as exhausted as I am, from our long travels. Perhaps you could see the Pikes inside, grand prince?"

Magnus barely keeps from glaring at me. I know he is highly suspicious. If I allowed him another month, I'm sure he'd have me give a full accounting of our journey east, before all the royals. I do not plan on giving him a month, and if he tries to have me give such a presentation, it likely will impact how soon I decide to travel back in time.

I do not have the energy for constant questions. I am only explaining my travels in full once, and only to Rian. I think he is the only one who deserves it, and who would understand.

The need to preserve image is what prompts Magnus to stalk off with Griffith Reach following him, to the Pikes. He pulls one of Vásan's arms away from Yvette so he might suggest they move inside the palace. Alo Pike is all too ready to assist with that. Vásan keeps a cool, neutral expression, as if what he has done is not at all out of character for him, and should have been expected. Yvette still looks as if she may be in a dream. She cannot take her eyes off him.

Vásan refuses to let go of her entirely.

"Well," Rian says, still partially watching as they all depart, "I suppose that means the trip was exceptional, if it has changed Vásan Pike, so."

"It was," I say. "Though I will admit, even I did not know he was going to do that. I am not sure why he would."

Rian shrugs it off and decides to give me his full attention, raising my hand to kiss it. I nearly chide him for that, given our still being in a public space, but we move on too quickly for me to conjure the right words.

"Regardless. We are glad you're back. The wait was agonizing," he says.

"I'm sure," I say, but cannot decide whether I want to reveal that it was equally difficult for me to spend so long away from him when I never have before in my life. Not in any timeline.

Ayla surges forward to take my hand away from Rian's.

"You should have seen him!" she insists. "He complained about you being away practically every single hour. Magnus was about ready to throttle him."

That makes me smile. "I see. And how have you been, princess?"

"I'm engaged!" Ayla cries happily. "To Soren! Isn't it wonderful?"

I am too startled to say anything.

"It is," Septimus answers first, joining Nissa and I at the top of the steps with Shinya hovering behind him. "Congratulations, princess."

His words remind me not to mention anything about the timelines in front of Ayla. It is good to see her so happy again, considering how she was when I left. I doubt an engagement alone has done that for her, but she and Soren have always been close. I hope she has spoken to him about things she could not bring herself to say in front of myself or Rian.

"I suppose that means you will be rather busy with preparations," I say. "Where is Soren?"

"He had a meeting," she says dismissively. "He apologizes for not being able to come and visit himself; he has been helping Grand Prince Magnus with the refugee issue, and since Magnus was here…"

"I understand completely," I say. "Please let him know I appreciate all he has done in my absence."

I need to thank several people, in fact. Seeing how well Rian and Ayla are means they have been well taken care of even without me. It reassures me, somehow, that if I had not returned, they would have had support.

"Septimus," Rian says, sternly, though possibly this is done in exaggeration. "I hope to hear nothing from my wife but how well you looked after her."

"I will pray for a positive review, then, your majesty," Septimus says.

"He did well," Nissa offers her own opinion. "They only antagonized one another every third day or so."

Rian laughs.

"Magicsmiths like to have their way, I think," he says, and then makes note of the last member of our party. "It looks like you picked up a stray while out east. Soleil's fault, I'm assuming," he adds.

"Not precisely. This is…Aiko Shinya," I say slowly.

Ayla covers her mouth with a hand, glancing at her father, but Rian only smiles, as I might have expected.

"I knew you looked familiar," he says cheerily. "Good to see you again, Lord Aiko. Welcome back to Isaaria."

"Thank you, sir," Shinya says, bowing to him. "But I am afraid I must disappoint you. I am not here formally, as a Lord Ambassador. I am only here to…to speak with Miss Resa Smith. Otherwise, I would not have come."

"Not to worry," Rian reassures him without pause. "Either way, you are more than welcome here. I am certain Teresa will see you, soon. Though if Naomi has her way, I'm afraid we will only be allowed to visit in rotation. She is most insistent we do not overwhelm the poor girl."

"I understand," Shinya says quietly.

"Where is my sister?" Septimus asks, looking more to Ayla than Rian. As the two women have undoubtedly become friends, she would know better.

"Miss Teresa is sleeping now," she admits. "She been quite tired, lately."

"But she is doing well?" I say.

Ayla bobs her head.

"Oh, yes. Extraordinarily well, I should say. She even starting asking for things for herself, like some western-style clothes. I think she is more comfortable in them after wearing them for so long, and that style suits her so well. But you can see her later. You should go and sleep! Magnus said you were all quite tired. That is why you did not come here straight away."

"We can get you dinner and a soft bed," Rian adds in promise. "Just say the word, and it will be done. We will have you all put away into rooms to relax, and leave all the messiness until tomorrow."

"That might be best," I agree, noting an ache in my lower back. More sleep sounds good, to me. "But first, I must speak with Korvaan and Naomi. If someone could please find them for me, and send them to my room, I would appreciate it."

"Oh, ahh. Well. Does it have to be your room?" Rian says.

"Why not?" I ask slowly.

"I may or may not have told the rest of the nobles about our…marital situation. So, they know, now. I'm sorry I could not ask you first, but it was unavoidable. You are queen of Isaaria, now."

I frown. "Then why did Magnus send my dress uniform?"

"We don't have any gowns fitted for you," Ayla points out.

That makes a fair amount of sense. So, I am queen of Isaaria officially, now, and still Captain Marson simultaneously. Strange.

I turn to Shinya, thinking of what to do with him. Usually, Soren would be here to arrange everything. Such a thing has never been my responsibility, and I am not certain how to go about organizing it.

"Nissa," I decide. "Could you accompany Lord Aiko and find a room for him, someplace? I'm sure Magnus could be of assistance, if needed."

Hopefully, that will subsequently rescue the Pikes from Magnus' pestering, as there is much to be discussed for their little family. Vásan has changed their dynamic entirely, and purposefully. Unavoidably. Nissa is clever enough to know my intentions instantly. Ayla picks it up as well.

"I would be all too happy to assist, your majesty," Nissa says.

"I will go as well," Ayla insists. "I know where Soren keeps everything in his office; I'm sure I can find a free room for Lord Aiko."

"And I think I shall see if I can convince Miss Qurvo if I might be allowed the first visit to my little sister, and her boys," Septimus says brightly. "Your majesty," he says to Rian, and offers to kiss Ayla's hand. She allows it.

Septimus hesitates a telling moment longer.

"Lord Aiko," he finally says, acknowledging Shinya, though he does not look at him. "Perhaps another time."

"Perhaps," Shinya murmurs.

Shinya leaves with Nissa and Ayla, whose bright and colorful dress and winter furs look out of place to me, somehow, though this is an Isaarian palace, and she a princess deserving of such fashions. It occurs to me, finally, that it is because her dress is winter-Alarkian in style. She wears a corset and numerous petticoats, in an Alarkian manner, her skirts wide and full. I see my cousin's presence here has set about some changes.

"Your majesty," Rian says, offering me his arm.

He escorts me inside, and ferries me up to his rooms, moving slowly, speaking of relatively trivial things. He tells me Mango has missed me. Vilaneau did well, though he clearly often wished for my advice. Teresa has found lovely friendships with Ayla, Yvette, and Irina Lundan, and Naomi has been fussing over her constantly. Damen and Aiden are the absolute darlings of the court. Soren requested Ayla's hand two weeks prior to our return, and Rian's acceptance of it has actually improved his parents' moods greatly.

It is a rare thing, but a fateful thing, Rian claims, that we should find our daughter with a marriage both suited to her, and to the political mechanisms of our country. The Carsans no longer feel slighted by their king and the other royals. Soren's mother, particularly, plans for the wedding to be quite grand, unavoidable, and, naturally, held on an important feast day.

I allow myself to hang on Rian's arm and lean against his shoulder. As I listen, I find it surprisingly easy to ignore any looks we are given, even if they are mainly innocent and curious in nature.

There is a fire lit in the king's chambers. I see that Rian has made it as comfortable as he can for me, knowing I would return soon. He is a good man. He brings me around and sits me in one of the chairs.

"I have missed you," I say.

He smiles and brings my hand up to kiss my knuckles.

"I'll have another chair brought," he promises. "And I will be in my study. Naomi and Korvaan will be here shortly."

His fingers linger against mine for a long while before he finally lets them drop, moving on behind the chair.

"Thank you," I say.

"Call for me when you need me," he says.

I agree to this, and sit before the fire, allowing myself to construct precisely what I would like to say to Naomi and Korvaan. I write myself a script, a truly repentant, understanding, well-meaning monologue. I set forth in my mind a schedule I intent to keep to: in my apology to Korvaan and Naomi, my explaining everything to Rian, taking a lunch with Ayla and Soren to give them my congratulations and having a spectacular time of it to give me the best of memories. Then there is the matter of reconciling Shinya and Teresa. I will need to have a conversation with Septimus, and set the record between the two of us straight before I start things over for the both of us.

And then, I think, I will possibly be ready to do it. To go back and never use my fluke again, but have the promise of a better life ahead.

I have it nearly all scripted by the time Naomi and Korvaan arrive, except the end, but I am more than willing to improvise. So, I begin the moment they enter, without any hesitation, barely breathing, barely allowing them a word in. I stand only to pull Naomi into the other armchair, and gesture for Korvaan to sit as well. He looks bewildered, but I do not take the time to think of Naomi's expression or what it means. I know she must still hate me. I do not care. I want to say my piece before either of them can bring up other ineptitudes on my part.

"Soleil," Naomi says, trying to interrupt.

"Yes," I say. "I know Korvaan has probably told you everything, and I know you are probably furious. You were angry last time, and I did not even give you the chance to be angry. Septimus asked me if I was willing to go back again and I said I was. I knew you did not want to, that you hated the entire concept of it, but I did not care. I did not ask."

"Soleil," she says again, and only manages to properly interrupt me this time because I realize she is trying not to laugh. "You can stop apologizing now."

"I'm not apologizing," I say. "Actually, well, yes, I am. But it is more than an apology. And I have much more to say."

"Honestly, Soleil, I think it might be better if we did not repeat ourselves over and over again," Korvaan adds.

"I am glad that we did not have this conversation before you left," Naomi admits. "I do not think I was ready to have it. I know you were not, either."

"I don't understand," I say.

Korvaan and Naomi exchange a look with one another.

"Soleil, I'm not angry anymore," she says. "Truly. I'm not. Korvaan and I had a great many conversations about it, and he told me...Many things. Things that he remembers and that I don't. I'm not angry anymore, about any of it."

"She means it," Korvaan adds on her behalf, almost laughing, too. "It has been a long time with you gone, Soleil. And, truly no offense intended, but it was easier to forgive you without you around to say something stupid."

I am stunned.

"You have good intentions," Naomi agrees. "But sometimes you say the worst possible thing in a conversation."

I look from one of them to the other. They appear to still be the Naomi and Korvaan I have known so many times over again. Yet I wonder if there is something in the air in the Summer Palace that is turning people into not themselves. First Vásan, and now these two.

I decide to fix my gaze on Naomi, finally, as she has been the one primarily irritated with me in cycles past.

"But you have a life, now, with Valor," I say. "Korvaan, you have Kaoli. You are both free. Free from being a part of a *khashak*. Who knows how things will happen, this final time. You could lose that. Just the same as I have made Taris lose Lune so many times."

"You did not cause that," Naomi says. "It simply happened. And you did not make me a member of any *khashak*. Our father decided that. He decided it long before you were old enough to come up with the idea. Before you rewrote history even once. So, how can I be angry with you for simply having us live a second or third or even forth time the lives we originally had?"

"I don't know," I must admit.

Her words strangely remind me of something Septimus said to me, a long time ago, now, toward the beginning of our journey. Something about how I am expected to hold myself responsible for decisions past versions of myself have made, even if I had no memory of it all, but no one else wanted to be held responsible in the same manner.

Naomi goes on.

"I know that Korvaan and I will be a part of a *khashak,* and that Nusk will train Taris to be Rian's *Khashtani,*" she says. "That Lune is supposed to be yours. But we can change some things, can we not? Maybe we will not get the lives we want right away, but…we can still work for them."

I frown, considering this. "You will not remember any of this," I warn Korvaan, as it occurs to me that they are only calm because they are operating under the assumption they will.

But Korvaan shrugs.

"So long as I'm a member of Rian's *khashak,* we will have a place at the palace," he reminds me. "If we do not, how would Naomi ever meet Valor? How would I chance upon meeting Kaoli?"

"That did not occur to me," I say.

"It didn't occur to us either, until recently," Naomi admits. "It was only because of your cousin, actually. Teresa. She said something, a while back, that struck me. About how, without having first met Kryto Grey, she would never have the chance to meet her sons, who she loves."

"She has said something similar to me," I mutter.

I recall that it made me think, as well, on concepts I had not previously considered. Perhaps it is because my own life, and destiny, is relatively charmed. I fall in love with Rian, a truly good man. I have Ayla, and am told I will have son destined to be as good a man as his father. I become a queen of an entire country.

While I am under no illusions that my life will be perfect, I had no choice in marrying Rian, really. It was decided for me. For people like Korvaan and Naomi, they chose their own spouses. In many ways, they are lucky to have ever chanced across someone to choose to love so much, in the vast expanse of the universe.

"It was selfish of you, to be willing to sacrifice so much of other people for the sake of just Rian," Naomi says. "But when we both thought about it, Korvaan and I realized we would be willing and are currently willing to risk certain things to keep the king and Ayla safe. Even if no one asked us to."

"Nusk will not ask you," I remind them. "It will be expected of you, same as Lune, and Taris."

Korvaan is unconcerned. "But we will not know we could have had any different. Besides, you are going to release Taris and Lune from any *Khashtani* bonds they may have, aren't you?"

"Hopefully I won't let them be *Khashtani* in the first place," I say. "But I do not know if that will happen. It may take some time before I have recognizable authority to say anything of that sort and be listened to. I will be a child. You will very likely have to spend at least a few years being trained for a position I will then strip from you under the intent of offering you freedom."

"Yes," Korvaan says, "but at that point, we will still have guaranteed positions in the palace."

"And I think we will likely want to stay," Naomi adds.

I have run out of ways to convince them of something I do not even want to convince them of in the first place.

"I don't know what I ever did to deserve having the two of you," I finally say. "But I promise, I will do my best not to interfere with what it is you say you want, in our final timeline. Even if those wants change."

"So long as you don't play pretend at being Fate, I'm sure we'll all be fine," Korvaan jokes.

I suppose my pride is what often gets me into trouble. I vow to do my best to curb it, and to be a reasonable person. If doing my best means being a good queen, friend, sister, wife, and mother, then I will dedicate my life to being that, knowing I am lucky the Almighty gave me a hundred chances over again to finally become the good person I have tried to be.

"I will do my best," I tell Korvaan.

Naomi stands, so the two of us do, too. I am surprised, then, that she leans forward to give me a meaningful embrace. I return it, wondering if and hoping that I can be a good sister to both Naomi and Lune one day, when I think I have not managed to do right by either of them, yet.

Well, by Naomi. I think rescuing Lune from the Dark ought to earn me some redemption for the poor choices of my past iterations.

"I do miss, and will miss, I think, growing up next to you," Naomi admits as she pulls away again. "From what Korvaan's said, you were like our sister. And since Lune was always more 'Carsans' than 'Marson', even originally, we never had that with her. I will miss having had a sister."

"I will miss that, too. Although, you know," I say, considering it, "if Taris happens to marry Lune one day, you will have two sisters."

"Three," Korvaan adds, feigning as if he is truly insulted. "What, does Kaoli not count simply because she was not there from the beginning?"

Naomi laughs. "Kaoli is lovely," she insists, soothing him. "Though, sometimes, I think, she is more terrifying than even Soleil."

"She ought to be," I say. "She has Soren to look after…You're really not angry?" I ask again.

Naomi sighs. "I cannot say that I wasn't," she says. "But you did not have to hear the king bemoan your absence. It is difficult to keep up hating a person he loves so obnoxiously. And he is a good man."

I must smile at that. "Yes," I agree. "Yes, Rian is the best of men."

"Valor and I both discussed it," she goes on. "And we figure, if we found one another at some point, in at least two different timelines, if the Almighty wants it, we will find a way to each other again. Yours and Rian's cannot be the only predestined love. You may be a Magicsmith, but even you do not get to claim a monopoly on that possibility."

That reminds me:

"Oh. Aiko Shinya," I say. "He is here to see Teresa. I know you have been helping to look after her, Naomi. Thank you for that. I think I will have him stop in tomorrow to see her. Before then, perhaps, do not mention his being here to her?"

Naomi suddenly adapts a shrewd look. "If I have it my way, he will have to do quite a lot of begging before I even consider letting him see her. After what he has done? He would be so lucky to be let in the same room."

"Do try to be nice to him," I say. "I think he is nervous about coming all this way to see her. He asked me to teach him to *pray.*"

Korvaan snorts a laugh.

Naomi purses her lips. "Well, I should hope so," she says.

Somehow, I do not think she plans on being charitable to Shinya. I would say there is some logic behind it, only I think he hates himself enough already without the rest of us adding to it. I wonder if, perhaps, Septimus is purposefully avoiding a confrontation with his sister's lover for Shinya's own sake, then. Septimus does not want to say something stupid, even if his opinions on the matter are completely valid.

I see the two of them out, Korvaan claiming he has tonight off from his duties and would like to spend the evening with Kaoli. Naomi wants to see Valor before returning to help Teresa, as she has been doing these past months. I think, in not having children, Naomi realizes she has missed a prime opportunity to mother someone. She was raised in Isaarian culture, after all; we Isaarian women are built for lecturing and teaching and simply being right.

After they are both gone, I feel pleasantly lightheaded. I had prepared myself for the possibility of some shouting, and some anger. I had hoped for reconciliation, but had not expected it.

I look around the room until I find the most Theebin icon possible hanging on the wall.

"Have I done something right for once?" I ask it, knowing I am not going to get an answer. "If you somehow made them more charitable toward me in my absence, I owe you…a month of novenas. I probably already do," I must admit. "Add it to the list of things I owe, I suppose…"

"Who are you talking to?" Rian asks, startling me.

I turn to see him leaning against the door frame.

"Ah. God. I suppose," I confess.

He considers this, then nods, and shrugs, as if this is a normal thing to admit to doing.

"Right," he says. "Mind if I move in?"

He holds up his work, stacked on a folding wooden desk. I believe Qhan had it purchased for him, at some point, so that Rian could have a portable surface and not always be trapped working in his office chair.

"No, please do," I say. "We've finished."

"And things went well?" Rian says, settling himself into what was formerly Naomi's chair.

Mango lazily pads into the room after him, circling Rian's right foot twice before deciding he would like to sit on top of it. Rian generously lets him.

"Shockingly so," I say.

"Mmm. So, you are not being generous to your foster siblings, today, dear wife," he teases.

"What?"

"You really thought they would not forgive you?" Rian points out. "That is a touch cruel, Soleil. You have not done anything damnable, and the Qurvos are intelligent enough to put that together on their own."

"I had not thought of it like that," I confess.

"Oh, I know. You are too hard on yourself, and, therefore, on everyone," he says, and buries his nose back into his paperwork.

I sit back into my own chair, for a time, and consider a great many things. Septimus said it was near impossible for me to imagine that, for once, what he was experiencing may have nothing to do with me personally. I suppose I do suffer from a lack of imagination when it comes to picturing things from another person's perspective. It is not as if I do not try, as I have actively made attempts, on several occasions. Only, I have, many times, come to the wrong conclusion.

Or, a partially wrong conclusion. To give myself some credit, I suppose it is difficult if not impossible to fully imagine another person's thoughts and experiences when you are the one still riding along in your own head, tainting the perspective somewhat. If I ask myself whether I would hold a permanent grudge against Korvaan and Naomi for something, ever, I must admit I would rather not. They are my foster siblings. I would not want to lose them, no matter how angry they made me. I suppose it is only natural Naomi might find it in herself to feel similarly.

Perhaps, before, she simply did not have enough time to consider it. She had been furious about it all last cycle, yes, justifiably. But she had still given me that hyssop concoction and the mint leaves, that saved Rian from the influence of *Dadj'zcha,* the witch in question likely Nexa or Jarrod Grey, I would suspect. They were both around and about the Pyrian Palace or the city at the time, after all.

So, even at her angriest with me, Naomi did not hate me.

I ought to give her more credit.

Though I am quite pleased with this newfound wisdom, though, it unfortunately does not offer me any decent insight into whatever has changed Vásan. I have come to understand Nissa, my cousins, my foster siblings, and even a portion of Aiko Shinya, but Vásan Pike remains a mystery to me, for now. He is such a strange man, at times. I still cannot imagine him ever marrying Lune.

Noting an ache in my legs, from spending so much time first cramped on a ship and then in a carriage, I stand and stretch.

"Rian? I think I would like to take a walk," I inform him.

He looks up from his work to smile at me. "Of course. Be back for dinner. Oh, and take Mango with you, could you? He will be restless. If Qhan is outside, could you tell him where you're going? Otherwise, he will worry."

"Oh?" I say, visibly surprised by this. "But…"

"Soleil, you are queen, now. And you are going to be for a long time, one day. Best get used to such things," Rian says.

So, while I do not think it entirely necessary given my still decent capabilities in the matters of self-defense, I inform Qhan that I would like to take a stroll in the winter gardens, and that I am taking Mango with me. He still insists on assigning me a guard, though he says they will keep their distance. If he or Rian did not insist first, then Vilaneau or Magnus would.

I do not know how long I walk for. Mango only manages a quarter hour before putting the effort in to flap up to my shoulders, and ride along. It is strange, knowing I technically have no responsibilities, now. I should, given my dual positions, yet it has all been taken care of in my absence, and no one has thought to discuss the transfer of these powers, yet.

I visit the dryad tree, which has been successfully implemented, here, and think of what Teresa and Damen and Aiden must have spent these past months amusing themselves with. I think it is clear from the clothing styles of Yvette and Ayla, both, that Teresa and her endearing fashion sense must be catching amongst the noble women. They all want to wear Alarkian clothes, now, which admittedly are probably warmer without always wearing a coat, given their layered petticoats. Teresa surely had no shortage of minders for the boys, either, given Ayla, Elodie and Sacha and Irina Lundan, and even Alo Pike.

I consider if I should call on anyone, for a visit, but finally decide against it, wanting to leave it all for another day. I have had enough social interaction, and do not want to risk having to encounter Magnus or his parents or, Fate's Fingers, the Carsans, at a time like this. I do not mind the Orams, but I feel it would be exhausting, now that I have the expectations of being and acting a queen. They will all want to discuss the east as well, undoubtedly, and I have yet to decide with Rian how much of that story we intend to share.

Besides, I have missed my husband.

So, I return to his rooms, and let him insist on me taking a warm bath to soothe my aching muscles, while he orders a private dinner for us. I come out dressed in one of Asmer's old robes, which only comes to my knees, but is still a comfortable wrap. It is almost funny, but knowing Asmer, and understanding what she must have remembered and how good a friend she was, I know she would not mind.

Oh, poor Asmer; I cannot imagine the embarrassment of being coerced into marrying Rian for political purposes while seeing him like her brother as much as he saw her as his sister, not a lover. She managed the whole affair with such queenly grace and dignity…

I resolve to listen to her better, when it comes to her advice and insistences on me properly learning how to be a queen to the Isaarian people. She will be a good advisor to have by my side.

I find Rian in our outermost room, in front of the fireplace again, and join him. He pulls me into his lap instead of next to him, and I allow it.

"When's dinner?" I say.

"Soon," he promises. "Enjoy the privacy while it lasts, darling; I have a stack of fat invitation cards for you that started fluttering in the moment I decided to announce we had married, officially."

"Mm," I say. "Well, perhaps we should make an announcement. I am only going to call on people who made my little cousin comfortably here in my absence. That ought to rule out the Carsans, save for Soren, and probably the Idos as well. That should make things more manageable."

Rian laughs, then leans forward to set his nose on my shoulder, his mouth at my back. "I have missed you," he mutters.

"I know," I say. "I missed you, too. I tried not to think about you and Ayla much, actually, because it only made it worse."

He groans. "I thought about you every day, and it was miserable. And do you know who was the only reasonable person about it all? Detrus Lundan! Everyone else insisted I was being overdramatic and childish, even Qhan!"

I consider this.

"You can be rather dramatic," I note.

Rian moans. "Oh, don't you start, too. It was a dangerous trip, and you know it. Any man would be concerned about his wife journeying half-way around the world just so she can take a quick jaunt through the Otherworld."

"It was not quick, for the record," I inform him. "By the end of things, it felt like the span of a great many years."

"Oh, well. Beg pardon," he teases.

"I'd tell you all about it," I say offhandedly, "but why bother when you will be forgetting it all shortly?"

"Will I, now?" Rian challenges.

"Aren't you?" I say. "…I did want to discuss that with you," I add, our conversation more serious, now.

"I'm afraid you missed that discussion, darling," he says, refusing to let me become grave. "I already had it with Korvaan."

"Did you?" I say.

"I will be remembering," he says with determination. "After experiencing a lifetime without knowing? And what I endured to remember? I cannot imagine living my true life not knowing all we have experienced together. Particularly not with you already knowing."

"But it will be painful for you," I insist. "It has been. I…do not want you to torture yourself."

Certainly not for my sake.

"It has been painful," Rian agrees. "But, once I thought on it, I realized it is perhaps better to know, and to have some suffering, than to be completely ignorant to what my own wife has experienced."

"I could bear it alone, for your sake," I say.

"And leave you to make all the sacrifice? Come, now, Soleil," he teases. "I am not so weak that I cannot manage to sacrifice some comfort. Besides, my experiences in our past lives will undoubtedly make me a better, wiser king. Who am I to deny Isaaria that?"

I consider this, and must concede. After all, I realized the same thing: I have become a better person, with all our lives and memories. Rian is right that he is wiser, now, than he ever was in our relative youth. He will be a young king with the experiences of several lifetimes. Perhaps that is what is needed, for the peace Isaaria has been promised.

"So, I will be knowing about your experience in the Otherworld, now," Rian insists.

"Will you, now?"

"Yes, my dear, I will. And leave nothing out."

He lets me take a few moments to myself, then, though I know he must be dreadfully curious about the Otherworld. We have announced we were successful in our efforts, after all, but aside from myself and partially Septimus, no one else truly knows what that means. I know Rian is the person who most deserves a full explanation, but I cannot pick where to start, yet.

"…I saw Mercer," I confess. "And Taris and Lune. Rian, I truly did go to the Otherworld. It's real. All of its real. And I saw it. I went."

"You did, mmm?" he muses.

I nod against his shoulder. "And I met a dragon, and we got shipwrecked, and, oh, the Mitaurus are in Isaaria. We think. They might have left, to try and find us someplace else, but they actually posed quite a threat, and perhaps next time around we should discuss whether something ought to be done about them. They have been around for so long, and everyone simply lets them be…"

Rian laughs. "It sounds as if you had a full trip," he notes. "So much has happened, with you gone. For both of us."

"Yes," I agree, and straighten up so I can move off his lap and fold my legs under me, seated across from him. "We have much to discuss. And, if you do not mind it, I think I shall go first."

I recognize the smile he uses, then. I know it is the one he has reserved especially and only for me.

"Soleil, I wouldn't have it any other way."

I AM WOKEN by a knocking on the door. Sharp, but polite, and not banging. Even without glancing at a clock, I know it has long since passed noon. The sun has already set once more and I have slept the length of an entire day away, and then some. Rian has let me rest, clearly, though we admittedly did stay up rather early into the morning, talking.

Despite my badgering and questioning him, unfairly testing him, he has stoutly agreed to remember everything with me, in the final timeline. I did not even bait him with the idea that I would choose to remember; he decided on his own. Even while waking, still tired, the concept pleases me. We will be like a set of ancient Fair, not unlike Kang and Aisling. I cannot wait for it.

I groggily call out platitudes and demands for patience while I force myself out of bed and stumble about, rubbing at my eyes and trying to dress. The knocking on the door is most insistent. I go to answer it half-dressed and am not prepared to hold up the weight of one Grand Princess Yvette Pike when she stumbles through the doorway and directly into me. She is still in her nightdress, with a robe over top. So, I suppose she and Vásan must have spent the day in private as well, and she did not bother to dress.

"Princess!" I manage to gasp out, worried at first that she is injured.

"Vásan told me everything!" she says, grabbing my shoulders as if her legs are about to give out from beneath her. "Everything! Please. You must promise me, if you go back again! You must promise!"

I manage to stammer something nonspecific regarding my confusion, as I have no idea what I am meant to promise.

"Promise you will not take Alo away from me!" she begs.

I am taken aback until I realize what she must have discussed with Vásan, at least in part. If Yvette understands I can rewrite timelines, and plan to at least once more, it stands to reason she and Vásan would also discuss the conception of their son, and the unfortunate circumstances that lead to it.

I realize, then, that Vásan has listened to me and Septimus talk enough to probably understand where my opinion on the matter lies.

Not that I intended for him to be listening. Or for Yvette to ever find out.

"If you want your son, you are asking me to allow something horrible to happen to you," I finally say.

"I don't care," Yvette says desperately, as if she thinks I will turn back time any second now. "You cannot change anything. Promise me. I want my son. Whatever needs to happen, simply let it. I do not care."

I make her loosen her grip on my shoulders. Yvette is perhaps half a hand shorter than me, and a small woman, but those fingernails of hers are like a banshee's digging into my skin, even if unintentionally.

"There is a chance, if I stop Bastien, you and Vásan could always still have Alo yourselves," I say.

"But you do not know that for certain," she says, accusatorily. "You cannot know for certain. I do not want you to take that chance. I only know I do not want to lose my son. Promise me."

I hesitate. It is one thing to promise myself I will try to do what is best for the world without exhausting myself, interfering. It is quite another to go ahead in my new life with the knowledge I have, and blindly turn away like Yvette wishes.

"I do not know if I can do that," I say.

"Bear that burden," she says sharply. "Because it is not your decision to make. I love Alo. I want my son."

It occurs to me that I cannot insist Yvette does not know what she is asking for, because she does. She has already lived it. In fact, if my cousin's children are any indication, there is some certainty in Alo needing to exist. I could potentially use that as an excuse for myself; that by interfering, and making it so that Alo is never conceived, I will have stopped the hand of Fate. But that is all it is: making an excuse; justifying why I could not stop Bastien Pike from doing something horrific.

Yvette sees my hesitation, the lack of conviction.

"Make me a solemn vow, right now," she demands. "Promise me that you will allow me to have my son. Promise you will not interfere with my life. Swear it!"

"How can you do this to yourself?" I ask.

She can hear in my tone all that I mean to say but cannot bring myself to.

"Because I have already lived it once," she says. "And while it was horrible, and painful, I know that I am strong enough to live with it. I already have. At the same time, I also know, now, the love that I feel for my son. All that will bring me joy to see him accomplish. I am living that, now, as well. And I know that I do not want to live without it."

I hear her, in all her desperation, but I do not know how to reconcile it with knowing what will happen to her. I understand her saying she can survive it, because she has, but what if she never had to?

"Please?" Yvette says again, sounding so small and girlish. "Please, just promise? Promise you will not take Alo away from me?"

Her eyes are watering, her lower lip trembling. I cannot imagine her ever looking like this before in her life. Considering what she is begging me for, I feel terrible. There are an infinite number of things she could be requesting, using such a pout to get, and this is what she is asking for.

Some tiny voice whispers in the back of my head, reminding me: I have rewritten the laws of time in order to meet my own son. How can I not expect Yvette to be willing to do whatever possible to the same effect?

"Your majesty, please?" she says again, and starts to cry. "Please?"

"If this is truly what you want," I say slowly, "and you are asking me to respect that, then…I suppose I have no right to try and tell you otherwise, or to make that choice for you. I…I will not interfere with your life."

Yvette falls completely into me again and begins to sob, her legs practically collapsing under her. Her deadweight is heavier than I would have expected, given how slight she is.

I am considering whether to put her down on the ground, or perhaps in a chair, when someone clears their throat from the open doorway. Vásan. I note that he has clearly taken the time to dress before coming after his wife. As though, while Yvette ran out to see me with great haste, Vásan still could not bring himself to appear before me wearing anything less than an ensemble worthy of a grand prince of Isaaria.

He has assumed his usual façade once more, as if we did not all see what happened yesterday. As I cannot gesture for his assistance, I am relieved he helps himself into the king's suite to take Yvette from me.

"I apologize for my wife's disruption of your rest," he says plainly.

But I can see him, now, for who he really is. This man holding his wife, whom he thought did not love him, could not love him, or even truly love their son.

Though, even from the version of the story I had heard, Yvette always was, somehow, attracted and rather interested in Vásan, even before they married. If given the choice, between the Pike brothers, and disregarding certain actions on Bastien's part, she would still choose Vásan. She would pick the Pike brother notably less publicly approved of at the time.

So, while I do not fully understand Yvette with regards to what she has asked me to do, I do know something else about her that it appears to have taken Vásan the better part of two decades to put together himself.

"For someone so smart, you are a stupid man, Vásan Pike," I tell him.

He does not break character. "Noted. Thank you, your majesty."

There comes a tentative knock at the door. Rian is there, with Qhan hovering behind him.

"Is this a bad time?" he asks, an eyebrow creeping up his forehead.

"Of course not, your majesty," Vásan says. "Please, excuse us."

He half-carries Yvette from the room, and does not say anything to comfort his sobbing wife, but he still came. He still spent last night discussing things with her much the same as how I did with Rian. So perhaps there is hope for the pair of them yet, even if it must be done all over again.

I wonder how their son is taking things.

Rian chases the thought away, for now, mainly because I see he has brought Aiko Shinya with him. Shinya had been pressed close to the wall until now, as if someone told him not to dare meet the eyes of Isaarian nobility. I'd suspect Naomi, except I do not believe she has met him again, yet.

"You let me sleep an entire day away," I accuse Rian.

"Well, yes," he agrees. "Which I now realize may have been foolish if we do not want to make a nocturnal creature out of you. But, nothing to be done about it. Now, if you would?"

I let him take my hand and pull me toward the door.

"I promised Lord Aiko here he could see Teresa sometime today, and he's been waiting an awfully long time," he says.

"You could have gone without me," I tell Shinya, who still will not meet my eye.

"I suspect not. Your majesty," he murmurs, mimicking how others have referred to me, though he would only know me as Captain Marson.

I suppose he has not gotten quite the reception I wished he might.

Rian hardly gives me time to ponder it. He is already off, walking down the hallway, and ferrying me with him.

"Tomorrow morning, I am setting up a breakfast for you and Ayla and Soren and me," he informs me. "So, I suppose that will force you to be up at a reasonable hour, even if you do not fall asleep until dawn. We will force some coffee into you."

"I do not require coffee," I insist. "Will we be discussing their marriage, then?"

"Oh, undoubtedly," he says. "After, I suppose we will need to have something of a rendezvous with Septimus about all this mess. Has he specified when would be best for us to…ah…"

"No," I say, understanding why he would not want to mention anything in front of Qhan or Shinya. "I believe it was made clear to the both of us that it would be my decision. Though we should still talk to him about having you and I remember things. I think I will need a certain piece of jewelry. Anyone else's, I suspect, will be made…null."

Fate implied it, after all. And perhaps he will be the one having a hand in allowing me to remember, even if he made no such direct promises, and certainly not for Rian at all. At this point, I suppose I trust the holy beings watching over us know what is best for us, and will do as they're told by the very essence of divinity.

"Ah, I see," Rian says, nodding to himself.

"…Maybe tonight," I say quietly, and I can see this has shocked him.

"What? So…so soon?" he says uneasily.

"I realized, yesterday, it should be done at the soonest opportunity," I say. "I started making a list, see. Of all the things I would want to see done, first. It occurred to me that perhaps I would simply keep adding things to the list. But those around us, for the most part, appear happy, now. I think I would like to go back thinking of everything in that way. Otherwise, I will put things off."

Rian considers this. I can tell, especially in light of the news about a breakfast he has put together, that this is mildly disappointing to him. But it is my decision. I know he will respect it, and support me in it.

He raises my hand to kiss my knuckles.

"Whatever you think is best," he says. "…Though that means we should speak with Septimus about that issue tonight, then."

"I plan on it," I confirm.

I am about to go on, to insist that if Rian truly thinks we should wait a few days longer, I would take his opinion into consideration. After all, I trust him more than anyone else in the world. But then I hear something, distantly. Something that I should have expected, but for some reason did not. Given what I have experienced with Widow and in the Dark's domain, for a moment I expect to see a ghost. An illusion.

When I do not, I realize those little cries must be real.

I stop, and Shinya almost walks into me.

"…What is that sound?" I ask, my voice barely a whisper.

"What? Oh. Rika!" Rian says, excited suddenly as he grins. "Teresa's baby came early! We forgot to say! Do you want to meet her?" he says, grabbing my hand and pulling me to the stairs. "Come, come, come—follow me!"

I blink, startled. I knew Teresa must be further along than she once was, now, given the time that has passed. I knew I wanted to reunite Shinya with her, and at least imply to him he could meet his daughter, so that he might stay. But I suppose, in a real sense, I did not realize Rika was already here.

I let Rian pull me along, and decide that this is a sign. We will go back, tonight. I think Fate has let me wait, and all others have let me return to Isaaria, when we truly did not need to. We only wanted to.

Now, I merely want to let Shinya meet his daughter, first. That will be enough.

Twenty-Three

SHINYA WALKS TWO PACES BEHIND ME, so silent that I occasionally must check to be sure he is still there. I would not be surprised if Shinya found himself without the courage to see Teresa again. But his expression remains unchanged, and he says nothing as we follow Rian up to Teresa's rooms. There is tension taunt in the atmosphere around us, and I realize I am somehow equally as nervous as Shinya is to see Teresa again.

Even if I tell myself that it does not matter in the end, I want their reunion to go well. I want there to be a precedence of hope to hold onto in the coming years, when I know I must allow my little cousin to marry a monster before finding her way to us. So long as, in one timeline, I know Rika exists and Shinya and Teresa reunite, it will be enough.

Instead of entering directly into Teresa's room, Rian instead takes us through the Smith's gathering room, where I am sure they have entertained many dinners when Teresa could not make it to a former occasion. Naomi slips out of Teresa's bedroom in time to meet us, quietly closing the door behind her. She frowns to see we have brought Shinya with, but does not comment on him.

"No need to stand guard, Naomi," Rian says cheerfully. "We have only come to meet the baby. Or, for Soleil and the child's father to meet her. I, of course, have already been formally introduced."

His lighthearted nature almost makes Naomi smile, but she purposefully restrains herself.

"Septimus is in there with her, now," she says, "as well as Grand Princess Irina. I'm asking him, first, if he will allow anyone...unexpected to visit."

She purposefully avoids even saying Shinya's name.

"How did she do in delivery?" I ask, wondering if there is a true reason that Naomi would potentially deny Shinya visitation. Is it that Teresa is merely as exhausted as any mother would be at this time, or is she too weak?

"We had to cut," Naomi admits. "The doctor did most of the work, I only helped stitch up afterwards."

Shinya frowns, and finally speaks. "Was there something wrong?"

"Nothing," Naomi promises. "The baby is healthy. But it seems that Aiden was taken out that way. So, we decided it would be easier to take Rika out the same way, instead of forcing Teresa to attempt the process naturally."

Shinya considers this, then nods slowly.

"It is a highly advanced technique," Naomi admits, pleased with herself. Perhaps she should be, despite her previous attempts at modesty. "And we were met with every possible success given the situation. She should recover entirely in a number of weeks."

Though I know this timeline will not even exist in said weeks, I am still pleased to hear this.

"Oh, she'll likely be bored to tears by then, even with all her drawing," Rian says brightly. "I suspect she will be pleased to have new visitors coming in and out."

His obvious hinting to Naomi does not change her opinion on Shinya, though, and she is back to frowning. So, the gatekeeper resumes her post. I decide it would be best if I came up with the solution to this and turn to Shinya.

"Wait here for a few minutes," I say, cautioning him. "I shall see if she is up to your visit."

"If she is not?" he poses.

"We will just have to wait," I say.

Thankfully, Shinya does not make a fuss over this and willingly finds a spot against the wall to stand and wait. Naomi gives me a small, approving nod before allowing Rian and I to pass through the door, and into the bedroom Teresa has been using these past months.

Irina Lundan is indeed there, as Naomi noted, seated in a chair beside the bed to keep my cousin company. Septimus is standing on the other side of the bed, surprising me by smiling for once as he watches his nephew and niece on the couch across the room from them.

Teresa looks tired, but much healthier than last I saw her. She managed to put on some amount of weight in the past few months, and looks happy. There are even roses in her cheeks. Her hair is pulled back prettily with that Kachin hairpin, and she is wearing a white lace nightgown that can open at the front, in Isaarian style. We Isaarians are rather practical about these things, after all, and she will need to feed the baby frequently. Additionally, I've no doubt Naomi has taken charge of Teresa's lying-in period, where we typically allow the mother to do no additional work while she looks after her new baby.

Teresa will have been brought specific foods, kept warm and comfortable, and told to do little more than rest, recover, and relax. Surely, she has had plenty of time to draw. Aiden, I expect, is quite happy with this arrangement; Teresa has rarely been healthy enough to play with him, anyways. But I do not see Damen anywhere. Perhaps, he is jealous of his new sister.

Rika herself has settled, since I first heard her. She has fallen asleep, laid against Aiden's chest. He is slumped down against the couch, so his little sister can sleep as comfortably as possible, and the way he looks at her is so tenderly innocent that it is almost heartbreaking. He is so gentle and loving with her. With his good arm, he strokes her head and puff of silky dark hair softly, looking down at her with the sort of open lovingness only someone so young can exude.

I already know Aiden will not want to let her go.

The baby is perhaps a few weeks old, now, depending on timing, but she still looks so small to me. Her complexion is fair, but with warmer undertones than her mother's, and her hair is solid black. As suspected, these traits alone identify her as another man's child. Aiko Shinya's.

"Your majesty," Teresa says when she sees Rian. "And Soleil! It…It is so good to see you again. To see you are safe."

"Likewise," I say.

There is more that I want to say, that I had planned to say. But even with a captive audience, all eyes on me, I cannot think of the right words.

"I will take my leave," Irina Lundan offers, with a knowing smile. "Teresa: so glad you have come to live with us. Your company, and your children's, are more than welcome here. Feel free to call upon me any time you like."

Teresa nods. "Thank you," she says. "And please extend my thanks to Grand Princess Pike as well. For your friendship, and for looking after me the way you all have."

Irina nods, curtsies to Rian, and then exists out the hallway door, a small smile still on her face.

"You look well," I tell Teresa.

"Yes," Septimus agrees, "and you look tired."

"Occupational hazard," I say, and move to take Irina's seat by Teresa. "I hear they cut you open."

"Only a little," she says. "Everyone has been most helpful in my recovery."

Across the room, Rika squawks, wriggling against her brother's chest.

"Mama!" Aiden cries, alarmed.

"Bring her here, darling," Resa says, holding her arms out.

Septimus moves to help Aiden with the baby, purely out of caution, given the boy's one good arm. Aiden makes it to the bed, scrambling up to get Rika into her mother's arms.

"When she's fussy, it means she has to eat," Teresa explains to her son.

"How do you know?" Aiden presses, in awe of his mother's ability, as Rika calms down instantly when taken to the breast.

"Because we already changed her, and you were cuddling her nicely for a long time, Aiden. So, she had plenty of love and care—she is only hungry."

The way she says that tells me that Aiden has wanted to hold Rika as much as possible since she was born.

"Can I stay here?" he asks, "And hold her again when she's done?"

Teresa gives him a look. "It is near bedtime for you," she warns him. "But you can lie down, and if she finishes soon, you can give her a kiss goodnight before you go off to bed. Yes?"

Aiden bobs his head excitedly.

"Lie down, then," Teresa insists, patting the pillow.

Aiden obeys instantly, too excited for him to fall asleep, but at least he is still a good listener. He will not be causing his mother any trouble with a new sibling. Lucky for Teresa.

"She is a strong eater," Septimus teases, and ruffles his nephew's hair playfully. "Unlike someone I could mention. Did you know you gave your mother quite a scare as a baby?"

"Really?" Aiden says.

"You were a tiny little scrap," Septimus confirms. "Your mother fretted over you often, for months, until you were strong enough to sit on your own."

"But I am much stronger, now," Aiden says. I have noticed his Alarkian has improved significantly. I have not heard a word of Lusch from him this entire time. "One day, I will be as strong as Damen, won't I?"

"Maybe so, darling," Teresa says.

Aiden continues to lay down as his mother commanded, but reaches over to play with the tufts of his little sister's hair.

"She is a very pretty baby, isn't she?" he says. "Probably the most perfect-est ever."

"Could be," Septimus says, and flashes me a look. "Would you say so, Soleil?"

"She," I start, and then must clear my throat and take in a sharp breath. "She is beautiful."

"Thank you," Teresa says. She is not beaming, exactly, but simply looks to her daughter with a gentle smile, and strokes the baby's cheek with a finger.

It occurs to me that while I have often drenched myself in my own anger, desperate not to feel anything else out of fear, all Teresa knows how to do is love. Even her husband, who has done so many horrible things to her, she cannot bring herself to hate. Perhaps I should be grateful, as I was hardly the most gracious of hosts when we first met, and Teresa does not hold anything against me for that.

"Do you want to hold her? She is nearly finished," Teresa says.

"H-H-Hold her?" I repeat.

"Of course," Teresa says, and gestures with a hand.

I creep closer to the bedside, wondering why I feel such dread. It is only a child, a mere infant. There is absolutely no threat here, no danger. Teresa separates the baby from her breast and Septimus helps her tuck her gown back in place.

"Say hello to your cousin, little Rika," Teresa says, turning her voice into a sweet croon.

Before I know it, the child is in my hands. I immediately pull her closer to my body, finding a natural way to hold the baby though I cannot imagine it having ever happened before.

She is not heavy enough. It is a strange thought, perhaps, but one that I cannot rid myself of. I have not held something this light and delicate before and it terrifies me. I need Rika to have more weight to her, something to constantly remind me that she is in my arms. Otherwise, I find, I cannot stop staring at her, telling myself repeatedly to hold her carefully and gently and not to drop her.

"I-I-I think I need to sit down," I stammer. "I need to sit down. I think I might drop her. She is too small. She is too damn small and—"

Before I can say anything else, Rian is there. I had just about forgotten about him, he has done so well to step back and allow me to take charge, here. He scoops the baby right up out of my arms and is already gushing over her so that Teresa's smile grows even larger. I am feeling a bit dizzy, and step backwards. Rian is saying for the hundredth time that Rika is a beautiful, perfect little girl.

All I can think of is the fact that Rian and I are meant to have three daughters, and two sons, including Ayla. I cannot help but picture holding two of my own dark-haired little girls as babies. Of helping Ayla hold them.

"She is such an adorable baby, Miss Teresa, you should be very proud," Rian claims. "In fact, you have very good-looking children, did you know that? They must get it from their mother!"

His teasing makes Teresa laugh.

"Ayla, Lisan, Thena, Artemis, Yeong-jun," I say suddenly.

The teasing stops. They all stare at me, including poor Aiden, who is merely curious and confused. He cannot fathom why I would blurt such a thing as that, suddenly.

"What?" Rian says, Rika still in his arms.

I am equally shocked by my own words. I am not myself. I feel oddly dizzy, and out of touch in my own body. It takes me too long to respond; I do not know how I know these things, but I do, and there is no forgetting them.

"…Those are our children's names."

Rian gently, slowly deposits Rika back in her mother's arms. He approaches me with care and takes my arms. I think he could see me shaking, but I was unaware of this myself until I felt his hands on me.

"Rian," I whisper. "We need to go back."

"I know."

"We must make things better. For our children."

"I know, I know."

He pulls me in against his chest and turns us around, so I do not have to face my cousins. He knows me well enough to understand I find most public emotions mortifying, unless they can be justified significantly. However, I find that, for some reason, I do not mind being here with a few tears brimming in my eyes. Out of everyone who could see me like this, those currently in the room are the most likely to understand.

"At least you already have it all planned out, hmm?" Rian says in Isaarian. "The number, the names, and everything."

I allow a short, watery laugh.

"I think Fate may have lent me a hand," I say.

Rian pulls back, looks me over, wipes away the tears threatening to fall and tucks back loose strands of hair.

"I look forward to the days I can meet them," he says. "And now, as long a road as it may be, at least we know those days are coming."

From his perspective, perhaps, yes. But I worry for the last cycle. I have promised Fate to cut my palms and heels and never use my fluke again. I have some experience living without a fluke, yes, but even in my ignorance, it often saved me. In the future, poison would work on me more easily. A fall from a great height, and I am dead and gone. Were someone to hurt Rian, hurt Ayla, hurt another one of our children, I could not make it be undone.

I will have to live with the hurt, the same as anyone else.

"We will need to sacrifice much for them," I say, still in Isaarian.

"I think we have already come to terms with that," he says. "And now? We will have Taris, and Lune. They will help."

I hesitate, but then say it. I know Rian needs me to. I know I need me to.

"And Mercer. Mercer will love them."

For a moment, he is stunned. I lock eyes with him and watch, and wait. But if the sins of a traitor can be erased by a divine power, I know I cannot possibly hold Mercer's good intentions against him.

This will be a new beginning for all of us, including him. I will have my family. Lune and Taris will have one another, and me, as the sister I should have been to them both. Mercer will have the chance to see that the world is not such a terrible place after all.

"Yes," Rian finally says, his voice softer. "Yes, he will."

This time, I smile first.

Behind me, Septimus clears his throat. I find that I am not annoyed with him, but have grown so used to his personality that I know I will miss him terribly. I am more than willing to turn from Rian, and stand beside him to face my cousins, knowing they are a part of the family I have always wanted.

"Well," Septimus says in Alarkian, "I may not have the greatest understanding of the Isaarian language, but I know names when I hear them. And it has occurred to me that we ought to finish up, here, and get moved on to the way things should be."

I keep one of my arms hooked through Rian's.

"I suppose you have it all worked out in terms of process?" Rian says.

"I'd given it some thought. And Fate may have presented an idea or two. I'm going to do some work on you," Septimus says, rolling and cuffing his sleeves. "You first, your majesty, and when I'm finished with you, Soleil. In the morning, she can stand outside in a peaceful spot, use the power of the sun, and we will go back. One final time."

Rian raises an eyebrow. "What kind of work?"

"Nothing nefarious," Septimus promises. "I think I owe it to the both of you to remember all this. Even if Fate did not imply you needed to know. But it is a difficult burden to bear. So, I am going to do my best to emotionally distance you from your more traumatic memories. You will recall they happened, but there will be no memory of suffering."

I glance over at Teresa, but she does not appear bothered by the fact she has barely met her daughter and now will need to start all over again. For me, it is reassuring to know that if Rika exists now, she will again. Somehow, some way, her soul will have its time in this world. I think that helps Teresa, too, and in a way—though her knowledge on the subject is considerably lesser—Yvette Pike. There will be some suffering for them, in their lives, but there will be for everyone. Rika existing means Teresa will leave the Greys, and somehow Aiko Shinya will find her. Fate has woven them that way, and his record is never wrong. Alo Pike existing means my son will have a best friend, and Yvette will have happiness again even after her suffering.

There is a wisdom in both these women that I do not have the temperament to entirely understand, though my time in the Otherworld has helped. Rian, however, does not have the luxury of our experience.

"So, all of this has been done for nothing," he sighs. "Going through everything over and over again."

"I would not say so," Septimus says. "Perhaps it may feel that way, and perhaps there is some truth to it. But one must also consider the people you both were, that first cycle, and the people you are, now. Perhaps you are the versions of yourselves, now, who are most needed. Who will do what is most good."

He exchanges a look with me. It is mind-boggling, in a way, but perhaps even the Dark's attempted machinations were meant to be. After all, ironic as it is, without his stealing of Taris, Lune, and Mercer, I would never grow closer to my sister. I would never become the better person I am, today, with all my experience. Without Septimus' power, I would never be able to remember it all in order to become that person.

There is a specificity in play that cannot be ignored. I suppose I cannot possibly forget ever again that the Almighty knows what he is doing. How laughable, that Original Soleil used her powers for purely selfish reasons, and in doing so, created the circumstances to make me who I am now: a much better person.

Of course, Rian will be a great king, preparing Isaaria for the golden age it will be for our son's reign. Not only because he is a good man, but because, as he has already said, now he has centuries of experience. Our son could not have a better mentor.

"You go," I tell Rian. "I will stay with Teresa for a while. And Rika."

He nods, knowing what I mean by that.

"See you in the morning, then," he says.

"And every morning after that," I remind him.

I stretch up to kiss the light smile that appears then.

"Miss Teresa," Rian says, and steps up to the bed to kiss her hand. "It has been a pleasure. I will look forward to when you find yourself in Isaaria again."

I think of the ghosts Widow tortured me with. It is not torture so much, anymore, to know that one day Rian and Taris will be there when Teresa needs them. She could not ask for better rescuers.

"Aiden," Rian says, and pats the boy's head. "Look after your mother until we can again, would you?"

Aiden lifts his head up and bobs it up and down.

"See you in the morning!" he says politely, brightly.

Rian laughs. Teresa does, too. Of course, Aiden does not understand, but nor should we expect him to. Perhaps he has the best attitude about all of this: why not expect the world to go on as usual.

Septimus gestures for Rian to lead the way as they cross the room, back to the door to the common area. I hesitate, deciding how I want to do this, before turning to Teresa once more.

"I'll just see them out," I tell her, and Teresa nods, smiling.

She does not suspect anything. Regardless of this being our last night in this timeline, I think a reunion between her and Shinya is good. Is deserved.

For both of them, and, for me as well. I do not know how things will go in the final loop, nor does anyone else save for Fate, I suppose. From what hints he gave, however, and from everything I've seen and heard, I think Shinya and Teresa are meant to be, beyond just Rika's conception.

They can be one another's redemption. Tonight, and moving forward.

Shinya has barely moved. He watches Septimus and Rian pass by, saying nothing to them, though Rian is already teasing Septimus about this and that. Naomi is still frowning at Shinya, as if she holds his past entirely against him and is dead-set on not changing. She does have reasons for that.

Despite her original opinion on the matter, however, she does not stand in the way of my decision-making when it comes to this visitation.

Shinya straightens, pushing himself off the wall as I approach. He does not say anything, but waits expectantly.

"I'm going to bring you in to see her and the baby, now," I tell him slowly. "One of her sons is in there, too. The one whose life you saved."

"Aiden," Shinya says quietly.

"Yes," I say, a little surprised he remembered, though perhaps I should not be. "I'm sure this will be something of a shock for her. Whatever way she reacts, please keep in mind that she did not expect to see you again. But she did say to me once that she wished you could meet your daughter. So, she likely will let that happen."

"I understand," Shinya says. Still so quiet.

"But if you say anything to upset her, you are leaving immediately," Naomi warns protectively.

She is miffed with Shinya, for essentially leaving Teresa to manage all this on her own, though there was no way for him to know about there being a child before now. I suppose the Qurvo children have always had bad luck when it comes to having only a single parent in their lives.

Still, protective as she is, Naomi merely follows behind Shinya as I lead the way back into Teresa's room. I know she will stay present the entire time, managing the situation, but likely will not interrupt unless she finds it absolutely necessary.

I rap gently on the door frame before re-entering, so that Teresa looks up from her children, and even Aiden picks up his head.

"Someone here to see you," I say, and then step aside, into the room, so that Shinya can enter behind me.

He does not approach her, but stands back near me, as if waiting for her permission. Teresa's eyes widen immediately. She blinks several times, as if she cannot believe this is happening. I understand the confusion; I, too, would not have expected such a thing. In a world of vast possibilities, the likelihood of this meeting, of my having found Shinya in the first place, is slim.

I suppose having such a small, flippant prayer of mine answered genuinely is a good lesson for me to learn.

"Resa," Shinya says softly.

She stares at him, her mouth agape, her bottom lip trembling as she struggles to decide what to say.

"I found him in Kacha," I explain cautiously, "and invited him to Isaaria, to see you again. And to meet his daughter. Based on the odds of all this happening, I would say Fate approves."

For a few more moments, Teresa struggles to find her tongue, and Aiden looks confused as he observes the strange man whose has such an effect on his mother. I know he is aware of the story, as Teresa told it to me right in front of him, but it occurs to me that Aiden might have been too sick to remember seeing Shinya before.

"I-I thought I would never see you again," Teresa manages to say.

Shinya practically flinches at the sound of her voice. "Would you like me to leave? If you prefer, I—"

"No, please, stay," she insists. "I suppose…you will want to meet Rika."

I catch sight of Shinya mouthing his daughter's name, repeating it, growing used to it. He gives a short nod to himself, approving. It is almost enough to make me smile, too.

"Mama?" Aiden says, questioning. He sits up.

"Aiden, this is Aiko Shinya. He…He is Rika's father," Teresa says, and then waits, nervous both with Shinya here, now, and because she isn't sure what sorts of questions Aiden might ask.

Aiden continues to look from his mother to Shinya, and finally to his half-sister.

"Oh. I know. You said before," he says.

Teresa is relieved. It is easy for her to slip back into mothering again.

"Remember your manners, Aiden," she tells him. "What do you say when you meet someone new?"

"Nice to meet you," Aiden says sweetly, slowly, in practiced Alarkian.

Shinya bows to him, as he would in the east. Usually, Aiden should bow, as the younger of the two. I suppose Shinya sees himself as lower in status, perhaps because of who he thinks he has become, in this world.

"I met you once already, in fact," Shinya says, his Alarkian also carefully pronounced. "But you were sick, then. I do not think you remember."

"That's when you gave Rika to Mama," Aiden says, in the practical, plain way that only a child could.

"…Yes," Shinya says, and glances at Teresa again.

Teresa is still as nervous as he.

"And now she is finally here. Will you hold her?" she offers.

Shinya hesitates. "You would allow me?"

That draws a smile. "Of course. You are her father."

Though Shinya still moves hesitantly, he accepts Teresa's offer and steps closer to the bed. I can feel the tension from him, and see it in his form as Teresa holds out their child.

But when Teresa carefully tucks Rika safely into his arms, the tension fades. Rika smacks her mouth and purses her lips, wriggling until she is curled against her father's chest, and then she settles again. Contrary to what one would expect, Shinya is more confident and natural with the baby than I was. She looks more like him than Teresa, and Rika's presence has softened him significantly from the man he was in the graveyard weeks ago.

Aiden crawls on the bed, across it, to watch Shinya with Rika.

Rika wriggles a little hand free and Shinya offers her a finger to grasp. She immediately pulls his finger closer, to her mouth, and Shinya allows a light sound that might have been a laugh.

"She's so...small," he says.

"Babies always start out small," Aiden offers, tentative but trying to be helpful the way Damen would be. "Mama said so," he adds, as if citing Teresa gives the fact more credence.

"Still," Shinya says. "She will need her brothers to look after her. I suppose you plan to take on this task?"

He acts so seriously while addressing Aiden. I cannot tell if he is humoring the boy or if this is how all Tourrannese act when their child has an elder sibling.

Aiden becomes serious, sitting up straight on the bed. "Yes!"

Shinya nods. "That is good," he says. "She will be well-protected."

Something occurs to him and he looks up to Teresa again.

"What made you think to name her how you did?" he asks.

Teresa shrugs. "I do not know. The name came into my head one day and I felt as if it would fit her. It was the same day I somehow knew she was a girl."

"Mm. You have chosen a strong name for her," Shinya says. "In Tourrannese. She will have a good life."

Teresa likes this prophecy. She smiles. The way she looks at her daughter, in Shinya's arms, tells me I have done the right thing.

He holds Rika for another few minutes, silently watching her every little fidget, likely feeling the fluttering of her butterfly heartbeats. I can only imagine what he is thinking, but I am certain he is committing every speck of her to memory from her tufts of black hair to her impossibly tiny fingernails to the curl of her delicate feet. It is only when Rika wriggles again in mild complaint that he hands the baby back to Teresa, to be swaddled properly for her own comfort.

This process, too, Shinya watches with care, as if he has already decided he will be spending enough time with his daughter to need to replicate it.

Once Rika is wrapped in her blanket, Teresa offers her to Shinya again, but he declines. That leaves Aiden to get another turn holding his sister, propped up safely against the pillows. He is so gentle and careful with her that Teresa does not appear at all worried.

"Thank you, for giving me this," Shinya says, bowing slightly to Teresa, out of habit, I think. "I…appreciate your generosity in this matter. Considering."

"Considering?" Teresa repeats.

"How things…came about."

He is careful to watch his word choice, with Aiden here. Teresa still understands perfectly.

"It took the two of us," she says simply. "So, there is nothing for you to feel wrong about. You did not make me do anything…that I did not want to."

She is watching him closely for his reaction. Shinya's eyes flick towards me, once, and I can tell he is embarrassed. Teresa is resolute in her continual insistence regardless of whom she is speaking to about the matter. There is a mixture of shame and responsibility felt on both sides, yet here they both are, doing what many would consider the right thing regardless. The best thing possible, perhaps.

I do not know much about Teresa's marriage, but while Kryto Grey may have charmed and romanced her as a young girl, that is no longer the ideal she is seeking. She wants someone who will choose responsibility, who will look after her and her children, and not simply expect her to obey them without cherishing her back.

For his part, I do not think Shinya came back out of obligation to his child, though he is doing what he can, now. Nor is he here because he expects another night with Kryto Grey's wife. Teresa does not merely make Shinya feel loved. She makes him repentant of who he became in the Tourrannese Civil War in a way no one else can. He needs that. Like everyone else in the world, he needs to be surrounded by people who make him want to be a better man.

"Will you stay?" Teresa asks quietly.

"No," he says.

I can see she is disappointed, but Teresa looks at the blankets in front of her instead of at him and nods.

"Then, do you think you will ever visit?" she asks.

Shinya gives her a confused look, so Teresa attempts to explain herself further. She is clearly embarrassed, as if she thought Shinya would want to stay, and does not know how to explain why she thought so.

"It is only, if you do not oppose, I think Rika may like to meet her father again. When she is older."

Shinya blinks. Understanding rushes into his features.

"No, I meant…I thought...I misunderstood. I meant I am not staying in this room with you. I thought it would be...inappropriate."

He reddens.

"But you would stay in Isaaria, then?" she asks for clarification, so hopeful as she looks up at him.

He nods.

The way Teresa smiles, as her entire figure straightens and the air about her lightens, is illuminating. I am certain Shinya must see this and understand how pleased she is to know he is going to stay. She knows that we are resetting time, but Shinya does not, and the idea that he would choose to stay with her and be her daughter's father pleases her greatly.

"That is…I would like that," she says. "I think…it would give us the opportunity to know one another better. And I'm sure Aiden would be happy to have someone in that role in his life, again. And Damen…"

It occurs to her, then, that she wants her eldest present. As things are, Damen likely is not close enough for Teresa to call for him.

"Could you find Damen for me, please?" she asks, her eyes pleading as if she thinks I might refuse her. "I am not meant to be up and about much, yet, and he keeps running off. There…There are a few things I need to talk to him about."

"Of course."

"I think he is not far," Naomi adds as I go to pass her. "I saw him sitting on the top of the stairs, last."

"I should be back soon, then," I say, and depart.

Part of me wants to know what Shinya and Teresa might discuss while I'm gone, but I suppose I cannot be privy to everything. Besides, it has been many weeks since I last saw Damen, and I strangely find that I want his company one last time. I have not known Damen and Aiden long, but I will still miss them. I will miss what they have brought out in me, and in Rian, in their innocence, and their potential.

They will be much younger than my children, I believe, but they will be a good influence on our entire family one day.

Damen is indeed still sitting on the steps, hunched over with his chin in his hands and his elbows on his knees. He is tucked against the side of the wall, so that he does not block this staircase, but he would not be big enough to anyway, even if he sat in the middle.

He can hear my footsteps approaching, so he is not startled to have my company. He does not look up at me, but glances to the side and appears to recognize my boots.

"Miss Ayla said you were back," he says. "She was very happy about it."

"It is always nice to see someone again when they have been gone for a long time," I said neutrally.

Damen ignores that.

"She came to see Rika," he says. There is not bitterness in his tone, but the simple sentence and the fact he felt the need to say it tells me all I need to know about his feelings.

"Many people will come to see Rika. She is a new person, and that is exciting for everyone. You, too. Did you want to hold her?" I ask, sitting down next to him. "Aiden has been clamoring to, almost every second he can."

Damen does not pick his head up, but shrugs.

"I know it is a strange time," I add. "Rika is going to recieve a lot of attention. I am certain you had plenty of attention, too, when you were first born. It will fade as people grow used to her. And she will undoubtedly love you as much as Aiden does."

"Aiden loves her," he says.

"Yes," I agree, careful in what I say. "And he loves you, too. Very much. You are his older brother, and you look after him wonderfully. Now he has someone to look after. That is all. Siblings love each other, and mothers love their children."

"…I think Mama loves her more than us. Or, at least, more than me," he finally whispers, and then sniffs.

I realize why he would think so, and my heart nearly breaks for him. It is a heavy realization for a child to manage on their own, even if it is an assumption, and even if it is not at all true.

"Why would you think that?" I ask gently.

I know it is not true, but I also understand that simply telling him that will not help him change his mind.

"Father loved me best. I'm his heir. I look like him. But Aiden hates him and looks more like Mama anyway, and Rika is only our half-sister. Mama's half. Mama hates our father, now," he says, his voice warbling and cracking. "So, she's going to hate me one day, too."

"I'm sure your mother does not hate anyone," I soothe. "She does not strike me as the sort of person capable of it. Some people are simply like that. And mothers could never hate their children. Trust me."

"How would you know?" he asks under his breath, small and quiet. "You don't. You don't know our family. You don't know how much better it would be if everything went back to normal."

"Normal?" I repeat. "Before Rika? Because then you would have your mother's attention again?"

"Because then we would be home!" he cries.

I nod. "You must miss it very much. I am sorry. We have done our best, but I know it is hard, being away from home. Would you say so?"

He sniffles again, aggressively wiping at his eyes. "I don't know."

"Is there anything at all you like better here?" I say, already knowing the answer but hoping it will put things in a positive light for him.

Damen frowns. "I…There are lots of things," he admits. "But…Father must miss us so, so much. We're happy here, and he misses us. I know he does. That's not fair. How can we be happy here without him if he loves us so much? How can Mama not love him any more when he misses us so much?"

Then it becomes clearer to me. There are two issues here, intertwined: Damen terrified his mother does not love him because he resembles his father, and Damen horrified by the idea that maybe he does not miss his father as much as he thinks he should. That leaves him with who, exactly? He can hardly choose one parent over the other if he thinks neither is a proper option anymore.

He does not miss his father so much as he misses knowing beyond a doubt that he is loved. He is afraid. So much is changing in his life, now. How does he know for a fact that his mother will not change her mind about loving him, too, if she can stop loving his father?

"You can be happy, Damen," I tell him, treading carefully. "You do not have to worry about what everyone else feels. Just how you feel. You can be happy. That does not mean you do not love your father. It means you also love your mother and Aiden and Rika. And they love you."

He is not convinced. "But what if Mama forgets to love me?"

I'm shocked by how Damen appears to think love works. I do not know if these are things someone taught him or if he has adapted this worldview by accident. I have seen portions of it before when speaking with him, yes, and I had hoped time would show him the truth. It seems, instead, to have only made him more confused.

"I only want her to still love me!" Damen cries.

He takes me by complete surprise, then, by throwing himself at me and clinging to my uniform front while starting to cry. I am hesitant, but then pull him closer and comfort him while letting him sob.

"Damen. Look at me," I say when he has resorted to sniffling again.

I am surprised when he does. The poignant hurt in his eyes tells me he is so terrified, yet desperately hopeful, that it reassures me he needs to hear what I'm about to say.

"You do not owe that man anything," I say. "Kryto Grey may be your father, but you do not owe him any part of yourself. You do not need to worry about being happy without him or about him missing you. You are here, now. You can be happy. Trust me, it will make your mother so happy to see you happy. And she will never, ever forget to love you."

"But Father said no matter how much Mama loves me, he will always love me more," he says.

"Now that is simply not true," I say. "You cannot measure love like that. And I know for a fact that your mother loves you. You are her son. While you do not remember it, she carried you for months just as she did for your siblings. Now: she might worry about you, yes, but that is part of a mother's love. She wants to do the best she can, to make sure she sets you up for the best life possible."

Damen still does not look convinced. I wonder if he is too young to understand, yet. All he knows is that Rika has his mother's attention, and he feels as if he belongs nowhere. He does not know how he fits into his own family anymore. Kryto Grey always told him he was the center of everything; any deviation of that therefore throws Damen's worldview into turmoil.

"Look at me. Look: She loves you, Damen," I promise. *"She loves you.* Trust me. A mother's love for her child is overwhelming. More than you know. More than you can possibly imagine. She could never, ever forget that. She would do anything for you."

"How do you know?" he whines again.

"I simply do."

"She forgot how to love Father."

"That is not the same," I say. "Now, let us see about getting you back with the rest of your family," I say. I stand and pick him up before he can protest. This is not an option. "Your mother wants to say goodnight. Tomorrow morning, everything will feel better. I promise."

He does not say anything but wraps his little arms and legs around me and buries his face in my shoulder. I wonder if Damen trusts me because he thinks I should have no reason to care about him at all, and yet, I appear to. It is the same with Rian, perhaps. With the two of us, and even Ayla and Naomi, he has nothing to lose and everything to gain.

In returning to the bedroom, I see Shinya has grown more comfortable in his reunion with Teresa. He does not smile, but his posture has relaxed; he has let his guard down, even with Naomi still present. There is still some wariness in him when he sees me carrying Damen in, but I think that is mainly because he does not know how Teresa's oldest son will react to him.

Teresa is drowsy, and does not notice me enter at first. Aiden does not either; he is still holding his little sister while flopped against the pillows, but both of the children are asleep. It is late for such a little boy to still be awake, after all, and much has happened for him in even the past hour alone.

"Mama?" Damen whispers.

Teresa's eyes immediately open.

"Baby, where were you?" Teresa asks sleepily. She pats the bed beside her. "Come join us. Come sit with me."

I carry him to the side of the bed and let Damen crawl across it to his mother. She pulls him into her lap immediately and looks him over as best she can as he wraps his arms and legs around her, same as he did me. He tries to hide his face.

"What's wrong, baby? Were you crying?" she says.

He does not answer at first, keeping his head against her shoulder. Teresa brushes his hair and kisses the top of his head.

"What's wrong, Damen? You can tell me."

"I miss Father," he whispers. "He is so sad without us."

I still do not think Damen knows how to articulate emotions accurately; he certainly does not appear to miss his father, but keeps insisting he does. After all, if he realizes he does not miss Kryto, it lends credence to his other fear. That perhaps you can forget how to love someone.

To her credit, Teresa is understanding even without this knowledge.

"That's fine," she soothes, still brushing his hair with her fingers. "You are allowed to miss him. He is your father. But…" She sighs. "It is not safe for us to stay with him, baby. Do you understand? I know it is hard, but…your father…is a very…complicated man."

"Why can't Father come here?" Damen mumbles, trying to hide the fact that he is crying. "Just to visit? It's not fair. He'd never hurt *me*."

I watch Teresa's mouth waver, and she swallows with some difficulty. It pains her, having to hear her son say something like that, but she will not say so. She does not want to manipulate him, or make him feel guilty over something completely natural.

"It's not fair," Damen cries. "I miss him, but I don't want to go home. It's not fair."

"I know it's not. I know. I am sorry," Teresa says, holding him tightly. "But I love you too much to leave you with him, Damen. He might not have ever touched you, but he hurt you, too. He hurt you by forcing you to grow up with a family that did not act like a family should. You have seen things and heard things you should have never had to witness. And I…I want to give you something better than that."

There are not many tears left for Damen to cry, but she still lets him. Teresa understands even better than I do the effect Kryto Grey has had on her sons. Damen is too young to understand that his current distress is his father's fault, but she does. Upsetting as it may be, Damen's reaction now is only further proof to her that she made the right decision.

Damen suddenly sits up in his mother's lap, as if he has come to a brilliant revelation.

"If he came here to say sorry, and he really meant it, would you love him again?" he asks desperately. "He misses us. He wants to say sorry."

Teresa considers this carefully. She does not want to say no.

"Maybe, one day, we can see him again, and see what happens," she says slowly.

"One day?" Damen repeats. "Like tomorrow? Could he say sorry and make it all better again tomorrow?"

"Probably not tomorrow, Damen."

"Oh."

"I'm so sorry, Damen," she whispers. "I hope that one day, maybe, you will understand why I had to do this. And then, perhaps, you can forgive me."

He does not say anything to this but snuggles himself back up against her. Teresa lets him, and says something to him in Lusch repetitively, soothingly. I suspect lines of a spoken lullaby. Eventually, Teresa flicks her eyes up at where Shinya is waiting and gives him a smile.

"I'm sorry," she mouths clearly in Alarkian, gesturing down at Damen with her chin. "Tomorrow?"

Shinya nods, understanding.

"Thank you," she mouths.

"Would you like me to take the boys to bed?" Naomi asks, quiet but not bothering to whisper.

"If you would not mind," Teresa says. "It is rather late. I think we should continue this at a later time. They are too tired."

Naomi agrees. She gently wakes Aiden and Damen both from sleep or drowsiness, speaking gently and sweetly as she offers to ferry them off to dreamland. Teresa takes Rika back so Naomi can slip Aiden down off the bed and offer her his little hand. Damen crawls off his mother's lap, sniffling and rubbing his eyes but happy to go to bed when he hears Aiden babble his name amidst something else in Lusch.

"Have sweet dreams. I love you. So much," Teresa whispers to Damen, and kisses him on the forehead before helping him down off the bed.

Naomi flashes me a smile, then offers to take Damen's hand, too. He surprises me by not ignoring her, but accepting the offer, and letting her lead him and Aiden off to their bedroom.

"I will leave, as well. For now," Shinya decides, quiet as usual. He bows to her, deeply. "Miss Resa. It…has been good to see you again. Please rest well. I will call on you tomorrow morning. If you like."

"I…I would like that," she confirms.

He nods to himself, several times, thinking. There is something on the tip of his tongue, I can tell. He is rewording it in Alarkian in his head, I'm sure, like a playwright, rehearsing it; an old habit of his.

"You are a good mother," Shinya finally adds, and then quickly leaves before she can respond.

Teresa beams in happiness the moment his words settle in, and she holds her daughter against her chest with almost childish glee. I hover near the bed with her for a few minutes. It is strange, but for once, there is nowhere for me to be, and nowhere I need to go. So, I decide, if Teresa does not mind my presence, I will wait with her until Septimus needs me.

We leave one another to our own thoughts for some time. Teresa looks comfortable holding her baby. She savors every second together knowing full-well that she will have to wait many years before she can hold Rika again.

I watch her and imagine holding my son. If I am willing to wait for that, I imagine Teresa is equally willing to wait for her daughter.

"I want to annul my marriage," she says suddenly. "Is there a way I can do that here? Is it…possible?"

She does not mean tomorrow. She means in the future, when she comes to Isaaria with no memory of Lune and me as her cousins, drawn here only by Fate. She will almost undoubtedly marry Kryto, she knows that, but she does not want to remain his wife.

"From what Septimus has told me, I do not think the Theebin church would accept your marriage as legitimate in the first place," I admit. Even without the factors of abuse and *Dadj'zcha*, Kryto Grey certainly is not the man Teresa thought he was when she married him whilst under the influence of unknown substances. "But I will make inquiries."

"Thank you," Teresa says quietly. "I know I have made many mistakes… Even though I know you and Septimus are going to go back again, soon, I want to work on fixing them in the meantime, even if it is only in my own head. I'm hoping it will somehow give me strength, in the next life. To do this all again."

I nod. I must always remember, despite my power to entirely destroy old timelines, some part of us must remember what has happened before. It must be enough for Shinya to remember, even after seeing her only once, how much he is in love with my cousin. So, my own actions, then, have mattered. Do matter. All of ours do.

"Would you marry Aiko Shinya then?" I cannot help but ask.

"I cannot say," Teresa sighs. "I do not know what he would want. But I want him to be here for Rika, at least. I want to know more about him."

I am impressed by her self-awareness and understanding.

"He is right about one thing," I say. "You are a good mother."

"Well, I am trying," she says. "I fear I have made many mistakes."

"I did not say perfect," I remind her. "Neither did he. But good, yes."

That makes her smile.

"Would you stay with me?" she asks. "I don't think I'll be able to sleep."

"Until Septimus comes back," I agree.

"Thank you."

She curls Rika's fine hair with her fingers. When the baby purses her lips, Teresa gives her a pinky to suck on.

I consider how naturally Shinya held his daughter. I always assumed mothers alone instinctively learned how to look after their children, somehow, someway. Shinya was completely different than expected, despite likely never holding a baby before. He was more at ease than I.

Septimus said Kryto was absolutely enamored when Damen was born. Did he ever hold his son the way Shinya held his daughter? If he reacted at all similarly, I can almost understand how Teresa convinced herself to love him.

"What was he really like? Kryto Grey?" I blurt.

Teresa looks up away from her daughter, almost shocked to hear me say anything let alone that.

"Do not feel obligated to answer," I say, but Teresa talks over me.

"No, I do not mind. Only, I'm finding I have no idea to describe him accurately to a stranger," she says. She gives a small, self-deprecating laugh. "I feel as if, no matter what I say, all you will see is a silly girl who let her heart run away with her."

"Everyone's heart runs away with them at one point or another," I allow.

"It did not help that he is charming," she confesses quietly. "Effortlessly. It sounds strange, but he genuinely is. Not the kind of charming where it feels as if he is trying too hard, or where you feel uncomfortable and unnerved. It is as if, when he speaks to you, you are the only person in the world who matters."

"Charming like a politician?"

She tries to make sense of this possibility.

"No? I could not say. I do not think so. There is a strange innocence in it. I could never tell if he was aware of it or not. It made me paranoid; trying to understand when he was manipulating me or what he truly meant."

I'm sure she can sense my skepticism.

"Septimus implied…" I start, but do not know how to say it. "He told me things about your lives."

Teresa accepts this.

"I know. I understand that Kryto did manipulate me, at least on some occasions. Perhaps many of them. Most of them. I do not know. But I think he loved me, too. I know he loved Damen. He is a monster," she says, "in many ways. But he is a man, too."

"I don't know if I have enough of an imagination to picture that," I admit. "At least not compared to the things I know are fact."

She understands.

"I know. Kryto is a paradox in many ways, even to me. Even more, I imagine, to a stranger. You understand, then, why I could not think of a way to describe him. If he walked in through that door right now, you would not believe me if I told you, 'That's him'," she says, stroking Rika's soft little cheek with a finger.

I frown, ready to refute. I am certain there would at least be some family resemblance between Kryto and his sons, especially given what Septimus said about Damen. However, I know my mentioning such a thing will not be pleasant for Teresa, so I merely nod and say nothing.

Then, a strange voice rasps from the doorway:

"Do you want to test that theory, darling?"

Twenty-Four

THE FEAR I ALLOW to spike in me is a grave mistake. If it had come down to a fair fight between us, I think I could have won; from even just the glimpse I get of him as I turn, I can tell, this man is not in good health. Despite his being bigger than me, the gauntness to his face and the way he leans against the doorframe betrays exhaustion that would have evened the field between us physically.

However, he is quick. Almost the moment I allow that fear in—what normally would drive me to move faster, more certain, more determined—I have lost. The emotion is sucked out of me so quickly, it makes my head spin, and I stagger. The fear is completely gone, but that is in no way a good thing. Confusion follows, but then that is taken away, too. It is as if I am no longer capable of those emotions, though I desire to be.

Reaching for that terror, that desperation, I am taken by surprise when it suddenly strikes back. Pure fear floods into me so quickly and furiously that I am frozen by it. Never before have I felt such fear, except in the realm of the Dark itself. Experiencing it in Samioth takes me utterly by surprise and forcibly reminds me of how helpless I was compared to such great power. I could only escape such a force of evil with divine assistance, after all. Logically, I must consider, what chance do I stand, here, on my own?

Before I can adjust, the fear is taken away again, and with it, most of my resolve. I am left woozy, my vision blurry. I stagger back against a wall and slide down it. It is similar to the utter exhaustion that sets in after a good cry, and all I want to do is fall asleep right there, on the floor.

I am helpless. The moment I begin to feel anger, or frustration of my circumstances, he can sense it, and takes that away from me, too.

Emotions, I recall. Septimus had mentioned it, at some point. He can do something or another with emotion. Or energy. Some form of manipulation, or channeling; it makes sense given what Septimus and Teresa have said about him. He can take one's emotions and use them. I do not know the mechanisms of such a thing precisely, but there is no doubt that my weakness, now, has strengthened him. His posture straightens, and some color returns to his face.

While using one's fluke generally exhausts them over time, Kryto Grey has found a way to replenish his energy using others', instead of relying on the sun, moon, and earth. Even I cannot do that.

I barely hear Teresa begin to scream when he is suddenly there, beside her on the bed. He looms over her with a hand tightly over her mouth, pressing her head against the wood behind her.

"Shh. Don't scream, now, little Dove," he says. His voice is warped, slightly, but sighing and chiding. He acts as if Teresa is a child, and he is tired of her whining. "I have such a dreadful headache. It has been so draining, chasing you all over the world…"

Teresa clamps one of her hands over his, the other pulling Rika tightly against her chest. I imagine she is trying to free herself, and scream for help, but he is stronger, and she cannot. She is already restricted, trying to keep her daughter safe, and he still has a free hand to pin her further.

He looks her over, hand still fastened over her mouth.

"You look well," he says. "It is such a relief. You cannot imagine how I worried, picturing you braving the wilds of the world. You Smiths are delicate creatures."

She continues to pull at his hand, her eyes wide.

"You want me to let go?"

Teresa nods. I wonder if it is difficult for her to breath with him covering her mouth and nose in such a manner.

"Promise not to scream?"

Teresa gives a weak whimper, her one free hand still over his, trying to dig her nails into his skin.

"Aw, why don't I believe you?" he tisks.

Yet, for some reason, it does not sound as if he is trying to purposefully mock her. It is more as if he intends to act playfully with her. As if he has caught his wife unawares with a well-meaning surprise and now wants a private moment alone.

"How about this," he starts after pretending to think of a solution. "I will let go, and you do not move a muscle. Agreed?"

Teresa nods. Held tight against her breast, Rika squawks, waking, and Teresa presses her even closer. I worry the baby will suffocate. Then, that emotional worry is stolen away, too, and a splitting headache takes its place. For several moments, my eyes grow spotty, and I can focus only on breathing, trying to force myself to stay conscious after such a shock. I am sure that if he were facing my direction, I would see Kryto Grey smirking, but his attention is seemingly solely on his wife.

"Don't move, now," he reminds her, sounding deceptively gentle.

He slowly removes his hand. Teresa whimpers, her chest heaving with each deep breath, but does not dare scream. I can see she is terrified of him. While I am sure he must be able to sense that, he does not take it away from her as he did me. Currently, Teresa's fear and consciousness serve him better.

He murmurs something to her in Lusch that sounds condescendingly approving, praising her for obedience.

He moves further onto the bed, before her. Though he may have been mocking her in saying so, Kryto Grey is right on one account: when beside him or his brother Amerson, Teresa does look small and delicate.

She sobs again when he reaches beneath the bedcovers and her nightgown to find her leg. It even takes me a moment to remember what he could be searching for, but Kryto must have a long memory, and knows his wife well. He finds the sheath for Teresa's Magicsmith knife around her thigh, unclasps it, and throws it off the bed. I watch where it slides under the wardrobe.

He does not touch the hairpin. He only stretches up again to kiss her neck. Teresa does not appreciate his intimacy, but she must be as relieved as I am that he does not touch Rika.

"It has been too long, little wife," he says. He speaks in Alarkian, again; her native language. "I have missed you so much. And the children. You cannot possibly imagine what it's been like…"

Teresa flinches violently as he touches her face.

What concerns me, more than how he does not react to her fear, is his tone of voice. I have heard that tone many times, from Rian. That is adoration. That is, at the very least, a man convinced he loves his wife.

"Oh, Teresa," he sighs, and leans forward to rest his forehead on her shoulder. "You have exhausted me. Now, at last, I can rest."

He stills for several long seconds. I can see how scared she is, but Teresa slowly reaches up and begins to comb her fingers through his hair. She whispers something I cannot hear that he responds to with a pleased sound. I'm curious as to what she plans, until I see how long she is taking between each stroke. She only has one hand available, still holding Rika, but she has found a way to bypass his suspicion.

To Teresa's credit, when she makes her attempt, she is quick about it. She finishes another stroke of his hair, then reaches up and snatches the blade out of the hairpin base and brings it down towards his neck.

Kryto is not fast enough to stop her from stabbing him entirely, but still grabs her arm and redirects her aim into his shoulder. Teresa struggles against him, but he is stronger and pins her arm up to try and relieve her of the weapon. I can see his shoulder bleeding through his clothes, but the wound is shallow.

Rika begins to cry. Teresa does her best, but there is not much she can do against a stronger opponent, as already proven with Amerson. Kryto takes the hairpin away from her. He does not use more force than necessary, but still keeps her pinned half-under him and ignores the baby completely.

"Teresa," he says. Playful with her, but well-meaning. Sincere. "I told you not to move. I thought you'd learned this lesson already: when you fight me, you only get yourself hurt. I know life can be frightening at times, but that is why you have me. You can depend on me for everything. You know that."

She has not given up on her struggling, but he counters her almost in a casual manner. It is as if he is trying his best to block out the fact his wife is terrified of him.

Teresa looks over his shoulder at me, hopeful and desperate. But where I had an idea of how to handle Amerson, and only needed the opportunity, I am out of ideas and stamina. I do not know where to go from here. I do not even know if I could manage to turn back time if I had an opportunity.

I cannot settle my thoughts and have no energy to spare. Kryto must know that. He pays me no mind, because he knows he has made me useless.

"Do not look at her, look at me," he laughs.

He still sounds as if he is merely teasing Teresa, craving her attention. He grabs her chin hard, and she flinches. She resists meeting his eyes for a few seconds, but gives up, and gives in. He waits, for her to understand, but then releases her face again. He even lets her comfort Rika without interruption or commentary; he is willing to play at being reasonable, as long as Teresa helps him to pretend they have a happy marriage.

"There," he says once Rika has quieted. "Much better. Now. Aren't you happy to see me?"

"How?" she whispers. "How? Did you…?"

"Our little Damen let me in," he claims, picking up her left hand to play with it, kissing where that dreadful burn reaches over her wrist.

His sleeve draws up. I see on his ungloved hand and wrist an intricate blue tattoo that starts behind his knuckles and must stretch up high on his arm. He pushes Teresa's sleeve up and looks woefully at her burn.

"Oh, darling," he sighs. "I know you think you were rid of me, doing this to yourself…But you could not bring yourself to burn Damen, could you? It was difficult to reach him instead of you, I will admit. But once we were close by, I called to him and he answered. He has missed me so much, Dove. You cannot even imagine."

Her face goes white. She jerks her hand away from him.

"I waited in their room," he goes on casually, "until they came to climb into bed. Then, I could not resist. I missed them."

Teresa sobs. Her chest is heaving and her body shakes with terror. I suppose she imagined stabbing Kryto, then retrieving her sons and running until she found help. She will not make a second attempt so long as he has their children. He knows that, as does she.

"They are my sons, Teresa," he reminds her. "You might have borne them, but do not forget who gave them to you."

He waits until she nods before continuing.

"Where is your brother? Where is our Septimus?" he asks gently. "Do not lie to me, sweetheart. We really don't have time for games."

"I don't know," she insists, crying so hard I can barely hear her.

So, regardless of how many men Kryto Grey may have brought with him, or what else is happening around the castle, they have not found Septimus. Either he is better at predicting catastrophe than he should be, or luck is on his side. Regardless, I need to find him and Rian and reach a safe place where I can regain my energy and turn back the clock.

As horrid as it seems, I cannot afford to worry about Teresa, now. The best I can do for her is to manipulate the timeline as quickly as possible.

"Then where is the great Isaarian King, Rian Yakarami, mmm?" Kryto asks. "Or do you not know that either?" he asks.

This is playful banter for him—something she is meant to respond to with a clever quip for them both to laugh off—but we all know that is not what will happen. It is difficult for me to observe his mannerisms because I cannot decide whether he is a madman who cannot conceive of her terror, or a monster who thrives off it.

After Teresa shakes her head in response to that, too, he reaches his third inquiry. He changes completely.

"And the bastard you let in our bed?" he hisses at her. "Is he here?"

Teresa shakes her head. "No," she insists hoarsely. "No. I have not seen him since. I do not know where he is."

There is relative quiet as he observes her, and I am sure he is trying to detect deception from her in any of the above three accounts. Years living with him must have strengthened her ability to emotionally detach from lying, however, because Kryto does not see through her words.

"What a shame," he says flippantly. "I so looked forward to having a discussion with him. Perhaps I could have given him some advice, for the next time you decided to entertain yourselves. I ought to know, shouldn't I?"

She flinches and will not meet his eyes. She hunches her shoulders like a cornered animal raising its haunches.

"I'm sorry, darling, I simply cannot stand the thought of him touching you," he says, sweet again. Concerned. Worried for his wife. "Of him giving you…that," he adds, then indicating Rika for the first time, with disgust.

Teresa holds Rika close to her chest and scrunches against the headboard in fear. The baby gives a cry of complaint, but Teresa is too scared to try and offer comfort. She cannot take her eyes off her husband.

"Please," she whispers. "Please. Please. *Please–*"

"Do you want to keep it?" he asks, his voice cold again.

Teresa bobs her head desperately. She begs him in Alarkian, and then switches to her best attempts at Lusch, as if she thinks that will please him.

"I suppose I will let you have it," he says. He continues before she can cry in relief. "I want you to be happy. I think it is clear you haven't been."

I have never hated someone as much as I hate him in these moments. Even knowing he has never been the one to kill Rian directly. Even knowing I am about to turn back time and start this all over again. I want to ignore my intellect, follow my instincts, and gut him. I am furious I am too weak to try.

"Are you still angry with me? For our first?" he asks Teresa, sounding so understanding and sympathetic. "Is that why you did this? You know I am sorry to have done it, darling, but you need to move on. Forget it. This child will not replace the one you lost."

Teresa's jaw trembles. She whispers, "She was our daughter."

He sighs.

"Oh, but sweetheart…being a female Grey-Smith would be miserable. A useless life. She would have suffered. Is it not better, then, to have kept her from that suffering entirely? That is merciful. That is what a father who loves his daughter should do for her."

He sounds like the sort of man who would say Ayla and the other orphans who endured what she did would be better off dead. He would say Soren Carsans would be better off dead instead of enduring a life without perfect legs. He would call it an act of mercy, just as he excuses the other things he has done.

"This thing's life will be miserable," he says. "By nature of the fact that it is a Smith and a bastard. But if you want to make it that miserable, I will allow you to make that choice. It is not *mine.*"

I hate that Teresa thanks him for this through her tears. However, she knows how to manipulate him somewhat; she has learned what he likes. He smiles to hear her pitiful gratitude. He kisses her forehead.

"Oh, Teresa. I need you to understand how much I love you. How much I will do to get you back, if ever you were taken from me.

"I know it is not your fault," he continues to soothe her, weaving a perfect lie for them both to believe. Giving her the opportunity to repent. "I know Septimus stole you away. I know it was his idea. He told you things to scare you, and you believed them. He always was the clever one. You are too weak, Dove. That is why I need to protect you."

Through the doorway enters a number of men I do not recognize, though they wear the Lusch military uniform. One of them is pushing Naomi in front of him. She glances my way, then flicks her eyes at Kryto and Teresa. I look her over in turn and while I detect a trickle of blood at her hairline, she is otherwise uninjured. I suppose Kryto is telling the truth, then. Damen did let him in. He did hide in the boys' room. I wonder at why they have left Naomi alive, but am grateful for it. Perhaps Kryto saw how much his sons like her. Perhaps he hopes she will know things Teresa does not.

Regardless, he ignores her, now. Teresa has noticed the additional company, but Kryto does not even glance their way.

"I understand. It was a moment of weakness. I left you all alone and you were frightened," he says. "Let us go home. I promise, I will not leave you alone again. Not even for a second."

He rises and holds his hands out to her.

"Let me have the baby, Dove," he insists, pretending to be cheerful and bright, teasing. However, the way he orders her is a warning, too.

He is giving her another chance. She had best not defy him ever again.

Still, Teresa hesitates, and Kryto forces a laugh.

"It is only for a moment, darling. Let me hold her so you can dress. And then we will all go home."

She nearly looks to me again, for help, but then changes course and casts her eyes down at the counterpane instead. I know she does not want to give in to Kryto, but cannot see an alternative, and does not want to risk him hurting Rika. So, she reluctantly hands her daughter over to him and chokes back sobs the entire time.

I have no power to stop any of this. Naomi, at least, attempts to. When Teresa trembles in trying to leave the bed, Naomi glares and steps forward. She slaps off the hand on her shoulder and curses at Kryto in Isaarian. It is enough to get his attention. He turns to her, still holding Rika placidly as if he would never threaten to kill her.

"She should not be up yet," Naomi snaps. "And certainly not traveling. She is still recovering."

Kryto glances at Teresa, who freezes in her attempts to leave the bed, frightened and wondering what he will do. He turns back to Naomi.

"Are you implying I do not know how to look after my own wife?" Kryto asks her. He does not sound angry, but I know that means nothing.

Naomi clenches her jaw but has the good sense not to answer that directly.

"She needs to rest," she insists. "And she will need medical care."

"So you say."

Naomi grinds her teeth in a way that reminds me of an old personal vice I broke years ago. "If you make her travel, and there is infection, you could kill her," she says. "Do you want that?"

I have no idea if this is true or not, but Naomi sounds convincing.

Kryto glances at Teresa again, then deftly pulls undergarments, petticoats, and a pale blue dress from the wardrobe, draping them over a chair. Teresa nearly says something, noting as I have that she will not be able to feed Rika dressed so. But she thinks better of it, and keeps her mouth shut.

"If rest and medical care are what my wife need, I will be sure she receives it," Kryto says. "I heard you are a physician of some sort, are you not?"

Naomi says nothing until one of Kryto's men takes a threatening step toward her. She flinches away, but speaks.

"I am. Of a sort."

"Then you will accompany us, as my wife's attendant. Go on, then. Help her. Teresa usually had lady's maids to assist, but I do not see any. Or would you have someone else here dress my wife?"

Naomi hesitates. I can tell she is thinking of asking to hold the baby, but she must know he will never agree to that. So, she crosses the room, flashes me a terse look, and begins to help Teresa out of bed. There is a folding panel decorated with pink blossoms, for privacy, but when Naomi begins to move Teresa behind it, Kryto gives a displeased sound in warning, and she stops. Naomi is discomforted by the other men in the room, but as Kryto merely stands there, watching her, she begins to untie Teresa's nightgown.

Kryto would rather force his wife to expose herself before his own men than let her out of his sight again. It is a minor concern compared to what else he has threatened, but that almost makes it worse. He knows Teresa will not attempt an escape so long as he is holding her daughter. He only wants to humiliate her.

I decide not to look. I am only one person out of this entire room, but no one here asked Teresa if she wanted to be watched by a dozen people while dressing. I will at least offer that courtesy.

Kryto, as well, only watches for a minute before the concept bores him. Teresa is keeping herself too composed, I think.

Instead, he crouches before me, his eyes flicking over me in an almost disinterested manner. Where his brother Amerson is mocking and disdainful, Kryto Grey is simply unimpressed by me; he cannot imagine how I could have possibly given all those who came before him so much trouble.

For once, I can get a good look at him, with him so close and my blurry vision clearing. He is younger than me, but older than Teresa by at least a good five years. I can see it in the silver flecks in his blue-black hair and the sharpness in his features. Possibly some of the latter is from weight loss; Septimus was not wrong when he told me Teresa and Kryto were connected. With Teresa in relatively good health, but far from him, her husband has undoubtedly suffered. There is still a sickly pallor over his olive skin, and I can imagine he once was physically larger than he is now.

However, what entrances me the most are those eyes of his.

Teresa's blue Fair eyes have compelled me and many others to help her, so long as she has asked. They endeared her to me, as did Aiden's. I never noticed how Damen did not have the same effect.

Sitting before his father, now I do. Damen truly does take after his father.

Kryto Grey's eyes are dark, but they remind me of Kang's. The angles to them, the sharpness. It is a family trait, I realize, but Amerson does not have them. Neither did Margo. These are dragon's eyes. I can feel that. From how he looks at me, I know: I am but another treasure to be added to the hoard. Simply a lesser one, now that he has Teresa and his sons back.

In another man, that may seem sweet: faced with his wife and the most powerful woman in the world, Kryto treasures Teresa more. But given our circumstances, I find it merely disturbing.

I want to loathe him. I want to glare and even spit at him. I force it all down, ignore the hatred, and try to keep myself as calm and unemotive as possible. I refuse to give him any more ammunition to use against us.

If I want to escape this, I need to be patient. I cannot fight everyone in this room; I do not even know how I would effectively fight Kryto, particularly not so long as he is holding Rika. So, horrifying as this is, I wait.

Kryto must feel my obstinate resolve and realize I am holding my emotions at bay, because he smirks.

"You learn quickly," he notes in approval. "So, you are smarter than Septimus always claimed. I used to tell him he was underestimating you, but he is set in his ways, our Septimus. He certainly does not like to admit when he is wrong."

For a second, I allow fear to creep in. An irrational fear that Septimus has been using me for some mere personal gain, despite all evidence to the contrary. Though I am quick to push it away, Kryto senses that shift.

"Oh, do not be dramatic," he sighs. "Septimus has not betrayed you. He is a traitor given how he has plotted against my family for decades, yes. But he is a coward. He desires allegiance to the winning side, and apparently, he seems to believe that is *yours.*"

He smirks. I am capable of speech but choose not to say anything yet. I know it will only succeed in making my blood boil, and I cannot allow that. I do my best to ignore him instead, but fail in this effort when he grabs my face.

"I suppose I should thank you for looking after my wife," he muses. "I'm sure you noticed; Teresa requires taking care of. Smiths are generally so delicate. But you are of a different breed, aren't you?"

"I am not a breed of anything," I say, keeping my tone as even as I can.

He considers this statement, and clearly has a rebuttal, but holds back.

"I suppose there is room for discussion, at some point," he says, and stands. "You look like a woman who enjoys arguing for its own sake. And you may be smart enough to offer an intellectually stimulating debate."

"Unlike 'most women', in your opinion?" I say.

I meant to insult him, but he laughs.

"I'm afraid I am not that type of man, Captain. I have known many intelligent women. I only meant compared to my wife."

As if that makes things any better.

Rika lets out a small mewl of complaint and Teresa nearly runs to her, still barely laced into her Alarkian undergarments. Naomi keeps her in place and continues to tie up the lacing at her back. She dares not whisper reassurances, but gives Teresa a comforting look. Kryto shushes the baby and rocks her, speaking soothingly to her in Lusch.

"It's all right, darling," he tells Teresa, using Alarkian for her. The baby's cry, and her reaction, have made those members of the room entertaining again. "Hurry along, now."

A horrendously exposed silence perpetuates as everyone in the room watches Teresa dress. She refuses to look at anyone and moves slowly, with habitual but lifeless actions. Before long, Naomi has trundled Teresa into western winter petticoats and is buttoning up the back of her blue silk dress.

It is only when Teresa sits to be helped with her little leather boots that Kryto finally speaks again, and it is only two words.

"Allow me."

He hands the baby off to Naomi then kneels to pull on his wife's stockings and to tightly lace up her tiny feet. I watch Teresa's shoulders drop. She looks faint in relief to see Naomi with Rika, and I am glad she is already seated. She completely ignores how reverently Kryto touches her legs, and keeps her eyes on either her daughter or cautiously flickering towards her husband's men.

Kryto finishes with her shoes. He kisses her right leg above the knee, and pulls down her skirts before helping her to her feet. Even with the heels of her shoes, Teresa looks no taller next to him. He looks her over in approval.

"See?" he says, smiling. "It is almost as if you never left. Now, do you want to go home, darling?"

Teresa keeps her head down so her tears drop on the carpet. She nods.

"Then come along, Dove. Damen is waiting for us," he says.

That makes her head jerk up. Her brow is furrowed in distress, and her lips part. It takes her several moments to manage speech.

"Damen…?" is all she says, but the rest of her question is clear.

Not Damen and Aiden? Why not Damen and Aiden?

Kryto adjusts his grip on her. She goes to take a step back but he does not allow it. Her breathing comes in quicker.

"Oh, sweetheart," he tisks. "He was weak. But fret not. You are still young. We will have more…"

There is a horrible moment when she stares at him with the same, frozen expression as before. Then the shock melts; she knows. She screams and screams. Naomi's eyes widen. She tries to stay composed to comfort Rika against her mother's bloodcurdling cries.

For my own part, I cannot think. I cannot breathe, because I know, too.

I know what it is Kryto Grey has done, that has caused Teresa to scream in such a manner. It is unthinkable, and yet, I am sure. Naomi looks caught between anger and horror, but lands on the latter, covering her mouth with a hand. She must have been apprehended just outside the boys' room, then, and did not witness their encounter with their father.

Kryto Grey is not a man. I do not care what Septimus says; to do what he has done, Kryto has abandoned whatever once gave him humanity. He must have. The fact that no one else in the room aside from Naomi and I look appalled only makes it easier for me to condemn them all.

"I know Amerson told you what your punishment was going to be," Kryto continues, as if Teresa is not succumbing to hysterics before him. "But I was angry, Dove. I realized, later, that it would simply be too cruel. I could never make you choose between one child or another; it would be much too hard for you. So, I chose for you. Because I love you."

Teresa gasps, trying to catch her breath.

"That's my son!" she screams. "My son! My baby!"

"It will be better for him this way," Kryto insists. "Better for him to be put to rest, now, and better for Damen. He will not need to spend his life looking after a crippled brother. Now he is free. You are, too."

Teresa's legs faulter under her, forcing Kryto to hold her up as she continues to scream and sob.

"Calm yourself, Dove," he soothes her. "You love me. You love me. Remember, you love me."

He repeats this chant several times over until he realizes, as I have, that she has fainted. I expect him to sigh at the inconvenience, as he will now have to carry her, but Kryto smiles instead. He bends to hoist Teresa in his arms, managing around her many skirts. The heels of her tiny shoes clink together like windchimes.

"She took it better than I expected," he says lightly.

I hear a number of laughs. I can tell Naomi wants to curse at him, but she is too horrified. She looked after Aiden and Damen both for so long; she is in mourning.

"What would you like to do now, sir?" someone asks.

"Let us be civilized about this," Kryto chides. "Find the Isaarian king and Septimus. Kill them both, quickly, but let Jarrod harvest the blood and bones. Only kill others if they get in your way. If they have a powerful fluke that you think may be useful, bring them with. Otherwise, I think I will tend to my wife. Do not interrupt me unless absolutely necessary."

Naomi wavers on her feet, like she, too, may faint. She recovers herself, and clutches Rika closer to her chest. Though neither of us know what Kryto plans, I know Naomi would die protecting Rika. I know she wishes she could have, for Aiden; that is why she is crying, now.

"Jarrod," Kryto adds in afterthought. "Take care of her."

He jerks his head at me, then hefts Teresa more securely in his arms. His men part from their cluster so he might sweep out the door with his wife. Someone shoves Naomi out behind him, as they begin to leave. N'omi tries to glance back at me, looking for reassurance, but she is forced to turn and look ahead of her so she can safely carry Rika.

Only one man does not move. He is smaller and slighter than Kryto, but still bigger than Septimus, and me. There is a resemblance between him and Kryto, though. Not in their eyes—I suspect few have eyes like Kryto Grey's—but their skin tones and facial features. The angular structure of their compositions.

This must be Jarrod Grey, Kryto's younger brother. He looks familiar to me, and I realize that I have met him before. Several times, I think. He is a sharpshooter. He is quite good at it, even as a young man. From what Kryto said, I think I can safely assume he is also a skilled practitioner of *Dadj'zcha.*

"Leave us," he says to the remaining four men. "Secure the hall."

They depart, closing the doors behind them, so that I am alone with Jarrod Grey. He tugs off a pair of gloves and unlatches a box hanging off his belt. It jangles with something metal inside.

I close my eyes and focus on my breathing, trying to ignore the sounds of him moving to my right. I would never have suspected that attempting to center myself in meditation would one day become so relevant.

"Tired, I see," Jarrod says. I barely hear him. "Kryto does tend to have that effect on people."

My breathing settles and I can feel my heartbeat slow into something natural and unperturbed. I force myself to feel every inch of my own body and the energy it takes to move even one toe. There is enough in me, still, to fight. Even if I am no longer young, and am not as reckless or quick-witted as I once was, it is in my nature to fight. I do not give up until I'm forced to.

As it so happens, that eventuality has yet to truly occur.

I feel my hair being moved and hear a snip. I open my eyes to see Jarrod Grey moving away from me again. He has opened his case, and taken out small silver scissors, a matching knife, needles, thread of varying colors and thickness, chalk, and one of several floppy little poppets.

The lock of my hair wraps around a poppet's neck. I am no fool; I can see Jarrod's silver knife. I am sure if he smudges my blood on that plain little doll, he will gain some control over me; at least the same amount they had over the other Crown Princes, last cycle.

I cannot afford to let that happen.

"Do not fear," Jarrod says, carefully plucking up his knife as he returns to me. "It will not hurt. But this will be easier for you if you embrace the inevitability of it all."

The angle of his approach is entirely relevant. I allow him to bend down to cut me. The moment I can reasonably reach with proper leverage, I grab him and turn my body sideways so I can flip my feet up and throw him over my head.

I scramble to my knees first, a clear goal in mind, but Jarrod grabs my ankle and yanks me back to the ground. I am sure he wants to pin me on my stomach while he collects the necessary blood for that poppet.

He is still attempting to find a decent position when I roll to one side and crunch up my knees, upsetting his balance. From there, it is easy to freely kick at him. I catch him once in the shoulder, and clip the side of his face with my boot heel. But he has held onto the knife, and even if it is a wild swipe, manages to cut my leg down from knee to ankle.

It is not deep, but it stings. It hurts.

Jarrod throws himself backward, the blood dripping down his knife surely enough. He leaves me to hasten towards the poppet, but he should have incapacitated me first.

It is not graceful, but I fling myself to my feet and throw myself onto his back, grabbed for his arms and wrenching them backwards. When I use my full weight, it not only pulls him back, but puts painful pressure on his arms as well. I hear the knife drop.

He must be in pain, but he spins around and under, forcing me to let go, then lunges. He grabs me around the waist to stop me from getting further leverage, and then straightens, my legs wrapped awkwardly, with one over his shoulder, the other under. But I can still use my fists.

Our unbalanced weight forces us to stagger forward towards the vanity. Jarrod Grey manages to pick me up higher and slam me down into it, shattering the many niceties on top of it and jabbing the shards into my back. He digs a hand into my hair to bang my head down. Thankfully, my skull misses the glass.

I ignore that pain and drive the heel of my hand up towards his chin. He manages to jerk away, lessening the effect, but I still feel bone crunch.

Unfortunately, a cracked jaw will not stop him, rendering my move pointless unless I wanted to infuriate him. With that hand still in my hair, he drags me backwards, off the vanity again. We may both be in pain, and panting, exhausted. But now I am on the ground, and he is not.

Nusk would kill me if he knew I ever let this happen.

I am forced to crawl, bit by bit, as Jarrod Grey kicks me. I feel like a whipped dog, and as he is smart enough to aim for my abdomen. I am constantly out of breath. There are swirling black spots in my eyes, and a well-timed kick lands just as I gasp, so that I am coughing and weakened.

My arm is flung ahead of me. I can feel the end of the carpet and the wood, underneath the furniture on the rims of the room.

My hand finds Teresa's Magicsmith knife under the wardrobe.

Fate always did love me, I think, because it is then that Jarrod decides to stop kicking me, to see if I am still conscious. The moment I see his boot, I force my aching body up and jab the knife into his thigh. Like most, his body curls forward against pain, to cry out. I yank the knife out again and slash it across his face.

This gives me enough time to stagger to my feet. He swings at me, but I can easily avoid that clumsy blow and counter with one of my own. I am dizzy, but competent, still. Between the two of us, I can stand straighter.

He tries to drive forward at me, to catch my waist like he did before, but I sidestep him and throw my body and his against the dresser. From there, I slam him down so his head connects with the side of the wood and he collapses. I do not care what his condition is, now; so long as he does not move, that is a victory for me.

I catch a glimpse of myself in the mirror; my wild hair, bloody nose, and bloodshot eyes. I am panting, exhausted, but Jarrod Grey does not get up. So, I am still capable of winning a fight when necessary. Now, I have several more monsters to manage.

The knife is slick in my hand, so I drag my palms against the bedsheets to dry them before gripping it tight.

The men Jarrod unwisely sent away to secure the hall must have heard the commotion on their way back, because they are entering Teresa's suite as I am leaving it. Whatever they expected, it was not a bloody, angry woman with a knife. I am able to catch the first man unawares and plant a kick directly at his abdomen, pushing him back into the one behind him and propelling me forward.

I do not need to get a good count on how many there are, though it is less than half a dozen. I am at my most brutal, despite the buzzing in my head and the exhaustion Kryto Grey left me with. I know I will need the sun before I can use my fluke again, but physically, I am still a threat.

It is not pretty, and I do not fight attempting to minimize casualties as a better woman might. My enemies may still have a sliver of humanity left about them, but I do not care anymore.

All I want, more than sunlight, and more than a chance to do things over again, is revenge. I crave revenge for Aiden.

I am determined to get that.

I make certain to keep a firm hold on Teresa's knife, as it is the only true weapon I have, now. I am practical, but deadly.

I manage to bleed two of my assailants before one of the men I kicked does not stay down, trying to attack me from behind. He grabs my arms and I let them go slack before pulling forward. He drags only my jacket off, and I can fight better without its stiffness. I spin back into a kick that catches him in the face and painfully traps him between my boot and the wall.

My knife flashes.

The last of them makes a grab for my hair. I jerk my hips back into him, whirl, and grab his arm, letting his momentum tip him forward, off-balance. I am in control. I twist his arm back and pop upwards, dislocating the elbow, then drop him to the ground.

I leave them behind and walk down the hall, wiping blood from my face.

My steps are staggering. I know I am weak from my encounters with both the brothers Grey, but I do not have the luxury of waiting for someone else to help. I allow myself to lean against the wall, dragging myself along it. My leg hurts, the cut stinging from knee to ankle, and I do my best to ignore the pain. When I hear footsteps approaching from ahead, I stop and take several deep breaths, prepared for the worst.

Never before would I likely think so, but it is a relief to see Vásan Pike. Yvette and their son Alo are close behind him.

The trio looks as shocked to see me as I am relieved to see them. When I stagger, Yvette manages to break from her reverie to help support my weight. I limp and hop a step to recover myself, admitting privately that the scratch on my leg may have been deeper than anticipated.

"What happened?" Vásan snaps.

"Kryto. Grey," I manage to rasp.

This does nothing to explain the situation to Alo or Yvette, but Vásan instantly understands. I watch his jaw tighten, and a muscle twitch, though those eyes of his stay as dead calm as always.

"Where is—" he starts.

He is cut off by a tremendous noise that makes my ears ring, and forces me to clap my hands over my ears, automatically crouching down to protect myself. When the ringing subsides enough for me to straighten and remove my hands, I catch a glimpse of Yvette and Alo and see that they, too, were affected by the noise.

Then Yvette screams. Vásan leaves a streak of blood against the wall as he slides against it to collapse on the ground.

I am quick to push Yvette into her son, away from the curve in the hall, so they are not in the direct line of fire. I lose my own balance and fall, shaking with exhaustion. Alo Pike leaves his mother to scramble forward and pull me out of the way as well, but I almost wish he had not. I can look after myself, I want to insist. He must protect his mother.

The smell of gunpowder is filling the corridor as I push Alo away, garbling something or another, trying to make him take Yvette and run. Footsteps approach, uncertain and stumbling: hurt, but not dead. Jarrod Grey. His head is bleeding, and his breathing is ragged, but he was not as unconscious as I should have ensured. I may want to be the queen of Isaaria, a woman who has never had to take a life, but I am not her. Not yet.

Yvette is whimpering and choking on her sobs, unable to decide what to do. She does not want to leave Vásan, I can tell, but still, she is terrified.

Jarrod Grey stops to watch Vásan struggle to breathe for a few moments. I tell myself I must rise and fight, but I cannot. Exhaustion hinders me. I cannot mentally overcome my physical barriers, and I now worry that it is going to get the entire Pike family killed.

"Shame," Jarrod says as he reloads methodically. "I hear you have an exception fluke, Grand Prince Pike. You would have been useful."

Vásan gives a wet cough but cannot find the support in his chest to speak.

Alo Pike takes the opportunity to rush the man who shot his father, but he is a slight boy. Jarrod pushes him off before knocking him in the face with the gun. Alo staggers, only to be grabbed by his shirtfront. When he continues struggling, Jarrod pushes him to the ground and levels the gun at him before Alo can try taking off his gloves.

For a few moments, I think Jarrod is going to kill him. So does Yvette, based on her attempts at begging in broken Alarkian. Jarrod Grey is thinking. He does not notice Vásan's arms slowly, painstakingly moving, but I do. I see him tugging at one of his gloves.

"We will bring you with, boy," Jarrod decides. "I'm sure you take after your father. You may prove your worth, yet."

The way he says it, I realize, Jarrod Grey does not mean Vásan. He means Bastien Pike. Alo must know this as well, because the blood drains from the poor boy's face.

"But you, little princess," Jarrod sighs, so casually waving his gun in Yvette's direction as he approaches her. "You, I am not so certain about."

He leans down and grabs her hair to pull her closer when she tries to scramble away from him. Yvette stifles a cry; her eyes are on that gun. In a manner that I am beginning to think typical of the family, Jarrod acts as if they are merely hosting a civil conversation.

"I know Bastien would like you back," he muses. "He has indicated as much. But Kryto said to kill anyone without a useful fluke and…Well. I do not think you would be worth the space you take up, princess. So, I—"

I throw Teresa's knife at him. It does not land at all where I intended, but still sticks in his side. Jarrod Grey is stunned. His hand with the gun wavers. He releases his grip on Yvette's hair and straightens. His free hand goes to touch at the blood beginning to pool at his side.

Vásan flings out an ungloved hand.

I do not know what he makes Jarrod Grey see. I do not know if I want such cursed knowledge, or if I even have the imagination or the stomach for it. But when the shock of it fades, Jarrod gives a choked scream. He stumbles back, away from Yvette. The blood drained from his face. He is suddenly desperate to get away from her. When he staggers toward Vásan, off balance, the grand prince kicks him toward the open stairwell.

Gravity takes over from there.

The gun goes off, but all I care about are the sounds of Jarrod Grey falling down the stairwell, and the fact that he does not even twitch, after that.

"He should not have touched them," Vásan rasps.

Yvette hesitates for a horrified moment, her face pale and hair askew. Then she scrambles over to his side, already getting her hands bloody trying to press at her husband's wound. Alo wipes the last of the blood away from his nose and crawls over to his father as well. But Vásan pushes Yvette's hands away and grabs his son to pull him as close as he can manage.

"Alo. Alo. Go. Take your mother," he rasps. "Get her out of here."

Alo is nodding repeatedly, so fast that I cannot tell if it is partially because his entire body is shaking or not. The poor boy knows his father is dying, and I can see tears pooling at the corners of his eyes.

Vásan then pushes his son away. There is not much strength behind the action, but there does not need to be.

"Leave," Vásan insists. "Leave. Now."

Alo is still nodding, mostly to himself I think, as he tries to pick his mother up under her arms and pull her away.

I do not help him. I am too busy using the wall to pull myself up again, already thinking of where I can acquire the weaponry I need, and how I might begin to summon the strength necessary. There are two Grey brothers dead, now, assuming the grave has appropriately claimed Amerson. The leaves one more.

I am not thinking ahead entirely. I have no plan and I do not care what I should do or what is meant to happen next; I am going to find and kill Kryto Grey. I am going to exact vengeance for the innocent child he slaughtered. I will do this for the boy who, not but an hour ago, tenderly held his infant sister and promised to protect her from the evils of the world. Who loved fish and fairy tales and his own family, so very much.

I only manage to take two steps away from the Pikes when I hear Vásan. Barely, as his voice has grown weak, but I still hear him.

"Soleil," he says, which stops me, mainly because I do not remember ever hearing Vásan say my name before. Perhaps he has, but I do not think so.

"Soleil," he says again. "Please. Please."

He does not need to say more. It makes me hesitate in abandoning them. I know Vásan must understand that, grandly speaking, it does not matter whether Yvette and Alo live, now. We are about to return to a different state of being, in a new timeline. He will not remember either of them. He is still asking. The pain of knowing some other villain may chance across them, with him in no state to defend them, is too much for him to bear.

I whirl back to help Alo pull Yvette to her feet. I am all but shaking the two of them, demanding their attention.

"Do you know where the queen's chambers are? They have not been in use since Asmer died, but do you know?"

Alo is nodding, still. I do not think he can make himself speak.

"There is a secret passage there. I do not mean the one to the king's rooms; there is another, that will lead you from Summer Palace directly. It is in her sitting room. A bookshelf. There is a mechanism, behind the Theebin Bible on the shelf, with the gold designs. *Go.*"

I pull them around and shove them forward, down the hall, away from myself and Vásan. I wait there, until I can no longer see them or hear their footsteps. Then I allow myself to lean back up against the wall and think. For a moment, I expect to hear a thank you whispered from Vásan, but I do not. If he is still alive, it will not be for long.

Though I know I should care, I do not. I cannot make myself care. I am too busy thinking about which direction Kryto Grey would have gone in. Where I can find him, now. How I can kill him.

He cannot be too far. Until they find Rian, their business here is unconcluded, and I suspect they need someone skilled in *Dadj'zcha* to harvest from him whatever is necessary from an Eye of Death. So even if Kryto has left the palace, he will not have left the city, or even the palace grounds, necessarily.

I consider his fluke. He can pull emotions from a person and absorb them as a form of energy. In return, it exhausts me, or anyone else he uses it on. From what I observed between him and Teresa, I am beginning to suspect that Kryto can use his fluke to specifically make someone feel something he wants them to feel. As long as I am as cold and mindless a killer as possible, I do not think he will be able to influence me.

However, this is admittedly conjecture, and I do not know what else he might do with the emotional energy he absorbs.

Pushing myself off the wall, I go back, first, to the Smith's rooms. Naomi carries a knife on her, usually, as well as a small pistol. I hope to retrieve them, assuming she was relieved of them. Unfortunately, I find neither; they must have been confiscated directly, then. But I do know where I might find another firearm.

I am headed to find Jarrod Grey's body, to see what I could utilize in terms of weaponry, when I hear something that draws my attention to the window in the room that was Septimus'. The way the Smith's suite is configured, he has a window facing south, to the front of the Summer Palace. It is with this view that I catch a glimpse of Kryto Grey. His hair is unmistakable, even from a distance, and he still carries Teresa. I cannot tell if she has woken again or not.

There appear to be more men of the Greys, here, than I originally anticipated. While they could not have executed a full assault on the palace in military fashion, they have not needed to. They have confiscated some of the palace's largest and grandest royal carriages, which I am certain Magnus would be furious about if he knew. Kryto is bringing his wife to one of them, now.

I can feel the direction of my breathing change, without my consent. The sight of this man infuriates me. A quick death would be too good for him. Torture with the Dark for eternity is still too good. I may have no right to, but I have decided that. And now I know where to find him.

What gives me pause, even if only for a few seconds longer, is that I see a small figure. The source of that noise I heard: some happy little cry.

Then I spot Damen. Damen, breaking off from where he had been waiting, with a small pack of Kryto's men, running to his parents. Kryto must stop, for a moment, as Damen hugs his leg, and though I cannot hear them, he speaks to the boy. Damen looks up at him, and his mother. He appears so joyous. So relieved.

He must not have seen what happened to Aiden, then. He cannot have. He loves Aiden. Damen would never want anyone to harm his little brother.

Damen walks along with his father, looking up to him with what I am certain is sheer adoration and admiration. Kryto braces himself on the carriage step and lays Teresa inside. She does not move once. After he sets her down on the cushioned seat, he turns back and pulls Damen up into his arms instead. Damen gives a happy cry, laughing, as his father props him up. But seeing how much this child loves his father only makes me hate Kryto more. I loathe how he has manipulated Damen into believing he is a good man. I despise how Damen can see his mother so unresponsive and not think to question it.

Kryto ambles around the carriage, chatting pleasantly with his son. I pray he hands Damen off to someone else so that he might attend to Teresa alone in the carriage, as he said he would. Some part of me still does not want to kill Kryto in front of his own child. But I tell myself I am willing to do so if I must.

I storm from the room and am almost immediately accosted. Perhaps that is not the correct term, as I am certain Septimus does not intend to hurt me. But he is stronger than me, now, and in this position. He traps my arms and pulls me back against him and the wall.

"What are you doing?" he hisses.

"Killing the man you love!" I snap.

I cannot avoid how shrill I sound, even to my own ears.

"Soleil. You cannot risk yourself," Septimus whispers in my ear. "If he thinks you are a threat, he will kill you. I think he has already proven that even in this weakened state, he is faster and more powerful than you are."

He. Kryto Grey.

"He killed his own son," I hiss. "A child. Aiden deserves vengeance."

Septimus hesitates. "Be careful with such things, Soleil…"

His words may have worked in other circumstances, but now, they only serve to enrage me further.

"He deserves to die!" I insist.

"Maybe so," Septimus says, his lack of conviction otherwise enough to halt my flow of anger. "But does he deserve it more than Aiden deserves to live?"

I am forced to consider this, giving him the opportunity to elaborate.

"Soleil, if you get yourself killed trying to take revenge on Aiden's behalf, he will never have another chance at life. You will have sacrificed that in the name of vengeance, regardless of whether it is deserved or not. But if you come with me now, we can turn back events this one last time, and make things right. We can stop this from ever happening."

I throw him off and Septimus surprisingly releases me without a fight. I hate that his words make sense.

"Killing Kryto will not do anything for Aiden. Especially not now," he warns me.

I glare at him. "You only say that because you love him," I snap.

"I love my nephew more," Septimus says.

He does not refute my statement. Unfortunately, this only serves to feed the growing seed of doubt in my mind; some part of me knows Septimus is correct, but I want to remain enraged. I want to punish Kryto for his evils, or else, how can I feel as if the world will ever be just?

"There are so many depending on us, Soleil," Septimus continues. "Who have put their trust in us. If you would risk yourself, you are also risking your own family. Your children. What about Lune and Taris and Mercer? Giving them the chance at a better life? What about Xerian, who would have followed you into the Otherworld if we asked it of him? Think of Vásan. Of Alo Pike. He has only just gotten his family back. Would you sacrifice all this, and the chance of having your family back, for meager revenge?"

"You are assuming I will lose," I say, though I am losing conviction.

"I am saying it is possible you could. It is not risking the world's future—our own futures—over that."

I let my shoulders slump. I can feel that there is not a fight with me, and certainly not a fight against so many. Not against Kryto Grey, without knowing what precisely his fluke is. I suspect, given his capabilities, he may be able to win. I know I should not risk the fate of the world in such a way.

Septimus takes advantage of the situation to continue trying to convince me I should leave with him.

"I have Rian, safe," he says. "He is waiting—he refused to leave without you. Go to him. Leave here. Allow yourself to recover your strength. Go back once and for all. End this. Give Aiden a chance to live. Give yourself the chance to have the family you were willing to face the Dark itself for. There does not need to be any more death in this cycle."

"Fate did not guarantee us a happy ending," I say.

"No," Septimus agrees. "But we should give ourselves the best chance to fight for one. You have the opportunity to do so. Do not let Kryto be the one to ruin that. He has committed a great act of evil, yes. I agree. But. Is your hatred for him in this moment worth more than the love you have for so many others?"

Unfortunately for revenge's sake, I cannot help but conjure examples. Korvaan, Naomi, Teresa. Taris, Mercer, Lune. I have promised all of them something beautiful. I even desire for myself the chance to see my children, to see how they change the world even in the smallest sense, knowing my son will befriend Alo Pike. I want to be here for them. I want to be here when Soren proposes to Ayla. When Lune and Taris marry. When Rian first holds our son. Perhaps I am not wrong that Kryto deserves punishment. But am I willing to risk all those other things for that?

He knows me too well; Septimus is correct. I would not. I cannot. Especially not when he himself is willing to fight for a better world, a better life, even one that may not be meant for him.

"…No," I finally agree. "It is not."

I see Septimus' shoulders lower, slightly. I realize that he was preparing himself, in case he could not convince me, and needed to take action against me. It does not matter, truly, whether some part of Septimus wants me to spare Kryto out of some remaining vestige of love for his own tormentor. He is still correct in what else he has said.

More than revenge, Aiden deserves life.

"Let us go, now," Septimus urges me quietly. "Put an end to all this, Soleil. It is what you were always destined to do."

"A gift for a reason," I murmur.

Only Septimus, having also gone to the Otherworld, would understand.

"Precisely," he says. His smile is sad.

I go to take a step forward, but stagger. Septimus catches my arms and helps to walk me down the hall. I feel dizzy enough to barely recognize how Septimus is glancing around, keeping an eye out for enemies. I feel as if I am leaning my weight against him more and more with each step.

Septimus leads me back towards the king's chambers. My feet stumble against one another. The closer we get, the more I am certain I could not best Kryto in a footrace, let alone a fight to the death.

"Where is Rian?" I demand as Septimus clumsily pulls me into the king's bedchamber.

The place has been raided, the furniture tipped over and all of Rian's things torn apart. Even Mango is nowhere in sight.

"He's here," Septimus says. "When Qhan came in to tell us there had been a breach, I knew. I hid them, in the passage between the king and queen's bedrooms. And then I came to find you."

"Qhan would not hide," I say.

"He did to help protect the king," Septimus says. "Particularly when I insisted this was a fight we could not win. But he sent Vilaneau, to get Ayla out of the palace without wait. Korvaan ought to be with his wife. I suspect the pair of them will go to protect Soren. That is the best we can do, now."

He lets me fall against the mattress that has been thrown to the ground.

"Where is the passage to the queen's chambers?" Septimus asks.

"Do you not know where the door is?" I ask.

"No. Help me, Soleil. We need to escape quickly."

"Let me sit for a moment," I sigh.

Septimus turns back to me, watches for a moment, then slings one of my arms over his shoulders and levers me back up to my feet.

"Kryto got to you, I see," he mutters.

"I feel drunk."

"Yes, he is very like that. It does not help you launched yourself into a fight after. Once we get you outside, you will feel much better."

"Ayla—" I start.

"Vilaneau is with her," Septimus promises again. "She is safe."

I do not know if I believe him, but I want to. I know that, if Ayla is captured, I could not save her. This time, trying to tell myself this cycle means nothing fails. I want to believe everyone is safe and well away from the danger, but I already know that is not true. Vásan, alone, has fallen as a casualty. I struggle to imagine Korvaan managing to escape with Kaoli and Soren, either.

I groan, my head pounding, but show Septimus where to open the clandestine passage between the king and queen's chambers in the Summer Palace. The queen's chambers will not have been used, even considering Rian's announcement of our marriage, and while Rian's rooms have been destroyed, it is evident no one found him or Qhan, here.

It is dark and musty inside the passage when Septimus pulls me inside. I am wary of the shadowy figures present, at first, but then both Qhan and Rian pull me from Septimus, and Qhan helps reseal the passage from the inside. I feel how tightly Rian pulls me against him and can tell he is relieved to see me safe. He holds me tightly against him, and I know he wants to never let me go. Mango mewls on his shoulder, and Rian shushes him.

"Are you hurt?" he whispers to me.

I make myself shake my head. It is a lie, but I do not want him to worry.

"Ayla—" I start.

"She is safe," Rian promises me. "I would not leave without you, but I promise you, Soleil, our daughter is safe."

I choke back a sob I did not realize was bubbling in my throat. I breathe in against his chest and allow the comfortable scent of him to chase some of the buzzing in my head away. Even if Septimus had not made a convincing argument to stop me from chasing after Kryto, I know now beyond a doubt that I could not have managed it. I do not know if I could have even made it down the stairs.

I hear Septimus take a deep breath in, and let it out heavily.

"Where should we go?" Qhan asks, and it takes me a moment to realize he is directing that inquiry at me.

I do not know. I close my eyes and rest my head against Rian's shoulder. I cannot do this.

"It does not matter," Septimus insists. "We need to buy ourselves enough time for sunrise. Once Soleil has spent hours in the sun, it should be enough."

Rian looks concerned. "I doubt we have that much time."

"Then she will have to use the moon," Septimus says shortly.

I want to protest; I prefer the sun greatly to the moon. I can feel its power exceptionally, and it would strengthen me faster. But I know they are both right. We do not know how much time the Greys are going to give us. The longer we wait, the more I know I will have to picture every one of their victims, imagining who else they may have killed.

Nissa? Soren? Magnus? Yvette and Alo? Irina and Detrus, their children? I do not want to consider it. If I do, I know, I will want to stay. I will insist on staying. The thought alone of them finding and hurting Ayla—of her terror, praying I arrive to save her, only for me to fail her—pains me. Wondering what Kryto might do to Teresa privately in that carriage infuriates me.

But Septimus was right; this is the best I can do for them.

Qhan leads the way through the passage to the queen's chambers, while Rian holds me up and Septimus watches behind us. I am almost concerned about the possibility of us being trapped in this passage, but before I can fully allow the panic to set, we are out again. Qhan intends to check the room, first, before letting us follow, but he does not need to. Even beforehand, I can hear who is there, and am no longer concerned. I almost, absurdly, smile.

"Where is it?" Alo Pike demands, sounded panicked and horrified. "She said it should be here, on the bookcase—where?!"

We exit the passage to see him throwing books off the shelf. Yvette is seated on the floor, staring blankly ahead, Vásan's blood still on her hands and nightgown. Aiko Shinya is standing there as well, a child hoisted in his arms, clinging to him. Alo continues to throw tomes from the shelves, hands still shaking, having completely forgotten my instructions.

"Calm yourself," Shinya tells him.

He turns, pulling the child higher against his shoulder.

I blink several times, and fall further into Rian, who barely manages to catch me again.

"Aiden!" I say. "Aiden! You're… You're alive!"

My voice is hoarse and horrifically meek. Aiden raises his head from Shinya's shoulder when he hears his name. He stares at me with those sweet blue eyes of his. I can see he is frightened, but he is comforted by Shinya's familiarity, and how he knows his mother trusts this man.

I stagger off of Rian and forward, nearly knocking Shinya and Aiden over.

"Your father," I say, "your father came. He…He said things…"

I cut myself off, realizing I cannot tell Aiden he is meant to be dead. But I still need to know.

"How," I ask. "How did you get here, Aiden?"

Rian is there to pull me back again, letting Shinya straighten.

"Damen's Ghost came," Aiden claims, scared, but still innocent enough to explain without bursting into tears.

"Damen's Ghost?" Rian prompts the boy. "And what did he do?"

He shrugs. "All I remember is waking up soon after I fell asleep, and seeing Daddy, and wondering what was happening. I thought it might have been a bad dream. But then Damen's Ghost came around and took me out of the room, and brought me to Rika's daddy. And now we're here."

I let Rian hold up my weight again. The meager relief he provided my headache is gone once more, and I am miserable in my confusion, but pleasantly astonished to see Aiden alive. Not having to imagine, any longer, how Kryto might have killed his son lifts a weight from my soul.

Qhan has gone to Alo Pike to pull the boy from the bookshelf and insist he see to his mother. Qhan instead will find the mechanism for the secret passage. I feel Septimus shutting the passage behind us, and then join me.

"Kryto may be a monster, but he would not kill his own son," Septimus whispers.

"You do not know that," I say, trying to at least keep my voice down for Aiden's sake. "You believed it, too, before you knew Aiden was safe."

But even then, I consider how Kryto went about things, how he appeared to purposefully do his best to terrify his wife. Perhaps that was only done for his own enjoyment, but now I must wonder if he had an alternative motive as well. Given how using my fear and anger strengthened him, he may purposefully, routinely use Teresa's emotional reactions for power. He might not even intend to harm Aiden, ever. He only wanted to regain the strength that Teresa took from him in the first place, in running away.

Qhan has the passage opened and indicates for us to go through. Rian assists me down the stairs, with my head continuing to swim with exhaustion. He is stronger than I remember. Septimus stays behind us all, keeping a hand hovering at his side, wishing he had his sword. The others follow between, Alo supporting his mother, Shinya still carrying Aiden.

I can only imagine what they are thinking, these companions of ours who do not know this world is not the one they are meant to live in. These events are ones they will never experience again, I pray.

Septimus was right. Killing Kryto will do nothing that matters. I need to live so that others may live. I owe it to them, now.

At the bottom of the passage, immediately after Qhan drags the stone door away, there is a blast of chilly air awaiting us. Outside, a winter storm has begun to pick up in the night. Snow falls into my hair and melts onto my clothing. Yvette shivers uncontrollably. There is snow up to my ankles and building. I do not look forward to taking off my boots and stockings to stand with my feet on the earth.

In fact, I recall having to flee from the Pyrian Palace, a cycle before. Only then, it was to eventually return, so sure I could still salvage that timeline. I was so hopeful I might. I cannot imagine, now, ever wanting to live in a world without Lune in it. Thinking of it, now, I am glad we are not intending to try and retake the Summer Palace.

Shinya puts down Aiden to remove his coat, and offers it to Yvette before picking Aiden up once more. Rian begins to remove his coat as well, insisting they drape it over the boy. Aiden is only in his nightwear, as is Yvette. Aiden does not even have stockings. Qhan removes his guard's jacket instead, insisting Rian keep his. Qhan also offers to carry me, if I cannot walk, but I promise him it is not necessary.

The feel of the cold air filling my lungs is painful, reminding my aching body of how broken it is, but I welcome it. It is a good pain.

We limp off at a pitiful pace into the city, as the winter storm picks up. The temperature thankfully drops no lower, but the snow falls in thick, fat flakes until Yvette's hair is completely coated. She and Alo are both still shaking, but I do not know what to say to either of them. At least Aiden manages to fall asleep and is no longer able to be distressed, or to ask questions about what is happening, or where his mother and brother are.

Shinya says nothing. He holds the boy up close against his chest and keeps his eyes forward. When he catches me looking at him, he gives me a short nod. I wonder what he thinks about. I wonder if he worries over Teresa and his daughter's safety as much as I do, having seen what Kryto is capable of.

Qhan brings us to a large public garden and its attached tea house. It is a business meant for those who have no natural space in their housing to experience the warmth of the sun or glow of the moon with the earth beneath their feet. I know we do not have much time, but Kryto will need to have the entire palace searched before it occurs to him that we have slipped away, and we have the city as our refuge.

Though it is late, the tea house is open with a night shift, for those who prefer the moon. Qhan goes in ahead of us, but given the wintery weather, most folk are staying home, tonight. We have the place to ourselves, save for the owners. Qhan takes care of anything that might need be said to them, and I am glad for it. I cannot think up an explanation, nor do I want to. Why lie? Why tell the truth, either, at a time like this?

Inside is warm. The owner's wife finds blankets and seats us by the fire, insisting on serving us warm drinks. She has questions, naturally, but manages not to ask them. I see her continually glance at Rian, though, and then me. So, she recognizes her king. But her attention is drawn by the still-bloodied Yvette, who breaks into tears and collapses in her son's arms, sobbing for Vásan. I allow the kindly woman to look after Yvette and Alo, certain she has, in her own mind, decided she can get answers later. As far as she knows, tomorrow will still come.

Shinya wraps Aiden up in wool blankets and places him in a chair, with Mango purring against the boy's chest, before coming to me.

"Miss Soleil," he says, and bows. "I am afraid I must leave you. I am going back to the palace. This boy cannot be without his mother. And…I must get my daughter back. I am sorry."

I glance at Rian, knowing this is a bad idea, but unsure how to stop him. I do not even know if I have a right to stop him, anymore. After purposefully creating a reunion for them, can I keep Shinya from wanting to rescue Teresa, even if it gets him killed?

"That is a noble pursuit," Rian says for me. "But could you wait an hour more, please? I need to discuss something with Soleil, and Septimus. We will not take longer than that, I promise you. Then you may leave. And we will look after Aiden, until you return."

Shinya nods. Though I know it does not matter, I am glad that this timeline will end with him here, with Aiden, instead of insisting on returning to the Summer Palace, where he would surely die.

The owner of the garden and shop lends us winter coats. Qhan, Septimus, Rian and I head to the back gardens, finding a patch of moonlight. Rian helps me remove my stockings and boots, and stands there beside me, letting me lean my weight on him once more. Qhan excuses himself, to ensure we are safe, here, and to keep a look out.

That leaves the three of us, in the moonlight.

My head has cleared, but my eyes continue to water, and I cannot stop them. I promise myself these are not tears. But I do not know that.

For a long time, no one speaks. I fill my lungs with frozen air, occasionally inhaling a snowflake. The moon is not as strong, for me, as the sun. I picture Lune as her namesake, lending me her strength. It makes me feel more capable. More able to utilize whatever strength this world is willing to give me.

I can feel my energy returning, even more than what Kryto took from me, the longer I stand in the moonlight. My feet are pained with cold, tinging each time I move them or clench my muscles.

I do not care. Like with the icy air, it is a good pain.

Eventually, I squeeze Rian's arm. He looks away from the moon and down to me once more. I wonder if he has been praying.

"Now?" he asks me gently.

"Soon," I say.

Septimus watches us, undoubtedly hears, then nods.

"I suppose this is goodbye, then," he says.

He tries to be as flippant as he usually is, but his voice breaks. I can tell that Septimus does not want this to be the end of things. Not in this way.

"Not forever," I say.

Septimus gives a sad smile.

"I am afraid it may be. In this final version of the world, I do not know who I will be," he warns us. "Remember—I will be raised by the Greys, as I was the first time around. It took me decades before deciding to betray them."

I frown. "And so?"

Septimus takes a deep breath. His sigh creates a cloud of frost in the air.

"You cannot try to rescue me. Or Teresa. Things must happen…as they should. You *must* let things be as naturally occurring as possible, now that we only have one chance left. If you try to intervene prematurely, then Damen and Aiden, or Rika, might never exist. That means that Teresa will eventually run from Kryto, with her children, and she will find her way to you. You can rest assured in that. But I do not know if I will ever join her. I may choose to remain loyal to the Greys. In which case, if necessary, you may have to face me one day. And kill me."

He looks directly at me as he says this. He watches closely, for my reaction. For Rian's.

"I'm afraid we are not going to do that, Septimus," Rian says first.

"You may have to," Septimus presses. "And I would like you to promise you will. Please. If it means stopping the Greys, with me so insistent on helping them, if it means saving Teresa and her children from them, then I want you to. I want you to do it before I can damn myself."

But even before I can answer, Rian is shaking his head.

"No," he says. "I'm sorry. I will not."

Septimus looks to me, instead. "Soleil?"

"I will find a way to save you," I promise. "Even if you do not want to be saved."

Septimus hesitates. "Soleil. That is not up to you."

"I don't care."

"Then I'm afraid...One more thing," he says, almost sadly, and before I can ask what, he reaches out to take Rian and I both by the wrist.

For a moment, it feels like there is a blank space in my head. It is quickly filled in, with reassurances to the contrary, but for a moment, it is almost as if I have forgotten something incredibly important.

And then I have forgotten the relevancy of its importance, too.

Septimus lets go of our wrists. I'm not sure why he was holding them in the first place, but I suppose it may have been for reassurance. Then he asks a strange question. I'm not sure where the thought came from.

"Soleil—do you remember who I said Teresa's husband is? The father of her children?"

I roll my eyes. "Aside from Aiko Shinya fathering Rika? No, how would I? You never told us. All you said was that he works for the Greys. One of their men. If he can even be called that," I add, recalling what I know Teresa's husband did to their second-born son.

I have some idea of what he looks like, but I do not even have the man's name. The fact Septimus is asking makes me vaguely suspicious and I frown at him.

"That is ***true at least, isn't it?"***

"...Yes," Septimus says sadly, looking down. "Yes, that is true at least. He really is naught but a pawn..."

"I have no idea what you mean," Rian admits.

The smile on Septimus' face is a melancholy one.

"...Excellent. Then things are how they should be. So that things can be as they should be."

He sounds so sad. I observe him closely, suspicious.

"Septimus. Is there something you need to tell me? About your nephews' father? Who he is?"

Septimus shakes his head and looks down. "No. You know he is a weapon of the Greys. You know what he is willing to do. That is enough."

I am confused by this. I have a vague memory of such a topic of conversation being important, but even that is beginning to fade. I cannot recall if Septimus ever told us who Teresa's husband is. I don't remember if it matters.

The only thought that wants to dominate in my mind is the reminder that Fate wants me to go back. We must go back. And we are going to.

We are going to make this a better world. Rian and I will, for our children.

Septimus looks up at the sky, at the snow falling.

"Well," he finally says. "If I knew they would remember me, I would ask you to tell Taris and Lune I'm sorry," he says. "…But I know you will tell them you love them. And that is better than anything I can offer."

"Septimus…" I start.

"Please," he interrupts. "Don't. I am going back inside, now. I am going to go and sit with Aiden, and tell Aiko Shinya to wait another few minutes, so you can come in and wish him well. Tell him the best point of infiltration for the palace. I don't know. I will think of something."

He gives a short laugh. It is sad. I am willing to admit, now, that these are tears on my cheeks. I know Septimus has resigned himself to being a villain in our lives, but I do not want him to be. I am going to miss him, infuriating as he can be. I do not want to let him go yet.

"You do what you must," he adds. "I do not think I can be here when you do it. But when you are ready…"

He hesitates, as if he is considering something more to say. Then he nods to himself and leaves us, standing there in the snow.

Rian pulls me tighter against him and kisses the top of my head. I count the seconds and tell myself that everything is as it should be, and if it is not, we will make it so. I do not know that for certain, but it is a comforting thought.

After another few seconds, I wriggle an arm free and dig into my pocket, pulling something out for Rian to see.

"…You. The pocket watch," he says in surprise. He laughs. "You have it."

"I have kept it on me for so long, now, it became habit," I confess. "I almost forgot it was here."

Rian puts a hand underneath mine to cup it, bringing my arm up higher so he can see the time. He does not read it out loud. We both watch the seconds-hand ticking, inching itself along. I feel as if my heart is beating along with it. I feel as if it is matching the beat I can feel in Rian's chest.

"You do it when you are ready," he tells me.

"I'm ready," I insist. "But I wish I did not have to do it alone."

"You don't," Rian says, though we both know I am the one with the power to make this happen. I am the one who will have to do it. To make us go back in time so far, and start all over again.

"Here," he tells me, and tucks us both comfortably together, holding the watch before us both. "We will watch it together. And exactly when those three hands align, you do it. You go back. We will count it down together."

"Together," I repeat.

I curl my frozen toes against the ground and feel them brush against a blade of petrified grass, or perhaps the petal of a flower, forgotten under the snow. The moon gleams off the chilly pinkness of my fingers next to Rian's, and I shiver. His breath is warm on the back of my neck. For a few moments, watching that second hand tick, I feel the panic in my stomach. I can feel the desire to sob.

But then it fades. I feel warm. There is nothing to see around us but flora and snow, but I can feel a tall, winged figure. I never saw the angel of fortitude while in the Otherworld. But he is the only one I imagine with wings. I can practically hear those wings flutter. I can hear them over Rian and I.

I know it is impossible for an angel to be here, and am certain I am only imagining it. But some part of me realizes the snow is no longer falling on us, only on the ground before us. It is as if a great pair of wings have been stretched out above us. I hear the wind whistle, but do not feel the biting cold.

The seconds pass by slowly. I watch them one by one, feel them and note each one in its individual importance. Rian sighs against my neck and presses his forehead down against me. I am no longer so afraid. I am prepared, I tell myself, to live the way we were meant to. I am ready to do that, with Taris, and Lune, and Mercer. I am willing to do that, and to trust.

I can do it, I know.

So, I watch the last few seconds tick, and enjoy them in the moonlight with Rian. And then we jump back.

Soleil's narrative ends here, but her story and Samioth's continues. Watch the final loop of reality unfold and explore the many tales of Samioth's cast, beginning with Lijimi prince and princess Castel and Emmelina Voskoss in The Magicsmiths Book One: *Of One So Magicblind.*

Cast of Characters

(alphabetical by first name)

ABRAM SONDUSHKI, Isaarian prince, Nissa's nephew and heir
ABSOLUM ORAM, Magnus' father, former king of Isaaria
ADRIAN RALHAN, Isaarian prince, Mercer's nephew and heir
AIDEN SMITH, second son of Teresa Smith and Kryto Grey
AISLING, Kang's wife, author of semi-autobiographical books
AMERSON GREY, eldest of the Grey brothers, with regenerative abilities
ALASTER T'CHOROT, one of the Greys' generals
ALDRICH WOLFF, last of the Wolffs, of whom there are many rumors
ALION CARSANS, Grand Prince, Crispin, Soren and Lune's father
ALOYSIUS PIKE I, Vásan and Bastien's father, a former Grand Prince
ALOYSIUS PIKE II, also called Alo, Vásan and Yvette's heir and only child
ANNA WOLFF, the only daughter of Mariana and Aldrich Wolff, deceased
ARGO NOX, one of the Greys' generals
ARTEMIS YAKARAMI, Rian and Soleil's daughter
ASMER AL'YIBNA, former queen of Isaaria, Rian's first wife, deceased
AYLA YAKARAMI, Rian's adopted daughter, princess of Isaaria
BASTIEN PIKE, one of the Greys' generals, Vásan's younger brother
BLUE, Charrion's third in command of the Mitaurus
BOGUN PARK, Kachin crown prince, cousin of Shinya, deceased
CAMILLA, a member of the Mitaurus, Charrion's younger sister
CASTEL VOSKOSS, prince of Lijimata, younger brother of Emmelina
CHARRION, the rumored blind and immortal leader of the Mitaurus
CHIMHWI PARK, Kacha's bastard princeling, cousin of Shinya, deceased
CLAIR ORAM, Magnus' mother, former queen of Isaaria
CLANAUGH, king of the Fae in the lands of Isaaria
COURAGE, the angel of courage/fortitude, hosts a male presence to Soleil
CRISPIN CARSANS, Grand Prince, son of Alion Carsans

DAMEN SMITH, elder son of Teresa Smith and Kryto Grey
DARK, the dark and fallen angel cast out of the Almighty's grace
DEATH, the angel of death, hosts a male presence to Soleil
DETRUS LUNDAN, Grand Prince of Isaaria, Irina's husband
EMMELINA VOSKOSS, Queen of Lijimata, elder sister of Castel
ELENA, presumably a friend of Castel's, mentioned by Wina
ELIATH MIRAK, the former king of the Fair folk, Seraphina's brother
ELIORA CARSANS, wife of Alion Carsans, Crispin and Soren's mother
ELODIE LUNDAN, Isaarian princess, Detrus and Irina's eldest child
EMMELINA VOSKOSS, the queen of Lijimata and Castel's elder sister
FABIAN, a member of Castel's Sunguard, mentioned by Wina
FAITH, the angel of faith, hosts a male presence to Soleil
FALISIA VOSKOSS, older half-sister of Emmelina and Castel
FATE, the angel of fate, hosts a male presence to Soleil
FAUSTUS, member of the Mitaurus
FOX, the newest and youngest member of the Mitaurus
GABRIEL MARSON, Soleil and Lune's father, Olivia's husband, deceased
HOPE, the angel of hope, hosts a female presence to Soleil
IRINA LUNDAN, Grand Princess of Isaaria, Detrus' wife
JAVIER VOSKOSS, cousin of Castel and Emmelina Voskoss
JARROD GREY, youngest of the Grey brothers
JAVIER VOSKOSS, Castel's older cousin, deceased, mentioned by Wina
JAXON GREY, Jarrod's younger twin, mentioned, deceased
JEAN VILANEAU, Soleil's eventual replacement in Rian's guard
KAETSCHA, sister of Clanaugh, princess of the Fae
KAOLI ADDER, Korvaan's wife, aid to Prince Soren Carsans
KANG, a mythical and misanthropic fellow cursed with dragon's blood
KORSIKO, an assassin for the Greys, formerly the 13th of the Mitaurus
KORVAAN QURVO, second son of Nusk, middle Qurvo child
KRYTO GREY, second of the Grey brothers, Teresa's husband
LISAN YAKARAMI, Rian and Soleil's son and heir
LOUISA ERIKSON, an Alarkian ambassador's daughter who was killed
LOVE, the angel of love, hosts a female presence to Soleil
LUC ERIKSON, former Alarkian ambassador to Lijimata, deceased

LUNE CARSANS, adopted daughter of Alion Carsans, Soleil's little sister
LURE, Charrion's second in command in the Mitaurus, not unlike a Fae
LYSANDRA GREY, Nexa's elder sister, mentioned, deceased
MAGNUS ORAM, Grand Prince of Isaaria
MALLIN CRUZ, underhanded but discreet apothecary
MANGO, Rian Yakarami's miniature sunblood dragon
MARGO GREY, Kryto, Amerson, Jarrod, and Nexa's aunt, Septimus' ally
MARIE SONDUSHKI, Isaarian princess, Nissa's niece
MERCER RALHAN, Grand Prince, Rian's former best friend, deceased
MI-SUN PARK, princess of Kacha, cousin of Aiko Shinya
NAOMI QURVO, only daughter of Nusk, youngest of the Qurvos
NEXA GREY, Kryto, Amerson and Jarrod's cousin, Dadj'zcha practitioner
NISSA SONDUSHKI, Grand Princess of Isaaria
NUSK QURVO, former Khashtani, Soleil's trainer,
OLIVIA SMITH, Soleil and Lune's birth-mother, deceased
PATRICE LUNDAN, Isaarian prince, Irina and Detrus' youngest child
PEACE, the angel of peace, hosts a female presence to Soleil
PHOEBUS KAGEN, one of Kryto Grey's generals
QHAN KHALEEM, Rian's favorite and most reliable bodyguard
RAUL, a member of the Mitaurus
RENKI AIKO, former Tourrannese-Kachin lord ambassador,
RIAN YAKARAMI, King of Isaaria, Soleil's husband
RIKA SMITH, daughter of Teresa Smith and Aiko Shinya
RISING SUN, a member of the Mitaurus
RIYONG JIN, friend of the late Princes Bogun and Chimhwi Park
RITTER, a member of the Mitaurus, known for using modern weaponry
RUSKIN, ally of Septimus and Margo Grey, deceased
SACHA LUNDAN, Isaarian prince, Detrus and Irina's elder son
SAKIA YAKARAMI, late grandmother of Rian Yakarami, former princess
SEBASTIAN, presumedly a friend of Castel's, mentioned by Wina
SEPTIMUS SMITH, elder brother of Teresa, uncle of Damen and Aiden
SERAPHINA MIRAK, the human sister of an ancient Fair king, Eliath
SHINYA AIKO, son of Aiko Renki, Teresa's lover and Rika's father
SOREN CARSANS, steward of the Summer Palace and Ayla's fiancé

SOLEIL MARSON, bodyguard to Rian and rightful queen of Isaaria
TANOGATTA, a member of the Mitaurus Soleil has seen at Mallin Cruz's
TARIS QURVO, eldest son of Nusk, half-sibling of Korvaan and Naomi
TERESA SMITH, sister of Septimus, mother of Damen and Aiden
THENA YAKARAMI, Rian and Soleil's daughter
VASÁN PIKE, Grand Prince of Isaaria, adoptive father of Aloysius II
VALOR ONDRA, Naomi's husband, one of Rian's guards
WIDOW, a member of the Mitaurus, a vampiric mind-magic wielder
WINA MURNINGSON, a member of Castel's Sunguard, deceased
XERIAN VICELL, a member of Septimus' alliance, from Rumshtama
YEONG-JUN YAKARAMI, youngest child and son of Rian and Soleil
YUUGO IDO, Grand Prince of Isaaria, the youngest of his peers
YVETTE PIKE, Grand Princess of Isaaria, Alo's mother, Vásan's wife
ZIERA, a member of the Mitaurus

www.ingramcontent.com/pod-product-compliance
Lightning Source LLC
Chambersburg PA
CBHW070541310726
48982CB00010B/1431/J

* 9 7 8 1 7 3 4 6 6 7 2 4 0 *